Praise for
Murder in the Supreme Court

"Her best job to date."
—*The New York Times Book Review*

"Truman keeps on turning out one bestselling mystery after another and you can see why in *Murder in the Supreme Court*. . . . An entertainment and good reading."
—*Los Angeles Times Book Review*

"If Margaret Truman keeps on writing murder mysteries about the Washington she once knew so well, it will become difficult to resist calling her the mistress of Capital crime. . . . *Murder in the Supreme Court* is not only a tight, well-written, cleverly plotted mystery fully professional in manner and matter, but one that suggests a whole series of Washington follow-ups ready and waiting for Margaret Truman's now practiced hand."
—*John Barkham Reviews*

Capital Crimes

By Margaret Truman

First Ladies
Bess W. Truman
Souvenir
Women of Courage
Harry S Truman
Letters from Father:
The Truman Family's Personal Correspondences
Where the Buck Stops
White House Pets
The President's House

IN THE CAPITAL CRIMES SERIES

Murder in Foggy Bottom
Murder at the Library of Congress
Murder at the Watergate
Murder in the House
Murder at the National Gallery
Murder on the Potomac
Murder at the Pentagon
Murder in the Smithsonian
Murder at the National Cathedral
Murder at the Kennedy Center
Murder in the CIA
Murder in Georgetown
Murder at the FBI
Murder on Embassy Row
Murder in the Supreme Court
Murder on Capitol Hill
Murder in the White House
Murder in Havana
Murder at Ford's Theater
Murder at Union Station
Murder at the Washington Tribune

Capital Crimes

Murder in the Supreme Court
Murder in the CIA
Murder in the House

Three classic novels of suspense

Margaret Truman

Ballantine Books New York

2005 Ballantine Books Trade Paperback Edition

Murder in the Supreme Court copyright © 1982 by Margaret Truman
Murder in the CIA copyright © 1987 by Margaret Truman
Murder in the House copyright © 1997 by Margaret Truman
Excerpt from *Murder at the Washington Tribune*
copyright © 2005 by Margaret Truman

Published in the United States by Ballantine Books,
an imprint of The Random House Publishing Group,
a division of Random House, Inc., New York.

BALLANTINE and colophon are registered trademarks
of Random House, Inc.

Originally published as three separate works entitled *Murder in the
Supreme Court,* published by arrangement with Arbor House
Publishing Company; *Murder in the CIA,* published by arrangement
with Random House; and *Murder in the House,* published by
arrangement with Random House, Inc.

In *Murder in the Supreme Court,* "As Time Goes By" by Herman
Hupfeld is reprinted by permission of Warner Brothers Inc.
© 1931 (renewed) by Warner Brothers Inc.

ISBN 0-345-48517-3

Printed in the United States of America

www.ballantinebooks.com

2   4   6   8   9   7   5   3

Murder in the Supreme Court

CHAPTER
1

"Oyez! Oyez! Oyez! All persons having business before the Honorable, the Supreme Court of the United States, are admonished to draw near and give their attention, for the Court is now sitting. God save the United States and this Honorable Court."

AS THE MARSHAL CHANTED THE OPENING RITUAL, NINE black-robed justices stepped through heavy burgundy drapes behind a winged Honduras mahogany bench and took their seats. Attorneys who would present the first set of oral arguments sat at a long counsel table in front of, and below, the bench. Before them were twenty ten-inch quill pens carefully crossed on writing pads, a tradition from the Court's

1

earliest days. An older attorney wore a morning coat; the rest were in dark, vested business suits.

"Let's begin," said Jonathan Poulson, Chief Justice, who sat in the middle of the bench. Bald except for tufts of white hair around the lower perimeter of his head, wire spectacles perched low on an aquiline nose, a long slender index finger pressed against his cheek, he listened as attorneys seeking admission to the Court were introduced.

"Admission granted," Poulson said. The clerk administered the oath. "Welcome, ladies and gentlemen," Poulson said. "Let's get on with the first case, *Nidel* v. *Illinois*."

A young attorney walked to the podium, cranked it higher, arranged long yellow legal sheets on it. His hair was thick and dark, and he had a sallow, slightly pockmarked face. "Mr. Chief Justice, and may it please the Court," he said in a strong voice, "two years ago, in the spring, the plaintiff sought to seek an abortion in her home state of Illinois . . ."

Poulson leaned back in his black leather chair and listened to the attorney's introductory remarks while looking out over the huge, majestic courtroom. It never failed to impress him, the dignity and beauty of it, walls and columns of white marble from Spain and Italy contrasting with carpet and drapes as red as blood. Directly in front of him, high on the west wall, was one of four thirty-six-foot marble Weinman friezes. Poulson absently identified each of the symbolic figures; the winged female figure of Divine Inspiration flanked by Wisdom and Truth. To the left stood the Powers of Good: Security, Harmony, Peace, Charity and Defense of Virtue. Evil was represented on the other side; Corruption, Slander, Deceit and Despotic Power.

The room was filled with spectators, as it usually was when a controversial issue was being argued. Those with special interest gathered in front of a gleaming brass rail. The press was in a designated section to the left. Behind the rail sat the general public. Every seat was occupied, and the line outside was long.

The Chief noticed a small boy looking up at the ceiling, a vast expanse of gold-leaf lotus blossoms, symbolizing Endurance, set against brightly lighted red and blue squares.

He returned his full attention to the attorney's words. He hadn't missed any of them despite his mental wandering. Years on the bench had honed that skill, first as an appellate judge in the Ninth Circuit, then with the U.S. Court of Claims until being nominated a little more than a year ago for Chief Justice by President Randolph Jorgens.

Jorgens, a conservative, had been swept into office on a nation's disenchantment with previous liberal, permissive administrations. He could have tapped an existing justice for the Chief's job but honored the tradition of not doing that for fear of upsetting the delicate balance that existed on the Court. Instead, he reached out to his old friend Jonathan Poulson, who, like the new president, espoused conservative ideology, a hard-nosed Constitutionalist, fiscally sound and overtly disdainful of changes that challenged time-proven American traditions.

The attorney was interrupted by the Court's only female justice, Marjorie Tilling-Masters, an attractive and brilliant woman who, besides bringing a moderate, reasoned philosophy to the bench, had been responsible, simply by virtue of being female, for changing the tradition of addressing justices as, "*Mr*. Justice Poulson," or "*Mr*. Justice Brown." Since her arrival, the *Mr*. had been dropped, although an occasional slip of the tongue still occurred.

The justice to Poulson's immediate right, Temple Conover, leaned close and said, "The attorney has a lisp."

Poulson smiled. As the oldest justice and the one with the most tenure on the Court, Conover took advantage of his seniority to display irreverence at times Poulson considered inappropriate. Conover had become a media char-

3

acter, irascible and argumentative, brilliant, foppish in his dress, flamboyant in his life-style. He'd recently married for the fourth time. His new wife was twenty-six; he was eighty-two. He was a devout liberal.

The justice to Poulson's left, Morgan Childs, leaned toward his microphone and said to the attorney, "Mr. Manecke, it's my understanding from your affidavits that the original appeal was based upon the refusal of the state to finance the plaintiff's abortion. That strikes me as vastly different from the argument you're presenting here today, that it is a woman's right to determine the fate of her own body."

The attorney looked up from his prepared statement and said, "Justice Childs, the issue is broader than simply one of fiscal decision making. That's why this case has reached this level. We're dealing with a basic issue of individual rights within a free society. To reduce it to . . ."

Childs waved his hand and shook his head. "That's my point, Mr. Manecke. I simply wish to keep things straight. Either we're arguing a woman's rights or the balancing of a checkbook."

A few of the spectators in the audience chuckled. Chief Justice Poulson looked up, which ended the momentary mirth.

Childs pressed, "We're being called upon to decide a national issue, Mr. Manecke. It would help if we knew what that issue was."

The attorney tried to get back to his prepared statement but another justice asked a question.

Poulson turned to his chief clerk, Clarence Sutherland, who sat behind him, and asked, "What is the substantive issue here?"

Sutherland smiled and shrugged. "Sex, I suppose."

Poulson drew a deep breath and returned his attention to the attorney's comments. Clarence disappeared through the

4

curtains, found a book he was looking for in a library housed behind the bench, returned and handed it to Poulson. "Page eleven, sir. It has relevance."

When the plaintiff's attorney had completed his hour, the older attorney in the morning coat stepped to the podium. He represented the state of Illinois. Poulson knew him well. They'd been classmates in law school.

"Mr. Chief Justice, and may it please the Court," he said, "I stand before you today as a representative of a confused and troubled American electorate. Concepts that have withstood the test of time are being rewritten by those with special, self-serving motives. The values that have provided the linchpin of the American dream, the fabric from which the American cloth has been woven, are being placed in deliberate jeopardy. In the case that has been brought here today . . ."

Justice Marjorie Tilling-Masters picked a piece of lint from her black robe. A security guard politely asked a spectator to remove his arm from the brass rail as the ancient Justice Conover mumbled to no one in particular, "The point, get to the point."

Chief clerk Clarence Sutherland walked behind the justices and handed a note to another clerk, Laurie Rawls. She read it, looked up and pouted. The note said he couldn't keep their dinner date. He shrugged and was about to return to his chair when a sharp, clear report crackled through the heavy silence of the room.

"Get down!" the marshal shouted.

All nine justices, robes awry, got down beneath the bench. Spectators looked around, and fell to the floor. Armed guards wearing white shirts and black ties ran to the bench. Clarence Sutherland had dropped to his knees next to Laurie Rawls. They looked at each other in shock.

"Stay low," a guard yelled.

Clarence poked his head up above the bench and saw a

5

security man walk into the courtroom carrying an unidentified object. He was smiling. "A lightbulb," he said in a loud voice. "Just a lightbulb that fell out of its socket."

"A lightbulb," Clarence said to Laurie as he helped her to her feet.

"It sounded like a gun," she said. "God, what a scare." She slumped in her chair and blew a strand of hair from her forehead.

Clarence leaned close to her ear. "Sorry about tonight but something came up."

"Who is it this time?"

"Come on . . ."

"Have a nice night." Her words were formed of ice.

Order was restored in the room. The old attorney stepped to the podium, tugged on his formal coat, cleared his throat and said, "Mr. Chief Justice, and may it please the Court, as I was saying . . ."

CHAPTER
2

JONATHAN POULSON SAT IN HIS CHAMBERS ON FRIDAY morning, three days after the lightbulb incident. "Where's Clarence?" he asked his other clerks.

"I don't know," one of them said. "Traffic, I suppose."

"Yes." Sutherland was often late, which always upset the Chief Justice. He believed in punctuality, felt those who didn't were attention-seeking bores.

A buzzer sounded at 9:25, five minutes before the Friday conference was to begin. Of all the rituals of the Court, the Friday conference meant the most to Poulson. Thousands of potential cases were presented to the Supreme Court each year under the concept of the Court granting a writ of certiorari, from the Latin *certiorari volumus*, meaning, "We wish to be informed." Most cases were dismissed by a clerk's written evaluation. Of those that survived a clerk's analysis, the Friday conference was crucial. Final decisions were made during it.

The nine justices gathered in a foyer off the main conference room where they engaged in the ceremonial act of helping each other on with their robes before shaking hands and entering the largest of four such conference rooms. Richly paneled in American quartered white oak, it contained a large conference table with a black leather inlay that was piled high with notebooks, memos and briefs. Poulson sat at the east end of the table, his customary place. Temple Conover, the senior associate justice, sat at the west end, again tradition. The junior associate justice, Morgan Childs, took his place nearest the door, where he would act as doorman and messenger, sending out for and receiving reference material.

"Good morning ladies and gentlemen," Poulson said. "The first matter we are to consider is . . ."

At ten minutes before ten there was a knock at the door. Poulson looked at the junior justice and raised his eyebrows. It was unheard of for anyone to intrude on the sanctity of the Friday conference. Temple Conover summed up everyone's feelings when he snapped, "Who the hell is that?"

"We'll see," Morgan Childs said.

The junior justice opened the door. Standing there was one of Conover's clerks, Laurie Rawls. "It had better be important," the Chief Justice said.

"It is, sir. It's . . ." She began to cry.

"What *is* it?" Poulson said, standing and going to the door.

"It's awful—"

"*What* is awful?" Poulson said. The eyes of the other justices were now on her.

"He's . . . oh, my God, he's dead . . ."

"Who's dead?" Childs put in quickly.

"Clarence . . ."

"Clarence Sutherland?"

"Yes . . . he's been . . ." And she broke down and collapsed against Poulson's chest.

He held her for a moment, then released her and moved into the hall, followed by the others. "Where is he?"

"In the Court."

Poulson briskly led the group down a broad hallway. They passed through the Great Hall's vast expanse of Alabama marble and rows of monolithic columns, collective footsteps ricocheting off the hard floor, black robes flowing behind them. A security guard snapped to attention. He'd never seen all nine of them walking as a group through a public area before.

They passed through huge double doors leading into the courtroom. The doors closed behind them with a heavy sigh. They rose and looked toward the bench, then tentatively moved up one of two interior aisles. There, seated in the Chief Justice's chair, was Clarence Sutherland. His head was cocked to one side, which caused wavy blond hair to droop in that direction. He appeared to be smiling, although it was more of a grimace. He was dressed in the same slate gray suit Poulson remembered him as having worn the previous day, green paisley tie neatly knotted against his Adam's apple, pale blue lisle button-down shirt curving to the contour of his vest. The only thing unusual was his forehead. In the center of it was a small, crusted hole from which blood had erupted over his right eye and down to his upper lip, where the beginnings of a moustache had trapped it and kept it from flowing further.

"He's dead," Morgan Childs said, stepping closer and craning his neck to get a better look.

"Murdered," Temple Conover said.

"In the Supreme Court," Chief Justice Jonathan Poulson added, like a judgment.

9

CHAPTER
3

LIEUTENANT MARTIN TELLER OF THE WASHINGTON MET-
ropolitan Police Department took a bite of prune Danish.
His phone hadn't stopped ringing since Clarence Sutherland's body was discovered. He'd just hung up on the head
of security for the Supreme Court, who had cleared him for
twenty-four-hour unlimited access to the court building until
the investigation was over. Now, he was talking to a reporter
from the Washington *Post*. "You know more than I do at
this stage," he said. "Yeah, that's right, it was a .22 and
he was sitting in the Chief Justice's chair when it happened.
Other than that . . . what? Who told you that? . . . Your sources
are privileged? Wonderful, so are mine. Sure, I'll get back
to you the minute we come up with something." How many
times over the years had he said *that*?

He hung up the phone and finished the Danish, washing it down with the cold remains of a container of coffee. He opened a file folder on his desk marked SUTHERLAND, C. HOMICIDE, and read the only two pieces of paper in it, then closed it and lighted a clove cigarette. He'd discovered cloves six months earlier while trying to quit smoking, his rationalization being that they tasted so bad he'd be reluctant to light one up. It hadn't worked. He was now a two-pack-a-day clove cigarette smoker.

The phone rang. "Detective Teller," he said.

"Good morning," a pleasant female voice said. "This is Susanna Pinscher at the Justice Department. I'm calling about the Sutherland matter."

"Matter?" he muttered to himself. At Justice even a murder was a legal "matter." "What can I do for you?"

"Well, I've been assigned to the case over here at Justice. I was told you'd be handling it at MPD and thought we should touch base."

Touch base...boy, she had all the lines. Still, it made sense. "Okay."

"Look, Lieutenant Teller, could we get together this afternoon? I'd like to set up a system to pool information."

"Do you have any?"

"Any what?"

"Information. I'm afraid I don't."

"Just background on the deceased, the circumstances of his being found, how he was killed."

"We're even."

Her sigh wasn't lost on him. He'd try to be more cooperative. "It's been a tough morning, Miss Pinscher. Sorry if I seem short. Sure, let's get together."

"How about three this afternoon?"

"No good for me. I'm interviewing Sutherland's family then." He silently debated it, then asked, "Want to come with me?"

"Well, I . . . yes, thank you, I appreciate the offer."

"I'll meet you in front of Sutherland's house at three. Know where it is?"

"I have the address. What kind of car should I look for?"

"Forget the car. You'll know me immediately."

"Really? How?"

"I'm the handsomest detective on the force, a cross between Paul Newman and Walter Matthau."

"And modest as all get out."

"Yeah, that's me. See you at three."

He hung up, stood, stretched and looked out his window over a blustery October Washington day. "Almost winter," he muttered as he rolled down his shirt sleeves. The right cuff flapped open. He'd noticed the missing button while dressing that morning but was running late. Besides, all his other shirts were missing buttons too. He slipped on his suit jacket and went to a small cracked mirror hanging crookedly near the door. Some days he felt younger than his forty-six years, but this wasn't one of them. His reflection in the cracked glass didn't help. He'd put on weight and was developing jowls beneath prominent pink cheeks. Loss of thin, brown, straight hair had advanced enough to cause him to start parting it lower so that the long strands could be combed up over the balding spot. "Moonface," he'd been called in high school. He smiled as he turned to retrieve the Sutherland folder from his desk. No matter what age had done to him, he looked better now than when he was in high school. At least the acne was gone.

Five minutes later he was seated around a small, scarred conference table with his superior, Dorian Mars, four years younger and possessing a master's degree in criminology and a Ph.D. in psychology. Also at the table were four other detectives assigned to the Sutherland case.

"This is the most important case in my career in law enforcement," Mars said, puffing on a pipe. He looked at

Teller. "It'll be a pressure cooker until it's solved, Martin. They're already talking bottom line. Which means our collective neck if we don't handle things well..."

Teller nodded solemnly and adjusted the buttonless cuff beneath his jacket sleeve. He opened the Sutherland folder and said, "We'll stay in the kitchen, Dorian, no matter how hot it gets," wishing he was able to curb a recent tendency to mimic his boss's penchant for the well-worn phrase.

HE WAS late getting to the Sutherland house, a huge and sprawling white stucco and red brick home set back on four acres in Chevy Chase. The original house had reflected the federal style of architecture popular during its construction in 1810. Numerous additions and wings had transformed it into a more eclectic dwelling.

Parked in front of a long, winding driveway was an MPD squad car. Two uniformed officers stood next to it. Another car was parked twenty feet further up the road. Teller pulled his unmarked blue Buick Regal behind the second vehicle. The door opened and Susanna Pinscher stepped out, a nicely turned pair of legs leading the way. Teller was immediately aware of her beauty. He judged her to be about five feet four inches tall but she carried herself taller. Clean, thick, black, gently wavy hair with errant single strands of gray fluttered in the breeze. Her face was definite and strong, each individual component prominent yet in sync with the others. She was fair, with full, sensuous lips etched in red, large expressive green eyes defined by an appropriate amount of mascara, rouge so expertly applied to her cheeks that the color seemed to emanate from within.

She extended her hand and smiled. He took it and said, "Sorry I'm late."

"It's okay. I just got here. You are Martin Teller?"

"You didn't know me right off?"

13

She cocked her head and narrowed her eyes. "Definitely Paul Newman. I don't see the Matthau, though."

"I think we can work together, Miss Pinscher. Come on."

They walked up the driveway. He allowed her to get ahead of him and took in her figure. A subtle pleated plaid skirt swung easily from her hips. She wore a blue blazer over a white blouse. She suddenly stopped, looked over her shoulder and asked, "Coming?"

"I'm with you." So far.

They told a uniformed black maid who they were, and she asked them to wait in the foyer. Teller looked around and whistled softly. "It's bigger than my whole apartment."

"He's a successful psychiatrist," Susanna said.

"There are poor ones?"

The maid returned and led them across a vast expanse of study and through another door, then along a corridor until reaching a separate wing. She knocked on heavy sliding doors. They opened and the maid stepped back to allow them to enter.

"Good morning, I'm Vera Jones, Dr. Sutherland's secretary. I hope you don't mind waiting. This dreadful thing has taken a toll on everyone, especially the immediate family."

"Of course," Susanna said.

The patient-reception area, which was also her office, was decorated in subtle earth tones, spacious and strikingly neat. Two sharpened pencils were lined up perfectly parallel to each other on top of a yellow legal pad on her polished desk. A large leather appointment book was squared with the corner of the desk.

Everything in order, like the woman, Teller told himself.

Vera Jones appeared the last word in a dedicated, organized secretary. Fortyish, tall and slender, her clothing was like her hair, matter-of-fact, nondescript, functional and not likely to detract from whatever business was at hand. She held herself erect and moved through the office like a blind person who knows her surroundings so intimately that a stranger would assume she was sighted. Her face was a series of sharp angles. Her mouth, wide and thin, was undoubtedly capable of being drawn even thinner under pressure.

Still, Teller thought, this could well be a sensuous woman. He'd come to the conclusion after his divorce that sexuality had nothing to do with sexiness. The overtly sexual female wearing provocative clothing, flirting, leading conversations into sexual innuendo was likely to be deceptive. He'd come to appreciate and trust subtlety, respond to it. He glanced at Susanna, who'd taken a leather wing chair next to Vera's desk, and wondered at her style.

Vera sat behind her desk and checked the pencils' alignment. She sighed; her breasts rose beneath a forest green sweater. Teller noticed their fullness. He took a matching chair across from Susanna and asked, "How long have you worked for Dr. Sutherland, Miss Jones?"

The turn of her head was abrupt, as though the question had startled her. "Twenty-two years," she said.

"That's a long time."

"Yes, it is." She paused, looked down at the desk top. "Is there any possibility of postponing this interview?"

"Why?" Teller asked.

"It seems so . . . so unnecessary considering the personal tragedy the family must face. The boy hasn't even been buried yet."

"That's tomorrow, isn't it?"

"Yes."

Teller looked at Susanna before saying, "I don't like it either, Miss Jones, but I don't make the rules."

A faint light came to life on a compact telephone console

15

on her desk, accompanied by a gentle bell. "Excuse me," she said. She got up and disappeared through a door.

"What do you know about him?" Teller asked Susanna.

"The doctor? Probably the most famous psychiatrist in Washington, confidant to the rich and powerful, a special advisor to the former administration on mental health issues, very rich and powerful, a world figure in his profession."

"What about his kid?"

"Clarence? Very little except that he's dead, murdered in the Supreme Court, of all places. He graduated from law school with honors and probably had a prestigious law career ahead of him."

"What else?"

She shrugged.

"I understand he was considered one of Washington's most eligible bachelors."

"That's natural in a city with more women than men."

Vera returned and said in a soft voice, "Dr. Sutherland will see you now."

His office was surprisingly small, considering the dimensions of the rest of the house. A glass coffee table in front of a beige couch served as his desk. Two orange club chairs faced the table. A comfortable brown leather recliner was in front of a draped window immediately to the couch's left. On the wall behind the club chairs was an ornate dark leather couch, its headrest curving up like a swan's neck.

"A relic," Dr. Sutherland said coldly from behind the glass table as he noticed Teller's interest in the couch. He hadn't stood when they'd entered.

Teller smiled. "You don't use it?"

"Seldom, only when a patient insists. Most don't. Please sit down. *You* can use that couch if you'd like."

Teller looked at the leather couch, turned to Sutherland and said, "Thanks, I think I will." He sat on it and extended a leg along its length. Susanna sat in one of the club chairs.

16

Dr. Sutherland leaned back on his couch and took in his visitors with restless eyes beneath bushy salt-and-pepper eyebrows. He had a full head of white hair that threatened to erupt any moment into disarray. He was deeply tanned —sunlamp or Caribbean vacations? Teller wondered. His dress was studied casualness, sharply creased twill riding pants, boots shined to a mirror finish, a blue button-down shirt and pale yellow cardigan sweater. He evidently was aware that he was being scrutinized because he said, "I've canceled all professional obligations since this tragedy with my son."

"Of course," Susanna said.

"My condolences," Teller said.

"Thank you."

"It was good of you to see us," Susanna said.

"I didn't expect both of you. Mr. Teller had made the appointment. Might I ask what official connection you have in this matter?"

"Oh, I'm sorry. I'm Susanna Pinscher. I'm with the Justice Department. Naturally, when something of this magnitude occurs, we're brought into it."

"The world is brought into it," he said, removing glasses that changed tint with the light, and rubbing his eyes. "Have either of you ever lost a child?" he asked.

"No," Teller said. "It must be tough. I have a couple of kids . . ."

Sutherland replaced his glasses on his nose and looked at Susanna. "Do you have children, Mrs. Pinscher?"

"Miss Pinscher. Yes, I have three. They live with my former husband."

"Very modern."

"It was best for both of us."

"Undoubtedly. It's a trend."

"Pardon?"

17

"Children being with the male partner. Biology has taken second place to social . . . progress."

Teller knew the tenor of the conversation was making Susanna uncomfortable. He sat up and said, "This is just the beginning, Dr. Sutherland. Nobody likes probing into a family in times of tragedy, but that's what's going to be happening until we get to the bottom line."

"Bottom line?"

"A cliché. I work for someone who uses those terms. Look, I'm not sure there's a hell of a lot to discuss today. It was important that we make contact because—"

"Because along with many other people, I am a suspect in my son's murder."

Teller nodded.

"I understand that, Mr. Teller."

"How about Mrs. Sutherland? Will she understand it?"

"To the extent she needs to. I didn't kill my son."

"I don't doubt it. Who else is in the family?"

"My daughter. She's in California working on her doctorate in English literature."

Teller asked, "Will she be here for the funeral?"

"There are some logistical problems with that, Mr. Teller." Sutherland stood and his height surprised his visitors. His posture on the couch indicated a shorter man, but he'd unraveled himself into over six feet. He extended his hand and said, "You will excuse me."

Teller asked as he shook hands, "What about Mrs. Sutherland, doctor? When can we see her?"

"Obviously not for quite a while. She's under heavy sedation. Perhaps later in the week."

"Of course," Teller said. "Well, thanks for your time. We'll be in touch."

"I suppose you will." He left through a door to the rear of his office.

18

Teller and Susanna went to where Vera Jones sat ramrod straight behind her desk, her hands crossed on the legal pad.

"Thank you for your time," Susanna said as she headed for the sliding doors.

Teller didn't follow her. He walked to a row of built-in bookcases and perused the books. "Has he read all of these?" he asked.

"I would imagine so," Vera said.

"I have a lot of respect for doctors, especially ones with Dr. Sutherland's reputation." He openly admired a large landscape that hung behind her. "That's a Sutherland, isn't it?" he asked.

"Yes."

"Graham Sutherland. I always liked his landscapes better than his etchings. Any relation to the family?"

"Distant." She led them to an outside door used by patients.

"Thanks for your time, Miss Jones," Teller said. "By the way, where were you the night Clarence was murdered?"

"Here with Dr. Sutherland. We were working on a paper he'd written for a psychiatric journal . . . he's widely published."

"I'm sure he is. Have a nice day."

Teller escorted Susanna to her car. Before getting in she looked back at the house, bit her lip and said, "Strange."

"Did you ever know a shrink who wasn't?"

"It's her. She bothers me. I feel sorry for her."

"Why?"

"I don't know, a type, a sadness in her eyes."

"I know what you mean. Say, how are you fixed for dinner tonight?"

He couldn't tell whether she legitimately wasn't sure of her plans or was groping for an excuse. She said, "I'm busy."

"Well, maybe another time. Let's keep in touch."

He watched her drive away, then drove back to MPD headquarters. At six he went to his apartment in Georgetown, where he fed his two cats, a male named Beauty, a female named the Beast, put a TV dinner in the oven and settled into his favorite reclining chair. Two paperback books were on a table next to him, a historical novel by Stephanie Blake and a collection of Camus's writings. He chose Camus, promptly fell asleep and awoke only when the odor of a charred TV dinner was strong enough to get through to him.

ACROSS TOWN in a large and tastefully decorated cooperative apartment, Susanna Pinscher said into the telephone in her bedroom, "I love you, too, honey. I'll see you this weekend. Okay. Pleasant dreams. Let me speak to daddy."

Her former husband came on the line. Their three children lived with him by mutual agreement, although Susanna visited freely and had taken them for the entire previous summer. The decision to give her husband custody had been a wrenching one but was, she continued to tell herself, the right one.

"Everything okay?" she asked.

"No problems. How about you?"

"Exhausted. They've assigned me to the Sutherland case."

"A biggie. That's all everyone talks about these days."

"I don't wonder. Murder in the Supreme Court. A first."

"Take care of yourself, Susanna. You'll be out this weekend?"

"Yes. Good night."

She prowled through the apartment, ending up in the kitchen, where she made herself an English muffin and coffee. She hadn't had dinner, had come straight home from the office, her briefcase bulging. She'd changed into a nightgown and robe and read until calling the kids.

She finished the muffin and went to the bedroom, where

she took an art book from a shelf. She climbed into bed and found an entry on the British artist Graham Sutherland. She read it, closed the book and turned out the light, wondering as she did why a detective from the MPD would know anything about a relatively obscure British artist.

What was law and order coming to?...

CHAPTER
4

SUPREME COURT JUSTICE TEMPLE CONOVER SAT IN THE sunny breakfast room of his home in Bethesda. He wore a pale blue flannel robe, blue terry-cloth slippers and a red wool scarf around his neck. Next to him was an aluminum Canadian crutch he'd used since his last stroke. The final draft of an article he'd written for *Harper's* magazine on the growing perils of censorship was on a place mat.

A grandfather clock in the dining room chimed out the time, 7:00 A.M. Conover poured what was left of coffee made for him by the housekeeper and looked out a window over formal Japanese gardens, a gift to his second wife, who was Japanese.

"Good morning, Temp," his current wife said from the doorway. Long blond hair flowed down over the shoulders of a delicate pink dressing gown secured at the waist by two buttons. A childlike, oval face was puffy with sleep. She leaned against the open archway, the toes of one foot curled over the top of the other, the bottom of the robe gaping open and revealing smooth white thighs.

"Hello, Cecily," Conover said. "Do you want coffee?"

She came to the table, saw that the glass carafe was empty. "I'll get more."

"Call Carla."

"I'd rather get it myself."

She returned ten minutes later with a fresh carafe, poured herself a cup and sat across from him, one shapely leg dangling over the other. He coughed. "How do you feel this morning?" she asked.

"Well. The article is finished." He slid it across the table. She glanced down at it, then sipped from her cup.

"How was the concert?" he asked.

"Boring."

"Where did you go after?"

"To Peggy's house for a nightcap."

"More than one. You didn't come home until almost two."

"We talked. Okay?"

"You might have called." He started coughing again. His eyes teared up and he gulped water. She started toward him but he waved her away. When he stopped coughing he asked, "Why didn't you call? I worry, you know."

"I didn't want to wake you."

"Who was there?"

"The usual group. Temp, I'm tired of the questions, of the suspicion every time I go out."

"Is it so without cause, Cecily?"

She exhaled a burst of air and returned her cup to the table with enough force to send its contents slopping over

23

the rim. "*Please* don't start on that again. One single incident doesn't—"

She was interrupted by the self-conscious clearing of a male throat. Standing in the doorway was a tall dark man of about thirty whose name was Karl. He wore tight jeans and a gray tee shirt stretched by heavily muscled arms and shoulders. A helmet of black curls surrounded a face full of thick features, heavy eyelids, a full sensuous mouth and a nose worthy of a prizefighter. He'd been hired six months earlier as a general handyman, gardener, and occasional chauffeur to Justice Conover. He lived in one of three garage apartments at the rear of the property.

"Sorry to barge in," he said with a trace of a German accent, "but I wondered if you needed me today to drive. You said yesterday that the Court limo might not be available."

Temple looked at the young man, whose attention was fixed on Cecily. "In an hour," he said. "I'll be ready in an hour."

"Yes, sir." Karl vanished from the doorway.

"What happened to your Court limo, Temp?"

"Maintenance, I think, or being used for the funeral."

"You're not going?" she asked.

"Of course not."

"You should. He was chief clerk."

He tried to control the trembling in his right arm but couldn't, and it quickly spread throughout his body. The crutch crashed to the floor and his hand hit the carafe.

"Are you all right, Temp?"

"Look at you."

"What do you mean?"

"Can't you at least have the decency to cover up when a man enters the room?"

She looked down, then up at him. "I'm wearing a *robe*, for God's sake."

24

"It has snaps, why don't you use them—?"

"This is ridiculous," she said as she pulled the hem of the robe over her bare legs and tugged the upper portion of it across her chest. "Excuse me, I have to get dressed for the funeral."

He placed the palms of his hands on the table and slowly pushed himself to his feet. She came around, picked up his crutch and handed it to him.

"Why do you have to go to that bastard's funeral, Cecily?"

"Because I think it's right—"

"Sutherland was a disgusting—"

"I don't want to discuss it, Temp." She left the room. He followed, his steps slow, labored, the rubber-tipped crutch preceding his right leg as he dragged it across the floor. He reached her bedroom, opened the door and said, "You insult me by going to Sutherland's funeral."

She tossed her robe on the bed and entered her private bathroom.

"You slut," he said just loud enough for her to hear.

She'd been leaning over the sink and peering at herself in the mirror. She straightened, turned and said, "And you, Mr. Justice, have the gall to talk about insulting someone?"

He tottered and grabbed the door for support. The trembling increased. It appeared he would topple over at any moment. She ran across the room and gripped his arm.

"Don't touch me," he said in a strong voice. She stepped back. He raised the crutch as though to strike her, lowered it. "All right, damn you, go to his funeral, Cecily, and *celebrate* his death for me."

CHAPTER
5

THE EPISCOPAL PRIEST CONDUCTING THE GRAVESIDE SER-
vice for Clarence Sutherland glanced at the thirty people
who'd come to pay their final respects. Clarence's mother
was near collapse and leaned against her husband. Their
daughter, Jill, who'd arrived on an overnight flight from
California, stood with her arm about her mother's shoulders.

A delegation from the Supreme Court headed by Associate Justice Morgan Childs stood together. Childs looked
up into an angry gray sky and blinked as the first drops of
rain fell. Next to him was Clarence's clerk colleague, Laurie
Rawls, who was crying.

Martin Teller turned up the collar of a Burberry trench-
coat. He'd awakened with the beginnings of a head cold.
He glanced at Dr. Sutherland's secretary, Vera Jones, who

stood behind the Sutherland family. She was the only person there, he realized, who'd dressed appropriately for the weather, right down to ankle-length Totes covering her shoes.

The corpulent, ruddy-faced priest still seemed to be catching his breath after the walk from the limousine. He looked down at *The Book of Common Prayer* he held in his beefy hands. *"Unto Almighty God we commend the soul of our brother departed, Clarence, and we commit his body to the ground . . ."*

Dr. Sutherland stepped forward, scooped up a handful of soil and sprinkled it over the coffin as cemetery workmen lowered it on straps. The rain fell harder and the priest held a hand over his head. He spoke faster.

Teller sneezed loudly, momentarily distracting attention from the grave site of three security men assigned by the Treasury Department to Justice Childs.

"The Lord be with you," said the priest.
"And with thy spirit," a few responded.
"Let us pray. Lord have mercy upon us."
"Christ have mercy upon us," was the reply.
"Lord have mercy upon us."

Teller watched the mourners return to their limousines. When they were gone, he approached the grave and looked down at the coffin. Who did you in, kid?

"Everybody has to leave," a workman said.

"Oh, yeah, right. Sorry."

There were several phone messages waiting for him when he returned to MPD headquarters, including one from Susanna Pinscher. He called her first.

"You were at the funeral?" she asked.

"Yeah. Very touching. And wet. I caught cold."

"So fast?"

"If it gets serious I can claim workman's comp. You know, Miss Pinscher, I was thinking about you last night."

"You were?" Her voice had a smile in it.

"Yes, I was. I finally figured out who you look like."

"And?"

"Candice Bergen."

"That's very flattering coming from Paul Newman."

"Definitely Candy Bergen."

"Do you always decide who people look like?"

"It's a hobby. How about dinner this week?"

"It might be hard. I—"

"To discuss the case. I have some thoughts."

"I'd like to hear them. Tell you what, Detective Teller, let's make it Saturday night. I have an appointment Saturday morning with Justice Childs. I might also be speaking with some of the other justices during the week. I'll be able to fill you in on those interviews."

"Sold. I'll pick you up at seven. Where do you live?"

There was a long pause. "Do you like Indian food?" she asked.

"No."

"How about Hungarian?"

"Of course I like Hungarian food, as long as I don't have to steal the chicken. I am Hungarian, at least half of me. My mother was a stoic Swede."

"Well, I have a favorite Hungarian restaurant, Csiko's, on Connecticut Avenue, Northwest. It's in the Broadmoor Apartment Building. How about meeting there at seven? I'll make a reservation."

"See you then, but give me a call if anything breaks sooner."

"I will. Talk to you soon."

It was true that Martin Teller was part Hungarian. It was

not true that he liked Hungarian food, especially goulash, or anything with paprika in it. As far as he was concerned, cooking Hungarian food for his father, and having to eat it, had sent his Nordic mother to an early grave.

CHAPTER
6

"WHAT ABOUT SUTHERLAND'S FRIENDS? HAVE THEY BEEN contacted?" Dorian Mars asked Teller.

"We're doing it now," Teller said.

"Not fast enough. The commissioner called. He's up in arms."

You sure turn a phrase, Dorian. Well, not to be out-done... "What does he expect, miracles?" Teller lighted a clove.

"I wish you wouldn't smoke those things in here, Marty. They're offensive."

"Not to me."

"Please."

"Okay." He carefully extinguished it, saving its expensive remains.

"Let's go over it," Mars said. "Everybody in the Court has been interviewed?"

Teller shook his head and eyed the cold cigarette. "Of course not, Dorian. Setting up interviews with people in the Supreme Court takes time."

"I understand that. What about the family?"

"Still working on it. The father, the shrink, is sort of impressive, strange but sure of himself, arrogant as hell, dresses good. The sister is getting her Ph.D. in California."

"California what? California politics, California geography?"

"California, Dorian. That's where she goes to school. She's studying literature."

"Classical? English?"

"Hungarian."

"A Ph.D. in Hungarian literature?"

"Something like that. I haven't met the deceased's mother yet."

"Why? Procrastination is the thief of time."

"Because her only son has been shot dead in the Supreme Court, which tends to give a mother headaches."

"Talk to her. Talk to anybody, but get something going fast. I'm under a hell of a lot of pressure from up top."

"I understand," Teller said.

"Are you coordinating with Justice?"

"Sure. We're in touch every day."

"Good. Marty, give me a gut feeling about this case. Who do you think?"

Teller shrugged. "It's wide open. I wish I had even a solid hunch to give you, but I don't. The only thing I will say is that it might be a woman."

"Why?"

"His life-style. The kid was handsome, smart, a dedicated swinger, broads all over the place, probably lots of them mad at him. I'm going over after this meeting to check out his bachelor pad in Georgetown. I had it sealed off the minute we heard he was dead."

"A woman, huh?"

"Maybe, maybe not. Sometimes it makes sense to me, but then it comes off too much like a dime novel, a woman coming into the Supreme Court in the middle of the night and putting a bullet in his head while he sits in the Chief Justice's chair. When I look at it that way, I end up leaning toward somebody who works in the Court. His coworkers didn't like him much, either."

"Why?"

"Power. He was on a power trip, from what I hear. Maybe he caught a justice in the john doing something he shouldn't be doing and held it over his head, if you'll pardon the visual.

"Don't be ridiculous."

"It's not ridiculous. Supreme Court justices are human, just like you and me. They go to the bathroom and—"

"I know, I know. Let's get back to family and friends. The father, you say he's strange. Is he strange enough to have killed his own son? And if so, why?"

Teller picked up his cigarette from the ashtray and put it between his lips.

"Don't, Marty."

"I won't light it. The father? What father kills his only son?"

"It happens. Life's a stage, and we're all players on it."

"You're so right, boss . . . Look, Dorian, too many could have killed Clarence Sutherland. There seem to be as many motives as there are alibis. I'll keep plugging. By the way, I ordered a wall chart for my office."

"A chart?"

"Yeah, a flow chart, it's called. I was getting confused with the Sutherland case so I thought I'd put it all on a chart. This chart has arrows and stars and even glitter letters to highlight things. It might not mean much to you but I wanted it. It was cheap."

"How cheap?"

"A hundred. I billed the Sutherland case number."

"A hundred?" Mars sighed. "I wish you'd cleared it with me first."

"Sorry."

"I'll approve it. I'll approve anything to see things move."

"Things'll move, believe me, Dorian."

"I want to meet every morning here at nine until the Sutherland case is wrapped up."

"Sure, bank on it, Dorian. Nine, right here, every morning."

"Good."

TELLER DROVE to Clarence Sutherland's Georgetown town house. A uniformed patrolman stood in front. Yellow tape had been strung across the entrance, and a sign on the door read NO ENTRANCE.

"How's things?" Teller asked the patrolman.

"Not bad, Lieutenant. How's with you?"

"Not bad. Anybody been around?"

"People from your division, that's about it. Say, Lieutenant Teller, if you're planning to be here for a little bit, how about letting me go for coffee?"

"Sure. Make it a half-hour. That's all the time I've got."

He entered a small foyer. To the left was a door leading to Sutherland's apartment. A staircase to the right led to another apartment upstairs. Teller fished out a key, opened Clarence's door and stepped inside.

The living room was large, lavishly decorated. A conversation pit formed by persimmon couches dominated the room. A large projection screen hovered over everything. Teller went to it and saw that it was linked to an elaborate television system that included a videotape recorder. Next to it was a long bookcase on which dozens of videotape cartridges were neatly stacked.

He went to the bedroom. It was the same size as the living room. A circular king-sized bed was made to appear even larger by a mirror that spanned the wall behind it. There was a television projection screen in that room too, as well as an expensive stereo system within arm's reach of the bed.

"What the hell is that?" he asked himself as he approached a panel of buttons and dials next to the bed. He pressed one button, and a small chandelier made of tiny pieces of mirror rotated above the bed. He turned one of the dials. A magenta spotlight came on. It was aimed at the chandelier, and its beam flashed off the mirror chips, creating a mosaic of twinkling light in every corner of the room.

"Lord," Teller muttered as he played with the other dials and knobs. Soon, he had the room spinning in multicolored light, reds and blues, even a strobe effect that caught everything, including the hand he injected into its field, in stop-motion.

He shut off the lights and opened a drawer in a table next to the bed. He didn't expect to find much. The initial search of the apartment had turned up an array of so-called recreational drugs, nothing of the hard variety but enough to send the kid to jail had it gone that way. A telephone book had been taken from the apartment and delivered to Teller at headquarters. He'd turned it over to another detective with instructions to contact every person listed in it.

He picked up the only item in the drawer, a diary of sorts. In it were dates and names, first names only, with initials following. What intrigued him were symbols next to each name. They'd been carefully drawn with a variety of colored pens, stars and circles, exclamation points, question marks, and an occasional "Dynamite...Dull...Promising..."

"A busy boy," Teller muttered to himself as he put the book in his raincoat pocket. In the good old days he'd have been called a cad.

He looked about the rest of the apartment, then returned to the living room, where he took a closer look at the videotapes on the bookcase. There were a few old movies, but most of them were disgusting corn porn. The label on a homegrown one read CINDY AND ME, APRIL. Touching stuff.

"Excuse me," a voice said from the front door that Teller had failed to close behind him.

"Yeah?"

"Are you a detective?"

"Who are you?"

"Wally Plum. I live upstairs."

"What can I do for you?"

"You can call off those goons outside. I live here, and I resent being stopped every time I come home."

"Oh, I'm sorry. They let you in, don't they?"

"That isn't the point."

Teller took a closer look at Wally Plum. He was thin and what was called good-looking, like many other young men around Washington. His features were angular, his skin surprisingly dark considering his blond hair and eyebrows. He'd begun balding prematurely; his hair was carefully arranged to maximize what he had. He wore a too-tight doublebreasted charcoal gray suit, and a blue shirt with a white collar that was pinched together by a thin gold bar beneath a solid maroon tie.

"Mr. Plum," Teller said, "I'm sorry for any inconvenience, but a murder has been committed—"

"I know that. Clarence was my friend."

"Yeah? How close were you?"

35

Plum laughed. "If I tell you, will that make me a suspect?"

"Could be."

"We were good friends. I rented my apartment from him."

"He owned this place?"

"Yes."

"Not bad on a law clerk's salary."

"He had help."

"Family?"

"Yes."

"Nice apartment. I was noticing his collection of tapes."

Another laugh. "He had some good stuff."

"What about this one?" He pulled CINDY AND ME, APRIL, from the shelf and handed it to Plum.

"Oh, that. We used to kid around sometimes."

"What'd you do, take movies of yourselves?"

"Sure."

Teller took the cartridge from Plum and returned it to the shelf. "The bedroom," he said. "It looks like a setup."

"It worked well for Clarence."

Teller shook his head and crossed the living room to the couch. He pushed on a cushion with his fingertips, then sat on it. "You know, Mr. Plum, I do believe the world has passed me by."

"How so?"

"All this sort of stuff. I don't understand any of it."

"Generation gap. Things change."

"I know." He lit a cigarette. "I have two daughters, and most of their talk is all Greek to me. Well, so long as you're here, tell me about Clarence Sutherland."

Plum sat in a chair near the door, crossed his legs. "What would you like to know?"

"Anything you can tell me. Start with what he especially liked to do."

36

"You've seen the apartment."

"I mean besides that."

"There was nothing besides that."

"Come on, he must have had hobbies, interests aside from chasing girls. Where did he like to hang out?"

"A lot of places."

"Did you hang around with him in those places? Were you drinking buddies?"

"Clarence didn't drink, maybe an occasional glass of wine."

"Drugs?"

"No."

"They found lots here in the apartment."

"I wouldn't know about that."

"I wish you did. I might be more inclined to cross you off as a potential suspect." And if he believed that, he'd believe in the tooth fairy. Hell, maybe Mr. Plum did...

Plum raised his eyebrows. "Oh, that's the way it is. Did Clarence use drugs? No, just soft stuff that everybody's into—"

"Like what? Pot?"

"Yes."

"Coke?"

"Once in a while. You *drink*. There's that generation gap again."

"I'm not in the mood to debate it with you," Teller said.

"Good. Anything else I can tell you about Clarence?"

"Other friends. Who'd he hang out with besides you?"

"We didn't hang out, Lieutenant."

"Whatever you want to call it."

"Clarence had many friends. Despite his prestigious family his friends included many sorts. Sometimes he enjoyed the low life. Clarence liked to get involved with strange types."

"Give me some of them."

37

"Names?"

"If you know them."

"I don't remember names. There were parties. He'd invite them, or meet them in a bar and—"

"Male, female?"

"Mostly female."

"Mostly? Was he—?"

"Gay? No. Bisexual? No. Clarence was straight."

"But sort of kinky."

"Depends on your point of view. Look, Lieutenant, Clarence in *my* view was a normal, healthy American male, having a good time before it was time to settle down."

"Did he have a steady girl friend? Somebody he saw regularly. Was he, forgive the expression, in love with anybody?"

"Not that I know of."

"Do you know any woman who might have wanted to take a shot at him?"

"No."

"Do you know any women who were in love with him?"

"Sure, a few. Clarence had charm to burn."

"Name one."

"Laurie Rawls."

"From the Court?"

"Right. She drove him crazy, calling at odd hours, showing up when he was with somebody else and making scenes. That lady has a problem. She played the game, but deep down all she wanted was to have a brood of kids and keep the apple pies coming out of the oven."

"Sounds like a nice girl."

"If you're into that."

"Clarence wasn't, I take it."

"You take it right. I already told you—"

"What else can you tell me?"

"Nothing really. Sometimes he saw older women. It's a

trend. Older women are into younger men these days. It makes them feel young."

"I'd think it'd make them feel older."

"Doesn't seem to work that way. At any rate, he saw a few from time to time."

"Names."

"Don't know them. Sorry."

Teller stood and took another look around the room. "Well, Mr. Plum, thanks for your time and talk. Very enlightening."

"My pleasure. You will talk to the men outside."

"Sure. By the way, they're not goons. They're police officers doing their job. End of speech."

"Don't take offense, it was just a phrase."

"Yeah, I know. By the way, what were you doing the night Clarence was killed?"

"I was in bed."

"Alone?"

"Of course not."

"An older woman? Sorry . . ."

"I'm not sure *how* old she was."

"Do you remember her name?"

"I . . . frankly I'm not sure . . . do you really have to know?"

"Not if you don't. Thanks again."

TELLER STAYED in his office until seven, then went home, where he put a frozen dinner in the oven and played a recording of *Der Rosenkavalier*. As waltz melodies drifted from his speakers he danced across the living room with an imaginary partner, who of course was Susanna Pinscher. "You look lovely tonight, my dear." She looked up into his eyes. "And you are the most attractive man I've ever known—"

Beast, his female cat, startled by a sound from outside, leaped from the couch and landed on the turntable. The needle dug into the vinyl record as it skated across the grooves, sending a cacophony of scratch and hiss into the room.

"Damn you," Teller yelled at her. She escaped the swing of his hand and scurried beneath a chair. He took a bottle of gin from the kitchen, poured himself a drink, sat in his recliner and offered a toast to the empty center of the room. "Here's to you, Miss Pinscher, wherever you are, and to you, Clarence Sutherland, whoever you were." He downed half the contents of his glass and added, "Generation gap, my ass."

CHAPTER
7

DAWN BROKE CRISP AND CLEAR THE FOLLOWING SATUR-
day. Susanna was up early. She did twenty minutes of
exercises, took a hot shower with the adjustable shower
head set at maximum pulsating pressure, dressed in a taupe
wool gabardine jumpsuit over a claret turtleneck sweater,
slipped into a pair of boots and got her car from the garage.
She had plenty of time to make her appointment with Justice
Childs, so she stopped in a neighborhood luncheonette,
bought the Washington *Post* and read it over coffee and
honeydew melon.

A half-hour later she exited the George Washington Memorial Highway at a sign that read NATIONAL AIRPORT
and found a road leading to the general aviation section of
that complex.

Morgan Childs's aviation background was well known to millions of Americans, and Susanna had boned up on the media reports that had created such public awareness. Childs was the most public of the nine Supreme Court justices. He'd been a combat ace in Korea, had been shot down and captured, escaping after six months of captivity. The dramatic details of his escape and subsequent heroism had captured the media's and public's attention. His picture had been on the cover of *Time*. Television crews followed him throughout Korea, sending back vivid images of that war's reigning hero. He'd returned to the United States much decorated, admired and in demand as a speaker and talk show guest. Eventually, public interest waned and he resumed private life as an attorney, then became a district court judge and, finally, was appointed to the highest court of the land, the youngest person ever to receive such an honor.

Susanna parked in a visitor's area and walked along a row of small aircraft. At the end was a hangar. Its door was open and she went inside. A young man in a three-piece suit stepped out of interior shadows and asked politely, "May I help you, ma'am?"

Her initial reaction was to question his authority but she reasoned that Justice Childs had probably been assigned security and that the young man represented it. "I'm Susanna Pinscher, I have an appointment with Justice Childs."

"Oh, yes, Miss Pinscher, the justice told me you'd be coming."

She looked in the direction of his finger. In a corner of the hangar and wearing olive green coveralls was Morgan Childs. His head and shoulders were lost inside the engine cowling of a 1964 vintage, fabric-covered, single-engine Piper Colt. He heard her approach, straightened up and smiled, which lit up a square, tanned, and rugged face. "Hi," he said. "I'd shake hands but no sense in two of us being covered with grease." His hands were black, and one cheek was smeared.

Susanna smiled. "You do your own repairs?"

"That's right. I always packed my own chute too. Besides, I like tinkering with this animal."

She touched the fabric on a wing. "It's yours?"

"Yes. I've had it a long time. I hope you don't mind meeting me out here, Miss Pinscher. I thought it would be less hectic and more private than the Court. Excuse me. I don't want to forget to replace this." He leaned into the engine and tightened something with a torque wrench.

Susanna leaned closer and watched him work. His fingers were thick and blunt, a workingman's hands. Like her father, she thought. She then realized how much Childs and her father had in common. Both had gray crewcuts, an anachronism. Her father, who'd retired to St. Helena, California, in the wine country north of San Francisco, had been an airline pilot with Pan Am for years. He too liked tinkering with mechanical things; nothing was beyond his ability to fix.

Childs straightened up, leaned against the plane and wiped his hands on a greasy rag. "Well, Miss Pinscher, let's talk. What do I know about Clarence Sutherland's murder? Not nearly as much as you do, I'm sure. I was with the other justices when the body was discovered, had the same shocked reaction, couldn't believe that not only had a Supreme Court clerk been murdered, but that he was sitting in the Chief Justice's chair, in the courtroom, when it happened."

"I would assume shock is an understatement."

"Yes, I suppose it is. I represented the other justices at his funeral."

"I read that and wondered why they all didn't attend."

"Too much pressing business in the Court."

She hesitated, then asked, "Were any of the justices . . . well, how shall I say it? . . . Were any of them . . ."

"Unwilling to attend the funeral because of animosity toward Sutherland? I doubt it."

"Why were you chosen, Justice Childs? Were you and Clarence Sutherland particularly close? I know he clerked for Chief Justice Poulson."

Childs shrugged and tossed the rag on a tool-laden table next to him. "R.H.I.P., Miss Pinscher."

"R.H.I.P?"

"Rank Has Its Privilege. I'm the junior justice. They asked for a volunteer and chose me."

"Like the military."

"Exactly."

"What about Clarence?" she asked. "I'm trying to piece together some sort of picture of him."

"Clarence Sutherland? Well, drawing an accurate picture of him isn't so easy. He was a rather enigmatic young man." A strong gust of chilled October air whistled through the open hangar doors and blew a set of engine specs for the Colt from the table to the floor. Childs picked them up, folded them carefully and put them into his coverall pocket. He looked toward the open hangar door and said, "I'd intended to get in an hour of flying this morning, Miss Pinscher. I'm afraid that's all the time I have, another hour. How about continuing this discussion up in the air?"

"In that?" she asked, pointing to the Colt.

"Yes. It's a fine airplane, stable, airworthy. Up to you."

"I'd love it . . . I think . . ."

They flew north at seven thousand feet. Childs talked a good deal about the aircraft—it had a Lycoming engine, a cruising range of 325 miles, a top speed of 120 mph and a service ceiling of twelve thousand feet.

Susanna had taken flying lessons years earlier but had stopped short of receiving her license. Flying with Childs brought back all the memories of those days, the intense feeling of freedom from earth's bonds, the exhilaration . . . She looked down at houses that seemed plastic symbols on a Monopoly board, tiny automobiles following slotted highways, racetracks that would fit into the palm of her hand.

"Enjoying it?" Childs asked.

"Very much," she said over the roar of the Lycoming.

"I'm happiest up here, Miss Pinscher. Things up here make more sense."

"I understand, but I have to make sense out of Clarence Sutherland's death."

"Of course. Fire away."

"Who didn't like him?"

Childs laughed and banked the aircraft into a tight left turn. "Time to head back," he said.

"Because of what I asked?"

"No, because of time. I have an appointment." He squinted as he scrutinized the instruments. "Who didn't like him? Lots of people, I'd say."

"Including you?"

"Yes, including me, I'm afraid. Clarence was . . . well, he was a bit of a spoiled brat. He had the attitude that he was born to the good life, and I suppose he was. Lots of money, family support, a good mind and a handsome face. Women fell in love with his boyish good looks, the vulnerable little boy in a man's body. He was a charmer, that's for sure, Miss Pinscher."

"Did you resent him for that?" Susanna asked.

Childs looked at her in surprise. "Resent him? Why would I do that? I didn't like him, but I didn't resent him. I think I felt more sorry for him than anything."

"Why, sir?"

"Because he was like so many young men today, Miss Pinscher. Put them in a tough situation and they can't figure out how to blow their own noses. They've been coddled, protected, sheltered. They never become men, although they

45

think they do because they wear suits and bed down a string of women." He pointed out the window. "There's the airport... Them's my sentiments, Miss Pinscher, they're children when they should be men. Too damn soft for my taste, however unjudicial that may sound."

Susanna watched as Childs set up the Colt for a landing, coordinating his approach with the ground controllers, flying parallel to the runway, then turning onto his base leg and, with a smoothly executed left turn, lining up with the long, wide strip of concrete.

"It was a nice ride," she said after they'd come to a stop at his tie-down spot. "Thank you."

"Glad you enjoyed it." He walked her to her car. "Can I give you an unsolicited opinion? We justices love to give opinions."

"I'd very much appreciate it."

"Clarence was very probably killed by a woman. It may be attractive to the media, but I'm afraid you'd be wasting your time investigating any man, including those on the Court. God knows we're not perfect, to put it mildly, but Clarence was a man who treated women badly. Common knowledge, I'm afraid. I've no evidence, no suspects for you, but it seems likely that one of his women got mad enough to seek her revenge."

"But you have nobody particular in mind?"

"No. As I understand it, you couldn't tell the victims without a scorecard."

She shook his hand and thanked him again for the flight.

"Please come back again, Miss Pinscher. I enjoyed having you aboard."

CHAPTER
8

"PRETTY FANCY FOR A HUNGARIAN JOINT," MARTIN TELLER said after joining Susanna at a table in Csiko's. "I feel like a prince."

She laughed. "It is a little overdone but I like it. Wait'll the gypsy violins start in."

They ordered drinks, a Bloody Mary for her, gin—*not* vodka—on the rocks for him. He settled back in an armchair and took in his surroundings; Austrian shades and draperies, burnished brass and polished wood, high ceilings with rococo plastering, a single red carnation on each table. "Very nice," he said, sipping his drink. "Are you Hungarian?"

"I'm a mixed bag, a little of this, a little of that, including a dash of Hungarian."

A waiter brought menus. "How did your interview with Childs go this morning?" he asked.

She put down the menu, glanced up over half-glasses. "Strange, maybe, but I find most people strange these days."

"Why is Childs strange?"

"Hard to say. He's very nice, friendly, open. He took me for a ride in his plane."

Teller put on a leer and wiggled an imaginary cigar in his fingers. "In his plane, huh? I thought he was married, four kids, nice quiet suburban life."

She removed her glasses. "Don't be silly. He was pressed for time and I got to ask a lot of questions while we were up in the air."

Teller waved his hands. "Don't mind me. I'm a little upset. I had to take Beauty to the vet today."

"Your dog?"

"Cat, one of two. He has hair balls."

"Oh." She replaced her glasses on her nose and returned to the menu.

He chose roast duck that was billed as a specialty of the house. "Careful of the red cabbage," she said, "it tastes like it's fermented." She ordered *szekely gulyas*, a pork and sauerkraut stew sprinkled with paprika and cooked with sour cream.

"So, Miss Pinscher, tell me about the rest of your week. Did you get to interview any of the other justices?"

"No, just Childs. He thinks a woman killed Clarence Sutherland, that he was a womanizer and evidently made at least one of them mad enough to kill him."

"I talked with a few employees at the Court and got the same picture."

She sat back. "A woman just walks into the main chamber of the United States Supreme Court and kills the chief clerk?"

"You can never figure women, Miss Pinscher. No offense. Can I call you Susanna?"

48

"Sure. Unless you prefer Candy."

"As the poet said, Candy's dandy but liquor's quicker."

"So true . . . Look, Lieutenant, I hate to be a party-pooper but a man is stone dead by hands other than his own. Maybe we ought to get back to cases."

He nodded gravely, but pleaded for a reprieve until they'd finished off apple strudel and coffee served in glasses resting in silver filigree holders.

"All right," he said, patting his stomach, "what do *you* think? Is Childs right about the perpetrator, as my boss would say? Did a woman do in young Sutherland?"

"—Certainly seems reasonable."

"What did Childs personally think of Sutherland?"

"Didn't like him, called him one of the soft generation."

"That wouldn't sit well with Childs. I did some reading up on him this week. A real hard-nose, military all the way. I never realized he came out of a poor background. Somehow I always assume people in his position were born right."

"Give him credit. He's a classic American success story."

"Yeah. I got a hold of that series *Life* did on him, the one written by Dan Brazier. It was good."

She nodded. "I read that series too. That was an interesting story in itself, the relationship between Childs and Brazier," she said, referring to a close friendship that had developed between the two men.

Brazier had been a UPI reporter assigned to Korea. Like Childs, he'd been captured by the North Koreans while covering a front-line skirmish, and they'd ended up in the same prisoner-of-war camp. The escape masterminded by Childs included five other prisoners, Brazier among them. They became inseparable after that, and Brazier had what amounted to an exclusive pipeline to the war's leading hero, the *Life* series representing only one of several rewards for that closeness.

After the war, Brazier ran into serious medical problems

directly linked to his captivity. One of his legs was amputated. A year later his other leg had to come off and he retired from journalism. As far as Susanna knew, he lived in obscurity in San Francisco.

"Does Childs still support him?" Teller asked.

"I don't know. The last I heard he did." Morgan Childs had sent a check to Dan Brazier every month for years. He'd tried to do it anonymously, but the press learned of it and reported on his generosity, which only added to his public image of a heroic, loyal and dedicated human being.

"An after-dinner drink?" Teller asked.

"Thank you, no. I really should get home. I was supposed to spend the weekend with my kids but this morning's meeting with Justice Childs threw a monkey wrench into my plans. I want to get out to see them first thing tomorrow."

"I don't see much of my kids. Two daughters, both in college. They come through once in a while, but most of their free time is spent with their mother in Paris."

Her eyes widened. "Paris, France?"

"Paris, Kentucky. She married some guy from there. Nice guy, takes good care of her, which got me off the alimony hook...By the way, I don't know what you like to do when you aren't working, but I've got two tickets to Cav-Pag at Kennedy Center next weekend."

"Cav-Pag?"

"Two one-act operas, *Cavalleria Rusticana* and *Pagliacci*. They usually play them together and call it Cav-Pag. Do you like opera?"

"I take it you do."

"Love it. I'm a hell of a tenor in the shower."

"Can I let you know later in the week?"

"Sure."

Her car was parked a short distance from the restaurant. He walked her to it.

"Thank you for a lovely dinner," she said. "I didn't intend for you to pay, especially since I chose the restaurant."

"You chose good. Besides, it was worth every penny. I like talking to you."

"Thank you. I don't know much about opera, but I'd like to go to... what's it called?"

"Cav-Pag. That's great. I'll talk to you during the week."

He watched her drive off, then got in his own car and drove to M Street, Northwest, in Georgetown. He parked illegally even though the new police commissioner had called for a crackdown on cops taking advantage of their position, walked a block and turned into Club Julie.

It was dark, smoky and crowded. The room was long and narrow, and a bar ran half its length on the right. In the center of the left wall was a tiny bandstand. Seated on it was the Julie of Club Julie, surrounded by keyboard instruments, an organ, acoustic and electric pianos and an electronic rhythm machine that duplicated the sound of percussion instruments.

"Hello, Marty," Julie said as Teller sat at the only empty stool at the piano bar. There were ten stools, seven of them occupied by middle-aged women, all of whom knew him. A waitress brought him gin on the rocks without being asked, and Julie launched into a medley of old sing-along tunes—"If You Wore a Tulip," "Down by the Riverside," "Ain't She Sweet,"...Teller sang along with the others. One hour and four gins later, he was holding a microphone and doing his best Frank Sinatra act, pulling notes up from the heart, closing his eyes and belting them out to the delight of the crowd.

"Good night, Marty," Julie said as Teller stood unsteadily and waved to hangers-on as he headed for the door.

"Sing 'My Way,'" a drunk at the bar muttered.

"Next time," Teller said. He took deep breaths of chilled night air, found his car and went home, singing "My Way" all the way to the front door.

"Generation gap, my ass."

CHAPTER
9

"LET'S GO OVER IT," TELLER SAID TO DETECTIVES GATH-ered in his office. A sizable contingent of them had de-scended on the Supreme Court and had taken preliminary statements from almost everyone, including the nine jus-tices.

"I felt like a fool asking a Supreme Court judge for his whereabouts the night of the murder," one of them said.

"What did he say?" Teller asked.

"It wasn't a he, it was a she, Justice Tilling-Masters."

"What did she say?"

"That she was at a party with her family."

"Did it check out?"

"Yup."

"Who else?" Teller asked.

They ran down a list. Of the nine justices, six had alibis that could be confirmed.

"Whose alibi has holes?" Teller asked.

"Conover, Poulson and Childs."

"They lied?"

"No, but they aren't solid," a hefty detective named Vasilone said. "For instance, Marty, Poulson was supposed to be at a party too, but I talked to somebody else who was there and he puts Poulson's departure at a different time than what Poulson told me. I'm still trying to get hold of other people who were there."

"What about Conover?"

"Says he was home alone working on a manuscript."

"Wife?"

"Out at a party, at least that's what her husband says. I asked him about household help and he told me he gave them all the night off."

Teller twisted a little finger in his ear. "How about Childs?"

Another detective reported on Childs. "He says he was tinkering with his airplane at the airport that night."

"At that hour?"

"That's what I said, Marty, but he told me it's the only time he can get away."

"Any corroboration?"

"An airport guard says he saw him earlier in the evening but doesn't know what time he left."

"Okay, that takes care of the top. What about everybody else in the Court?" He was handed a list of people who could not definitively account for their activities.

"There's lots more to interview," Vasilone said. "You can only do so much."

"I know," Teller said. "Keep plugging. I want daily reports."

When they were gone from his office he sat back, feet

on the desk, and closed his eyes for a moment. When he opened them he looked at framed photographs of his daughters on his desk. "If you knew what I had to do for a living you wouldn't be so quick to ask for money." Which reminded him that they were due their monthly allotment. He wrote each of them a check, included a note in the envelopes which he signed "Love, Dad," and mailed them in a box just outside MPD.

He hoped they appreciated him.

CHAPTER
10

CHIEF JUSTICE POULSON WALKED BRISKLY THROUGH HIS reception area, nodding to secretaries and clerks as he passed. He entered his main chamber, tossed a stack of files on the desk and looked at a clock-barometer on a shelf behind his chair. The meeting of the judicial conference had run a half hour longer than planned, and everything else that afternoon would be affected, pressured, compressed.

Poulson hated the administrative aspect of being Chief Justice. He'd thought about it when offered the position by President Jorgens. There were many advantages to being an associate rather than the Chief. The other eight justices concerned themselves only with law, but the administrative details of running the Court fell to him, all the bureaucratic nitty-gritty. He was also expected to preside over such organizations as the judicial conference, which in reality was nothing more than a lobby of federal judges.

On the other hand, he thought as he opened a small walnut-faced refrigerator and took out a bottle of Bailey's Irish Cream, there were compensating factors. Because he was Chief, the Court was known as the "Poulson Court." He officially ranked third in federal government protocol, although there were those who felt that because of the vice-president's political impotency, the chief justice was actually second in power only to the president.

Then again, he told himself as he poured a small portion of the liqueur into a glass and replaced the bottle in the refrigerator, there was a price to be paid for that power. The other justices were relatively anonymous, could live their private lives without gawkers and autograph seekers, all except Marjorie Tilling-Masters, of course, whose appointment to the Court had garnered wide media attention.

There was a knock on his door. "Come in," he said.

A secretary entered carrying a yellow legal pad. She came around behind him and placed the pad on the desk. "Justice Poulson, these are the phone calls that came in while you were gone."

"Thank you," he said. He glanced at the names on the paper. "Pinscher? She called again?"

"Yes, sir."

"All right."

"And Mr. Smithers is waiting."

"What's that about?"

"The film, sir."

"Oh, right. Give me a minute, then send him in."

"Yes, sir."

He waited until she was gone before draining the glass. He took a tissue from a desk drawer and wiped the glass clean, then placed it in its customary spot on the shelf behind him, where the cleaning crew would find it. He rubbed a

57

flat area of his right thumb with his other fingers. His wife, Clara, referred to his right thumb as his built-in worry stone. He massaged his nose where his glasses had left their mark, told his secretary, "Send him in."

Walter Smithers came through the door. Tall, and carrying the leather attaché case, he represented the American Bar Association.

"Mr. Smithers," Poulson said, standing and offering his hand.

"It's a pleasure, Mr. Chief Justice. It's good of you to find time for me."

"I'm afraid I don't have much of that commodity this afternoon. I try to keep to a tight timetable, but things can sometimes get out of hand."

Smithers sat and opened his case. He handed a set of papers to Poulson and said, "I think this accurately sets forth our proposal, Mr. Chief Justice. When I heard that you were interested in having the visitor film replaced, I immediately took it up with our public-information people. There was unanimous agreement that the new film should reflect the Court as it is today. After all, it no longer is the Burger Court. It's now the Poulson Court."

Poulson glanced at the proposal. "Mr. Smithers," he said, "the cooperation and support of the ABA is gratifying. I've been at the receiving end of some good-natured kidding about replacing the film. A few of my colleagues, in their more whimsical moments, accuse me of what seems to be called ego-tripping. My goal is to present to the American people the most accurate and up-to-date portrait of the nation's highest court. The Supreme Court has changed dramatically, not only in its faces but in its philosophy, a philosophy which, I might add, accurately reflects the sense of the American people, as I believe it should. Since assuming office I've brought about a number of changes within the Court that reflect this new philosophy, and I feel the visitor film should too. However, I have a reservation."

"What is that, sir?"

"It seems to me inappropriate for the American Bar Association to finance this new film. Even though a conflict of interest obviously does not exist, certain factions might take exception. That's why I expressed the idea to you on the phone of having the ABA work with the Supreme Court Historical Society in producing a new and more up-to-date motion picture. I'd prefer that the society receive credit for having produced it."

"We have no problem with that, Mr. Chief Justice."

"Good. I'm anxious to see the project get underway, and I assure you the full cooperation of the Court."

Smithers realized Poulson had effectively ended the meeting. He rose, shook hands and promised to get back shortly with a more detailed schedule. After he left the chambers, Poulson took a toothbrush and toothpaste from a cabinet and went to a private lavatory, where he enthusiastically brushed his teeth. He returned to his chambers, checked his appearance in a mirror and buzzed his outer office. "Please have the Court limousine wait in the basement for me," he said.

"Yes, sir."

Minutes later he climbed into the back seat. "The Treasury Department," he told the uniformed driver.

A young man met them, and Poulson followed him to an elevator leading to Treasury's basement. The young man led him along a dimly lit steam tunnel until reaching the White House. They rode an elevator to a higher floor and stood in front of the Oval Office.

"Please wait, sir," the young man said as he crossed a large carpeted area and spoke in hushed tones to a woman behind a desk. He returned to the Chief and said, "He'll see you in a moment, sir."

A few minutes later the woman said, "Please follow me." She opened the doors and he stepped into the Oval Office.

President Jorgens was behind his desk. He smiled, stood and came around to shake Poulson's hand. "Good to see you, Mr. Chief Justice. I appreciate your taking time out from a busy schedule."

"Any time, Mr. President. How have you been?"

"Splendid. The sharks may proliferate but I still know how to swim. Sit down, make yourself comfortable."

"Thank you."

Jorgens touched an American flag as he passed it, settled in a large leather chair and propped his feet on the desk. "Jonathan, what's happening with the abortion case?"

The directness of the question took Poulson aback. He shifted his legs and squeezed the tip of his nose. After a few moments he said, "It's very close, Mr. President. No one, on the Court or in public life, is *for* abortion. But there is a legal issue here as defined by *Nidel* v. *Illinois*. Individual philosophies are rendered mute—"

"Lawyer talk. Legalese, Jonathan. I campaigned on a promise of righting wrongs in society, of returning to basic values. We had a president who was supposed to do that and didn't. I thought you understood all that."

"I do, of course, Mr. President, but the individuals on the Court carry with them their own views of the law. I talked with Justice Childs this morning. I'd assumed he'd be in favor of Illinois, but after our conference I realized that the legal question bothers him. Unlike Congress, one cannot depend upon a man's predisposition to a given issue on the Court."

"Or a woman's?"

"Yes, but I think Justice Tilling-Masters will support the state's position. That's my reading of her, at least."

"I hope so."

The President put his hands behind his head and stretched.

Poulson noticed the beginnings of wear in the sole of his shoe. He considered mentioning it, then thought better of it. After all, that was the late Adlai Stevenson's trademark, and the association would hardly, he thought, amuse the President. Instead, he said, "I've ordered a new visitor film be produced."

"Film?"

"The one visitors watch in the Court's small theater. I'm having it updated."

"That's nice, Jonathan. Let's get back to the abortion question. Is there anything that I can do, or my people, to help shape a rational decision in *Nidel* v. *Illinois*?"

Poulson searched the President's face as he formulated a reply. Randolph Jorgens was a self-assured man. He stood well over six feet and kept himself in good physical condition in the White House gym. Leathery, lined, tan skin testified to his Arizona heritage. His smile was wide and appealing, always at the ready. His cool gray eyes missed little while building a vast industrial empire, or after having entered the political arena. *Smart*, was the operative word around Washington—smart, and hard, and shrewd.

"I don't know of anything that might come from the executive branch, Mr. President, that would especially help in this matter." What Poulson wanted to say was that the entire conversation was inappropriate. The Court was supposed to be sacrosanct, a bastion of independent thought and judgment without influence from any other part of government, including the President of the United States.

Poulson's appointment by Jorgens to the Chief Justice's chair had been energetically debated during confirmation proceedings. An exhaustive FBI investigation, along with the Senate's own probe, had been nerve-racking for the entire family. Poulson was aware that the President had ordered his own secret investigation utilizing the IRS and, it was rumored, certain CIA personnel. There had also been long, in-depth conversations between the two men before Jorgens announced his choice. Those conversations had concentrated on relative political and social positions. Poulson had evidently satisfied the President's perception of what the new Chief Justice should believe in and espouse from the bench.

Questioning during the Senate Judiciary Committee's confirmation hearings had been spirited and, at times, hostile, depending on the questioner. One liberal senator had expressed his concern over the extent to which Poulson could function independently of the new administration, to which Poulson had replied, "I am, after all, Senator, a human being. I am subject to all the foibles of other human beings, including distinguished members of the United States Senate. I am, at the same time, a man who has devoted his life to the law. I believe in law above all else. Without law we cease to function as a civilized society. There have been many times in my career when my personal beliefs were placed in direct conflict with the larger issue of jurisprudence. In each of those instances law prevailed, just as it will should I be confirmed Chief Justice of the United States Supreme Court."

He'd meant every word of it.

"I'd like to be kept informed on a daily basis," Jorgens said.

"Of course, Mr. President."

"What about Conover, Jonathan? I assume he'll vote in favor of the plaintiff."

"It's likely, Mr. President."

"Damned old fool."

Poulson said nothing. As much as he disliked Temple Conover's life-style and persistent, in his view, misguided, liberalism, he did respect the senior justice for his rock-solid adherence to his convictions.

"Is there anything else, Mr. President?"

"This Sutherland matter, Jonathan. Where does it stand?"

"I just don't know. All we can do is to cooperate fully with the investigative agencies assigned to the case—"

"I don't like what I've heard about it."

"Such as, Mr. President?"

"The bastard's success in compromising people before he was killed."

"That was unfortunate, as we all know. I certainly was never in favor of accepting him as one of my clerks to begin with."

"Then why did you?"

Poulson winced against the question. The President knew why he had, and to ask the question was provocative. Still, Poulson felt compelled to answer. "As you know, his father was instrumental in that decision. Besides, no matter what Clarence Sutherland was personally, he was a brilliant young man. I don't think there's ever been a clerk here, during my term, with his skill at writing briefs. But of course if I had known about his other side . . ."

"Hindsight is a waste of time, Jonathan. I just wish you had been a little quicker to see what was happening beneath your eyes, in your own chambers. By the time you did, and reported it to me, the barn door had been open one hell of a long time."

"It seems to me, sir, that—"

"There are serious questions of governmental operations and even national security involved up in this mess, damn it." His face reddened. "Our highest intelligence echelons may have been compromised, at least potentially, by his actions, as has this very office. I had a briefing this morning by the CIA, and the threat of his knowledge . . . through his father . . . is a real one."

He suddenly stood and smiled, came around the desk and slapped Poulson on the back. It was all there again, the infectious grin, the warmth, the sense of being your best friend. "Let's keep on top of it, Jonathan, really on top of it."

"Of course. Thank you, Mr. President."

"Thank *you*, Jonathan. Please give my best to Mrs. Poulson."

"I certainly will, sir, and the same to the First Lady."

Poulson retraced his steps through the steam tunnel to the Treasury Building, where his car was waiting. "The Court, sir?" asked the driver.

"No, home, please. I'm tired, very tired." He leaned back and closed his eyes, his shirt clammy and cold against his skin.

VERA JONES knocked on Dr. Chester Sutherland's office door. He told her to enter. He was with a patient, a high-level administrator in the Department of Agriculture. "I'm sorry to disturb you, doctor, but Mr. L. is on the phone. He says it's urgent."

Sutherland looked at his patient, said, "Excuse me, please." He went through the door at the rear of his office and picked up a phone on which there were three buttons, one of which was lighted. "Hello, Mr. L.," he said.

"Hello, Dr. Sutherland. There's a meeting at ten tomorrow morning."

"Of course, I'll be there. Thank you for calling."

The man who'd placed the call gently hung up his phone, left his office and walked down a long, carpeted corridor until reaching the Oval Office's oak doors. He knocked, was told to enter.

"The meeting is set, sir," he said.

"Thank you, Craig."

Craig departed. President Randolph Jorgens stood, scratched his belly through his shirt and ran his hand over a leather horse on his desk. "I need a vacation," he said.

CHAPTER
11

SUSANNA PINSCHER WAS WITH MATT MITCHELL, HER SU-
perior at the Justice Department. Large drops of rain splat-
tered against the window in his office; a cold front had
invaded the city from the north. It was three o'clock in the
afternoon but was dark enough outside to be night.

"Are you sure you don't want some tea, Susanna," Mitchell asked. "You're soaked. You'll catch pneumonia."

"Okay, some tea."

"And put this on." He dropped a beige wool cardigan
sweater in her lap as he passed. "I keep it around for when
I get all wet. Which is too much of the time." Brief smile.

She draped the sweater over her shoulders and shivered.
She'd gotten caught in the storm while walking back from
a meeting in Chief Justice Poulson's chambers. She'd used

an underground tunnel as far as it extended down Constitution Avenue, but was exposed the rest of the way.

Mitchell returned carrying a steaming cup of tea. He handed it to her, looked down at her feet and said, "You're making puddles on my floor."

"I can't help it."

He laughed. "Puddles beat waves."

The hot cup felt good in her hands. She inhaled the tea's aroma, sipped it.

"So, Susanna, how did it go with Poulson?"

"He's pleasant enough, seems anxious to cooperate. The only sticky point is where the interrogations should be conducted."

"I take it he doesn't want them held in the Court."

"He feels the Court has been violated enough and questions why follow-up investigations can't be held outside the building."

"He has a point. The first thing Poulson did after becoming Chief was to slap an even tighter lid on everything that happens inside the Court. Any clerk who's even seen talking to a reporter is fired, no excuses, no explanations. They can't even say no comment. Opening up the Court to a full-scale MPD investigation is like inviting every reporter in town to a public meeting. Cops are biologically incapable of keeping their mouths shut."

"Matt, I realize the Supreme Court is a special place, but a murder happened there. My training has always said that you investigate where the crime occurred."

"This is different, Susanna. In the first place, we don't get involved in murders very often. In the second place, the MPD has already interviewed everyone in the Court and did it inside the building. The place has been gone over with the old fine-toothed comb, and if the President decides to go ahead with appointing a special prosecutor, there'll be that much more disruption to the Court's activities." He sat

66

on the edge of his desk. "There's another aspect to all this, Susanna, and maybe you haven't considered it. If a Supreme Court justice had been murdered it would make sense. The fact is that a clerk was killed, and if he'd been shot anyplace else other than the Supreme Court it would be just another routine MPD investigation."

"If."

"Okay, but the fact remains that there are more important considerations than Clarence Sutherland's murder. There's the law of the land to preside over. That's the Court's job, after all."

"What about if a murderer is sitting on the Supreme Court, presiding over the law of the land?"

He started to respond, pulled back, shook his head, stood and went to the window. "Miserable day." He turned and said to her, "You don't really believe that, do you?"

"That Clarence Sutherland's murderer might be one of nine justices? I don't like to believe it but it's a real possibility, isn't it?"

"No."

"Then who?"

He returned to the desk and leaned close to her. "Susanna, you go around spouting theories like that and your days in this city, and on this job, are numbered."

She placed the empty teacup on the desk and closed the gap between them. "I thought the name of the game was to solve Sutherland's murder, Matt, no matter where or what."

"That's true, but let's not go beyond Justice's scope. We're at least partly in this for show . . . I spoke with the assistant attorney general this morning and he—"

"*Show*? I quit."

"Quit? That's ridiculous."

"Like hell . . . not only am I told by my superior that my assignment is a kind of sham, I'm told that this big, wonderful Department of Justice that I broke my buns to join is in show business."

"Calm down."

"Then say something to help me."

"Keep working on the Sutherland case. Go after it full steam ahead, but also please don't lose perspective. There are other things that share parity with Sutherland's death."

"I'll try." She handed him his sweater, picked up her water-soaked pumps and went to the door. "Matt," she said, "I don't mean to be a pain in the neck, I really don't, but I have to feel that what I'm doing is important."

"It is. I was shorthanding the situation, Susanna. Ignore it."

She'd try.

CHAPTER
12

Susanna Pinscher and Martin Teller stood in the Grand Foyer of the Kennedy Center's Opera House, one of three large theaters contained in the vast and sprawling arts complex. The performance of *Cavalleria Rusticana* was over and it was intermission.

"Did you enjoy it?" Teller asked.

"Very much."

"It's some theater, isn't it?"

"I've been here before."

"To see an opera?"

"No. Chinese acrobats. I had the same impression of the place then that I have tonight. It's big, formal and sort of stuffy."

"Opera buffs seem to like it that way. Makes them feel

elegant or something. But every time that chandelier dims I get goose bumps. How about a drink?"

"It's so crowded," she said, pointing to a mob surrounding a small bar.

"Don't worry about that," he said. "I belong to the Golden Circle society."

"What in God's name is that?"

"A bunch of people who pay a *thousand* bucks a year for the privilege of not standing in line for a drink during intermission. You wouldn't think a cop could manage it, but I wash my own socks and make out with the finer things."

"I'm impressed, socks or no socks."

They were served cognac in snifters. They clicked rims and he said, "Here's to indulgence."

She smiled. "Tell me, Detective Teller, why does a man who spends his working days dealing with the low life lay out a thousand dollars a year to rub shoulders with opera buffs?"

"You have it wrong." He leaned close to her ear. "I can't stand these people. The fact is that dealing with what I deal with every day makes me sort of crazy for a change. What I get out of opera is a beautiful change. Fantasy after eight hours of reality. Makes sense?"

"It does." She clicked her glass to his and drank.

The second half of the evening, *Pagliacci*, was less inspiring than the first.

"I believe they call this kind of writing *verismo*," Teller said as they left the ornate red theater and headed for his car. "It means 'realism' but it doesn't work as well as traditional opera. Puccini trumped all of them, including his fellow Italians."

"You're a very interesting...man," she said as they drove from the parking garage.

"You were about to say character."

70

"No, I wasn't, but I guess it would fit."

"I also get my shoes shined instead of doing them myself, and I send my laundry out."

"A typical bachelor."

"Typical?"

"No, I'm sorry. I enjoyed tonight. Very much. Thank you."

"Where to now?"

"Home."

"Hungry?"

"No."

"Feel like singing?"

"After hearing those wonderful voices?"

"They weren't so great. I have V-discs that are better."

"I wouldn't know from better, I'm afraid. Damn little opera in my upbringing."

"Ditto. I got the taste for it late in life ... Look, I know a nice place in Georgetown. A bunch of crazies hang out there but they're basically nice people, just like to sit around and drink and sing. The owner and I are friends. He plays the piano. He made a million in frozen French fries and then dumped the whole business to open a club. I don't know whether you'd like the place or not but they serve steak sandwiches on garlic bread until closing, and sometimes the music is good and—"

"Do they serve French fries?"

"The best in D.C."

"Let's go."

Instead of sitting at the piano bar, Teller took her to a corner far from the bandstand. They said little to each other as she observed the Saturday night crowd.

"Well, what do you think?" he asked after their drinks and sandwich platters had been served.

"I don't know yet, I haven't tasted it."

"I mean the place. Nice atmosphere, huh?"

71

"Yes, it's—"

"What's the matter?"

"It's sort of sad, seeing people in a singles bar—"

"Singles bar? This isn't a singles bar. If it were I wouldn't come here."

"Don't be touchy. It's just that I wish those women sitting around the piano bar were *with* someone..."

"But that's what's nice about Club Julie, Susanna. It's *like* a club, no hassles like in real singles bars. Women can come here and feel safe."

"I suppose you're right. Funny, but it makes me think of Dr. Sutherland's secretary...Vera Jones."

Teller sliced into his steak and took a bite. "Good. Don't let it get cold."

"Do you think she's ever been married?"

"Vera Jones? Most people have been, although she does come off like one of those who hasn't. But I don't figure her for the singles'-bar scene. Not her style—"

"What is her style?"

"Quiet, a one-on-one type, maybe a twenty-year affair with a married man."

"Dr. Sutherland?"

"Not likely, but you never know. I do think she's loyal and discreet enough to be a twenty-year mistress, don't you?"

"Yes. Do you find her attractive?"

"Yes, in a cold sort of way."

"Hidden passion, as they say in the purple romances?"

"Could be."

"A legitimate suspect?"

"Everybody is at this point."

"Including the nine justices?"

"Including the nine justices. Do you know who interests me?"

"I'm afraid to ask."

He grinned. "That court clerk, Laurie Rawls. She was at the funeral and bawled all through it. I figure there was more to her relationship with Sutherland than just a co-worker."

"*Cherchez la femme...*"

"Huh?"

"Justice Childs's advice to me. Look for the woman. Have you interviewed Laurie Rawls?"

"One of my people did. Uneventful. She said she liked Clarence, enjoyed working with him. Her alibi is shaky, but so are a lot of other people's."

"If you'd like, I'll talk to her. She might open up to another woman."

"Could be. I understand she's been temporarily assigned to the Chief Justice. She'd worked for the old man, Conover."

"I'll call her Monday morning."

Julie, the owner, came to the table and asked Teller if he wanted to sing. Teller shook his head, but Susanna insisted. "I've never heard a singing detective before."

"You still won't have," he said as he went to the bandstand, and picked up a microphone while Julie played an introduction to "As Time Goes By."

"*You must remember this, a kiss is still a kiss,*
A sigh is just a sigh.
The fundamental things apply, as time goes by."

He smiled at Susanna as he ventured into the second stanza. She nodded her approval and leaned her chair back against the wall, her thoughts divided between attention to his resonant voice and the thing that had led them to spend the evening together—Clarence Sutherland's murder. She felt overwhelmed. The number of suspects and the com-

73

plication of it having happened in the United States Supreme Court.

The smell of garlic filled her nostrils, and chatter at adjoining tables deafened her. She closed her eyes against a pain that had started at the back of her neck and was now creeping up over her head and toward her forehead. She opened her eyes and saw a blurry Martin Teller.

"...*the world will always welcome lovers,*
As time goes by."

He held the last note and Julie rolled off a rich chord. Applause, applause. Teller put the microphone on top of the piano and made his way to the table.

"I warned you."

"It was terrific."

He sat down and looked at her closely. "You don't look so good, do you feel sick?"

"I...it's a migraine coming on, damn it. I get them once in a while."

"I'm sorry. Let's go, I'll take you home."

"I'm sorry to ruin the evening."

They pulled up in front of her building. Teller put his hand on the ignition key but didn't turn off the engine. "I'll walk you in."

"No, please don't. I'll be fine. Thank you for a really wonderful evening."

"I just wish you felt better." He turned, leaned close. "I'd like to kiss you."

"Well, then, Lieutenant, for God's sake *do* it."

CHAPTER
13

TEMPLE CONOVER SAT IN HIS CHAMBERS WEARING AN OLD,
loose, nubby gray sweater. He'd changed from black shoes
to worn carpet slippers as soon as he arrived that morning.
It was almost noon. He was to attend a luncheon at the
British Embassy on Massachusetts Avenue, known as
Washington's "Embassy Row," at which he was to receive
a plaque from England's equivalent of the American Bar
Association for his years of "dedication to upholding the
principles of freedom and justice." Cecily would join him
there, and after lunch she was to drive him to the airport
for a flight to Dallas, where he would address the Texas
Bar Association's annual formal dinner.

He turned to his typewriter and quickly wrote a memo
to Chief Justice Poulson.

Jonathan—Despite my consistent harping that we have too many clerks as it is, taking Miss Rawls from me at the peak time of cert petitions is intolerable. I know you lost Sutherland, but I'd appreciate your reconsideration of the transfer, as "temporary" as it might be.—Temple C.

He called out the open door to his senior secretary, a heavy, middle-aged woman named Joan who'd been with him for six years. She stepped into his chambers.

"Have this envelope delivered right away to the chief." He handed it to her. "Where's Bill and Marisa?" he asked, referring to two of three remaining clerks on his staff.

"In the library."

"Get them down here right away."

"Yes, sir."

They arrived minutes later and took seats across the desk from him. He waved a hand over piles of petitions for certiorari, requests to the Supreme Court to review decisions handed down by lower courts. Of five thousand such requests received each year, only about two hundred were accepted for review. Each justice was expected to analyze the five thousand petitions, then vote on which of them to accept. A minimum of four out of the nine justices was necessary for a cert to be granted.

Shortly after becoming Chief, Poulson had attempted to establish a cert pool, ostensibly to relieve the workload on each justice, but he'd been voted down, with Conover leading the opposition. The senior justice felt it had been a move on Poulson's part to gain additional control of the Court, something he felt had been happening with regularity.

In reality, it was the clerks who reviewed most petitions for cert and condensed them to one- or two-page summaries for their justices.

Conover picked up a thick file of cert reviews his clerks

felt warranted his special consideration. "I've read these and agree with your views, but what good are they if we can't get three of the others to go along with us?"

"I think we can, sir, on the job discrimination and ecology petitions," Bill said. "I spoke this morning with Justice Tilling-Masters's clerks, and they feel she'll be in favor of accepting them this term. We know the Chief's position. Justice Childs won't bend, but..."

The other clerk added, "Peg O'Malley, who works for Justice Sims, told me that he might go along with us on the job discrimination case if it's narrowed to the pension issue and doesn't include sexual discrimination."

Conover twisted in his high-backed leather chair and groaned as a sharp pain shot from his hip to his shoulder. "I don't see how that's possible," he said, his voice mirroring his discomfort.

"I'll keep working on her," Marisa said.

"Don't bother. I'd rather press on the ecology issue and the two petitions on church and state."

"Yes, sir."

Fifteen minutes later, and after Bill's help with his shoes and jacket, Conover stood by Joan's desk while she assisted him on with his overcoat. "Would you like me to walk down with you?" she asked.

"No."

She handed him his crutch and he slipped his forearm into its metal sleeve. "I want those opinions ready to be circulated when I come back."

Another of his secretaries, Helen, wished him a safe and pleasant trip. He thanked her, then said, "Mrs. Conover will be coming by to pick up theater tickets that are being sent over this afternoon. Please see that she gets them."

"Of course, sir."

Both secretaries watched him slowly and painfully leave the room.

"Poor man," Joan said aloud.

"It's awful to see him in such pain," Helen said.

"I sometimes think of Justice Douglas when I see him," Joan said.

"I do, too, especially when his wife comes in."

Joan shook a finger in the air and said emphatically, "The *only* thing they have in common as far as *that's* concerned is that they ended up with young wives. Justice Douglas's wife was a lady, a tremendous and loyal help to him before he died. I wish I could say the same for Mrs. Conover."

Helen started to say something but Joan cut her off. "Enough of this. Justice Conover's personal life is his own business. I just hope this dreadful thing with Mr. Sutherland doesn't open up that can of worms. Come on, let's get going on those opinions. If they're not on his desk when he gets back from Dallas we'll all be looking for jobs at Foggy Bottom."

CHAPTER
14

"I'M DELIGHTED YOU COULD GET FREE FOR LUNCH," Susanna Pinscher said to Laurie Rawls after they'd met inside
the front door of the American Cafe's Capitol Hill branch
on Massachusetts Avenue. Susanna had called Laurie to set
up an interview and suggested lunch. The clerk declined
lunch, then called back the following day and accepted.

They were seated at a blond wooden table in a corner.
Susanna settled into her chair and looked across at her young
luncheon guest. She'd liked Laurie Rawls from the moment
they met. There was an openness and brightness about her,
a wide-eyed inquisitiveness. She wore no makeup to mask
her translucent, fair skin that gave off the same healthy glow
as her short, straight brown hair. She was dressed in a
pleated gray flannel skirt, a dusty rose blouse that buttoned

to the neck and a blue blazer with the crest of her alma mater, George Washington University.

"I was surprised when you called back and agreed to lunch," Susanna said after ordering a white wine for herself and a kir for Laurie.

"Why? Because I'm a suspect? The fact is, Miss Pinscher, I'm interested in you. You've obviously succeeded in a field I'd like to get into. I thought lunch might be helpful for *me*."

Susanna liked her candor. "Well, the Justice Department isn't very glamorous, but it does have its interesting moments..."

"I'm sure."

"As I assume the Supreme Court does for you."

"I love clerking there. Some of my friends are clerking other places, but being in the nation's highest court is... well, it's kind of awesome."

"I understand you've been assigned to Chief Justice Poulson since Clarence's murder. It must have been tough... I mean losing someone you've worked closely with, and in such a violent way..."

"Yes." She took a long, deliberate drink, put down her glass, picked up a menu. "I'm famished. What do you recommend?"

"Some days the meat pies are good, and—"

"I think I'll have a California salad."

"I'll stick with turkey. Another drink?"

"Thank you, no, but you go ahead."

Susanna ordered another wine, and said to Laurie, "How well did you know Clarence Sutherland?"

Laurie hesitated a beat before saying, "About as well as anyone else on the Court, I guess." It was delivered too offhandedly, Susanna thought. Laurie added, "Clarence could be... difficult."

"How so?"

"He worked for Chief Poulson, he was chief clerk. Sometimes he made the other clerks pretty mad. Some of them thought he was cruel—"

"I see . . ." And rather obviously, Susanna thought, Laurie was one of them. She decided to pursue that sideways . . . "I've seen pictures of Clarence Sutherland. He certainly was a handsome man."

Laurie's face had seemed to sag, her buoyancy flatten out.

Their lunch was served. Susanna chatted about her job at the Justice Department, about her background and the events that led her to Washington and to her present position. Finally, almost abruptly, she decided it was time . . . "Laurie, were you in love with Clarence Sutherland?"

It was as though she had kicked her. Laurie's face turned to stone, she looked abstractedly around the crowded restaurant.

"Shouldn't I have asked?"

"You can *ask* anything you wish. You're investigating a murder and I understand I'm a suspect. I also know you know I haven't an alibi. I was caught in the traffic at what I'm told was the approximate time of the murder. I was by myself."

"Yes, I do know that, and it's true you, *along with many others*, are a suspect. But I also want you to know that I'm not interested in hurting people in the process of helping to solve this thing—"

"I'm sure . . . All right, you've asked a question . . . as one lawyer to another, I'll tell you our relationship was more than professional."

"As one woman to another," Susanna said, "was he in love with you?"

She grimaced. "Clarence was immune from such weakness, vulnerability . . ."

"I'm told Clarence was a womanizer."

81

"How quaint, old-fashioned..."

"Choose your own poison."

"Immature might be closer."

Susanna smiled. "Yes . . . well, he was young—"

"He's a dead young man now." Laurie's voice was cold, her face ice. "If it's all right with you, I think I've had enough discussion about Clarence Sutherland."

"I'm sorry if I've pried too much into your personal relationship."

"I realize full well your job, but . . ." Laurie stared at the tabletop, then looked up, a smile applied like makeup now on her face. "Look, Miss Pinscher, I'm sorry . . . I'm a grown lady . . . I've got degrees that say so, and I am a clerk of a Supreme Court judge. Fire away, ask anything you want. I'll try to be as truthful as I know how."

Susanna took the check from the waiter. "All right, Laurie. Did you kill Clarence?"

She started to answer, lost the words, then said with a short laugh, "Of course not."

"Good. Any notion who did?"

"None."

"Possibilities? I mean at least in theory?"

"Do we have time?"

"He was that disliked—?"

"Hated, I'm afraid, would be more accurate."

"But not by you."

"They say the two emotions are close—sometimes indistinguishable."

"Laurie, do you think a woman killed him, a woman who'd been hurt by him as you obviously have been?"

"I don't know. There were so damn many. But there were plenty of men who hated Clarence's guts too."

"Husbands?"

"I guess, but I wasn't thinking about them especially

...Frankly—" her tone became more confident, and confidential—"It was a mystery that Clarence was even able to stay on as chief clerk."

"Oh? My understanding was that, whatever else, he was brilliant, competent and knowledgeable."

"He was all those, one of the brightest people I'd ever met. He had a sadistic side that set others against him. The things...he could be cruel for no reason...even toward his superiors...The other clerks constantly expected Chief Justice Poulson to fire him, but of course it never happened—"

"Why not?"

She hesitated. "Justice Poulson is a gentleman, a decent human being. But, in confidence, he's also weak. Some said that Clarence played on his weaknesses to keep his job."

"What weaknesses?"

Laurie shrugged. "Clarence knew things about Justice Poulson that evidently could have proved embarrassing to him. What they were I don't know." She was not being entirely truthful with Susanna. Her thoughts went back to the night in the Court when she and Clarence were together in her office. She'd just finished reading an analysis of a case he'd written...

"I envy you," she'd said.

"Why?"

"Your ability to take something as complex as this case, dissect it so quickly and put it all on paper in such a cogent, literate way."

He laughed. "Just a combination of genes, superior intellect, sensitivity, native talent and inherent survival instincts."

"Justice Conover feels differently about you," Laurie said, rolling her chair closer to him so that she could see what he was reading. It was one of many briefs filed in the *Nidel* v. *Illinois* abortion case.

"What else is new?" he asked, not looking up.

"He said you were ruthless and unprincipled."

Clarence looked at her and smiled. "What do you care what that senile old creep says?"

He leaned back in his chair and slowly shook his head. "These justices... They get their butts plopped down in a lifetime job because they spent their careers attending the right political functions, meeting the right people and saying the right things. Then they put on their black robes and make laws, at least when they're not fighting with their wives or playing footsie with some senator or seeing their shrink."

"Like your father—"

"Yes, like dear old dad, analyst to stars, confidant of the powerful, stroking their egos to make them feel worthy of their exalted positions... Do you know what, Laurie? These same people can be made to squirm when you push the right buttons." He turned to her and cupped her chin in his hand. "Give us a kiss."

"Not here."

"Nobody's around. Come on."

He tried to fondle her. She pushed him off. "Clarence, take it easy... later..."

"Why, because we're in these hallowed halls? Listen, Laurie, let me tell you a secret. Poulson's got a closetful of skeletons. I know which closet they're in and what they look like. He came down hard on me this afternoon and I reminded him, nicely of course, about one of them. He backed down. Oh, he kept his dignity. After all, Chief Justice Jonathan Poulson is, if nothing else, dignified. I loved it. And you can tell that old fool you work for that if he says anything else about me I'll broadcast his wife's top-secret erogenous zones."

84

Laurie stood, smoothed her dress and said she had to leave.

Clarence looked at his watch. "I have an hour." He stood and put his arms around her. "Plenty of time for us to—"

She slipped away from him, even though she was tempted in spite of herself, opened the door and went out, trying to shut out the sound of his laughter that trailed her down the corridor. . . .

Susanna put cash on the check, picked up her handbag from the floor. "What about the other justices, the other clerks? Did any of them feel strongly enough about Clarence to . . ."

It seems inconceivable . . . Clarence was provocative, difficult, but that a justice would . . . she shook her head.

They parted on the sidewalk and promised to keep in touch.

Susanna returned to her office, where she made notes of what had been said during lunch.

Further down Constitution Avenue Laurie Rawls closed the door behind her in Chief Justice Jonathan Poulson's chambers and sat herself in a chair. Poulson was behind his desk. He smiled warmly. "Well, how did it go at lunch?"

"Fine, sir. She's very nice, very bright, and doing her job."

"Yes, well, I hope you don't mind my encouraging you to accept the luncheon date with Miss Pinscher. When you mentioned it to me, my initial reaction was to counsel against it. After all, there's a limit to what people should be put through, murder or no murder. But it seemed a good chance to find out just what progress Justice and the MPD were making. I want this matter cleared up as soon as possible so that the Court can get back to normal. What did she have to say about the investigation?"

"Not too much, really, but it was evident to me, Justice

Poulson, that little progress has been made. Apparently the suspect list is as wide open as it was the first day."

"I see . . . well, sorry to hear that."

"Would you mind if I left early, sir? I'm not feeling so well."

"Of course."

She gathered her things from her office and walked down the back stairs to the Great Hall, impressive in its marble splendor. A frieze decorated with medallion profiles of lawgivers and heraldic devices looked down on her as she approached the courtroom. Two members of the Court's special security force stood at the doorway. "Hello, Miss Rawls," one of them said.

"Hello," she answered vaguely as she stood a few feet away and peered into the vast, empty arena where so many of a nation's great legal battles had been fought. She wanted to leave, but her feet felt as though they were set in the marble floor. She started to tremble, or feel as though she were, and her eyes filled with tears in spite of all her resolutions *not* to let that happen.

An abrupt sound rang out behind her.

"Sorry," one of the security men said as he bent over to pick up a clipboard he'd dropped. "You really jumped, Miss Rawls."

"Yes, I'm on edge these days. I suppose we all are."

CHAPTER
15

HE HEARD HER FOOTSTEPS ON THE STAIRS, THE FUMBLING
in her purse, a key being inserted into the lock. The door
swung open and she stepped into the small, cluttered apartment.

"Where have you been?" Dan Brazier asked. He was in
his wheelchair near a window. Outside, on Broadway, in
San Francisco's North Beach district, the transition from
day to night was in progress and day's final warm glow
bathed everything in yellow. It was the time of day when
the dirt on the windows was most evident, years of accumulation on the outside, a murky brown film of tar and
nicotine on the inside.

Sheryl Figgs, who lived with Brazier, placed a bag of

groceries on a butcher block table in the middle of the living room and handed him the mail.

"Where have you been?" Brazier repeated as he flipped through the envelopes.

"I bought food on the way home from work. How are you feeling?" She noticed that a bottle of gin she'd bought yesterday was almost empty.

Brazier ripped open an envelope and looked at a check from Supreme Court Justice Morgan Childs. As usual, it had been drawn on his personal account in Maryland, and the envelope contained only a box number as a return address.

"You got your disability check," Sheryl said.

Brazier opened that envelope, too, then dropped both checks to a threadbare, imitation Oriental rug.

"I asked you how you were feeling," she said, kicking off her shoes and pulling a purple sweater over her head. She was not an unattractive woman, although an almost perpetual downturn to her mouth created a sad moue. Her hair was blond and seemingly unkempt; no matter how often she washed it, it appeared to be dullish. Her face was thin, pinched, and very pale. Remnants of teenage acne had left a tiny cluster of scars on both cheeks, which she covered with makeup. She was tall and slender. White skin on her arms, legs and belly was soft and loose, like that of an older person. "Damn stretch marks," she often said when they were in bed. "That's what having four kids will do to you."

Once when she'd said it, Brazier had reacted angrily. "You're complaining about marks on your belly. I don't have any legs." He seldom mentioned his disability, and she felt guilty for days about provoking him to bring it up.

She fetched him more ice and he poured the remains of the gin into his glass. She made herself a bourbon and water and sat at the table. "I brought the newspaper," she said.

"You read it." He continued to stare out the window, the gin and ice cubes shimmering in light from outside.

She unfolded the paper on the table and started to read. "Hey," she said, "there's a whole story here about your buddy Childs."

Brazier turned, grimaced. "What's it say?"

She read in silence for a few moments. "Well, it's not really about him. It's about that Sutherland murder case. Listen to this. The woman who's investigating the murder for the Justice Department—her name is Pinscher, Susanna Pinscher—interviewed him up in his airplane."

Brazier grunted.

"Nobody'll make any public comments, it says here, but the reporter claims to have an inside source. He says the investigation is narrowing down to the women in Sutherland's life . . . he was a real swinger."

"What else does it say about Childs?"

"Nothing. Oh, it does say that all the justices are trying to keep a lid on the investigation inside the Court." She lowered the paper and looked at Brazier. "I don't blame them. Who wants people snooping around the Supreme Court—?"

"Let me see it," Brazier said. She gave him the paper and he read the article, then dropped the paper on top of the checks and wheeled himself to the table. "What's for dinner?"

"I thought I'd make a meat loaf. Do you want a salad?"

"No. I'm going out for a little while. How long does a meat loaf take?"

"I don't know. I'll look it up in the cookbook. About an hour, I guess. Where are you going?"

"Around the corner for a drink. I'll be back. Help me downstairs."

She knew it was useless to argue. She would have liked him to stay while she prepared dinner. Sometimes, when he hadn't had too much to drink, they'd be together in the tiny kitchen and talk. She loved talking to Don Brazier when he was sober. He was the smartest man she'd ever met, and even though she knew he didn't mean it, he often made her feel like an intellectual equal, someone he respected and listened to. When he was sober.

She took a red-and-black flannel jacket from a closet and helped him on with it, then wheeled him through the door to the top of a short, straight and narrow set of steps leading one flight down to the street. She watched as he pulled himself out of the chair and, using banisters on either side, literally walked down them with his hands. She followed with the chair, avoiding the scene with her eyes and keeping up a conversation to make his difficult journey go faster. "Mr. Valente talked to me today," she said. "He told me that they're going to rewrite all the software manuals and that he'd be interested in talking to you about doing some of the work. He remembers the things you wrote in magazines and says he'd like to meet you. I told him I'd see about having you come by someday for lunch and—"

He reached the bottom and she hurriedly slipped the chair beneath him. "If I wanted to write again I'd get a damn agent, Sheryl. I don't need you hustling for me, and you can tell your friend Valente to mind his own business. What are you doing, coming on with him?"

"Oh, for God's sake, Dan, he's my boss. He's married and—"

"Open the door."

She did, and he wheeled himself out to the street.

"An hour," she said.

"Yeah, an hour."

She prepared the meat loaf, kneading the bread crumbs, onions and seasoning into the meat, topping it with two strips of bacon and putting it in the oven. She placed two lettuce wedges on plates and brought them to the butcher block table, carefully folded two paper napkins next to the plates and placed silverware on them. Satisfied that she'd done all she could until the meat loaf was done, she sat in the living room and turned on local news on a black-and-white television set. She watched for a few minutes before her attention wandered, first to the flashing, garish red-and-green neon light on the window from a topless club two doors down the street, then to a row of framed photographs lined up on a small table next to her chair. She picked up one of the photos, held it close. Two men were in the picture, Dan Brazier and Morgan Childs, the latter now a Supreme Court justice. It had been taken in Korea shortly after they'd returned from their captivity. Both were grinning broadly. Their arms were around each other and Childs held two fingers in the air, forming a *V*-for-victory sign. "How handsome," Sheryl thought, meaning both of them. Brazier was still handsome, she felt, maybe even more so than when the picture was taken. They looked somewhat alike, Brazier and Childs, rugged, masculine, square faces and strong, forceful chins, clear eyes that saw through you, muscular bodies belonging to men of action, sort of like cowboys, it sometimes occurred to her.

Brazier's upper body had increased in strength since the loss of his legs. He refused to wear any type of prosthesis: "I don't want phony legs," although she knew that when he lived in Washington following the war he had gone to a hospital and tried a set. He never talked much about those years, and she knew not to ask many questions. He could become explosive when pressed for answers, which was why she hadn't asked about Dr. Chester Sutherland, father of the murdered law clerk.

Once, while rummaging through a dresser drawer, she'd come across old, pocket-size appointment books. One of them went back to Brazier's Washington days, and in it was written Dr. Chester Sutherland's name, address and phone

91

number. On subsequent pages the entry "Dr. S." appeared next to times of the day. It had meant nothing to her when she'd first read the books. Brazier had seen a myriad of doctors in an attempt to save his legs. But after reading about the murder of Clarence Sutherland in the local paper, she'd returned to the dresser drawer and confirmed what she'd remembered.

The newscaster introduced a story about a love triangle in the Bay area that had resulted in one of the lovers being bludgeoned to death. It made her think of Brazier's comment about her boss, Mr. Valente. He often accused her of seeing other men, although it wasn't true. She understood, though. A man without legs felt only partially a man. He was wrong, though. Dan Brazier was more of a man than anyone else she'd ever known in her life . . . strong and wise, a sensitive and pleasing lover . . . When he was sober.

The aroma of meat loaf drifted from the kitchen and she felt good. Sheryl liked to cook, especially for Dan. She went to the kitchen, opened the oven and peered in at the bubbling loaf. "Looks pretty good." Then, in a markedly sadder voice . . . "Please come on home, Dan. Please don't make me eat this alone."

As she had too many meals too many times before.

CHAPTER

16

IT WAS THE SORT OF BLEAK, COLD DAY THAT PRESAGED winter. The last leaves had fallen from the trees, and things formerly hidden by them were now visible.

Dr. Chester Sutherland looked through a tinted window in a limousine that had picked him up at his house. He watched Georgetown University's spires slowly glide by, the Potomac patterned by a cold, gray chop. Ahead, through skeletal branches of bare trees, a stark white, neocolossal building surrounded by miles of twelve-foot-high chain link fence came into view. A large sign on the George Washington Parkway identified it—CENTRAL INTEL-LIGENCE AGENCY. Until 1973 the sign had read FAIRBANK HIGHWAY RESEARCH STATION. But then, ironically, President Nixon, in the spirit of more open government, had ordered signs telling it like it was, and, some said, the CIA has never been the same.

The limousine was met at a gate by a team of General Service Administration guards. Credentials were scrutinized before it was allowed to proceed to the next checkpoint. Eventually the long black vehicle entered an underground garage where Sutherland was greeted by a dour young man in a blue suit who wore his ID badge on a chain around his neck. They went upstairs, their route taking them past unmarked doors until reaching a dining room that overlooked the woods of Langley, Virginia. A table covered with pale blue linen and set with expensive silver and china was prepared to seat four people. Sutherland's guide, who'd mentioned that he was with the agency's public-affairs office, excused himself and quietly left the room. Moments later another door opened and a tall man in his fifties entered, moved across plush, thick royal blue carpet and extended his hand. "Roland McCaw, Dr. Sutherland, deputy director of science and technology."

Sutherland shook his hand. "Yes, Mr. McCaw, Bill Stalk mentioned you to me. He said you'd come over from the navy."

"That's right. I'm still trying to get my land legs here at the Company. Drink?"

Sutherland shook his head.

McCaw went to a rolling liquor cabinet and poured himself a stiff shot of rye and a glass of club soda on the side. Sutherland observed him. He carried himself like a military man, held himself a little too erect, which would account for the way his suit fit him, like a garment on a rack instead of on a body.

"Bill will be joining us shortly, doctor. Please have a seat." He indicated the chair he wanted Sutherland to take. Sutherland sat and crossed his legs, careful to preserve a precise crease in his gray flannel trousers, topped by a straw-

94

colored cashmere sport jacket, a blue button-down Oxford cloth shirt and a maroon knit tie. It was Saturday, and he resisted a suit on the weekend. Besides, he knew the people he'd be meeting with would all wear suits. He wanted to stand a bit apart.

William Stalk, director of the CIA's science and technology division, came through the door, "Sit, Chester," he said as Sutherland started to get up. "Hello, Roland. I see you got the jump on us." He went to the liquor cabinet and poured a vodka and tonic. "Terrible tragedy about your boy, Chester. I am so sorry."

"Thank you."

The fourth man at lunch was a small, thin Indian with thick glasses, Dr. Zoltar Kalmani. Sutherland knew of his work through professional and technical journals. His primary recognition was in the field of behavior modification using pharmacological agents, including drugs. He drank white wine and smoked thin brown Sherman cigaretellos, which, he commented in a high-pitched, singsong voice, did not contain saltpeter and thus did not interfere with his sexual life. His laugh was more a giggle.

The conversation stayed on everyday topics while two white-jacketed waiters served shrimp cocktails, a choice of filet of sole almondine or London broil, a bib lettuce salad with vinaigrette dressing, tiny boiled potatoes, coffee, and lemon or raspberry sherbet. (The CIA prided itself on gentlemen's manners—if not always substance.)

Once the table had been cleared Bill Stalk went to the door and locked it. "Cognac?" he asked. McCaw took him up on the offer, the others did not.

Stalk returned to the table, took a small note pad from his breast pocket and opened to a page on which six terse lines were written, each of them numbered. He removed a mechanical pencil from the same pocket, clicked a button on its tube and said, "Item One. Dr. Kalmani has been

95

continuing with some of the research that came out of MKULTRA, a lot of which can be directly credited to your work, Chester."

Sutherland reversed his legs, nodded. "I believe I will have some cognac."

Stalk served the drink, then returned to his note pad. "Naturally, we've had to narrow our focus where experimentation is concerned, but that's probably all to the good. The public scrutiny the program came under prompted a closer evaluation of certain of its elements. Much of what we did was wasted, which, I might add, is no criticism of your work, Chester."

"I understand."

"It was a time when every avenue of interest had to be explored. It would have been a shame to ignore a potential area of legitimate research. But now that public probing has lessened, we would be derelict in not pushing ahead with the valid findings that came out of those previous efforts. Wouldn't you agree, Chester?"

He nodded.

What Sutherland really was thinking was that he wished he weren't there. He didn't understand why he'd been summoned to the meeting in the first place. He'd met with President Jorgens a week ago, and the matter of proceeding with the research had been thoroughly discussed. It was no longer his concern. He'd been out of CIA research for six years.

At the time of his recruitment it had made sense to him. His orientation in medicine had followed the same route as most of his colleagues—research. That was where the action was, and the scramble for funding was an ongoing one. He'd been flattered when the CIA had approached him, and for eight years he'd devoted a portion of his time to the project known as MKULTRA, a top-secret program in which drugs and hypnosis were utilized in a search for effective

96

mind-and-behavior control. Hypnosis had been his specialty, although he'd taken part in many of the pharmacological studies as well. He'd been given carte blanche in the study; money was no object. National security was at stake, or so he'd been told.

But then newspaper probes uncovered the use of drugs on unwitting subjects. Books were written that further laid it open to the public. The families of subjects, some of whom had been killed by the experiments, brought suits against the government. The program was hastily scrapped, and those physicians involved with it quietly returned to their private practices, their names deleted from records released under the Freedom of Information Act.

Sutherland had been relieved when it happened. As much as he believed in the research, he'd found its demands an increasing intrusion into his practice and personal life. Above all, he did not want public knowledge of his involvement in government research. National security aside, there was still something inherently unsavory about it, he'd decided.

Bill Stalk moved to the second item in his note pad. Sutherland listened patiently, forcing his mind to focus on what the director of the agency's most secret division was saying. Eventually, he covered all six items.

"It sounds as though you've developed a solid research program based on the past," Sutherland said. "I wish you well."

"Thanks to you, Chester, and others like you, we have the foundation to build on. The dead ends identified themselves, which leaves us free to pursue more fruitful avenues of inquiry."

"People do not understand the necessity of such research," Dr. Kalmani said. "The future of a free world depends upon being in the forefront of controlling human behavior."

Stalk told a joke which was met with polite laughter.

97

McCaw lighted a cigar and puffed contentedly. Sutherland checked his watch. It was time to leave.

"Anyone for a little skeet shooting?" Stalk asked. "I reserved the range at three."

"I have to get back," Sutherland said. "I have weekend patients later in the day."

"You work too hard, Chester."

"The curse of my WASP heritage. If there's nothing more to discuss, I'll be leaving. Thank you for filling me in on future plans. They have no direct bearing on me, but as an old hand in the project it's gratifying to be kept informed. Dr. Kalmani, it was a pleasure."

"For me, too, Dr. Sutherland. I trust we shall see more of each other in the future."

Bill Stalk stood, shook Sutherland's hand and said in a lowered voice, "Chester, would you mind coming to my office for a few moments?"

Sutherland glanced at the others. He did not want to linger, yet couldn't deny the director his wish. "Yes, of course," he said.

Stalk's office was in a corner of the building. It was austere; the desk was bare, and a single set of bookshelves contained only leather-bound volumes of literary classics.

"I really have to get back," Sutherland said.

"I know, Chester, but asking you out here had very little to do with what we discussed at lunch."

"I gathered that."

"I'm sure you did. Of all the people of your professional caliber in the program, you're the one whose instincts I most trust."

"That's flattering, Bill, but to be frank with you I'm damn glad to be out of it. Why did you ask me back? Is there a problem that involves me?" He knew what the answer was but didn't want to acknowledge it.

"Security, Chester, that's the question. The continuation

of the research depends on security. Naturally, we released what we could of the files under the Freedom of Information Act. Hell, we had no choice, and we sanitized them as best we could. I've received information from . . . well, let's just say very high and reliable sources that there might be a weak link in the future chain . . . and that that link might be you."

"Because of my son—?"

"Precisely. That's another thing I've always admired about you, your ability to cut through the skin and get to the marrow." He frowned and cleared his throat. "Chester, there's a very legitimate concern about your files."

"Why?"

"Because certain members of your immediate—"

"Family?"

"Yes, and others, might have had access to them and could potentially compromise our position."

"My son, sir, is dead."

"Was he the one who gained access to them?"

"To what?"

"Your MKULTRA files."

"There weren't any."

"That's not what I've been told."

"Who told you otherwise?"

"A reliable source."

"*I'm* a reliable source."

"Of course you are, Chester. When I heard about your son I was shocked. I'd met him once and was very impressed with his intelligence. He was a son any father could be proud of, I would have been pleased to have called him my own . . ."

Sutherland resisted the temptation to respond sharply. Instead he said, "Clarence's death was a tragic loss to all of us close to him, and we're trying to cope with the horror

99

of it as best we can. If there isn't anything else, Bill, I'd just as soon get back to my family."

Stalk came around the desk and draped his arm around Sutherland's shoulders. "Chester, I'm sorry if I've intruded on sensitive ground. There's no need for that, national security or no national security. But I have an obligation to explore any possible area of weakness. You understand, I'm sure."

"Yes, of course. I enjoyed lunch, Bill, it was good seeing you again."

Stalk pushed a buzzer on his desk, then walked Sutherland to the door, his arm still over his shoulder. "You know, Chester," he said, "I realize we've discussed this before, and I promise you this will be the last time. Are you certain you didn't keep files of your own on MKULTRA?"

Sutherland placed his hand on the doorknob and turned it. He looked into Stalk's eyes and said flatly, quietly, "Yes, I'm certain. Enjoy the skeet shooting."

CHAPTER
17

Eight of the nine Supreme Court justices sat in the main conference room. Missing was Temple Conover. He had called to say he was ill but promised to come in later in the day.

Jonathan Poulson had presented his argument in favor of the state of Illinois in the *Nidel* v. *Illinois* case. Much of what he said had been contained in a long memorandum from him earlier in the week. It was a typical Poulson memo, long and rambling, filled with redundancies and lacking in clarity of writing and thought. At least that was the way most of the clerks viewed his written work, and their justices tended to agree.

What some of the justices found particularly upsetting about the memorandum was its stress on achieving a unanimous decision within the Court so that a clear and strong message on abortion would be available to lower courts across the nation. Poulson seemed to be saying that in this particular case it mattered less what each individual justice believed represented the facts of law in *Nidel* v. *Illinois* than a need to reflect the administration's antiabortion posture, which in turn reflected the nation's morality. "It's ridiculous," was the way one justice put it to his clerks. "If there's ever been a case that didn't lend itself to unanimity, this is it."

When Poulson had completed his arguments in the conference, the senior justice was next to speak. Since Conover wasn't present, his turn was passed on. One after another the justices presented their views of the case based on their reading of the briefs and the oral arguments heard in open court.

"I don't understand why we continue to deal with this matter beyond the scope of the legal issue," Justice Tilling-Masters said. "If it's the intention of members of this Court to render a sweeping opinion on abortion from legal, philosophical and moral perspectives, *Nidel* v. *Illinois* is not the case to base it on. I said that from the beginning. That's why I voted against accepting it for review."

"I agree," Morgan Childs said from his chair near the door. "This case is too narrow for that. In accepting it for review we're being asked to determine whether the federal government has a right to tell a state what it must do with its funding for health care. It isn't federal money we're discussing, it's state money." He picked up law books that had been opened to specific pages and quoted from previous cases he felt had bearing on *Nidel* v. *Illinois*. "It's my view that the state of Illinois has a right to determine its policies on state-funded medical care. Naturally, if an individual's rights are in question another

102

element would be introduced, but I find that situation lacking in this instance."

Poulson nodded enthusiastically. "Can we take a preliminary vote?"

They went around the table, beginning with the Chief. It ended up four to four.

"I'm afraid I can't accept this," Poulson said. "Perhaps there are overlooked factors that we might reconsider." He started to present his views again when another of the justices, a thin, scholarly man named Ronald Fine, who was second in seniority to Temple Conover, and who often voted with the senior justice on social issues, interrupted. "Chief Justice," he said in a quiet, level voice tinged with a southern accent, "I believe we have a preliminary vote on this case. Naturally, Justice Conover's vote will be the deciding one, and I'm sure we are all...well, shall we say, relatively certain how the senior justice will vote."

Poulson knew Fine was right on both counts. Still, he did not want to leave the conference in the minority.

"Let me call Justice Conover," Fine said, "and inform him of the vote."

"Yes," Poulson said. A wave of anxiety had swept over him; he was anxious to return to the quiet of his chambers.

There was silence in the room as Fine placed the call to Conover's house. "Yes, Justice Conover, that's the way the vote went...Pardon?...Of course, I'll pass that information on to the others...Oh, just a second, Justice Poulson wants to speak with you."

He handed the phone to Poulson. "Temple, how are you feeling?...Good, glad to hear it. You're voting for Nidel I take it...Yes, I understand. I would like to speak with you when you come in this afternoon...Yes, thank you, you too."

"That makes it five to four," Childs muttered, "for the

plaintiff. Somehow, I can't help but feel that this won't represent a final vote."

"It usually doesn't," said Justice Augustus Smith, the Court's only black member. Known as "Gus" to his friends, he was the most easygoing of the nine; quick-witted and filled with gentle humor. "With Temple writing the majority opinion," he said, "there's no way somebody won't see some light on the other side. Did he say he'd write it himself?" he asked Fine.

"No, but it's a fair assumption."

Under the rules of the Court, the senior justice in the majority was empowered either to write the initial opinion or assign it to another member of the majority. Had Chief Justice Poulson been in the majority, that authority would have gone to him. As it now stood he would assign the minority opinion, and each justice was free to write a personal, dissenting judgment.

Poulson hid his anger until reaching his chambers. He realized that his failure to gain unanimity was not particularly relevant in light of the way the initial vote had gone. Not only would the Poulson Court fail to utter a call to the nation that would reflect President Jorgens's campaign promise to return decency to American life, but a distinct blow would be delivered to that pledge, resulting in an important victory for the social libertarians he and Jorgens abhorred.

But as he sat back in his high-backed leather chair and soaked in the calm of his office, his initial anger and anxiety faded. This was only the beginning. If there were ever a time for a chief justice to effectively lobby his colleagues on the Court, this was it. He thought about Augustus Smith's comment and realized how accurate it had been. Temple Conover would write a majority opinion that would go too far. Conover couldn't help it. His zeal for social reform, combined with the influence of age and his natural irascible personality, would see to it, and more moderate justices who'd voted in the majority just might shift their final votes.

Poulson lunched with an old friend from law school and his friend's son, also an attorney, at the National Lawyer's Club. The young man asked questions, which pleased Poulson. Poulson told him that of all the institutions in America, it was the Court that stood apart from political wheeling and dealing. It was, he said, a body of nine individuals who, by virtue of their backgrounds, education and experience could interpret the Constitution without being mortgaged to any person or group. He ended up by giving the young man what had become a canned speech, but as he continued, checking now and then to measure the son's interest, he felt genuine pride. He'd always revered the sanctity of the law, which was why he'd worked as hard as he had to gain his first appointment to a bench to escape practicing law with all its deals and bargaining, its infighting and corruption.

The young man asked about Poulson's views of secrecy in the Court. He phrased the question carefully so as not to hint at recent media criticism of the Poulson Court as being the most secretive in history.

Poulson smiled. "I'll answer that by quoting my predecessor, Chief Justice Warren Burger. I always remember a speech he gave to the Ohio Judicial Conference about ten months before being sworn in as chief. I may not have it 100 percent correct, but it will be close enough. Justice Burger said, 'A court which is final and unreviewable needs more careful scrutiny than any other. Unreviewable power is the most likely to engage in self-indulgence and the least likely to engage in dispassionate self-analysis.' But these words really sum up Justice Burger's feelings, and mine. 'In a country like ours no public institution, or the people who operate it, can be above public debate.'"

The young attorney's father kept his smile to himself. His friend, now Chief Justice, had, in fact, clamped a heavy lid on the Court far beyond anything experienced in the past. He couldn't help thinking back to his younger days when he and Poulson were struggling to get started. A mutual friend had termed Poulson "the most paranoid guy I've ever met." When told of the comment, Poulson had laughed and said, "Just because you're paranoid doesn't mean they aren't following you."

"Well, I really must be getting back," Poulson said. "Good luck to you, young man, in your career. If there's anything I can do for you, please feel free to ask. Your dad and I go back a long way together."

As they prepared to leave the dining room Poulson's friend asked about major cases pending at the Court. Poulson hurriedly listed a few, including *Nidel* v. *Illinois*.

"How does that one look?" his friend asked.

A laugh from Poulson. "You know better than that, Harold. If there's one thing in the Court that demands secrecy it's the voting on cases. You'll have to read the papers like everybody else."

Poulson had his driver stop at a drugstore on the way back to the Court to buy Preparation H and a bottle of aspirin. They were for different problems. Once back in his chambers he took two aspirins for a headache that had begun during lunch, instructed his secretary that he did not want to be disturbed, settled in his chair and picked up a private phone. He dialed. It was answered on the first ring. "The office of the attorney general," a woman said.

"Hello, this is Chief Justice Poulson. Is Mr. Fletcher available?"

"Just a moment, Mr. Chief Justice."

A few moments later Attorney General Walter Fletcher came on the line. "Good afternoon, Mr. Chief Justice," he said. "What can I do for you?"

"Nothing at the moment, Walter. I just thought I'd better call and tell you that preliminary voting on the abortion case did not go well."

There was a pointed silence on Fletcher's end.

"I'm not discouraged," Poulson said. "These things shift, especially something as sensitive as this. I wouldn't be surprised if we ended up with an almost unanimous decision in favor of Illinois once the dust settles."

"But as of now, it doesn't look good. Is that what you're saying?"

Poulson tried to act nonchalant. "No need to worry, Walter. You might tell the President that we've got things under control."

"Can I tell him that with conviction, Mr. Chief Justice?"

"Absolutely." (Well, you can tell him, but it's not in the bag.)

"Fine. Thank you for calling. By the way, if the President wants to discuss this with you, will you be available later today or tomorrow?"

"I'll make myself available any time that's convenient for him, Walter."

It was appropriate, but these were difficult times, he told himself, rationalizing. If the nation under President Jorgens's leadership were to regain its former balance and prestige—and the need for that he *was* unequivocal about—it would take definite, even bold steps by every governmental institution to bring about that change.

"'The law, wherein, as in a magic mirror, we see reflected not only our own lives but the lives of all men that have been,'" Poulson said aloud, quoting Oliver Wendell Holmes, Jr., and felt a sense of relief displace his doubting mood. He poured himself a glass of vodka and sternly addressed himself. "You've been appointed Chief Justice of

the Supreme Court by the President of the United States,"
he said, "and you'll do what's *right*, damn it, for the President, for the Court, and for the American people. *No matter
what . . .*"

CHAPTER
18

"WHO?" TELLER ASKED THE DESK SERGEANT WHO'D CALLED from downstairs the following morning.

"Mrs. Temple Conover. She wants to see you, says it's urgent."

"Send her up."

He couldn't imagine the senior justice's young wife visiting MPD headquarters unless she had something that related to the Sutherland murder. Well and good. He'd just come from his nine o'clock meeting with Dorian Mars and it hadn't been pleasant.

Cecily Conover was ushered into Teller's office.

"I'm sorry to barge in on you this way," she said, "but it couldn't wait."

"Please sit down, Mrs. Conover. Now, what couldn't wait?"

She crossed her legs, fussed at her blonde bangs. Teller couldn't help but react to her sexiness. She was a naturally attractive woman who seemed to feel a need to reinforce what came naturally. She also acted nervous; acting or for real, he wondered?

"I'm not sure I should be here," she said, "but I didn't know what else to do."

He leaned forward on his desk and smiled. "Whatever brings you here, Mrs. Conover, I'm sure we can talk about it."

"I've never been so confused in my life," she said as she shifted her weight in the chair, her skirt riding up on her thighs.

"How is your husband?" Teller asked.

"Fine, just fine. He's an amazing man, Lieutenant Teller, but I'm sure you know that. Every American knows of my husband's contributions to the law . . . and justice."

"True. I don't know how he does it. Somebody told me the other day he's written more than twenty books. I see things by him in magazines too. I hope I'm half that active when I get—"

It was a smile intended to put him at ease. "Yes, my husband is old, detective, and has his physical problems, but he doesn't stop for a moment. He's a very virile man."

He wished she hadn't used the word *virile*. Why mention something so intimate to a stranger? He shifted gears and asked her whether she enjoyed being in the public eye.

"No, I hate it. I'm a very simple person, a very private one."

"I'm sure you are."

He was getting fed up with her posturing. He wished she'd get to the point. When she didn't, and after a few more meaningless exchanges, he put it to her. "Why did you come here this morning, Mrs. Conover? Does it by any chance have to do with the Sutherland case?"

She pursed her lips and looked away.

"If you have something to contribute, anything, you might as well do it now. Frankly, I can use all the help I can get, even if it's painful for you. We can talk frankly and privately."

She looked at him. "Can we? I mean, can I discuss things with you and be *sure* it will stay in this room?"

Teller sat back and lit a clove. "That depends," he said as a blue cloud of smoke headed for the ceiling. "If you want to share a confidence with me, I'm sure there'll be no problem in keeping it confidential, but if it has a bearing on the investigation, I can't promise. I guess you'll just have to trust me."

"Funny, but I do trust you, detective. You have that kind of face."

"Thank you." (What the hell kind of face was *that*?)

"I'm concerned about how I'll be seen by you . . . and others. After all, a wife is supposed to stand by her husband for better or for worse. A wife can't testify in court against her husband, can she?"

"She can't be forced to. Can if she wants to."

"Then you understand my dilemma."

"No, I don't. You haven't told me anything yet."

"I'm sorry." He couldn't see any tears but she dabbed a corner of her eye with a tiny embroidered handkerchief. "All right, Detective Teller. Here." She reached into a floppy oversized purse, pulled out a brown paper bag and handed it to him. "Go ahead, look at it," she said.

He pulled a handkerchief from his pocket, reached inside the bag and pulled out a Charter Arms Pathfinder .22-caliber pistol with a seventy-six millimeter barrel.

"Yours?" he asked.

111

"My husband's."

"And?"

She looked down at her lap. "It might be the gun used to kill Clarence. It's the same kind of pistol described in the newspapers."

Teller weighed the pistol, examined it. "It's easy to ascertain whether it was the murder weapon."

"Yes, you can do that sort of thing, can't you?"

"That's right. But before we get to the technology, Mrs. Conover, I'd like to know more about why you think this weapon might be the one used in Clarence Sutherland's murder?"

"I told you, it fits the description in the papers."

"So do thousands of other .22-caliber handguns. If everybody who owned one turned it in after reading about Sutherland, we wouldn't have room to store them."

"But those other people don't work in the Supreme Court, nor did they know about Clarence or have a reason to—" She stopped abruptly.

"Are you actually telling me you think that your husband might have used this weapon to kill Clarence Sutherland?"

She gasped, opened her eyes, then shook her head. "*No*, I'm not suggesting anything like that. He kept the gun in his chambers. I guess someone who knew that took it to kill Clarence."

"If it's the murder weapon."

"Well...but you can find that out, can't you?"

Teller shrugged. "How did *you* know your husband had this weapon, Mrs. Conover?"

"I...Justice Conover and I once had an argument, a silly spat. He waved the gun at me. It was over as fast as it started."

"You argued in his chambers?"

"Yes."

"And he waved a gun at you?"

112

"It was all so silly, just—"

"Maybe life has passed me by, Mrs. Conover, but from where I sit a man waving a gun at his wife sounds like more than just a silly spat."

She stamped her foot. "I'm sorry I ever *mentioned* it. God . . . I thought it was right to bring the gun to you. I was just trying to help . . ."

"Did that *spat* with your husband involve Clarence Sutherland, by any chance?"

"Of course not. I don't remember what it was about."

Teller looked at her hard. "All right, I'll have ballistics check this out."

"There's something else . . . I'm afraid . . ."

"You think your husband is capable of killing you?"

"He's . . . he can be volatile at times. He's very jealous and imagines things—"

"Was he jealous of Clarence Sutherland?"

She opened her eyes and dabbed at them with her handkerchief. "He's jealous of *everyone*."

"I'm going to take the pistol to ballistics now, Mrs. Conover. You're free to stay if you'd like, but you don't have to."

"I think I'd like to leave," she said. "I do ask that if it is the murder weapon you let me know before anyone else."

"We'll see."

He helped her on with her coat and held the door open. "It was gutsy of you to come forward like this," he said, not meaning it but feeling he had to say it.

"I had to," she said. "Thank you for being so decent about everything . . ."

He watched her move off to the elevators, then went to the ballistics lab, found its director and handed him the pistol. "The Sutherland case," he said. "It's hot." . . .

The chief of ballistics came to Teller's office immediately

113

after the tests. "It's the weapon," he said. "Perfect match. Bullet and muzzle. No question."

"Prints?"

"Partials, maybe enough for a positive ID, maybe not. But there's no doubt about the weapon itself, Marty. Sutherland was shot with it."

Teller spun around in his chair and looked out his window over a gray, wet Washington.

"Who's it belong to?" the lab chief asked.

"Somebody I wish it didn't. Keep this cool until I have a chance to talk to Mars. Not a damn word to anybody."

"Okay, Marty, but move fast. These things are hard to sit on for very long."

Ten minutes later Teller was meeting with Dorian Mars. He told him about Cecily Conover's visit, her handing over the murder weapon. Mars listened, no change of expression. After Teller had finished, Mars lit his pipe, clicked the stem against his teeth and said, "Silence is golden, Marty."

"So I've heard. The lid stays on?"

"Tight."

"How long?"

"I'll get to the commissioner right away. Hey, this guy is the senior justice of the United States Supreme Court—"

"Owning the gun doesn't mean he used it, Dorian. His wife says someone must have taken it from his chambers. Maybe she did. Implying her husband just might have done it...a jealous man, and really diverting suspicion from herself...after all, she's a few light-years younger than he is. Maybe he was getting in her way. The bloom was off the rose of playing a justice's wife?..."

Mars dropped the pipe on his desk and picked up his phone. "I'll call you later, Marty. Stay available."

As Teller was leaving he heard Mars say into the phone, "...I don't care what he's doing or where he's doing it, this can't wait, and if you make *me* wait you'll be a new statistic on the unemployment rolls."

CHAPTER
19

Susanna Pinscher called Martin Teller at three that afternoon.

"You promised to keep me informed about any developments on your end. You didn't."

"Don't know what you're talking about—"

"Yes, you do. I'm talking about the gun you got into your hot hands this morning."

It took him a moment, finally, "I don't believe it."

"Come on, do you think something that important can be kept a secret?"

"Who told you?"

"It doesn't matter, somebody here at Justice."

"It does matter, damn it. If there's a leak from here I want to plug it."

"Later. The important thing is that you have the murder weapon. What now?"

"It's being discussed. It's not like your run-of-the-mill murder weapon, Susanna. The damn thing belongs to Justice Temple Conover. Not only that, his wife brings it to MPD, which is not what a run-of-the-mill wife does."

"Can we get together?"

"Sure. When?"

"A drink, dinner."

He was about to leave his office at six to meet her when Dorian Mars came through the door.

"I was just leaving," Teller said.

"It'll take a minute. Look, Marty, first of all the commissioner, along with other heavy rollers, wants the Conover thing hushed up for a few days."

"It's probably all over town already," Teller said. He didn't mention his conversation with Susanna.

"Maybe so," Mars said, "but I want it kept tight to our vest."

"Tight to? . . . Right. I really have to run."

"One more minute, Marty. You told me that you were working close with Justice."

"I have a contact."

"Maybe you should find another one."

"Why?"

"The scuttlebutt is that Justice has developed an important lead in the case."

"What is it?"

"I don't know, but I sure as hell want to. It's still MPD's responsibility to resolve this case and I'll be damned if I'll stand still for those people over at Justice doing our job and rubbing our noses in it."

"I'll see what I can find out."

"Fill me in at the nine o'clock meeting."

"I'll do my best."

* * *

HE MET Susanna at Coolbreeze's, a neighborhood bar on Eleventh Street, where they ordered Italian specials of the day from a blackboard and a bottle of Corvo red. Teller told her about Cecily Conover's visit. When he was finished, she asked what the MPD intended to do with the evidence.

"Nothing for the moment. Conover will have to be questioned again, but right now everybody's bracing for a confrontation with the Court's senior justice over the fact the murder weapon belongs to him."

"I think everybody at MPD is very naive," she said.

"Why?"

"I guarantee you that by noon tomorrow the gun will be front-page material. It's already all over Justice, and I'm sure it's the same at MPD."

Teller nodded. "You're right, but it sure isn't going to come from me. Now, let's talk about you and Justice. You sounded annoyed on the phone that I hadn't called you with the gun story. You do understand why, don't you?"

She shook her head and sipped her wine. "No, I don't. We agreed to share information. Telling me isn't like telling a reporter from the *Post*."

"I know that, but I was in a spot. While we're on the subject of sharing information, what's the so-called big breakthrough at Justice?"

She shrugged. "What big breakthrough?"

Teller held up his index finger. "No games, Susanna. I leveled with you—"

"Only after I called you on it."

"Doesn't matter. I've filled you in about Conover's gun. Your turn."

"What I came up with is minor league compared to the gun. I've been assigned a couple of nice bright young interns to help with the investigation. I had them go back over

118

everything ever written about public figures in the case, Conover, Childs, Poulson, Dr. Sutherland, anybody who piqued a journalist's interest."

"Why?"

"Because I didn't know what else to have them do. Frankly, Marty, it's all been a dead end for me. I envy you having the murder weapon plopped in your lap."

Teller bit his lip and poured the last of the wine into their glasses. He hated to admit she was right. He hadn't done a thing to bring about possession of the pistol, couldn't point to painstaking digging or innovative thought.

She continued. "At any rate, one of my interns came up with an intriguing bit."

"Go ahead."

"Chief Justice Poulson has been a patient of Dr. Chester Sutherland. What do you think?" she asked.

"A man is entitled to see a doctor, including a shrink."

She looked annoyed. "But if that shrink's son was his murdered clerk, and the patient happens to be Chief Justice of the Supreme Court?"

"Sure, it's an interesting linkup—"

"What if Clarence Sutherland knew about Poulson's psychiatric problems through his father and held it over his head? Remember I told you about my lunch with Laurie Rawls, how she said no one could understand why Clarence wasn't fired? Even granted his ability. Maybe that's how he kept his job."

Teller said, "And maybe Poulson killed his law clerk to keep his mouth shut?"

"Maybe."

"If so, the kid must have come up with some pretty damaging information. Do you think Poulson's gay?"

She shook her head, then changed tack. "Who knows? Stranger things have come out. A homosexual Chief Justice would blow the lid off the whole nation, not to mention the

119

career of the President who appointed him, a President awash in moral rectitude and a Chief Justice who publicly is known to share his sentiments..."

Teller nodded. Farfetched, but so was Watergate and the idiotic Bay of Pigs... "By the way," Teller said, "when you mentioned Laurie Rawls it reminded me of something. I talked to a close friend of Clarence Sutherland, a guy named Plum. Plum says Laurie was crazy in love with Clarence, called him at all odd hours, made huge scenes when he was with somebody else."

"It seems to fit his pattern. I want to see her again. I think I could keep our relationship going. I must say I like her—I'd hate to see her come up guilty."

"Come on, lady, you're investigating a murder. I'll take whatever, whoever I can get. You get that way after a few years in this business."

He paid the check and they went outside. "How are your kids?" he asked.

"Fine. How are yours?"

"Good, last I heard. Nightcap?"

"Okay."

"I'd suggest my place but the cleaning woman hasn't been in for six months."

She took his arm. "Mine was in this morning."

They sat in her living room for several hours, talking about their lives, families, exchanging gossip about people in Washington, and some of the cases they'd been involved with.

She yawned. "I guess I'd better call it a night—"

He slid close to her, took her in his arms and kissed her, gently at first, then more urgently. She fell back into soft corduroy cushions, her arms around his neck, their bodies pressed tight together...

Afterward he said, "If I wanted to be flip, I'd say something brilliant like, 'Thanks I needed that.' What I'd like to say, if you can stand it, counselor, is 'Thanks, and you're quite a woman.'"

She smiled. "And thank you, Teller. And, not being flip, I'll say I really did need that . . . and enjoyed it . . ."

As he was leaving her apartment at two in the morning he said, "Something bothers me about this info on Poulson being a patient of Dr. Sutherland."

"What?" She was now wearing a purple velour robe and slippers.

"How your interns came up with it by reading old newspaper clippings. It's not the sort of thing that makes the papers."

She kissed him on the cheek. "Elementary, my dear Teller. One of the interns has a father who owns a pharmacy frequented by the high and the mighty, including Chief Justice Poulson. He's had prescriptions filled there that were prescribed by Sutherland. And I'll let you in on another shocking revelation."

"Yeah?"

"Somebody in the Chief Justice's family has hemorrhoids."

"I see. Good night, Susanna."

"Good night, Teller. Sleep tight."

CHAPTER
20

MORGAN CHILDS RECEIVED CLEARANCE TO LAND AT NEW York's Kennedy Airport. He banked his Piper Colt into a tight left turn, slipped into the prescribed landing pattern and set down smoothly on Runway 21 Right. He braked the small aircraft to a quick stop, turned off the runway and taxied to a designated small-plane area.

After arranging for tie-down facilities he asked a dispatcher to call him a cab. "I'm catching American's nine o'clock flight to San Francisco," he told him.

"Are you Judge Childs?" the dispatcher asked.

"Yes."

"Happy to drive you over myself, sir."

The dispatcher, a gregarious fellow, did not stop talking all the way to the American Airlines terminal. Childs half listened; his thoughts were on recent events in the Court and on the purpose of his weekend trip to California. He was scheduled that night to address a western regional meeting of Sigma Delta Chi, the journalism fraternity, on the subject of freedom of the press. He'd originally turned down the invitation, but called the program chairman a week before the meeting. The chairman was delighted. "It'll be quite an honor, Mr. Justice, and a pleasant surprise for our members," he'd said.

Childs boarded a 747 through Gate Three and glanced inside the flight deck as he passed it on the way to his seat in First Class. The three-man crew was busy preparing for departure, and Childs wished he could be up there with them rather than strapped in as a passenger. Nothing relaxed him more than being at the controls of an airplane in the vast ocean of air above the earth, the problems of everyday life far below and losing importance with every foot of altitude. He could have made a connection later in the day to San Francisco from Washington, but opted for the New York flight because it gave him a little solo time aloft.

"Good morning, Justice Childs," a flight attendant said. "We've been expecting you aboard."

"Good morning. Nice day for flying."

"Yes, beautiful. Can I get you anything?"

"No, I'm fine, thank you."

He settled back in his seat, opened a briefcase and took out a handwritten draft of the speech he would give. The doors to the aircraft were closed and, engines whining, the huge aircraft rolled away from the gate. Fifteen minutes later it lifted off the ground and began its long, carefully prescribed journey west.

Childs had a Bloody Mary before breakfast and worked on the speech, deleting paragraphs, inserting new ones. Satisfied that the notes did not contain inappropriate references to pending cases, he returned them to his briefcase.

He peered out the window at the panorama thirty thousand feet below, then looked across the aisle where another passenger was reading a paperback book. A copy of that morning's New York *Times* was next to him. He noticed Childs and said, "Help yourself."

Childs took up the paper and scanned the front page. He'd left his house that morning before his Washington *Post* had been delivered, and had deliberately avoided turning on his car radio on the way to the airport. With so little time for silence and reflection, he husbanded every moment he could find.

He started to turn the page when an item at the bottom from United Press International caught his eye. The headline read: SUTHERLAND MURDER WEAPON FOUND.

He read the lead:

The .22-caliber pistol used in the killing of Supreme Court clerk Clarence Sutherland has been uncovered by the Washington Metropolitan Police Department, it was learned last night. The report, unconfirmed by MPD spokespeople but attributed to a reliable source within the department, claims that the pistol has been subjected to ballistics testing and that it is, in fact, the murder weapon.

The story, which was continued inside the paper, went on to recount the details of Sutherland's death. It ended: *Dorian Mars, chief of detectives for the MPD, refused to comment when reached at his home, but promised a statement later today.*

The flight arrived in San Francisco at 12:15 California time. Childs went to a phone booth and placed a credit-card call to his home in Virginia. His wife answered.

"What have you heard about the weapon being found?" he asked.

"It was on the news this morning. Some reporters have called."

"Why would they call me?"

"They're trying to find out more about it, I suppose. Morg, I'm very concerned."

His laugh was forced. "Why?"

"Why did you call about it?"

"Curious, that's all. I read about it on the plane and thought you'd have picked up more than the initial dispatch I read." There was silence on the other end. He asked, "Has there been any word on how the MPD got hold of the weapon, or who it belonged to?"

"Not that I know of. Are you all right?"

"I'm fine. I just arrived and am heading for the hotel. I'll call you from there."

"All right."

"Peg."

"What?"

"I wish you were with me."

"I should have come."

"Yes, you should have. If another reporter or someone from the police call, tell them nothing. Understand? Just say, 'No comment.'"

"All right. Call me later."

"I will."

The SDX dinner committee had booked Childs into a suite on the fifteenth floor of the Mark Hopkins Hotel. A bouquet of flowers, a basket of cheese and two bottles of wine had been sent up by the hotel's assistant manager, who had escorted Childs to the suite.

"Is there anything you need, Mr. Justice?" he asked before leaving.

"No, thank you, everything looks fine."

"Have a pleasant stay with us. We're honored to have you."

125

Childs stepped onto a glassed-in terrace that overlooked the city. Bright sunlight streamed through the windows and created a small rainbow in one corner. It was silent in the suite, and very calm. Yet, in the midst of beauty and peace, he was apprehensive. It was a feeling he hated, one that said weakness, loss of control.

He did what he usually did when anxious. He exercised. He stripped off his clothes and in his boxer shorts went through a half-hour of knee-bends and push-ups, stretching and pulling. He observed himself in a full-length mirror. He was in excellent shape for his age, which made him feel better. He tended to be scornful of people who didn't take care of themselves. He'd survived his Korean captivity because he'd been mentally and physically strong, and if the need ever arose again to survive, he intended to still be ready.

The banquet chairman called to inquire whether everything was satisfactory, and to go over the schedule for that night's dinner, which would be held downstairs in the Peacock Court. He invited Childs to have drinks with the officers of the organization but Childs declined, claiming he had reading to do on matters before the Court.

He showered, napped for an hour, then called home. Sue, the youngest of his four children, answered. They chatted for a minute before Childs asked to speak with her mother.

"Mom's not here, dad. She had a fashion show to go to, at Garfinckel's, I think."

"Yes, I forgot. By the way, honey, anything new about the report I heard that they found the gun that killed Clarence Sutherland?"

"Gee, I don't know. Somebody from NBC called and asked to talk to you, but I told them you were gone until Sunday. I guess it was about the gun. Mom told me not to say anything to anybody."

"That's right, honey. Well, take care. I'll see you tomorrow night."

"Okay, dad. Give a good speech."

"I'll try."

He turned on television and searched for a newscast. It was too early in the day; he'd have to wait until that night to pick up new information about the gun.

He looked at the phone, then at the TV screen. A college football game was in progress. He turned down the sound, picked up the phone and dialed a number. A woman answered.

"Hello," Childs said, "may I speak to Dan Brazier?"

"He's not here. Who's calling?"

"A friend. Who is this?"

"Sheryl. I expect Dan back in an hour or two. Give me your name and—"

He dropped the phone in its cradle, got up, dressed in tan corduroy slacks, a white shirt and a dark brown crewneck sweater and rode the elevator to the lobby. He entered a waiting cab and gave the driver an address in North Beach.

He walked along Broadway, stopping to peer in shop windows and to read large, garish signs extolling sexual favors available inside. His reaction to them was visceral. He hated pornography, and had voted in a number of cases to curtail its proliferation. The First Amendment, he felt, did not grant the right to create and prosper from materials that were blatantly offensive, that degraded women, victimized those who were exposed to it and generated revenue for mob-controlled interests to feed a mushrooming drug traffic. His eldest daughter had recently joined a women's march against porn in New York's Time Square, and he'd been very proud of her.

Still, he deeply believed in the First Amendment and, in most court cases, had focused on the distribution of pornography rather than the curtailing of its production. If there

127

were those in society who needed pornography to compensate for inadequate personal lives, all right, so be it, but no one should be exposed to it who did not want to be...

He glanced up at a number above a doorway, crossed the street and looked at it from that perspective. He tried to see through the windows of an apartment on the second floor but a reflection made it impossible.

He stayed for a half-hour, watching, checking his watch, leaning against a building. He might have stayed longer if a teenage girl dressed in a pea coat, jeans and wearing a purple feather in her hair had not approached him and asked, "Want to party?" Childs walked away from her, found a cab and returned to the hotel, where he read briefs until it was time to dress for dinner.

There were two hundred people gathered in the Peacock Court. Childs was warmly welcomed by the officers of the group, who led him to the dais, where he was seated in the center of a dozen people.

"I hope you don't mind the publicity, Mr. Justice," a woman to his immediate right said. "We were so excited when we heard you'd decided to accept the invitation that we crowed about it."

"I haven't seen any," he said.

"It was in the papers today," she said, "and on radio and television. We have working press here tonight to cover your speech."

"Well, I hope I say something worth their trouble."

She laughed and touched his forearm.

The banquet chairman asked whether he'd consider holding a brief press conference with reporters, informal, of course, and guaranteed not to take more than fifteen minutes. He agreed and followed the chairman to a tight knot of men and women at the end of the dais. One of the group, a bearded young man with an intense expression on his face, said, "Justice Childs, we'd like to ask you a few questions."

"Go ahead," Childs said, "but first let me ask you one." They laughed. "What's this rumor I've heard about the gun used to kill Clarence Sutherland being found?"

"We wanted to talk to you about that," a young woman said. "I was told as I was leaving the office that the gun belongs to Justice Conover, and that his wife was the one who delivered it to the police."

"I didn't..." Childs held back words that would betray his shock at what she'd just said. He smiled. "I hadn't heard that, and naturally would not want to comment on it until I had a chance to confirm the facts."

"But what if it's true, Justice Childs? You've sat on the bench with Justice Conover for quite a long time now. Do you think he's the sort of man who would be capable of—?"

"I think that's an inappropriate question, young man. I don't want to discuss the Sutherland matter any further. If you have questions about my appearance here tonight, please ask them."

"Do you have an advance copy of your talk?" another journalist asked.

"No. I work from notes."

"Please, Mr. Justice, just one more question about the gun that was found. Were you aware that Justice Conover kept a weapon in his chambers, and if so, do you—?"

"I'd better get back to my seat," Childs said. "Thank you for coming."

He returned to the center of the dais. His speech went well. He was confident he'd struck the right note, combining a stated reverence for the First Amendment with a call for responsibility among the media.

Afterward he took advantage of the first lull to excuse himself, said good-night to his hosts and made his way toward the door. Eventually, after being stopped numerous times enroute, he reached the lobby. Piano music drifted from the lower bar, and Childs recognized the familiar strains of "Tomorrow." He paused in the center of the lobby, unsure whether to return to his suite or to go outside for a walk. He decided to go upstairs and call Peg. As he walked toward a bank of manually operated elevators, an anachronistic nicety he always enjoyed about the Mark Hopkins, a voice from behind said, "Play ball."

Childs stopped in his tracks, the words ringing in his ears.

"Home run," the voice said.

Childs slowly turned his head. Ten feet away in a wheelchair was Dan Brazier, dressed in a brown suede jacket, flowered open shirt and khaki pants pinned over the stumps of his legs.

"Dan?"

"In the flesh, Morgan." He closed the gap between them and extended his right hand. Childs took it, held it for a moment, then vigorously shook it.

"What are you doing here?" Childs asked.

"Waiting for you. Hell, when my old buddy hits town to give a speech I figure I have to catch him. Your picture was in the paper today. Thanks for looking me up."

"I called."

"She told me, but you didn't leave a name."

"I was ... Well, it doesn't matter. How've you been, Dan? You look good."

"I feel great, ready to run the mile."

Childs winced, then stepped back a few paces and said, "When I heard you say, 'Play ball,' I couldn't believe it."

"I figured it would grab your attention."

They had used the phrase "play ball" to signal their escape from the North Korean prisoner-of-war camp. Baseball terms had been used as a code throughout their days of internment, and the system had worked, their captors having little idea of what they were saying to each other.

"How'd your talk go?" Dan asked.

"Fine."

"I used to belong to SDX but dropped out years ago. If I was still a member I would have been there."

The initial shock at seeing Brazier was now replaced by awkwardness, a need to escape to the solitude of his suite. But he knew he couldn't simply shake hands and walk away, not after so many years, and memories.

"Buy me a drink," Brazier said.

"Sure," Childs said. "In there?" He pointed to the lower bar, which was just off the lobby.

"Why not?"

They found a table and ordered. Childs was quickly aware that Dan was a little drunk. He slurred some of his words, his eyes had a hard, glassy cast to them. After they'd been served, Childs asked, "What's new, Dan?"

"What can be new for a former hack without legs? I keep going."

"Who's Sheryl?"

"The woman I live with."

"You look good, Dan. You live around here?"

"You know where I live, Morgan, the place you stood across from and watched this afternoon."

Childs started to protest but Brazier added, "Sheryl told me about this guy standing across the street and looking at the place for an hour."

"What makes you so sure it was me?"

"Old newshawk's intuition. It's like a woman's. It was heartwarming to know that you cared enough to check out where you've been sending the checks. The neighborhood ain't great but it has its advantages. By the way, Mr. Justice, you should have taken the kid up on her offer."

"What kid?"

"Bobbi, the hooker who sent you hightailing it from the street. Word is she's good, gives—"

131

Childs cut him off. "Are you doing any writing?" he asked.

"No. I decided sitting at a typewriter and putting little marks on paper is a dumb way for a grown man to spend his day. No, I just sit and watch the flow go by my window and live the retired life, thanks to a little help from the United States Government and my friends."

The bitterness was not lost on Childs. He held up his glass of bourbon. "Here's to baseball, Korean style."

Brazier looked at him without picking up his own glass. His stare was hard, unremitting. A thin smile formed on his lips.

"Please, join me," Childs said.

"Why not?" Brazier lifted his glass and clicked it against Childs's. "Here's to life, Mr. Justice, or to what passes for a reasonable facsimile."

Childs looked over his glass. "I'm sorry you're so bitter, Dan."

"Bitterness is in the mouth of the taster. I've tasted. It's bitter. Period."

The pianist returned and launched into a medley of Broadway show tunes.

"What can I do for you, Dan?" Childs asked. "I often wish we'd stayed close, but it was your decision to put space between us. I've continued to do what I think is right—"

"And necessary? You always were the ultimate pragmatist, Morgan, a survivor above all else—"

"Is that so wrong? We all survived, didn't we—?"

Brazier looked down to where his legs should have been.

"Forgive me, Dan, and I know it's easy for me to say, but it beats being dead." Childs slowly turned the glass in his hands and gazed into its amber contents. "I remember a story about Louis Armstrong. He had an old black fellow who traveled with him. They called him Doc because his only job was to see that Armstrong took his medication while on tour. Artie Shaw came backstage during an intermission, noticed that Doc wasn't around and asked where he was. Armstrong said, 'Doc's dead.' Shaw asked what was wrong, and Armstrong said, 'When you're dead, *everything's* wrong.'"

"Jesus, Morgan, you're a little too old to play Pollyanna. I don't need parables, especially from you."

"What do you need from me, Dan? More money?"

Brazier shook his head. "No, I don't need more money. It may not look it to you but I live pretty good. Sheryl's a good woman, takes good care of me. I eat good, drink good, even make love good, and..." He held his index finger in the air. "And, Morgan, I sleep good. How are you sleeping these days?"

Childs glanced around the lounge, which had filled up. He said firmly, "I sleep fine."

"The survivor at the height of his powers. I need another drink."

"I have to go. I'm catching an early flight."

Brazier gripped his arm. "Another drink, Morgan, for old times. Who knows, we may never see each other again."

Childs checked his watch. A woman at a nearby table recognized him, came to their table and asked for his autograph.

"I really don't give autographs," he said. "I think—"

"Don't disappoint your public, Mr. Justice," Brazier said, tightening his grip on his arm.

Childs scrawled his name on a slip of paper the woman handed him. "Thank you, sir," she said. Childs forced a smile as Brazier caught a waitress's attention and ordered another round.

Brazier talked about the Jorgens presidency. He didn't like Jorgens. Childs said little, neither agreeing nor disagreeing.

133

Eventually, the conversation shifted to Clarence Sutherland's murder.

"I heard on the news they found the weapon. Know anything about it, Morgan?"

"Just what I read."

"Sounds like a break in the case." Before Childs could respond, Brazier added, "When I heard it, I immediately thought of you."

"Oh? Why?"

"You've been a big gun collector since the service. I saw your collection when I was in Washington. Very impressive."

"If you're wondering whether the gun belonged to me, it didn't. Apparently it belonged to Justice Conover."

"I know. Who do you figure killed Sutherland?"

"I have no idea."

"He called me, you know."

"I heard."

"From him?"

"Who else? You didn't bother telling me."

"He was a nasty little bastard," Brazier said.

"He wasn't exactly liked."

"What did he tell you about the call to me?"

"It doesn't matter."

"Of course it doesn't. He's dead, which is good for you."

"I resent that."

"Resent it, but it's true, isn't it?"

Childs downed the remaining bourbon and ran his fingers over his mouth. "It was good seeing you again, Dan. Best of everything."

"Don't dismiss me, Mr. Justice."

"Call me Morgan. We're friends."

"That's right, Morgan, maybe even more so these days. Sutherland saw to that."

"I don't see how."

"Yes, you do. Do you have a nice room here? They give you the bridal suite? By the way, how's Peg and the kids?"

"They're fine."

"Are you staying in a big suite?"

"Dan . . ."

"I'd like to see it."

"Another time, Dan."

"How about now, buddy?"

"Don't push me, *buddy*."

"I'm not pushing. Dr. Sutherland would term it being assertive, stating my needs and wishes, being up-front. He taught me to take stock of my assets and to ignore my failings—"

"Damn it," Childs muttered as he searched the crowded room for a waitress.

"Calm down, Morgan. You were always so calm in Korea."

Childs ignored him and continued looking for the waitress. He found her, literally yanked the check from her hands and put down cash on the table. "I have to be leaving."

"There's more to talk about," said Brazier. He tipped over his empty glass.

"Another time."

"Now, damn it."

The people who'd recognized Childs were aware of the rising voices at his table, which embarrassed him. He turned his back to them and looked at Brazier, who smiled and said, "Invite me up, Morgan. Like I said, we have more to talk about."

They rode up in the elevator, Brazier in his wheelchair, Childs standing rigidly in a corner. The operator called their floor and wished them a good night. Childs opened the door to the suite and held it as Brazier wheeled himself inside.

"Very nice," Brazier said as he pivoted in the center of the living room.

135

Childs took off his suit jacket and tossed it on a chair. "There's only wine," he said.

"We can order up."

"I'd rather not." He turned around and leaned over Brazier, his hands on the wheelchair's arms. "Get it out, over with, Dan. The only reason I accepted this speaking engagement at the last minute was because I intended to look you up. I tried, said the hell with it. Fine, *you* looked me up and here we are. I'm tired. I have an early flight in the morning and there are things I need to do tonight before turning in. Get to the point you want to make and then get out."

"Wine always gives me heartburn. If you have Tums around I don't mind. If you don't, I'd just as soon have a bottle of gin, on me, of course."

"I don't need Tums."

"Looks like gin it is." He went to the phone and called room service. "A bottle of Beefeater, two glasses and some cold shrimp." He turned in his chair, raised his eyebrows at Childs, then said into the phone, "And a bottle of Old Grand Dad, lots of ice."

"I have to call Peg," Childs said after Brazier had hung up.

"Let me say hello when you do. I always liked Peg. She's real people."

Childs dialed the number and, after preliminaries, said, "There's an old friend here with me, Peg. Dan Brazier. He wants to say hello."

It was obvious to Brazier that Peg said something that would have been awkward for Childs to respond to. He took the phone and said, "Hello, Peg, a voice from the past."

"Hello, Dan, what a surprise."

"Well, when I heard Morgan was going to be out here I couldn't resist seeing him again. We're having a hell of a time, living it up, telling war stories, recapturing our youth."

"That sounds nice, Dan. I'd love to see you again the next time you're in Washington."

He almost commented on the icy tone of the invitation but didn't. Instead, he said, "I'll take you up on that offer, Peg. In this whole world my two favorite people are Justice Morgan Childs and his lovely wife Peg. Good talking to you. Here's the judge."

Childs ended the conversation quickly. Room service arrived with an elaborately adorned cart, ice in a silver bucket, a mound of shrimp on a bed of lettuce and iced bottles of gin and bourbon. Brazier fished two dollars from his pocket and handed it to the young man who'd delivered it. "Looks great," he said as he wheeled himself to the cart and poured gin for himself, bourbon for Childs. "This is the way to live, ol' buddy." He handed Childs his glass. "To us, Morgan, to being friends and respecting the dark side of our lives." He downed his gin and poured another. "You know, Morgan, there's something nice about friends sharing a secret. It's like kids pricking fingers and becoming blood brothers, if you know what I mean."

"I know what you mean."

"It's good, positive, binds people together, especially when one of the friends has so much to lose."

"Are you talking about you, Dan?"

"Hell, no, Morgan, we know who I'm talking about."

Childs removed his tie, unlaced his shoes and put them under a desk, then unbuttoned the cuffs of his shirt and rolled the sleeves up to his biceps.

"You look like you're getting ready for a fight," Brazier said.

"Maybe I am."

"Really? Who are you going to fight with, the guy who

137

delivered the booze or your old friend? If it's me, I'm ashamed of you. I'm sort of at a disadvantage."

"All that means is that you can't run."

"But I wheel a mean hundred-yard dash. Look, Morgan, there's no need for you to get antsy with me. I've proved ever since Korea that I'm a true friend, discreet and trustworthy. If I hadn't been, things might have been a lot different in the life of Morgan Childs, justice of the Supreme Court, American hero, inspiration to youth—"

"Shut up!"

"It's *okay*, buddy, I understand. You're under the gun with this Sutherland thing, pardon the pun . . . You know something, Morgan, the way I see it, mankind was done a service by whoever knocked off Clarence Sutherland."

"I'm not sure I look at it that way, Dan, and I am sorry for blowing up—"

"Hey, we all have our moments, even a Supreme Court justice . . . Sutherland was a *big* moment for you, wasn't he?"

"I don't know what you mean."

"Well, you knew he called me and asked me all those questions about Korea. He didn't need answers—he already had 'em. What did he say to you, that he had the goods on you and would spill unless you did him a favor—"

"Of course not. Don't be melodramatic—"

"Never kid a kidder, Morgan. Frankly, if I'd been in your shoes I would have killed him myself."

"Enough, Dan. You've had too much to drink."

"I'm just getting started."

"Not here, you haven't. It's time to leave."

"Some way to treat a friend. He knew everything, Morgan, all the nitty-gritty—"

"He knew what you'd told his father during your therapy."

"Who would have figured that being open with a shrink

would cause trouble? When I told his father things about Korea, I assumed it stayed with him. I only went to him because the orthopedic doctors thought I could benefit from psychiatric counseling to . . . how did they put it? . . . 'to help resolve my inner feelings about loss of limbs.' Ain't that a hot one?"

"You didn't *have* to get into Korea with him, did you? There was no need to talk about it—"

"Come on, Morg, free association is the ticket in therapy. You sit there and everything is so calm and relaxed, so nonjudgmental. It's pretty easy. I knew the minute I started talking about us and Korea that I was getting into deep water, but what the hell, he's a doctor and I'm a patient. It's all confidential, unless . . . unless your shrink happens to have a son who manages to snoop through his father's records."

"He knew a good deal about a good many, it seems."

"I know. You walk around with that kind of information and somebody's liable to take a shot at you."

"I didn't."

"Duly noted, your honor . . . Anyway, somebody did. Who else did his father treat and keep records on?"

"I wouldn't know."

"Good stuff. Even though I don't write anymore, the old instincts keep coming through. It's a hell of a story, a Supreme Court clerk whose father is a psychiatrist treating big shots reads his father's files and holds trump cards over the big shots. That's power, Morgan, like J. Edgar Hoover had."

"Not worth murder."

"Depends. Have you ever told Peg about Korea?"

"It doesn't matter."

"Of course it does."

"Not to you."

139

"I'm your closest friend, Mr. Justice, except for your wife, but that's a different friendship—"

"Very different."

"All I'm saying is that we're in this together. No matter what you had to do to handle the Sutherland thing, I want you to know that you can trust me to the grave."

"I never doubted that, Dan. If I did—"

"That's what I like to hear, still the hard-nosed survivor to the core."

Childs poured himself another drink. He was beginning to feel the effects of the alcohol. His thoughts at that moment were ambivalent—he wanted Brazier to leave, yet was enjoying a certain pleasure at having him there. Acute, painful images of Korea flashed through his mind . . . the rotting flesh of prison camp, the sounds of North Korean guards laughing as they beat a prisoner . . .

"You're an important man, Morgan," Brazier said. "Think about it. There's only nine of you in the world."

"I'm aware of that."

"But what is true importance, Morgan? I mean, take away the black robes and you're like everybody else, getting old, losing touch, dying."

"I don't see it exactly that way."

"Nobody likes to, but it's reality. Remember how we used to talk about staying ready every minute until the break came? You were obsessed with that, which is probably what saved us. You'd hop off that straw cot every morning, yell for us to wake up and start your damn calisthenics, and I'd curse at you through every push-up and every step of running in place. But you were right, Morgan, you got us up and kept us ready. And here we are. Well, more or less. Are you still ready?"

Childs smiled at the challenge. "As ready as ever, Dan. Remember, I'm a survivor."

Brazier slipped out of his jacket, unbuttoned his shirt,

yanked off his tie and tossed them to the floor. His naked torso was thick and heavily muscled.

"What are you doing?"

"Getting ready, Morgan. Come on." He slid from the chair and assumed a position on the carpet from which to do push-ups. "Thirty minutes worth, Morgan. We'll count. The winner gets . . . well, how about a hundred?"

"Don't be silly."

"Lost it, Morgan? Sorry to hear that. I read once that some guy did almost two thousand push-ups in a half hour, world record. Count 'em off for me."

Brazier began, massive arms lifting his body easily from the carpet and lowering it again, up and down, the tempo increasing. At first Childs didn't count, and Brazier picked it up at ten. When he got to fifty Childs took over.

"Check your watch," Brazier said.

"A hundred and twenty. Don't worry, I'll keep time." He refilled his glass and continued to count as Brazier raised and lowered himself in a steady cadence. A half hour later he'd done nine hundred push-ups. His body glistened with sweat, and strands of black hair hung down over his face. He lay on his back, arms spread to the sides, and started to laugh. After a while, there was no way for Childs not to join him.

"What'd I do, nine hundred?" Brazier asked. "Want to take a shot at breaking the Dan Brazier middle-aged, legless record?"

"No, I think it's time we called it a night."

"I guess you're right." Childs held the wheelchair as Brazier lifted himself into it. "You know, Morgan, this has been a sort of historic night. Here I am, former newspaperman and starmaker doing push-ups in a fancy suite while a Supreme Court justice counts 'em off. Who'd believe it?"

"It was good to see you again, Dan. I'd just as soon keep this evening between us."

"Hey, you know me, Mr. Closed Mouth. I've been proving that for years, right, ever since Korea."

"What happened wasn't so terrible—"

"Of course not. They used us both for a so-called greater good, the war effort, patriotism, victory over the gooks. You came out of it a hero, Morg, and I'm proud as hell to have helped create you." He put on his clothes. "I'm also glad Sutherland got it," he said when he was dressed.

"Are you?"

"Yup. It brings it back to the way it always was, just you and me against the world."

Childs started to say something, held the words that had formed on his lips and said only, "You know, Dan, that if you ever need anything you just have to give a yell."

"Oh, yeah, Morgan, I've always known that. Don't worry, you'll hear me all the way across the country." He wheeled himself to the door, opened it, looked back and said, "It was good seeing you again, Mr. Justice. Best to the wife and kids."

CHAPTER
21

TWO PRESS CONFERENCES WERE HELD ON MONDAY.

In the morning Senior Supreme Court Justice Temple Conover, his wife at his side, sat before a bank of microphones and television cameras in a room in the Department of Justice. He wore a dark gray vested suit, white shirt and muted green tie. He'd removed his topcoat but kept his red wool scarf around his neck throughout the session.

He began by reading a short statement he'd written that morning:

I understand that the Metropolitan Police Department has in its possession the weapon used to kill court clerk Clarence Sutherland. That weapon, a .22-caliber pistol, belonged to me. Until now I was not aware that it had been used in the commission of a crime, nor do I know who took it and under what circumstances. This represents the sum and substance of my knowledge of the matter.

One of fifty reporters in the room outshouted the others and asked, "Is it true that your wife, Mr. Justice, was the one who gave the gun to the MPD?"

"I have no comment other than the one I have given you."

Another reporter called out to Cecily Conover, "Did you bring the gun to the MPD, Mrs. Conover?"

Cecily, who wore a tight straw-toned cashmere-and-silk dress, responded, "The circumstances under which my husband's pistol was uncovered are not a matter of public record. It was a pistol he's owned for some time and—"

Conover glared at her, then said to the questioners, "You were told that I would not answer questions, that my appearance here this morning was solely for the purpose of making the statement I have just read. Thank you for coming. Good day." He stood, turned so that an aide could help him on with his coat and limped toward the door, his right arm securely in his crutch, his face tight and pained.

Cecily smiled at reporters who pressed close and fired questions at her. She held up her hand and said, "Not now, please, not now." She joined her husband at the door, took his arm and they disappeared into the hallway.

Susanna Pinscher had been standing at the rear of the room. She felt a kind of sadness about what she'd witnessed. There sat an old, brilliant and distinguished jurist dishonored by his young and beautiful wife. Bringing his pistol to the MPD had been, to put it mildly, an unfaithful act, more than her rumored infidelities. Susanna found herself actively disliking Cecily Conover. A real little bitch . . .

An old friend from CBS-TV spotted her and asked if she

144

knew whether Cecily Conover had turned in the gun. "I can't get a confirmation from MPD," he said.

"I have no idea," Susanna said, wondering who at MPD had leaked the story. It couldn't be Teller...

The second press conference took place at three in the afternoon. It was held in the White House. President Jorgens announced he had named a well-known Texas trial attorney, Donald Wishengrad, as special prosecutor in the Sutherland case.

Jorgens delivered a long statement, ending with, "... *this unfortunate murder and resulting developments have threatened to shake public faith in our highest institutions and officials. By naming a special prosecutor, I hope to bring this matter to a swift and just conclusion and to restore that shaken faith.*"

He took a limited number of questions, one of which was whether he was referring to justice Conover when he spoke of shaken public faith in high officials. He quickly replied, "I referred to *no* specific individual. The Supreme Court is our highest tribunal, and anything, or anyone, who puts a cloud over it does a profound disservice to the nation."

After Jorgens left the room reporters buzzed about whether Temple Conover was, in fact, being singled out. Jorgens's feelings about the senior justice were a matter of public record. He'd attacked Conover's liberal stance on many occasions, and once had commented during a televised fireside chat, "Some of our more dedicated liberal thinkers, such as the distinguished Justice Conover, see nothing wrong about turning the country over to pornographers, dope addicts and criminals in the name of freedom. I don't call that freedom for anyone, except for a small, zealous number of social misfits. Indeed, I call that license." He'd then added, "I forget the sage who said it, but I think he was onto something when he said, 'there's nothing older than an old Liberal.'"

Conover had sent Jorgens a letter following the telecast, chiding him for his lack of good taste. He did not receive a reply.

"The real question," said one of the reporters to her colleagues, "is whether Conover might have killed Sutherland."

"It depends on whether his wife is the piece of business they say she is, and whether she and Sutherland ever got it on together," said another.

"And," put in a third, "whether the old man had the goods on them and cared enough to do something drastic."

AT SIX o'clock that evening Susanna Pinscher circled a block in Washington's northwest district. A car vacated a parking spot and she quickly took it. She looked around to get her bearings, then walked in the direction of an address written on a small slip of paper, stopped in front of an older building that had recently been converted into apartments, confirmed the number over the door and stepped inside a small lobby. Mailboxes and buzzers were to the left. She leaned close to them and squinted in the dim light. L. RAWLS—2C. She pressed the buzzer. The answering signal tripped a lock on the lobby door.

"Hi," Laurie Rawls said when she answered Susanna's knock.

"Hi. Sorry I'm late, but I had trouble parking."

"Everybody does. Come in."

The apartment was small but airy. She'd entered directly into the living room. A kitchen was immediately to the right and there was a pass-through to the living room. A dozen hanging plants covered a picture window. The room was painted a pale yellow and trimmed with white. The furniture was green, which, with the plants, gave the space a pleasant outdoorsy feeling.

"Sit down," Laurie said. "I don't have much in the way

146

of booze but I do have wine. I think there's some Scotch, too, maybe a little vodka."

"Wine would be fine, Laurie, red or white."

Susanna sat on the couch. A glass-topped coffee table was piled high with books, including *The Brethren*, a former best-seller that provided unflattering insight into the Supreme Court.

"Must have been required reading," Susanna said of the book when Laurie returned with the wine.

"I guess so. Bacon and eggs all right for dinner?"

"Sounds fine." She raised her glass. "Here's to better days."

"I'll drink to that."

"I love your plants. Your thumb is decidedly green."

"They grow in spite of me." She sipped her wine. "I appreciate your coming here, Susanna."

"When you called this afternoon I was a little confused, not about the call but about how you sounded, and that you wanted to avoid public places. Why do you feel that's necessary?"

Laurie shrugged. "Maybe I'm getting paranoid. They say that if you hang around Washington enough you get that way."

"Especially when you're involved in a murder investigation."

"Yes, that helps. Did you see the press conference today?"

"I was at Justice Conover's. I heard about the President's."

"I saw them on the early news. I'm back clerking for Justice Conover."

"Really? How did that happen?"

"He complained about the Chief taking me away from him, and I guess he won."

"How do you feel about it?"

147

"Ambivalent, especially now that the gun has been found."

It was obvious that Laurie wanted to talk about the gun but had some reservations. Susanna decided not to push, and switched to chitchat about the Washington Redskins.

"I don't follow football," Laurie said, "although it's hard not to in this town. Everything is so hard in *this town*. Excuse me." She went to the bathroom, returning with a smile on her face, her voice reflecting a new, although determined, lightness. "I think I'll get dinner going."

"Can I help?"

How about doing the eggs? I usually manage to mix in the shells. I hope you're better at it."

They went into a small white kitchen where Laurie handed Susanna an apron. "One of these days I'm going to get my kitchen act down and become Earth Mother. I always wanted to be a good cook but was told it was old-fashioned and that the way to a man's heart these days definitely isn't through his stomach." She said it with a lilt, but there was a touch of bitterness mixed in.

"Have the rules changed that much?" Susanna said as she gathered things to set the table. "I'm just enough older than you to have experienced something different." She turned, shoved her hands in her apron's large front pocket. "I happen to think it's okay if a woman wants to cook and bake and make a man happy. I guess I'm not much of a feminist. At least not orthodox."

"But you don't live your life that way."

"A matter of choice, and circumstances. Laurie, I do think, though, that a woman who makes the other choice ought to be respected, not be accused of having sold out."

"What about abortion? It's the hot topic even in this town, as you know. I mean the case before the Court..."

"Well, I don't see how anyone can be *for* abortion, but I also believe in a woman's right to make a choice..."

148

"I think the Court will rule in favor of a liberal position. I mean in *Nidel v. Illinois*."

"Why do you think it will go that way?"

Laurie whipped eggs in an aluminum bowl with a whisk. "Being a clerk in the Supreme Court puts you on the inside of a lot of things, Susanna... sometimes I wish I didn't know—"

"Puts a burden on you, doesn't it?"

"You might say that... They've taken a preliminary vote on *Nidel v. Illinois*." When Susanna said nothing, Laurie added, "It was five to four in favor of Nidel."

"Why are you telling me this? Should you be?"

Laurie dropped the whisk in the bowl, turned and rubbed her hands on her apron. "Probably not, but it's all *relevant*, Susanna. So many things happening in the Court are related to what happened to Clarence."

"Do you want to talk more about it?"

"Yes and no."

Susanna let it go at that during dinner. There were times when she wanted to reach out and tell Laurie how much she liked her, that she could consider her a friend, but knew she shouldn't. She was there because Laurie had called and asked her to be there, had gotten her to the apartment with the promise of revealing further information about the Sutherland case. Stick to the ground rules, she told herself.

"More wine?" Laurie asked when they were finished.

"Coffee, I think."

They had coffee in the living room. Laurie put on a recording of *Die Zauberflöte*, Mozart's *Magic Flute*. "He was commissioned to write it," she said, "by a theater owner in Vienna who wanted a magic opera. Mozart approached it as light clowning but the more he worked on it the more it became a kind of serious celebration of man."

Susanna laughed. "If anything positive comes out of the

149

Sutherland case it will be an education for me in opera."
Teller first and now Laurie.

They listened to one side of the record in silence. Laurie turned over the disc and returned to the couch, where Susanna had leaned her head back and closed her eyes. Susanna asked without moving, "What did you want to tell me, Laurie?" She almost added, You can trust me, but didn't, knowing that would be unprofessional.

"The gun..."

"What about it?" She opened her eyes and turned so that they faced each other.

"Justice Conover threatened his wife with it."

"I'd heard that."

"From whom?"

"That's not important. Nothing stays secret very long in this town."

"Justice Conover threatened his wife with it because she'd been having an affair with Clarence. Did you know that too?"

"There's been a lot of speculation—"

"It's true. When Justice Conover found out about it he went sort of berserk, broke things in his chambers and..."

"And what?"

"And said... said he'd kill both of them."

"How do you know this? Were you actually there?"

"I was close enough to hear. It was an awful scene, the judge pulled out the gun... God... for a moment I really thought he was going to shoot her."

"But of course he didn't."

"No."

"What about Clarence? Did Justice Conover confront him about it?"

"Yes."

"Did you hear that conversation too, Laurie?"

She shook her head. "Clarence told me."

150

Susanna sat up straight. "He did? Why would he do that?"

"I never knew . . . unless it was another way to hurt me . . ."

Susanna reached out and touched her shoulder. Damn it, she could be *human*, couldn't she? "I'm sorry, Laurie, it must be very painful to drag this up."

"It's all *right*." Except obviously it wasn't. In spite of herself tears formed in her eyes. "Clarence liked to make sure I knew about his other women. I wouldn't have minded so much, I think, if he'd actually fallen in love with someone else, but that was never the case. It was always the sex he'd brag about, somebody he'd picked up in a bar or at a party, or someone . . ."

"Someone like Cecily Conover."

No answer. But the silence spoke volumes. "How long did their affair last?"

"I don't know if it ever ended. He'd tell me . . . they'd meet at his apartment or a hotel or even in the Court—"

"In the *courtroom*?"

"No . . . in Clarence's office. The only time I think he ever did anything like that in the actual courtroom was . . . I'm embarrassed to tell you . . . was with me. Pretty sick, right? Was this what my parents put their darling daughter through law school for . . ."

Susanna's natural reaction was sympathy, but she also wanted Laurie to go on. She didn't have to prompt her.

"It only happened once," Laurie said, "and it really isn't quite as terrible as I've made it sound. We didn't go all the way in the courtroom, but we came damn close. Clarence had a pixyish—some might say quirky—side to him. He often worked late and liked to go into the courtroom and pretend to be chief justice. He'd sit in the middle chair and issue proclamations to the room, which, obviously, was empty and dark, except when I was with him."

"Was that often?"

"No, just once in a while—"

"And one night you made love there?"

"He did become affectionate, and we, to use an old-fashioned term, necked, petted. I was worried that one of the building's security people would come in but Clarence didn't seem at all worried. If it had been up to him we probably would have—"

Susanna smiled. "Another old-fashioned term...gone all the way?"

"Right."

The second side of the record ended. Laurie stood up and asked, "More of the same, or something lighter?"

"Something lighter."

She put on George Shearing with strings and went to her plants, touched them with exaggerated tenderness, turned and said, "I'm pretty damned frightened, Susanna."

"Of what?"

"Of being there."

"In the Court?"

"Yes. Oh, God, I don't want to come off strange or nutsy, paranoid, but, after all, somewhere in the United States Supreme Court it seems there's a murderer..."

Susanna went to her. "Is there something you aren't telling me? Did Clarence confide something to you—?"

She started to deny it, then nodded. "Yes, he did..."

"And?"

"I think one of the justices must have done it..."

Susanna pointed to the couch. "Let's sit down. Now, go ahead."

"Clarence used to say how he had a key to every lock, to every person on the Court. He knew compromising things about the justices."

"How, specifically?"

"I don't really know, although I suppose just being close to them, listening, would account for it. He'd worked closely

152

with Justice Poulson, and claimed Poulson was nothing but a puppet of President Jorgens and that he could prove it."

"Lots of people have said or implied that about Poulson, Laurie. In fact, that sort of charge has been made about chief justices for years."

"I think there was more to it than that," Laurie said. "It's one thing for a justice to be influenced by the political philosophy of a president who's appointed him to the bench, but it's another to have the White House play a direct role in your decisions on specific issues."

"Has that happened with Poulson?"

"Clarence claimed it had, and he told me he had documents to prove it. He said that if they were released they'd blow the lid off the Court, and maybe the Presidency too."

Susanna whistled. "I'd like more coffee," she said. "And some brandy if you've got any."

"I do."

They continued to talk about Justice Poulson and his links to the White House. Laurie didn't have much more to offer because she hadn't actually seen the proof Clarence had referred to, but she seemed convinced that it represented a real threat to the Chief Justice, and even to the President. Enough to provide a motive for murder.

"What about the other justices?" Susanna asked. "You've told me about Justice Conover and his wife's affair with Clarence. Are there others whose private lives might have been compromised by Clarence?"

"He seemed to have something on *all* of them, Susanna. I remember him once talking about Justice Childs. He laughed and said, 'Some hero. He's a phony.'"

"Justice Childs? His heroism in Korea is well documented—"

"I don't have any answer for that. All I know is that I wake up in the middle of the night and see the justices' faces. I dream that all nine of them stand in front of the

153

bench. Clarence sits in the Chief's chair...just like he did when he was killed. He laughs at them, calls them fools and fakes. Each justice has a pistol, and one fires and hits Clarence in the head—"

"Which one?"

"I don't *know*. It's a dream, I wake up, thank God."

"If you had to go with your gut instinct, Laurie, which would it be?"

A nervous laugh. "I wouldn't know, Susanna, but if I had to narrow it down, I'd say Conover, Poulson or Childs. From what I know, they had real motives. I know how much has been made of Clarence's relationships with women, but I don't think a woman killed him. I'd turn the old saying around, look for the man, Susanna..."

Twenty minutes later Susanna sat in her car. She started the engine, gripped the wheel and said to herself, "Look for the man. Look for the woman. Look somewhere else but, of course, don't look at me..."

In Chevy Chase, a two-man team finished searching Dr. Chester Sutherland's offices.

"That's it," one of them said.

"Right," said the other. "We've got the MKULTRA files. Whatever the hell they are. That's what they wanted. Let's go."

CHAPTER
22

"I'M CERTAIN OF IT," VERA JONES TOLD DR. CHESTER Sutherland the following morning. "Look..."

He looked over her shoulder at an unlocked file drawer with the label MNOP. "Are you sure you locked it last night before you left?" he asked.

She looked at him. "I have locked and checked these files for twenty-two years, doctor, and last night was not an exception."

"Yes, of course, I'm sorry. Have you found out whether anything is missing?"

"Not yet. I thought you should know before I did anything."

"Have you checked my office?"

"No."

155

Sutherland, who'd been eating breakfast when she called from the office, and who still wore a robe over silk pajamas, entered his private office, Vera at his heels.

"Everything looks in order," he said. "Have you gone through the unlocked file?"

"I told you—"

"Yes, yes, I know. Why don't you do that now. I want to check in here."

She started to leave, then turned, hands on hips. "Should I call the police?" she asked.

"No. First let's see what's missing, if anything."

She closed the door behind her. Sutherland went to the paneled wall behind the curved couch, touched a spot and a section opened. Built into the wall behind the concealed door was a safe and two locked, wood-grained file cabinets. He turned the dial on the safe; it was secure. So were the cabinets. He fished a key from a pocket in his robe and inserted it into the top cabinet. The drawer slid out easily on nylon casters, and a row of red plastic file folders with typed labels stared at him. He did not have to touch them to know some were missing. The supporting bracket behind them had always been in the right position to hold them erect and neat. Now they slumped against one another.

"Damn it, god*damn* it."

Vera knocked.

"Just a minute," he said, locking the file and closing the wall's hinged panel. "Come in."

"I've checked," she said. "Nothing seems to be missing. Perhaps I did forget to lock it after all."

"That would be uncharacteristic of you."

"I'm human."

He took a step toward her, then stiffened and went to the glass coffee table that was his desk.

"Was anything disturbed in here?" she asked.

"No . . . no, nothing at all. Are you sure everything outside is secure?"

"Yes."

"That file that was unlocked . . . it contained the Ps. Was Justice Poulson's file there?"

"Yes, of course."

"Good. Vera, perhaps we should talk."

"About what?"

"About Clarence's murder."

"Why? What is there to discuss?"

"I'd call that denial and resistance."

"Please doctor . . . Clarence's death was a tragic blow to us all. We grieve, we try to recover, retrench and get on with our lives."

"Come, sit down." He patted a spot on the couch next to him. "Please, sit a minute."

She uneasily joined him on the couch, long, slender fingers smoothing her skirt over her knees. He put a hand over one of hers and smiled. "We've been together a long time, Vera, been through a good deal . . ."

She said nothing.

"People who share as we have tend, inevitably, to become close, sometimes closer than even blood relations." She continued to look straight ahead, her breasts rising and falling beneath her blouse that was buttoned to her neck, her hand, though, rested perfectly still on her knee beneath his hand.

"Life is an accumulation of episodes, Vera. We all tend to function day by day, and what we do is shared by a limited number of people that we let into our lives. These are the people we most trust with our secrets."

She turned now so that she faced him. "If this is your way of finding out whether my loyalty to you and to *your* secrets is intact, I must say I resent it—"

He started to say something but she went on quickly.

"No, Chester, you don't have to worry about me, and I think you know that. We've been sucked into something that ended up destroying Clarence. It's over now. His death, as tragic as it was, has at least seen to that."

Sutherland sat back, straightened out his fingers and examined his nails, positioning them on the palm of his other hand like a jeweler creating a scrim for his gems. Apparently satisfied with their condition, he looked at her and said, "It will all work out, won't it, Vera?"

"Of course it will, doctor."

"Thank you, Vera."

"There's nothing to thank me for," she said, going to the door. "We do what we have to do . . . I mean, we go on . . ."

Sutherland sat on his couch after she was gone and stared at that portion of the wall where the file cabinets and safe were hidden behind. He went to the phone in his smaller office, consulted a small black book he'd taken from his desk, dialed a number. William Stalk, director of the Central Intelligence Agency's science and technology division, who at the moment happened to be playing a video space-invader game with his son, answered. "Good morning, Chester. To what do I owe the pleasure of this *early* morning call to my home?"

"I'm sure you know why I'm calling, Bill."

Silence.

"There's been a break-in at my office. It happened last night."

"I'm sorry to hear it. Any damage?"

"No, but my files were invaded."

He laughed. "I hope they didn't snitch anything juicy about your patients. That could be embarrassing for a lot of people."

Sutherland started to mention the missing MKULTRA

158

files but held back his words, saying instead, "I'd like to see you, Bill."

"I'll be at home all morning. My wife reminded me a few weeks ago that I'd been spending too little time with my boy, so I blocked out part of today. We've been playing one of those games on TV where electronic enemy blobs keep coming at you fast and furious. He's a lot better at it than I am, but then again he gets more practice. The damn things are addictive."

"When can I see you?"

"How about this afternoon, at my office? Three o'clock."

"I'll be there, count on it."

VERA JONES sat behind her desk. A lighted button on the telephone went out. She picked up a pencil and began writing on a pad. Moments later Sutherland came into her office. "Cancel any patients I have today," he said.

"All right. There were only four. I'll call them."

"And you might as well go home after you've made the calls. I'll be gone all day."

"Perhaps I will. Thank you."

She stayed at the office the rest of the day, rearranging files, typing dictated notes of patient sessions left for her by Sutherland and doing what was an obsession with her— retyping pages in a master telephone book that contained not a single handwritten entry or cross-out.

At six-thirty, after washing her coffee cup, she took from a concealed compartment in her desk a file folder with a typed label at the top that read, POULSON, J., opened the cover and read the first page, then went through a dozen additional pages, each filled with lines of pristine typing. Had someone taken the time and interest to compare the pages in Poulson's file with materials in other files, they might have wondered why his pages, presuming to cover months of sessions and resulting notes, were all freshly typed, as though they'd been done in a single sitting, which was the case. Vera was aware of the inconsistency and wished it weren't so, but there had been no other way to duplicate the missing file. She'd typed the new pages from what she'd remembered of the originals, the doctor's comments and analytic perceptions. It was the best she could do and, she reminded herself, the chances of it being discovered were remote. The Poulson file was a dead one. He hadn't been a patient in a long time. There was no reason for Dr. Sutherland to review his case, which was why his asking about it concerned her. She'd kept the reconstructed file in her special hiding place ever since making it, reluctant to put it to the test in the MNOP drawer. Now, she knew she would have to. She double-checked every lock in the office, turned out the lights and went to her car, where she sat for some ten minutes, the motor running, her body trembling against the cold and inner anxiety. Once the heater had come to life she drove off to her apartment. She sat for a moment in front of it, trying to decide whether to go inside or to go on. The thought of spending a long night alone was nearly unbearable. She shifted into DRIVE and headed down the Rockville Turnpike, south on Wisconsin to Connecticut Avenue and down Connecticut to Lafayette Park, where she sat at a red light and stared at the White House. Most of its windows were alive with pale yellow light, and the porte-cochere designed for Thomas Jefferson that covered the north entrance, and that was favored by visiting heads of state, was illuminated by spotlights. The traffic light turned green; she continued to stare. A motorist behind her blew his horn. She came erect, glanced in her rearview mirror and proceeded through the intersection.

She felt the onset of panic. She drove by rote, passing corner after corner, wanting to turn at each of them. Eventually she crossed the Kutz Memorial Bridge and parked along the Tidal Basin under Japanese cherry trees that were waiting for spring.

"My God, what's happening to me," she said as she gripped the wheel and tried to squeeze control into her body. She hated herself when she allowed this to happen. It was weak, pathetic, dangerous. It always frightened her to become confused. She was usually the one who could see things clearly in the midst of chaos, focus on the real issues, make crucial decisions to restore order and resolve conflicts.

But now she sat alone and afraid, and desperately wished there was someone to comfort her, to grab hold of, to touch and be touched by. The sense of weakness was overwhelming. She started the car and drove to M Street, Northwest, in Georgetown, where after considerable searching she found a parking spot. As she walked up the street the sound of loud community singing and a piano came through the partially open front door of Club Julie. She almost turned and retraced her steps to her car but the pull of the music, the human voices, laughter, drew her inside.

The club was unusually crowded for a weeknight. The smoke was thick, which was why the front door had been propped open.

She'd decided that if she couldn't find a secluded place at the bar she wouldn't stay. She wasn't one for joining in community sing-alongs, although she rather enjoyed listening and watching others indulge. She'd felt uncomfortable the last time she'd been here, which was the only other time. Her escort had insisted on sitting close to the piano. She thought about that night and winced.

She glanced nervously about. A stool at the corner of the bar nearest the front door appeared to be vacant, so she went to it. A reasonably well-dressed man on the next stool smiled and said, "Hello there."

"Is this seat taken?" she asked. She noticed an empty beer glass in front of it.

161

"I think he left," the man said. "It's all yours."

She sat and waited to be served.

"Let me buy the lady a drink," the man told the bartender.

"Thank you, no," Vera said. To the bartender: "A vodka and tonic, please."

When the bartender returned with her drink he said, "Haven't seen you in a long time."

She was startled by the comment. "I've been very busy," she said, wishing he hadn't spoken to her.

"Yeah, right," said the bartender. "Anyway, good to see you again. Enjoy."

Julie played a song familiar to the man next to her, who began to sing, turned to her and said between the lines, "Know this one?"

She shook her head.

He stopped singing. "I've never seen you here before."

"I was only here once, a long time ago."

"Nice place. I don't get here much myself but I was coming home from a meeting and thought I'd stop in for a pop and a little music."

She sipped her drink.

"You live around here?"

"No."

"Work in the neighborhood?"

"No."

"I'm vice-president of a computer company. We're not very big but . . ." He pulled out a business card and shoved it at her. She tried to read it in the dim light.

"Name's George Jansson," he said, extending his hand.

She took it. "My name is Vera."

"Vera? Nice name, very old-fashioned." He scratched his head. "I don't think I've ever met a Vera before." He laughed. "Lots of Georges around, though. Can I buy you a refill?" He held up both hands to offset a negative reply. "No strings, no ulterior motives. I just enjoy talking to you."

He looked down the length of the bar and called out, "Robbie, another round here."

He shouldn't have had any additional drinks, Vera decided twenty minutes later. He'd become tipsy, not less of a gentleman, just sillier. She didn't dislike him. His hair was close cropped and gray at the temples, he had kind eyes.

"Another?" he asked.

"No, thank you, I really must go."

"It's too early. Come on, hang in, or at least keep me company."

"I'm sorry but it's been a rather difficult day and tomorrow will be the same..."

Julie announced that he was about to play a request and that a favorite regular patron would sing it. A portly man wearing a shirt collar too tight for him, and carrying a drink, stepped to the microphone and waited for Julie to play the introduction to "Chicago." He sang with gusto, pronouncing the title, "Chick-cargo, Chick-cargo."

Vera's bar companion called for another round of drinks.

"No, please, I can't stay—"

"How about a nightcap someplace else?"

"I'm sorry..."

He put his hand on her arm and looked at her. "Look, you don't have to worry. I'm a pretty nice guy, if I do say so. I just...well, I like being able to talk to a woman. I'm not hustling you, please believe me. We could just go and have coffee, just sit a little longer, that's all."

It was, of course, just what she wanted, in fact badly needed... "Well, all right, but just for a bit..."

"Do you have a car?"

"Yes."

"Tell you what. There's an all-night place six blocks straight up M Street. I'll meet you there. They have great cheesecake. You like cheesecake?"

163

"Yes, matter of fact I do." She found herself able to smile. He *was* nice.

"Good." He paid the checks, helped her on with her coat, said good night to the bartender and held the door open for her. The cold night air felt very good on her face.

"Where's your car?" he asked.

She pointed. "Two blocks up."

"I'll walk you."

"That's not necessary."

"My pleasure. Never mind what they say, chivalry isn't dead, and it doesn't cost a dime." He took her arm and they started up the street.

Their progress did not go unnoticed. Detective Martin Teller had pulled up at the curb across from Club Julie as they were leaving. He recognized Vera immediately. "What the hell is she doing here?" he asked himself. He considered following them but saw that they'd stopped at a car. The man opened the door and Vera got in.

"And who is that?" Teller asked himself as he got out of his car and went into his favorite club. The seats previously occupied by Vera and the computer executive were still vacant, and he took one. "Robbie," he called to the bartender.

"Hiya, Marty," Robbie said, "good to see you."

"Same here. Robbie, that woman who just left with the guy in the suit. Do you know her?"

Robbie shrugged, shook his head.

"Did she come in with the guy?"

"No. He bought her a couple of drinks and they took off. He comes in regularly, though."

"You never saw her before?"

Robbie leaned on the bar. "Yeah, I've seen her before, once, I think."

"In here?"

"Yeah, months ago."

"Tell me about it."

Robbie made another customer's drink, filled a waitress's order at the service end of the bar, then returned to Teller. "What can I tell you, Marty? I can't remember every woman who comes in here."

"Try."

"Important?"

"Maybe. Give me a gin while you go down memory lane."

He came back with the drink. "Okay, I do remember more about her than I might some others. She's a type, you know, very uptight, sort of prissy, pinched face like she kind of disapproves of everything. For some reason she didn't strike me as the sort who'd enjoy our place. Most everybody's pretty loose here, right?...Let me see. Oh yeah, there's another reason for remembering her. The real reason, I guess...She had a tiff with a guy at the bar and left."

"The same guy as tonight?"

"No, no, a lot younger."

"She pick him up here?"

"Nope. They came in together, and that was another reason I remember them. He didn't look like he belonged here either. He was young, a sort of snotty character if I remember right. Good-looking guy, though, dressed nice. They didn't fit in here, and they didn't seem to fit together either. Still, who knows who fits with who anymore? Anyway, they sat down there." He pointed to the end of the bar nearest the piano. "I served them and everything was okay for a while, but then they started arguing. I think I tried to finesse them out of it, offered a drink on the house, something like that."

"How'd it end up?"

"*That* I remember. She left and he stayed. I think he ended up leaving with another girl."

165

Teller drank half his drink. Robbie started to walk away but Teller said, "Wait, Robbie. Tell me what the guy looked like."

"I don't really remember. Like I said, he was young, blond, snotty, looked down his nose all night."

"Remember the picture of the Supreme Court clerk who was murdered?"

The bartender rubbed his chin. "Sure, what was his name?"

"Sutherland."

"Right . . . Jesus . . ."

"What?"

"That's right, that could have been the guy she was with that night. It looked like him . . ."

Teller sat back and threw up his hands. "Here I am investigating the most important murder case in Washington history, aside from Lincoln, and you, a trained observer of mankind, miss something like this. Was it the same guy or not, damn it."

"Could be. I'd have to see a picture."

Teller went to his car, took an eight-by-ten glossy photo of Clarence Sutherland from his briefcase in his trunk and returned to the bar. He led Robbie into the kitchen, where there was more light. Robbie examined the photograph.

"Well?"

"Yeah, I think it's the same one."

"You think?"

Robbie looked at Teller. "Come on, Marty, this place isn't a lineup. Lots of guys come through. I can't be *sure*, but if I had to lay a bet on it I'd say it's the same guy."

Teller leaned against a sink, drew a deep breath. "Don't tell anybody about this, Robbie."

"Why should I?"

"Just don't."

The chef, an illegal alien named Juan, grinned at Teller. "Hey, detective, you want something to eat?"

166

"Yeah, fries and a Julieburger, medium, and easy on the anchovies. But not too easy."

VERA PASSED the all-night diner and saw George, the computer executive, get out of his car. She didn't want to disappoint him, go back on her word, but any guilt about that took second place to a compelling need to be home. She accelerated, and the diner became a red neon dot in her rearview mirror.

CHAPTER
23

CHESTER SUTHERLAND DECIDED AS HE APPROACHED HIS house in Chevy Chase to drive around the back and then enter through his office. He noticed as he came up the long driveway that all lights in the house were off with the exception of his bedroom.

He did not immediately get out of his car. The last seven hours were a blur to him. After leaving the two-hour meeting with Bill Stalk at CIA Headquarters he'd gone to his club, where he had dinner alone. He then did something he had not done in years, went to the movies. He hadn't liked the film, an attempt at comedy by names he was only vaguely familiar with from having once watched "Saturday Night Live." The young people in the audience loved it though. It didn't matter, though, whether he liked the film or not.

It was something to do, a way to blot out what had happened during the two hours with Stalk.

The meeting had started pleasantly enough, Stalk again telling of his fascination with video electronic games and how he'd decided to take a few days off in the future and spend them practicing so that he could better compete with his son. Sutherland had listened politely, even offered comments of his own on the subject, but he knew the badinage would soon be over and the serious subject that had brought him there would take its place.

"So," Stalk said as he sat behind his desk and propped his feet on it, "you wanted to talk to me, Chester. You sounded upset on the phone, although I suppose if someone had broken into my office I'd be upset too." He laughed. "It's a good thing for us that you never did keep files on the MKULTRA Project. If you had I'd be concerned that whoever broke into your office might have taken a peek."

Sutherland knew Stalk was playing with him. If he'd had any doubts earlier about who had broken into his files, they no longer existed.

"Did the Company do it, Bill?"

Stalk assumed an expression of surprise, shock. "The Company? Why would we do such a thing to someone who's been an important, trusted part of our operation?"

Sutherland, who hadn't eaten since breakfast and then had only partially finished because of Vera's call, suddenly was hungry and would have liked a drink. He was, he knew, in a touchy position. If the CIA hadn't taken the files, his admitting that he had in fact kept them, despite his constant denials, would brand him a liar and, worse, a fool. Still, if it hadn't been someone from the Company, he felt obliged to report it to the man and the agency most jeopardized by the theft.

He decided to admit he'd kept files and that they were now missing, hoping that his candor would bring a parallel

169

honesty from Stalk. It did not work that way . . . After Sutherland finished telling Stalk the truth, the director stood, brought his fist down sharply on the desk. "Damn it, I knew it." He quickly went to the expanse of windows overlooking the woods, and for a moment Sutherland thought that he was going to put his fist through the glass. Instead he rolled the fingertips of both hands over the pane.

"I'm sorry, Bill," Sutherland said, standing and coming halfway across the room. "You must understand that I had several motives for involvement in the project. I do care about serving the country when and as I can, but I'm also an individual. I'm a scientist, or at least I'm involved with science, and for someone like me the payoff is in the excitement of discovery, of breaking new ground, creating understanding where it hasn't existed before. I couldn't devote all that time and knowledge without having something to show for it personally. I've never talked about it to anyone, and the files have been secured in my private office for as long as they've existed. But it was important to me that I at least had them."

"Like Nixon keeping the tapes," Stalk said. He was not amused. In fact, his face looked like granite. He went back to his desk, opened a drawer and pulled out a sheaf of file folders. Sutherland recognized them immediately as the ones taken from his office.

"It *was* you," Sutherland said.

"Of course it was us, Chester, and a damn lucky thing it was. A few years ago if we'd known these files existed we'd have done the same thing, only we would have been rather less discreet about it. The American public has seemed to demand more discretion these days with their break-ins."

Sutherland leaned forward. "But why take them now? I told you that no one has ever seen them except me. Every entry was made personally by me."

Stalk slapped the files back in the drawer and closed it hard.

Sutherland sat in a chair and drew a deep breath. He was afraid he knew what was coming.

"You weren't the only one to have access to those files, Chester, and you know it. Your son did too."

Sutherland looked at the floor. "Whatever my son might have been, or might have done, he's paid for it, Bill. Do we need to attack him now? Whatever he knew . . . about people, other things, whatever he might have done to hurt . . . God knows, he's been punished, and with no chance for appeal, no chance of parole. My son, sir, is dead. Isn't that *enough*?"

Stalk nodded. "I do sympathize with you, Chester. I was thinking about your son this morning while I was playing that video game with my boy. I suppose there's no greater loss than the death of a child, no matter the age."

Sutherland felt his stomach clutch.

"Are you all right, Chester?"

"Yes . . . I'm not happy with what your people did, but I suppose I can understand it—"

"Chester, it's been a very difficult period for us. We've been hit on from all sides, which does not exactly make our mission any easier. There have been so many leaks that damaged us, and we were forced to release some of MKUL-TRA under the Freedom of Information Act. Sure, we sanitized everything we could and held back more than some think we should have, but you know as well as anyone how compromised this nation would be if the entire project had been laid open. When we realized that material we hadn't released was beginning to surface, we became, to put it mildly, concerned. Our first assumption was that the leak was within the division, and we went to a good deal of trouble to find it and shut it off. But then we looked outside and uncovered that *your son* was making it known in certain

171

places he had access to his father's files. Naturally, I can't reveal the source of that information. What a shame, was what I said, and felt, when the picture became clearer. What a damn bloody shame."

Along with everything else, Sutherland found himself annoyed at Stalk's use of the British usage. That was something he'd always noticed about CIA brass, the tendency to affect the language and manner of their British counterparts.

Stalk locked Sutherland's files in the drawer, dropped the key into his jacket pocket, stood, came around the desk and slapped the psychiatrist on the back. "You know, Chester, this is a strange world we live in, and it sometimes takes extraordinary people, and acts, to inject some sanity into it. There is no clear-cut good or bad, Chester. Mostly it's a matter of survival. Some understand that, some don't." He removed his hand from Sutherland's back and went to his door. The point was made, the meeting was over.

At the door Stalk shook Sutherland's hand. "I'd be happy to have you back in the program, Chester, but I would understand if that should prove rather too difficult for you. If that is the case, I think it best that you never come here again."

The notion of ever returning to the CIA's top secret research program almost made Sutherland laugh. Still, he needed to ask, "Why would you invite me back into the program in the light of what's happened with the files?"

"Well, Chester, no offense, but once a man has made the mistake you have, he does tend to become rather more easy to control. I've enjoyed knowing you, Chester. Good luck in all your future endeavors. By the way, I'd heartily recommend getting one of those video games. A wonderful way to get your mind off real problems..."

Sutherland now got out of his car and went through the back door to his office. As usual, Vera had left a night-light on, a large translucent plastic goose he'd given her as

172

a gift five years ago. A small bulb in the base illuminated the entire figure and cast a warm glow over the room.

He flipped on the overhead lights, took a key from his pocket and opened the file drawer marked MNOP. He touched the top of a folder marked *Poulson, J.*, almost removed it to read its contents, then closed the drawer and locked it. He made his way to the house, glanced at mail that had been left on a table near the staircase, then slowly climbed the stairs to the second floor, where he opened the door to his bedroom.

His wife Eleanor was on the chaise, reading.

"You're home," Chester said. "I thought the fundraiser would go later."

"I didn't go," she said, removing her glasses and looking up at him through narrowed eyes.

"Why not?"

"I couldn't get up the interest or strength." She didn't sound weary, her voice was strong.

He took off his jacket and hung it in the closet, took off his shoes and sat on the edge of their king-sized bed.

"Where were you?"

"I had a meeting, grabbed some dinner at the club and then went to the movies."

"The movies? You went to the movies? You haven't been to the movies for as long as I can remember."

"I needed a little diversion," he said as he unbuttoned his shirt.

"I'm impressed."

"Impressed with what? What's so unusual about going to a movie?"

"I don't mean the movies, Chester, I mean the need for diversion. I've never known you to express such a human need."

He understood too well that she was looking for an argument. He went to a bathroom off the bedroom, closed the door, took a fast hot shower, put on a terry-cloth robe and returned to where Eleanor stood in front of an eighteenth-century French escritoire. She held in her hands what she'd been reading on the chaise, a thick batch of letters. She was especially beautiful at the moment, her face etched with a sadness that had been perpetual since Clarence's murder. Champagne blonde hair was pulled up into a loose chignon on the top of her head, stray tendrils framed a full, lovely face.

"What are you reading?"

She answered so quietly that he didn't catch it. He asked again.

She turned. "Letters from Clarence, Chester, letters he wrote while in college and that you never had the time to read."

He abruptly crossed the room to his bureau. "Nonsense," he said over his shoulder, "I read everything he ever wrote us—"

"Only because I insisted on it. You'd sit and pretend to take in his words, pretend to respond to what he'd said, but the fact is none of it really mattered to you. You were never interested in your own son . . . Too bad he wasn't one of your patients—"

"That's enough, Eleanor. We've gone over this too many times before."

He watched as she lowered the letters to the desk, as though putting them in a fire. There was a discernible trembling to her hands as she gripped the edge of the writing desk for support. When she turned and faced him her blue eyes shone with anger. "He's dead, Chester, and I think you killed him—oh, you didn't have to pull the trigger, Chester. There are other ways to assassinate a human being without being the one at the other end of the gun—"

"I've heard *enough*, Eleanor. Have you been drinking?"

"Isn't that typical of you, Chester, and how *unanalytic*, to look for an external reason for something that displeases you. Have I been drinking? Should I be literary and say that I've been drinking the words of the son that I no longer have, that I'm drunk with the loss of him?"

"I'm tired, Eleanor, we can discuss this in the morning—"

Her action took him by surprise. She swept the letters from the desk, ran across the room and pushed them in his face. "Read them, Chester," she shouted. "Read them now that it no longer matters. Listen for the first time to what was in your son's heart."

The corner of one of the letters nicked his eye. He put his hand to it, turned and crouched in pain. "What *heart*?" he said.

She came up behind him, placed her hands on his shoulders and spun him around. "Why did you hate him so?" she asked. Tears now flowed down her cheeks.

He straightened, his hand still over his eyes. "I didn't hate him, Eleanor, I loved him, damn it . . . no, damn *him*. He was no good . . ."

"Is that an appropriate way for a psychiatrist to talk?"

"Maybe it is. Sometimes I think we do a disservice using so much jargon to describe behavior. There are people in this world, Eleanor, who are no damn good, and as much as it breaks my heart to say it, our son was one of them—"

He knew it was coming, didn't avoid it. Almost welcomed it. She brought her right hand across his face. When he didn't react she did it again, then grabbed his neck with both hands and dug her nails into his flesh. He took hold of her wrists and pulled himself free. Tiny rivulets of blood sprung from where her nails had broken the skin and ran down to the collar of his robe.

175

"Oh God . . . I'm sorry, Chester . . ." Her body was heaving.

"We're all sorry, Eleanor. Sorry . . . I'll sleep downstairs . . ."

CHAPTER
24

MARTIN TELLER GLANCED AT A WALL CLOCK AS HE MOVED through the bull pen at MPD headquarters. It was a quarter to nine, fifteen minutes until his morning ritual with Dorian Mars.

A detective assigned to the Sutherland case stopped him and said, "Got a new Polish joke, Marty."

"Not interested. Besides, Polish jokes are in bad taste these days."

The detective looked at a colleague and shrugged. "*Sorry*," he said. Teller continued toward his office, entered it and slammed the door behind him.

It had been a bad morning. His cats had gotten into a fight during breakfast and spilled his coffee all over the rug. A few minutes later his ex-wife called from Paris, Kentucky, to inform him that their younger daughter was dropping out of college because she was pregnant. "Who did it?" Teller asked, now knowing what else to say. "I don't know, Marty, she's coming home in a few days and I'll let you know." Then, as he was leaving his apartment building, he read a notice posted on the wall that there would be no hot water for three days while the boiler was being serviced.

The detective who'd offered the Polish joke opened the door and asked, "You playing tonight, Marty?" He was referring to an intrasquad poker game.

"No, and instead of playing poker I suggest you and the rest of the brilliant young sleuths assigned to me spend the night hitting every bar in town, especially the singles' joints, with Clarence Sutherland's photo in hand."

"*Every* bar?"

"Start in Georgetown. Ask the bartenders, the broads hanging out, guys on the make. I want a list tomorrow morning of every joint you hit, and I want it before nine o'clock.

"That's a lot of overtime, Marty."

"You complaining?"

"No. What's with you? How come you're so uptight this morning?"

"The position of the moon relative to my sun."

"No kidding."

"No kidding. You got any kids?"

"None that I know of."

"They break your heart. Get moving."

"Yeah, have a good day."

Teller picked up a coffee cup stained from the day before, went into the bull pen and poured from a communal pot, leaving a quarter in a dish. He returned to the office, hung up his jacket and sat behind his desk. It was now 9:10. He punched in Dorian Mars's extension on his phone. "Marty?" Mars said. "Where are you? I'm waiting."

178

"Let's skip the meeting this morning, Dorian. I've got nothing to report. It would be a waste of time."

"Doesn't matter. We should meet anyway, every day. Brainstorming can open things up. You run a case like this through a grinder enough times and out comes the perfect hamburger."

"What?"

"Come up, Marty."

"No. I've got a lot of sorting out to do. Let's catch up later."

Mars sighed loudly. "All right, Marty. By the way, are you okay? You sound strange."

"I'm terrific, Dorian, tip-top, at peace with my fellow man. Life is truly a bowl of cherries, a virtual perpetual cabaret."

"Take it easy, Marty."

Teller called the desk and instructed the sergeant on duty to hold all calls until further notice.

"One just came in for you, detective. I was about to put it through."

"Who is it?"

"Your Miss Pinscher, from Justice."

"*My?* Oh, all right, I'll take it, but that's it for a while."

"Good morning," Susanna said.

"Good morning. How've you been?"

"All right. I thought you might have called me."

"I've been busy as hell. Sorry."

"That's not what I called about, though. I wanted to fill you in on a conversation I had with Laurie Rawls."

Teller found a pad of paper and uncapped a pen. "Go ahead," he said.

"Remember when I said I thought I might be able to establish a sort of big-sister relationship with her? Well, it happened . . . I had dinner at her apartment and she opened up."

179

"What did she say?"

She read from notes she'd made right after leaving Laurie's apartment—Laurie back clerking for Conover, the preliminary vote in *Nidel v. Illinois* in Nidel's favor, confirmation that Cecily Conover and Clarence had had an affair and that Justice Conover had confronted both of them about it. Teller listened, made his own notes until she got to the part about Clarence sitting in the Court at night and playacting, and that he and Laurie had almost made love there.

"In the Supreme Court? That is mighty high-level making out."

"Well, his liking for the Chief's chair could explain why Clarence was there the night he was killed. No one had to entice him into the room. He went there on his own almost as a matter of routine..."

"Go on."

"Laurie says that Clarence once bragged to her that he had...How did she put it?...He had the key to every lock and person in the Court. Evidently Clarence knew something damaging or embarrassing about everyone. At least that's what he told her."

"Where'd he get the information?"

"I asked her that too. She says he picked it up while working as closely as he did with the justices."

"What about his father? Did he come up?"

"In what context?"

"The fact that he treated the high and mighty, and that Clarence might have learned things through that connection."

"We didn't discuss it."

"Okay, anything else?"

"Laurie says that Justice Poulson is sort of a puppet of President Jorgens and that the White House plays a direct role in most everything Poulson does on the Court. She also claims that Clarence had documents to prove it that would...here's exactly what she said...'had documents to prove it that would blow the lid off the Court.'"

"Is the phone you're using secure?"

"I think so—"

"Don't think. Be sure."

"I'm in my office at *Justice*."

He wanted to tell her that a telephone in the Justice Department was probably as unsecured as any phone in Washington, but didn't. He wanted her to go on.

"There's not much more," she said. "She told me that Clarence knew that Justice Childs was a phony hero and that he could prove it."

"How?"

"I don't know and I don't think she does either. Anyway, her advice was to look for a man—"

"Seems I've heard that before."

"Childs said look for a woman. Remember?"

"Yeah...Do you think she did it?"

"Laurie? No, but my opinion doesn't mean anything. What do you think?"

"Who knows? You can't tell the players in this thing without a scorecard." He glanced up at his empty flow chart on the wall.

"Well, Detective Teller, I've shown you mine. Now, it's your turn."

"I'd love to, but I've never found that the phone was a substitute—"

"*Teller*...cut it out...have *you* learned anything new?"

"Not a thing."

"Sure? I'd hate to think this was a one-way street, my telling and your holding back."

"Free for dinner this week?"

"No. I'm taking a few days off and going with one of my kids to California to visit my father. By the way, did you know that Mozart wrote *The Magic Flute* because a theater owner in Vienna commissioned it?"

"Yeah."

"You did?"

"Sure. He started off writing a light piece but it turned out to be a serious work—"

"Damn."

"Call when you get back."

From the carton that had contained the wall chart he took an assortment of colored, magnetic plastic symbols and labels, spread them on his desk, then used an erasable marking pen to write the names of each suspect. He considered categories to group the names under—*personal* and *Professional, male* and *female, Court* and *family*. He decided on the last, wrote the words on the largest of the magnetic labels and put them on the board. He added a third heading, *personal*, to include those not in the Court or family.

He ran into a snag grouping names beneath headings. Those from the Court, people like Poulson, Conover and Childs, might well have had personal rather than professional reasons for killing Clarence. Or both? He'd let it go, at least where the chart was concerned.

When he was finished, the chart was resplendent in red, green, yellow and blue:

COURT	FAMILY	PERSONAL
Justices Poulson	Dr. C. Sutherland	Friends
Childs	Mrs. Sutherland	(Male)
Conover	Sister	(Female) C. Conover
Clerk L. Rawls		

He considered where to place Vera Jones. Seeing her at Club Julie and convinced that she'd had a personal relationship with Clarence certainly made her a good suspect. He started to put her name under *Personal*, then changed it to *Family*. A close call.

He narrowed his eyes and took in the chart as a blur of color. He slapped colored magnetic arrows on the board to link the names, realized it accomplished little. Besides, he wanted more room next to each name to write comments. He rearranged the board into a vertical configuration.

COURT

Justices Poulson

Childs

Conover

Clerk L. Rawls

FAMILY

Dr. C. Sutherland

Mrs. Sutherland

Sister

Vera Jones

PERSONAL

Friends

(Male)

(Female) C. Conover

He wrote Clarence's name in large letters and put it at the top of the chart, then took it down, changed it to DE-CEASED and returned it to the board. Next he sat at his desk and wrote out motives to be put next to each suspect.

Poulson—father's patient, White House sellout.

Childs—phony hero???? (He found orange magnetic

question marks and strung four of them next to his comment.)

Conover—jealousy, wife and deceased.

Dr. C. Sutherland—violation of his files???? (Again, a string of question marks.)

*Mrs. Sutherland??—*He didn't know, and had used up the supply of question marks. He took two from the other lines and placed them after her name.

Sister—nothing.

Vera Jones—woman scorned, possible affair.

*Friends—*He'd taken Laurie Rawls's name from the Court list and put it here. Next to her name he put *Jealousy.*

He created another heading, MISC. No suspects yet here; he left it blank, a category-in-waiting.

He decided he didn't want the others to see the chart so he called around the department until he found a large roll of brown paper that he taped over the chart. Finally he went downstairs to a public phone booth and called Paris, Kentucky. His ex-wife answered.

"Anything new?" he asked.

"She called. She'll be home tomorrow."

"What'd she say?"

"She was crying."

"Look, be sure she tells whoever this guy is that her father's a cop."

"Why?"

"What do you mean, why? Maybe he won't run so fast if he knows I'm a cop."

"Or maybe he'll run faster...except I don't think he's trying to run anywhere, Marty. She says they're in love."

"Wonderful. Call me the minute she gets home."

"I will. Please don't get all riled up about this. I'm sure it will all work out."

"Sure it will...just like everything else."

CHAPTER
25

SUSANNA, FEELING BETTER THAN SHE HAD IN WEEKS, RE-veled in her first day at her father's modest, yellow stucco home in St. Helena. She sat on the patio, a tart, icy banana daiquiri from the blender on a wrought-iron table next to her, her feet in sandals, sunglasses shielding her eyes from a blinding afternoon sun as she watched her father and her son toss a baseball about in the backyard.

Later, after a barbequed chicken and corn-on-the-cob feast, she sat with her father on the patio, illuminated by a single flattering gas lamp. They sipped coffee and caught up on their lives.

"I wish you could stay longer," he said. "It's good having you here."

"Me, too..." And she told him about the Sutherland investigation and the strain she was under.

"Do you think you'll ever find out who did it?"

"We'd better...I thought I'd spend part of tomorrow looking up Dan Brazier." She'd told him about Brazier's link with Morgan Childs and her hunch that the former journalist just might be able to shed a little light on the case.

"Is a Supreme Court judge really a suspect?"

"Could be." She cut it short, not saying that not one but at least three, Childs, Conover and Poulson, were legitimate suspects.

"By the way, who's *we*?"

"People working on the case, including a detective from the Metropolitan Police Department named Martin Teller." She told him a little about Teller. When she was through, he smiled. "What's funny?"

"It sounds like you're falling a little for a cop."

She laughed. "Who knows? He's not your everyday cop...loves opera, calls his female cat Beast and male cat Beauty."

Her father shrugged, changed the subject, as he most always did when she began to talk too much about men in her life. "This Dan Brazier," he said. "Do you have an appointment with him?"

"No. I was going to call but decided I'd just drop in. I have his address."

"I don't like it."

"Don't like what?"

"Any of it, you involved in investigating a murder. Why don't you get out of it, get out of Washington for that matter, come back here."

"I couldn't be that far from the kids, dad."

"Bring 'em with you. They belong with their mother anyway."

"Please, let's not get into that again."

186

He touched her hand. "Okay, but I'll tell you this, Susanna. No one will ever convince me that a judge of the United States Supreme Court could kill someone, let alone in cold blood in the courtroom and, as I understand it from the papers, in the Chief Justice's chair."

"Truth's stranger than fiction, dad. Which I guess is why fiction is rarely the truth. I mean, who would believe it . . . Anyway I don't *know* whether one of the justices did it. It could have been an old lover, a coworker, even someone from the family."

As he stood and stretched, she noted the beginning of a potbelly. "*If* it's any one of 'em, Susanna, I'd put my money on the old one, Conover. Jealousy . . . it's one damn powerful emotion, and destructive as hell. Some states automatically acquit a man for killing his wife's lover, did you know that?"

"I do now." They watched television with her son until ten, when she announced she was turning in. "Don't worry about tomorrow," her father said. "Rich and I will make out just fine." He cuffed his grandson on the head.

"Thanks," Susanna said. "I know you will."

SHE LEFT the house at ten the following morning, driving her father's 1976 Mercury station wagon. She passed through towns that made up California's wine country—Rutherford and Napa, Pleasanton and Mission San Jose, down through flat and dusty plains on either side of Route 680, past the vineyards of Charles Krug and Beringer, Beaulieu and Christian Brothers until traffic thickened as she neared the Bay Bridge linking San Francisco to Oakland. It was a short drive up the Embarcadero to Broadway in North Beach. She found Brazier's apartment and rang the downstairs bell. No response. She decided to walk, and to call Brazier's number from time to time.

She strolled the length of Fisherman's Wharf, stopping

in shops along the way, buying a leather address book from a sidewalk artisan, a nubby cotton pullover from another. She tried Brazier's number a few times, always without success. She lunched at the Buena Vista, where Irish coffee had been introduced into the United States, and had espresso late in the afternoon in one of Ghirardelli Square's cafes.

She took a cab back to her car. Since it was parked only two blocks from Brazier's apartment, she decided to try again. This time the bell ring resulted in Sheryl Figgs opening the upstairs door.

"Hello," said Susanna. "I'm looking for Dan Brazier." She wasn't sure whether Sheryl's face reflected disappointment or confusion or both.

"He's not here."

"Will he be back? I'm sorry, I'm Susanna Pinscher. I work for the Justice Department in Washington and—"

"Yes, I know you, I know your name. I read about you."

"Oh? Well, I'm here visiting my father in St. Helena and . . ." She realized she was shouting up the flight of stairs, and so did Sheryl.

"I'm sorry," Sheryl said. "I don't mean to be rude. Would you like to come up?"

"Yes, thank you."

Susanna stepped into the small, cluttered apartment.

"You'll have to excuse the mess," Sheryl said. "I got home from work an hour ago and decided to do some cleaning. Once I get in that mood I lose my head. Dan's not here, but I expect him home pretty soon."

Sheryl, wearing a soiled red apron decorated with sewn felt knives and forks, wiped her hands on the apron. "I read the article about you and the Supreme Court murder not too long ago. You interviewed one of the judges up in his plane."

"Yes . . . Look, I'm sorry to barge in on you this way but I did try to call."

"I was at work. I work with computers. Dan must have . . . well, he likes to get out in the fresh air."

"It's beautiful weather."

"I know, I hate to be cooped up too." She raised her eyes. "What a mess. I wanted to have it all put back together before Dan came home. He's a neatnik, a regular Felix. I'm an Oscar, I'm afraid."

Susanna glanced into the bedroom. On a double bed that took up most of the room were dresser drawers. Sheryl quickly said, "I wanted to straighten them out before Dan got home. I get in this mood sometimes and—"

"Me, too," Susanna said, "but not often enough."

Sheryl, whose responses always seemed to be a delayed reaction, said, "I shouldn't have started it so late in the day. I have to start supper."

Susanna looked at photographs of Brazier and Morgan Childs. "These are interesting pictures," she said.

"They were such good friends . . . Dan went to see him when he was out here a few weeks ago."

Susanna turned. "He did?"

"Yes. Justice Childs gave a speech and Dan had a drink with him after. More than one, actually." She smiled. "They got sort of drunk together, Dan said, and he ended up doing push-ups while Judge Childs counted . . . Dan should be home soon. I'm sure he'll be happy to meet you. I . . ."

Susanna looked at her. If she read Sheryl's expression accurately, maybe Dan Brazier would not be too happy to meet her. She considered leaving, decided not to. She wasn't in a popularity contest. She was on a murder investigation. "Could I use your phone? I'd like to call my father and tell him I'm running late. My son is with him and they're probably wondering where I am."

"Oh, sure, it's in the kitchen." She butted her forehead against her hand. "Sorry . . . it's not working and I promised Dan I'd call the phone company and report it. You can use the one in the bedroom, if you can find it under all that mess."

Susanna started for the bedroom.

"Miss Pinscher."

She stopped. "Yes?"

"Would you like to stay for supper? I don't know where Dan is but sometimes he gets talking and doesn't quite make it home for dinner. It's always a waste. I cook for two and it ends up just me. Anyway, if he does come home . . . well, I don't think he'd mind some company." (Again, she didn't sound very convincing on that score.) "Please stay, I'll make meat loaf."

"One of my favorites."

"I'll get it going right away." She snapped her fingers. "I knew I forgot something. I *always* forget things. I need some ingredients . . . I'll run out and get them. Only be a minute."

Susanna waved and said, "Please, don't go to any trouble. I really should be heading back and have dinner with my family—"

"No, I insist. You just stay and make yourself comfortable until I get back. Only take a few minutes. Would you like a drink? There might be some gin left. I drink wine and don't even like that much, but I like to keep Dan company. I'll pick up some wine." She put on a tan raincoat, slung her purse over her shoulder and opened the door. "I'll be back before you know it."

The slam of the door reverberated throughout the apartment. Susanna looked into the bedroom, where a princess phone could be detected beneath a pile of sweaters. She picked it up and dialed her father's area code and number. "My long-lost daughter," he said. "Where are you?"

"At Dan Brazier's apartment. Dad, I've been invited to stay for dinner. Do you mind?"

"Sure you want to?"

"Yes. He isn't here but his girl friend . . . I guess that's what she is . . . his girl friend has invited me and I'd like to take her up on it."

A long pause. "Why don't you come home, Susanna? It's a long drive, I worry about you."

"I won't stay long, I promise." She looked at the pile of things on the bed. One drawer that had been emptied of clothing contained a pile of small, leather-bound books. She picked one up and opened it . . .

"Well, Susanna, if you insist, Rich and I will fend for ourselves," her father was saying. "He'll have to suffer through my cooking but I suppose it won't kill him."

"What?"

"I said my cooking won't kill him."

But she heard nothing he said. Staring up at her from one of the pages she'd been almost idly flipping through was: *Dr. Chester Sutherland, Psychiatrist*, followed by his Chevy Chase address.

"He doesn't want chicken again, I don't know what else I have here, I don't cook much for myself and—"

"Dad, I'll see you later."

She snapped the book closed and was about to drop it back into the drawer when a presence in the bedroom doorway made her spin around.

She dropped the book.

"Who the hell are you?" he asked.

"I'm . . ."

He turned his head, said to an unseen man, "Yeah, thanks for the help upstairs, Harry. See you tomorrow." The door slammed shut. Brazier returned his attention to Susanna. "Like I said, who are you? And what the *hell* are you doing in my bedroom?"

Susanna forced a smile. "Both very good questions . . . I'm Susanna Pinscher, Mr. Brazier. Your . . . Miss Figgs invited me to stay for dinner. She went out to—"

191

"What do you think you were looking at?"

"What? Oh . . . I wasn't really looking at anything. I called my father to tell him I'd be late, he lives in St. Helena—"

"Come off it. You had something in your hand when I came in. One of those books from the drawer—"

She looked down into the drawer. "Books? No, I wasn't looking at anything." She took a few steps toward the door, which was blocked by Brazier and his wide, metal chair. She extended her hand. "I'm visiting from Washington," she said. "I'm working on the Clarence Sutherland murder case for the Justice Department and thought that while I was out here I'd look you up."

"Why?"

"Because you were close to Justice Morgan Childs . . . and he's, well, after all, he's a member of the Court—"

"Get out." His voice was ragged, he even raised a fist. She knew he was drunk. "Get out *now*."

"All right, but I can't go anywhere unless you move."

He glared at her with watery eyes, his fist still in the air. He seemed unsure whether to vacate the doorway or stay there, blocking her. Susanna took a deep breath, took a step closer to him. "I'm leaving," she said. "Excuse me."

He hesitated, then rolled his chair backward, providing just enough room for her to pass. She went quickly to the front door, opened it. Sheryl was on her way up the stairs, her arms full of brown bags.

"I'm sorry," Susanna said, "but I have to go. My son isn't feeling too well and my father thinks I ought to head back right away—"

"I bought steaks and wine—"

"I am sorry. Another time." She waited for Sheryl to reach the landing, then quickly descended the stairs and burst through the outside door to the street. Had she lingered for another minute or two she would have heard the sound

192

of Dan Brazier's hand hitting Sheryl across the face, and the thud of her body slamming against a wall.

She ran to her car and drove as fast as she could back to St. Helena. Her father and son were deep in a game of checkers.

"Quick dinner," her father said.

"Yes. And I'd love a drink."

"Daiquiri?"

"Bourbon. Straight."

CHAPTER
26

"WHY CAN'T YOU TRUST ME?"

Temple Conover, who'd just come downstairs for breakfast, brought his cane across the back of a chair. "Trust you, Cecily? *Fide, sed cui vide.*"

"You and your damn foreign words. What does that mean?"

"Trust, but take care *whom* you trust."

The argument, which had erupted upstairs in the bedroom, was precipitated by a phone call from Martin Teller asking for another interview with Cecily.

She came around behind her husband and touched his neck. He twisted in his chair, grimaced at her. "How could you have done that?" His voice was raspy.

"I told you, Temp, I was frightened, scared to death,

matter of fact. You *threatened* me with that gun, I didn't know what to do..."

He sipped his orange juice while she came around the other side of the table and plopped down in a chair.

"Get that pout off your face," he said.

"Don't tell me what to do with my face."

He grabbed the cane that was resting against his chair and extended it toward her. She got to her feet and screamed at the top of her lungs, "Don't ever raise that thing at me again. Don't ever threaten me again, Temple, ever, ever again." Tears. "God, I hate you."

His voice was calm. "Yes, I know that. You took the gun to the police, you've been unfaithful and let me know it. This house is my Gethsemane. You serve me hemlock with my juice."

"I don't understand your damn fancy talk and you know it—"

"You understand betrayal, though, that comes easy as pie, not to mention lying and cheating." The palms of his hands slapped against the tabletop. Juice slopped over the rim of Cecily's glass, staining the pale blue linen tablecloth.

She had been standing with her back to the table as he spoke, her arms around herself. Now that she had stopped crying, her face, which he could not see, was relaxed. She heard him take another drink of his juice, then the sound of his fork against his plate as it scooped up scrambled eggs. Without turning she said, "I turned in the gun, Temple, because you killed him."

His second forkful was halfway to his mouth. It remained poised there as he looked up over his glasses.

"Did you hear me, Temp? I said—"

"I heard you. Along with all your other sterling qualities, you're pretty stupid."

She turned slowly. "Am I? Temple, you're so full of hate. You couldn't stand having Clarence walk the same

195

earth with you. What had he done to you, Temple, provided a little warmth and fun for a woman you claim to love, or at least used to . . ." She stopped and waited for the invariable outburst, the cane, thrown dishes. It did not come. He sat back and actually smiled.

"Maybe it was his ambition you couldn't stand, a young man on the way up, making you feel so old? . . ."

"Go on."

She wasn't sure how to react, what to say next. She sat down and drank cold black coffee. "Was it his White House job, Temple, that broke the camel's back?"

"Having someone like Clarence Sutherland considered for an important job in the administration of our government would be more than most decent people could bear."

She shook her head. "You love to rub it in that I'm not as smart or *decent* as you, don't you, Mr. Justice. Well, maybe I'm not so dumb after all."

He reached for a buzzer that would sound throughout the house, part of a system installed after his first stroke so that he could summon aid from any room. Moments later Karl appeared in the doorway.

"Call the Court motor pool and tell them not to send a car this morning. You drive me, Karl."

Karl glanced at Cecily, nodded and disappeared.

Conover pushed against the arms of his chair and stood. His ability to walk had improved over the past few months, and he'd been able to shuck the elaborate Canadian crutch for a more conventional cane, which he took in his right hand. "My best to the detective," he said. He paused, then added, "You may be interested in my plans . . ."

"What plans?"

"First, we're conferencing this morning about the abortion matter. I intend to see that a free choice means something in this country, even for poor women. Afterward I shall resign from the Court and spend whatever time I have

196

left *alone*, what's left of my peace of mind intact. My resignation from the Court will coincide with my action for divorce from you."

"Well, Temple dear, I surely wouldn't fight either decision. I would only expect my fair share as a dutiful and loving wife for more than five years."

He managed to hold his anger in check as he slowly crossed the room.

"I'll *fight* for what's mine," she said.

He paused, turned, leaned on his cane. "Cecily, for the past six months your every move has been noted by a firm of private investigators—"

"You had me *followed*? How *tacky*, Temple."

"Yes, I agree, but sweets to the sweet. Well, like they say, have a good day."

He took his coat from a hall closet, put it on and stepped out to the front of the house, where Karl waited behind the wheel of a shiny red cadillac. Conover said nothing as he settled into the back seat and looked at the house. Cecily stood at the window. "So damned beautiful," he murmured. "Damned is the word . . ."

As Karl drove off, Martin Teller pulled up in his car. Conover looked at him, turned away and closed his eyes. Karl glanced in the rearview mirror. Conover often fell asleep on the way to the Court, which was fine with Karl. He didn't like talking to the old man.

Teller rang the bell. A housekeeper answered it, took his card and returned a few moments later. "Mrs. Conover will see you," she said in an Irish brogue.

Cecily was seated at the breakfast table in the sunroom. "Good morning," she said. "Coffee?"

"No, thanks. I appreciate you seeing me like this, Mrs. Conover. Usually I try to schedule things further in advance but I needed to talk to you today."

"My pleasure, sit down."

Teller, who'd given his coat and hat to the housekeeper, took the chair that had been occupied by Justice Conover.

"Any progress on the case?" Cecily asked.

"It never works fast, Mrs. Conover. You go day by day, put a piece together now and then, here and there. If you're lucky you end up with enough of the puzzle to recognize the face."

"I see. Well, what can I do for you?"

The folds of her robe had fallen open and the upper part of her breasts was looking at him. He looked away as he asked, "Why did you bring me your husband's gun, Mrs. Conover?"

"I told you why. I was afraid. Temple had threatened me with it—"

"Because of Clarence Sutherland?"

She began an answer but he cut her off. "Look, Mrs. Conover, I'm a cop but I don't enjoy poking into people's personal lives. What people do is their own business, unless it affects me, my job ... Your relationship with Clarence Sutherland had nothing to do with me personally, but it might with my murder investigation. Did you have an affair with Sutherland?"

"Yes."

"That simple."

"What else do you want me to say?"

"I guess I'm used to people beating around the bush over questions like that. Okay, let's get back to you turning in your husband's weapon. You say you were afraid of him using it on you. Is that the only reason?"

She opened her eyes wide, started to say something, then cried softly, a perfect teardrop running down each rouged cheek. "Excuse me," she said, standing and getting a tissue from a table. She dabbed at her eyes, wiped her nose and sat down again. "I suppose you deal with weepy women all the time in your profession."

198

"Sometimes," Teller said, waiting for the act to finish.

She looked down at her lap. "I haven't been completely honest with you, Detective Teller."

"Well, you're only human."

"Yes. I'm sure you'll understand why when I tell you what I've held back."

"I'll try my best, Mrs. Conover."

"I delivered the gun to you because . . . because my husband murdered Clarence Sutherland." (No change in her tone of voice.)

Teller looked around the room, ran his finger under his shirt collar. A very cool little lady. "You're sure?"

"Yes, I'm sorry to say, but I am."

"Proof?"

"If you mean did I see him do it, no. Did he tell me he did it? Well, not exactly, but he surely hinted at it enough times."

"Why do you think he did do it, because of your affair with Sutherland?"

"Of course, that, but Clarence's rise to power inside the Court, his success, the offer to him of a job on President Jorgens's staff . . . they all contributed—"

"Sutherland was offered a job in the White House?"

"Yes, in so many words. It wasn't definite, but he was very excited about it."

"What sort of job?"

"Something to do with legal affairs, I guess. Imagine, someone that young going up so fast. My husband couldn't *bear* it. It ate away at him like a cancer—"

"Because a young man was getting ahead?"

"That young man had slept with his wife, Detective Teller."

"Are you willing to testify that your husband killed Clarence Sutherland?"

"How testify?"

"Make a formal statement. If you do, it at least will be enough to ruin him, even if it doesn't stick in court. It'll be front page in every newspaper in the country, the world. Sure you want to do that to him, Mrs. Conover?"

She drew a deep breath, rubbed her forehead. "This may be hard to swallow, I know...after what I've said and done, but I care about Temple...I really do...but if you lived with a person you knew in your heart had killed another person, well...what would you do?..."

"We're talking about you, Mrs. Conover. Is there anything else you can give me by way of proof?"

"I'm afraid not, but I'm sure if you question him it will come out...I wish I could be more helpful. I'm trying...this is very difficult, as I'm sure you understand..."

"Oh, I think maybe I do, Mrs. Conover. And thank you." He stood up and extended his hand.

A thin smile crossed her lips. Her robe had fallen even further open, one bare leg now dangled over the other. "Please keep in touch," she said. "This is the most difficult thing I've ever faced in my life, and I'm not an especially strong person..."

"I'm sure...well, thanks for your time. And have a good day..."

No sooner was he gone than she picked up the phone and dialed her husband's office. Laurie Rawls answered. "Miss Rawls, this is Mrs. Conover."

"Good morning," Laurie said. "How are you?"

"Not too well, I'm afraid."

"I'm sorry, anything I can do?"

"Yes...Justice Conover is on his way to the office. I would appreciate your not telling him that I called."

Silence.

"Miss Rawls, of all the clerks my husband has had work for him, you've always been my favorite. I don't wish to

200

sound as though I'm, so to speak, currying favor, but it happens to be true."

"Thank you."

"Are you alone?"

"Yes, I am. Why do you ask, Mrs. Conover?"

"Miss Rawls, let's talk woman to woman. I'm sure you're aware that certain . . . tensions between Justice Conover and myself have existed during our relationship—"

"Mrs. Conover, I'm not sure whether this sort of conversation is appropriate. I—"

"Please, hear me out. Things have reached a very bad point . . . I'm even afraid for my safety—"

"Again, I think that—"

"Miss Rawls, there's a file in my husband's office that relates to me and our marriage. I'm at my *wits'* end. *That* file contains, well, what could be damaging personal information about me. I suppose there have been times during my marriage when I might not have been quite as careful as I should have been . . . Miss Rawls, I *need* that file."

"Mrs. Conover, Mrs. Conover I couldn't—"

"*Please*, I'm begging you. I understand your position, but you must understand mine too. I'm talking to you not as an employee of the Court. I'm talking to you as one woman to another . . ."

"Mrs. Conover, I sympathize with you, but it's still out of the question. I have no idea what file you're talking about, and I don't want to. I'm a clerk on this Court. That's a position of unique trust, as you know. I can't compromise it for *any* consideration, regardless of personal feelings," (which include not liking you, lady).

The importuning abruptly stopped. "All right. You will forget that I called?"

"I can assure you of that. It never happened."

"Thank you."

Laurie heard the phone click on the other end, slowly

hung up, leaned over and looked down at a red file folder on her desk. She opened it and, once again, looked at the many pages lying within. On top, the very top, was a picture of Cecily Conover entering a motel with Clarence Sutherland.

KARL PULLED the Cadillac up in front of the justices' entrance to the Supreme Court building. His passenger, Senior Justice Temple Conover, appeared to have slept throughout the trip.

Karl got up and opened the back door. Conover did not move. "Justice Conover," he said. Still no reply. He reached inside, gently shook Conover's shoulder. It was only then that he noticed that the justice's tongue protruded at a peculiar angle from a mouth twisted grotesquely. He stepped back as the judge slumped toward the door, his head coming to rest over the curb, his red woolen scarf dipping into stagnant water in the gutter.

Sic transit gloria mundi, Judge Conover might have said, if he were talking.

CHAPTER
27

SOME TWENTY MINUTES LATER A DETECTIVE ASSIGNED TO
the Sutherland case walked into Martin Teller's office. "Did
you hear, Marty?"

"Hear what?"

"Justice Temple Conover had a stroke right in front of
the Supreme Court."

"I just left his house... Dead?"

"No, but close. In a coma."

"Where'd they take him?"

"Capitol Hill, on Mass."

"Have somebody monitor his progress," Teller said. "And
round up everybody for the meeting."

Teller and four detectives sat in his office, three coffees,
one tea and one chicken soup. They reviewed the Sutherland

case from the beginning, each man contributing what information his area of investigation had uncovered. There wasn't all that much, and Teller knew it. He sat with his feet up on his desk and twisted his toes in his right shoe. The inner leather lining had split and curled up in the front of the shoe. "Excuse me," he said, removing the shoe, pressing the lining flat, then quickly slipping his foot inside. "That's better," he sighed. "Okay, let's go over the logs from the surveillance."

A detective picked up a thick sheaf of papers, handed portions of it to the others, "I've got the log on Justice Poulson."

"Go ahead, read," Teller said. "And everybody listen up. If something rings a bell, yell."

The detective recited the entries on the first page of the log on Poulson, stopped and laughed.

"What's funny?"

"Putting a tail on the Chief Justice of the Supreme Court. You could get arrested for that."

"Just read," Teller said. He hadn't lightly made the decision to put a twenty-four hour surveillance on three Supreme Court justices. But what else could he do? And Dorian Mars had added to the squeeze when he said during one of their 9:00 A.M. meetings, "Marty, all the line is out. Unless we get a fish on the hook damn soon we're all going back on foot patrol." To which Teller had replied, "What if it's a big fish, Dorian?" And Mars had said, "Just as long as the net we use is strong enough." And Teller had said, "There's plenty of fish in the sea, Dorian. Too damn many." And the conversation had ended with Mars, lover of the extended metaphor and cliché, saying, "Then stop trolling and get out the harpoon."

Justice Poulson's movements under surveillance didn't provide much. He divided his time between home and the

Court, with time out for two speaking engagements in Washington, one in Virginia and three visits to the White House.

"Is that a lot of visits for a Supreme Court Justice to the White House?" Teller asked.

The detective shrugged. "Why should it be? They're top guys in the same business. Telling the rest of us what's up."

"What about Childs?"

The log on Morgan Childs's movements were also not especially revealing.

Pretty much the same for Temple Conover, except that the officer assigned to cover Conover had made a note that it was his opinion that Mrs. Conover was also being followed. He'd asked whether someone from MPD was on her case and was told no.

"You didn't have a tail on her, did you, Marty?" one of the men in his office asked.

He shook his head. "Maybe her husband had her followed."

"From what I hear about her, it probably wouldn't be a bad idea," someone said, which started a series of lewd comments about Cecily Conover.

"Knock it off," Teller said. "Let's get on with the rest of them. What about Dr. Sutherland?"

Sutherland's surveillance log was read. The detective reading the log said, "The doc makes house calls at the CIA. Makes sense, a shrink making house calls to the crazies at Central Intelligence."

Teller scratched under his arm and lit an odious clove.

"Come on, Marty, please."

"Hold your breath if you don't like it... Let's look at this a minute. Why *would* he be going to the CIA?"

"Maybe *he's* a spook. Remember those stories a couple of years back about all the strange drug experiments the CIA was into? Lots of doctors involved, if I remember right, civilian doctors... maybe he was one of them."

"Go back over those stories," Teller said. "See if he's mentioned anywhere."

When they'd finished with the logs, Teller asked for a review of background checks on the suspects.

The voices droned on, and Teller found himself at one point on the edge of nodding off. He struggled against it, even resorted to digging a fingernail into the palm of his hand. His mind wandered—the last opera he'd seen, Puccini's *La Fanciulla del West*, "The Girl of the Golden West," which he hadn't liked . . . a former girl friend calling and suggesting they get together for "old times' sake," which he'd declined to do . . . the lyrics to "You're the Top," which he'd forgotten while trying to sing it at Club Julie . . . bills that were overdue . . . his younger daughter, she'd come home and told her mother everything. She was planning to marry the father of the child as soon as he finished college, which was two years down the road. She planned to have the baby, live with her mother and find a job until the wedding. Teller had asked his former wife for the young man's name. She reluctantly gave it to him on his promise that he wouldn't call and make trouble. "I saw his picture," she said. "He's blond, adorable . . ." "Wonderful," Teller had said.

He came out of his reverie as the detective reading from the report said, "There's this one year while Poulson was sitting on the Court of Claims that's hard to nail down."

Teller sat up. "Why?"

"Well, he took a year's leave of absence and according to what I can piece together, used it to write a book."

"What kind of a book?"

"About suing the United States government. It's a textbook."

"Was it published?"

"Sure. I got a copy. You approved it on my expense sheet."

"What's this court about?"

"It only hears cases against the United States, I'm told."

"So what's so strange about that year? He takes a leave of absence and writes a book."

"Right, but he didn't stay at home to write it. The first four months of the year he sort of disappeared."

"Sort of?..."

"Yeah, his family was home, but he holed up in a place called Sunken Springs, Delaware."

"Why? Do they own a summer place there?"

"No."

"Where did he live in Sunken Springs?"

"Nobody seems to know. Four months later he comes home and goes on with his work on the book. Then he's back on the bench, the book's published and everything else is laid out clean for the record."

"Check it out."

"How?"

"Troll the waters. Let out all the line. Use a strong net..."

"Huh?"

"Just do it, Maurice."

He spent the rest of the day rearranging his flow chart, taking phone calls and thinking about his daughter, and about Susanna Pinscher...

He stopped in a music store on the way home and bought the sheet music to "You're the Top," committed the lyrics to memory over a dinner of frozen Welsh rarebit, toast and bacon, talked on the phone with someone from MPD who reported that Justice Conover was still in a coma and might not survive, took a nap, then went to Club Julie, where he sang loud and bad until the wee hours.

207

CHAPTER
28

NEWS OF TEMPLE CONOVER'S STROKE PERMEATED EVERY corridor and filtered through every door, open and closed, in the Court. His secretaries, Joan and Helen, cried, as did a black cleaning woman who said, "Lord have mercy on him." Conover had been the Court's leading champion of minority rights ever since coming to the bench.

A conference that had been called for that morning by Chief Justice Poulson to discuss *Nidel v. Illinois* was delayed an hour. When it was finally convened in the main conference room, Morgan Childs was absent. Justice Tilling-Masters asked where he was.

"He's running late," Augustus Smith said. "He'll be here shortly."

Poulson couldn't hide his annoyance at Childs's absence. He slapped a pencil on the table and looked at his watch.

"How's Justice Conover?" Justice Fine asked.

"The same, I suppose," Poulson said. "One of his clerks is at the hospital and is keeping in touch. I'm afraid it doesn't look too good."

"He's survived them before," Smith said. "He comes from hardy stock. And we certainly can't afford to lose him." Smith meant lose a liberal's vote on the Court, and Poulson knew what he meant.

Poulson looked sharply at him, then at Tilling-Masters. "Have you had a chance to go over my memo?" he asked.

"I'll need another day."

The door opened and Morgan Childs entered the room. "Sorry," he said as he took his seat and opened a folder.

"Well, we can begin," Poulson said. "Naturally, we all share grief over what has happened to Justice Conover, and we pray that his recovery will be swift and complete."

No one in the room said what he, or she, was thinking. It wasn't a matter of doubting the Chief Justice's sincerity about Temple Conover. Despite what some considered his inadequacies on the bench, he was not without compassion . . . There were no formal rules to deal with the sudden and complete incapacitation of a justice. It was up to the remaining eight justices to decide the disposition of cases that were pending before the condition. Were Conover to recover sufficiently to be able to communicate his thoughts, his final vote on the abortion issue could be cast from the hospital by phone, through a clerk or another justice. But he was in a coma, and the prognosis was not good.

"We might as well address the immediate issue," Poulson said. "Justice Conover is not in a position to vote on pending cases. I think we agree that of all the cases before this court, *Nidel v. Illinois* is the most pressing. I wonder whether—"

"I'm not certain that's true," Justice Fine said. "Sorry to

interrupt, Mr. Chief Justice, but because *Nidel v. Illinois* does have importance as a precedent-setting decision that will influence social programs in this nation for generations to come, it might be prudent to hold it over until Justice Conover has recovered."

"If he recovers," Justice Tilling-Masters said. "And what if he doesn't?"

"We could hold over the case for next term," Augustus Smith said. An action he personally did not favor. Smith's problem as a liberal was that if Conover was unable to return to the bench, President Jorgens would appoint a more conservative replacement. *Any* stalemated vote held over for the arrival of the new justice would, in all likelihood, mirror the administration's views. As for the abortion issue, well, he wasn't sure . . .

"I'm against that," said Poulson. "The nation is waiting for this Court's decision on abortion. To delay will only indicate indecision on our part." He didn't state the real reason for wanting to push forward on a vote. His personal lobbying efforts had resulted in what he perceived as a wavering on Augustus Smith's part. Smith had voted in favor of Nidel during the initial vote. Now, with the vote four to four, if he had a change of heart it would make it five to three in favor of Illinois and against abortion.

There was more discussion about what to do in Conover's absence. Finally Poulson suggested another preliminary vote.

"Are we really ready for that?" Smith asked.

"I think so," said Poulson. "Let's see where we stand."

Tilling-Masters said, "It seems to me that we know where we stand. It obviously still falls four-to-four, now that Justice Conover can't vote. Perhaps we should hold the case over until the next term."

Poulson knew that holding it over until the President could appoint a conservative to the bench was, on the face of it, safer. But one could never be sure. Judges sometimes changed stripes once they got to the Supreme Court . . . look at Black, a Klu Kluxer turned liberal, and Eisenhower surely never expected Earl Warren to lead the fight to strike down the "separate but equal" doctrine . . . *And* if his instincts about Smith were right, *Nidel v. Illinois* could be settled quickly, and the way he wanted. The Poulson Court would have acted, the nation would have clear guidelines on a nasty, divisive issue, the administration's pledge would be fulfilled and he, Poulson, would have delivered what he'd promised.

"Let's vote," Justice Fine said, removing wire spectacles and rubbing his eyes. "If there's been a change, we might as well find out."

Morgan Childs cleared his throat, held up a finger. "I think another vote is premature," he said.

"Why?" Poulson asked.

"I'm not ready, Mr. Chief Justice."

"Not ready?" Poulson couldn't help but smile. Childs's conservative views were well known, solid. Certainly, Poulson reasoned, Childs couldn't be considering changing his vote in favor of the plaintiff Nidel.

Childs went on, "I've read every position paper that's been generated since the last vote, along with a stack of related materials. This is the sort of issue that naturally stirs up very personal feelings that tend to influence sound legal reasoning. I'd be less than honest if I didn't admit that this has happened to me, but when I strip away my private views, I keep coming back to a very narrow and clearly defined legal issue. I haven't reached a firm decision as yet, but my reaction to the legal aspects of this case is different from what it was earlier."

"I'm surprised," said Poulson. It was the mildest reaction he could manage.

"Well," Childs said, "surprised or not, that's where I stand at this moment."

211

Justice Smith, a wry smile on his face, asked, "What if you had to vote right now, Justice Childs? What would it be?"

"Hypothetical votes don't interest me," Childs said.

"They don't count, but they're interesting," Smith said, still smiling.

They spent another half-hour discussing other pending cases and deciding what to do in light of Conover's situation. Eventually it was decided to table voting on all cases until a clearer picture of the senior justice's physical condition could be determined.

Poulson went to his chambers and slumped in his chair, his stomach a knot, his nerve ends alive. He tried to calm down, took deep breaths, considered having a drink.

It was inconceivable to him that Childs might vote for Nidel. How many times had they sat together over lunch or dinner and discussed their views on life, not as Supreme Court justices but as men, husbands and fathers, observers of society and of the moral deterioration it had suffered at the hands of liberal gurus? A man doesn't change that much, he told himself, and if he did, it would surely be to become even more concerned about the shredding of the American fabric, to become even more conservative. He refused to acknowledge, even to himself, that Childs's narrow legal focus on the case might be sound. It didn't matter what the legal technicalities were. There was a greater issue at stake, one beyond strict legal considerations. There was decency to be upheld, moral leadership to be exercised...and a President in the White House who had appointed him and expected him to live up to his commitments.

Anger displaced anxiety. He picked up the phone and dialed a number in the White House. It rang in the office of Craig Lauderman, special assistant to the President. A secretary answered, told Poulson to hold and entered Lauderman's private office. "Sir, the Chief Justice wishes to speak with you."

Lauderman, thirty-five years old, thick brown hair neatly combed over a thin, patrician face and wearing tortoiseshell glasses, raised his eyebrows, and then his patrician face. "Thank you, I'll take it."

"Mr. Lauderman," Poulson said when he came on the line, "I hope I'm not interrupting some important affair of state." He laughed a tentative laugh.

Lauderman did not laugh, or smile. "Is there something I can do for you, Mr. Chief Justice?"

His coldness was not lost on Poulson, who hesitated before saying, "I'd like to speak to the President."

"He won't be available to anyone until tomorrow afternoon."

"That's a shame."

"Is it urgent?"

"Yes."

"Perhaps I can help."

"I don't think so, Mr. Lauderman."

"Try me, Mr. Chief Justice."

Poulson resented the tone used by the younger man. Who the hell was he, just another middling bright and over-weeningly ambitious young man with a position of influence in Jorgens's administration, lording it over everyone in Washington—senators and congressmen, cabinet officials and even Supreme Court justices. He wanted to tell him what he thought of him and his kind. Instead he said, "It has to do with *Nidel v. Illinois*."

"I suspected that was the purpose of your call, Mr. Chief Justice. The President is on top of it and is taking steps he considers appropriate—"

"I don't think you understand, Mr. Lauderman. There have been developments that—"

"How is Justice Conover?"

213

"The last we heard, he was still in a coma and the prognosis is guarded."

"It was a shock . . . Well, perhaps the President could get back to you, Mr. Chief Justice. As I said, he's quite up to date on the case, and so am I."

Poulson's voice now filled up with anger. "Perhaps you'd better tell the President, Mr. Lauderman, that it seems Justice Childs is considering changing his vote. Perhaps you could suggest that thought be given to Justice Childs and his vote—"

"I will, Mr. Chief Justice. Thank you for calling."

The line went dead. Poulson took his coat from a closet and headed into the hallway. He needed time to think. Maybe a walk would help. As he proceeded down the corridor Laurie Rawls came around a corner. "Good morning, Mr. Chief Justice," she said.

"Good morning, Miss Rawls."

"Any word on Justice Conover?" she asked.

"Nothing new," Poulson said. "We're all hoping. Good day," and he walked past her.

LAURIE RAWLS left the building and drove home, where, after rummaging through closets, she chose a tailored brown tweed suit, taupe blouse with a button-down collar, stockings and plain brown pumps. She checked herself in a mirror, playing with her hair and makeup. Finally, apparently satisfied, she returned to her car and drove slowly toward the center of Washington, checking her watch every few minutes and varying her speed accordingly. She parked in a garage on Eighteenth Street near the General Services Building and walked toward the White House. She'd been told to enter through the south portico, which she did. A guard took her name and checked a list, then called Craig Lauderman's office. "Yes, Miss Rawls, you're expected," the guard said. "Someone will be here to escort you in a minute."

Lauderman's office was large, free of clutter. He was in shirt sleeves. He stood up and offered his hand. "Nice of you to stop by, Miss Rawls."

"I appreciate your finding the time for me—"

"Don't be modest. The President is impressed with you and what you've offered us."

She seemed almost embarrassed. "Thank you, that's very flattering."

"Yes, well, I know what you mean. I sit close to the most powerful leader in the Free World. Few people have that opportunity. Right here is where the buck stops."

Well, almost, she thought. Like more than one top presidential aide, Lauderman tended to so identify himself with the top man that he began to think he *was* the man. No question, though, that he had the President's confidence, and that no one had access to Jorgens unless cleared by the Jorgens Militia, a cadre of arrogant, aloof young men with ambition in their veins and steel in their hearts. This one tended to frighten her, as he did so many others...but he also attracted her. Montesquieu said power corrupts... well, it also seduces, she thought...

"I want you to know, Miss Rawls, that I speak for the President when I say to you we appreciate the information you have offered us about Dr. Chester Sutherland's research files. I don't think I overstate it when I say that those files, were they to end up in the wrong hands, would have posed a grave threat to national security."

"Well, Mr. Lauderman, when I learned...through his son...that such files existed, I knew something needed to be done. It wasn't an easy decision. Clarence Sutherland was a friend and...and close colleague. Were he still alive, I would not, to be perfectly honest with you, have informed the White House of the existence of the files. But once he

215

was gone I did what I thought was right. I hope I made the right decision."

"You did, Miss Rawls. One must follow one's best instincts in these things . . . Tell me about yourself, Miss Rawls."

"What would you like to know?"

He smiled. It was not really much of a smile. Tight-lipped. She wondered whether he ever let go, laughed out loud.

"Tell me about the essential Laurie Rawls, the Laurie Rawls who might end up working with me every day and who, in that event, would work at the right hand of the President of the United States."

She shifted in her chair, organized her thoughts. Be precise, she told herself, and she was. He listened impassively, his eyes never leaving hers, his mind like a computer taking in her words and committing them to chips to be instantly replayed when and if needed.

"Very impressive," he said when she was through.

"Thank you." Good, he'd been impressed with her performance. She felt more in control now and actually felt his peer, every bit as bright, and calculating, as he was. An even match.

He offered her a glass of water. She declined. He poured himself a glass from a crystal pitcher wrapped in glove leather. "Do you drink?"

"Drink? Alcohol?"

"Yes."

"I like wine." And quickly added, "with meals."

"Drugs? Smoke pot?"

"No."

"Never?"

"Well, I did once or twice a long time ago but . . ."

"Any skeletons in the Rawls closet? Sordid romances, insanity in the family, cheating on college exams, unpaid

216

parking tickets or college loans, people holding something over your head..."

"No."

"Good." He leafed through a file folder, looked up and said, "You do know, Miss Rawls, that this job can be yours if things progress as we hope they will."

"I'm not sure I understand exactly what you mean, Mr. Lauderman. Clarence Sutherland and I were close. He told me about your interest in having him come to work here at the White House and—"

"How close were you?"

"Will honesty ruin my chances?"

"Honesty will help insure them."

"We were very close. Very..."

"And you're understandably upset by his death...but you still have your priorities in order. I like that, Miss Rawls. You're a pragmatist." He leaned on his elbows as he said, "Your late friend, Clarence Sutherland, was close to being named to our team here at the White House. At first I balked at the suggestion. After all, what could he offer us that any bright law graduate couldn't offer? Bright law school graduates are a dime a dozen, and being a clerk in the Supreme Court doesn't mean all that much. We know how he got the appointment, which, I might add, is no crime. His father, because of his *close* relationship with Justice Poulson, did what any caring father might have done, used a delicate relationship to benefit a son. I would do the same thing. Would you?"

"I think so."

"Well, the important thing is that Clarence Sutherland had certain information, because of his father's profession, that was valuable to this administration. Does that offend you?"

"Why should it?"

"It would some. I'm glad it doesn't you."

"As you said, I'm a pragmatist."

"And ambitious."

"Yes. I would imagine you would understand that."

He allowed a grin. "Yes, I do. When you first came here with the information about Dr. Sutherland's files, I was skeptical of you. I asked myself what you wanted, what your game was, what your price was. That's what I'm paid for."

"Was it because I'm a woman?"

"Why should it be? I'm no sexist. Just a realist. Miss Rawls, you want the job Clarence was being considered for and I admire you for that. You say you have the same information he had because of your—"

"Because I was very close to him. Yes. When you're that close to someone, you tend to share everything..."

"Yes... well, I'm aware of that. But can you stop the sharing if necessary. I'm speaking of what you would learn here at the White House?"

"Absolutely." She looked directly at him when she said it.

"Good. Now... we need a... continuing factor inside the Court. Mr. Sutherland held that out to us. Now, he's no longer in a position to provide it. Perhaps you are."

"I think I am."

"As I said, I'm a realist, Miss Rawls. Give me some results to convince me."

"Such as?" Actually she knew the answer.

"Help insure that the vote on *Nidel v. Illinois* goes the way it should. The way the administration, *and* the American people believe it should."

"That isn't easy—"

"Sutherland said it was."

"I'm not Clarence Sutherland."

"But you're peddling the same thing."

"I'm not *peddling* anything."

218

"Sorry, Miss Rawls. I'm afraid I'm not as good at the legal niceties as you are. Let me put it this way. Justice Childs may be a problem. I understand you might know something about him to help moderate his perhaps overly rigid *legal* principles."

"I might."

"If you want this job, Miss Rawls, you'd better."

"It comes down to that?"

He nodded.

"Well, there are certain inconsistencies in Justice Childs's background that might be helpful in persuading him to—"

"See the light?"

"Yes."

"You know what they are?"

"Yes."

"Can you prove them?"

"I think so."

"Childs is swaying in his position. His vote, I understand, is now crucial to the outcome of *Nidel v. Illinois*."

"I thought he was solidly for the state of Illinois."

"Not as of this morning. Can you do something about that?"

"Yes."

"Glad to hear it. As I told you at the beginning of this meeting, the job of judicial liaison can be yours, provided you can contribute to certain conditions within the Court—"

"Count on me, Mr. Lauderman. There is nothing Clarence Sutherland knew that I don't know. Nothing he could do that I can't do."

"I'm going to enjoy working with you, Miss Rawls. I have a good sense of people. You're good people, and I intend to tell President Jorgens exactly that."

"Thank you."

They stood and shook hands. "Maybe we could have

dinner some night," he said. "Since we're likely to be working together for what I hope is a long time, we really should get to know each other. Don't you agree?"

"I certainly do. Thank you. You'll hear from me shortly, Mr. Lauderman."

"I look forward to it."

CHAPTER
29

THE BRIEF, VOLATILE CONFRONTATION WITH DAN BRAZIER had left Susanna temporarily shaken, and by the following morning, highly annoyed with herself for having exited so hastily before asking the questions that had brought her to the apartment in the first place.

She'd told her father about the incident the night it happened. He was adamant about her getting off the Sutherland case. When confronted with her decision to return to see Brazier, he became angry.

"I have a job," she said.

"Your job is *also* to be a mother to your children." Which once again started all the business of her having given custody to her former husband. By the time she left the house

221

for Brazier's apartment, a thick cloud of tension trailed behind.

She deeply regretted that but forced herself to forget about the argument and to concentrate on what she would say to Brazier. She knew that ordinarily she was not a particularly brave person, tended to avoid confrontation ... Except, damn it, that wasn't completely true, she reminded herself as she passed over the Bay Bridge. It had taken real courage, no matter what anyone said, to end her bad marriage and especially to give up physical possession of her children. She'd stood up to it, had made a good career in a male-dominated world without sacrificing herself as a woman, without forgetting that she was a woman. Or a mother. She was still a good mother, even though she did not have everyday possession of her children. But their relationship was better than it had ever been. No, she had nothing to apologize for, feel guilty about, and was not about to create something now by avoiding Dan Brazier.

She planned her approach, went over it a dozen times. It didn't matter how he reacted, whether he hit out at her, just as long as she got to ask her questions.

She rang the downstairs buzzer. Sheryl Figgs opened the door at the top of the stairs and squinted against a shaft of bright sunlight that backlit Susanna. "Who is it?" she asked.

"Susanna Pinscher. I'd like to speak to Mr. Brazier."

"Oh, no, I don't think that's—"

Susanna quickly climbed the stairs. "Please, Miss Figgs, I won't stay long. I'm sorry about dinner the other night, but it was a difficult situation."

Sheryl glanced nervously into the apartment. She was wearing a faded pink robe and was barefoot, her hair was tousled. Obviously she'd just gotten out of bed.

"Is he here?" Susanna asked, looking past her.

"He's ... we just ..."

"I'll only stay a minute," Susanna said, stepping around her and into the living room.

"Who is it?" Brazier called from another room.

"It's me, Susanna Pinscher. I'd like to speak with you."

Sheryl came up behind her. "I really don't think it's a good idea. He was so angry after you left last time he—"

Brazier wheeled himself from the bedroom, chest bare, a dollop of shaving cream still beneath his right earlobe.

"Why did you come back?" he asked, wiping water from his neck with the towel.

"To ask you a few questions." Susanna looked into his gray eyes, at his powerful upper body that could have belonged to a weight lifter. "I won't stay long, no longer than the last time," she said, determined not to wilt under his intense gaze.

"I have nothing to say to you."

"I really think you do." She summoned up the line she'd rehearsed in the car. She had nothing to back it up, only Laurie Rawls's comment based on something Clarence had told her. She'd decided not to ask it as a question, she'd challenge and hope for the best. "Morgan Childs isn't what he's cracked up to be—"

"What the hell are you talking about?"

"About his so-called heroic deeds in Korea? I understand that was all made up, and you helped."

He started to respond, then wiped the back of his hand across his square, lined face as though to dismiss the subject, and her.

"Why?" Susanna pressed.

"What do you know?" he said, turning his chair and wheeling to the window. "What the hell does anybody know any more about heroes?"

"I know I like them better if they're legitimate."

Sheryl Figgs approached him. "Dan," she said, "if you'd rather have her leave—"

He waved her away, fixed Susanna with a look and pointed his index finger at her. "How do you know what you say you know?"

"It's my job, Mr. Brazier. I'm investigating a murder, and this could be relevant."

"How?"

She couldn't backtrack now. He'd all but acknowledged it, at least he hadn't denied it. "Clarence Sutherland knew about Justice Childs's so-called exploits in Korea. Sutherland was a man who used information for power. If he held damaging knowledge over Childs's head, it might have provided a real motive for your friend to have killed him—"

"Don't be ridiculous. Whatever Morgan Childs is or isn't, he's not a murderer."

"And Nixon wasn't a crook, and the boy next door who killed his family was always so polite and nice...It's an old story, Mr. Brazier. Appearances can deceive...anyway, the fact is that a substantial part of Justice Childs's public image revolves around his having performed all sorts of heroic deeds in Korea, which isn't exactly true."

"So?"

"So? Is that all you can say? A whole country was misled by a fantasy *you* wrote. Why did you do it?" She hoped she hadn't gone too far...after all, she wasn't really certain how much he was involved in Childs's Korean scenario.

He tugged on the arms of his wheelchair as though not sure which way to move, then looked up and asked, "What's your politics, Miss Pinscher? Liberal, conservative? Don't give a damn?"

"Moderate, I suppose."

"What does that mean?"

"I try to go by the issues. Sometimes I come down on what's considered to be the liberal side, other times the conservative."

Brazier looked at Sheryl, who leaned against a wall. "Get

me a shirt, will you?" She returned from the bedroom with a wrinkled red plaid shirt that he slipped over his massive shoulders, leaving it unbuttoned.

Susanna said, "My politics really haven't any bearing on this, Mr. Brazier. What I'm wondering about is why you and Justice Childs would get together on a sham—?"

"That's your word."

She pulled out a chair from the desk, sat down and said as calmly as she could, "Mr. Brazier, I'm not here to make trouble. What happened in Korea between you and Justice Childs is no one's business but your own, unless, of course, it bears on Clarence Sutherland's murder. I'm not your antagonist. I'm doing my job, or trying to..."

"Then you should understand."

"Understand what?"

"That we did what we had to do."

"I'm sorry, I don't follow you."

"Korea needed a hero. *Before* Vietnam. Maybe if we'd been more successful there'd have been no Nam. Anyway, nobody quite understood what was going on. It was a United Nations action, mostly manned by the U.S. MacArthur got everybody confused about not being allowed to win the war —Harry Truman had to fire him for insubordination...for forgetting who was Commander in Chief. Harry was right. But the country badly needed something to be proud of, we made the most of a brave man...Childs...who was a natural for the hero's role—a kind of rallying point for back home. Hell, the flag-raising photo on Iwo Jima that hit every front page in America during World War II was a phony too, a sham to use your word, staged by a military public relations guy to give the folks back home a sense of the glory and courage of their troops—which was no sham. So..."

"I think I understand," she said, "but when something

is that calculated, it seems to me it loses its value. I mean, I can't quite buy the end justifies the means—"

"*Okay*, Miss Pinscher, enough."

"Mr. Brazier, again, I tell you I'm not trying to stir up trouble, but I'm sure you can understand that—"

He lit a cigarette and wheeled himself into the kitchen, returning with a bottle of gin. "Drink?" he asked.

"No, thank you."

"We have wine," Sheryl called from the bedroom, where she'd gone to dress.

"You look like a wine drinker," Brazier said as he poured himself a tumbler full of gin.

"If that means what I think it means—"

"It means I'm tired of your judging me, or Childs, Miss Pinscher. All right, so you've discovered the deep dark secret of Korea and Morgan Childs. Where'd you get it, from that scum Sutherland?"

"Clarence, or his father?"

He cocked his head and closed one eye. "You're pretty good, lady."

"What do you mean?"

"You've got me talking too damn much." He shook his head and drank down more of the gin. "Where *did* you get the story about Childs and me?"

She was relieved *he'd* mentioned Sutherland and decided to go with it. "Clarence Sutherland found out about it from his father's files." She remembered having seen Sutherland's name in Brazier's old appointment book. "I take it you were a patient, and you told Dr. Sutherland about Childs and Korea. The son picked up the information somehow from his father's confidential files and used it to blackmail Childs . . ."

It was pretty much all supposition on her part, but Brazier's expression seemed to confirm it. He again filled his glass and looked toward the window. Sheryl came from the

226

bedroom, dressed in slacks and sweater. "You've done a job, Susanna Pinscher. I toast you." He raised his glass. "Here's to Sherlock Holmes, Philip Marlowe, Travis McGee and Susanna Pinscher, sleuths of a feather, and so forth . . . so you know a deep, dark secret . . . what are you going to do with it?"

"Nothing, unless, as I said, it bears on the Sutherland case—"

"And if it does?"

"It it does, I'll have to—"

"Look, what if Morgan Childs did kill the Sutherland kid, which of course I'm not saying he did . . . I mean, what did we lose except a cheap, venomous, blackmailing snake ready and willing to sell a national hero down the tubes for his own private gain? Think about it, lady, put them on a balancing scale. Sutherland was filth. Morgan Childs represents to millions of Americans the sort of man we hardly ever see anymore. Name someone these days who's worth being called a hero, someone to look up to, to *stand* for something good in America. Athletes? That's a laugh. The only thing they've left kids to look up to are the size of their contracts. Movie stars? Forget it. Politicians? Those that aren't under indictment, or taping illegally, are busy getting rich in payoffs from the folks that financed their election campaigns . . ." He leaned forward in his chair. "Morgan and I have our problems, but they're ours, not yours or anybody else's. He means something to you, to me, to every person in America. He sits on the highest court in the land and votes his convictions about whether something is or isn't constitutional. He hasn't mortgaged himself to anybody. He stands for decency and honor, things we don't have much of anymore. There's a network of boys' groups in America that goes by Morgan Childs's name and that exists because he raises millions every year for them—"

"I understand all this, Mr. Brazier, and I happen to agree

227

with much of what you say. My father often talks the same way. I have three children of my own, and I worry about who they'll be able to look up to. I've met Justice Childs, went flying with him, matter of fact. I liked him, he reminds me of my father... *but* if Clarence Sutherland threatened him enough to drive him to murder, that's obviously overriding—"

"Leave it alone," Brazier said.

"I can't—"

"*Drop* it," he said, not turning. "There's a bigger picture to be considered—"

"Mr. Brazier, a person has been killed, and—"

He spun the chair around so fast that his glass flew from his hands and landed at Sheryl's feet. She picked it up, scooping ice cubes into it with her hand. Brazier shouted, "Morgan Childs counts for something, damn it. He means something to America, and to me. He saved my life in Korea and—"

"I understand what you're saying and I sympathize with it, but I've got to ask... did your good friend Morgan Childs murder Clarence Sutherland?"

His words came slowly, measured by the anger he was suppressing. "Just...get...*out. Before I do something violent.*"

She backed into the hall, followed by Sheryl, who closed the door behind her.

"I'm sorry, Miss Pinscher. Dan is...well, he's very difficult at times, especially when it involves this country and Korea and Morgan Childs. He really cares so much, has such deep convictions that sometimes it gets the better of him."

"I understand," Susanna said. She touched her arm.

"I love him so much," she said. "He's been through a lot. He's a decent, fine man in pain. I've had pain in my life, but nothing like what he's suffered."

228

"I respect him," Susanna said. "Please believe that."

"I do." She wiped her eyes. "You know, he could have been an important man, Susanna."

"He was. His by-line was in every magazine in America."

"But he could have been even bigger."

"Why didn't it happen?"

"He became so bitter, so terribly negative. I tried to snap him out of it, tried to encourage him to write again but he refused."

"He hasn't written anything in how long?"

"Years. When we first met he was almost finished with a book, but he never finished it. It just sits under the bed collecting dust."

"What sort of book?"

"It's about how the CIA tested drugs on people years ago." She partially swallowed the final words.

"I'd read newspaper reports about it when the CIA was forced to release its files. How did Dan get interested in it?"

"Oh, it doesn't matter...he'll never finish it...He's so damned worried about protecting people and his country. Even the doctors that were involved in the experiments—"

"Doctors? Dr. Sutherland, for example?"

Sheryl quickly shook her head. "I don't know," she said. "Dan got involved in the project when he was at a clinic somewhere in Delaware, a place called Sunken Springs."

"Was Dr. Sutherland mentioned in Dan's manuscript, Sheryl? Is that why Dan had his name in his appointment book?"

"What book?"

"The one in your bedroom, the one he saw me looking at the last time I was at your apartment."

"He didn't tell me that."

"Oh. I thought—"

229

"He just said he didn't want anybody snooping around his life. He was so mad at me for letting you in..."

"I'm sorry I've caused you grief."

"You haven't. I accept what goes with being in love with someone like Dan. I know lots of men who wouldn't cause such problems, but they also wouldn't give me what Dan gives me."

"Yes...well, thanks again, Sheryl, for taking me into your confidence. It's been a real...experience meeting you, and Dan Brazier..."

CHAPTER
30

SUSANNA AND HER SON ARRIVED BACK HOME IN WASH-ington at eight in the evening. She delivered him to his father's house, drove to the Justice Department, went to her office and, by the light of a desk lamp, reviewed notes she'd made during the flight. She dialed Martin Teller's home number. No answer. She tried MPD headquarters. An officer at the desk said he thought Detective Teller was still in the building. After a few minutes Teller came on the line.

"Martin, I'm back. I need to see you. Are you free?"

"Come on over, I'll be in my office."

It was close to eleven when she arrived. Teller was in shirt sleeves, wearing a dark five-o'clock shadow. He closed the door, sat in his chair. She perched on the edge of the desk.

"Okay, let's have it."

She did, at first leaving out items that might link her two meetings with Brazier to the Sutherland murder.

"Brazier sounds a little *crazy*. How does it relate to the case?"

"Here's how. First, Morgan Childs isn't quite what he's cracked up to be, although I don't think any the less of him because of it, at least not from Brazier's version of the whys. What matters, though, is that Childs was vulnerable because of charming Clarence Sutherland's knowledge of his true Korean background. Dan Brazier laid it on a bit thick in his stories once they got back home and Childs went along. Was, I gather, persuaded to go along by Brazier, who felt the country deserved a hero out of that war and Childs was ideal material. He did apparently save Brazier's life, but I didn't get the details on that. Anyway, reluctant hero or not, Childs is open to a journalistic field day if what Brazier did and he went along with ever comes out. It could indeed be made to look like he's been a fraud, he might well face impeachment by the Congress . . . it's sure as hell a motive for murder and makes him a suspect. Even good guys panic when they see their life going up in smoke. Agreed?"

Teller nodded slowly. "How did Clarence get the information?"

"From his father's psychiatric files. Brazier had been his father's patient while he was in Washington."

"Go on."

"I found out from Brazier's girl friend, Sheryl Figgs, that he'd been working on a book exposing the CIA's mind-control experiments. Evidently he'd been institutionalized as Sutherland's patient in a place called Sunken Springs, in

232

Delaware. I can't prove this right now, Martin, but I know that—"

"That Dr. Sutherland was connected with the CIA experiments?"

"Yes...how did you know?"

"We've been working on Dr. Sutherland, some things broke while you were away."

"What? You've nailed down Sutherland's role with the CIA?"

"Yeah...I'll tell you something else. Chief Justice Poulson was probably in that same Sunken Springs funny farm. At first Sunken Springs meant nothing to me. We were supposed to believe that Poulson had spent some time there writing a book. We did a little checking. Besides a drugstore, meat market, shopping center and a movie theater open on the weekends, Sunken Springs has a very private and protected facility where the rich and famous can get their heads together when they start to come unglued. And rumor has it that the CIA uses the place as a halfway house, a retreat for spooks who've come in from the cold and need a rest, not to mention it's a research clinic for CIA experiments. I just got the report in late this afternoon. According to it there's a—"

"Are you *sure* Justice Poulson was there? Was he a patient?"

"It's a pretty reasonable assumption, wouldn't you say?"

"Then busy busy Clarence would have had *that* to hold over his head. If it had come out that Poulson had been institutionalized, he never would have been confirmed as Chief Justice. Or kept the job if it came out afterward. Did the White House know?"

Teller shrugged. "If I were writing this script, I'd have them knowing it...Clarence Sutherland was offered a job on President Jorgens's staff."

"He was? Wow..."

Teller got up and walked to the wall chart, untaped the brown paper and stepped back.

"What's that?" Susanna asked.

"My wall chart, obviously. Cost a hundred bucks. It's sort of comforting to me. Makes me feel less confused than I really am. Now...you may ask why would Clarence be offered a job in the White House..."

"Not to be a wise guy, Mr. Detective, but I think it's now fairly clear. Clarence used his knowledge of Poulson's institutionalization to pressure the President and his men to give him a job. Poulson was and is Jorgens's man."

"Right, but maybe there's more. If Clarence had the goods...you should forgive the expression...on Childs, he could have used that to swing weight inside the Court on the President's behalf. I mean with Childs."

She nodded.

"He was a nasty little bastard, wasn't he?" Teller said.

"Worse...what else have you learned since I was away?"

"That's about it."

"You're sure?"

"I'm sure. Now let's get organized."

She joined him in front of the chart. "There they are," he said, "the suspects all laid out. Time to refine it."

"Who are you ruling out?"

He folded his arms and squinted. "Let's see. Laurie Rawls. Aside from her anger at Clarence for his fooling around, is there any other reason to suspect her?"

"That might be good enough reason to keep her on the list."

"It might be, but I really think we should focus in. There's too many players with a maybe motive. I vote for taking her out of the game."

"All right."

234

He moved her magnetized nameplate from the board. "Who else?"

"Dr. Sutherland?"

"Why?"

"He was Clarence's father. Do fathers kill sons in cold blood? It happens in fits of anger or passion, but this killing was premeditated."

Teller nodded. "Except what if the son were blackmailing his own father over involvement in CIA drug experiments on people who didn't know how they were being used, some of whom died from the experiments? We went back through the files the CIA released, the MKULTRA files. The people in that business come up with some real screwy names for their little projects... *Artichoke, Bluebird*... grown men playing cloak-and-dagger games... Anyway, I don't figure papa shrink doing it, though with a son like Clarence he might have done himself in out of guilt for what he perpetrated on the world. I vote for taking him from the board."

"All right. It's your board."

"Don't be a wise guy." But he smiled when he said it, and removed Sutherland's name. "Next?"

"Justice Conover?"

"You heard?"

"About his stroke? Yes. How is he?"

"Last word he was still in a coma."

"Poor man."

"Yeah. I interviewed Cecily Conover again. 'Poor man' is right."

"If *Cecily* were the victim I'd have to vote him to the top of the list."

"Is he coming down from the board?"

"What do you think?"

"Yes..."

"Done." Conover's name joined Sutherland's and Laurie Rawls's on the desk.

"Cecily Conover?"

"As much as I'd like to see her *numero uno* I don't think so. That lady, and I use the term loosely in her case, really covers her tail. She'd get someone else to do it."

Susanna reached out and took Mrs. Sutherland's and Clarence's sister's names down. "Any argument?" she asked. "I'd say they're more to be pitied for having been related to Clarence. Especially Mrs. Sutherland."

"I agree."

"What about the 'friends' category?" Susanna said.

"Off with 'em."

Susanna started to remove Vera Jones's name from the board.

"Hold on."

"Why? From what we have on her she's not in the running." When he didn't respond she asked, "Are you holding out on me about her, Martin?"

"You know what I like about you, Susanna, along with a few other things?"

"What?"

"That you call me Martin. With most people it's plain Marty. Like the poor character in Paddy Chayefsky's play. You and my mother...Martin...except she did it when she was sore at me."

Susanna laughed and told him to stop being so adorable or she'd have to break off business and take him to her apartment.

"Sorry," he said. "And *adorable* nobody ever called me."

He told her about meeting up with Vera Jones at Club Julie, and about what the bartender said.

"But that would only put her in the same category as Laurie Rawls. Another woman spurned. Is that enough?"

He shook his head. "No, she has more going for her than that. She's been with Sutherland for years, must know all

236

about a lot, including his CIA games. I'd like to leave her on the list . . . and I think we have to add a few."

"I thought we were trying to make the list smaller."

"We are, but that doesn't mean ignoring live ones."

"Who do you want to add?"

He muttered something under his breath.

"What?"

"How would you categorize the White House and the CIA on the board?"

"The White House?"

"If Jorgens appointed Poulson Chief Justice knowing he'd been in a mental institution, well . . . that speaks for itself. And if Jorgens has been exerting improper influence on Supreme Court business through what is in effect blackmail, courtesy of Clarence's access to his old man's files, that makes the President of the United States an accomplice to blackmail, to say nothing of violating the concept of separation of powers—"

"I'm not sure I can deal with it—"

"We have to . . . and the same with the CIA. If Clarence knew about the drug experiment programs and was holding that kind of information out for grabs, the friendly folks at our Central Intelligence Agency wouldn't mind seeing him . . . removed. Maybe they call it neutralized, or terminated, but it all spells death." He sat behind his desk, took out two strips of paper, uncapped his marking pen. "Do we lump them together under *Government* or do we make separate plates for *CIA* and *WH*. White House. I wouldn't want to spell it out on the board. Might get people shook up if they looked under the brown paper."

"Make them separate, *CIA* and *WH*."

He did and put them on the board. "There, how's it look?"

They stood back and took another look at the revised chart before he covered it.

DECEASED

POULSON—*blackmail*

CHILDS—*blackmail*

VERA JONES—*personal, and access to same knowledge as deceased*

CIA—*secrets compromised*

WH—*blackmail*

Teller walked her to her car.

"Want to come back to the apartment?" she asked.

"I'd like to, but I'm not going to."

"Why?" She touched his cheek.

"Tired, stuff on my mind. My youngest kid is pregnant. She dropped out of school."

"Oh, I'm sorry, Martin."

"Yeah, well, like they say, life is what happens while you're making other plans. Give me a rain check, okay?"

"You got it. Good night." She kissed him lightly on the lips. He pulled her close and pressed his mouth hard against hers. When they came apart, and she was about to open the door to her car, he said, "How about going out to see Dr. Sutherland and Vera Jones tomorrow?"

"Good idea. Confront them. It worked pretty good for me with Dan Brazier. What time?"

"I'll call them in the morning." He shrugged. "It is morning."

"Just let me know when, Martin. And get some sleep."

238

CHAPTER
31

IT WAS TWO DAYS BEFORE TELLER AND SUSANNA WERE able to see Dr. Chester Sutherland and Vera Jones. If Teller hadn't pressed hard during his third call to Vera it probably would have taken even longer.

Vera escorted them now into Sutherland's inner office and turned to leave.

"I'd like to have both of you here," Teller said.

"I have work to do—"

"So do we, Miss Jones."

Vera looked at Sutherland, who nodded, then sat down in a straight-backed cane chair, hands folded on her knees, eyes straight ahead, her pale, cameo face empty of expression. She wore a brown tweed skirt that flared wide below the knees. A beige cashmere sweater with a large, thick collar seemed to prop her head up above her shoulders. Her hair was drawn back into a severe chignon. She wore no makeup.

"Well, Mr. Teller, how are you progressing in the investigation?" Sutherland asked. He sounded pretty damn detached, Teller thought, considering that the investigation happened to involve his murdered son.

"Pretty good, doctor. Matter of fact, the last few days have given us some important new information." He glanced at Vera, whose face grew even stonier.

Even Sutherland reacted. He sat forward on his couch and asked, "What sort of information, Detective Teller?"

"We'd like to ask you and Miss Jones some questions."

Sutherland smiled. "Go ahead and ask. I've tried to be completely candid with you, as I'm sure Miss Jones has."

When Teller didn't immediately follow up with a question, Susanna, remembering her experience with Dan Brazier, said flatly, "We know, Dr. Sutherland, about your involvement with the CIA's experimentation programs, and that Clarence also knew about it and let you know that he knew..."

Sutherland, who'd relaxed into the couch's cushions, uncrossed his legs and said without looking up, "That's nonsense, Miss Pinscher, and you know it."

"It's fact," Teller said. "But there's more than that, Dr. Sutherland. We know that Chief Justice Poulson was a patient of yours, and that you institutionalized him in Sunken Springs, Delaware—"

"Now, look here...I resent this intrusion into a confidential area." Sutherland stood up abruptly.

Susanna put in quickly, "Dan Brazier was also a patient, Dr. Sutherland, and Clarence learned the truth about Justice Childs's Korean War record through *those* files—"

"*Damn it*," Sutherland said, crossing the room.

"Take it easy," Teller told him. "How these things relate

240

to your son's murder is speculative, but it's our job to follow through on them, see where, if anywhere, they lead to."

"This is horrible," Vera Jones said.

"It sure is," Teller said. "Look, neither Miss Pinscher nor I have any personal interest in either of you. All we're interested in is who killed your son, Dr. Sutherland. Now, if your son was blackmailing people on the Court, if he had information to make that blackmail a genuine threat, well, that makes for a motive for murder."

Sutherland, who'd had his back to Teller, turned now and said, "You pry into people's private lives. I am a physician. My relationship with patients is privileged under time-honored ethics and, I might add, under law. My patients—"

Vera broke in now, obviously capable of staying cooler when the heat was on than the good doctor. "None of this matters," she said. "If you've come here to ask Dr. Sutherland or me direct questions, please do, then leave. Anything else, any*one* else is none of your concern."

"That's your opinion," Teller said. "Everything seems to link back to this office, to the files you keep, and as long as that link exists, I intend to pursue it. I think I speak for Miss Pinscher too."

Vera glared at Susanna. "Do you need someone to speak for you, Miss Pinscher?"

"No, Miss Jones, not usually, but in this case it happens to be true."

"Let's get back to it," Teller said.

"Please, leave this office," Sutherland said.

"Not just yet," Susanna said more calmly than she felt.

"Didn't you hear me?" Sutherland said. "You're trespassing on private property. Do I have to call—"

"The police?" Teller said.

"I'll report you," Sutherland said, his hand poised above the phone, then slowly lowered it to his side. "Detective

241

Teller, are you seriously suggesting that my own son was blackmailing me?"

"We're not suggesting anything," Susanna said, "but we are *saying* that Clarence's murder is connected, in some way we don't fully understand yet, back to you, his father, and to this office. Surely in light of what we've found out about Justices Poulson and Childs, and your involvement with the CIA, the logic in what we're saying is evident."

"If you'll excuse me," said Vera Jones, standing and going to the door.

"Not yet," Teller said. "What about the psychiatric files on Poulson and Dan Brazier?"

Sutherland was now markedly calmer, more self-assured. Presumably he'd administered some tranquilizing therapy to himself, Susanna thought with amusement. "Did your son take them?" she asked.

"Of course not."

"How secure are your files?" Teller asked.

"Very," said Vera, and she said it with genuine conviction.

Sutherland nodded vigorously. "You're making assumptions about Justice Poulson and Mr. Brazier. You're wrong. I can sympathize with your frustration. This, after all, was my son who was killed—"

"Sure . . . well, look, doctor, we *know* Poulson was your patient, ditto Brazier. What goes on between you and a patient is private. We respect that, don't want to know what problems Poulson had that made you put him into an institution for treatment. Same for Brazier's therapy. All we're saying is that your son got those people pretty damn mad at him, very possibly the Central Intelligence Agency too, which is not exactly an outfit to have mad at you. Whoever killed your son may well have done it because of something he learned and took with him from this office . . ."

Silence.

242

"Would you excuse us, Miss Jones," Sutherland finally said. Teller and Susanna looked at each other, then at Vera, who stood ramrod straight, hands at her sides, then slowly reached for the door, opened it and was gone.

"Miss Jones has been with me a very long time," Sutherland said when she had gone. "She's loyal, efficient and . . ."

"And? . . ." Susanna nudged. She was getting a bellyful of Dr. Sutherland. The man's son was a creep, but he seemed singularly unaffected by his murder.

"People like Miss Jones are wonderful, loyal, but sometimes just a little too set in their ways—too rigid—for, I hasten to add, all the right reasons. In any case, I've decided to do something she would hardly approve of and I'm not sure I do either. Still, sometimes we need to bend. You've found out that Jonathan Poulson, Chief Justice of the United States Supreme Court, was once a patient of mine. You've also learned that Dan Brazier was treated by me, and that his relationship with another justice of the Court was discussed. There are things that, no matter how hard we try, become known to others—"

"Dan Brazier isn't really important," Susanna broke in, "but what he had to say about Justice Childs is."

"Yes, Miss Pinscher, I understand that . . . By the way, while your information about certain people having been patients of mine is correct, you're wrong about Clarence. I mean to say, even if he wanted to do what you've suggested, he could not possibly have gotten into my files. My files are secure. There are two sets of keys to them, and two sets alone. I have one, Miss Jones the other."

"What about Miss Jones?" Teller asked.

"Please, don't be ridiculous. You've seen how she is, how even more rigid about confidentiality than I am—"

"Did Clarence and Miss Jones have an affair?" Susanna asked abruptly.

"From the ridiculous to the absurd. But even if that were

243

true, she would never compromise those files...not for anyone. I would entrust my very life to Miss Jones. And I say that as a psychiatrist whose job it is to know a little something about people. She is just too conditioned to loyalty and honor to deviate. Sometimes this may not always be to her advantage, but there it is, and it is certainly to my advantage and that of my patients. Past and present...But as I said, I am going to bend a little so as to convince you without question of this, which should allow you to then concentrate your efforts in more promising areas...I'm going to show you the files on Mr. Brazier and Justice Poulson..."

Teller and Susanna looked at each other, not quite believing what they were hearing.

"Surprised, I see. Don't be. I wish to cooperate and indeed *help* you in a meaningful way. So I will show you the files but *not* allow you to *read* them. You'll see they exist. You'll see they're intact and therefore played no part in the death of my son."

Sutherland buzzed Vera Jones, said into the phone, "Please bring me the files on Dan Brazier and Jonathan Poulson." She obviously balked because he said in a firmer voice, "Just do it, Miss Jones. Thank you."

She entered the office carrying two thick file folders, her face mirroring her displeasure, handed them to Sutherland, turned around and left the room. Without a word.

Sutherland first took up Brazier's file. "Here." He removed sheets of typewritten paper and spread them on the coffee table. "All here, all my notes and observations, my comments about treatment and how it was progressing, copies of letters between myself and other physicians. Mr. Brazier was not a seriously ill person. Losing one's legs is, of course, traumatic, and he needed psychological support. Which is what I tried to give him, the support to accept his

244

physical problems and to push ahead in spite of them, using, by the way, a quite intelligent and indeed creative mind."

"He isn't succeeding too well," Susanna said.

"I'm sorry to hear that. But of course that's only your opinion, Miss Pinscher. Well . . . so much for Dan Brazier's files. All here, intact, just as they were compiled. Nothing changed, nothing out of order. My son did not, on the evidence, ever remove them, nor did anyone else."

"Are his comments about Justice Childs in that file?" Susanna asked.

"Good question, that, after all, is at the core of your interest. Here, see for yourself." He took three sheets from the pile and turned them on the table so that they faced Teller and Susanna. On top of each was typed in capital letters: KOREA-CHILDS RELATIONSHIP. Just as Teller and Susanna leaned forward to get a better look, Sutherland shuffled the pages together and returned them to the folder. "Sorry," he said, "but I told you I would not go along with actually having these files read by you . . . All right, now for Justice Poulson." He opened the Chief Justice's file and almost casually spread its pages on the table. Teller and Susanna again came forward in their seats. Teller started to ask a question, when Sutherland's face suddenly tightened. He forced a smile, collected the pages from the table and put them back into the folder. "Satisfied?"

"I suppose we have to be," Teller said.

"I think I've demonstrated beyond any question not only my willingness but my desire to cooperate." He stood, the folders under his arm. "Now, I'm afraid I really must ask you to leave. The files you place such importance on are here, as you've seen. I must trust that even my showing them to you in the limited fashion I have will remain between us, and that you will appreciate the confidentiality of *our* relationship."

Teller and Susanna stood, shook hands with him and left

245

through Vera Jones's office. She did not acknowledge their good-byes, just sat at her desk, hands folded on it, eyes straight ahead. . . .

They'd driven to Chevy Chase in Teller's car. When they were on their way back to Washington he asked, "Did you notice what I noticed?"

"I did, or at least I think I did. When he started looking at the sheets in Poulson's file he seemed at least for a minute there upset. He recovered quickly, but it seemed he was surprised. I think it was because the sheets in Poulson's file didn't look like the ones in Brazier's. Right? . . ."

"Go ahead. I may make you a member of the force."

"The sheets in Poulson's file all looked the same, like they'd been typed in one sitting. Brazier's were different. Obviously, Sutherland's notes on Brazier were taken and typed over a long period of time. Not so Poulson's. Maybe Clarence cleaned out the file and the loyal, honorable Miss Jones made up a new one."

"I think you're right," Teller said. "And if you are, it was the first time the shrink knew about it. He was clearly surprised, even though, like you said, he put back the old professional suave double time. . . ."

Teller pulled up in front of the Department of Justice. Susanna started to open the door, paused. "And now?"

"Good question. I'll consult my magic wall chart and see if it yields the answer. Also, I'll call you later. Okay?"

"You'd better."

MEANWHILE, IN Chevy Chase, Dr. Chester Sutherland slowly got up from his couch and approached the door leading to his outer office. He'd been sitting there for ten minutes reading through Jonathan Poulson's file. Vera had come into his office the moment Teller and Susanna were gone, but Sutherland had waved her away. "Let me explain," she'd said. "Get out, Vera."

Vera now straightened at her desk as the door opened. She looked up at him. "I did what I had to do."

"Damn it," he said, flinging the files across the room in a highly unpsychiatric fashion. "Where is Poulson's original?"

"I don't know."

"You told me he gave it back to you."

"I lied . . ."

"Do you realize the position this puts us in?"

"Did they notice?"

"I don't think so, but I'm not sure."

"Why did you ever show the files to them? It was stupid."

"I wanted them off my back. Besides, I only *showed* the files to them. I didn't allow them to see anything specific—"

"Then there's really nothing to worry about."

Sutherland gathered up the papers from the floor and put them on her desk. "I hope you're right," he said. "I just wish—"

"Just wish it hadn't happened, doctor. Yes, how much we both wish that."

CHAPTER
32

LAURIE RAWLS SAT AT HER DESK IN JUSTICE CONOVER'S chambers, the phone wedged between her shoulder and ear. "Yes, I understand," she said to the caller. "Yes, that's wonderful news. I'll let everyone know immediately. Thanks."

She hung up and doodled the outline of a frame house on a yellow legal pad. When she'd added a chimney from which a thin curl of smoke twisted up to the top of the page, she picked up the phone and dialed Chief Justice Poulson's extension. His secretary Carla answered.

"Laurie Rawls, Carla. I'd like to see the Chief right away."

"He's busy, Laurie. He left word not to be disturbed."

"I think he'll want to see me, Carla. I have something

very important to discuss with him concerning Justice Con-over and the abortion vote."

"How is Justice Conover?" Carla asked. "Any news?"

"No change. Please, tell Justice Poulson that I need ten minutes with him, no more."

Moments later Carla came back on the line. "Come on over now, Laurie, but make it fast, for my sake."

POULSON SAT behind a desk piled high with legal briefs. The remains of an egg salad sandwich he had brought in for lunch topped one pile of folders, two stained paper coffee cups another. He was in shirt sleeves, his face was drawn. He did not get up when she entered, simply waved to an empty chair.

"I know you're busy, Mr. Chief Justice, but I was certain you'd want to hear what I have to say."

"Carla said it was about Justice Conover?"

"Yes. Marisa called from the hospital. He briefly came out of his coma. She said he slipped back into it, but the doctors are now optimistic that he will at least partially recover."

"That's good news. Have you told the others?"

"No, only you."

His smile was fatherly, concerned. He sat up, gestured at the materials on his desk. "I feel as though I'm drowning in paper . . ."

Laurie smiled. "We all feel that way at times, sir. Justice Poulson, there's something else I'd like to discuss with you."

"Oh? Well . . . how about another time, Miss Rawls? As you can see, I'm—"

"This is the time, I think," she said, her voice deter-minedly firm. "Justice Poulson, I know what Clarence knew . . ."

"I beg your pardon . . ."

249

"I have the files, sir."

"What *files*?"

"About you... and your stay in the place in Delaware... about how the White House has known this and used it ever since you became Chief Justice..."

Face flushed, he came half out of his chair. The half-eaten sandwich slid to the floor. "How *dare* you?"

"Please, Mr. Chief Justice, try to understand. There's no need for upset over this, provided we can talk about it. Sort of man to man, sir?..."

He slumped back in his chair. Blood seemed to drain from his face, leaving it with the appearance of having been dusted with gray powder. He looked toward the door leading to the outer offices.

"Don't worry, sir," said Laurie, "no one else knows about this. It can stay that way."

He looked at her, face expressionless. Eerie, she thought to herself. Well, press on... She stood up, picked up a pitcher and poured ice water into a glass. "Here you are, sir," she said, placing the glass on the desk. "Go ahead. Drink it."

Poulson did.

Laurie sat down again. "As I said, Mr. Chief Justice, there's really no need for any of this to leave this room. I admire you very much, I always have. I think people become, well, sort of victims of circumstance and just do their best under the circumstances... sir, you've done that, I respect people who can do that..."

"Do you?" Strength had returned to his voice, along with color to his cheeks.

"Yes, I do. So did Clarence, only he went too far, didn't he?"

"Did he, Miss Rawls?"

His new-found calm bothered her. Before, when it appeared that he might fall apart, she felt in control. Now her heart tripped as she said, "I have great compassion for your...dilemma, Justice Poulson. You must be under tremendous pressure from many quarters, especially with the abortion vote so imminent—"

"That too?"

"Well...yes, it's all there in the file Clarence took from his father's office, sir. How difficult it must be to be forced to make a decision on something as sensitive as abortion...when your own daughter has had one..."

He squinted at her as though she'd gone out of focus.

"I'm sure whatever decision she made was the right one, Mr. Chief Justice."

His silence was damned unnerving.

"I understand, sir, I really do..."

"Do you, Miss Rawls?"

"Yes, sir, I do. An entire life ruined over one indiscretion, one mistake. It just isn't fair."

"Since you've been so busy reading, I assume you know I encouraged it."

"Yes, sir...the guilt, I read about it in the files."

His mood changed. He was no longer the angry, grieving, guilty father. Now he sounded like a public person... "Miss Rawls, I know many people don't agree with my position, but I feel my daughter is also a symbol of what must not be allowed to go on in this nation. It's not just a matter of morals, of self-determination. The same *attitude* that got my daughter into such trouble—(and you too? Laurie thought)—has gotten this nation into trouble...live for the moment, forget the consequences, the future...it's *not* just a legal matter, this case, though it comes up in a legal forum. It is a question that transcends legalisms. Because of its implications it goes to the heart of the question of our own national survival. I *believe* that, Miss Rawls, we have a President who believes it, for which I'm grateful—(not to mention that he appointed you, she thought)—I am proud

251

of where I stand, Miss Rawls, and intend to use every power at my disposal to make that stand prevail."

She assured him she was touched by what he'd said. It surely was quite a speech. "That's why we can help each other, Justice Poulson," she said. "I too want to make a contribution. As you know, sir, Clarence was offered a job on President Jorgens's staff."

"Yes, matter of fact I tried to stop it."

"You did?"

"Of course. The notion of someone like Clarence Sutherland serving the President was anathema to me—"

"Why didn't you succeed?"

"Circumstances. I don't want to talk about it, Miss Rawls."

"I've been offered the same job."

His face showed authentic surprise.

"I'm not Clarence Sutherland, Mr. Chief Justice. I'm no saint, but I want to advance *and* contribute at the same time. I believe in the late Ayn Rand's theory of selfishness. It's *not* a negative word. By being selfish, self-interested, I can achieve the sort of personal freedom and power that will enable me to help others."

"Rather oversimplified, Miss Rawls, but I suppose there's a point there . . . Well, so the job is yours, with, I take it, the same conditions as applied to Sutherland."

"Yes . . . that the abortion vote goes the way the White House wants it to."

"As I said, I believe in the President's position in this matter. Do you?"

"My personal feelings are beside the point, sir."

He grunted, leaned on the desk. "What do you want, Miss Rawls?" (Of course knowing full well the answer.)

"Support for me in getting the job I want. And support inside the Court on the abortion vote."

"My position is well known, I've never wavered. I'm for Illinois in *Nidel v. Illinois*—"

252

"But what about Justice Childs? They say his commitment isn't so strong . . . that his vote was supposed to be for the state's position against abortion but now he's leaning the other way on strict constitutional grounds . . . I'm a law clerk here, sir, all us clerks know from the research we do for you justices how you're leaning on a particular case . . . or at least we have a good clue or two. I'm familiar with Justice Childs's research lately . . ."

"Yes, well, an effort is being made to convince him to hold to his original position in favor of Illinois."

"Yes, sir, and if he does that the vote will stay at four to four. If Justice Conover recovers he would vote for the plaintiff, which I gather is your reason for pushing for an early vote, but if Justice Childs shifts there's no question your position will lose."

And, Poulson thought, if Childs holds firm and Justice Smith changes to our side, we're home free . . . Damn Childs . . . can't he see this isn't just a matter of the state intervening in a private citizen's choice. It goes way *beyond* that . . . If Childs had a daughter like mine—

"Sir, with all due respect, isn't the one essential, the most immediate concern Justice Childs? His position has to be solidified . . . I do believe I—"

"You can do that, Miss Rawls?"

"With your help, sir . . ."

Poulson shook his head. This woman was a little terrifying . . . "My help? Such as, Miss Rawls?"

"Make a phone call and arrange a meeting."

"With whom?"

"Miss Jones . . . Dr. Sutherland's secretary."

He turned in his chair so that he faced the window. "I don't wish to have any contact with that office—"

"Just a phone call, Mr. Chief Justice. You certainly needn't meet with anyone, but the weight of a call from you will accomplish far more than one from me. All I need, sir, is a chance to talk to Miss Jones. Here, in these chambers."

"I'm not sure I understand, but in any case, why not go to her office?"

"Because here, in this building, in these chambers, matters take on a different, an added dimension, sir. Mr. Chief Justice, if you would call and ask her to meet you here in your chambers tonight, at seven, she will certainly not question you about reasons . . . You can be gone when she arrives, but I'll be here. I have a . . . a proposition for her, an exchange that I believe will benefit everyone . . . you, her, me, the White House, this Court, indeed, the nation . . ."

"And if I refuse?"

"Well, sir, then I suspect you jeopardize a great deal . . . personally and professionally, including the outcome of *Nidel v. Illinois*."

He wanted to strangle her. What he did was to nod and turn away.

"Good. I'll be going back to Justice Conover's office. Will you call and let me know about tonight? Sir?"

"Thank you for stopping in, Miss Rawls."

Twenty minutes later she received a call in Justice Conover's chambers.

"It is arranged for seven." And then the phone was hung up.

"Thank you, *sir*," she said to the dial tone.

CHAPTER
33

MARTIN TELLER LOOKED AT HIS WATCH. HE HAD BEEN parked near the Sutherland house in Chevy Chase for nearly three hours. He had decided to renew the tail on Dr. Sutherland and Vera Jones that afternoon, and elected to take one of the shifts himself. Sutherland had left the house an hour ago and had been picked up further down the road by one of Teller's men. He would wait for Vera.

His stomach growled with hunger. He was out of cigarettes. It had turned bitterly cold, and he started the engine from time to time to keep warm. He had just turned it off again and was watching a mongrel dog cross the road when Vera Jones came out of the Sutherland driveway and turned left, in the opposite direction from which he faced. He started the car, turned and drew close enough to keep her in view. It was quite dark.

She found a parking spot near Union Station, got out and walked down First Street in the direction of the Supreme Court. Teller parked illegally and walked behind her, always ready to turn away should she decide to look back. She did not.

He stood at the foot of the steps leading up to the Supreme Court's massive front doors and watched her go up to terrace level, then veer left to a visitor-and-staff entrance at the side of the building. He looked at his watch—6:50.

LAURIE RAWLS left Justice Conover's area and walked down the long, wide corridor toward Justice Poulson's chambers. As she came abreast of Justice Childs's chambers he came through the door. "Hello, Miss Rawls," Childs said. "Working late?"

"Yes," she replied pleasantly. "You too?"

"Afraid so. I've got some time to put in before the conference in the morning on *Bain v. Paley*."

"Well, not too late, Mr. Justice."

"I'll try not to. Have a nice night."

She headed toward Chief Justice Poulson's chambers.

MOMENTS EARLIER the Chief had left his chambers, carrying with him a set of legal briefs and a law book. A guard at the end of the hall greeted him.

"Hello, John," he said.

"Be here late, Mr. Chief Justice?"

"Not too late, I hope."

He continued walking until he reached the doors that led to the main courtroom. They were open; a guard who usually stood in front of them was at the far end of the corridor drinking from a public fountain. Poulson stepped into the courtroom. It was dark except for lights playing off the

256

fountains in the courtyard that cast flickering, erratic flashes of white across the huge chamber.

LAURIE RAWLS saw Vera Jones standing outside the entrance to Poulson's office suite. She had never actually met her before but recognized her from descriptions Clarence had given her... "looks like a bird... Miss Prim... a hatchet face... not bad in the sack, though... Laurie's face, and stomach, tightened at the memory of these last words.

Vera turned at the sound of Laurie's shoes on the marble floor.

"Miss Jones?" Laurie asked.

"Yes... I have an appointment, with Chief Justice Poulson..."

"Yes, I know. I'm Laurie Rawls, a law clerk here."

Vera gave no sign that she knew about Laurie through Clarence. She stood stiffly, without expression, as Laurie offered her hand and said, "Actually, I'm afraid Justice Poulson won't be able to be here for your meeting. He was called away, but I can fill in, with his approval."

"I don't understand..."

"Please, come in." Laurie entered the outer office and flipped on the overhead lights.

Vera remained in the hallway. Laurie turned. "Come on in, Miss Jones, it's just like any other office. No dragons."

Vera still did not move.

"Miss Jones," Laurie said, hands on hips, "I really don't have all night. If you'll just come in I'll get to the point right away."

Vera looked to her left and right before moving across the threshold.

"Have a seat," Laurie said, pointing to a leather chair against the wall.

"I'll stand. I'm not sure I approve of this. Justice Poulson said nothing about you—"

"It's *okay*, Miss Jones, I assure you. Justice Poulson and I discussed it at length this afternoon. What I'm about to suggest, as I said, has his approval."

When Vera still didn't take the chair Laurie shrugged, leaned back against a desk and said, "I have something you need, and you have something we need."

"We?"

"Here, at the Court."

"What could I possibly have that—"

"The file on Dan Brazier."

"I don't know what you're talking about—"

"Oh, of course you do. Dan Brazier was a patient of your boss, Dr. Sutherland, just as Chief Justice Poulson was. I don't intend to beat about the bush, Miss Jones. The fact that you and Clarence had an affair . . . an amusing word for something between people of such different ages . . . is not my concern now, nor is your reason for allowing Clarence to take certain files from his father's office. What *is* important is that I've come into possession of Justice Poulson's file. I assume you'd like to have it back. At the same time, there are things in Mr. Brazier's file that are of interest to—"

"You are sick, Miss Rawls."

"Only of you and your posturing, Miss Jones. Let's get down to it . . . I'm offering you an even swap that will benefit everyone—"

"Everyone? You mean you."

"I mean everyone. I'm not at liberty to discuss Court business, but the importance to this Court of having Mr. Brazier's file, the importance to the administration itself and to the nation is substantial, I assure you. It is not just a matter of individuals. There's a greater good—"

"Greater good?" Vera said, shaking her head and now sitting on the edge of the chair. "My God, what would you

or Clarence know about a greater good, or any good? Those files represent a sacred trust—"

"You should have thought of that when you gave them to him."

"I didn't *give* Clarence anything. He *took* advantage of a situation—"

"Yes," —Laurie smiled— "he was very good at that, wasn't he? What did he do, Miss Jones, steal the keys while you lay next to him on the office couch—?"

"You're disgusting."

"Please, let us be ladies . . . now, back to business. You give me Brazier's files, or a true copy of them, and I'll return Justice Poulson's files."

"After you've copied them?"

"Trust me."

The laugh burst from her.

"What choice do you have, Miss Jones?"

". . . I'll have to think about it—"

"After consulting with your employer?"

"Leave Dr. Sutherland out of this. He was as much a victim of his son as I was."

"A convenient way to get off the hook."

"Think what you will—" Suddenly Vera felt an intense, enveloping heat. She took off her cap and unbuttoned the top of her coat.

"Are you all right?" Laurie said. "Would you like some water?"

"No, I feel fine . . . Is that all you have to say to me?"

"That's all. Brazier for Poulson. I need to know first thing tomorrow morning."

"Why?"

"Not your concern, Miss Jones."

Vera stood, touched the back of the chair for support. She felt light-headed, her legs were weak. She clenched her

259

cap at her side, squeezed it as hard as she could, her long, sinewy fingers pushing through the loosely knitted fabric.

"I'll walk you out," Laurie said.

Vera's body seemed to go rigid, as though the words had physically touched her. "No, stay away from me. You're no different than he was—"

"Oh, we're very different, Miss Jones. We're in the same business, of course, but Clarence is dead and I'm alive. Quite a difference, I'd say. I intend to carry on in Clarence's memory at the White House...I've been offered the position Clarence would have had...if he'd lived. Isn't that good news?"

"God, you are so vile—"

"Miss Jones, I'll be at my desk in Justice Conover's chambers by eight in the morning. Here's my extension." She scribbled a number on a slip of paper.

"Go to hell."

"Whatever you say, Miss Jones. Good night...."

Laurie waited a few moments, then turned off the lights and stepped into the hall. Vera was gone. She returned to Conover's chambers, where a shaft of light came from beneath the door to the justice's private chambers. Laurie was sure she had turned off all the lights before meeting with Vera Jones. She thought of calling the security office, then decided to investigate for herself. She went to the door, listened, heard something slam shut. She opened the door.

Cecily Conover was hunched over her husband's desk. She jumped to attention, lost her balance and fell into her husband's large leather chair.

"What are you doing here?" Laurie demanded.

"I was...God, you scared me. I was looking for that file—"

"How dare you search through his desk."

Cecily got to her feet. "I called and asked you to help me find that file. It has nothing to do with the Court, with government, with anything except my life...can't you understand that? I'm trying to survive, just like he is."

"And it looks like he will?"

"Yes, it does, enough to make sure of a divorce that will strip from me everything that's rightfully mine—"

"Since when does a wife who sleeps around deserve anything in a divorce?"

"Coming from *you*—"

"Get *out*."

"Please, Miss Rawls...I'll pay you. If I have that file at least the settlement will be decent for me. I'll share it with you, I promise...I'll do anything you want, only get it for me—"

Laurie snapped off the lights and went to the outer office, leaving Cecily standing in the dark next to the desk. Slowly Cecily crossed the carpeted room and joined Laurie. "Won't you listen to reason, Miss Rawls? Clarence told me you were the brightest female he'd ever met—"

Laurie, whose back had been to Cecily, quickly turned. "Clarence told you that?"

"Yes. I suppose it was his way of making me feel stupid. He used to tell me I was dumb—"

"I know," Laurie said, taking satisfaction in the look on Cecily's face. "Mrs. Conover...I suppose I can call you that a little while longer...the record your husband collected about you is very safe—"

"It is? Where is it?"

"I have it. Clarence gave it to me."

"Then for God's sake give it to me. What good is it to you?"

"Maybe we can work something out. Meanwhile, be assured that we share what's in it, just you and me and, of course, your husband. But it really isn't of much value to him unless he has it, now is it?"

"You're blackmailing me."

261

"It was your suggestion. Look, all you have to do is make sense with me from time to time...We could have lunch, perhaps even dinner. Relax, Mrs. Conover, we can be good friends. We have quite a lot in common."

Yes...we have Clarence—"

"*No*, we don't have him in common, Mrs. Conover. Clarence loved me. For him, you were just a temporary diversion. Good night, Mrs. Conover, you know the way out."

HE ENTERED the darkened courtroom and stood next to the bench, his fingertips resting lightly on it. Here was America's highest *concilium*, where in daylight eight men and one woman decided the various fates of millions of people. Their power was as great as the tons of lactescent marble used to create the arena. Greater.

Words. Millions of words spoken here on behalf of men condemned to die, the disenfranchised seeking justice, corporations in conflict with individuals, the issues always more important than the individuals bringing them for adjudication. For here, truly, was the court of last resort.

It was operatic, he thought, the room a slumbering giant, sated with that day's offerings and waiting for another sun to rise, for another case to be debated and decided in favor of plaintiff or defendant, hero or villain, Christian or lion.

Above him the justices' nine chairs, each a different height and shape, stood empty and facing in different directions. He smiled. The Court ran with precision, yet the chairs were never lined up. Appropriate. There were few unanimous, orderly decisions either.

He climbed the few steps leading to the bench and slowly walked behind the chairs until he reached the middle one. It faced to its left. He sat in it, not turning, simply accepting the direction in which it pointed him, toward the windows and fountains. The chair did not feel comfortable to him....

She entered the courtroom and stood just inside the door. Light from the fountains played across pews and benches, off the long brass rail and silent microphones, occasionally reaching the ceiling.

There was one nearly constant pool of light that splashed across the lectern, causing its burnished finish to glisten. She felt calmer than she had minutes ago, although she knew it was misleading. Until her collapse, which thank God had occurred in private, she'd felt very much in control of herself. But then it had happened, as though plugs had been pulled from her body, allowing every drop of control and resolve to pour from her, leaving her drained and shaking, feeling as though she would break into a thousand pieces. Laurie Rawls . . . that horrible woman had been the catalyst to her coming undone . . . God, she was Clarence reincarnate—worse, if that was possible . . .

She fixed her attention on the lectern, something to lean on. She walked to it, touched its illuminated surface, then its dark part, as though there might be a tactile difference.

She heard something, looked up at the nine black leather chairs. Had the middle one moved? Darkness played tricks . . . sound was exaggerated, light created bizarre shapes.

Another sound, this time from behind. She turned slowly and peered into the section of the courtroom reserved for the press. Nothing. She started to tremble again and gripped the lectern, head lowered, legs threatening to collapse under her. This was where it had happened . . .

Another sound from the bench, metal against metal. "Is someone there?"

No response.

Her purse dropped to the floor. She did not pick it up. . . .

Teller, who sat in the shadows of the press section, wasn't sure for a moment whether to stand up and let her see him. He had followed her to the building, used his earlier security clearance, as detective in charge of the investigation of

263

Sutherland's murder, to gain access and note her being met by Laurie Rawls; noted too Chief Justice Poulson leave his chambers and walk to the courtroom. Teller had decided the best he could do was to trail the Chief Justice, which he had done, followed him to the courtroom, watched him take his accustomed seat at the bench. Did he expect to see the woman who now was behaving so erratically? No, actually he had intended to wait a few minutes, see what, if anything, Poulson was up to, and then go outside the courtroom to wait for the woman who had disappeared into Poulson's chambers with Laurie Rawls. Yet here they both were, and it was clear that the end of this bizarre, in so many ways unsavory, case was about to take place where it had begun —with the discovery of the chief clerk, dead from a gunshot wound in the chair of the highest judicial personage of the land.

Now Teller watched, with sadness and a shivery feeling that he was somehow invading the sanctity of a very troubled human being's innermost feelings. She struck the lectern's side with clenched fists, muttered, barely audibly, "And what was it for? Was it all for nothing? . . ."

As if in eerie answer, the leather chair at the center of the bench turned slowly to face the front. She could not make out the figure in the chair clearly, little more than a hand on the chair's arm was clear. But Teller knew who it was . . . the same man who regularly occupied that chair during the proceedings of the Court . . . the Chief Justice of the Supreme Court of the United States. Both he and the woman, for reasons that obviously compelled them, had returned to the scene of the crime, and in their separate but related fashions were principal players in the final act of this crime's resolution . . . Teller shook his head, reflected with some frustration but also with a sense of the appropriateness of it all, that when this murder, like so many others, was solved, it would be the principals rather than the police—whatever their contribution—that brought it to its finale. Well, at least he was here on the scene, which was more than he was able to be in most cases he'd worked on. At least he had, thanks in large part to Susanna's digging and smart evaluations, pretty much figured out who the guilty party was, and it was what he knew and suspected that had brought him here for the denouement...

"It was not for nothing." The voice came from the Chief Justice's chair. And now Chief Justice Jonathan Poulson leaned forward so that his face was illuminated by the light that came in through the windows. "But let me tell you, young lady, you have no obligation to say anything more—"

"I want to, though. I need to...It wasn't just that he was so cruel to me, and he was...but he was cruel to other people too, I know that. He was so damn clever, and more than that, unscrupulous. That was really what made it all possible, his willingness to do anything, say anything to get what he wanted—"

"I repeat," Poulson interrupted, "you really should not say anything more. You have your rights, and you will be well defended—"

Teller decided it was time to show himself. Leaving the shadows of the press section, he crossed halfway to the lectern, looked up at the bench. "Good evening, Mr. Chief Justice." Poulson did not reply, only nodded to him, clearly annoyed that there was a witness to this scene, one that he felt was uniquely private, one that he and the troubled woman at the lectern had a right to share alone, at least for now.

Teller turned to her. "Miss Jones, I'm sorry to break in on you like this. Believe that. But I'm also afraid that I have to tell you that you're under arrest." Feeling almost ridiculous, he proceeded to read her her rights, as he was obliged to do—after all, some judges in this very Court had prescribed them, or at least sanctioned them.

"Listen to him," Poulson said. "It's in your interest—"

But she was not yet through. Speaking slowly, as though not quite hearing either Teller or Poulson, she said, "I thought it was the right thing to do, he had hurt so many, and was threatening so many more. My God, he had things to hurt the Chief Justice of the Supreme Court, to ruin the reputation of another justice, a national hero even, to get to the President . . . he was going to use his rotten influence, influence based on filth, poking into other people's lives . . . to make laws about having babies . . . abortion . . . *he* was an abortion . . . even his father, his own father, a doctor, said so . . ."

Poulson came down from the bench, asked Teller to leave, that he would see that Vera Jones came to headquarters later, but Teller, much as he would have liked to go along with that, knew he could not properly do it. Sometimes Supreme Court judges, especially the Chief Justice, tended to forget the nitty-gritty of lowly police procedure. They could afford it. He couldn't.

As he began to lead Vera out of the courtroom, he asked her what she meant by saying, "Was it all for nothing?"

She shook her head. "I mean that terrible Laurie Rawls . . . I know people will say I hate her because we both had affairs with Clarence, but it's not just that." She looked at Teller now, seemed to come back from the remote state she'd been in. "Detective Teller . . . yes, you and Miss Pinscher were right to come to the office, to wonder about the Poulson file. God knows, I only wish I had it when you came, that I hadn't been such a damned miserable fool as to believe him about what he said he felt for me. Did I really believe him? I'm afraid I did . . . because I so much *wanted* to. You never knew him, but he could be the most charming, loving, even . . . yes, loving . . . At first it was the looks, some people said a Robert Redford look-alike. He could convince you that you were the only woman alive . . . yes, he convinced me of that, and of course I badly wanted to believe it, like I said. I'm not the most desirable woman to most

266

men, I was flattered, excited, felt like a real woman for the first time since I could remember...Oh, there are no excuses, not really..."

"Well, that's right, Vera, but there are explanations, and you've got them, if anybody in a case like this ever did. I don't know what will happen, but I'm damned if I'm not going to do what I can to see that those explanations aren't forgotten when it counts..." He was about to say "when you come to trial," but maybe that wouldn't happen, maybe they'd get her off on grounds of temporary insanity, which would be okay by him in one sense, but in another, damned unfair. What the lady had done was murder and nobody could say that was okay...but if ever there was a justification...and not saying there was...Vera Jones sure had it...

"Thank you," and she almost smiled, "but there's still Laurie Rawls. Now she has the file on the Chief Justice, just like Clarence did. She just now tried to get Justice Childs's file too, threatening me. Well, at least she won't get that. But Justice Poulson's file..."

"I wouldn't worry too much about that now," Teller said, although he was plenty worried. Whatever Vera Jones said would be discounted by Laurie. That tough little lady would deny everything, say Vera was cracked, had gone around the bend because Clarence gave her a tumble and then dumped her, and so forth. And some might be inclined to believe her. Well, by God, Clarence hadn't given him a tumble, and he hadn't gone round the bend...well, not yet anyway, but if he hung around this city much longer who could predict? Sooner or later it seemed to get to everybody, even to a wonderful opera-loving gourmet cop like Martin Teller...

"But I am worried," Vera was saying. "I know people won't believe me. I know what they'll say about me. And if that woman ever gets a job close to the President, like Clarence was going to do and like she says she's after—"

267

"We'll work on that, Vera . . . Tell me, what happened that night . . . I mean, if you can talk about it now, maybe it will help me to help you . . ."

She nodded, shrugged. "I'd called Clarence and pleaded with him to return the files on Justice Poulson that he'd gotten from me. My God, along with everything else, I'd betrayed his father, a man I've worked for and respected for years. Clarence told me to come to his office, we'd talk about it. When I got there he laughed at me, called me names . . . some of which I deserved . . . especially about being dumb. Anyway, after a while we came into this court-room—"

"Why?"

"He liked it here, said he'd be sitting in one of the chairs up there one day, maybe even the chair in the Oval Office. God, isn't that scary?"

Teller nodded. "It surely is, Miss Jones . . . Well, what happened then?"

"I knew that there was more than idle threat in what he said. He had so much on so many people . . . I asked him for the file, for *my* sake . . . that will show you how dumb I was, all right . . ."

"Go back a moment, Miss Jones. That night with Clarence before you came to the courtroom. Did anything else happen there?" He was wondering about the gun.

"Yes, he had a file of material that Justice Conover had collected about his wife. Clarence had found it in Justice Conover's chambers and took it, along with a gun. He laughed about how he had found out about the file, that Mrs. Conover had told him about it, that she was sure her husband was keeping tabs on her . . . she and Clarence had been . . . intimate . . . too. And so Clarence went to the judge's office and found it, got into his locked files . . . and we know how he got the key, don't we? From Laurie Rawls. Clarence brought the gun with him into the courtroom. He told me

268

not to worry, that he'd take good care of me, just as his father had done for years. Imagine, trying to compare himself with his father . . . He also laughed at Justice Conover, said how hypocritical it was for a great liberal and anti-guncontrol man to keep a gun in his office. I didn't think much about it at the time, but now I wish I had said something, that maybe a man like Justice Conover had made enemies in his career by his courageous stands, maybe he had good reason to keep a gun. Clarence, though, said it was to scare away all the men sniffing around the old boy's . . . those were his words . . . wife. And I knew then what I'd known but never admitted to myself . . . that Clarence had been one of those men, that he'd had an affair with Mrs. Conover too. And then he started in about all the other stuff he had to keep other people in line . . . justices of this Court, his own father, even the President . . . Oh yes, he said, he'd be in the White House sooner than anybody thought . . ."

Teller stopped her just as they came to the courtroom door. He led her back, gently holding her arm, and up to the raised area of the bench. Poulson, as he expected, had gone. He followed now just behind her, letting go of her arm. He removed his .38 from its holster beneath his armpit, emptied the bullets into his pocket. He offered her the gun when she reached the middle chair, the Chief Justice's chair. "Vera, show me what happened. Was Clarence sitting here?"

She nodded.

Leave it to paranoid Clarence to pick the Chief Justice's chair. Crazy, but crazy like a fox . . . Teller sat in the chair. "Go ahead, Vera."

She resisted taking the gun at first, then did and quickly placed it on the bench in front of Teller. "He began one of his speeches about how grateful he was for all the stupid, corrupt people who made themselves so conveniently vulnerable to him. How in a way they were all working for him, and maybe someday he'd have a reunion, when he

269

made it to where he was going . . . He went on like that, until I just couldn't stand it. Oh yes, he included me in his group, but it was more than the awfulness of what he said, it was the way he said it so calmly, like it was already done, like nothing could stop him . . . it took hold of me then, my own part in what he had done and even worse what he would do . . . all because of my own stupidity and weakness . . . And then, you won't believe this, but then he actually tried to make love to me, grabbed hold of me and I picked up that gun"—she picked up the gun now—"and . . . I did it . . ." And as she said those last words she squeezed the trigger, and the only sound in that august courtroom was the sound of metal striking metal, a sound that the late Clarence Sutherland never heard.

Gently he took the gun from her hand, returned it to his holster, and led her out of the courtroom, out of the building and into the dark Washington night.

CHAPTER
34

THEY LEFT THE KENNEDY CENTER AFTER A PERFORMANCE of Puccini's *La Bohème*.

"It was great," Susanna said. "So much...passion."

"That's Puccini," Teller said as he let go of her hand and fumbled for his car keys. "Where to now?"

"Up to you. No, I take that back. You picked the entertainment, so far, now it's up to me." She looked straight ahead, and said, straight faced, "We go to your place."

And just as straight faced, he said, "The cleaning woman hasn't been in, joint's a mess—"

"You don't have a cleaning woman."

"I surrender."

* * *

IN HIS apartment, which was fully as much of a mess as he'd warned it would be, he took an old blanket off of the couch. "Keeps the cat hairs off. Sit, but watch out for the middle, a bad spring." He put on the stereo. "Drink?"

"Love one."

When they'd settled in with their drinks, he said, "Vera told me Clarence looked like Robert Redford. Not in the morgue he didn't. I didn't go into that. I'd already put her through enough in the courtroom. God, it was eerie, Poulson there, then her showing me how she shot Sutherland . . ."

They sat on one end of the couch, drinks in hand. One of the cats rubbed against her leg.

"Martin," she said, "do you think it's over?"

"Yes . . . well, our part in it anyway. Tell me about your scene with Laurie Rawls." After he had told Susanna what Vera had said about Laurie, Susanna had approached Laurie. To try to talk her out of what she intended to do . . .

"I went to her apartment. Of course she was very different from what she'd been the other times we'd been together. All self-assured and hard. Until I told her that you were ready to press blackmail charges against her."

"What did she say?"

"At first she hung tough, said I was bluffing. I told her that besides having enough evidence to make a solid case, a few leaks to the media would ruin her White House chances anyway."

"And?"

"She quickstepped into Miss Sugar again, even managed a few tears. Told me as a woman I ought to *under-stand* . . . she was only trying to look out for herself in a tough man's world."

"And?"

"I'm afraid I almost hit her. What I told her was to stuff it, that if she didn't resign from the Court, turn down the

White House job and get out of town I'd make it my career to make sure she went to jail. I think she believed me."

"Good deal. And of course the White House wouldn't touch her now anyway, and she knows it."

"Do you know what still bothers me, Martin? Jorgens is still President and Poulson is still Chief Justice."

"Susanna, we solved a murder. After that, it's life goes on. Speaking of which," and he reached for her.

"Hold it, detective. I'm still *talking* . . ."

"I know. All right, look, you could leak the story to some buddy reporter about Poulson having been in an institution and that President Jorgens knew about it when he nominated him for Chief Justice."

"I couldn't—"

"Of course you couldn't."

"Besides, there's Childs. He's still an inspiration to millions of people. His story would come out, and in the worst possible light." She sipped her drink. "Do you think Dr. Sutherland knew Vera Jones had killed his son?"

"I think so. Boy, what a rat he was, his own father wouldn't turn in his murderer."

"Did she say so to you? I mean that the doctor knew?"

"She as much as said it, and it was pretty clear anyway. But what do I do with that kind of information? I could bring charges against him for obstructing justice by withholding information about a murder investigation, but that's not in the cards. It's been billed as a crime of passion. That way nobody's boat gets rocked. And it's a better defense for Vera . . . God knows, she deserves all the breaks she can get. Besides I've got other things to worry about, like a pregnant daughter, my pension and two mangy cats . . . What about you, counselor?"

"I'm thinking of taking off."

"You just got here. And this was your idea, remember?"

"I mean to California, idiot. And I do remember—"

273

"No, damn it."

"I talked to my ex. It hasn't been so easy for him, trying to start over again, taking care of three kids. It's time I took them on, grew up. I think a new start might be good for all of us."

He didn't know what to say except, "Want another drink?"

"Please."

When he came back from the kitchen with the refills, she asked him more about what Vera Jones had told him before her formal interrogation.

"I really felt for her," he said. "Still do. She snapped in the courtroom when she was with Clarence that night, like she did at first the night she confessed. Funny, she lost control, shot him, then collected herself enough to return the gun to Conover's chambers, using keys Clarence had with him. More, she goes back to the courtroom and puts the keys in his pocket. It's ironic that Clarence had Poulson's file with him that night, only she didn't know it. She thought he only had the file Justice Conover had built on his wife. Vera returned it to Conover's chambers too, along with the gun and Poulson's file, which is now back in Dr. Sutherland's office where it belongs. She could have taken it that night but didn't have her wits about her enough for that. Or maybe she was scared to be stopped going out and having it found on her. I guess that was it . . .

"Well, after seeing the phony file Sutherland showed us. I thought so. He was surprised, you'll remember, so that left Vera as the only one who could have taken it, and then tried to cover her tracks with retyped stuff. That's why I decided to follow her myself. I got lucky."

"Not so lucky . . . for a cop you're pretty smart . . . By the way, what did you think about the decision in *Nidel v. Illinois*?"

"What did you think?"

"Well, you know my sentiments, but more than anything,

274

I think I was especially pleased to see Justice Conover get well enough to vote. He's a good man and has had a rough time."

"Must be a blow to the White House," he said.

"I guess, but like you say, there are more important things —like your kids, mine, our lives—speaking of which, detective, enough of this talk, let's get down to cases." She moved over close to him on the couch.

"Not here, the spring..."

"Doesn't a bachelor detective have a bedroom?"

He did, and after shoving the cats from their way, proceeded to show her, and to put thoughts of California, at least for the moment, far, far out of her mind.

Murder in the CIA

1

THE BRITISH VIRGIN ISLANDS, NOVEMBER 1985

Her name was Bernadette, eighteen, tall, a classic island "smooth skin," as they say there—very dark and with a velvety texture—hair the color of ink and falling to her shoulder blades, a full, rounded body defined beneath a clinging maroon jersey dress, a true *mantwana*, the island word for voluptuous woman.

They'd been teasing her since the launch left Anguilla Point on Virgin Gorda for its morning run to Drake's Anchorage on Mosquito Island. She'd started seeing a popular young man from Virgin Gorda, which prompted the gentle ribbing. Although she protested, she enjoyed it. She was proud of her new boyfriend and knew the other girls were jealous. "Gwan tease me, marrow deh," she said, a defiant smile on her lips. Tease all you want; tomorrow will be my day.

There were fifteen of them on board; waiters and waitresses, the bartender, kitchen help, chambermaids, and gardeners. Most of the help lived on Virgin Gorda and were brought in by launch. Drake's Anchorage was the only resort on Mosquito Island (named for a Colombian Indian tribe, not the dipterous insect), and there was only one house for staff, which was occupied by two engineers.

Bernadette was the assistant manager. Her English was excellent; so were her number skills. Her father, a bone fisherman, waded out into the shallow flats of Murdering Hole at dawn each morning in search of the indigenous fish, the so-called ladyfish. Her parents had a hard life, one they hoped she wouldn't inherit. She was their only child.

She turned her face into the wind and thought of last night with her new love. Spray from the intensely blue water stung her face. Life was good now. Last week she'd been depressed, wondered whether she would have to spend the rest of her life in this one place, as beautiful as it might be. Now, *he* was there and the glass was half full again.

The resort had been booked exclusively for two days by a Canadian businessman who'd done the same thing three months earlier, to hold seminars for key people, his assistant had said. The top echelon stayed in two magnificent villas overlooking Lime Tree Beach. Lesser managers occupied ten white-clapboard oceanfront cottages built on stilts and facing Gorda Sound. They all ate together in the thatch-roofed, open-air restaurant where the chef served up vol-au-vent stuffed with escargots, dolphin baked with bananas, West Indian grouper done with spices, herbs, and white wine, and deeply serious chocolate mousse from a guarded recipe.

Bernadette remembered the rules that had been laid down by the Canadian the last time he'd been there. The two villas were to be off-limits to everyone except his people, and resort workers were to come to them only when specifically invited. The villas were to be cleaned while their occupants were breakfasting. Always, the younger men who occupied the smaller cottages would be present in the villas when the chambermaids cleaned, or when busboys delivered food and whiskey.

Although secrecy had been the byword during the Canadians' first visit on Mosquito Island, there were those inevitable, human moments when the shroud was lifted, like the day on the beach when Bernadette saw one of the younger men sitting in a brightly striped canvas chair while cleaning a handgun. When he realized she was watching, he returned the weapon to its holster and quickly entered his cottage.

After that, Bernadette's friends noticed that others in the party carried revolvers in armpit holsters, although they took pains to conceal them. "Businessmen," the chef had said to her. "Serious business, I would say."

While the Canadian and his three senior colleagues had met in the villas, the younger men, always dressed in suits, sat on terraces surrounding the villas, saying nothing, their eyes taking in everything. They seemed pleasant enough men but kept to themselves. One had been a little more open and Bernadette had had a few friendly conversations with him. He was handsome and had a nice smile. Bernadette assumed he was in charge of communications because he frequently talked into a small portable radio to two yachts anchored offshore. Three of the four older men had arrived on those yachts. A float plane had delivered the fourth.

The radioman seemed to enjoy talking to Bernadette and she'd openly flirted with him. Once, she'd asked why there was so much secrecy surrounding a business meeting. She'd asked it lightly, giggled actually, and touched his arm. He'd smiled and said quietly, matter-of-factly, "We're about to launch a new product that our competitors would love to learn more about. That's all. Just taking precautions."

Bernadette didn't ask about the guns because it was none of her business, but she and other staff gossiped about them, speculated, eventually came to the conclusion that big mucky-mucks from up north attached more importance to them-selves and to what they did than was necessary. "Silly boys," they said. One thing was certain: The silly boys tipped big. Everyone from Drake's Anchorage was happy to see them return.

On this day, a single yacht carrying three of the group's leaders arrived a few minutes past two. The float plane touched down a half hour later and slowly taxied toward the long, thin dock.

Bernadette had greeted those who'd disembarked from the yacht, and had been disappointed when the handsome young radioman wasn't among them.

Now, as she waited for the float plane's three passengers to step onto the dock, she saw his face through a window. He was the last one out of the aircraft, and she gave him her biggest welcome. He simply nodded and got into a motorized cart with the two older men. The native driver pulled away from the dock and proceeded along a narrow path that followed the contour of the sea. Bernadette watched it disappear around the curve of a hill and wondered why he'd been so curt. "Strange people," she told herself, happy that she had her new boyfriend back on the bigger island.

The arrival of the yacht and plane had been witnessed, and generally ignored, by people on yachts in the surrounding waters. Yachts in the British Virgins are as common as yellow cabs on New York City streets. One man, however, watched the comings and goings through a telescope from his 46-foot Morgan. He'd been anchored a mile offshore since early morning and had cooked breakfast on board. He had sandwiches for lunch accompanied by a Thermos of rum punch, and had just put on a pot of coffee. A pad of paper at his side was filled with notes. He wore cut-off jeans, brown deck shoes, a T-shirt that said EDWARDS YACHT CHARTERS, and a white canvas hat with a large, floppy brim on which was sewn a blue, red, and yellow patch—BRITISH NAVY: PUSSER'S RUM

He looked up and checked wind conditions. It'd be slow going back to base on Tortola. No sense raising the sails. It'd be engine all the way. He debated staying longer, decided there was nothing to be gained, hauled in the anchor, took a last look toward Mosquito Island, and headed home on a course that took him past a tiny island on which a single structure stood, an imposing, three-story concrete house surrounded by a tall chain-link fence. Two Doberman pinschers ran on the beach. A float plane and a pair of large, fast powerboats bobbed in a gentle swell against a private dock.

The man on the Morgan with his name on his T-shirt smiled as his boat slowly slid by the island. He poured rum into his coffee, lifted the cup toward the island, and said, "*Za vashe zdarov'ye!*" He laughed, put his cup down, and extended the middle finger of his right hand to the island.

4

2

"What's new with the audio rights on Zoltán's new book?" Barrie Mayer asked as she entered her office on Georgetown's Wisconsin Avenue.

Her assistant, David Hubler, looked up at her from a desk piled high with manuscripts and said, "Not to worry, Barrie. We'll have contracts this week."

"I hope so," Mayer said. "You'd think we were negotiating for a million the way they drag their feet drawing papers. A lousy thousand bucks and they treat it like they were buying rights to Ronald Reagan's guide to sex after seventy."

She entered her inner office, tossed her attaché case onto a small couch, and opened the blinds. It was gray outside, threatening. Maybe a storm would clear out the hot, humid Washingtonian weather they'd been having the past few days. Not that it mattered to her. She was on her way to London and Budapest. London was always cool. Well, *almost* always cool. Budapest would be hot, but the Communists had recently invented air conditioning and introduced it to their Eastern bloc countries. With any luck she could spend her entire stay inside the Hilton.

She sat behind her desk and crossed long, slender, nicely molded legs. She wore a favorite traveling outfit: a pearl gray pants suit that had lots of give and barely wrinkled. Sensible burgundy shoes and a shell-pink button-down blouse completed the ensemble. Hubler poked his head through the door and asked if she wanted coffee. She smiled. Not only was he remarkably talented and organized, he didn't mind serving his boss coffee. "Please," she said. He returned a minute later with a large, steaming, blue ceramic mug.

She settled back in her leather chair, swiveled, and took in floor-to-ceiling bookcases that lined one wall. The center section contained copies of many books written by the writers she represented as literary agent. There were twenty writers at the moment; the list swelled and ebbed as their fortunes shifted, but she could count on a hard core of about fifteen, including Zoltán Réti. Réti, the Hungarian novelist, had recently broken through and achieved international acclaim and stunning sales due, in no small part, to Barrie Mayer's faith in him and the extra effort she'd put into his latest book, *Monument*, a multi-generational novel that, according to the *New York Times* review, "touches the deepest aspects of the Hungarian, indeed the human, spirit."

Timing had been on the side of Réti and Mayer. The Soviets had recently loosened restrictions on Hungarian writers and artists, including travel. While Réti's manuscript had gone through a review by officials of the Hungarian Socialist Workers' Party under the leadership of János Kádár, it had emerged relatively unscathed. Réti had skillfully wrapped criticism of Hungary since its "liberation" in 1945 by the Soviet Union into innocuous passages, and reading between the lines said more than his Socialist readers had caught.

Monument was snapped up by publishers around the world and sat on best-seller lists for weeks. It was gratifying to Barrie Mayer because she'd put her all into the book. Now the major dilemma was what to do with the large sums of money Réti was earning from its success. That problem was still being addressed, and one of the reasons for Mayer's trip to Budapest was to confer with Réti and with a ranking member of the Hungarian Presidium who, according to Réti, "could be persuaded" to bend some rules.

Barrie had to smile when she thought of what "could be persuaded" meant. It translated into graft, pure and simple, money under the table to the right Hungarian officials, New York City style, a capitalist solution to a Socialist problem.

On a previous trip to Budapest, Barrie had been introduced to the Presidium member with whom she would meet again this time. He'd sustained a hard, incorruptible façade throughout most of that initial confab, referring to Réti as "a writer for the Hungarian people, not motivated by commercial success." To which Barrie had responded, "If that's the case, sir, we'll keep his millions in our account until there is a shift in policy."

"We have restrictions on foreign currency entering Hungary," said the official.

"A shame," said Mayer. "We're potentially talking millions of U.S. dollars. That would be good for your economy—*any* economy."

"Yes, a good point, Miss Mayer. Perhaps . . ."

"Perhaps we can pursue this another time." She got up to leave.

"I might be able to think of a way to create an exception in this case."

Barrie smiled. What did he want for himself, one of the new condos going up in the Buda hills that only went to Hungarians with a fistful of hard currency, a new car in months instead of the usual four-year wait, a bank account of his own in Switzerland?

"When will you return to Budapest?" he asked.

"Whenever you've . . . 'created your exception.' "

That meeting had taken place a month ago. The official had informed Réti that he'd "smoothed the way for Réti's funds to reach him in Budapest." He'd added, "But, of course, Mr. Réti, there must be some consideration for the time and effort I have expended in your behalf, to say nothing of the risk in which I place myself."

"Of course," Réti said.

7

"Of course," Barrie Mayer said to Réti when he relayed the official's message.

"Of course," she said to herself, grinning, as she sipped the hot, black coffee in her Washington office and allowed her eyes to wander to other books on the shelves written by foreign authors. Funny, she thought, how things in life take their own natural course. She'd never intended to become a literary agent specializing in foreign writers, but that's what had happened. First one, then another, and soon a blossoming reputation as an agent especially sensitive to the needs of such artists. She enjoyed the status it gave her within the publishing industry and in Washington, where she'd become a "hot name" on party invitation lists, including foreign embassies. There was the extensive travel, which, at times, was fatiguing but stimulating as well. She seemed to live out of suitcases these days, which displeased people like her mother who made no effort to conceal her disappointment at seeing so little of her only child.

Barrie's mother lived in a town house in Rosslyn, far enough away for Barrie's sanity, but close enough to see each other occasionally. Mayer had stayed at her mother's last night, an accommodation because of the trip she was about to begin that morning. They'd had a pleasant dinner at Le Lion d'Or, then sat up talking at her mother's house until almost 2:00 A.M. Barrie was tired; it would be good to get on the Pan Am flight from New York to London, sink into a first-class seat, and nap.

She pulled a box of scented pink notepaper from her desk and wrote quickly in broad, bold strokes:

I know I shouldn't bother writing because in the frame of mind you've been in lately, the sentiment behind it won't register. But, that's me, always willing to take another shot and lay *me* on the line. You've hurt me again and here I am back for more. The only reason you're able to hurt me is because I love you. I also suspect that the *reason* you hurt me is because you love me. Fascinating creatures, men and women. At any rate, I'm about to leave and I wanted to say that when I get back we should book some private time, just the two of us, go away for a few days and talk. Maybe this time the words won't get in the way. London and Budapest beckon. Be good, and miss me, damn you.

Hubler came in again. "Got everything?"

"I think so," Mayer said, putting the pages in an envelope, sealing and addressing it, and slipping it into her purse. "Thanks to you."

"You'll be gone a week?"

"A day shy. I'll be at Eleven, Cadogan Gardens in London, and the Hilton in Budapest."

Hubler laughed. "So, what else is new?"

Mayer smiled and stood, stretched, blinked green eyes against sleepiness. "Is the car here?"

"Yeah." The agency had a corporate account with Butler's Limousine, and a stretch was waiting downstairs. "Barrie, a question."

"What?"

"You uncomfortable with this meeting with the Commie big shot in Budapest?"

"A little, but Zoltán says 'Not to worry.' " They both laughed. "He's been talking to you too much, David."

"Maybe he has. Look, I know *you* know your business, but greasing palms in a Socialist country might not be the smartest thing to do. You could be set up. They do it all the time."

Mayer grinned, then picked up her attaché case from the couch, came to where Hubler stood, and kissed him on the cheek. "You, David, are a dear. You also worry more than my mother does, which puts you in the Guinness class. Not to worry, David. Call me if you need me. I'll check in with you a couple of times. By the way, where's Carol?" Carol Geffin was one of two secretaries at the agency. The other, Marcia St. John, was on vacation. The only other two people on Mayer's staff were away on business, one in Hollywood following through on film rights to Réti's novel, the other in New York attending a conference.

"Must have been another heavy night at the Buck Stops Here," Hubler said. Carol Geffin's favorite disco closed at 6:00 A.M., sometimes.

Mayer shook her head. "You tell Carol that she's got to

9

make a choice between working and dancing. One more late morning and she can dance all day on her money, not mine. Give me a hand, huh?''

Hubler carried her briefcase and a suitcase Mayer had dropped off in the reception area to the waiting limo. "See you in a week," she said as she climbed inside the back of the Fleetwood Brougham. The driver closed the door, got behind the wheel, and headed for National Airport and the shuttle to New York. She glanced back through the tinted glass and saw Hubler standing at the curb, his hand half raised in a farewell. One of many things Mayer liked about him was his disposition. He was always smiling, and his laugh was of the infectious variety. Not this day, however. His face, as he stood and watched the limo become smaller, was grim. It bothered her for a moment but quickly was displaced by thoughts of the day ahead. She stretched her legs out in front of her, closed her eyes, and said to herself, "Here we go again."

Her suitcase had been checked through to London, leaving her free to grab a cab from La Guardia into the city, where she was let off at the corner of Second Avenue and 30th Street. She walked toward the East River on 30th until she reached a brownstone with a series of physicians' names in black-on-white plaques.

JASON TOLKER—PSYCHIATRIST. She went down the steps and rang the bell. A female voice asked through an intercom, "Who is it?"

"Barrie Mayer."

A buzzer sounded and Barrie opened the door, stepped into a small carpeted reception area, and closed the door behind her. She was the only person there except for a young woman who came from an office in the rear and said, "Good morning."

"Good morning," Mayer said.

"He's not here, you know," the nurse said.

"I know, a conference in London. He told me to . . ."

"I know. It's here." The nurse, whose face was severely chiseled and whose skin bore the scars of childhood acne, reached behind a desk and came up with a black briefcase of the sort used by attorneys to carry briefs. Two straps

10

came over the top, and a tiny lock secured the flap to the case itself.

"He said you'd been told about this," the nurse said.

"That's right. Thank you."

The nurse's smile was a slash across her lower face. "See you again," she said.

"Yes, you will."

Mayer left, carrying the new briefcase as well as her attaché case, one in each hand. She checked into a room at the Plaza that David had reserved from Washington, had lunch sent up, and perused papers from her attaché case until three, when she placed a wake-up call for five, stripped naked, and took a nap. She got up at five, showered, dressed again, took a cab to Kennedy Airport, and checked in at the Clipper Club, where she had a martini and read a magazine before boarding Pan Am's seven o'clock 747 to London.

"Can I take those for you?" a flight attendant asked, indicating the two briefcases.

"No, thank you. Lots of work to do," Mayer said pleasantly.

She slid both cases under the seat in front of her and settled in for the flight. It left on time. She had another martini, and then caviar and smoked salmon, rare beef carved at her seat, and blueberry cheesecake; cognac to top it off. The movie came on, which she ignored. She put on slippers provided by the flight attendant and a pair of blue eyeshades from a toiletry kit given to each first-class passenger, positioned a pillow behind her head, covered herself with a blue blanket, and promptly fell asleep, the toes of her left foot wedged into the handle of the briefcase she'd picked up at Dr. Jason Tolker's office.

The cabbie from Heathrow Airport to her hotel was an older man who took more delight in chatting than in driving. Mayer would have preferred silence but he was a charming man, as all the older London cab drivers seemed to be, and she thought of the difference between him and certain New York cabbies, who not only were rude and uncaring but malicious, nervous, opinionated, hyperactive, and who curbed any tendency toward humanity by driving insanely.

11

"Here we are, ma'am," the driver said as he pulled up in front of a row of brick houses on Cadogan Gardens. There was no indication of a hotel on the block. Only the number 11 appeared above a polished wooden door that Mayer went to. She rang a bell. Moments later a hall porter in a white jacket opened the door and said, "Welcome, Miss Mayer. Splendid to see you again. Your room is ready."

She signed the guest book and was led to the suite she usually reserved—Number 27. It consisted of a living room, bedroom, and bath. The white ceilings were high, the walls of the living room bloodred. Victorian furniture was everywhere, including a glass-fronted bookcase, an armoire, a dressing table in front of French windows in the bedroom that overlooked a private park across the street, and a gracefully curved chaise and chairs upholstered in gold.

"Would you like anything, ma'am?" the porter asked.

"Not this minute, thank you," Barrie said. "Perhaps tea at three?"

"Of course."

"I'll be leaving tomorrow for a few days," she said, "but I'll be keeping the room for my return."

"Yes, ma'am. Tea at three."

She slept, and later watched BBC-TV while enjoying scones with clotted cream and jam with her tea. She had dinner at seven at the Dorchester with a British agent, Mark Hotchkiss, with whom she'd been exploring a business link for the past few months, and was back in bed at the Cadogan by ten.

She arose at seven, had breakfast sent up to the room, dressed and left the hotel at eight. She arrived at Heathrow's Terminal Number 2 and joined a long line of people waiting to go through a security section leading to a vast array of flights by smaller foreign airlines, including Malev, the Hungarian National Airline.

She'd been through this before. How many trips had she taken to Budapest in the two or three years? Fifteen, twenty? She'd lost track. Only her accountant knew for certain. The line at Terminal 2 was always impossibly long and slow, and she'd learned to be patient.

She glanced up at a TV departure monitor. Plenty of time.

An older man in front of her asked if she'd "protect" his place while he went to buy a pack of cigarettes. "Of course," she said. A woman behind her ran the wheel of a suitcase caddy into Mayer's heel. Mayer turned. The woman raised her eyebrows and looked away.

The line moved in spurts. Mayer carried her briefcases, and pushed her suitcase along the ground with her foot.

A loud voice to her right caused Barrie, and everyone else in the line, to turn in its direction. A young black man wearing an open white shirt, black trousers, and leather sandals had gotten up on a trash container and began screaming a protest against British policy in South Africa. Everyone's attention remained on him as two uniformed airport-security officers pushed through crowds of people in his direction.

"Barrie."

She didn't immediately react. Because she, and everyone else in the line, had turned to her right, her back was to a row of counters. The mention of her name had come from behind her.

She turned. Her eyebrows went up. She started to say something, a name, a greeting, when the hand came up beneath her nose. In it was a metal tube that might have held a cigar. The thumb on the hand flicked a switch on the tube and a glass ampule inside it shattered, its contents blown into Mayer's face.

It all happened so quickly. No one seemed to notice . . . until she dropped both briefcases to the floor and her hands clutched at her chest as a stabbing pain radiated from deep inside. She couldn't breathe. The airport, and everyone in it, was wiped away by a blinding white light that sent a spasm of pain through her head.

"Lady, are you . . . ?"

Her face was blue. She sank to her knees, her fingers frantic as they tried to tear open her clothing, her chest itself in search of air and relief from the pain.

"Hey, hey, over here, this lady's . . ."

Mayer looked up into the faces of dozens of people who were crouching low and peering at her, in sympathy or in horror. Her mouth and eyes opened wide, and rasping sounds

13

came from her throat, pleas without words, questions for the faces of strangers so close to her. Then she pitched forward, her face thudding against the hard floor.

There were screams now from several people who saw what had happened to the tall, well-dressed woman who, seconds before, had stood in line with them.

The man who'd gone to get cigarettes returned. "What's this?" he asked as he looked down at Mayer, sprawled on the floor of Terminal Number 2. "Good God," he said, "someone do something for her."

3

BUDAPEST—TWO DAYS LATER

"I just can't believe it," Collette Cahill said to Joe Breslin as they sat at an outdoor table at Gundel, Budapest's grand old restaurant. "Barrie was . . . she'd become my best friend. I went out to Ferihegy to meet her flight from London, but she wasn't on it. I came back to the embassy and called that hotel in Cadogan Gardens she always stays at in London. All they could tell me was that she left that morning for the airport. Malev wouldn't tell me anything until I got hold of that guy in operations I know who checked the passenger manifest. Barrie was listed as a reservation, but she hadn't boarded. That's when I really started worrying. And then . . . then, I got a call from Dave Hubler in her Washington office. He could barely talk. I made him repeat what he'd said three, four times and . . ." She'd been fighting tears all evening and now lost the battle. Breslin reached across the table and placed a hand on hers. A seven-piece roving Gypsy band dressed in bright colors approached the table but Breslin waved them away.

Collette sat back in her chair and drew a series of deep

15

breaths. She wiped her eyes with her napkin and slowly shook her head. "A heart attack? That's ridiculous, Joe. She was, what, thirty-five, maybe thirty-six? She was in great shape. Damn it! It can't be."

Breslin shrugged and lighted his pipe. "I'm afraid it can, Collette. Barrie's dead. No question about that, sadly. What about Réti, her writer?"

"I tried his house but no one was there. I'm sure he knows by now. Hubler was calling him with the news."

"What about the funeral?"

"There wasn't any, at least nothing formal. I called her mother that night. God, I dreaded it. She seemed to take it pretty well, though. She said she knew that Barrie wanted immediate cremation, no prayers, no gathering, and that's what she had."

"The autopsy. You say it was done in London?"

"Yes. They're the ones who labeled it a coronary." She closed her eyes tightly. "I will not buy that finding, Joe, never."

He smiled and leaned forward. "Eat something, Collette. You haven't had a thing for too long. Besides, I'm starved." Large bowls of goulash soup sat untouched in front of them. She took a spoonful and looked at Breslin, who'd dipped a piece of bread in the hearty broth and was savoring it. Cahill was glad she had him to lean on. She'd made many friends since coming to Budapest, but Joe Breslin provided a stability she needed at times like this, perhaps because he was older, fifty-six, and seemed to enjoy the role of surrogate father.

Breslin had been stationed with the American Embassy in Budapest for just over ten years. In fact, Collette and a group of friends had celebrated his tenth anniversary only last week at their favorite Budapest night spot, the Miniatur Bar on Budai Läszlö Street, where a talented young Gypsy pianist named Nyári Károly played a nightly mix of spirited Hungarian Gypsy melodies, American pop tunes, Hungarian love songs, and modern jazz. It had been a festive occasion and they'd closed the bar at three in the morning.

"How's the soup?" Breslin asked.

"Okay. You know, Joe, I just realized there's someone else I should call."

"Who's that?"

"Eric Edwards."

Breslin's eyebrows lifted. "Why?"

"He and Barrie were . . . close."

"Really? I didn't know that."

"She didn't talk about it much but she was mad about him."

"Hardly an exclusive club."

The comment brought forth the first smile of the evening from her. She said, "I've finally gotten old enough to learn never to question a relationship. Do you know him well?"

"I don't know him at all, just the name, the operation. We had some dispatches from him this morning."

"And?"

"Nothing startling. Banana Quick is alive and well. They've had their second meeting."

"On Mosquito?"

He nodded, frowned, leaned across the table, and said, "Was Barrie carrying anything?"

"I don't know." They both glanced about to make sure they weren't being overheard. She spotted a table four removed at which a heavyset man and three women sat. She said to Breslin, "That's Litka Morovaf, Soviet cultural affairs."

Breslin smiled. "What is he now, number three in the KGB here?"

"Number two. A real Chekist. Drives him crazy when I call him Colonel. He actually thinks not wearing a uniform obscures his military rank. He's a pig, always after me to have dinner with him. Enough of him. Getting back to Barrie, Joe, I didn't always know whether she was carrying or just here on business for her agency. She'd tightened up a lot lately, which made me happy. When she first got involved, she babbled about it like a schoolgirl."

"Did she see Tolker before leaving?"

"I don't know that, either. She usually contacted him in Washington but she had time to kill in New York this trip,

so I assume she saw him there. I don't know anything, Joe—
I wish I did."

"Maybe it's better you don't. Feel like dinner?"

"Not really."

"Mind if I do?"

"Go ahead, I'll pick."

He ordered *Fogasfile Gundel Modon*, the small filets of
fish accompanied by four vegetables, and a bottle of Egri
Bikavér, a good red Hungarian wine. They said little while
he ate. Cahill sipped the wine and tried to shake the thoughts
that bombarded her about Barrie's death.

They'd become friends in college days. Collette was raised
in Virginia, attended George Washington University, and
graduated from its law school. It was during her postgrad-
uate work that she met Barrie Mayer, who'd come from
Seattle to work on a master's degree in English literature
at Georgetown University. It had been a chance meeting.
A young attorney Cahill had been seeing threw a party at
his apartment in Old Town and invited his best friend, another attorney who'd just started dating Barrie Mayer. He
brought her to the party and the two young women hit it
off.

That they became close friends surprised the attorneys
who'd introduced them. They were different personalities,
as different as their physical attributes. Mayer, tall, leggy,
had a mane of chestnut hair that she enjoyed wearing loose.
She seldom used makeup. Her eyes were the color of mal-
achite and she used them to good advantage, expressing a
variety of emotions with a simple widening or narrowing, a
partial wink, a lift of a sandy eyebrow, or a sensuous cloud-
ing over that she knew was appealing to men.

Cahill, on the other hand, was short and tightly bundled,
a succession of rounded edges that had been there since
adolescence and that had caused her widowed mother sleepless nights. She was as vivacious as Mayer was laid-back,
deep blue eyes in constant motion, a face punctuated by
high cheekbones that belied her Scottish heritage, a face
that seemed always ready to burst apart with enthusiasm
and wonder. She enjoyed using makeup to add high color
to her cheeks and lips. Her hair was black ("Where did that

18

come from, for heaven's sake?" her mother often asked), and she wore it short, in a style flattering to her nicely rounded face.

Their initial friendship was rooted in a mutual determination to forge successful careers. The specific goals were different, of course. For Mayer, it was to eventually head up a major book-publishing company. For Cahill, it was government service with an eye toward a top spot in the Justice Department, perhaps even becoming the first female Attorney General. They laughed often and loudly about their aspirations, but they were serious.

They remained close until graduation, when the beginning stages of their work moved them away from each other. Cahill took a job with a legal trade journal published in Washington that kept tabs on pending legislation. She gave it a year, then took a friend's advice and began applying to government agencies, including Justice, State, and the Central Intelligence Agency. The CIA was first with an offer and she accepted it.

"You *what*?" Barrie Mayer had exploded over dinner the night Cahill announced her new job.

"I'm going to work for the CIA."

"That's . . . that's crazy. Don't you read, Collette? The CIA's a terrible organization."

"Media distortion, Barrie." She had smiled. "Besides, after training, they're sending me to England."

Now Mayer's smile matched Collette's. "All right," she said, "so it's not such a terrible organization. What will you be doing there?"

"I don't know yet, but I'll find out soon enough."

They ended the dinner with a toast to Collette's new adventure, especially to London.

At the time of Collette Cahill's decision to join the Pickle Factory, as CIA employees routinely referred to the agency, Barrie Mayer was working at a low-level editorial job with *The Washingtonian*, D.C.'s leading "city" magazine. Her friend's decision to make a dramatic move prompted action on her part. She quit the magazine and went to New York, where she stayed with friends until landing a job as assistant to the executive editor of a top book publisher. It was during that experience that she took an interest in the literary agent's side of the publishing business, and accepted a job with a medium-size agency. This suited her perfectly. The pace was faster than at the publishing house, and she enjoyed wheeling and dealing on behalf of the agency's clients. As it turned out, she was good at it.

When the founder of the agency died, Mayer found herself running the show for three years until deciding to strike out on her own. She ruled out New York; too much competition. With an increasing number of authors coming out of Washington, she decided to open Barrie Mayer Associates there. It flourished from the beginning, especially as her roster of foreign authors grew along with an impressive list of Washington writers.

Although their careers created a wide geographical distance between them, Barrie and Collette kept in touch through occasional postcards and letters, seldom giving much thought to whether they'd ever renew the friendship again in person.

After three years at a CIA monitoring station in an abandoned BBC facility outside of London, where she took raw intercepts of broadcasts from Soviet bloc countries and turned them into concise, cogent reports for top brass, Cahill was asked to transfer to a Clandestine Services unit in the Hungarian division, operating under the cover of the U.S. Embassy in Budapest. She debated making the move; she loved England, and the contemplation of a long assignment inside an Eastern European Socialist state did not hold vast appeal.

But there was the attraction of joining Clandestine Services, the CIA's division responsible for espionage, the *spy* division. Although space technology, with its ability to peek into every crevice and corner of the earth from miles aloft, had diminished the need for agents, special needs still existed, and the glamour and intrigue perpetuated by writers of spy novels lived on.

What had they said over and over during her training at headquarters in Langley, Virginia, and at the "Farm," the handsome estate a two-hour drive south of Washington? "The CIA is not essentially, or wholly, an espionage organization. It has only a small section devoted to espionage, and agents are never used to gain information that can be obtained through other means."

Her instructor in the course "Management of the Espionage Operation" had quoted from British intelligence to get across the same point. "A good espionage operation is like a good marriage. Nothing unusual ever happens. It is, and should be, uneventful. It is never the basis of a good story."

Her cover assignment would be the embassy's Industrial Trade Mission. Her real responsibility would be to function as a case officer, seeking out and developing useful members of Hungary's political, industrial, and intelligence communities into agents for the United States, to "turn" them to our side. It would mean returning to Washington for months of intensive training, including a forty-four-week language course in Hungarian at the Foreign Service Institute.

Should she take it? Her mother had been urging her to return home from England and to put her law training to the use for which it was intended. Cahill herself had been considering resigning from the Pickle Factory and returning home. The past few months in England had been boring, not socially but certainly on the job as her routine became predictable and humdrum.

It was not an easy decision. She made it on a train from London after a weekend holiday of good theater, pub-crawling with friends she'd made from the Thames Broadcasting Network, and luxuriating in a full English tea at Brown's.

She'd take it.

Once she'd decided, her spirits soared and she enthusiastically prepared for her return to Washington. She'd been instructed to discuss it with no one except cleared CIA personnel.

"Not even my mother?"

An easy, understanding smile from her boss. "*Especially* your mother."

"You will hear two things from Hungarians," her language instructor at Washington's Foreign Service Institute told the class the first day. "First, they will tell you that Hungary is a very small country. Second, they will tell you that the language is *very* difficult. Believe them. Both statements are true."

Friday.

Cahill's first week of language classes had ended, and she'd made plans to spend the weekend with her mother in Virginia. She stopped in the French Market in Georgetown to pick up her mother's favorite pâté and cheese, and was waiting for her purchases to be added up when someone behind her said her name. She turned. "It can't be," she said, wide-eyed.

"Sure is," Barrie Mayer said.

They embraced, stepped apart, and looked at each other, then hugged again.

"What are you doing here?" Mayer asked.

"Going to school. I'm being transferred and . . . it's a long story. How are you? The agency's doing well? How's your . . . ?"

"Love life?" A hearty laugh from both. "That, too, is a long story. Where are you going now? Can we have a drink? Dinner? I've been meaning to . . . "

"So have I. I'm going home for the weekend . . . I mean, where my mother lives. God, I can't believe this, Barrie! You look sensational."

"So do you. Do you have to go right now?"

"Well, I—let me call my mother and tell her I'll be late."

"Go tomorrow morning, early. Stay with me tonight."

"Ah, Barrie, I can't. She's expecting me."

"At least a drink. My treat. I'm dying to talk to you. This is incredible, bumping into you. Please, just a drink. If you stay for dinner, I'll even send you home by limo."

"Things are good, huh?"

"Things are *fantastic*."

They went to the Georgetown Inn where Cahill ordered a gin and tonic, Mayer an old-fashioned. There was a frenetic attempt to bring each other up to date as quickly as possible, which resulted in little information actually being absorbed. Mayer realized it and said, "Let's slow down.

You first. You said you were here to take classes. What kind of classes? What for?"

"For my job. I'm"—she looked down at the bar and said sheepishly—"I can't really discuss it with . . . with anyone not officially involved with the Company."

Mayer adopted a grave expression. "Heavy spy stuff, huh?"

Cahill laughed the comment away. "No, not at all, but you know how things are with us."

"*Us?*"

"Don't make me explain, Barrie. You know what I mean."

"I sure do."

"Do you?"

Mayer sat back and played with a swizzle stick. She asked, "Are you leaving jolly old England?"

"Yes."

"And?"

"I'll be . . . I've taken a job with the U.S. Embassy in Budapest."

"That's wonderful. With the embassy? You've left the CIA?"

"Well, I . . ."

Mayer held up her hand. "No explanations needed. I read the papers."

What had been an exuberant beginning to the reunion deteriorated into an awkward silence. It was Cahill who broke it. She clutched Mayer's arm and said, "Let's get off the cloaks and daggers. Barrie, your turn. Tell me about *your* agency. Tell me about, well . . ."

"My love life." They giggled. "It's stagnant, to be kind, although it has had its moments recently. The problem is that I've been spending more time on airplanes than any-where else, which doesn't contribute to stable relationships. Anyway, the agency is thriving *and*, coincidentally, you and I will probably see more of each other in Budapest than we have for the past five years."

"Why?"

She explained her recent success with foreign authors, including the Hungarian, Zoltán Réti. "I've been to Buda-pest six or eight times. I love it. It's a marvelous city despite Big Red Brother looking over your shoulder."

"Another drink?"

"Not for me. You?"

"No. I really should be heading off."

"Call your mother."

"All right."

Cahill returned and said, "She's such a sweetness. She said, 'You spend time with your dear friend. Friends are important.' " She delivered the words with exaggerated gravity.

"She sounds wonderful. So, what is it, dinner, stay over? You name it."

"Dinner, and the last train home."

They ended up at La Chaumière on M Street, where Mayer was given a welcome worthy of royalty. "I've been coming here for years," she told Cahill as they were led to a choice table near the center fireplace. "The food is scrumptious and they have a sense of when to leave you alone. I've cut some of my better meals and deals here."

It turned into a long, leisurely, and progressively introspective evening, aided by a second bottle of wine. The need to bombard each other with detailed tales of their lives had passed, and the conversation slipped into a comfortable and quiet series of reflective thoughts, delivered from their armchairs.

"Tell me more about Eric Edwards," Cahill said.

"What else is there to say? I was in the BVI meeting with an author who'd recently hit it big. Besides, never pass up a chance at the Caribbean. Anyway, he took me on a day cruise, and the charter captain was Eric. We hit it off right away, Collette, one of those instant fermentations, and I spent the week with him."

"Still on?"

"Sort of. It's hard with my travel schedule and his being down there, but it sure ain't dead."

"That's good."

"And . . ."

Cahill looked across the candlelit table and smiled. "That's right," she said, "there was something you were dying to tell me."

"Eric Edwards isn't enough?"

"Only if you hadn't hinted that there was something even bigger. Lay it on me, lady literary agent. That last train home isn't far off."

Mayer glanced around the restaurant. Only two other tables were occupied, and they were far away. She put her elbows on the table and said, "I joined the team."

Cahill's face was a blank.

"I'm one of you."

It dawned on Cahill that her friend might be referring to the CIA but, because it didn't make much sense—and because she had learned caution—she didn't bring it up. Instead, she said, "Barrie, could you be a little more direct?"

"Sure. I'm working for the Pickle Factory." There was mirth in her voice as she said the words.

"That's . . . how?"

"I'm a courier. Just part time, of course, but I've been doing it fairly regularly now for about a year."

"Why?" It was the only sensible question that came to Cahill at the moment.

"Well, because I was asked to and . . . I like it, Collette, feel I'm doing something worthwhile."

"You're being paid?"

Mayer laughed. "Of course. What kind of an agent would I be if I didn't negotiate a good deal for myself?"

"You don't *need* the money, do you?"

"Of course not, but who ever has too much money? And, finally, some earnings off the books. Want more specifics?"

"Yes and no. I'm fascinated, of course, but you really shouldn't be talking about it."

"To *you*? You're cleared."

"I know *that*, Barrie, but it's still something you don't chit-chat about over dinner and wine."

Mayer adopted a contrite expression. "You aren't going to turn me in, are you?"

Collette sighed and looked for a waiter. Once she'd gotten his attention, she said to Mayer, "Barrie, you have ruined my weekend. I'll spend it wondering about the strange twists and turns my friend's life has taken while I wasn't around to protect her."

They stood outside the restaurant. It was a crisp and clear

evening. The street had filled with the usual weekend crowds that gravitated to Georgetown, and that caused residents to wring their hands and to consider wringing necks, or selling their houses.

"You'll be back Monday?" Mayer asked.

"Yup, but I'll be spending most of my time out of town."

"At the Farm?"

"Barrie!"

"Well?"

"I have some training to take. Let's leave it at that."

"Okay, but promise you'll call the first moment you're free. We have a lot more catching up to do."

They touched cheeks, and Collette flagged a cab. She spent the weekend at her mother's house thinking about Barrie Mayer and the conversation at the restaurant. What she'd told her friend was true. She *had* spoiled her weekend, and she returned to Washington Monday morning anxious to get together again for another installment of Barrie Mayer's "other life."

"This restaurant isn't what it used to be," Joe Breslin said as he finished his meal. "I remember when Gundel was . . ."

"Joe, I'm going to London and Washington," Cahill said.

"Why?"

"To find out what happened to Barrie. I just can't sit here and let it slide, shrug and accept the death of a friend."

"Maybe you should do just that, Collette."

"Sit here?"

"Yes. Maybe . . ."

"Joe, I know exactly what you're thinking, and if what you're thinking bears any relationship to the truth, I don't know what I'll do."

"I don't know anything about Barrie's death, Collette, but I do know that she assumed a known risk once she got involved, no matter how part time it might have been. Things have heated up since Banana Quick. The stakes have gotten a lot bigger, and the players are more visible and vulnerable." He added quickly, in a whisper, "The schedule's been moved up. It'll be sooner than planned."

"What are you saying, Joe, that this could have been a Soviet wet affair?" She'd used Russian intelligence slang for blood, for an assassination, which had been picked up by the intelligence community in general.

"Could be."

"Or?"

"Or . . . your guess. Remember, Collette, it might have been exactly what it was labeled by the British doctors, a coronary pure and simple."

A lump developed in Cahill's throat and she touched away a tear that had started down her cheek. "Take me home, Joe, please. I'm suddenly very tired."

As they left Gundel, the Soviet intelligence officer at the table with three women waved to Collette and said, "*Vsyevó kharóshevo*, Madam Cahill." He was drunk.

"Good night to you, too, Colonel," she responded.

Breslin dropped her at her apartment on Huszti ùt, on the more fashionable Buda side of the Danube. It was one of dozens of apartments the U.S. government had leased to house its embassy personnel, and although it was extremely small and three flights up, it was light and airy and featured a remodeled kitchen that was the best of all the kitchens her embassy friends had in their subsidized apartments. It also came with a telephone, something Hungarian citizens waited years for.

A flashing red light indicated Cahill had two messages on her answering machine. She rewound the tape and heard a familiar voice, his English heavily laden with his Hungarian birthright. "*Collette, it is Zoltán Réti. I am in London. I am shocked at what I have heard about Barrie. No, shocked is not the word to describe my feelings. I read about it in the paper here. I am attending a conference and will return to Budapest tomorrow. I am sorry for the loss of your good friend, and for my loss. It is a terrible thing. Goodbye.*"

Cahill stopped the machine before listening to the second message. London? Hadn't Réti known Barrie was coming to Budapest? If he hadn't—and if she knew he wouldn't be here—she had to be on CIA business. But that broke precedent. She'd never traveled to Budapest without having him there as the reason for her visit which, in fact, was legitimate. He was a client. The fact that he happened to be Hungarian and lived in Budapest only made it more plausible and convenient to perform her second mission, carrying materials for the Central Intelligence Agency.

She started the second message:

"Collette Cahill, my name is Eric Edwards. We've never met, but Barrie and I were quite close, and she talked about you often. I just learned about what happened to her and felt I had to make contact with someone, anyone who was close to her and shares what I'm feeling at this moment. It seems impossible, doesn't it, that she's gone, like that, this beautiful and talented woman who . . ." There was a pause, and it sounded to Cahill as though he were trying to compose himself. *"I hope you don't mind this long and convoluted message but, as I said, I wanted to reach out and talk to her friend. She gave me your number a long time ago. I live in the British Virgin Islands but I wondered if . . ."* The line went dead. He was cut off, and the machine made a series of beeping noises.

His call set up another set of questions for her. Didn't he know that *she* would know who he was, that he lived in the British Virgins, was a CIA operative there whose primary mission had to do with Hungary? Was he just being professional? Probably. She couldn't fault that.

She made herself a cup of tea, got into her nightgown, and climbed into bed, the tea on a small table beside her. She decided three things: She would request time off immediately to go to London and Washington; she would look up everyone who was close to Barrie and, at least, be able to vent her feelings; and she would, from that moment forward, accept the possibility that her friend Barrie Mayer had died prematurely of a heart attack, at least until there was something tangible to prove otherwise.

She fell asleep crying silently after asking in a hoarse, low voice, "What happened, Barrie? What *really* happened?"

4

Collette: Please see me as soon as you come in. Joe.

The note was taped to the telephone in her office on the second floor of the embassy. She got a cup of coffee and walked down the hall to Breslin's office. "Come in," he said. "Close the door."

He took a sip of his coffee which, Cahill knew, contained a healthy shot of akvavit, compliments of a buddy in the U.S. Embassy in Copenhagen who always included a bottle in his diplomatic pouch. "What's up?" she asked.

"Feel like a walk?"

"Sure." He wasn't suggesting it because he needed exercise. What he had to say was important and private, and Breslin was a notorious paranoiac when it came to holding such conversations inside the embassy.

They went down a broad staircase with worn red carpeting, through a door tripped electronically by a young woman at the front desk, past a Hungarian Embassy employee who was running a metal detector over a visitor, and out into bright sunshine that bathed Szabadság tér and Liberation Square.

A group of schoolchildren gathered at the base of a huge

memorial obelisk dedicated to Soviet soldiers who'd liberated the city. The streets were bustling with people on their way to work, or heading for Váci utca and its parallel shopping boulevard from which all vehicles were banned. "Come on," Breslin said, "let's go down to Parliament."

They walked along the Danube's shoreline until they reached the domed, neo-Gothic Parliament building with its eighty-eight statues depicting Hungarian monarchs, commanders, and famous warriors. Breslin looked up at it and smiled. "I would have liked being around here when they really did have a Parliament," he said. Since the Soviets took over, the Parliament continued to function, but in name only. The *real* decisions were made in an ugly, rectangular building farther up the river where the MSZMP—the Hungarian Socialist Workers' Party—sat.

Cahill watched boat traffic on the Danube as she asked, "What do you want to tell me?"

Breslin pulled his pipe from his jacket, tamped tobacco into its bowl, and put a wooden match to it. "I don't think you'll have to ask for time off to chase down what happened to your friend Barrie."

"What do you mean?"

"Based upon what Stan told me this morning, you're going to be asked to do it officially." Stanley Podgorsky was chief-of-station for the CIA unit operating out of the embassy. Of two hundred Americans assigned there, approximately half were CIA people reporting to him.

"Why me?" Cahill asked. "I'm not a trained investigator."

"Why not? How many Company investigators have you known who were trained?" It caused her to smile. "You know how it works, Collette, somebody knows somebody who's been compromised and they get the assignment, instant investigator. I think that's you this time around."

"Because I knew Barrie?"

"Exactly."

"And it wasn't a heart attack?"

"Not from what I hear."

They approached a construction crew that was using jackhammers to tear out an old dock. When they were close enough so that even sophisticated, long-range microphones would fail to distinguish their words from the din, Breslin said, "She *was* carrying, Collette, and evidently it was important."

"And it's gone?"

"Right."

"Any ideas?"

"Sure. It was either us or them. If it was them, they have the material and we're in a panic. If it was us, one of our people has what she had in her briefcase and maybe is looking to sell it to the other side." He drew on his pipe and said, "Or . . ."

"Or wanted what she had for other reasons, personal maybe, incriminating, something like that."

"Yes, something like that."

She squinted against the sun that popped out from a fast-moving cloud and said, "Joe, we're down here for more than just a preliminary warning to me that Stan might ask me to look into Barrie's death. He told you to feel me out, didn't he?"

"Not in so many words."

"I'll do it."

"Really? No hesitation?"

"None. I wanted to do it on my own time anyway. This way I don't blow what leave I have coming to me."

"That's pragmatic."

"That's working for the Pickle Factory too long. Do I go back and tell him, or do you?"

"You. I have nothing to do with this. One final bit of advice, Collette. Stan and the desk people back at Langley really don't give a damn how Barrie died. As far as they're concerned, she had a heart attack. I mean, they know she didn't but *she* doesn't count. The briefcase does."

"What was in it? Who was it from?"

"Maybe Stan will tell you, but I doubt it. Need-to-know, you know."

"If I'm trying to find out who ended up with it, I'll need to know."

"Maybe, maybe not. That's up to Stan and Langley. Let

them lay out the rules and you stay within them." He looked over half-glasses to reinforce his point.

"I will, and thanks, Joe. I'll go see Stan right now."

Podgorsky occupied an office that had a sign on the door that read TYPEWRITER REPAIR. Many CIA offices within the embassy had such signs which, the thinking went, would discourage casual visitors. They usually did.

He sat behind a battered desk with a row of burn marks from too many cigars perched on the edge. Stanley was short and stocky, with a full head of gray hair of which he was inordinately proud. Cahill liked him, had from the first day she arrived in Budapest. He was shrewd and tough but had a sentimental streak that extended to everyone working for him.

"You talked to Joe?" he asked.

"Yes."

"Make sense to you?"

"I guess so. We were close. I was supposed to meet her flight."

He nodded and grunted, rolled his fingertips on the desk. "Were you meeting her for us?"

"No, strictly personal. I didn't know whether she was carrying or not."

"She ever talk to you about what she was doing?"

"A little."

"Nothing about this trip."

"Nothing. She never got specific about any trip she took here. All she ever got into was her meetings with her agency clients like Zoltán Réti."

"He's not here."

"I know. He called me last night from London and left a message on my machine."

"You find it strange he isn't here?"

"As a matter of fact, yes."

"She was supposed to meet with him and a Party big shot about clearing Réti to get the money his books are making in the West."

"How much was *that* going to cost?"

Podgorsky laughed. "Whatever the *papakha* needed to

buy one of those condos up on the hill, or to get himself a fancy new car quick."

"Palms are all the same."

"So's the grease and the way it goes on." His face became grim. "We lost a lot, Collette."

"What she was carrying was that important?"

"Yeah."

"What was it?"

"Need-to-know."

"*I* need to know if I'm going to be digging into what led up to her death."

He shook his head. "Not now, Collette. The assignment is clear-cut, no ambiguities. You go home on leave and touch base with everybody in her life. You're grieving, can't believe your good friend is dead. You find out what you can and report it to a case officer at Langley."

"How cynical. I really do care what happened to my friend."

"I'm sure you do. Look, you don't have to do this. It's not in your area, but I'd suggest you think six times before turning it down. Like I said, the stakes are big here."

"Banana Quick?"

He nodded.

"Am I really taking leave?"

"It'll be on the books that way in case somebody wants to snoop. We'll make it up to you later. That's a promise from me."

"When do you want me to start?"

"Leave in the morning."

"I can't. You know I have a meet set up with Horgász."

"That's right. When?"

"Tomorrow night."

Podgorsky thought for a moment before saying, "It's important?"

"I haven't seen him for six weeks. He left word at one of the drops that he had something. It's been set, can't be changed."

"Then do it, leave the next morning."

"All right. Anything else?"

"Yeah. Go easy. Frankly, I tried to veto having you assigned to this. Too close. Good friends usually get in the way. Try to forget who she was and concentrate on business. A briefcase. That's all anybody cares about."

She stood and said, "I really do hate this place, Stan."

"Gay ol' Budapest?" He laughed loudly.

"You know what I mean."

"Sure I do. Everything set for Horgász?"

"I think so. We're using the new safehouse."

"I still don't like that place. I should have stuck to my guns and killed it when it was suggested. Too close to too many other things."

"I'm comfortable with it."

"That's good. You're a trouper, Collette."

"I'm an employee. You said I'll be on leave, which means no official status. That makes it tough."

"No it doesn't. The only thing having status would give you is access to our people. You don't need them. They don't have any answers. They're *looking* for answers."

"I want to retrace Barrie's steps. I'll go to London first."

He shrugged.

"I want to talk to the doctors who did the autopsy."

"Nothing to be gained there, Collette. They used cleared personnel."

"British SIS?"

"Probably."

"How was she killed, Stan?"

"Beats me. Maybe prussic acid if it was the Soviets."

"We use it, too, don't we?"

He ignored the question by going through a slow, elaborate ritual of clipping, wetting, and lighting a cigar. "Forget the British doctors, Collette," he said through a cloud of blue smoke.

"I still want to go to London first."

"Nice this time of year. Not many tourists."

She opened the door, turned, and asked, "How's the typewriter repair business?"

"Slow. They make 'em too good these days. Take care, and keep in touch."

She spent the remainder of the day, much of the night, and all of the next day preparing for her meet with a man, code name Horgász, Hungarian for "Fisherman." He represented Collette Cahill's coup since being in Budapest. Horgász, whose real name was Árpád Hegedüs, was a high-ranking psychologist within the KGB's Hungarian intelligence arm.

Cahill had met Árpád Hegedüs the first week she was in Budapest at a reception for a group of psychologists and psychiatrists who'd been invited to present papers to a Hungarian scientific conference. Three Americans were among the invited, including Dr. Jason Tolker. Cahill's dislike for Tolker was instantaneous, although she hadn't thought much about it until Barrie Mayer confided in her that he was the one who'd recruited her into the part-time role of CIA courier. "I didn't like him," Cahill had told her friend, to which Mayer replied, "You're not supposed to like your shrink." Mayer had been his patient for a year before hooking up with Central Intelligence.

Árpád Hegedüs was a nervous little man, forty-six years old, who wore shirt collars that were too tight and wrinkled suits that were too large. He was married and had two children. Most of his training in psychology had been gained at the Neurological and Psychiatric Clinic on Balassa utca, near the Petőfi Bridge linking the Pest and Buda sides of the Grand Boulevard. He'd come to the attention of Soviet authorities after he'd developed and instituted a series of psychological tests for workers in sensitive jobs that were designed to flag personality traits that could lead to dissatisfaction, and perhaps even disloyalty. He was taken to Moscow, where he spent a year at VASA, the Soviet military intelligence school that constitutes a special department of the prestigious Military Diplomatic Academy. His intellect shone there and he was brought into the Sovietskaya Kolonia, the KGB's arm responsible for policing the loyalty of the Soviet's colonies abroad, in this case its Hungarian contingent. That was the job he held when Cahill met him at the reception, although his official position was with the teaching staff of his Hungarian alma mater.

Cahill bumped into him a few more times over the ensuing months. One night, as she ate dinner alone in Vigadó, a downtown brasserie on Vigadó Square, he approached the table and asked if he might join her. They had a pleasant conversation. He spoke good English, loved opera and American jazz, and asked a lot of questions about life in the United States.

Cahill didn't attach any significance to the chance meeting. It was two weeks later that the reason for his approach became obvious.

It was a Saturday morning. She'd gone for a run and ended up at the former Royal Palace on Castle Hill. The palace had been completely destroyed during World War II. Now the restoration was almost completed and the baroque palace had been transformed into a vast museum and cultural complex, including the Hungarian National Gallery.

Cahill often browsed in the museum. It had become, for her, a peaceful refuge.

She was standing in front of a huge medieval ecclesiastical painting when a man came up behind her. "Miss Cahill," he said softly.

"Oh, hello, Mr. Hegedüs. Nice to see you again."

"You like the paintings?"

"Yes, very much."

He stood next to her and gazed up at the art work. "I would like to speak with you," he said.

"Yes, go ahead."

"Not now." He looked around the gallery before saying so softly she almost missed it, "Tomorrow night at eleven, at the St. Mary Magdalene Church in Kapisztrán tér."

Cahill stared at him.

"In the back, behind the tower. At eleven. I will wait only five minutes. Thank you. Goodbye." Cahill watched him cross the large room, his head swiveling to take in the faces he passed, his short, squat body lumbering from side to side.

She immediately returned to her apartment, showered, changed clothes, and went to Stan Podgorsky's apartment.

"Hi, Lil," Cahill said to his wife when she answered the door. "Sorry to barge in but . . ."

"Just a typical Hungarian Saturday at home," she said. "I'm baking cookies and Stan's reading a clandestine issue of *Playboy*. Like I said, just your run-of-the mill Hungarian weekend."

"I have to talk to you," Cahill told him in the crowded little living room. "I've just had something happen that could be important."

They took a walk and she told him what had transpired in the museum.

"What do you know about him?" he asked.

"Not much, just that he's a psychologist at the hospital and . . ."

"He's also KGB," Podgorsky said.

"You know that for certain?"

"I sure do. Not only is he KGB, he's attached to the SK, the group that keeps tabs on every Russian here. If he's making an overture to us, Collette, he could be playing games—or he could be damn valuable. No, Christ, that's an understatement. He could be gold, pure gold."

"I wonder why he sought me out," she said.

"It doesn't matter. He liked the way you looked, sensed someone he could trust. Who knows? What matters is that we follow up on it and not do anything to scare him off, on the long shot that he might be turned—or *has* turned." He looked at his watch, said, "Look, go on home and pack a small overnight bag. I'll meet you at the embassy in two hours, after I get hold of some others we need on this. Take a circle route to the embassy. Make sure nobody's tailing you. Anybody look interested in your conversation with him at the museum?"

"I really wasn't looking for anyone, but he sure was. He was a wreck."

"Good. And for good reason. Okay, two hours, and be ready for a marathon."

The next thirty-six hours were intense and exhausting. By the time Cahill headed for the square of St. John Capistrano, she'd had a complete briefing on Árpád Hegedüs provided by the station's counterintelligence branch, whose job it was to create biographical files on everyone in Budapest working for the other side.

A gray Russian four-door Zim with two agents was assigned to follow her to the street-meet with Hegedüs. The rules that had been laid down for her were simple and inviolate.

She was to accept nothing from him, not a scrap of paper, not a matchbook, *nothing*, to avoid being caught in the standard espionage trap of being handed a document from the other side, then immediately put under arrest for spying.

If anything seemed amiss (*"Anything!"* Podgorsky had stressed), she was to terminate the meeting and walk to a corner two blocks away where the car would pick her up. The same rule applied if he wasn't alone.

The small Charter Arms .38-caliber special revolver she carried in her raincoat pocket was to remain there unless absolutely necessary for her physical protection. If that need arose, the two agents in the Zim would back her up with M-3 submachine guns with silencers.

She was to commit to nothing to Hegedüs. He'd called the meet, and it was her role to listen to what he had to say. If he indicated he wished to become a double agent, she was to set another meeting at a safehouse that was about to be discarded. No sense exposing an ongoing location to him until you were sure he was legit.

Cahill lingered in front of a small café down the street from the Gothic church. She was grateful for its presence. Her heart was beating and she drew deep breaths to calm down. Her watch read 10:50. He said he'd wait only five minutes. She couldn't be late.

The gray Zim passed, the agents looking straight ahead but taking her in with their peripheral vision. She walked away from the café and approached the church, still in ruins except for the meticulously restored tower. She had a silly thought—she wished there were fog to shroud the scene and to give it more the atmosphere of spy-meeting-spy. There wasn't; it was a pristine night in Budapest. The moon was nearly full and cast a bright floodlight over the tiny streets and tall church.

She went behind the church, stopped, looked around, saw no one. Maybe he wouldn't show. Podgorsky had raised that possibility. "More times than not they get cold feet," he'd told her. "Or maybe he's been made. He's put his neck way out on a limb even talking to you, Collette, and you may have seen the last of him."

She had mixed emotions. She hoped he wouldn't show up. She hoped he would. After all, that's what her new job with the CIA in Budapest was all about, to find just such a person and to turn him into a successful and productive counterspy against his own superiors. That it had happened so fast, so easily, was unlikely, was . . . "Life is what happens while you're making other plans," her father had always said.

"Miss Cahill."

His voice shocked her. Although she was expecting him, she was not ready for his voice, any voice. She gasped, afraid to turn.

Hegedüs came out of the shadows of the church and stood behind her. She slowly turned. "Mr. Hegedüs," she said in a shaky voice. "You're here."

"*Igen*, I am here, and so are you."

"Yes, I . . . "

"I will be brief. For reasons of my own I wish to help you and your country. I wish to help Hungary, my country, rid itself of our most recent conquerors."

"What sort of help?"

"Information. I understand you are always in need of information."

"That's true," she said. "You realize the risk you take?"

"Of course. I have thought about this for a very long time."

"And what do you want in return? Money?"

"Yes, but that is not my only motivation."

"We'll have to talk about money. I don't have the authority to . . . " She wished she hadn't said it. It was important that he put his complete trust in her. To suggest that he'd have to talk to others wasn't professional.

It didn't seem to deter him. He looked up at the church tower and smiled. "This was a beautiful country, Miss Cahill. Now it is . . . " A deep sigh. "No matter. Here." He pulled two sheets of paper from his raincoat pocket and thrust them at her. Instinctively, she reached for them, then withdrew her hand. His expression was one of puzzlement.

"I don't want anything from you now, Mr. Hegedüs. We'll have to meet again. Is that acceptable to you?"

"Do I have a choice?"

"Yes, you can reconsider your offer and withdraw it."

It was a rueful laugh. "Pilots reach a point in their flight that represents no return. Once they pass it, they are committed to continuing to their final destination—or crashing. It is the same with me."

Cahill pronounced slowly and in a clear voice the address of the safehouse that had been chosen. She told him the date and time: exactly one week from that night, at nine in the evening.

"I shall be there, and I shall bring what I have here to that meeting."

"Good. Again, I must ask whether you understand the potential ramifications of what you're doing?"

"Miss Cahill, I am not a stupid man."

"No, I didn't mean to suggest that. . . . "

"I know you didn't. You are not that kind of person. I could tell that the moment I met you, and that is why it was you I contacted."

"I appreciate that, Mr. Hegedüs, and I look forward to our next meeting. You have the address?"

"Yes, I do. *Viszontlátásra!*" He disappeared into the shadows. Somehow, his simple "Goodbye" was inadequate for Collette.

If the meet went smoothly, she was not to get into the Zim but return to her apartment by public transportation. A half hour after she'd arrived, there was a knock on the door. She opened it. It was Joe Breslin. "Hey, just in the neighborhood and thought I could buy you a drink."

She realized he was there as part of what had gone on at the church. She put on her coat and they went to an outdoor café, where he handed her a note that read, *"Tell me what happened without mentioning names or getting specific. Use a metaphor—baseball, ballet, whatever."*

She recounted the meeting with Hegedüs as Breslin lighted his pipe and used the match to incidentally ignite the small slip of paper he'd handed her. They both watched it turn to ash in an ashtray.

When she was done, he looked at her, smiled his characteristic half-smile, touched her hand. "Excellent," he said. "You look beat. These things don't take a hell of a lot of time, but they drain you. So drain a *hosszúlépés* and I'll take you home. If anyone's tail is on us, they'll think we're having just another typical, torrid, capitalistic affair."

Her laugh caught, became almost a giggle. "After what I've been through, Joe, I think we should make it a *fröccs*." Two parts wine to one part soda, the reverse of what he'd suggested.

Now, two years later, she prepared for another meet with the Fisherman. How many had there been, fifteen, twenty, maybe more? It had gotten easier, of course. She and "her spy" had become good friends. It was supposed to end up that way, according to the handbook on handling agents-in-place. As Árpád Hegedüs's case officer, Cahill was paid to think of everything that might compromise him, threaten him, *anything* that conceivably could jeopardize him and his mission. So many rules she had to remember and remind herself of whenever a situation came up.

Rule One: The agent himself is more important than any given piece of information he might be able to deliver. Always consider the long haul, never the immediate gain.

Rule Two: Never do anything to jog his conscience. Never ask for more than his conscience will allow him to deliver.

Rule Three: Money. Small and steady. A change in basic lifestyle tips off the other side. Make him come to depend upon it. No bonuses for delivering an especially important piece of information, no matter how risky it was to obtain. Among other reasons, don't reveal how important any one piece of information might be.

Rule Four: Be alert to his moods and personal habits. Be his friend. Hear him out. Counsel when it's appropriate, hear his confessions, help him stay out of trouble.

Rule Five: Don't lose him.

This meet had been arranged like all the others. When Hegedüs had something to pass on, he left a red thumbtack in a utility pole around the corner from his home. The pole was checked each day by a Hungarian postman who'd been on the CIA payroll for years. If the tack was there, he called a special number at the American Embassy within ten minutes. The person answering the phone said, "International Wildlife Committee," to which the postman would respond, "I was thinking of going fishing this weekend and wondered about conditions." He would then abruptly hang up. The person who'd taken the call would inform either Stan Podgorsky, Collette Cahill, or the station's technical coordinator and second-in-command, Harold "Red" Sutherland, a hulk of a man with sparse red hair, feet that had broken down years ago beneath his weight, and who was fond of red suspenders and railroad handkerchiefs. Red was an electronics genius, responsible for video and audio eavesdropping for the Budapest station, including an elaborate recording operation in the safehouse where Cahill and Hegedüs met.

It was understood that a meet would take place exactly one week from the day the tack was found, at a predetermined time and place. Cahill had informed Hegedüs at their last get-together of the change in safehouses, which was acceptable to him.

Cahill arrived an hour before Hegedüs. The recording and photographic equipment was tested, and Cahill went over a set of notes she and others at the station had developed. Hegedüs's desk officer back at Langley, Virginia, had transmitted a series of "RQMs," intelligence requirements, that they wanted met from this most recent meet. They all involved the operation known as Banana Quick. Primarily, they needed to know how much the Soviets knew about it. Cahill had given the requirement to Hegedüs at their last meeting and he'd promised to come up with whatever he could.

When Árpád Hegedüs walked into the room, he chuckled. A table was set with his favorite foods, which had been brought in that afternoon—*libamáj*, goose liver; *rántott gombafejek*, champignon mushroom caps that had been fried in the kitchen by Red Sutherland shortly before Hegedüs's arrival; a plate of cheeses, Pálpusztai, Márványsajt, and a special Hungarian cream cheese with paprika and caraway seeds known as körözött. For dessert there was a heaping platter of *somlói galuska*, small pieces of sponge cake covered with chocolate and whipped cream—they were a passion for Hegedüs. Everything would be washed down with bourbon. He'd been served vodka early in the game, but one night he expressed a preference for American bourbon and Red Sutherland arranged for Langley to ship in a case of Blanton's, the brand Sutherland, a dedicated bourbon drinker, claimed was the best. An hour-long meeting on the subject of which bourbon to sneak into Hungary had been held behind embassy closed doors and, as often happened, it became a project with a name—"Project Abe," referring to Abraham Lincoln's pre-political career as a bourbon distiller.

"You look well, Árpád," Cahill said.

He smiled. "Not nearly as good as you, Collette. You're wearing my favorite outfit." She'd forgotten that at a previous meeting he'd complimented her on the blue and gray dress she had on again this night. She thanked him and motioned toward a small bar in the corner of the room. He went to it, rubbed his hands, and said, "Splendid. I look forward to these evenings for seeing Mr. Blanton almost as much as for seeing you."

"As long as I'm still the most important, the highest proof, you might say" she said. He seemed puzzled; she explained. He grinned and said, "Ah, yes, the proof. The proof is always important." He poured himself a full glass and dropped an ice cube from a silver bucket into it, causing the amber liquid to spill over the sides. He apologized. Cahill ignored him and poured herself an orange juice, almost as rare in Budapest as bourbon.

"Hungry?" she asked.

"*Always*," he answered, his eyes lighting up as if there were candles on the table. He sat and filled a plate. Cahill took a few morsels and sat across from him.

Hegedüs looked around the room, as though suddenly

realizing he was in a new place. "I like the other house better," he said.

"It was time to change," Cahill said. "Too long in one place makes everyone nervous."

"Except me."

"Except you. How are things?"

"Good . . . bad." He waved his pudgy hand over his plate. "This will be our last meeting."

Cahill's heart tripped. "Why?" she asked.

"At least for some time. They are talking of sending me to Moscow."

"What for?"

"Who knows how the Russian mind works, what it's for? My family packs now and will leave in three days."

"You won't be with them?"

"Not immediately. It had occurred to me that sending them has other meanings." He answered her eyebrows. "It has been happening to others recently. The family is sent to Russia and the man stays behind expecting to join them but . . . well, he never does." He devoured two of the mushrooms, washed them down with bourbon, put his elbows on the table, and leaned forward. "The Soviets become more paranoid every day here in Hungary."

"About what?"

"About what? About security, about leaks to your people. Having the families in Russia is a way to control certain . . . how shall I say? . . . certain questionable individuals."

"Are you now considered 'questionable'?"

"I didn't think so, but this move of my family and talk of moving me . . . Who knows? Do you mind?" He indicated his empty glass.

"Of course not, but put the ice in first," she said lightly. She'd been growing increasingly concerned about his drinking. Almost the entire bottle had been consumed last time, and he was quite drunk when he left.

He returned to the table and sipped from his fresh drink. "I have news for you, Collette. What did you call your request last time—an RQM?"

"Yes, a requirement. What is the news?"

"They know more than your people perhaps realize."

"About Banana Quick?"

"Yes. That island they've taken has been doing its job. The surveillance equipment on it is their best, and they've recruited native people who have been passing on information about your activities."

The Russians had leased the private island in the British Virgins from its owner, a multimillionaire British real estate developer who was told it was to be used as a rest-and-recreation area for tired, high-ranking Soviet bureaucrats. The U.S. State Department, upon learning of this and after hurried conferences with the CIA, approached him and asked that he reconsider. He wouldn't. The deal went through and the Russians moved in.

A further assessment was made then by State and Central Intelligence. Their conclusion: The Soviets could not move in enough sophisticated equipment and staff in time to effectively monitor Banana Quick, nor had they enough agents in place to build an effective corps of citizen-spies.

"Can you be more specific?" Cahill asked.

"Of course." He pulled papers from his rumpled black suit jacket and handed them to her. She laid them flat on the table and started reading. When she was done with the first page, she looked up at him and allowed a tiny whistle to come through her lips. "They know a lot, don't they?"

"Yes. These dispatches arrived from the island outpost. It was all I felt I could safely take—and bring with me. I return them in the morning. However, I have seen many more and have done my best to commit them to memory. Shall I begin?"

Cahill looked to the wall that concealed the cameras and recorders. Hegedüs knew they were there and often joked about them, but they remained shielded from his view, the sight of such instruments providing neither inspiration nor incentive. She prompted him to start before more of the bourbon disappeared and his memory with it.

He talked, drank, ate, and recalled for three hours. Cahill focused on everything he said, making notes to herself despite knowing every word was being recorded. Transcripts seldom provide nuance. She pushed him for details, kept him going when he seemed ready to fade, complimented, cajoled, stroked, and encouraged.

"Anything else?" she asked once he'd sat back, lighted a cigarette, and allowed a permanent smile of satisfaction to form on his thick lips.

"No, I think that is all." He suddenly raised his index finger and sat up. "No, I am wrong, there is more. The name of a man you know has come up."

"What man? I know him?"

"Yes. The psychiatrist who is involved with your *Company*."

"You mean Tolker?" She was instantly furious at herself for mentioning the name. Maybe he didn't mean him. If so, she'd given the name of a CIA-connected physician to the other side. It was a relief to hear him say, "Yes, that is the one. Dr. Jason Tolker."

"What about him?"

"I'm not really sure, Collette, but his name was mentioned briefly in connection with one of the dispatches from our island listening post about Banana Quick."

"Was it positive? I mean, were they saying that . . . ?"

"They said nothing specific. It was the tone of the voices, the context in which it was said that led me to believe that Dr. Tolker might be . . . *friendly*."

"To you. To the Soviets."

"Yes."

Cahill had forgotten about Barrie during the session. Now her image filled the room. She wasn't sure how to respond to what Hegedüs had said, so said nothing.

"I am afraid I am becoming an expensive friend to you and your people, Collette. Look, the bourbon is all but finished."

She resisted mentioning that it always was, said instead, "There's always more to replace it, Árpád. But not to replace you. Tell me, how are things with you personally?"

"I shall miss my family but . . . perhaps this is the time to bring up what is on my mind."

"Go ahead."

"I have been thinking, I have been feeling lately that the time might be approaching for me to consider becoming one of you."

"You are. You know that. . . ." She observed him shaking his head. He was smiling.

"You mean time to defect to our side?"

"Yes."

"I don't know about that, Árpád. As I told you when that subject came up before, it isn't something I deal with."

"But you said you would talk to those in charge about the possibility."

"Yes, I did." She didn't want to tell him that the discussion with Podgorsky and with two people from Langley had resulted in a flat denial. Their attitude was that Árpád Hegedüs was valuable to them as long as he remained ensconced in the Hungarian and Soviet hierarchy and could provide information from the inner councils. As a defector, he was useless. Of course, if it meant saving him in the event he'd been uncovered by his superiors, that would create a different scenario; but Cahill had been instructed in no uncertain terms that she was to do everything in her power to dissuade him from such a move, and to foster his continued services as an agent.

"It was not met with enthusiasm, I take it," he said.

"It isn't that, Árpád, it's just that—"

"That I am worth more where I am."

She drew a breath and fell back in her chair. It was naive of her to think he wouldn't know exactly the reason without being told. He worked for an organization, the KGB, that played by the same rules, operated from the same set of needs and intelligence philosophies.

"Don't look worried, Collette. I do understand. And I intend to continue functioning as I have. But, if the need arises, it would be comforting to me and my family to know that the possibility was there."

"I appreciate your understanding, Árpád, and I shall bring it up with my people again."

"I am grateful. Well, what do you say, 'One for the road'?

I shall have one, and then the road, and then home."

"I'll join you."

They sat in silence at the table and sipped from their drinks. His smile was gone; a sadness that pulled down the flesh of his face had replaced it.

"You're more upset about your family going to Moscow than you want to admit," she said.

He nodded, eyes on his glass. He grunted, looked up, and said, "I have never told you about my family, about my dear children."

Collette smiled. "No, you haven't, except that your daughter is very beautiful and sweet, and that your son is a fine boy."

There was a flicker of a smile, then gloom again. "My son is a genius, a very bright boy. He is sensitive and loves artistic things." He leaned forward and spoke with renewed animation. "You should see how the boy draws and paints, Collette. Beauty, always such beauty, and the poetry he writes touches me so deeply."

"You must be very proud," Collette said.

"Proud? Yes. And concerned for his future."

"Because—"

"Because in Russia, he will have little chance to develop his talents. For the girl, my daughter, it is not so bad. She will marry because she is pretty. For him . . ." He shook his head and finished his drink.

Cahill was tempted to come around and hug him. Any initial thoughts of the chauvinistic attitude he'd expressed were tempered by her understanding of the society in which he, and his family, functioned.

She thought, then said, "It would be better for your son here in Hungary, wouldn't it?"

"Yes, there is more freedom here, but who knows when that will end? America would be best. I am not a religious man, Collette, but I sometimes pray to someone that my son will be allowed to grow up in America."

"As I said before, Árpád, I'll try to . . ."

He wanted to continue, and did. "When I first came to you and offered my services, I talked about how my beloved Hungary had been destroyed by the Soviets. I talked of disgust with their system and ways, of how this wonderful country has been forevermore changed by them." He sighed deeply, sat back, and nodded in agreement with whatever he was thinking at the moment. "I was not completely honest, Collette. I came to you because I wanted to find a way to see my family—my son—reach America. Instead, he goes to Moscow."

Cahill stood. "Árpád, I will make every effort to help bring that about. No promises, but a decent effort."

He stood, too, and extended his hand. She took it. "Thank you, Collette. I know you will do what you say. I have been here a long time. I must go."

He was paid and she escorted him to the door. She said, "Árpád, be careful. Don't take risks. Please."

"Of course not." He looked back to the center of the room. "The tape and camera are off?"

"I assume they are. The main show is over."

He motioned her into the hall and spoke in a whisper, so close to her ear that his lips touched it. "I am in love."

"In . . . love?"

"I have met a wonderful woman recently and . . . "

"I don't think that's a good idea," Cahill said.

"Good idea, bad idea, it has happened. She is very beautiful and we have commenced . . . an affair."

Collette wasn't sure what to say, except, "What about your family, Árpád? You say you love them so much and . . . "

His grin was sheepish, a little boy caught in a quandary. His eyes averted her and he shuffled his feet. Then he looked at her and said, "There are different forms of love, Collette. Surely, that reality is not a Socialist aberration." He cocked his head and waited for a response.

Cahill said, "We should meet again soon and discuss this. In the meantime, take extra care. Discuss what you're doing with no one. No one, Árpád."

"With her?" His laugh was guttural. "We have so little time together that discussion is the last thing on our minds. *Köszönöm*, Collette."

"Thank *you*, Árpád."

"Until the next time a tack appears in the pole. *Viszontlátásra!*"

Rule Six: Do anything you can to keep your agent from having an affair—at least with anyone else.

5

Collette Cahill got off a Malev flight in London, went to a phone booth, and dialed a number. A woman answered, "Eleven, Cadogan Gardens."

"My name is Collette Cahill. I was a close friend of Barrie Mayer."

"Oh, yes, what a tragedy. I'm so sorry."

"Yes, we were all terribly shocked. I've just arrived in London for a few days' vacation and wondered if you had any available rooms?"

"Yes, we do, a few suites as a matter of fact. Oh, goodness."

"What?"

"Number 27 is available. It was Miss Mayer's favorite."

"Yes, that's right, she always talked about it. That would be fine with me."

"You wouldn't mind . . . ?"

"Staying where she'd stayed? No, not at all. I'll be there within the hour."

She spent the first hour sitting in the Victorian living room and imagining what Barrie had done the last day and night of her life while in London. Had she watched television,

51

gone across to the private park, read, called friends, napped, walked the pretty, quiet streets of Chelsea and Belgravia, shopped for relatives back home? It eventually became too sad an exercise. She went downstairs to the main drawing room and flipped through an array of magazines and newspapers, then caught the attention of one of the hall porters. "Yes, ma'am?" he said.

"I was a very good friend of Miss Mayer, the lady who'd stayed in Number 27 and who recently died."

"Poor Miss Mayer. She was one of my favorite guests whenever she was here, a real lady. We're all terribly sad at what happened."

"I was wondering whether she did anything special the day she arrived, the day before she died?"

"Special? No, not really. I brought her tea at three . . . let me see, yes, I'm quite certain it was three o'clock the afternoon she arrived. We made a reservation for her that evening at the Dorchester for dinner."

"For how many people?"

"Two. Yes, for two. I can check."

"No, that's all right. Did she take a taxi, or did someone pick her up?"

"She took the limousine."

"*The* limousine?"

"Ours. It's available to our guests twenty-four hours a day."

"Did the limousine pick her up at the Dorchester?"

"I don't know, madam. I wasn't here that evening when she returned, but I can ask."

"Would you mind?"

"Of course not."

He returned a few minutes later and said, "To the best of recollection, Miss Mayer returned a little before ten that evening. She arrived by taxi."

"Alone?"

He looked at the floor. "I'm not sure, madam, whether that would be discreet to comment upon."

Cahill smiled. "I'm not snooping. It's just that we were such good friends and her mother back in the States asked me to find out what I could about her daughter's last hours."

"Of course. I understand. Let me ask."

He returned again and said, "She was alone. She announced she was going straightaway to bed and left an early call. That was the morning she was leaving for Hungary, I believe."

"Yes, that's right, to Budapest. Tell me, didn't the police come and ask questions about her?"

"Not to my knowledge. They came and took her things from the room and . . ."

"Who's *they*?"

"Friends, business colleagues, I think. You'd have to ask the manager about that. They spoke to her. They took everything and were gone within ten minutes. The other one . . . there were three chaps . . . he stayed behind for at least an hour. I remember he said he wanted to sit where Miss Mayer had spent her last hours and think. Poor chap, I felt terrible for him."

"Did any of them have names?"

"I feel like I'm getting a proper interrogation," he said, not angrily but with enough of an edge to cause Cahill to back off. She smiled. "I guess so many people knew and loved her that we're not behaving in our usual manner. Sorry, I didn't mean to ask so many questions of you. I'll check with the manager a little later."

He returned the smile. "No problem, madam. I understand. Ask me anything you wish."

"Oh, I think I've asked enough. Did they have names, the men who came here and took her things?"

"Not that I recall. They might have muttered something or other but . . . Yes, one of them said he was a business associate of Miss Mayer. I believe he said his name was Mr. Hubler."

"David Hubler?"

"I don't think he used a first name, madam."

"What did he look like? Was he fairly short, dark, lots of black curly hair, handsome?"

"That doesn't quite fit my memory of him, madam. Tall and sandy would be more like it."

Cahill sighed and said, "Well, thank you so much. I think I'll go back upstairs and take a nap."

"May I bring you anything? Tea at three?"

Like Barrie, Cahill thought. "No, make it four," she said.

"Yes, madam."

She called David Hubler a few minutes before tea was scheduled to arrive. It was almost eleven in the morning in Washington. "David, Collette Cahill."

"Hi, Collette."

"I'm calling from London, David. I'm staying in the same hotel Barrie always used."

"Eleven, Cadogan. What are you doing there?"

"Trying to sort out my mind about what happened. I took a vacation and am heading home, but thought I'd stop here on the way."

There was silence.

"David?"

"Yeah, sorry. I was just thinking about Barrie. Unbelievable."

"Have you been here in London since she died?"

"Me? No. Why?"

"Someone at the hotel thought you might have been the one who picked up her things from the room."

"Not me, Collette."

"Were any of her things sent back to you at the office?"

"Just her briefcase."

"Her briefcase. Was it the one she usually carried?"

"Sure. Why?"

"Oh, nothing. What was in it?"

"Papers, a couple of manuscripts. Why are you asking?"

"I don't know, David. My mind just hasn't functioned since you called me with the news. What's happening back there? The agency must be in chaos."

"Sort of, although not as bad as you might think. Barrie was incredible, Collette, but you know that. She left everything in perfect order, right down to the last detail. You know what she did for me?"

"What?"

"She had me in her will. She left me insurance money, one of those key-man policies. In effect, she left me the agency."

Cahill was surprised, enough so that she wasn't quite sure what to say. He filled the gap with, "I don't mean she left it all to me, Collette. Her mother benefits from it, but she structured things so that I'm to run it for a minimum of five years and share in the profits. I was flabbergasted."

"That was wonderful of her."

"Typical of her is more like it. When will you be back in Washington?"

"A day or two. I'll stop by."

"Please do, Collette. Let's have lunch or dinner. There's a lot we can talk about."

"I'd like that. By the way, do you have any idea who she might have seen here in London before . . . before it happened?"

"Sure, Mark Hotchkiss. They were scheduled for dinner the night she arrived."

"Who's he?"

"A British literary agent Barrie liked. Why, I don't know. I think he's a swine and I told her so but, for some reason, she kept talking to him about linking up. With all Barrie's brights, Collette, there were certain people who could con her, and Hotchkiss is one."

"Know how I can reach him while I'm here?"

"Sure." He gave her an address and phone number. "But watch out for him, Collette. Remember, I said swine, *co-chon*."

"Thanks, David. See you soon."

She replaced the phone in its cradle as the porter knocked. She opened the door. He placed the tea tray on a coffee table and backed out of the suite, leaving her sitting in a gold wingback chair. She wore a light blue robe; shafts of late-afternoon sunlight sliced through gaps in the white curtains and across the worn Oriental rug that took up the center of the room. One beam of light striped her bare foot and she thought of Barrie, who was always so proud of her feet, gently arched and with long, slender toes that were perfectly sized in relation to each other. Cahill looked at her own foot, short and stubby, and smiled, then laughed. "God, we were different," she said aloud as she poured her tea and smeared clotted cream and black cherry jam over a piece of scone.

She caught Mark Hotchkiss just as he was leaving his office, introduced herself, and asked if he were free for dinner.

"Afraid not, Miss Cahill."

"Breakfast?"

"You say you're Barrie's friend?"

"Yes, we were best friends."

"She never mentioned you."

"Were you that friendly that she would have?"

His laugh was forced. He said, "I suppose we could meet for something in the morning. You have a decent place near you on Sloane Street, right around the corner. It's a café in back of the General Trading Company. Nine?"

"Fine. See you then."

"Miss Cahill."

"Yes?"

"You do know that Barrie and I had entered into a partnership arrangement just prior to her death?"

"No, I didn't know that, but I was aware it was being discussed. Why do you bring it up now?"

"Why not bring it up *now*?"

"No reason. You can tell me all about it in the morning. I look forward to it."

"Yes. Well, cheerio. Pleasant evening. Enjoy London. The theater season is quite good this year."

She hung up agreeing with David Hubler. She didn't like Hotchkiss, and wondered what aspect of him had seduced Barrie into entering a "partnership agreement," if that claim were true.

She called downstairs and asked if they could get her tickets to a show. Which one? "It doesn't matter," Cahill said, "something happy."

The curtain went up on *Noises Off* at seven-thirty, and by the time the British farce was over, Cahill's sides hurt from laughing, and the unpleasant reason for her trip had been forgotten, at least for the duration of the show. She was hungry, had a light dinner at the Neal Street Restaurant, and returned to the hotel. A porter brought cognac and ice to her room and she sat quietly and sipped it until her eyes began to close. She went to bed, aware as she fell asleep of the absolute quiet of this street and this hotel, as quiet as the dead.

6

Cahill arrived on time at the General Trading Company, whose coat of arms heralded the fact that it had provided goods to at least one royal household. She took a table in the rear outdoor area. The morning had dawned sunny and mild. A raincoat over a heather tweed suit made her perfectly comfortable.

She passed the time with a cup of coffee and watching tiny birds make swooping sorties on uncovered bowls of brown sugar cubes on the tables. She glanced at her watch; Hotchkiss was already twenty minutes late. She'd give it ten more minutes. At precisely nine-thirty, he came through the store and stepped onto the terrace. He was tall and angular. His head was bald on top, but he'd combed back long hair on the sides, giving him the startling appearance of—not swine, David, she thought, duck—he looked like a duck's rear end. He wore a double-breasted blue blazer with a crest on its pocket, gray slacks, a pair of tan Clark's desert boots, a pale blue shirt with white collar, and a maroon silk tie. He carried a battered and bulging leather briefcase beneath his arm. A similarly well-worn trench coat was slung over his shoulder.

"Miss Cahill," he said with energy. He smiled and extended his hand, his teeth markedly yellow, and she noticed immediately that his fingernails were too long and needed cleaning.

"Mr. Hotchkiss," she said, taking his hand with her fingertips.

"Sorry I'm late but traffic is bastardly this hour. You've had coffee. Good."

Cahill stifled a smile and watched him ease into a white metal chair with yellow cushions. "Not chilly?" he asked. "Better inside?"

"Oh, no, I think it's lovely out here."

"As you wish." He made an elaborate gesture at one of the young waitresses, who came to the table and took their order for coffee and pastry. When she'd gone, he sat back, formed a tent beneath his chin with his fingers, and said, "Well, now, we're obviously here to discuss Barrie Mayer, poor dear, may she rest in peace. You were friends, you say?"

"Yes, close friends."

"She never mentioned you, but I suppose someone like Barrie had so many friends or, at least, acquaintances."

"We were close *friends*," Cahill said, not enjoying his inference.

"Yes, of course. Now, what was it you wished to discuss with me?"

"Your relationship with Barrie, what she did the night before she died, anything that might help me understand."

"Understand? Understand *what*? The poor woman dropped dead of a heart attack, coronary thrombosis, premature certainly but Lord knows what life has in store for any of us."

Cahill had to remind herself of her "official" role in looking into Mayer's life. She was a grieving friend, not an investigator, and her approach would have to soften to reflect that. She said, "I'm actually as interested for Barrie's mother's sake as I am for my own. We've been in contact and she asked me to find out anything that would . . . well, comfort her. I'm on my way to Washington now to see her."

"What do you do for a living, Miss Cahill? I know that's

hardly a British question, more what you Americans seem always to ask at first meeting, but I am curious."

"I work for the United States Embassy in Budapest."

"Budapest! I've never been. Is it as gray and grim as we hear?"

"Not at all. It's a lovely city."

"With all those soldiers and red stars."

"They fade into the background after a while. You had dinner with Barrie the night before she died."

"Indeed, at the Dorchester. Despite the Arabs, it still has London's finest chef."

"I wouldn't know."

"You must let me take you. Tonight?"

"I can't, but thank you. What mood was Barrie in that night? What did she say, do? Did she seem sick?"

"She was in the pink of health, Miss Cahill. May I call you Collette? I'm Mark, of course."

"Of course." She laughed. "Yes, call me Collette. You say she seemed healthy. Was she happy?"

"Irrepressibly so. I mean, after all, we forged a partnership that evening. She was bubbling."

"You mentioned on the phone that you'd become partners. I spoke with David Hubler in Barrie's Washington office. He had no idea it had gone that far."

"David Hubler. I dislike being indiscreet but I must admit Mr. Hubler is not my favorite person. Frankly, I thought he was a stone about Barrie's neck, and I told her so."

"I like David. I always understood from Barrie that she was extremely fond of him, and had great professional respect for him."

"Besides being a consummate businesswoman, Barrie Mayer was also gullible."

Cahill thought of Hubler saying the same thing. She said to Hotchkiss, "Mark, are you aware of Barrie's will and what it contains relative to David Hubler?"

"No." He laughed loudly, revealing the yellowed teeth. "Oh, you mean that nonsense about ensuring that Hubler runs the Washington office if she should die. A bone, that's all, a bone tossed at him. Now that the agency . . . *all of it*

. . . passes to me, the question of Mr. Hubler's future has little to do with a piece of worthless paper."

"Why?"

"Because the agreement Barrie and I entered into takes precedence over what was decreed before." He smiled smugly and formed the finger tent again. The waitress delivered their coffee and pastry and Hotchkiss held up his cup. "To the memory of a lovely, talented, and beautiful woman, Barrie Mayer, and to you, Miss Collette Cahill, her dear friend." He sipped his coffee, then asked, "Are you truly not free this evening? The Dorchester has a very nice dance band and, as I said, the chef is without parallel in London these days of mediocre food. Sure?" He cocked his head and elevated one bushy eyebrow.

"Sure, but thank you. You signed a paper with Barrie that night?"

"Yes."

"May I . . . I know this is none of my business, but . . ."

"I'm afraid it would be inappropriate at this time for me to show it to you. Are you doubting me?"

"Not at all. Again, it's just a matter of wanting to know *everything* about her just before she died. Did you go to the airport with her the next morning?"

"No."

"I just thought . . ."

"I dropped Barrie back at the hotel. That was the last time I saw her."

"In a taxi?"

"Yes. My goodness, I'm beginning to feel as though you might have an interest beyond that of a close friend."

Cahill grinned. "The hall porter at the hotel said the same thing. Forgive me. Too many years of asking stranded American tourists where they might have lost their passports."

"Is that what you do at the embassy?"

"Among other things. Well, Mark, this was extremely pleasant."

"And informative, I trust. I'll be coming to Washington

soon to tidy up things at the agency. Do you know where you'll be staying?"

"With my mother. She lives outside the city."

"Splendid. I shall call you there."

"Why not contact me through David Hubler? I'll be spending considerable time with him."

"Oh, I think I've placed one foot in one very large mouth."

"Not at all." She stood. "Thank you."

He stood, too, and accepted her hand. They both looked down at the check the waitress had placed on the table. "My treat," Cahill said, knowing it was what he wanted her to say.

"Oh, no, that would be . . ."

"Please. I initiated this. Perhaps I'll see you in Washington."

"I certainly hope so."

Hotchkiss left. Cahill stopped on her way through the large store to buy her mother a set of fancy placemats, and a book for her nephew. She walked around the corner to the hotel, where she made a series of calls to the physicians who'd performed the autopsy on Barrie and whose names she'd gotten from Red Sutherland before leaving Budapest. The only one she reached was a Dr. Willard Hymes. She introduced herself as Barrie Mayer's closest friend and asked if she could arrange to meet with him.

"Whatever for?" he asked. He sounded young.

"Just to put my mind, and her mother's mind, at rest."

"Well, Miss Cahill, you know I'm not at liberty to discuss autopsy findings except with designated authorities."

Pickle Factory authorities, Cahill thought. She said, "I understand that, Dr. Hymes, but it wouldn't breach any confidences if you were to tell me the circumstances of the autopsy, your informal, off-the-record reactions to her, what she looked like, things like that."

"No, Miss Cahill, that would be quite out of the question. Thank you for calling."

Cahill said quickly, "I was concerned about the glass that was found in her face."

"Pardon?"

Cahill continued. She'd read up on past cases in which prussic acid had been used to "terminate" agents on both sides. One of the telltale signs was tiny slivers of glass blown into a victim's face along with the acid. "Dr. Hymes, there was glass in her face."

She was guessing, but had drawn blood. He made a few false starts before getting out, "Who told you about the glass?"

That was all she needed, wanted. She said, "A mutual friend who'd been at the airport and saw her just after she died."

"I didn't know there was a friend with her."

"Were you at the airport?"

"No. She was brought here to clinic and . . ."

"Dr. Hymes, I really appreciate the chance to talk with you. You've been very generous with your time and I know Barrie's mother will appreciate it."

She hung up, sat at a small desk near the French windows, and wrote a list of names on a piece of the hotel's embossed buff stationery:

KNEW BARRIE CARRIED FOR THE CIA

Dr. Jason Tolker
Stanley Podgorsky
Red Sutherland
Collette Cahill
Langley Desk Officer
Dr. Willard Hymes
Mark Hotchkiss ???
David Hubler ???
Barrie's mother ???
Eric Edwards ???
Zoltán Réti ???
KGB ???
Others ??? Other boyfriends—Others at literary agency—Others
   at Budapest station—The World.

She squinted at what she'd written, tore the paper into tiny pieces and ignited them in an ashtray. She called downstairs and told the manager on duty that she'd be leaving the following morning.

"I hope you've enjoyed your stay," the manager said.

"Oh, yes, very much," Cahill said. "It's every bit as lovely as Miss Mayer always said it was."

7

TORTOLA, BRITISH VIRGIN ISLANDS

The twin-engine turboprop Air BVI plane from San Juan touched down on Beef Island and taxied to the small terminal. Thirty passengers deplaned, including Robert Brewster and his wife, Helen. Both looked tired and wilted. There had been a delay in San Juan, and the Air BVI flight had been hot; tiny fans installed in the open overhead racks had managed only to stir the warm, humid cabin air.

The Brewsters passed through passport control and Customs, then went to a yellow Mercedes parked behind the terminal. Helen Brewster got in. Her husband said to the native driver, "Just a few minutes." He went to a pay phone, took out a slip of paper, and dialed the number on it. "I'm calling Eric Edwards," he told the woman who answered. "He's dining with you tonight."

A few minutes later, Edwards came on the line.

"Eric, it's Bob Brewster."

"Hello, Bob. Just get in?"

"Yes."

"Pleasant trip?"

"Not especially. Helen isn't feeling well and I'm beat. The heat."

"Well, a nice week's vacation down here will straighten you out."

"I'm sure it will. We're looking forward to seeing you again."

"Same here. We must get together."

"I was thinking we could catch up for a drink this evening. We'll go to the hotel and freshen up and . . ."

"I'm tied up this evening, Bob. How about tomorrow? I have a free day. We'll take a cruise, my treat."

Brewster didn't bother, nor did he have the energy to argue. He said, "I can't speak for Helen. Call me in the morning. We're staying at Prospect Reef."

"Give my best to the manager there," Edwards said. "He's a friend, might even buy you a welcoming drink."

"I'll do that. Call me at eight."

"It'll have to be later. I'm in for a long evening."

"Eric."

"Yes?"

"Life has become very complicated lately."

"Has it? That must be why you and Helen are so tired. Simplicity is far less fatiguing. We'll talk about it tomorrow."

Eric Edwards returned to a candlelit table in the Sugar Mill Restaurant, part of a small and exclusive resort complex on Apple Bay. Across from him sat a tall, stately blond woman of about thirty-five who wore a low-cut white silk dress. Because her skin was deeply tanned, it contrasted sharply with the white dress, like teeth against the natives' dark skin. It had taken her many hours in the sun to become that color. Her skin, especially the tops of her breasts, hinted at the leathery texture it would turn to by sixty.

Her nails were long and painted an iridescent pink. Her fingers held large rings, and ten slender gold bracelets covered each wrist.

Edwards was dressed in white duck slacks, white loafers sans socks, and a crimson shirt worn open to his navel. His hair—sun-bleached blond with gray at the temples so perfectly blended that it might have come from a Hollywood makeup expert—swirled casually over his forehead, ears, and neck. The features on his tanned face were fine and angular, yet with enough coarseness to keep him from being pretty. There was sufficient worldly weariness and booze in his gray eyes to give them substance and meaning.

Eric Edwards was a handsome man, no matter what the criterion. Ask Morgana Wilson who sat across from him. Someone had, recently. "He's the most sensuous, appealing male animal I've ever known," she told a friend, "and I've known a few in my day."

Edwards smiled up at the waiter as he removed bowls that had contained curried banana soup, a house specialty. Edwards ordered another rum punch, reached across the table, and ran his fingers over the top of Morgana's hand. "You usually look beautiful. Tonight, you look spectacular," he said.

She was used to such compliments and simply said, "Thank you, darling."

They said little as they enjoyed their entrees—pasta with lime cream and red caviar, and grilled fish with fennel butter. There was little to say. Their purpose was not to exchange thoughts, only to establish an atmosphere conducive to the mating game. It wasn't new to them. They'd spent a number of intimate evenings together over the past four or five years.

She'd met Edwards during a trip to the BVI with her husband, a successful New York divorce lawyer. They'd chartered one of Edwards's yachts for an overnight cruise. Her husband returned to New York after only a few days in the islands, leaving Morgana behind to soak up a few additional days of sun. She spent them with Edwards on one of his yachts.

Six months afterward, she was divorced, and Edwards was cited as having been caught in *particeps crimini*—a corespondent to the action. "Ridiculous," he'd told her. "Your marriage was damn near over anyway." Which was true, although his powerful attraction had certainly played a role.

They saw each other no more than three or four times a year, always when she visited him in the BVI. As far as she knew, he never came to New York. In fact, he never called her when he was there. There were others to contact on those trips.

"Ready?" he asked, when she'd finished the soursop fruit ice cream and coffee.

"Always," she said.

The alarm clock next to Edwards's bed buzzed them awake at six the next morning. Morgana sat up, folded her arms across her bountiful bare breasts, and pouted. "It's too early," she said.

"Sorry, love, but I've got a charter today. I have to provision it and take care of some other things before my guests arrive." His voice was thick with sleep, and raspy from too many cigarettes.

"Will you be back tonight?"

"I think so, although you never know. Sometimes they fall in love with the boat and decide to stay out overnight."

"Or fall in love with you. Can I come?"

"No." He got out of bed and crossed the large bedroom, tripping over her discarded clothing on the floor. She watched him as he stood before one of two large windows with curved tops, the first rays of sunrise casting interesting patterns over his long, lean naked body.

"I have to leave tomorrow," she said in a little girl's voice that always grated on him.

"Yes, I know. I'll miss you."

"Will you?" She joined him at the window and they looked down from his hilltop villa to Road Harbor, the site of his chartering operation. Edwards Yacht Charters was a small company compared to the Moorings, the reigning giant of island chartering, but it had managed to do well, thanks to some innovative PR a one-man agency in New York had conceived and implemented for it. Edwards currently owned three yachts—a Morgan 46, a Gulfstar 60, and a recently purchased, Frers-designed 43-foot sloop. Finding customers in season for them wasn't difficult. Finding experienced, trustworthy captains and mates was.

She turned him so they faced and wrapped her arms about his body. She was tall; the top of her head reached his nose, and he was over six feet. The warmth of her naked body, and the damp, sweet smell of sex in her hair radiated powerfully in surges through him. "I really have to go," he said.

"So do I. I'll be back in a flash," she said, heading for the stone bathroom that was open to the sky. When she returned, he was back in bed and ready for her.

Edwards's mechanic, a skinny Tortolian named Walter who was capable of fixing anything, was on board when Edwards arrived. Native *kareso* music blared from a large portable cassette recorder. As Edwards poked his head down into the engine room, Walter said, "*Laam*, I work on this engine all night long."

Edwards laughed and mimicked him. "*Laam*, I really don't care, and I'm not paying you extra. How about that, my conniving friend?"

Walter laughed and closed a cover over the engine. "How about the boat don't run so good today, huh? How about that, my rich boss?"

"*Laam*, or Lord, or whatever it is you say, don't do that to me, and turn down the bloody radio."

The good-natured banter was standard. Edwards knew that Walter would turn himself inside out to please him, and Walter knew that Edwards appreciated him, and would slip him extra pay.

Edwards had called Robert Brewster and arranged to meet him at the dock at ten. Brewster arrived wearing madras Bermuda shorts, a white button-down shirt, high-top white sneakers, and black ankle socks. He carried a canvas flight bag. His legs were white; this would be the first exposure to sunlight they'd received all year.

"No snorkeling equipment today, huh?" Walter said to Edwards after observing the new arrival.

"No, not today," Edwards said. "Where's Jackie?"

"I see her at the coffee shop. She be down." Jackie was a native girl Edwards sometimes used to crew smaller charters. She was willing, energetic, a good sailor, and almost totally deaf. They communicated through a pidgin sign language they'd developed. She arrived a few minutes later and Edwards introduced her to Brewster, who seemed distinctly uncomfortable standing on the deck. "She doesn't hear anything," Edwards said. "If her father only owned a liquor store I'd be tempted to . . ."

"Could we get on with it?" Brewster said. "I want to get back to Helen."

"Sure. She still under the weather?"

"Yes. The heat."

"I like heat," said Edwards. "It makes you sweat—for the right reasons. Let's get going."

Fifteen minutes later, after they'd cleared the channel, Edwards hoisted sail with Jackie's help. Once everything was trimmed, he turned to Brewster, who sat next to him at the helm, and said, "What's up? What did you mean things are getting complicated?"

Brewster smiled at Jackie as she delivered a steaming cup of coffee from the galley. Edwards shook his head when she offered one to him and told her with his hands that he and his guest needed time to be alone. She nodded, grinned at Brewster, and disappeared down the galley ladder.

Brewster tasted his coffee, made a face, and said, "Too hot and too strong, Eric . . . and I don't intend to say it reflects you. All right, what's going on down here?"

"With what?"

"You know what I mean. With Banana Quick."

"Oh, *that*." He laughed and turned a winch behind him to take up slack in a sail. "As far as I'm concerned, everything's just wonderful with Banana Quick. You hear otherwise?"

"It isn't so much what I hear, Eric, it's more a matter of what's blatantly visible. The death of Miss Mayer has a lot of people upset."

"None more than me. We were close."

"Everyone knows that, and that's exactly what has people back at Langley wondering."

"Wondering about what? How she was in bed?"

Brewster shook his head and shifted on his seat so that his back was to Edwards. He said over the gentle rush of wind and whoosh of water against the keel, "Your cuteness, Eric, doesn't play well these days."

Edwards had to lean close to him to hear. Brewster suddenly turned and said into his face, "What was Barrie Mayer carrying to Budapest?"

Edwards leaned back and frowned. "How the hell would I know?"

"It's the opinion at Langley, Eric, that you damn well might know. She'd been down here to see you just before she died, hadn't she?"

Edwards shrugged. "A couple of days, something like that."

"One week exactly. Would you like her itinerary?"

"Got videos of us making love, too?"

Brewster ignored him. "And then *you* disappeared."

"Disappeared where?"

"You tell me. London?"

"As a matter of fact I did pop over there for a day. I had a . . ." He smiled. "I had an appointment."

"With Barrie Mayer?"

"No. She didn't know I was there."

"That's surprising."

"Why?"

"It's our understanding that you had become serious."

"You understand wrong. We were friends, close friends, and lovers. End of story."

Brewster chewed his cheek and said, "I don't want to be the rude guest, Eric, but you'd better listen to what I have to say. There is considerable concern that Banana Quick might have been compromised by Barrie Mayer, with your help."

"That's crap." Edwards pointed toward the private island on which the Russians had established their supposed R & R facility. "Want to stop in and ask them what's going on?"

Brewster moved to the side of the yacht and peered at the island. Edwards handed him a pair of binoculars. "Don't worry," he said, "they're used to me looking down their throats. See all that rigging on the roof? They can probably hear us better than we can hear each other." He laughed. "This game gets more ridiculous every day."

"Only for people like you, Eric." Brewster held up the binoculars and watched the island slip past. He lowered them, turned, and said, "They want you back in Washington."

"What for?"

"For . . . conversation."

"Can't do it. This is the busy season down here, Bob. How would it look if I . . . ?"

"The end of the week, and don't give me 'busy season' dialogue, Eric. You're here because you were put here. This wonderful boat of yours, and the others, are all compliments of your employer. You're to be back by the end of the week. In the meantime, they want us . . . you and I . . . to spend a little time together going over things."

"What things?"

"What's been going on in your life lately, the status of your mission here, the people you've been seeing . . ."

"Like Barrie Mayer?"

"Among others."

"How come they sent you down, Bob? You're a desk jockey . . . what's it called, employee evaluation or some nonsense like that?"

"Helen and I decided to come here on vacation and they thought—"

"No, they thought you and Helen should come here on vacation and, while you're here, have these little talks. More accurate?"

"It doesn't matter. The fact is that I'm here, they want, and you are expected to give. What do you think, Eric—that the Company set you up here in the British Virgin Islands because it likes you, felt it owed you something? You pulled off what I consider the biggest coup . . . no, let's call it what it is, the biggest scam anyone has ever pulled on the agency."

Edwards's laugh was more forced this time.

"What did they put up to get you started, Eric, a half a million, three quarters of a million?"

"Somewhere around there."

"It hasn't been cost-effective."

"Cost-effective?" Edwards guffawed. "Name me one agency front that's cost-effective. Besides, how do you measure the return?"

72

Brewster stared straight ahead.

"Whose idea was it to use the BVI as headquarters for Banana Quick?" He didn't wait for Brewster's reply. "Some genius up there at Langley decides to direct an Eastern European operation from down here. Talk to me about cost-effective. The point is that once that decision was made, there had to be a surveillance unit in place, and that's me."

"You were here before Banana Quick."

"Sure, but I have to figure it was already in the planning stages when the deal was made to send me here. What was the original reason, to make sure that these idyllic islands weren't infiltrated by the bad guys? I had to laugh at that, Bob. What they really wanted was to keep tabs on our British cousins."

"You talk too much, Eric. That's something else that has them worried. You operate too loose, get close to too many people, drink too much. . . ."

"What the hell have they appointed you, Company cleric? I do my job and I do it well. I did twelve years of dirty work while you guys basked in air conditioning at Langley, and I keep doing my job. Tell them that."

"Tell them yourself at the end of the week."

Edwards looked up into a scrim of pristine blue sky, against which puffs of white clouds quickly moved across their bow. "You had enough?" he asked.

"I was just beginning to enjoy it," Brewster answered.

"I'm getting seasick," Edwards said.

"Want a Dramamine? I took one at breakfast."

"You're getting sunburned, Bob."

"Look at you, a prime candidate for skin cancer." The two men stared at each other before Edwards said, "Tell me about Barrie Mayer."

"What's to tell? She's dead."

"Who?"

"Mother Nature. A clogged artery to the heart, blood flow ceases, the heart cries out for help, doesn't get it, and stops pumping."

Edwards smiled. Jackie came up from the galley and gestured. Did they need anything? Edwards said to Brewster, "You hungry? I stocked a few things."

"Sure. Whatever you have."

"Lunch," Edwards said to the slender native girl, using his hands. "And bring the Thermos." He said to Brewster, "It's full of rum punch. We can get drunk together and get candid."

"Too early for me."

"I've been up a while. Barrie Mayer, Bob. Why did you ask me what she was carrying? Her principal's the one to ask. It's still that shrink, Tolker."

"That bothers me."

"What bothers you?"

"That you know who her principal was. What else did she tell you?"

"Damn little. She never said a word about signing on as a courier until . . ."

"Until what?"

"Until somebody told her about me."

"That you're Company?"

"Yeah."

"Who was that?"

He shrugged.

Edwards thought back to the night Barrie Mayer told him she was aware that he was more than just a struggling charter boat owner and captain.

She'd come to the BVI for a week's vacation. Their affair had been in progress for a little more than a year and they'd managed to cram in a considerable amount of time together, considering the physical distance that separated them. Mayer flew to the BVI at every opportunity, and Edwards made a few trips to Washington to see her. They'd also met once in New York, and had spent an extended weekend together in Atlanta.

Seeing her get off the plane that day jolted him with the same intense feelings she always raised in him. There had been many women in his life, but few had the impact on him she did. His first wife had had that effect. So did his second, come to think of it, but none since . . . until Barrie Mayer.

He recalled that Barrie was in a particularly giddy mood that day. He asked her about it in his car on their way to his villa. She'd said, "I have a secret to share with you." When he asked what it was, she said it would have to wait for a "very special moment."

The moment occurred that night. They'd gone out on one of his yachts and anchored in a cove where they stripped off their clothes and dove into the clear, tepid water. After their swim—more aquatic embracing than swimming—they returned to the yacht and made love. After that he cooked island lobsters and they sat naked on the bleached deck, legs crossed, knees touching, fingers dripping with melted butter, a strong rum swizzle burning their bellies and tripping the switches that cause incessant laughter.

They decided to spend the night on the yacht. After they'd made love again and lay side by side on a bundle of folded sails, he said, "Okay, what's this big, dark secret you have to share with me?"

She'd dozed off. His words startled her awake. She purred and touched his thigh. "Eurosky," she said, or something so softly that he couldn't catch it. When he didn't respond, she turned on her side, propped her head on her elbow, looked down into his face, and said, "You're a spy."

His eyes narrowed. Still, he said nothing.

"You're with the CIA. That's why you're here in the BVI."

He asked quietly, "Who told you that?"

"A friend."

"What friend?"

"It doesn't matter."

"Why would anyone tell you that?"

"Because . . . well, I told . . . this person . . . about you and me and . . ."

"What about you and me?"

"That we've been seeing each other, that I . . . really want to hear?"

"Yes."

"That I'd fallen in love with you."

"Oh."

75

"That seems to upset you more than my knowing about what you do for a living."

"Maybe it does. Why would this *friend* even bring it up? Does he know me?"

"Yes. Well, not personally, but knows of you."

"Who does your friend work for?"

She started to feel uncomfortable, hadn't expected the intense questioning from him. She tried to lighten the moment by saying with a laugh, "I think it's wonderful. I think it's silly and wonderful and fun."

"What's fun about it?"

"That we have a mutual interest now. You don't care about my literary agency, and I don't care about your boats, except for enjoying being on them with you."

His raised eyebrows asked the next question. Mutual?

"I work for the CIA, too."

His eyebrows lowered. He sat up and looked at her until she said, "I'm a courier, just part time, but it's for the Company." She giggled. "I like the Pickle Factory better. It's . . ." She realized he was not sharing her frivolity. She changed her tone and said, "I can talk about it to you because . . ."

"You can talk about it to nobody."

"Eric, I . . ."

"What the hell do you think this is, Barrie, a game, cops and robbers, an exercise to inject more excitement into your life?"

"No, Eric, I don't think that. Why are you so angry? I thought I was doing something worthwhile for my country. I'm proud of it and I haven't told anyone except you and . . ."

"And your friend."

"Yes."

"And your friend told you about me."

"Only because she knew I was seeing you."

"It's a woman?"

"Yes, but that doesn't matter."

"What's her name?"

"I think under the circumstances that . . ."

"Who is she, Barrie? She's breached a very important confidence."

"Forget it, Eric. Forget I even mentioned it."

He got up and sat on the cabin roof. They said nothing to each other. The yacht swayed in the soft evening breeze. The sky above was dark, the stars pinpoints of white light through tiny holes in black canvas. "Tell me all about it," Edwards said.

"I don't think I should," she said, "not after that reaction."

"I was surprised, that's all," he said, smiling. "You told me you had a big surprise to share with me at an appropriate time and you weren't kidding." She stood next to him. He looked into her eyes and said, "I'm sorry I sounded angry." He put his arm around her and kissed her cheek. "How the hell did you end up working for the CIA?"

She told him.

8

SAN FRANCISCO

Dr. Jason Tolker sat in his suite at the Mark Hopkins and dialed his Washington office. "Anything urgent?" he asked his receptionist.

"Nothing that can't wait." She read him a list of people who'd called, which included Collette Cahill.

"Where did she call from?" he asked.

"She left a number in Virginia."

"All right. I'll be back on schedule. I'll call again."

"Fine. How's the weather there?"

"Lovely."

It was two in the afternoon. Tolker had until six before his meeting in Sausalito. He put on a white cable-knit sweater, comfortable walking shoes, tossed his raincoat over his arm, posed for an admiring moment before a full-length mirror, then strolled down California Street to Chinatown, where he stopped in a dozen small food shops to peruse the vast array of foodstuffs. Among many of his interests was Chinese cooking. He considered himself a world-class Chinese chef, which wasn't far from true, although, as with many of his hobbies, he tended to over-value his accomplishments. He also boasted a large collection of vintage jazz recordings. But, as a friend and devoted jazz buff often said, "The collection means more to Jason than the music."

He bought Chinese herbs that he knew he'd have trouble finding in Washington, or even in New York's Chinatown, and returned to the hotel. He showered, changed into one of many suits he had tailored by London's Tommy Nutter, went to the Top of the Mark, sat at a window table with a glass of club soda, and watched the fog roll in over the Golden Gate Bridge on its way to obscuring the city itself. Nice, he thought; appropriate. He checked his watch, paid, got into his rented Jaguar, and headed for the bridge and his appointment on the other side.

He drove through the streets of Sausalito, the lights of San Francisco across the bay appearing, then disappearing through the fog, and turned into a street that began as a residential area, then slowly changed to light industry. He pulled into a three-car paved parking lot next to a two-story white stucco building, turned off his engine and lights, and sat for a moment before getting out and approaching a side door that was painted red. He knocked, heard footsteps on an iron stairway, and stood back as the door was opened by an older man wearing a gray cardigan sweater over a maroon turtleneck. His pants were baggy and his shoes scuffed. His face was a mosaic of lumps and crevices. His hair was gray and uncombed. "Hello, Jason," he said.

"Bill," Tolker said as he stepped past him. The door closed with a thud. The two men walked up a staircase to the second floor. Dr. William Wayman opened a door to his large, cluttered office. Seated in it was a woman who Tolker judged to be in her mid-thirties. She was in a shadowed corner of the room, the only light on her face coming through a dirty window at the rear of the building.

"Harriet, this is the doctor I told you about," Wayman said.

"Hello," she said from the corner, her voice small and conveying her nervousness.

"Hello, Harriet," Tolker said. He didn't approach her.

79

Instead, he went to Wayman's desk and perched on its edge, his fingers affirming the crease in his trousers.

"Harriet is the person I told you about on the phone," Wayman said, sitting in a chair next to her. He looked at Tolker, who was illuminated by a gooseneck lamp.

"Yes, I was impressed," Tolker said. "Perhaps you'll tell me a little about yourself, Harriet."

She started to talk, then stopped as though the tone arm on a turntable had been lifted from a record. "Who are you?" she asked.

Wayman answered her in a calm, patient, fatherly voice. "He's from Washington, and is very much involved in our work."

Tolker got up from the desk and approached them. He stood over her and said pleasantly, "I think it's wonderful what you're doing, Harriet, very courageous and very patriotic. You should be extremely proud of yourself."

"I am . . . I just . . . sometimes I become frightened when Dr. Wayman brings other people into it."

Tolker laughed. It was a reassuring laugh. He said, "I'd think you'd find that comforting, Harriet. You're certainly not alone. There are thousands of people involved, every one of them like you, bright, dedicated, *good* people."

Tolker saw a small smile form on her face. She said, "I really don't need a speech, Dr. . . . what was your name?" Her voice was arrogant, unfriendly, nothing like the sweet quality it had when they'd been introduced.

"Dr. James. Richard James." He said to Wayman, "I'd like to see the tests, Bill."

"All right." Wayman placed his hand on Harriet's hand, which was on the arm of her chair. He said, "Ready, Harriet?"

"As ready as I'll ever be," she said in a voice that seemed to come from another person. "It's showtime, Dr. J-a-m-e-s."

Wayman glanced up at Tolker, then said to her in a soothing voice, "Harriet, I want you to roll your eyes up to the top of your head, as far as you can." He placed his forefinger on her brow and said, "Look up, Harriet." Tolker leaned forward and peered into her eyes. Wayman said, "That's right, Harriet, as far as you can." Her pupils disappeared, leaving only two milky white sockets.

Tolker nodded at Wayman and smiled.

Wayman said, "Now, Harriet, I want you to keep your eyes where they are and slowly lower your eyelids. That's it . . . very slowly . . . there you are. You feel very relaxed now, don't you?" She nodded. "Now, Harriet, your arm, the one I'm touching, feels light, buoyant, as though a dozen helium-filled balloons were attached to it. Let it rise, let it float up. That's it, that's wonderful." Her arm drifted into the air and hung there as though suspended by an invisible wire.

Wayman turned to Tolker and said, "She's a perfect 'five,' the best I've ever seen."

Tolker grunted and leaned close to her face. "This is Dr. James, Harriet. How do you feel?"

"I feel good."

"I have something I want to ask you to do."

"I . . . I won't."

Wayman said, "She responds only to me. What do you want her to do?"

"Learn a phrase, and be told I'm the one she's to repeat it to."

"All right. Harriet, I want you to remember what I'm about to say to you. You'll never repeat it to anyone else except someone who says to you, 'The fog is thick.' All right?"

"Yes," she said in a dreamy voice.

"I want you to remember, 'There are four people. Two of them are good, and two of them are bad. The bad ones are Bill and Sally.' Do you understand?"

"Yes."

"When I tell you to come out of the pleasant, relaxed state you're enjoying now, you'll remember that phrase and only repeat it to someone who says, 'The fog is thick.' "

"Yes."

"I'm going to count backwards from five to one. When I reach one, you'll open your eyes and feel very good, very relaxed. Ready?"

"Yes."

"Five—four—three—two—one."

She blinked open her eyes and a placid smile crossed her face.

"Feel good?" Wayman asked.

"Yes. I feel good."

"You look very relaxed, at peace," Tolker said.

"Who are you?" she asked.

Tolker laughed. "You know who I am. I was introduced to you only a few minutes ago."

"Yes, I remember. You're Dr. James."

"That's right. I was wondering, Harriet, about the four people we've been discussing."

She looked at Wayman and frowned.

"You know who I mean," Tolker said, "the four people we're concerned about. We want to know which ones we can trust and which ones we can't trust."

"I don't understand," she said.

"Of course you don't," Wayman said. He looked at Tolker and said, "Go ahead."

Tolker said to her, "Harriet, the fog is thick."

She closed her eyes, opened them, and blinked rapidly.

"Did you hear me, Harriet? I said the fog is thick."

Her eyes continued to flutter. They rolled up in her head, and her arm began to tremble. She said in a halting, tentative voice, "There are . . . four people. Some of them are good and . . . two of them are bad. The bad ones are . . . Bill . . . and . . . Sally."

"Excellent," Wayman said. He sat back and looked to Tolker for approval. Tolker returned to the desk and resumed his seat on its edge.

Wayman said to Harriet, "That was very good, Harriet. You're not in your relaxed state anymore. You can open your eyes now. You've done a very good job."

Tolker watched her come out of her hypnotic state. She shook her head and rubbed her eyes.

"What do you remember?" Wayman asked her.

"I remember . . . I was feeling very good. Is there something else I should remember, *Doctor*?" It was the same angry, scornful voice she'd used earlier.

"No," Wayman said. He stood and held out his hand to

her. "Why don't you wait in the other room. I won't be long. I just want to talk to my colleague for a few moments."

She got up and ran her hands over the front of her dress. Tolker observed that she was attractive, a little overweight but with a frank sensuality she was used to displaying. She watched him, openly inviting him as she crossed the room, opened a door, and went out.

"Impressed?" Wayman said. He'd gone to his chair behind the desk and lighted a cigarette.

"Yes. She's good. I'm not sure she's a five, though."

"I test her that way," said Wayman.

"I'd have to look again. Her upgaze is, but the eye roll might not be."

"Does it really matter?" Wayman asked, not bothering to mask the amusement in his voice. "This search for the perfect five is probably folly, Jason."

"I don't think so. How long have you been working with her?"

Wayman shrugged. "Six months, eight months. She's a prostitute, or was, a good one, highly paid."

"A call girl."

"That is more genteel. We came across her by accident. One of the contacts arranged for her to bring men to the safehouse. I watched a few of the sessions and realized that what I was seeing in *her* was far more interesting than the way the men were behaving under drugs. I mentioned it to the contact and the next time she was up, we were introduced. I started working with her the next day."

"She was that willing?"

"She's bright, enjoys the attention."

"And the money?"

"We're paying her fairly."

Tolker laughed. "Is this the first time she's been put to the test?"

It was Wayman's turn to laugh. "For heaven's sake, no. I'd started planting messages with her and testing the recall process within the first month. She's never failed."

"I'll have to see more."

"Tonight?"

"No." Tolker walked to a window that was covered by

heavy beige drapes. He touched the fabric, turned, and said, "There's something wrong with using a hooker, Bill."

"Why?"

"Hookers are . . . Christ, one thing they're *not* is trust-worthy."

Wayman came up behind and patted him on the back. "Jason, if one's basic morality were a criterion for choosing subjects in this project, we'd all have abandoned it years ago. In fact, we'd all have been ruled out ourselves."

"Speak for yourself, Bill."

"Whatever you say. Shall I continue with her?"

"I suppose so. See how far you can take her."

"I'll do that. By the way, I was sorry to hear about Miss Mayer."

"I'd rather not discuss it."

"Fine, except it must rank as a loss, Jason. If I understood you correctly the last time we met at Langley, she represented one of your best cases."

"She was all right, a solid four, nothing special."

"I thought she was . . . "

"Just a solid four, Bill. I couldn't use her to carry mentally. She worked out as a bag carrier."

"Just that?"

Tolker glared at him. "Yes, just that. Anything else for me to see while I'm out here?"

"No. I have a young man in therapy who shows potential, but I haven't made up my mind yet."

Wayman showed Tolker out of the building and to his car. "You drive her home?" Tolker asked.

"Yes."

"She live in San Fran?"

"Yes."

"She still turn tricks?"

"Only for us. We have a session set up for tomorrow night. Care to join us?"

"Maybe I will. Same place?"

"Yes. Good night, Jason."

"Good night, Bill."

Dr. William Wayman closed the door behind him and muttered "Slime" as he climbed the stairs.

Tolker returned to the city, called his wife from the room at the Hopkins, had a brief conversation. Their marriage had deteriorated to an accommodation years ago. He called another number. A half hour later a young Oriental girl wearing a silk dress the color of tangerines knocked at the door. He greeted her, said, "It's been too long," and sprawled on the bed as she went into the bathroom. When she returned, she was nude. She carried a small plastic bag of white powder, which she placed on the bed next to him. He grinned and absently ran his hand over her small breast.

"I brought the best," she said.

"You always do," he said as he rolled off the bed and started to undress.

At eleven o'clock the next night Jason Tolker stood with Dr. William Wayman and two other men in a small apartment. A video camera was positioned against an opening through the wall into the adjoining apartment. A small speaker carried audio from the other apartment.

"Here we go," one of them said, as what had been a static picture of the next room on the monitor suddenly came to life. The door to the next room opened. Harriet, the woman from Wayman's office the night before, led a rotund man through the door. She closed and locked it, turned, and started to undo his tie. He was drunk. A large belly hung over the front of his pants, and his suit jacket was visibly wrinkled even in the room's dim light.

"Drink?" she asked.

"No, I . . . "

"Oh, come on, join me in a drink. It gets me in the mood."
She returned from the kitchen with two glasses.

"What's she using?" Tolker asked.

"That new synthetic from Bethesda," Wayman said.

It turned out to be a wasted evening, at least scientifically. The man Harriet had brought to the apartment was too drunk to be a valid subject, the effects of the drug she'd placed in his drink compromised by the booze. He was too drunk even to have sex with her, and fell asleep soon after they'd climbed into bed, the sound of his snoring rasping from the speakers. The men in the next room continued to watch, however, while Harriet pranced about the room. She examined her full body in a mirror, and even hammed for the camera after a cautious glance at the sleeping subject.

"Disgusting," Tolker muttered as he prepared to leave.

"Harriet?" Wayman asked.

"The fat slob. Tell her to pick better quality next time." He returned to the hotel and watched Randolph Scott in a western on TV before falling asleep.

9

VIRGINIA, TWO DAYS LATER

It was good to be home.

Collette Cahill had slept off her jet lag in the room that had been hers as she grew up. Now she sat in the kitchen with her mother and helped prepare for a party in her honor that night, not a big affair, just neighbors and friends in for food and drinks to welcome her back.

Mrs. Cahill, a trim and energetic woman, had gone to an imported food store and bought things she felt represented Hungarian fare. "That's all I eat now, Mom," Collette had said. "We get a lot of Hungarian food."

To which her mother replied, "But we don't. It's a good excuse. I've never had goulash."

"You still won't have had it, Mom. In Hungary, goulash is a soup, not a stew."

"Pardon me," her mother said. They laughed and embraced and Collette knew nothing had changed, and was thankful for it.

Guests began to arrive at seven. There was a succession of gleeful greetings at the door: "I can't believe it." "My

87

God, it's been ages!" "You look wonderful." "Great to see you again." One of the last guests to arrive was, to Collette's surprise, her high school beau, Vern Wheatley. They'd been "a number" in high school, had dated right through graduation when they promptly went their separate ways, Collette staying in the area to attend college, Wheatley to the University of Missouri to major in journalism.

"This is . . . this is too much," Cahill said as she opened the door and stared at him. Her first thought was that he'd grown more handsome over the years, but then she reminded herself that every man got better-looking after high school. His sandy hair had receded only slightly, and he wore it longer than in his yearbook photo. He'd always been slender, but now he was sinewy slim. He wore a tan safari jacket over a blue button-down shirt, jeans, and sneakers.

"Hi," he said. "Remember me?"

"Vern Wheatley, what are you doing here? How did you . . . ?"

"Came down to Washington on assignment, called your mom, and she told me about this blast. Couldn't resist."

"This is . . ." She hugged him and led him to the living room where everyone was gathered. After introductions, Collette led him to the bar where he poured himself a glass of Scotch. "Collette," he said, "you look sensational. Budapest must be palatable."

"Yes, it is. I've had a very enjoyable assignment there."

"Is it over? You're coming back here?"

"No, just a leave."

He grinned. "You take leaves, I take vacations."

"What are you doing these days?"

"I'm an editor, at least for the moment. *Esquire*. It's my fifth . . . no, seventh job since college. Journalists have never been known for stability, have we?"

"Judging from you, I guess not."

"I do some free-lancing, too."

"I've read some of your pieces." He gave her a skeptical look. "No, I really have, Vern. You had that cover story in the *Times* magazine section on . . ."

"On the private aviation lobby helping to keep our skies unsafe."

"Right. I really did read it. I said to myself, 'I know him.' "

"When."

"Huh?"

"I knew him when. I'm still in my when stage."

"Oh. Do you like New York?"

"Love it, although I can think of other places I'd rather live." He sighed. "It's been a while."

"It sure has. I remember when you got married."

"So do I." He chuckled. "Didn't last long."

"I know, Mom told me. I'm sorry."

"I was, too, but then I realized it was good it fell apart so soon, before there were kids. Anyway, I'm not here to talk about my ex-wife. God, I hate that term. I'm here to celebrate Collette Cahill's triumphant return from behind the Iron Curtain."

She laughed. "Everybody thinks Hungary is like being in the Soviet Union. It's really very open, Vern. I suppose that bothers the Soviets, but that's the way it is, lots of laughter and music, restaurants and bars and . . . well, that's not entirely true, but it's not as bad as people think. The Hungarians are so used to being conquered by one country or another that they shrug and get on with things."

"You're with the embassy?"

"Yup."

"What do you do there?"

"Administration, dealing with trade missions, tourists, things like that."

"You were with the CIA."

"Uh-huh."

"Didn't like it?"

"Too spooky for me, I guess. Just a Virginia country girl at heart."

His laugh indicated he didn't buy it but wasn't about to debate.

Collette drifted to other people in the room. Everyone was interested in her life abroad and she did her best to give them capsule responses.

By eleven, just about everyone had gone home, except for her Uncle Bruce who'd gotten drunk, a next-door neighbor who was helping Collette's mother to gather up the debris, and Vern Wheatley. He sat in a chair in the living room, one long leg casually dangling over the other, a beer in his hand. Collette went to him and said, "Nice party."

"Sure was. Feel like escaping?"

"Escaping? No, I . . ."

"I just figured we could go somewhere, have a drink and catch up."

"I thought we did."

"No we didn't. How about it?"

"I don't know, I . . . just a second."

She went to the kitchen and said she might go out for a cup of coffee with Wheatley.

"That's nice," said her mother, who then whispered, "He's divorced, you know."

"I know."

"I always liked him, and I could never understand what he saw in that other woman."

"He saw something—a ring, a marriage, a mate. Sure you don't mind?"

"Not at all."

"I won't be late. And, Mom, thanks for a wonderful party. I loved seeing everyone."

"And they loved seeing you. The comments, how beautiful you are, what a knockout, a world traveler . . ."

"Good night, Mom. You're spoiling me." She said goodbye to the neighbor and to her Uncle Bruce, who was hearing or feeling nothing, but would in the morning, and she and Wheatley drove off in his 1976 Buick Regal.

They went to a neighborhood bar, settled in a corner booth, ordered beers, and looked at each other. "Fate," he said.

"What?"

"Fate. Here we are, high school sweethearts separated by fate and together again because of fate."

"It was a party."

"Fate that I was here when the party was thrown, fate that you came home at the right time, fate that I'm divorced. *Fate.* Pure and simple."

"Whatever you say, Vern."

They spent two hours catching up on their lives. Cahill found it awkward, as usual, that there was much she couldn't talk about. It was one of the limitations to working for the CIA, particularly in its most clandestine division. She avoided that aspect of her recent life and told tales of Budapest, of the nights at the Miniatur and Gundel, of the Gypsy bands that seemed to be everywhere, of the friends she'd made and the memories she'd developed for life.

"It sounds like a wonderful city," Wheatley said. "I'd like to visit you there someday."

"Please do. I'll give you a special tour."

"It's a date. By the way, your former employer made a pass at me not too long ago."

Cahill tried to imagine someone she'd worked for doing that. A homosexual former boss?

"The Pickle Factory."

"The CIA? Really?"

"Yeah. Journalists used to be big with them. Remember? Then all the crap hit the fan back in '77 and it was 'cool it' for a while. Looks like they're back with us."

"What did they want you to do?"

"I was heading off for Germany on a free-lance assignment. This guy in a cheap suit and raincoat got to me through a friend who lives in the East Village and sculpts for a living. This guy wanted me to hook up with a couple of German writers, get to know them, and see what they knew about the current situation in Germany."

Cahill laughed. "Why didn't they just ask them themselves?"

"Not enough intrigue, I guess. Besides, I figured that what they really want is to have you in their pocket. Do them one favor, then another, collect a little dough for it and start depending upon more. You know what?"

"What?"

"I'm glad you aren't with them anymore. When I heard you'd taken a job with the CIA, all I could think of was what I wrote in your yearbook."

She smiled. "I remember it very well."

"Yeah. *To the one girl in this world who will never sell out.*"

"I really didn't understand it then. I do now."

"I'm glad." He sat up, rubbed his hand to signal that that phase of the conversation was over, and asked, "How long will you be home?"

"I don't know. I have . . ." She had to think. "I have two weeks' leave, but I'm spending a lot of it trying to run down what happened to a very dear friend of mine."

"Anybody I know?"

"No, just a good friend who died suddenly a week or so ago. She was in her mid-thirties and had a heart attack."

He made a face. "That's rough."

"Yes, I'm still trying to deal with it, I guess. She was a literary agent in Washington."

"Barrie Mayer? I didn't know you were friendly."

"You know about it?"

"Sure. It made the New York papers."

"I didn't read anything about it," Cahill said with a sigh. "I know her mother real well and promised her I'd try to find out as much as I could about what Barrie was doing right up until she died."

"Not a great way to spend a vacation. Leave. I forgot."

"Holiday. I like the British approach."

"So do I, in a lot of things. I'm sorry about what happened to your friend. Having friends die is for . . . for older people. I haven't started reading the obits yet."

"Don't. You know, Vern, this was great but I'm pooped. I thought I was slept out but my circadian rhythms are still in chaos."

"Is that like menopause?"

"Vaguely." She laughed. "I should get home."

"Sure."

They pulled up in front of her mother's house. Wheatley turned off the engine and they both looked straight ahead. Cahill glanced over and saw that he was grinning. She thought she knew what he was thinking, and a grin broke out on her face, too, which quickly turned into stifled laughter.

"Remember?" he said.

She couldn't respond because now laughter took all her breath. She tried. "I . . . I remember that you . . ."

"It was you," he said with equal difficulty. "You missed."

"I did not. You had your coat collar turned up because you thought it was cool and when I went to kiss you good night, all I hit was . . . the . . . coat collar."

"You ruined the coat. I never could get the lipstick off."

They stopped talking until they'd gotten themselves under control. She then said to him, "Vern, it was great seeing you again. Thanks for coming to my party."

"My pleasure. I'd like to see you again."

"I don't know if . . . "

"If we should, or if you'll have time while you're home?" She started to reply but he placed his finger on her lips. "I've never forgotten you, Collette. I mean . . . I'd like to see you again, go out, have dinner, talk, just that."

"That'd be nice," she said. "I just don't know how much time I'll have."

"Give me whatever you can spare. Okay?"

"Okay."

"Tomorrow?"

"Vern."

"Are you staying here?"

"At the house? Another night, I think. Then I'm going to stay in the city. I really should have dinner with Mom tomorrow."

"Absolutely. I remember what a hell of a cook she is. Am I invited?"

"Yes."

"I'll call you during the day. Good night, Collette."

He made a deliberate gesture to flatten his jacket collar. She laughed and kissed him lightly on the lips. He tried to intensify the kiss. She resisted, gave in, resisted again, and opened the door. "See you tomorrow," she said.

10

Jason Tolker's Washington office was located in a three-story detached house in Foggy Bottom, next to the George Washington University campus and with a view of the Kennedy Center from the third floor.

Cahill arrived precisely at 6:00 P.M. Tolker's secretary had told Cahill that he would see her after his last patient.

She rang, identified herself through an intercom, and was buzzed through. The reception area was awash in yellows and reds, and dominated by pieces of pre-Columbian and Peruvian art. Her first thought was to wonder whatever happened to the notion of decorating therapists' offices in soothing pastels. Her second thought was that Dr. Tolker was a pretentious man, not the first time she'd come to that conclusion. Her only other meeting with him, which occurred at the scientific conference in Budapest a week after she'd arrived there, had left her with the distinct impression that his ego was in direct proportion to the outward manifestations of his personality—movie-star handsome (Tyrone Power?), expensive clothing on a six-foot frame built for designer suits, money (it was as if he wore a sandwich board with a large green dollar sign on it). But, and probably more

94

important, there was a self-assuredness that many physicians seemed to carry with them out of medical school but that was particularly prevalent with those who dealt with a patient's emotions and behavior, a godlike view of the world and fellowmen, knowing more, seeing through, inwardly chuckling at how the "others" live their lives, scornful and bemused and willing to tolerate the daily brush with the human dilemma in fifty-minute segments only, payment due at conclusion of visit.

The receptionist, a pleasant, middle-aged woman with a round face, thinning hair, her coat and hat on, ready to leave, told Cahill to be seated: "Doctor will be with you in a few minutes." She left, and Cahill browsed a copy of *Architectural Digest* until Tolker came through a door. "Miss Cahill, hello, Jason Tolker." He came to where she was sitting, smiled, and offered his hand. Somehow, his gregarious greeting didn't match up with what she'd remembered of him from Budapest. She stood and said, "I appreciate you taking time to see me, Doctor."

"Happy to. Come in, we'll be more comfortable in my office."

His office was markedly subdued compared to the waiting room. The walls were the color of talcum; a soothing pastel, she thought. One wall was devoted to framed awards, degrees, and photographs with people Cahill didn't recognize at first glance. There was no desk; his wine leather swivel chair was behind a round glass coffee table. There were two matching leather chairs on the other side of the table. A black leather couch that gracefully curved up to form a headrest was against another wall. A small chair was positioned behind where the patient's head would lie.

"Please, sit down," he said, indicating one of the chairs. "Coffee? I think there's some left. Or maybe you'd prefer a drink?"

"Nothing, thank you."

"Do you mind if I do? It's been an . . . ." A smile. "An interesting day."

"Please. Do you have wine?"

"As a matter of fact, I do. Red or white?"

"White, please."

She watched him open a cabinet, behind which was a bar lighted from within. Her reaction to him was different than it had been in Budapest. She began to like him, finding his demeanor courteous, friendly, open. She also knew she was responding to his good looks. For a tall man, he moved fluidly. He was in shirtsleeves; white shirt, muted red tie, charcoal gray suit trousers, and black Gucci loafers. His dark hair was thick and curly, his facial features sharp. It was his eyes, however, that defined him: large, saccadic raven eyes that were at once soothing and probing.

He placed two glasses of wine on the coffee table, sat in his chair, lifted his glass, and said, "Health."

She returned the salute and took a sip. "Very good," she said.

"I keep the better vintages at home."

She wished he hadn't said it. There was no need to say it. She realized he was staring at her. She met his gaze and smiled. "You know why I'm here."

"Yes, of course, Mrs. Wedgemann, my secretary, told me the nature of your visit. You were a close friend of Barrie Mayer."

"Yes, that's right. To say I was shocked at what happened to her is one of those classic understatements, I suppose. I've been in touch with her mother who, as you can imagine, is devastated, losing her only daughter. I decided to take . . . to take a vacation and see what I could find out about things leading up to Barrie's death. I promised her mother I'd do that but, to be honest, I would have done it for myself anyway. We *were* close."

He pressed his lips together and narrowed his eyes. "The question, of course, is why come to me?"

"I know that Barrie was in therapy with you, at least for a while, and I thought you might be able to give me some hint of what frame of mind she was in before she died, whether there was any indication that she wasn't feeling well."

Tolker rubbed his nose in a gesture of thoughtfulness before saying, "Obviously, Miss Cahill, I wouldn't be free to discuss anything that went on between Barrie and me. That falls under doctor-patient confidentiality."

"I realize that, Dr. Tolker, but it seems to me that a general observation wouldn't necessarily violate that principle."

"When did you meet Barrie?"

The sudden shift in questioning stopped her for a moment. She said, "In college. We stayed close until we each went our separate ways for a number of years. Then, as often happens, we got back in touch and renewed the friendship."

"You say you were close to Barrie. How close?"

"Close." She thought of Mark Hotchkiss, who'd exhibited a similar skepticism of the depth of her relationship with Mayer. "Is there some element of doubt about my friendship with Barrie or, for that matter, my reason for being here?"

He smiled and shook his head. "No, not at all. I'm sorry if I gave you that impression. Do you work and live in the Washington area?"

"No, I . . . I work for the United States Embassy in Budapest, Hungary."

"That's fascinating," said Tolker. "I've spent some time there. Charming city. A shame the Soviets came in as they did. It certainly has put a lid on things."

"Not as much as people think," Cahill said. "It's got to be the most open of Soviet satellite countries."

"Perhaps."

It dawned on Cahill that he was playing a game with her, asking questions for which he already had answers. She decided to be more forthright. "We've met before, Dr. Tolker."

He squinted and leaned forward. "I thought we had the minute I saw you. Was it in Budapest?"

"Yes. You were attending a conference and I'd just arrived."

"Yes, it comes back to me now, some reception, wasn't it? One of those abominable get-togethers. You're wearing your hair different, shorter, aren't you?"

Cahill laughed. "Yes, and I'm impressed with your memory."

"Frankly, Miss Cahill, when more than a year has passed since meeting a woman, it's always safe to assume she's changed her hair. Usually, it involves the color, too, but that isn't the case with you."

"No, it isn't. Somehow, I don't think I was born to be a blonde."

"No, I suppose not," he said. "What do you do at the embassy?"

"Administration, trade missions, helping stranded tourists, run-of-the-mill."

He smiled and said, "It can't be as dull as you make it sound."

"Oh, it's never dull."

"I have a good friend in Budapest."

"Really? Who is that?"

"A colleague. His name is Árpád Hegedüs. Do you know him?"

"He's . . . he's a colleague, you say, a psychiatrist?"

"Yes, and a very good one. His talent is wasted having to apply it under a Socialist regime, but he seems to find room for a certain amount of individuality."

"Like most Hungarians," she said.

"Yes, I suppose that's true, just as you must find room for other activities within the confines of your run-of-the-mill job. How much time do you devote to helping stranded tourists as opposed to . . . ?"

When he didn't finish, she said, "As opposed to what?"

"As opposed to your duties for the CIA."

His question startled her. Early in her career with Central Intelligence, it would have thrown her, perhaps even generated a nervous giggle as she collected her thoughts. That wasn't the case any longer. She looked him in the eye and said, "That's an interesting comment."

"More wine?" he asked, standing and going to the bar.

"No, thank you, I have plenty." She looked at her glass on the table and thought of the comment Árpád Hegedüs had made to her during their last meet in Budapest: "Jason Tolker might be friendly to the Soviets."

Tolker returned, took his seat, sipped his wine. "Miss Cahill, I think you might accomplish a lot more, and we might get along much better, if you practiced a little more candor."

"What makes you think I haven't been candid?"

"It isn't a matter of thinking, Miss Cahill. I *know* you haven't been." Before she could respond he said, "Collette E. Cahill, graduated cum laude from George Washington University Law School, a year or so with a legal trade journal, then a stint in England for the CIA and a transfer to Budapest. Accurate? Candid?"

"Am I supposed to be impressed?" she asked.

"Only if your life to date impresses you. It does me. You're obviously bright, talented, and ambitious."

"Thank you. Time for me to ask you a question."

"Go ahead."

"Assuming the things you've said about me were correct, particularly my supposed continuing employment with the CIA, how would you know about that?"

He smiled, and it quickly turned into a laugh. "No argument, then?"

"Is that Shrink School 101, answer a question with a question?"

"It goes back further than that, Miss Cahill. The Greeks were good at it. Socrates taught the technique."

"Yes, that's true, and Jesus, too. As a learning tool for students, not to evade a reasonable question."

Tolker shook his head and said, "You're still not being candid, are you?"

"No?"

"No. You know, either through Barrie or someone else in your organization, that I have, on occasion, provided certain services to your employer."

Cahill smiled. "This conversation has turned into one with so much candor that it would probably be upsetting to . . . to our employers, *if* we worked for them."

"No, Miss Cahill, your employer. I simply have acted as a consultant on a project or two."

She knew that everything he'd said up to that moment was literally true, and decided it was silly to continue playing the game. She said, "I'd love another glass of wine."

He got it for her. When they were both seated again, he looked at his watch and said, "Let me try to tell you what it is you want to know without you having to ask the questions. Barrie Mayer was a lovely and successful woman, as you're well aware. She came to me because there were certain aspects of her life with which she was unhappy, that she was having trouble negotiating. That, of course, is a sign of sanity in itself."

"Seeking help?"

"Of course, recognizing a problem and taking action. She was like most people who end up in some form of therapy, bright and rational and put together in most aspects of her life, just stumbling now and then over some ghosts from the past. We worked things out very nicely for her."

"Did you maintain a relationship after therapy was finished?"

"Miss Cahill, you know we did."

"I don't mean about what she might have done as a courier. I mean a personal relationship."

"What a discreet term. Do you mean did we sleep together?"

"It would be indiscreet for me to ask that."

"But you already have, and I prefer not to answer an indiscretion with an indiscretion. Next question."

"You were telling me everything I need to know without questions, remember?"

"Yes, that's right. You'll want to know whether I have any information bearing upon her death."

"Do you?"

"No."

"Do you have any idea who killed her?"

"Why do you assume someone killed her? My understanding is that it was an unfortunate, premature heart attack."

"I don't think that's really what happened. Do you?"

"I wouldn't know more about that than what I've read in the papers."

Cahill sipped her wine, not because she wanted it but because she needed a little time to process what had transpired. She'd assumed when she called and asked for an appointment with Tolker that she would be summarily turned down. She'd even considered seeking an appointment as a patient but realized that was too roundabout an approach.

It had all been so easy. A phone call, a brief explanation to the secretary that she was Barrie Mayer's friend—instant appointment with him. He'd obviously worked fast in finding out who she was. Why? What source had he turned to to come up with information on her? Langley and its central personnel files? Possible, but not likely. That sort of information would never be given out to a contract physician who was only tangentially associated with the CIA.

"Miss Cahill, I've been preaching candor to you without practicing it myself."

"Really?"

"Yes. I'm assuming that you're sitting here wondering how I came up with information about you."

"As a matter of fact, that's right."

"Barrie was . . . well, let's just say she didn't define close-mouthed."

Cahill couldn't help but laugh. She remembered her dismay at her friend's casual mention of her new, part-time job as courier.

"You agree," Tolker said.

"Well, I . . ."

"Once Barrie agreed to carry some materials for the CIA, she became talkative. She said it was ironic because she had this friend, Collette Cahill, who worked for the CIA at the American Embassy in Budapest. I found that interesting and asked questions. She answered them all. Don't misunderstand. She didn't babble about it. If she had, I would have ended the relationship, at least that aspect of it."

"I understand what you're saying. What else did she say about me?"

"That you were beautiful and bright and the best female friend she'd ever had."

"Did she really say that?"

"Yes."

"I'm flattered." She sensed that a tear might erupt and swallowed against it.

"Want my honest opinion about how and why she died?"

"Please."

"I buy the official autopsy verdict of a coronary. If that

101

isn't why she died, I'd assume that our friends on the other side decided to terminate her."

"The Russians."

"Or some variation thereof."

"I can't accept that, not today. We're not at war. Besides, what could Barrie have been carrying that would prompt such a drastic action?"

He shrugged.

"What *was* she carrying?"

"How would I know?"

"I thought you were her contact."

"I was, but I never knew what was in her briefcase. It was given to me sealed, and I would give it to her."

"I understand that but . . ."

He leaned forward. "Look, Miss Cahill, I think we've gotten off onto a tangent that goes far beyond the reality of the situation. I know that you're a full-time employee of the CIA, but I'm not. I'm a psychiatrist. That's what I do for a living. It's my profession. A colleague suggested to me years ago that I might be interested in becoming a CIA-approved physician. All that means is that when someone from the agency needs medical help in my specialty, they're free to come to me. There are surgeons and OB-GYN men and heart specialists and many others who've been given clearance by the agency."

She cocked her head and asked, "But what about being a contact for a courier like Barrie? That isn't within your specialty."

His smile was friendly and reassuring. "They asked me somewhere along the line to keep my eye out for anyone who might fit their profile of a suitable courier. Barrie fit it. She traveled often to foreign countries, particularly Hungary, wasn't married, didn't have any deep, dark secrets that would jeopardize her clearance, and she enjoyed adventure. She also appreciated the money, off-the-books money, fun money for clothes and furniture and other frills. It was a lark for her."

His final words hit Cahill hard, caused her to draw a deep breath.

"Something wrong?" Tolker asked, observing the pain on her face.

"Barrie's dead. 'Just a lark.' "

"Yes. I'm sorry."

"Do you feel any . . . any guilt about having recruited her into a situation that resulted in her death?"

For a moment, she thought his eyes might mist. They didn't, but his voice had a ring of pathos. "I think about it often. I wish I could go back to that day when I suggested she carry for your employer and withdraw my offer." He sighed and stood, stretched, and broke his knuckles. "But that's not possible, and I tell my patients that to play the what-if game is stupid. It happened, she's dead, I'm sorry, and I must leave."

He walked her to the office door. They paused and looked at each other. "Barrie was right," he said.

"About what?"

"About her friend being beautiful."

She lowered her eyes.

"I hope I've been helpful."

"Yes, you have, and I'm appreciative."

"Will you have dinner with me?"

"I . . ."

"Please. There's probably more ground we could cover about Barrie. I feel comfortable with you now. I didn't when you first arrived, thought you were just snooping around for gossip. I shouldn't have felt that way. Barrie wouldn't have a very close friend who'd do that."

"Maybe," she said. "Yes, that would be fine."

"Tomorrow night?"

"Ah, yes, fine."

"Would you mind coming by here at seven? I have a six o'clock group. Once they're gone, I'm free."

"Seven. I'll be here."

She drove home realizing two things. One, he'd told her everything that she would have known anyway. Two, she was anxious to see him again. That second thought bothered her because she couldn't effectively separate her continuing curiosity about Barrie Mayer's death from a personal fascination with him as a man.

"Have a nice night?" her mother asked.

"Yes."

"You're staying in the city tomorrow night?"

"For the next few nights, Mom. It'll be easier to get things done. I'm seeing Barrie's mother tomorrow for lunch."

"Poor woman. Please give her my sympathy."

"I will."

"Will you be seeing Vern?"

"I don't know. Probably."

"It was fun having him at dinner last night, like when you were in high school and he used to hang around hoping to be invited."

Cahill laughed. "He's nice. I'd forgotten how nice."

"Well," said her mother, "the problem with pretty girls like you is having to pick and choose among all the young men who chase you."

Cahill hugged her mother and said, "Mom, I'm not a girl anymore, and there isn't a battalion of men chasing me."

Her mother stepped back, smiled, and held her daughter at arm's length. "Don't kid me, Collette Cahill. I'm your mother."

"I know that, and I'm very grateful that you are. Got any ice cream?"

"Bought it today for you. Rum raisin. They were out of Hungarian flavors."

11

Cahill drove a rented car into the city the next morning and checked into the Hotel Washington at 15th and Pennsylvania. It wasn't Washington's finest, but it was nice. Besides, it had a sentimental value. Its rooftop terrace restaurant and bar offered as fine a view of Washington as any place in the capitol. Cahill had spent four glorious Fourth of Julys there with friends who, through connections, had been able to wangle reservations on the terrace's busiest night of the year, and were able to view the spectacular festivities that only Washington can provide on the nation's birthday.

She went to her room, hung up the few items of clothing she'd brought with her, freshened up, and headed for her first appointment of the day: CIA headquarters in Langley, Virginia.

The person she was seeing had been a mentor of sorts during her training days. Hank Fox was a grizzled, haggard, wayworn agency veteran who had five daughters, and who took a special interest in the increasing number of women recruited by the CIA. His position was Coordinator: Training Policy and Procedures. New recruits often joked that his title should be "Priest." He had that way about him—ignoring his five issue, of course.

She whizzed along the George Washington Memorial Parkway until reaching a sign that read CENTRAL IN-TELLIGENCE AGENCY. It hadn't always been marked that way. In the years following its construction in the late 1950s, a single sign on the highway read BUREAU OF PUBLIC ROADS. Frequent congressional calls for the agency to be more open and accountable brought about the new sign. Behind it, little had changed.

She turned off the highway and onto a road leading to the 125-acre tract on which the Central Intelligence Agency stood. Ahead, through dense woods, stood the modernistic, fortress-like building surrounded by a high and heavy chain-link fence. She stopped, presented her credentials to two uniformed guards, and explained the purpose of her visit. One of them placed a call, then informed her that she could pass through to the next checkpoint. She did, submitted her identity again to scrutiny, and was allowed to proceed to a small parking area near the main entrance.

Two athletic young men wearing blue suits and with re-volvers beneath their jackets waited for her to approach the entrance. She noticed how short their hair was, how placid the expression on their faces. Again, a show of credentials, a nod, and she was escorted through the door by one of them. He walked slightly in front of her at a steady pace until coming to the beginning of a long, straight white tunnel that was arched at the top. Royal blue industrial-grade car-peting lined the floor. There was nothing in the tunnel except for recessed lights that created odd shadows along its length. At the far end was an illuminated area where two stainless-steel elevator doors caught the light and hurled it back into the tunnel.

"Straight ahead, ma'am."

Cahill entered the tunnel and walked slowly, her thoughts drifting back to when she was a new recruit and had first seen this building, had first walked this tunnel. It had been part of an introductory tour and she'd been struck by the casualness of the tour guide, a young man who demonstrated what Cahill, and others in her class, considered strangely irreverent behavior considering the ominous image of the CIA. He'd talked about how the contractor who'd built the building wasn't allowed to know how many people would occupy it, and was forced to guess at the size and capacity of the heating and air-conditioning system. The system turned out to be inadequate, and the CIA took him to court. He won, his logic making more sense to the judge than the "national security" argument presented by the agency's counsel.

The guide had also said that the $46-million building had been approved in order to bring all agency headquarters personnel under one roof. Until that time, the CIA's divisions had been spread out all over Washington and surrounding communities, and Congress had been sold on the consolidation because of problems this created. But, according to this talkative, glib young man, whole divisions began moving out shortly after moving in when construction was completed. When this came to the attention in 1968 of then director Richard Helms, he was furious and decreed that no one was to make a move without his personal approval. Somehow, that didn't deter division chiefs who found being under one roof to be stifling and, if nothing else, boring. The exodus continued.

Cahill often wondered how you ran an organization with that kind of discipline, and whether the young tour guide's loose tongue had cut short his agency career. It wasn't like the FBI, where public relations and public tours were routine, conducted by attractive young men and women hired solely for that purpose. The CIA did not give tours to outsiders; the guide was obviously a full-fledged employee.

She reached the end of the tunnel where two other young men awaited her. "Miss Cahill?" one asked.

"Yes."

"May I see your pass?"

She showed him.

"Please take the elevator. Mr. Fox is expecting you." He pushed a button and a set of the stainless-steel doors slid open quickly and silently. She stepped into the elevator and waited for them to close. She knew better than to look for a button to push. There weren't any. This elevator knew its destination.

Hank Fox was waiting for her when the doors opened a floor above. He hadn't changed. Though older, he'd always looked old, and the changes weren't quickly discernible. His craggy face broke into a smile and he extended two large, red, and callused hands. "Collette Cahill. Good to see you again."

"Same here, Hank. You look terrific."

"I feel terrific. At my age you might as well or, at least, lie. Come on, Fox's special blend of coffee awaits you." She smiled and fell in step with him down a wide hallway carpeted in red, its white walls providing a backdrop for large, framed maps.

Fox, Cahill noticed, had put on weight and walked with a slower, heavier gait than the last time she'd seen him. His gray suit, its shape and material testifying to its origins in a Tall and Big (read Fat) Man's clothing shop, hung gracelessly from him.

He stopped, opened a door, and allowed her to enter. The corner office's large windows looked out over the woods. His desk was as cluttered as it had always been. The walls were covered with framed photos of him with political heavyweights spanning many administrations, the largest one of him shaking hands with a smiling Harry S. Truman a few years before the President's death. A cluster of color photographs of his wife and children stood on his desk. A pipe rack was full; little metal soldiers stood at attention along the air-conditioning and heating duct behind the desk.

"Coffee?" he asked.

"If it's as good as it used to be."

"Sure it is. The only difference is that they told me I have a fast and irregular pulse. The doc thought I was drinking too much coffee and said I should use de-caf. I compromised. I mix it half and half now, half the amaretto from that fancy coffee and tea shop in Georgetown, the other half de-caf. Never know the difference." Hank Fox's special blends of coffee were well known throughout the agency, and being invited to share a pot carried with it the symbolism of acceptance and friendship.

"Sensational," Cahill exclaimed after her first sip. "You haven't lost your touch, Hank."

"Not with coffee. Other things, well . . ."

"They moved you."

"Yeah. That's right, the last time I saw you was when I had that office in with Personnel. I liked it better there. Being up here in Miscellaneous Projects is another world. The director said it was a promotion, but I know better. I'm being eased out, which is okay with me. Hell, I'm sixty."

"Young."

"Bull! All this crap about being only as old as you think is babble from people who are afraid of getting old. You may feel young, but cut you open and the bones and arteries don't lie." He sat in a scarred leather swivel chair, propped his feet on the desk, and reached for a pipe, leaving Cahill staring at the soles of his shoes, both of which sported sizable holes. "So one of my prize pupils has returned to see the aging prof. How've you been?"

"Fine."

"I got a BIGOT from Joe Breslin saying you were coming home." Fox often used intelligence terms from his early days, even though they'd passed out of common usage over the years. "BIGOT" stemmed from secret plans to invade France during World War II. Gibraltar had been established as a planning center, and orders for officers being sent there were rubber-stamped "TO GIB." BIGOT was the reverse, and the term came into being: Sensitive operations were known to be *bigoted*, and personnel given knowledge of them were on the *bigot list*.

"Any reason for him doing that?" she asked.

"Just an advisory. I was going to call but you beat me to it. This your first leave from Budapest?"

"No. I took a few short ones to Europe, and got back home once about a year ago for a favorite uncle's funeral."

"The boozer?"

She laughed. "Oh, God, what a memory. No, my hard-drinking Uncle Bruce is still very much with us, rotted liver and all. Having him in the family almost blew my chances here, didn't it?"

"Yeah. That prissy little security guy raised it during your clearance investigation." He belched and excused himself, then said, "If having an alky in the family ruled you out for duty around here, there'd only be a dozen temperance-league types running intelligence for the good ol' U.S. of A." He shook his head, "Hell, half the staff drinks too much."

She laughed and sipped more coffee.

"Let me ask you a question," he said in a serious tone. She looked up and raised her eyebrows. "You here strictly for R & R?"

"Sure."

"The reason I ask is that I thought it was strange . . . well, maybe not strange, but unusual for Joe to bother using a BIGOT to tell me you were coming."

She shrugged. "Oh, you know Joe, Hank, the perpetual father figure. It was nice of him. He knows how fond I am of you."

" 'Fond.' Pleasant term to use on an old man."

"*Older* man."

"Thank you. Well, I'm fond of you, too, and I just thought I'd raise the question in case you were involved in something official and needed an inside rabbi."

"Rabbi Henry Fox. Somehow, Hank, it doesn't go with you. Priest, yes. They still call you that?"

"Not so much anymore since they shifted me."

His comment surprised Cahill. She'd assumed he'd only been physically moved, but that his job had remained the same. She asked.

"Well, Collette, I still keep a hand in training, but they've got me running an operation to keep track of the Termites and Maggots. It's an Octopus project."

Cahill smiled, said, "I never could keep it straight, the difference between Termites and Maggots."

"It really doesn't matter," Fox said. "The Termites are media types who don't carry a brief for the Communists, but who always find something wrong with *us*. The Maggots follow the termites and do whatever's popular which, as you know, means taking daily shots at us and the FBI and any other organization they see as being a threat to their First Amendment rights. Between you and me, I think it's a waste of time. Take away their freedom to write what they want and there goes what the country's all about in the first place. Anyway, we've got them on the computer and we plug in everything they write, pro or con." He yawned and sat back in his chair, his arms behind his head.

Cahill knew what he'd meant by it being an "Octopus project." A worldwide computer system to track potential terrorists had been termed Project Octopus, and had become a generic label for similar computer-rooted projects. She also thought of Vern Wheatley. Was he a Maggot or a Termite? It caused her to smile. Obviously, he was neither, nor were most of the journalists she knew. It was a tendency of too many people within the CIA to apply negative terms to anyone who didn't see things their way, a tendency that had always bothered her.

She'd debated on her way to Langley whether to open up a little to Fox and to bring up Barrie Mayer. She knew it wasn't the most prudent thing to do—need-to-know coming to the fore—but the temptation was there, and the fact that Joe Breslin had alerted Fox to her arrival gave a certain credence to the notion. There were few people within the Pickle Factory that she trusted. Breslin was one; Fox was another. Mistake! Trust no one, was the rule. Still . . . how could you go through life viewing everyone with whom you worked as a potential enemy? Not a good way to live. Not healthy. In Barrie Mayer's case, it had worked the other way around. Whose confidence had she trusted that turned against her? Had Tolker been right, that her death might have been at the hand of a Soviet agent? It was so difficult to accept, but that was another rule that her employer instilled in every employee: "It's easy to forget that we are at war every day with the Communists. It is their aim to destroy our system and our country, and a day must never pass when that reality isn't at the forefront of your thinking."

"You know what I was just thinking, Collette?" Fox asked.

"What?"

"I was thinking back to when this whole organization was started by President Truman." He shook his head. "He'd never recognize it today. I met Truman, you know."

She glanced at the photograph on the wall before saying,

111

"I remember you talked about that during training." He'd talked about it often, as she recalled.

"Hell of a guy. It was right after those two Puerto Ricans tried to assassinate him in 'fifty. They did their best to do him in, botched it, got death sentences, and then Truman turns around at the final minute and commutes their sentences to life. I admired him for that."

Along with cabinet building, winemaking, jewelry design and crafting, and a dozen other interests, Hank Fox was a history buff, especially the Harry Truman presidency. During Cahill's training, it was obvious that the Truman hand in creating the CIA in 1947 was being deliberately glossed over. She hadn't understood the reasons for it until Fox had sat down with a few favorite recruits over dinner at Martin's Tavern in Georgetown and explained.

When Truman abolished the OSS following World War II, he did so because he felt that such wartime tactics as psychological warfare, political manipulation, and para-military operations that had been practiced during the war by the OSS had no place in a peacetime, democratic society. He did, however, recognize the need for an organization to coordinate the collection of intelligence information from all branches of government. As he said, "If such an organization had existed within the United States in 1941, it would have been difficult, if not impossible, for the Japanese to have launched their successful attack on Pearl Harbor."

And so the Central Intelligence Agency was born—to collect, assimilate, and analyze intelligence, not to engage in any other activity.

"He got snookered," Fox had told his handful of students that night at dinner. "Allen Dulles, who ended up running the CIA six years later, thought Truman's views on intelligence were too limited. Know what he did? He sent a memo to the Senate Armed Services Committee undercutting Truman's view of what the CIA was supposed to be."

Fox had produced a copy of that memo for his students:

Intelligence work in time of peace will require other techniques, other personnel, and will have rather different objectives. . . . We must deal with the problem of

112

conflicting ideologies as democracy faces communism, not only in the relations between Soviet Russia and the countries of the West but in the internal political conflicts with the countries of Europe, Asia, and South America.

Dulles went on to contribute a concept to what would eventually become intelligence law, and which gave the CIA its ultimate power. It called for the agency to carry out "such other functions and duties related to intelligence as the National Security Council may from time to time direct." This took it out of the realm of congressional control and helped establish the atmosphere under which the CIA could function autonomous from virtually all control, including manpower and financing. The director had only to sign a voucher and the funds were there, something President Truman had never envisioned happening.

Cahill and the other students at that dinner with Hank Fox later discussed his somewhat irreverent view of the agency and its history. It was refreshing; everyone else with whom they'd come into contact seemed rigidly bound to a party line, no room for deviation, no patience with frivolity or casual remarks that could be construed as less than sanctified.

"Well, on to other functions and duties," Cahill said. "I lost a very good friend recently."

"I'm sorry. Accident?"

"No one is sure. It's been ruled a heart attack but she was only in her thirties and . . ."

"She work with us?"

Cahill hesitated, then said, "Part-time. She was a literary agent."

He removed his feet from the desk and replaced them with his elbows. "Barrie Mayer."

"Yes. You know about her, about what happened?"

"Very little. The rumor mill swung into full gear when she died, and the word was that she did some part-time carrying for us."

Cahill said nothing.

"Did you know she was affiliated?"

"Yes."

"Did she carry to you in Budapest?"

"Not directly but yes, she carried to Budapest."

"Banana Quick."

"I'm not sure about that, Hank."

"Is that what you're on these days?"

"Yes. I turned someone."

"So I heard."

"You did?"

"Yeah. Whether you know it or not, Miss Cahill, your Hungarian friend is viewed around here as the best we've got at the moment."

She resisted a smile of satisfaction and said, "He's been cooperative."

"That's a mild way to put it. Your girlfriend's demise has a lot of people reaching for the Tums bottle."

"Because of Banana Quick?"

"Sure. It's the most amibitious project we've had since the Bay of Pigs. Unfortunately, it has about half as much chance of succeeding, and you know how successful the Cuban fiasco was, but the timetable's been pushed up. Could be anytime now."

"I wouldn't know about the overall project, Hank. I get information from my source and I feed it back. One spoke. I'm not privy to what the wheel does."

"Operation Servo?"

"Pardon?"

"Haven't heard of it?"

"No."

"Just as well. Another act of genius by our army of resident geniuses. I hope death is final, Collette. If it isn't, Harry S. Truman has been twisting and turning ever since he left us the day after Christmas, 1972." He drew a deep breath and his face seemed to sink, to turn gray. He pressed his lips together and said in a low voice lacking energy, "It's no good here anymore, Collette. At best, it's disorganized and ineffectual. At worst, it's evil."

She started to respond but he quickly said, "You'll have to pardon a tired, disgruntled old man. I don't mean to corrupt your enthusiasm with my jaded grumbling."

"Please, Hank, no apologies." She glanced around the office. "Are we secure?"

"Who knows?"

"You don't care?"

"No."

"Why?"

"It's a perk of becoming old. Lots of things don't matter anymore. Don't get me wrong. I do my job. I give them my best effort and loyalty for the check. I want to retire. Janie and I bought a pretty house on some land down in West Virginia. Another year and that's where we head. The kids are doing nicely. We bought another dog. That's three. The five of us, Janie, me, and the canine trio, need West Virginia."

"It sounds great, Hank," Cahill said. "Should I leave now?"

"You have to?"

"I have a luncheon appointment in Rosslyn."

" 'Appointment.' " He smiled. "Not a date?"

"No. I'm meeting Barrie Mayer's mother."

"Only kid?"

"Yes."

"Tough."

"Yes."

"Come on. I'll walk you out. I need fresh air."

They stood next to her small, red rented car and Fox looked up at the building, then out over the woods that shielded other buildings from view. "Rosslyn? I spend a lot of time over there."

"Really?"

"Yeah. One of the Octopus computer centers moved to Rosslyn. Half this joint is empty now."

Cahill laughed as she thought of the tour guide who'd talked about that. She mentioned him.

"I remember him," Fox said. "He was an idiot which, we've all come to realize, doesn't preclude you from working here. He was a running joke around here, and his boss was told to get him out. He hit him with fifty demerits in a week, and you know what that means. Fifty in a *year* is automatic dismissal. The kid was really broken up. He came to me

115

and begged for another chance. I felt sorry for him but he *was* an idiot. I told him I couldn't do anything and he slunk away. He's probably a millionaire four times over now."

"Probably. Hank, it was wonderful seeing you, touching base like this."

"Good to see you, too, kid. Before you take off, listen carefully to me."

She stared at him.

"Watch that pretty little rear end of yours. The Barrie Mayer thing is hot. So's Banana Quick. It's trouble. Watch who you talk to. Banana Quick is a mess, and anybody associated with it goes down the tube along with all the rest of the dirty water." He lowered his voice. "There's a leak in Banana Quick."

"Really?"

"A big one. Maybe that's why your friend isn't with us anymore."

"Oh, no, Hank, she'd never . . ."

"I didn't say she'd do anything, but maybe she got too close to the wrong people. Understand?"

"No, but I have a feeling you're not about to continue my education."

"I would if I could, Collette. I've been kicked upstairs, remember? Need-to-know. I don't have that need anymore. Be careful. I like you. And remember Harry Truman. If they could screw the President of the United States, they can screw anybody, even bright, pretty girls like you who mean well." He kissed her on the cheek, turned, and disappeared inside the building.

12

"It was sweet of you to come," Mrs. Mayer said as they sat at a window table in Alexander's III in Rosslyn, just over the Key Bridge from Georgetown. Rosslyn had grown rapidly. Their view of Georgetown and Washington from the penthouse restaurant was partially obscured by the latest in a series of high-rise office and apartment buildings.

"Frankly, I dreaded it, Mrs. Mayer," Collette said, running a fungernail over the starched white linen tablecloth.

Melissa Mayer placed her hand on Collette's, smiled, and said, "You shouldn't have. It means a great deal to me that one of Barrie's closest friends cared enough to see me. I've felt very lonely lately. I don't today."

Her words boosted Cahill's spirits. She smiled at the older woman, who was impeccably dressed in a light blue jersey suit, white blouse with lace at the neck, and mink stole. Her hair was white and pulled back into a severe chignon. Her face had a healthy glow, aided by makeup that had been expertly applied. She wore a substantial strand of pearls around her neck and pearl earrings with tiny diamond chips. Her fingers, gnarled by arthritis, supported heavy gold and diamond rings.

"I had all sorts of things I'd planned to say when I saw you but . . . "

"Collette, there really is very little to say. I'd always heard that the saddest thing in life was to have a child predecease a parent and I never debated it. Now I *know* it's true. But I am also a believer in the scheme of life. It was never meant to be perfect. The odds are that children will outlive their parents, but it certainly isn't set in stone. I've grieved, I've cried, I've cried a great deal, and now it's time to stop those things and continue with my life."

Cahill shook her head. "You're an amazing woman, Mrs. Mayer."

"I'm nothing of the sort, and please call me Melissa. 'Mrs. Mayer' creates too wide a gap."

"Fair enough."

A waiter asked whether they'd like another drink. Cahill shook her head. Mayer ordered a second perfect Manhattan. Then Collette said, "Melissa, what happened to Barrie?"

The older woman frowned and sat back. "Whatever do you mean?"

"Do you believe she died of a heart attack?"

"Well, I . . . what else am I to believe? That's what I was told."

"Who told you?"

"The doctor."

"Which doctor?"

"Our family doctor."

"He examined her, did an autopsy?"

"No, he received confirmation from a British physician, I believe. Barrie died in . . . "

"I know, in London, but there's . . . there's some reason to question whether it really was her heart."

Mayer's face hardened. She said in a voice that matched her expression. "I'm not sure I understand what you're getting at, Collette."

"I'm not sure what I'm getting at either, Melissa, but I'd like to find out the truth. I simply can't buy the notion that Barrie had a coronary at her age. Can you?"

Melissa Mayer reached into an alligator purse, took out

a long cigarette, lighted it, seemed to savor the smoke in her lungs and mouth, then said, "I believe that life revolves around accepting, Collette. Barrie is dead. I must accept that. Heart attack? I must accept that, too, because if I don't, I'll spend the rest of my days in torment. Can't you accept *that*?"

Cahill winced at the intensity in her voice. She said, "Please don't misunderstand, Melissa, I'm not trying to raise questions that would make Barrie's death more painful to you than it is right now. I realize losing a friend is not as traumatic as losing a daughter, but I've been suffering my own brand of torment. That's why I'm here, trying to lessen my own pain. I suppose that's selfish, but it happens to be the truth."

Cahill watched the older woman's face soften from the hard mask it had become, for which she was thankful. She was feeling an increasing amount of guilt. There she was sitting with a grieving mother under false pretenses, pretending only to be a friend but, in actuality, functioning as an investigator for the CIA. That damned duality, she thought. It was the thing that bothered her most about the work, the need to lie, to withhold, to be anything but the basic person that you were. Everything seemed based upon a lie. There was no walking in the sunshine because too much was conducted in shadows and safehouses, messages written in code instead of plain English, strange names for projects, a life of looking over your shoulder and watching your words, and suspicions about everyone with whom you came in contact.

"Melissa, let's just have a pleasant lunch," Cahill said. "It was wrong of me to use this occasion to salve my own feelings about losing my friend."

The older woman smiled and lighted another cigarette. "Barrie was always chiding me for smoking. She said it would take ten years off of my life but here I sit, very much alive, smoking like a chimney and talking about my health-conscious daughter who's very much dead." Collette tried to change the subject but Mrs. Mayer shook her off. "No, I would like to talk about Barrie with you. There really hasn't been anyone since it happened that I could turn to, be open with. I'm very glad you're here and were close to her. There didn't seem to be many people close to her, you know. She was so outgoing, yet . . . yet, she had so few friends."

Cahill looked quizzically at her. "I would have thought the opposite was true. Barrie was so gregarious, full of life and fun."

"I think that was more show than anything, Collette. You see, Barrie had a lot of nasty things to deal with."

"I know she had occasional problems but . . . "

The smile on Melissa Mayer's face was a knowing one. She said, "It was more than just normal problems, Collette. I'm afraid I'll go to *my* grave regretting those aspects of her life in which I played a part."

Cahill felt uncomfortable at what seemed to be Mayer's apparent intention to delve into some cavern of secrets about Barrie and her. Yet she was as curious as she was uncomfortable, and did nothing to hinder the conversation.

Mayer asked, "Did Barrie ever mention her father to you?"

Cahill thought for a moment. "I think so but I can't remember in what context. No, I'm not even sure she did." In fact, it had struck Cahill a few times during her years of friendship with Barrie Mayer that she didn't mention her father. She remembered a conversation during college with Barrie and some other girls about fathers and their impact on daughters' lives. Barrie's only contribution to the conversation had been sarcastic comments about fathers in general. Later that night, Cahill asked about her own father and was met with the simple response, "He's dead." The tone of Barrie's voice had made it plain that the conversation was over.

Cahill told Melissa Mayer about it and the older woman nodded. Her gaze drifted across the dining room as though in search of a place to which she could anchor her thoughts.

"We don't have to talk about this, Melissa," Cahill said.

Mayer smiled. "No, I was the one who introduced the subject. Barrie's father died when Barrie was ten."

"He must have been a young man," said Cahill.

"Yes, he was young and . . . he was young and not missed."

Cahill said, "I don't understand."

120

"Barrie's father, my husband, was a cruel and inhuman person, Collette. I wasn't aware of that when I married him. I was very young and he was very handsome. His cruelty started to come out after Barrie was born. I don't know whether he resented that a child came between us or whether it just represented a warped aspect of his character, but he was cruel to her, abusive physically and psychologically."

"That's terrible," Cahill said.

"Yes, it was."

"It must have been terrible for you, too."

A pained expression came over Mrs. Mayer's face. She bit her lip and said, "What was terrible was that I did so little to stop it. I was afraid of losing him and kept finding reasons for what he was doing, kept telling myself that he would change. All that did was to prolong it. He . . . *we* virtually destroyed Barrie. She had to find ways to escape the pain of it and went into her own private little world. She didn't have any friends then, just as she didn't as an adult—except you, of course, and some love interests—so she created her own friends, imaginary ones who shared her private world which was, Lord knows, better than her real one."

Collette felt a lump develop in her throat. She thought back to spending time with Barrie and tried to identify some sort of behavior that would indicate such a childhood. She came up empty, except for Barrie's tendency sometimes to drift off into her own thoughts, even in the middle of a spirited conversation with a group of people. But that hardly constituted strange behavior. She'd done it herself.

Melissa Mayer interrupted Cahill's thoughts. "Barrie's father left on her ninth birthday. We had no idea where he went, didn't hear from him again until Barrie was ten and we received a call from the police in Florida. They told me that he'd died of a stroke. There wasn't even a funeral because I didn't want one. He was buried in Florida. I have no idea where." She sighed. "He certainly lived on in Barrie, though. I've carried the guilt and shame of what I allowed to be done to my daughter all these years." Her eyes filled up and she dabbed at them with a lace handkerchief.

Collette felt a twinge of anger at the woman across from

her, not only because of her admission that she did nothing to help her daughter, but because she seemed to be looking for sympathy.

She quickly told herself that wasn't fair and motioned for a waiter. They both ordered lobster bisque and Caesar salads.

The conversation took a decided upturn in mood. Melissa wanted Cahill to talk about experiences she'd had with Barrie, and Collette obliged her, some of the stories making Melissa laugh heartily, aided, in Cahill's mind, by the second drink.

When lunch was over, Cahill brought up the subject of the men in Barrie's life. Her question caused Barrie's mother to smile. She said, "Thank God the experience with her father didn't sour her on men for the rest of her life. She had a very active love life. But you must know more about that than I do. It's not the sort of thing daughters routinely share with their mothers."

Cahill shook her head. "No, Barrie didn't tell me about her male friends in great detail, although there was one, a yacht charter captain from the British Virgin Islands." She waited for a response from the mother but got none. "Eric Edwards. You didn't know about him?"

"No. Was it a recent relationship?"

Cahill nodded. "Yes, I think she was seeing him right up until the day she died. She shared her feelings about him with me. She was madly in love with him."

"No, I didn't know about him. There was that psychiatrist she was seeing."

Cahill almost said the name but held herself in check. "Seeing professionally?" she asked.

The mother made a sour face. "Yes, for a while. I was very much against it, her going into therapy where she'd have to bear her soul to a stranger."

Cahill said, "But, considering Barrie's childhood, that might have been the best thing she could do. Hadn't she had any professional help up until seeing this psychiatrist? You said his name was . . . ?"

"Tolker, Jason Tolker. No, I never saw the need for it. I think I was the one who should have had therapy, considering the grief it caused me all these years, but I don't believe in it. People should be able to handle their own emotional lives. Don't you agree?"

"Well, I suppose . . . I gather from what you've said that Barrie saw him socially as well."

"Yes, and I found that appalling. Imagine going to some-one like that for more than a year and telling your most intimate secrets and then going out with him. He must have considered her a fool."

Cahill thought for a moment, then said, "Was Barrie in love with this psychiatrist?"

"I don't know."

"Did you meet him?"

"No. Barrie kept her personal life very separate from me. I suppose that goes back to her childhood needs to escape her father."

"I really don't know of any other men in Barrie's life," Cahill said, "except for fellows she dated in college. We fell out of touch for a while, as you know."

"Yes. There is that fellow at the office, David Hubler, who I think she was interested in."

That was news to Cahill, and she wondered whether the mother had it straight. She asked whether Barrie had ac-tually dated Hubler.

"Not that I know of, and I suppose the fact that she freely introduced him to me means there was not romantic in-terest." She suddenly looked older than she had at the be-ginning of lunch. She said, "It's all water over the dam, isn't it, now that she's dead? All so wasted." She sat up straight, as though she'd suddenly realized something. She looked Cahill in the eye. "You really don't believe Barrie died of a heart attack, do you?"

Cahill slowly shook her head.

"What, then? Are you saying someone killed her?"

"I don't know, Melissa, I just know that I can't accept the fact that she died the way they say she did."

"I hope you're wrong, Collette. I know you're wrong."

"I hope so. I'm glad we could get together for this lunch. I'd like to keep in touch with you while I'm back here in Washington."

123

"Yes, of course, that would be lovely. Would you come for dinner?"

"I'd like that."

They went to the basement parking garage and stood next to Melissa Mayer's Cadillac. Cahill asked, "When was the last time you saw Barrie?"

"The night before it happened. She stayed with me."

"She did?"

"Yes, we had a nice quiet dinner together before she took off on another journey. She traveled so much. I don't know how she managed to keep her sanity with all the trips."

"It was a hectic schedule. Did she have her luggage with her at your house?"

"Her luggage? Yes, she did, as a matter of fact. She was going to go directly to the airport but decided to stop at the office first to take care of some things."

"What kind of luggage did Barrie have?"

"Regular luggage, one of those hang-up garment bags and a nice leather carry-on. Of course, there were always the briefcases."

"Two of them?"

"No, only the one that she always used. I bought it for her birthday a few years ago."

"I see. Did she act different that night at your house? Did she complain about feeling ill, display any symptoms?"

"Goodness, no, we had a delightful evening. She seemed in very good spirits."

They shook hands and drove off in their respective automobiles. A third car left the garage at the same time and fell in behind Cahill.

She returned to the hotel and called David Hubler. They made a date for drinks at the Four Seasons at four. She then called the British Virgin Islands, got the number of the Edwards Yacht Charter Company, and reached a secretary who informed her that Mr. Edwards was away for a few days.

"I see," Cahill said. "Do you have any idea when he'll be back? I'm calling from Washington and . . . "

"Mr. Edwards is in Washington," said the young woman, whose voice had an island lilt.

124

"That's wonderful. Where is he staying?"

"At the Watergate."

"Thank you, thank you very much."

"What did you say your name was, ma'am?"

"Collette Cahill. I was a friend of Barrie Mayer." She waited; the name didn't trigger a response from the girl.

She hung up, called the Watergate Hotel, and asked for Mr. Edwards's room. There was no answer. "Would you like to leave a message?"

"No, thank you, I'll call again."

13

Cahill sat in the lavish lobby of Georgetown's Four Seasons Hotel waiting for David Hubler. A pianist played light classics, the delicate notes as muted as the conversations at widely spaced tables.

Cahill took in the faces of the well-dressed men and women. They were the faces of power and money, cause and effect, probably in reverse order. Dark suits, furs, highly polished shoes, minimal gestures, and comfortable posture. They belonged. Some people did and others didn't, and nowhere was the distinction more obvious than in Washington.

Were the people around her involved in politics and government? It was always assumed that everyone in Washington worked in its basic industry, government, but that had changed, Cahill knew, and for the better.

It had seemed to her during her college days that every eligible young man worked for some agency or congressman or political action committee, and that all conversation gravitated toward politics. It had become boring for her at one point, and she'd seriously considered transferring to another college in a different part of the country to avoid becoming too insular. She didn't, and ended up in government herself.

What if? A silly game. What was reality for her was that she worked for the Central Intelligence Agency, had lost a friend, and was now in Washington trying to find out what had happened to that friend, for herself and for her employer.

She realized as she waited for Hubler that she'd been forgetting or, at least, ignoring that second reason for being there.

Her official assignment to take "leave" and to use it "unofficially" to find out more about Barrie Mayer's death had been handed her so casually, as though it really didn't matter what she discovered. But she knew better. Whatever underlying factors contributed to Mayer's death, they had to do with Banana Quick, perhaps the most important and ambitious clandestine operation the Company had ever undertaken. The fact that it had been compromised in some way by Mayer's death, and its implementation had been accelerated, added urgency—an urgency that Cahill now felt.

She lost track of time, and of the Four Seasons as she reflected on what had transpired over the past few weeks, especially what had been said to her by her Hungarian agent, Árpád, and what Hank Fox had said that morning about a leak in Banana Quick.

Tolker? Hegedüs had hinted that he might be "friendly" to the other side. But, she wondered, what information could he have on Banana Quick that would threaten the project and, if he did, where did he get it?

Barrie Mayer? It was the only source that made any sense to her, but that raised its own question—where would Mayer have learned enough about the project?

Eric Edwards? Possible. They were lovers, he was CIA, and he lived in the British Virgins.

If Mayer *was* killed because of what she was carrying that pertained to Banana Quick, who had the most to gain, the Soviets, or someone working with or within the CIA with something to hide?

She checked her watch. Hubler was a half hour late. She ordered a white wine and told the waitress she had to make a phone call. At Barrie's agency, Marcia St. John answered.

Margaret Truman

"I was supposed to meet David at the Four Seasons a half hour ago," Collette said.

"I don't know where he is," St. John said. "I know he planned to meet you but right after you called, he got another call and tore out of here like an Olympic sprinter."

"He didn't say where he was going?"

"No. Sorry."

"Well, I'll wait another half hour. If he doesn't show and checks in with you, ask him to call me at the Hotel Washington."

"Shall do."

As Collette resumed her seat in the Four Seasons and quietly sipped her wine, David Hubler parked his car in front of a hydrant in Rosslyn, got out, locked the door, and looked up the street. He had to squint, finally to shield his eyes with his hand from the harsh, direct rays of a blazing setting sun that was anchored at the far end of the busy road. There was a heavy, dirty haze in the air that compounded the blinding effect.

He said aloud the address he'd been given by the caller who'd prompted him to run from the office, and to break his date with Collette. He checked his watch; he was ten minutes early. Street signs at the corner told him he was within half a block of his destination, an alley between two nondescript commercial buildings.

A group of teenagers passed, one carrying a large portable radio and cassette player from which loud rock 'n' roll blared. Hubler watched them pass, turned, and started for the corner. The sidewalk was busy with men and women leaving their jobs and heading home. He bumped into a woman and apologized, circumvented a young couple embracing, and reached the corner. "What the hell," he said as he turned left and walked halfway down the block until reaching the entrance to the alley. He peered down it; the sun was anchored at its end, too. He cocked his head, focused his eyes on the ground, and took a few steps into the narrow passageway. It was empty, or appeared to be. Steel doors that were rear entrances to businesses were closed. Occa-

128

sional piles of neatly bagged garbage jutted out into the alley; two motorcycles and a bicycle were securely chained to a ventilation pipe.

Hubler continued, his eyes now searching walls on his left for a large red sign that would say NO PARKING. He found it halfway into the alley, above a bay of sorts. A narrow loading dock with a roll-down corrugated door was below the sign. Large drums, probably having contained chemicals or some other industrial product, were stacked three high and five deep, creating a pocket invisible to people on the streets at either end.

He looked at his watch again. It was time. He skirted the drums and went to the loading dock, placed his hands on it, and listened. The alley was a silent refuge from the distant horns of the streets, the boom boxes, and the animated conversations of people happily escaping nine-to-five.

"On time," a male voice said.

Hubler, hands still on the loading dock, raised his head and turned in the direction of the voice. His pupils shut down as his eyes tried to adjust from shadows to the stream of sunlight pouring into the alley. The man to whom the voice belonged took three steps forward and thrust his right hand at Hubler's chest. A six-inch, needle-thin point of an ice pick slid easily through skin and muscle and reached Hubler's heart, the handle keeping it from going through to his back.

Hubler's mouth opened wide. So did his eyes. A red stain bloomed on the front of his shirt. The man withdrew the pick, leaned his head closer to Hubler, and watched the result of his action, like a painter evaluating an impetuous stroke of red paint on his canvas. Hubler's knees sagged and led his body down to the cement. His assailant quickly knelt and pulled Hubler's wallet from his pants pocket and shoved it into his tan rain jacket. He stood, checked both ends of the alley, and walked toward the sun, now in the final stage of its descent.

When Hubler didn't arrive, Cahill paid for her drink and returned to her hotel. There were two messages, one from

Vern Wheatley, the other from the British literary agent, Mark Hotchkiss. She tried Dave Hubler at home. No answer. Hotchkiss, the message said, was staying at the newly renovated Willard. She called; no answer in his room. Vern Wheatley was staying in his brother's apartment on Dupont Circle. She reached him.

"What's up?" she asked.

"Nothing much. I just thought you might be free for dinner."

"I'm not, Vern, wish I were. Rain check?"

"Tomorrow?"

"Sounds good. How's the assignment going?"

"Slow, but what else is new? Trying to pin down bureaucrats is like trying to slam a revolving door. I'll give you a call tomorrow afternoon and set things up."

"Great."

"Hey, Collette?"

"Huh?"

"You have a date tonight?"

"I wouldn't call it that unless the fact that I'm having dinner with a man makes it so. Business."

"I thought you were home to relax."

"A little relaxation, a little business. Nothing heavy. Talk to you tomorrow."

She hung up and chided herself for the slip. As she took off her clothes and stepped into the shower, she found herself wishing she were on a vacation. Maybe she could tack on a week of leave when she was done snooping into Barrie Mayer's death. That would be nice.

After her shower, she stood naked in front of a full-length mirror and looked herself over from head to toe. "Strictly a salad, no bread," she said to her reflection as she pinched the flesh at her waist. She certainly wasn't overweight, but knew the possibility was always there should she neglect her sensible eating habits and go on a binge.

She chose one of two dresses she'd brought with her from home, a mauve wool knit she'd had made for her in Budapest. Her hair had grown longer and she debated with herself whether she liked it that way. It didn't matter at the moment. She wasn't about to get a haircut that evening.

She completed her ensemble with tan pumps, a simple, single-strand gold necklace, and tiny gold pierced earrings, a gift to her from Joe Breslin on the first anniversary of her assignment to Budapest. She grabbed her purse and raincoat, went to the lobby, and told the doorman she needed a cab. She wasn't in the mood to drive and have to search for parking spaces.

It had started to rain, and the air had picked up a chill from a front that was passing through Washington. The doorman held a large golf umbrella over her as he opened the door to a taxi that pulled up. She gave the driver Jason Tolker's address and, a few minutes later, was seated in his reception area. It was six forty-five; Tolker's group session was still in progress.

Fifteen minutes later, the participants in the group filed past her. Tolker emerged moments later, smiling. "Spirited group tonight. You watch them argue with each other over trivialities and understand why they don't get along with colleagues and spouses."

"Do they know you're that cynical?"

"I hope not. Hungry?"

"Not especially. Besides, I've put on a few pounds and would just as soon not compound it tonight."

He looked her up and down. "You look perfect to me."

"Thank you." He didn't waste time, she thought. She'd never responded to men who came up with lines like that, found them generally to be insecure and immature. Vern Wheatley flashed through her mind, and she wished she hadn't accepted Tolker's dinner invitation. Duty! she told herself, smiled, and asked what restaurant he had in mind.

"The best in town, my house."

"Oh, wait a minute, Doctor, I . . ."

He cocked his head and said in serious tones, "You're stereotyping me, Miss Cahill, aren't you, assuming that because I suggest dinner at my place the seduction scene is sure to follow?"

"It crossed my mind."

"Mine, too, frankly, but if you'll come to dinner at my house, I promise you that even if you change your mind,

131

you'll get no moves by me. I'll throw you out right after coffee and cognac. Fair enough?''

"Fair enough. What's on the menu?''

"Steaks and a salad. Skip the dressing and you'll lose a pound or two.''

His champagne-colored Jaguar was parked outside. Cahill had never been in one; she enjoyed the smell and feel of the leather seats. He drove swiftly through Foggy Bottom, turned up Wisconsin Avenue and passed the Washington Cathedral, then took smaller streets until reaching a stretch of expensive houses set back from the road. He turned into a driveway lined with poplar trees and came to a stop on a gravel circle in front of a large stone house. A semicircular portico decorated with egg-and-dart detail protected the entrance. There were lights on in the front rooms that shed soft, yellow illumination through drapes drawn over the windows.

Tolker came around and opened Collette's door. She followed him to the front door. He pushed a buzzer. Who else was there? she wondered. The door opened and a young Chinese man wearing jeans, a dark blue short-sleeved sweatshirt, and white sneakers greeted them.

"Collette, this is Joel. He works for me.''

"Hello, Joel,'' she said as she entered the large foyer. To the left was what looked like a study. To the right was a dining room lighted by electrified candelabra.

"Come on,'' Tolker said, leading her down a hall and to the living room. Floor-to-ceiling windows afforded a view of a formal Japanese garden lighted by floodlights. A high brick wall surrounded it.

"It's lovely,'' Cahill said.

"Thanks. I like it. Drink?''

"Just club soda, thank you.''

Tolker told Joel to make him a kir. The young man left the room and Tolker said to Cahill, "Joel's a student at American University. I give him room and board in exchange for functioning as a houseboy. He's a good cook. He's been marinating the steaks all day.''

Cahill went to a wall of books and read the titles. They

all seemed to be on the field of human behavior. "Impressive collection," she said.

"Most of them pop garbage, but I wanted them all. I'm a collector by nature." He came up beside her and said, "Publishers have been after me to write a book for years. Frankly, I can't imagine spending that much time on anything."

"A book. I imagine that would be an ego-booster, not that . . ."

He laughed and finished her sentence. "Not that I need it."

She laughed, too, said, "I sense you're not lacking in it, Doctor."

"Ego is healthy. People without egos don't function very well in society. Come, sit down. I'd like to learn more about you."

She wanted to say that she was the one who wanted to learn something from the evening. She sat on a small, gracefully curved Louis XV sofa upholstered in a heavy bloodred fabric. He took a seat on its mate, across an inlaid leather coffee table. Joel placed their drinks in front of them and Tolker said, "Dinner in an hour, Joel." He looked to Cahill for approval, and she nodded. Joel left. Tolker lifted his glass and said, "To dinner with a beautiful woman."

"I can't drink a toast to that, but I won't argue."

"See, you have a healthy ego, too."

"Different from yours, Doctor. I would never toast myself. You would."

"But I didn't."

"It wouldn't have offended me if you had."

"All right, to a beautiful woman *and* to a handsome, successful, bright, and impossibly considerate gentleman."

She couldn't help but laugh. He got up and started a tape that sent soft sounds of a modern jazz trio into the room. He sat again. "First of all, how about calling me Jason instead of Doctor?"

"All right."

"Second, tell me about your life and work in Budapest."

"I'm on leave," she said.

"Spoken like a true Company employee."

133

"I think we ought to drop any conversation along those lines."

"Why? Make you nervous?"

"No, just aware that there are rules."

"Rules. I don't play by them."

"That's your choice."

"And your choice is to rigidly adhere to every comma and period. I'm not being impudent, Collette. I just find it amazing and wonderful and damned ironic that you and Barrie and I have this uncommon common bond. Think about it. You and your best friend both end up doing work for our country's leading spook agency, you because of a sense of patriotism, or the need for a job with a pension and a little excitement, Barrie because she became close to me, and I, as I've already acknowledged, have been a consultant to the spooks a time or two. Remarkable when you think of it. Most people go through their lives not knowing the CIA from the Audubon Society and never meeting a soul who works for them."

"Small world," she said.

"It turned out that way for us, didn't it?"

He arranged himself comfortably on his couch, crossed his legs, and asked, "How well did you know Barrie?"

"We were good friends."

"I know, but how well did you know her, *really* know her?"

Cahill thought of her luncheon conversation with Mayer's mother and realized she didn't know her friend well at all. She mentioned the lunch to Tolker.

"She was more disturbed than you realize."

"In what way?"

"Oh, what we call a disturbed myth-belief pattern."

"Meaning?"

"Meaning that she lived by a set of troublesome beliefs caused by childhood myths that were not tied to normal childhood patterns."

"Her father?"

"Her mother mentioned that to you?"

"Yes."

He smiled. "Did she indicate her role in it?"

134

"She said she felt guilty for not putting a stop to it. She was very candid. She admitted that she was afraid to lose her husband."

Another smile from him. "She's a liar. Most of Barrie's adult problems stemmed from her mother, not her father."

Cahill frowned.

"The old lady's a horror. Take it from me."

"You mean from Barrie. You've never met the mother."

"True, but Barrie was a good enough source. What I'm suggesting to you, Collette, is that you become a little more discriminating about who in Barrie's life you turn to for information."

"I'm not looking for information."

"You said you were trying to find out what went on with her just before she died."

"That's right, but I don't consider that 'looking for information.' I'm curious about a friend, that's all."

"As you wish. More club soda?"

"No, thank you. You obviously aren't including yourself in that restricted list."

"Of course not. I was the best friend she had . . . excluding you, of course."

"You were lovers, too."

"If you say so. Barrie didn't have any trouble attracting men."

"She was beautiful."

"Yes. Her problem was she couldn't tell the white hats from the black. Her choice in men was terrible, self-destructive to say the least."

"Present company excepted."

"Right again."

"Eric Edwards?"

"I wondered whether you knew about Barrie's macho yacht captain."

"I know a lot about him," Cahill said. "Barrie was very much in love with him. She talked about him a great deal."

"Excuse me, I need a drink." He returned a few minutes later. "Joel's started the steaks. Let me give you a quick tour before dinner."

The house was unusual, an eclectic assortment of rooms,

135

each decorated in a different style. The master bedroom had been created from three rooms. It was huge. While the other rooms in the house smacked of an Early American influence, this room was modern. The thick carpet was white, as was the bedspread on a king-size round bed that stood in the middle of the room like a piece of sculpture, spotlights in the ceiling focusing all attention on it. One wall housed a huge projection screen television and racks of state-of-the-art sound equipment. Besides a black lacquered nightstand that held controls for the audio and video equipment, the only other furniture was black leather director's chairs scattered about the room. There wasn't a piece of clothing, a shoe, or a magazine.

"Different, isn't it?" he said.

"From the rest of the house, yes." She pictured Barrie Mayer in the bed with him.

"My apartment in New York is different, too. I like different things."

"I suppose we all do," she said, walking from the room at a pace just under a run.

Dinner was relaxed, the food and talk good. The subject of Barrie Mayer was avoided. Tolker talked a great deal about his collections, especially wine. When dinner was finished, he took Cahill to the basement where thousands of bottles were stored in temperature-controlled rooms.

They came upstairs and went to his study, which had the look of a traditional British library, books on three walls, polished paneling, carpet in warm earth tones, heavy patinated furniture, pools of gentle light from floor lamps next to a long leather couch and leather armchairs. Tolker told Joel to bring them a bottle of cognac, then told him he was finished for the night. Cahill was glad the young Chinese man wouldn't be around any longer. There was something unsettling about him, and about the relationship with Tolker. Joel hadn't smiled once the entire evening. When he looked at Tolker, Cahill could see deep anger in his eyes. When he looked at her, it was more resentment she sensed.

"Brooding young man, isn't he?" she said, as Tolker poured their drinks.

Tolker laughed. "Yes. It's like having a houseboy and guard dog for the price of one."

They sat on the couch and sipped from their snifters. "Do you really think you're overweight?" Tolker asked.

Cahill, who'd been staring down into the dark, shimmering liquid, looked at him and said, "I know I can be if I'm not careful. I love food and hate diets. Bad combination."

"Ever try hypnosis?"

"No. Oh, that's not true. I did once, in college. So did Barrie."

It had been a fraternity party. A young man claimed to know how to do hypnosis and everyone challenged him to try it on them. Cahill was reluctant. She'd heard stories of how people can be made to act foolish at the hands of a hypnotist. It represented giving up control and she didn't like the idea.

Mayer, on the other hand, eagerly volunteered and convinced Cahill to give it a try. She eventually agreed and the two of them sat next to each other on a couch while the young man dangled his fraternity ring from a string in front of their eyes. As he talked about how they would begin to feel sleepy and relaxed, Cahill realized two things: She was feeling anything except sleepy, and was finding the whole situation funny. Mayer, on the other hand, had sagged into the couch and was actually purring. Cahill diverted her eyes from the ring and glanced over at her friend. The hypnotist realized he'd lost Cahill and devoted all his attention to Mayer. After a few more minutes of soothing talk, he suggested to Mayer that her hands were tied to helium balloons and would float up. Cahill watched as Mayer's arms began to tremble, then slowly drifted toward the ceiling. They remained there for a long time. Others in the room were watching intently. They were quiet; only the hypnotist's voice invaded the silence.

"I'm going to count from one to five," he said. "When I reach five, you'll be awake, will feel real good, and won't remember anything from the last few minutes. Later, someone will say to you, 'The balloons are pretty.' When you hear that, your arms will feel very light again and they'll float up into the air. You won't try to stop it because it will feel good. Ready? One—two—three—four—five."

Mayer's eyes fluttered open. She realized her arms were high in the air, quickly stretched them, and said, "I feel so good and rested."

Everyone applauded and the beer keg became the center of attention again.

Twenty minutes later, a friend of the hynotist who'd been prompted casually said to Mayer, "The balloons are pretty." Others at the party knew it was coming and were watching. Barrie Mayer yawned. A contented smile crossed her face and her arms floated up toward the ceiling.

"Why are you doing that?" someone yelled.

"I don't know. It just . . . feels good."

The hypnotist told her to lower them. "No," she said, "I don't want to."

He quickly went through the induction again, then told her that her arms were normal and that there weren't any balloons filled with helium. He counted to five, she shook her head, and that was the end of it.

Later, as Collette and Barrie sat in a booth in an all-night diner drinking coffee, Collette said, "You're such a phony."

"Huh?"

"That business with hypnosis and your arms being light and all. You were going along with it, right?"

"I don't know what you mean."

"You were acting. You weren't asleep or hypnotized."

"No, I really was hypnotized. At least I *think* I was. I don't remember much about it except feeling so relaxed. It was great."

Collette sat back and looked closely at her friend. "The balloons are pretty," she said softly.

Barrie looked around the diner. "What balloons?"

Collette sighed and finished her coffee, still convinced that her friend had been playacting for the sake of the hypnotist.

When she was finished telling the story to Jason Tolker, he said, "You shouldn't be so skeptical, Collette. Just because you weren't receptive doesn't mean Barrie wasn't. People differ in their ability to enter an altered state like hypnosis."

138

"Barrie must have been *very* receptive. It was incredible what that student was able to get her to do unless . . . unless she was just going along with it for fun."

"I don't doubt you're not hypnotizable, Collette," Tolker said, smiling. "You're much too cynical and concerned about losing control."

"Is that bad?"

"Of course not, but . . . "

"Did you ever hypnotize Barrie?"

He paused as though thinking back, then said, "No, I didn't."

"I'm surprised," Cahill said. "If she was that susceptible and . . . "

"Not susceptible, Collette, receptive."

"Whatever. If she was that receptive, and you use it in your practice, I would have thought that . . . "

"You're crossing that line of doctor-patient confidentiality."

"Sorry."

"You might be more hypnotizable than you think. After all, your only brush with it was with a college amateur. Want me to try?"

"No."

"Could help you resist fattening food."

"I'll stick to willpower, thank you."

He shrugged, leaned forward, and said, "Feel like turning on?"

"With what?"

"Your choice. Pot. Coke. Everything I have is the best."

An invitation to drugs wasn't new to Cahill, but his suggestion offended her. "You're a doctor."

"I'm a doctor who enjoys life. You look angry. Never turn on?"

"I prefer a drink."

"Fine. What'll you have?"

"I don't mean now. I really should be going."

"I really *have* offended you, haven't I?"

"Offended? No, but I am disappointed you choose to end the evening this way. I've enjoyed it very much. Would you take me home now?"

"Sure." His tone was suddenly surly, his expression one of annoyance.

They pulled up in front of her hotel and shut off the engine. "You know, Collette, Barrie wasn't the person you thought she was. She enjoyed drugs, used them with some frequency."

Cahill turned and faced him, her eyes narrowed. "One, I don't believe that. Two, even if it's true, it doesn't matter to me. Barrie was tall, slender, and her hair was sandy. I'm short, could be chubby, and have black hair. Thanks for a nice evening."

"I kept my promise, didn't I?"

"Which one?"

"Not to put moves on you. Can I see you again?"

"I don't think so." It swiftly crossed her mind that maybe she should keep in touch with him as a potential source of information. She had learned things about Barrie that were previously unknown to her and that, after all, was the purpose for her being in Washington. She softened her rejection with, "Please don't misunderstand, Jason. I'm a little confused these days, probably a combination of lingering jet lag, still grieving about Barrie's death, and a lot of other things. Let me see how my schedule goes the next few days. If I'm free, I'll call you. All right?"

"Don't call us, we'll call you."

She smiled. "Something like that. Good night."

"Good night." His face was hard and angry again, and she could see a cruelty behind his expression that caused her to flinch.

She stepped from the car—he didn't bother getting out to open the door for her this time—and started toward the hotel's entrance where the doorman, taken by surprise by her sudden exit, quickly pushed open the door for her. Across the lobby, she could see Vern Wheatley. He was seated in a wing chair facing the door. When he spotted her, he jumped up and met her just inside.

"Vern, what are you doing here?" she asked.

"I have some news, Collette, and I think we'd better discuss it."

140

14

Cahill sat with Vern Wheatley the next morning in his brother's apartment. "Good Morning America" was the program on television. The morning paper sat on a coffee table. The lead story on page one seemed to be set in gigantic type; it virtually sprang off the page at Cahill.

D.C. LITERARY AGENT MURDERED

David Hubler, 34, a literary agent with the Georgetown firm of Barrie Mayer Associates, was found murdered last night in an alley in Rosslyn. A spokesman for the Rosslyn Police Department, Sergeant Clayton Perry, said that the cause of death appeared to be a sharp object driven into the victim's heart.

According to the same police spokesman, robbery was the apparent motive. The victim's wallet was missing. Identification was made from business cards in his pocket.

The story went on to provide sketchy details about Hubler. Barrie Mayer's death was mentioned in the final paragraph: "The agency for which Hubler worked suffered another recent loss when its founder and president, Barrie Mayer, died in London of a coronary."

Collette sat on a couch in the living room. She wore Wheatley's robe. Her eyes were focused on the newspaper. Wheatley paced the room.

"It could be a coincidence," Cahill said in a monotone.

Wheatley stopped at the window, looked out, rolled his fingertips on the pane, turned, and said, "Be reasonable, Collette. It can't be. Both of them within such a short period of time?"

A local news cutaway came on TV and they turned their attention to it. It was the second lead story. Nothing new. Just the facts of Hubler's death—apparent robbery—a thin, sharp object the weapon. No suspects. "Back to Charles Gibson in New York and his guest, a former rock star who's found religion."

Collette clicked off the set. They'd been up all night, first in her room at the hotel, then to the apartment at 4:00 A.M. where Wheatley made coffee. She'd cried, much of it out of sympathy for David Hubler, some of it because she was frightened. Now her tear tank, she thought, was empty. All that was left was a dry throat, stinging eyes, and a hollow feeling in her stomach.

"Tell me again how you found out David was dead."

"That's a *real* coincidence, Collette. I happened to be over at Rosslyn police headquarters trying to run down some leads for this assignment I'm on. I was there when the report came in about Hubler. Because of you, I knew right away who he was. You talked a lot about him the night of your party, how that guy Hotchkiss claims he ended up owning the agency and what it would mean to Hubler."

"You just happened to be there?" There was disbelief in her voice.

"Yeah. The minute I heard, I came looking for you at the hotel."

She blew a stream of breath through her lips and pulled on a clump of her hair. "It's scary, Vern, so scary."

"You bet it is, which is why you can't go around viewing it as some dumb coincidence. Look, Collette, you don't buy the fact that your friend Barrie dropped dead of a heart attack. Right?"

"I never said that."

"You didn't have to. The way you talked about it said it all. If you're right—if she was killed by someone—Hubler's death means a hell of a lot more. Right?"

"I don't know how Barrie died. The autopsy said . . ."

"What autopsy? Who did it, some London doctor, you said? Who's he? Did anybody back here connected with her family confirm it?"

"No, but . . ."

"If Barrie Mayer didn't die of natural causes, who do you think might have killed her?"

"Damn it, Vern, I don't know! I don't know anything anymore."

"More coffee?" Wheatley asked.

"No."

"Let's view it rationally," Wheatley said. "Whoever killed Hubler might have killed Barrie, right? The motive could have to do with the agency, with a client, a publisher, or with this character Hotchkiss. What do you know about him?"

"That I didn't particularly like him, that he had dinner with Barrie in London the night before she died, and that he claims to have entered into a partnership agreement with her."

"Did he show you papers?"

"No."

"Do you know where he lives, where his office is in London?"

"I have it written down. He's not there, though. He's in Washington."

Wheatley's eyes widened. "He's here."

"Yes. He left a message for me. He's at the Willard."

"You talked to him?"

"No. He wasn't there when I returned his call."

Wheatley started pacing again. He paused at the window. "Let me talk to Hotchkiss," he said.

"Why would you want to do that?"

"I'm interested."

"Why? You didn't know any of these people."

"I feel like I did because of you." He sat next to her and put his hand on her arm. "Look, Collette, you check out of the hotel and come stay here with me. My brother won't be back for another couple of weeks."

"I thought . . ."

"So did I, but he called from Africa yesterday. He finished the photo assignment but he wants to do some shooting for himself."

She pondered his suggestion. "You seem to think *I* might be in danger," she said.

He shrugged. "Maybe, maybe not, but you're a link, too, to both of them. You've met Hotchkiss. He knows you were close to Barrie and that you know about Barrie's will that sets Hubler up to run the agency. I don't know, Collette, I just think being safe is better than being sorry."

"This is all silly, Vern. I could go back to Mom's house."

"No, I want you here."

She looked up into his slender, chiseled face and realized he was giving an order, wasn't suggesting anything. She got up, went to the window, and watched people on the street below scurrying to work, briefcases and brown paper bags of coffee and Danish in their hands. There was something comforting about seeing them. It was normal. What was happening to her wasn't.

Wheatley said, "I'm going to take a shower. I have some appointments this morning. What are you up to?"

"I don't have any definite plans. I have some calls to make and . . .."

"And we check you out of the hotel. Right?"

"Okay. Can I use the phone?"

"Use anything you want. And let's get something straight right now, up front. You stay here, but it doesn't mean you have to sleep with me."

She couldn't help but smile. "Did you really think I'd assume that?" she asked.

"I don't know, but I just want it understood."

"Understood, sir."

"Don't be a wise guy."

"And don't you be a male chauvinist."

144

"Yes, ma'am. I'll do my best."

She heard the shower come on, picked up the phone in the living room and called her mother.

"Collette, where have you been? I tried you many times at the hotel and . . ."

"I'm okay, Mom, just a change of plans. I'll tell you all about it when I see you. Is anything wrong with you?"

"No, but Mr. Fox called. He was the one you liked so much, wasn't he?"

"Yes. What did he want?"

"He said it was very important that you call him. I promised I'd get the message to you but I couldn't reach you."

"That's okay, Mom. I'll call him this morning. Anything else new?"

"No. Your Uncle Bruce fell last night. He broke his arm."

"That's terrible. Is he in the hospital?"

"He should be but he wouldn't stay. That's the problem with drinking like he does. He can't go to the hospital because he can't drink there. They set his arm and sent him home."

"I'll call."

"That would be nice. He's such a good man except for all the drinking. It's a curse."

"I have to go, Mom. I'll call you later in the day. By the way, I'll be staying at Vern's brother's apartment for a few days."

"With him?"

"Vern? Well . . ."

"His brother."

"Oh, no. He's in Africa on a photo assignment. Vern will be here but . . ."

"You be careful."

"Of Vern?"

"I don't mean that, I just . . ."

"I'll be careful."

"Give him my best. He's a nice boy."

"I will." She gave her the apartment phone number.

Wheatley came from the shower wearing a big, fluffy red towel around his waist. His hair was wet and fell over his forehead. "Who'd you call?" he asked.

"My mother. She says hello."

"The bathroom's all yours."

"Thanks."

She closed the bathroom door, hung the robe on the back of it, and turned on the shower. A radio inside the stall was tuned to a light rock station. She reached through the water and steam and found WGMS-FM, where Samuel Barber's *Adagio for Strings* was being performed by the New York Philharmonic. She turned up the volume, withdrew her hand, stood in front of the mirror, wiped condensation from it with her palm, and peered at herself.

"Out of control," she said. "Everything's out of control."

The poignancy of the music drew her into the shower, where she eased herself under the torrent of hot water until her body had acclimated, then thrust her face beneath it. As fatigue was driven from her by the pulsating stream, she thought of her decision—*his* decision—to stay with him. Maybe she shouldn't. There was no need. She wasn't in any danger.

She absently wondered why Wheatley was so interested? Of course . . . how stupid not to realize it immediately. There's a story in it, possibly a big one. He wanted her close in case she could contribute to it by knowing Mayer and Hubler. She'd undoubtedly be finding out more about their deaths, and he could use that knowledge. It didn't anger her that she might be used by him. In fact, it set her mind at ease.

She took a plastic bottle of shampoo from a white wire rack, poured some into her hand, and vigorously worked it into her hair. It relaxed her; she felt ready to start the day. She'd call Hank Fox, then go to Barrie Mayer's agency where she'd find out what she could from her associates. There was Mark Hotchkiss to call, and Eric Edwards. It would be a busy day but she welcomed it. She'd been floundering too long, flopping between the role of concerned, grieving friend and unofficial investigator. It was time to pull everything together, accomplish what she could, grab a legitimate week's vacation and get back to Budapest where, no matter how much intrigue existed, there was a sense of order and structure.

She didn't hear the door open. It was only an inch at first, then wider. Wheatley stuck his head inside the bathroom and said softly, "Collette."

The water and music blotted out everything for her.

"Collette," he said louder.

She sensed rather than heard him, looked through the glass door and saw him standing there. She gasped; hot water instantly filled her throat and caused her to gag.

"Collette, I have some clean Jockey shorts if you want a pair. Socks, too."

"What? *Shorts?*"

"Yeah. Sorry to barge in." He backed out and closed the door.

She quickly finished showering, stepped out and stood immobile, her heart pounding, her lips quivering. "Shorts," she said. "Jockey shorts." She began to calm down and started to laugh as she dried her hair. He'd left a clean pair of shorts and white athletic socks on a hamper. She put them on, slipped the dress she'd worn the night before over her head, and went to the bedroom where he was finishing dressing in jeans, a turtleneck, and a corduroy sport jacket.

"Thanks for the shorts and socks," she said. "They don't exactly go with the dress, but they'll do until I can get back to the hotel."

"We'll go right now," he said. "Hope I didn't scare you?"

"Scare me? Of course not. I thought you were making a move."

"I promised, remember?"

She thought of Jason Tolker's similar promise. She tried to slip her pumps over the heavy socks, gave up, and slipped bare feet into them. "Can't use these," she said, tossing the socks on the bed.

They drove to the hotel in her rented car, checked out, and an hour later were back in the apartment. "Got to go," Wheatley said. "Here's an extra key to the place. Catch up later?"

"Sure."

"Who are you seeing today?"

"I'm going over to Barrie's agency."

147

"Good idea. By the way, who was that guy you were with last night?"

"Just a friend. A doctor, friend of the family."

"Oh. We're on for dinner tonight, right?"

"Right."

"Take care. Maybe I'm being paranoid but I'd move easy," he said. "Don't take chances."

"I won't."

"Not worth it. After all, murder isn't your business. You help stranded tourists, right?"

"Right." There was a playful, disbelieving tone in his voice, and it irked her.

After he'd gone, she picked up the phone and called Hank Fox in Langley.

"You took your time," he said.

"I just got the message. My mother couldn't track me last night."

"One of those nights, huh?"

"Not in the least. Why did you call me?"

"A need to talk. Free now?"

"Well, I . . ."

"Be free. It's important. You have a car?"

"Yes."

"Good. Meet me in an hour at the scenic overlook off the G.W. Parkway, the one near the Roosevelt Bridge. Know it?"

"No, but I'll find it."

"An hour."

"I'll be there."

15

Collette dressed in a gray skirt, low shoes, red-and-white striped button-down shirt and blue blazer. She went to a coffee shop around the corner from the apartment and had bacon and eggs, then got in her car and headed for her rendezvous with Hank Fox.

She kept to the speed limit on the George Washington Memorial Parkway, but her mind was going faster. Had Fox found a link between Barrie Mayer's and David Hubler's deaths? That possibility opened up another avenue of thought—David Hubler might have been involved with the CIA, too. That hadn't occurred to her before but, now that it had, it didn't seem far-fetched. Hubler and Mayer worked closely together at the agency. Mayer's frequent trips to Budapest, and the constant contact with authors like Zoltán Réti, could easily have opened up areas of discussion between them. Even if it hadn't, there had to be some tangible vestige of Mayer's part-time work for the CIA kicking around the office. Maybe she'd actually recruited Hubler into her second life. If that were the case, Cahill hoped she'd done it with agency blessing. Taking others into the fold without being ordered to do so was bound to cause major trouble, big enough, she realized, to have caused their deaths. She'd heard of agents who'd been "terminated" by the CIA itself, not for revenge or punishment as with the Mafia, but as an expedient means of closing leaks on a permanent basis.

Traffic was light this morning, so light that she noticed a green sedan that had fallen in behind her as soon as she turned onto the parkway. It stayed a considerable distance from her, but occasional glances in the rearview mirror confirmed that it was still there. She decided not to proceed to the location given her by Hank Fox until the green sedan was no longer an issue. She reached the scenic overlook Hank Fox had mentioned but passed it, her eyes quickly surveying the area. There were two cars, one a four-door pale blue Chevrolet Caprice, the other a white station wagon with paneling. A young woman holding a baby on her hip walked a dalmatian on a leash. A pit stop for the dog, Cahill thought, as she got off at the next exit and made a series of sharp turns on local streets until finding her way back onto the parkway. She checked her watch; she was ten minutes early but that time would be eaten by having to exit the parkway again and circling back. She checked behind her in the mirror. No green sedan. So much for that.

Precisely an hour after she'd talked to Fox she turned into the parking area. The woman, baby, and dog were gone, leaving the Caprice sitting by itself. Cahill pulled up next to it, put her car into PARK, turned, and peered into the Caprice. Hank Fox looked back at her through the glass. She noticed there was someone else in the car. She stiffened; why would he bring someone else? Who was it? She tried to see, but glare on the window left only a vague image in the passenger seat.

Both doors on the Caprice opened. Hank Fox stepped out of the driver's side, Joe Breslin the other. Collette breathed a sigh of relief, and surprise. What was Breslin doing there?

Fox slid in next to her and Breslin got in the rear.

"Joe, what a surprise," Cahill said, turning and smiling.

"Yes, for me, too," Breslin said, slamming the door.

"Let's go," Fox said.

"Where?" asked Cahill.

"For a ride, that's all. Head out toward the airport."

Cahill did her turnaround again and headed south on the parkway, along the Potomac, until reaching National Airport. Fox told her to pull into the metered parking area. When she was at a meter and had turned off the engine, he said, "You two go inside. I'll stay with the car."

They entered the terminal and Breslin led the way to the observation deck entrance. They paid, went through the door, and stood at a railing. Below them was the aircraft ramp area and active runways. A brisk wind whipped Collette's hair. She gently pressed her middle fingers against her ears to muffle the whine of jet engines.

"Just right," Breslin said.

"What?"

"Just the right amount of ambient noise." He moved closer to her, turned, and said inches from her ear, "Plans have changed."

Cahill looked quizzically at him.

"How would you like a little time in the sun?" he asked.

"Sounds nice. I was going to ask about a vacation."

"It's not a vacation. It's an assignment."

When he didn't say more, she asked.

"They want you in the BVI."

"Why?"

"To get to know Eric Edwards. They want you to get close to him, see what he's up to."

Cahill looked to the runway where a Boeing 737 was slicing into a gray sky. Breslin, his hands shoved into his raincoat pockets, a dead pipe clenched in his teeth, paused for what he'd said to sink in, then removed the pipe and leaned toward her. "Banana Quick has been badly compromised, Collette. We have to know how and why."

"Edwards is in Washington, not the BVI," she said.

"We know that, but he'll be returning there in a couple of days. They want you to make contact with him here and do whatever you have to do to . . . to get inside him. See if you can wangle an invitation from him to go down there."

"Wait a minute," she said, her face reflecting her anger, "you want me to sleep with him?"

"The orders don't stipulate that. They just say . . ."

151

"To do anything I have to do to 'get inside him.' No dice, Joe. Hire a hooker. The Pickle Factory's ripe with them."

"You're overreacting."

"I'm underreacting," she said sharply.

"Call it what you will, the order has come down and you're it. You don't have a choice."

"Ever hear of quitting?"

"Sure, but you won't. I don't want you to. You don't have to sleep with anybody, just get to know a little about his operation and tell us about it. He's too independent, not enough controls."

"What if he doesn't invite me to the BVI?"

"Then you will have failed. Try not to let that happen."

"Where are you getting your information about the leak?"

Breslin glanced around before saying, "From your man in Budapest, Árpád Hegedüs."

"It's definitely Edwards?"

"We don't know, but he's a logical place to start. He's our eyes and ears down there. We know he's a drinker and a talker. Maybe he's been drinking and talking with the wrong people."

"The Russians know everything?"

Breslin shrugged. "They know too much, that's for sure." Some other people came onto the observation deck and stood close to them. "There are two tickets at the Concert Theater box office for some dance recital tomorrow night at the Kennedy Center," Breslin told her. "Go to it. I'll be on the terrace at intermission. Check in with me then."

Collette let out a deep sigh and placed her hands on the railing. "Why did they send you all the way from Budapest to tell me this?" she asked.

"Why do they do anything, Collette? Besides, sending me indicates how important the project is. When the stakes are big, they care enough to send their very best." He smiled.

She couldn't help but smile, too. "They sent you because they knew you could get me to do it."

"Did I?"

"I'll do my best, no promises."

"Can't ask for more than that," he said, touching her arm and turning.

A half hour later they were back at the overlook. Before Fox and Breslin got out of her car, Fox asked, "How was your evening with Jason Tolker?"

"You know about that?"

"Yes."

"It was pleasant enough. He and Barrie were close. I wanted to find out what I could from him."

"Did you? Find out anything?"

"A little."

Breslin said from the back seat, "Save it for tomorrow night on the terrace, Collette." He slapped Fox on the shoulder and said, "Let's go."

They got into Fox's car and drove off, neither man looking back. When they were gone, Cahill felt alone and vulnerable. She gripped the bottom of the steering wheel and saw her eyes in the rearview mirror. Somehow, they didn't belong to her. She tapped the mirror so that it no longer reflected her face, started the engine, and drove as quickly as she could to the apartment, remembering to check her mirror a few times. No green sedan.

16

"Eric Edwards?"

"Yes."

"This is Collette Cahill, Barrie Mayer's friend."

"Hi, how are you? My secretary told me you'd called. I assume you got my message in Budapest?"

"Yes, I did. I'm sorry I didn't contact you sooner but I've been busy."

"I understand."

"I still can't believe she's dead."

"Hard for any of us to believe it. Barrie talked a lot about you. I suppose you were her best friend?"

"We were close. I was wondering if we could get together for a drink, or lunch, or whatever works for you. Will you be in Washington long?"

"Leaving tomorrow. You on vacation?"

"Yes."

"How's things in Budapest?"

"Fine, except for when I heard about Barrie. Are you free for lunch?"

"No, unfortunately I'm not. I'm on a tight schedule."

"Time for a fast drink this afternoon? I'm free all day."

"Well, I suppose . . . how about six? I have a dinner date at seven."

"That'd be fine." She realized she was not about to generate enough interest from him in an hour to result in an invitation to the BVI. "Actually," she said, "I'm not being completely honest. I do want to talk to you about Barrie, but I also would love some good advice on the BVI. I'm spending part of my vacation there and thought you could recommend a good hotel, restaurants, that sort of thing."

"Happy to. When are you leaving?"

Some quick thinking. "In a few days."

"I'll give it my best shot when we meet tonight. On a budget?"

"Sort of, but not too tight."

"Fine. Like sailing?"

Collette had never been out in a sailboat. "Yes," she said, "I love it." She knew she should qualify her answer. "I really don't know much about it, though. I've only been a few times."

"Let's see if we can't arrange a day trip for you. I'm in the yacht-chartering business."

"I know. It sounds . . ." She laughed. "It sounds wonderful and romantic."

"Mostly hard work, although it does beat a suit and tie and nine to five, at least for me. Any suggestion where to meet tonight?"

"Your choice. I've been away from Washington too long."

"Might as well come over here to the Watergate. Would make my life a little easier. Come to my room. I'll have something sent up. What do you drink?"

"Scotch and soda?"

"You got it. See you at six, Room 814."

She drove to Barrie Mayer's literary agency where Marcia St. John and Carol Geffin were behind their desks. Tony Tedeschi, one of the associate agents, was burrowing through a file cabinet in the corner.

St. John, a lanky, attractive mulatto, who'd been there the longest, greeted Cahill soberly.

"I heard," Cahill said.

St. John shook her head. "First Barrie, now David. It's incredible."

Tedeschi said, "How are you, Collette?"

"Okay, Tony. The question is how are *you*?"

"We're holding up. Have you heard anything new about David?"

"No, just the TV and newspapers. What are the funeral plans?"

"Not set yet," St. John said. "How's Budapest?"

"Fine, last I saw it." Collette looked at the door leading to Barrie's private office. It was open a crack and she saw a figure cross the room, then disappear. "Who's in there?" she asked.

"Our new leader," St. John said, raising her eyebrows.

"New leader?"

"Mark Hotchkiss."

"Really?" Cahill went to the door and pushed it open. Hotchkiss, in shirtsleeves, bow tie, and yellow suspenders, was seated behind what had been Barrie Mayer's desk. A pile of file folders were on his lap. He looked up over half-glasses, said, "Be with you in a minute, Miss Cahill," and went back to leafing through the files.

Cahill closed the door and stood at the edge of the desk. She waited a few moments before saying, "I find this arrogant, at best."

He looked up again and smiled. "Arrogant? I'd hardly call it that. Due to unforeseen circumstances, there's been a dreadful gap created at this agency. I'm being decisive. If that represents arrogance, so be it."

"Mr. Hotchkiss, I'd like to see the partnership agreement you and Barrie signed."

He smiled, exposing his yellow teeth, pushed the glasses up to the top of his head and leaned back in Mayer's chair, arms behind his head. "Miss Cahill, I have no reason whatsoever to show you anything. The partnership arrangement Barrie and I constructed is quite sound, quite legal. I suggest that if your curiosity is that strong, you contact Barrie's solicitor . . . attorney, Richard Weiner. Would you like his address and phone number?"

"No, I . . . yes, I would."

Hotchkiss found a slip of paper on the desk and copied it onto another slip. "Here you are," he said, a smug smile on his face. "Call him. You'll find that everything is quite in order."

"I'll do that."

"Now," he said, standing and coming to her, "I believe we had tentative plans for dinner here in Washington. What night is good for you?"

"I'm afraid I'm all booked up."

"Pity. I'm sure we have a great deal to talk about. Well, if you change your mind, give me a call. I suspect I'll be here day and night trying to sort things out." His face suddenly sagged into a sympathetic expression. "I am so sorry about that poor chap, Hubler. We had our differences, but to see such a personable young man snuffed out at such an early age is bloody awful. Please give my deepest sympathies to his family."

Cahill's frustration level made further talk impossible. She spun around and left the office. Tedeschi was the first to see her. "You, too, huh?"

"This is absurd," Cahill said. "He just walks in and takes over?"

"Afraid so," Tedeschi said. "He's got the piece of paper. He ran it through Dick Weiner. Weiner doesn't believe it, either, but it looks legit. Why Barrie would have hooked up with this bozo is beyond me, but it looks like the lady made a mistake."

"She made it, we live with it," said Marcia St. John, who'd overheard the conversation.

"Barrie had a will," Cahill said. "She turned things over to David in the event of her death."

Tedeschi shook his head. "The will's invalid, according to Weiner. The partnership agreement takes precedence for some legal reason, the way it was worded, who knows? It's all foreign language to me."

"I'm going to see Weiner."

"You know him?" Tedeschi asked.

"No, but I will."

"He's a nice guy and a good lawyer, but you're wasting

your time. Hotchkiss has the agency as the surviving partner. Excuse me, Collette, I gotta work on my résumé."

"I just don't believe this," Collette said, shaking her head and knowing it was a pathetically ineffective statement.

"Life in the fast lane," Carol Geffin said.

"How's David's family holding up?" Collette asked.

"The way they're supposed to, I guess. God, he was young." St. John started to cry and went to the ladies' room.

Collette asked again about funeral arrangements, and was told a decision was to be made later that afternoon. She left the office and went to a phone booth from which she called the attorney, Richard Weiner. She explained her relationship; he was on the line in seconds.

"This can't be right," she said. "Barrie would never have signed an agreement with Hotchkiss making him a full partner so that he'd inherit the agency if she died."

"I feel the same way, Miss Cahill, but the papers do seem in order. Frankly, I can't take any further steps without the prompting of her family. They'd have to challenge it, go after expert handwriting analysis, probe the background of the deal."

"Her only family is her mother."

"I know that. I spoke with her earlier this morning after hearing about David Hubler."

"And?"

"She said she was too old to become involved in something like this."

"What about Dave's family? Her will took care of him. Wouldn't it be in their interest to challenge Hotchkiss?"

"Probably not. Barrie didn't leave the agency to him. She simply stipulated that he be retained on a specified compensation package for five years. She left him key-man insurance, too, fifty thousand dollars."

"Who gets that now that *he's* dead?"

"The agency."

"Hotchkiss."

"Ultimately, not directly. It goes in the corporate coffers. He's the corporation."

She banged her fist against the booth and said, "First her, now David. Do you think . . . ?"

"Think what, that Hotchkiss might have killed David? How can I think that, Miss Cahill?"

"I can. I have."

"Well, I suppose you're . . . but what about Barrie? She died of natural causes."

Cahill had to fight with herself to keep from telling him that Barrie hadn't died of natural causes, that she'd been murdered. Instead, she said, "I'm glad I had a chance to talk with you, Mr. Weiner."

"Let's talk more. If you come up with any information that bears on this, call me day or night." He gave her his home phone number. She pretended to write it down but didn't bother. She knew she wouldn't be calling him at home, or at his office again either. Barrie Mayer's business affairs really didn't interest her, unless Mark Hotchkiss were involved in both deaths. She doubted it. Weiner was right; Hotchkiss wasn't the type.

Still, there was the question of how he'd enticed Mayer into signing such a binding partnership agreement. Had he held something over her head? What could it be? Wrong road, Cahill decided. She'd pursue it later, after taking care of primary business, her initial meeting with Eric Edwards.

That brought up another whole series of thoughts as she returned to the apartment, stopping first at a bookstore to buy a travel guide to the British Virgin Islands.

Did Edwards know for whom she was working? That was one of the biggest problems in tracking Mayer's life prior to her death. Who knew what? Tolker knew. She had to assume that Edwards knew, too. He hadn't indicated it on the message he left on her answering machine in Budapest, or during their brief telephone conversation that morning. But *he knew*; she had to operate under that assumption.

It also began to lean heavily on her that she'd been hopelessly naive in this matter. She'd never once questioned the motives or activities of people like Joe Breslin, Hank Fox, Stan Podgorsky, or any of the others with whom she'd developed a "father-daughter" relationship. The fact was that they responded to a higher calling than Collette Cahill's personal needs and future. They were Company men, fully capable of selling anyone down the river to further the cause

159

for which they'd been hired, or to perpetuate their own careers and lifestyles. "Damn it," she mumbled as she parked the car and headed for Vern Wheatley's brother's apartment, "I hate this."

Those feelings were forgotten as she spent an hour reading the travel guide and formulating questions for Eric Edwards about her "vacation." It took her into the early afternoon. She called Mayer's office and asked whether there'd been any word on funeral plans for David.

"Private," St. John told her. "Just family."

"Why?"

"Because that's the way they want it."

"Who's in the family?"

"His mother and father, a sister who's flying in from Portland, cousins, others, I guess."

"You were his family, too, at least part of it."

"Collette, I only work here. There's a man in Barrie's office with a funny way of talking and yellow fangs. One of the nicest guys I ever knew is being buried. Tony's grinding out résumés like they were the State of the Union address, and Carol is dwelling on which disco will have the best collection of hunks tonight. I miss David. I'd be there if they let me. Understand, Collette?"

"Sure. Sorry. I can keep in touch?"

It was a hollow laugh. "P-l-e-a-s-e," St. John said. "Make sure *I'm* alive on a day-to-day basis."

Collette hung up and wrapped her arms about herself as the meaning of St. John's final remark sent a chill through her body. Two dead out of the same office. That realization caused her to begin rethinking everything that had happened. Maybe Barrie Mayer's death had absolutely, positively nothing to do with spies and governments. Maybe it had to do with commerce, pure and simple. Maybe . . . maybe . . .

There were so many of those.

17

Edwards answered his door wearing a white hotel-provided terrycloth robe with a "W" on the breast pocket. "Miss Cahill, come in. I'll only be a minute. I managed to get in a little workout at the end of the day." He disappeared into the bedroom, leaving her alone in the suite's living room.

A small set of barbells rested on towels on the floor. Written on them in black was PROPERTY OF WATERGATE HOTEL. A rock station blared the day's latest hits. Clothing was strewn on every piece of furniture.

She answered a knock on the door. A young Hispanic bellhop rolled a cart into the room, opened its leaves, fussed with napkins and silverware, and handed Collette the check. ".I'm not . . . Sure." She signed Edwards's name and included a dollar tip.

Edwards came from the bedroom wearing slacks. Cahill couldn't help but take immediate note of his bare upper body—heavily muscled arms and chest, trim waist, and all of it the color of copper. "It arrived," he said. "I owe you anything?"

"No. I signed."

"Good. Well, let me finish dressing. Help yourself."

"Can I pour you something?"

"Yes, please. Just gin on the rocks. The bottle's over there." He pointed to a cabinet on which a half-empty bottle of gin sat. He returned to the bedroom and Cahill fixed the drinks. When he again joined her he'd put on a monogrammed white silk shirt and yellow loafers. She handed him his glass. He held it up and said, "To the memory of Barrie Mayer, one hell of a fine lady." He drank. She did, too, the Scotch causing her mouth to pucker.

"I'm sorry to be in a rush." He cleared clothing and magazines from the couch and they sat on it. "Tell me, is there anything new about Barrie?"

"New? No. I assume you heard about her associate being murdered last night?"

"No, I didn't. Which associate?"

"David Hubler."

"I don't believe it. She really liked him. He was murdered?"

"That's what the police say. It happened in Rosslyn. Somebody rammed a sharp object into his heart."

"Jesus."

"They say robbery was the motive because his wallet and credit cards were missing, but that doesn't prove anything to me."

"No, I guess not. What irony, the two of them dying so close together."

Collette nodded.

He looked directly at her and said, "I miss Barrie. We were getting close to making it official."

Cahill was surprised. "You were planning marriage?"

"Maybe 'planning' isn't the word, but we were headed in that general direction." He smiled. It was a charming, engaging, little boy's smile. "You must have thought I was some college sophomore with that message I left on your answering machine. It took me forever to get a line to Budapest. When I did and was faced with that infernal machine, I just started babbling. I was very upset. *Very* upset."

"I can imagine," said Cahill. "When had you last seen her?"

"A week or so before. Frankly, we'd been having a few problems and were looking forward to getting away for a few days to straighten things out. She was planning a trip to the BVI when she got back from Hungary. She'll never make that trip now, will she?"

Cahill reacted by filling up. She took a deep breath and forced a smile. Her thoughts were on the situation that existed at the moment, the same old one that characterized every meeting she'd had during the past few days. Did he know she worked for the CIA? She reminded herself that *she'd* decided the answer to that earlier in the day. He knew. Still, should she bring everything up, Barrie's courier life, Jason Tolker, her job in Budapest, and her knowledge of his job in the British Virgins?

Not yet, she decided. The wrong time.

"So, to get onto a lighter note," Edwards said, "you're coming to my little part of the world for a rest."

"Yes, that's right." She'd forgotten that aspect of her visit.

"Made any plans yet?"

"Not really. It's a last-minute decision. I thought I'd go to a travel agent but then I remembered you. Barrie said you know the BVI better than anyone."

"That's not true, but I have learned a lot sailing those islands. Want to go posh? Peter Island, Little Dix, Biras Creek. Want a little more action? The Tradewinds, Bitter End. Looking for a real native feel? Andy Flax's Fischer's Cove, Drake's Anchorage on Mosquito Island. Lots of choices, with even more in between."

Mosquito Island, she thought, the site of Banana Quick's highest-level meetings. "What would you recommend?"

"There's always my place."

Would it be this easy?

"Or," he said, "one of my yachts, if one is available. I promised you a day's sailing. Might as well stay on board and save yourself some money."

"That's much too generous."

"I wouldn't be offering it to just anyone. Barrie stayed

with me so many times, at my house and on the yachts. I'd really be privileged to have you, Collette. I can't promise I'll be around much. It depends on bookings, but we're still out of season down there and, at least when I left, things were slow." He stood and refilled his glass. "Another?"

She checked her watch. "You have to leave," she said, "and I have things to do. I feel as though I should be doing something to repay your generosity."

"Don't be silly," he said, walking her to the door.

"If you weren't going back tomorrow, I'd invite you to join me at the Kennedy Center. I ended up with two tickets to a marvelous performance and there's just me to use them."

"Damn, I wish I could," he said, "but it's impossible. I have appointments back home in the afternoon. You'll find somebody else."

She was glad he turned her down. It had been an impetuous offer, one she thought might help bring them closer together in a hurry. But then, she realized, it would be awkward, if not impossible, to meet with Joe Breslin at intermission. Did Edwards know Breslin, and Hank Fox? Probably by name, not by sight. Agents like Edwards operated as rogues, seldom coming into contact with administrative types. They had their single contact in Langley, some operatives in place, and that was it. The nature of the beast. Whether he knew about her was another matter, a bridge to be crossed when . . .

"How's things at the embassy?" he asked as they stood at the door.

"Fine, last I heard."

"You still with the same division?"

What division was that? She said, "Yes."

"When are you planning to come to the BVI?"

"I thought maybe . . . maybe Saturday." It was Wednesday.

"Great. Pan Am goes into San Juan and you can catch an Air BVI flight from there. There's a new direct service out of Miami, too."

"I'd rather leave from New York." She made a mental note to check out the Miami flight. "Thanks for the offer."

"I look forward to it. You have my phone number. Let me know when you're due to arrive and I'll have you picked up."

"This is all overwhelming."

"It's for Barrie. See you in the sun in a couple of days."

18

The Dance Theatre of Harlem ended its first act to thunderous applause from twenty-five hundred people in Kennedy Center's concert hall. Cahill joined in enthusiastically from her twelfth-row-center seat. She picked up her raincoat from the empty seat next to her and moved with the crowd as it spilled out into the Grand Foyer, the Hall of States, and the Hall of Nations. It had been raining when the audience arrived, but had stopped during the first act.

She went to one of the doors leading to the broad terrace on the Potomac and looked out. A few people had gone outside and stood in small groups separated by puddles. She looked toward the railing on the river side and saw Joe Breslin. His back was to her. Blue smoke from his pipe drifted up into the damp night air.

She came up behind him. "Hello, Joe."

He didn't turn as he said, "Nice night. I like it just after it rains."

She joined him at the railing and they looked out over the river and toward National Airport. A jet screamed over them as it sought the solid safety of the runway, its landing gear extended like a large bird's talons reaching for a tree branch. After its engine noise had faded, Breslin asked, "Enjoying the performance?"

"Very much. You?"

"It's not my favorite entertainment but I suppose it has its place."

She started to discuss the dance troupe but knew it wasn't why they were standing there. "I made contact with Eric Edwards," she said.

"And?"

"I'm joining him in the BVI on Saturday."

He swiveled his head and stared at her, smiled, raised his eyebrows, and returned his gaze to the river. "That was fast," he said, sounding disapproving.

"It was easy," she said. "Barrie paved the way."

"Barrie?"

"The common bond between us. I didn't have to do any seducing. We're a couple of friends because of her."

"I see. Are you staying with him?"

"Yes, either at his home or on one of his yachts."

"Good. How did you meet up with him?"

"I called. He invited me for a drink at his suite at the Watergate. Actually, I invited myself. I told him I was planning a vacation in the BVI and asked for recommendations."

"Good tactic."

"I thought so. Anyway, it worked. Now, what's the next step?"

"Meaning what?"

"Meaning, what are you looking for while I'm there?"

Breslin shrugged and drew on his pipe. "I don't know, anything that looks interesting."

"It can't be that vague, Joe."

"I don't mean it to be." His sigh was deep and prolonged. He looked around at others on the terrace. The nearest people were fifteen feet away—two couples who'd come to the railing to see the river. Breslin positioned his body so that he leaned on the rail with his back to them, and was facing Cahill. "Why are you staying with your former boyfriend?"

His directness took her aback. "Vern Wheatley? How do you know about him?"

"It's not so much knowing about him, Collette, it's knowing about you."

"I'm being followed?"

"You're being protected."

"From what?"

"From harm."

"I resent this, Joe."

"Be grateful. What about Wheatley?"

"What about him? We went together in high school, that's all. When I came home, my mom threw a party and he showed up. He's down here on assignment for *Esquire* magazine."

"I know that. Why are you staying with him?"

"Because . . . Christ, Joe, what business is it of yours?"

"You're right, Collette, it's not my business. It's the Company's business."

"I'd debate that."

"Don't bother."

He looked at her and said nothing. She said, "Vern was the one who told me about David Hubler being killed."

"And he convinced you to leave the hotel and move in with him for . . . for your own safety?"

"Yes, as a matter of fact, that's exactly what happened." She shook her head and made a sound by blowing air past her lips. "Boy, I am some protected girl, huh, Joe? What are you doing now, trying to get me to distrust Vern, too? Trust nobody, right? Everybody's a spy or a double agent or a . . ."

Breslin ignored her rising emotions and said flatly, "You do know that your high school beau is in Washington researching a story on us?"

It hit her in the chest like a fist. "No, I did not know that," she said in a controlled voice.

"Hank Fox's unit has been tracking your friend."

"So?"

"Maybe he wants you close to him for information."

"I doubt that."

"Why?"

"Because . . ."

"I think you should be aware of the possibility."

"Thank you." She wasn't proud of the snippy way she answered, but it was the best she could manage.

"About Edwards. There's a possibility that he's the leak in Banana Quick."

"So I heard."

"If so, he's potentially dangerous."

"In what way?"

"Physically. To you. It's something else I thought you'd appreciate knowing."

"Of course I do."

"It's possible he's been turned."

Another fist in the chest. "I thought it was just a matter of drinking too much and a loose tongue."

"Could be those things, too, but the possibility of a turn can never be overlooked. It isn't prudent to overlook such possibilities."

"I certainly won't. Anything else you think I should know?"

"Lots of things. Your man, Árpád Hegedüs, is on his way to Russia."

"He is? They did it?"

"Yes. We had one final meeting with him before he left. It wasn't easy. He wouldn't talk to anyone except 'His Miss Cahill.' We managed to convince him that it was in his interest to talk with somebody else."

"How is he?"

"Frazzled, afraid of what's in store for him once he's back in Mother Russia. He almost bolted, came over to us."

"He wanted that."

"I know, I went over the transcript of the session with Stan. The woman he's met complicated things for him. He was ready to defect and bring her with him."

"He didn't."

"We dissuaded him."

"Because we need him." Now it was scorn she didn't intend to come from her mouth.

"We suspect he'll be all right. There's nothing to indicate he's in trouble."

"The woman?"

"She's a clerk in a Hungarian food-processing plant. No use to us."

169

"I don't think we'll ever see Hegedüs again."

"We'll see. What's really important is that casual, last-minute comment he made at the end of your session with him about Dr. Tolker."

"I know. I never had a chance to discuss it with anyone before I left. I figured the transcript would tell the tale."

"We think Tolker's okay."

"Why?"

"Because . . . because he's never done anything to raise anyone's doubts. Still . . ."

"Still, he was Barrie Mayer's contact, and she was intimate with Eric Edwards which, according to Logic 101, means a link with Banana Quick. Maybe Tolker's the leak."

"Maybe, maybe not. We're watching him. What concerns us more at the moment is his link with your former beau, Mr. Wheatley."

The fists to the breastbone were beginning to hurt. "What link?" she asked.

"Wheatley is digging into a program that we abandoned years ago. Project Bluebird? MK-ULTRA?"

"Means nothing to me."

"It was covered in your training. Mind control. Drug experimentation."

"Okay, I remember vaguely. Why would Vern be interested if it's past tense?"

Breslin hunched his shoulders beneath his raincoat against a sudden cool breeze that whipped in from the river. "That's what we'd like to know. Maybe you could . . . ?"

"Nope."

"Why not? He's using you as a source of information for *his* ends."

"That's your interpretation, not mine."

"Do him a favor, Collette, and ask some questions. He's swimming in deep water."

"Why do you say that?"

"Look at Mr. Hubler."

Cahill started to respond, pushed away from the railing, and took steps toward the door leading back into the Kennedy Center. Breslin said, "Collette, come here."

She stopped; lights flashed indicating the second act was

about to begin. She turned, hands in her blazer pockets, head cocked, eyes narrowed.

Breslin smiled and made a small motion with his index finger for her to return to him. She looked down into a wavy reflection of herself in a large puddle on the terrace, brought her eyes back up to him, and retraced her steps. Another jet, this time taking off from National, shattered the moment with its crescendo of full throttle.

Breslin said once she was again at his side, "David Hubler came over to Rosslyn because he'd been told there was a book to be offered on an inside story about us." She started to say something but he raised his finger to silence her. "He was to meet someone on the corner where we have a facility. This unnamed person was to talk to him about selling inside information which, in turn, would be turned into a book, a best seller no doubt."

Cahill just stared at him and blinked.

"This facility in Rosslyn is the one Hank Fox directs."

Another blink. Then, the question, "And David was killed by this person who was going to sell him information?"

"David was killed by . . . we don't know."

"Not robbery?"

"Not likely."

"Us? Someone from . . . *us*?"

"I don't know. Your friend, Vern Wheatley, was there when it happened."

"He was with the Rosslyn police looking for information on a story he's doing about Washington and . . ."

"He was there." His words were stone-hard.

"Good God, Joe, you're not suggesting that Vern had anything to do with David's murder?"

"I stopped suggesting things a long time ago, Collette. I just raise possibilities these days."

"You're damn good at it."

"Thanks. By the way, one of Barrie Mayer's clients, Zoltán Réti, was in to see us." He laughed. "Talk about a poor choice of words. He contacted Ruth Lazara from Cultural Exchange at a party, said he had to talk to someone. We arranged a meet."

"What did he say?"

"He said that he was convinced that he'd been sent to London for a conference because they knew he was supposed to meet Barrie Mayer when she arrived in Budapest."

"Meaning what?"

"Meaning . . . that the Soviets evidently knew not only that she was carrying something important, but that they wanted her point man out of the way."

"You think the Soviets killed her?"

"No idea."

"Joe."

"What?"

"What was Barrie carrying?"

"As far as I can ascertain, nothing."

"*Nothing?*"

"Nothing."

"She was killed for *nothing*?"

"Looks like it."

"Great. That gives real value to her life."

He re-ignited his pipe.

"We have to go in," Cahill said. "It's starting again."

"Okay. One more thing, Collette. Keep these things in mind. One, choosing you to follow up on the Banana Quick leak isn't a frivolous choice. You have the perfect reasons for asking questions, and now you've got an invitation from one of our primary people. You've met Tolker. Don't drop that contact. You're living with someone who's poking his nose into our affairs, which means you have as much access to him as he has with you. Be a pro, Collette. Drop all the personal reactions and do the job. You'll be rewarded."

"How?"

He grunted. "You want figures?"

"No, I want some sense of being able to return to a routine life."

"Meeting Hungarian turncoats in secret safehouses?"

"Right now, Joe, that's like working nine to five as a switchboard operator."

"Do the job and you can have what you want. They told me."

"Who?"

"The brain trust."

172

"Joe."

"What?"

"I don't know you."

"Sure you do. When this whole thing settles, it'll be like old times, dinners at Gundel, the Miniatur, heartburn, out-of-tune violins. Trust me."

"They say that in L.A."

"Trust me. I'm a fan."

"I'll try."

Cahill skipped the second act and returned to the apartment where Vern Wheatley was waiting. He was in his shorts, a can of beer in his hand, his bare feet propped up on the coffee table. "Where've you been?" he asked.

"The Kennedy Center."

"Yeah? Good concert?"

"Dance recital."

"Never could get into dance."

"Vern."

"What?"

"Let's talk."

19

By the time Saturday rolled around and Cahill was settled into a seat on a Pan Am flight to San Juan, she was more than ready to escape Washington, and to spend some time on an island. She had no illusions. Her trip to the BVI was just an extension of everything else she'd been doing since returning from Budapest but, for some reason (probably the concept of hitting your foot with a hammer to make you forget a headache), there was a vacation air to the trip.

There hadn't been time to visit her mother before leaving, but she did squeeze in a frantic shopping spree in search of warm-weather clothing. She didn't buy much; sunny islands didn't demand it—two bathing suits, one a bikini, the other a tank suit, both in shades of red; a multicolored caftan, white shorts, sandals, a clinging white dress, and her favorite item, a teal blue cotton jumpsuit that fit perfectly, and in which she felt comfortable. She wore it that morning on the plane.

Once airborne, and breakfast had been served, she removed her shoes, reclined in her seat, and tried to do what she'd promised herself—use the flight to sort things out without interruption, off by herself, some time alone in her own private think tank.

She'd had one additional contact with Langley before leaving. It was with Hank Fox. During their meeting on the Kennedy Center's terrace, Breslin had verbally given her a special telephone number to call, and suggested she check in each day, saying to whoever answered, "This is Dr. Jayne's office calling for Mr. Fox." She did as instructed and Fox came on the line a moment later. All he said was, "Our friend's gone back to Budapest. You're all set to go south?"

"Yes, Saturday."

"Good. In the event you get homesick and want to talk to someone, there's always a large group of friends at Pusser's Landing. They congregate in the deck bar and restaurant. Feed the big bird in the cage between noon and three. You'll have all the conversation you need."

She'd been on the receiving end of enough double-talk since joining the CIA to understand. Obviously, they kept a bird in a cage at this place called Pusser's Landing, and if she fed it at the right time, she'd be approached by someone affiliated with the CIA. It was good to know.

"Call this number when you get back," Fox said. "I'll be here."

"Right. Thanks."

"My best to Dr. Jayne."

"What? Oh, yes, of course. He sends his regards, too."

Silly games, she used to think, until she was in the field and understood the thinking behind such codes. *Need-to-know*; unless the person receiving the call was certain to answer, there was no need for whoever else picked up the phone to know who was calling. They carried it to extremes at times, especially those who loved intrigue, but it made sense. You had to adopt that attitude, she'd reasoned during her training, or you'd never take anything seriously, and that could get you in trouble.

Had Barrie Mayer not taken it seriously enough? Cahill wondered. She had been shockingly cavalier at times, and Cahill had called her on it. Had she joked at the wrong time, when the thing she was carrying was no joke? Had she taken too lightly the need to use a code name, or failed to contact someone through circuitous routes rather than directly?

The possible link between Mayer's and Hubler's deaths remained at the top of her list of thoughts. Dave Hubler had been killed in an alley adjacent to a CIA facility in Rosslyn, the one run by Hank Fox. Supposedly, Hubler had gone there to meet with someone who'd indicated he, or she, was willing to sell inside Company information that could be used in a book. That certainly drew Hubler in enough to validate a possible *mutual* reason for both murders.

She tried to stretch her mind to accommodate all the possibilities. She was hindered in this exercise by the most pervasive thought of all, the last thirty-six hours with Vern Wheatley.

She'd returned from the dance recital and decided to force a conversation. They talked until three o'clock the next morning. It was a frustrating discussion for Cahill. While Wheatley had been open to an extent, it was clear that there was more he was holding back than offering.

Collette had started the discussion with, "I'd like to know, Vern, exactly what this assignment is you're on for *Esquire*."

He laughed; Rule Number One, he told her, was never to discuss a story in progress. "You dilute it when you do that," he said. "You talk it out and the fire's gone when you sit down to write it."

She wanted to say, "Rule Number One for anyone working for the CIA is to stay far away from journalists." She couldn't say that, of course. As far as he knew, she'd left Central Intelligence for a mundane job with the United States Embassy in Budapest.

Or *did* he believe that? If Hank Fox's insinuations were correct, Wheatley had made contact with her again not to rekindle their romance, but to get close to a potential inside source to feed the story he was working on about a program that had been dropped long ago.

There it was again, *the* dilemma. Who knew what about whom? On top of that, could she believe Hank Fox? Maybe Wheatley wasn't pursuing a story about the CIA. The agency's paranoia wasn't any secret. There were people within it who found conspiracies behind every garage door in Georgetown.

She realized as she sat with Wheatley that night in his brother's apartment that she'd have to be more direct if anything near the truth were to be ferreted out. She took the chance and said, "Vern, someone told me today that you weren't in Washington doing a story on social changes here. This person told me you were digging into a story about the CIA."

He laughed and shook his empty beer can. "I think I'll have another. Can I get you something?"

"No, I . . . sure, any Scotch in there?"

"Probably. My brother has been known to take a drink now and then. Neat?"

"A little water."

She used his absence to go to the bedroom, where she undressed and got into one of his brother's robes. Three of her could have been enfolded in it. She rolled up the sleeves and returned to the living room where her drink was waiting. Wheatley raised his beer can. "Here's to the basic, underlying distrust between man and woman."

Cahill started to raise her glass in a reflex action. She stopped herself and looked at him quizzically.

"Great scenario, Collette. Some clown tells you I'm down here doing a story on the CIA. You used to work for the CIA so you figure I showed up at your house to get close to a 'source.' That's my only interest in Collette Cahill, hoping she'll turn into a Deep Throat—hey, maybe that wouldn't be so bad—and now she confronts me with the naked facts." He threw up his hands in surrender. "Your friend is right."

Wheatley put his beer can down on a table with considerable force, leaned forward, and said with exaggerated severity, "I've come into information through a highly reliable source that the Director of the CIA is not only having a wild affair with a female member of the Supreme Court—naturally, I can't mention her name—but is, at the same time, engaged in a homosexual liaison with a former astronaut who has been diagnosed at a clinic in Peru as having AIDS."

177

"Vern, I really don't see . . ."

"Hold on," he said, his hand raised as a stopper. "There's more. The CIA is plotting the overthrow of Lichtenberg, has permanently wired both of Dolly Parton's breasts, and is about to assassinate Abe Hirschfeld to get control of every parking lot in New York City in case of a nuclear attack. How's it play for you?"

She started to laugh.

"Hey, Collette, nothing funny here."

"Where's Lichtenberg? You meant Liechtenstein."

"I meant Lichtenberg. It's a crater on the moon. The CIA wouldn't bother with Liechtenstein. It's the moon they want."

"Vern, I'm being serious," she said.

"Why? You still work for our nation's spooks?"

"No, but . . . it doesn't matter."

"Who told you I'm working on a CIA story?"

"I can't say."

"Oh, that's democratic as hell. I'm supposed to bare my soul to you, but the lady 'can't say.' Not what I'd expect from you, Collette. Remember the yearbook line I wrote."

"I remember," she said.

"Good. Anything new about your friend Hubler?"

"No."

"You talk to that Englishman, Hotchkiss?"

"Yes, I ran into him at Barrie's agency. He's taken over. He owns it."

"How come?"

She explained the partnership agreement and told him of her call to Mayer's attorney.

"Doesn't sound kosher to me."

"To me, either, but evidently Barrie saw fit to make such a deal."

"She was that impetuous?"

"Somewhat, but not to that extent."

He joined her on the couch and put his arm around her. It felt good, the feel of him, the smell of him. She looked up into his eyes and saw compassion and caring. He lightly brushed her lips with his. She wanted to protest but knew she wouldn't. It was preordained, this moment, in the cards, an inevitability that she welcomed. . . .

They slept late the next morning. She awakened with a start. She looked over at Vern, his face calm and serene in sleep, a peaceful smile on his lips. Are you being legit with me? she questioned silently. All thoughts of their discussion the night before had been wiped away by the wave of passion and pleasure they'd created for themselves in bed. Now sunlight came through the windows. The passion was spent, the reality of beginning another day took center stage. It was depressing; she preferred what she'd felt under the covers where, someone once said, "They can't hurt you."

She got up, crossed the room, and sat in a chair for what seemed to be a very long time. It was only minutes, actually, before he woke up, yawned, stretched, and pushed himself to a sitting position against the headboard. "What time is it?" he asked.

"I don't know. Late."

Another yawn, legs swung over the side of the bed. He ran his hand through his hair and shook his head.

"Vern."

"Yeah?"

"I loved last night but . . . "

He slowly turned his head and screwed up his face. "But *what*, Collette?"

She sighed. "Nothing. I guess I just hate having to wake up, that's all. I'll be away a few days."

"Where you going?"

"The British Virgin Islands."

"How come?"

"Just to get away. I need it."

"Sure, I can understand that, but why that place? You know people there?"

"One or two."

"Where are you staying?"

"Ah . . . probably on a chartered yacht a friend of mine is arranging."

"You have rich friends." He stood, touched his toes, and disappeared into the bathroom.

Cahill realized she was sitting in the chair naked. She picked up her robe from where she'd tossed it on the floor and started a pot of coffee.

When he returned, he'd turned cold. He'd showered and dressed. He went through papers in a briefcase and started to leave.

"Don't you want coffee?" Cahill asked.

"No, I have to go. Look, I may not see you before you leave."

"Won't you be back tonight?"

"Probably, only I may end up going out of town overnight. Anyway, have a nice vacation."

"Thanks, I will."

He was gone.

He didn't return that night, and it bothered her. What had she done to turn such a warm, loving night into a frosty morning? Because she was going away? He was jealous, imagining that she'd be sleeping with someone else, an old or current boyfriend in the BVI. She wished she could have confided in him about the nature of her trip, but as that thought caused a jolt of sadness and frustration in her, it was tempered by knowing that he probably wasn't being open with her, either.

She got up early Saturday morning and packed. At the last minute she looked for a paperback book to take with her. There were piles of them everywhere. She picked up a half dozen from a nighttable next to the bed and scanned the covers. One immediately caught her eye. Its title was *Hypnotism*, by someone named G. H. Estabrooks. She put it in a shoulder bag she intended to carry on board, called a local cab company, and was on her way to National Airport.

After the Pan Am flight attendant had served Collette a cup of coffee, she pulled the book from her bag and opened it to a page on which was a brief biographical sketch of the author. Estabrooks had been a Rhodes Scholar, held a 1926 doctorate in educational psychology from Harvard, and was a professor of psychology, specializing in abnormal and industrial psychology at Colgate University. The book she held was first published in 1943, and had been revised in 1957.

The first few pages dealt with a murder trial in Denmark in which a man had hypnotized another to commit a murder. The chief state witness, Dr. P. J. Reiter, an authority on hypnotism, stated that any man is capable of any act while hypnotized.

She continued skimming until reaching page sixteen, where Estabrooks discussed the use of hypnotism in modern warfare. She read his thesis carefully.

Let us take an illustration from warfare, using a technique which has been called the "hypnotic messenger." For obvious reasons the problem of transmitting messages in wartime, of communication within an army's own forces, is a first-class headache to the military. They can use codes, but codes can be lost, stolen or, as we say, broken. They can use the dispatch carrier, but woe betide the messages if the enemy locates the messenger. They can send by word of mouth, but the third degree in any one of its many forms can get that message. War is a grim business and humans are human. So we invent a technique which is practically foolproof. We take a good hypnotic subject in, say, Washington, and in hypnotism we give him the message which we wish transferred. This message can be long and complicated, for his memory is excellent. Let us assume the war is still on and that we transfer him to Tokyo on a regular routine assignment, say, with the Army Service Corps.

Now note a very curious picture. Awake, he knows just one thing as far as his transfer to Tokyo is concerned; he is going on regular business which has nothing whatever to do with the Intelligence Department. But in his unconscious mind there is locked this very important message. Furthermore, we have arranged that there is only one person in all this world outside ourselves who can hypnotize this man and get this message, a Major McDonald in Tokyo. When he arrives in Tokyo, acting on posthypnotic suggestion, he will look up Major McDonald, who will hypnotize him and recover the message.

With this technique, there is no danger that the subject in an off-guard moment will let drop a statement to his wife or in public that might arouse suspicions. He is an Army Service Corps man going to Tokyo, that is all. There is no danger of getting himself in hot water when drunk. Should the enemy suspect the real purpose of his visit to Tokyo, they would waste their time with third-degree methods. Consciously, he knows nothing that is of any value to them. The message is locked in the unconscious and no amount of drugs, no attempts at hypnotism, can recover it until he sits before Major McDonald in Tokyo. The uses of hypnotism in warfare are extremely varied. We deal with this subject in a later chapter.

Collette went to the chapter on using hypnotism in warfare but found little to equal what she'd read on page sixteen. She closed the book, and her eyes, and replayed everything having to do with hypnosis and Barrie Mayer. Their college experience. Mayer had been such a willing and good subject.

Jason Tolker. He obviously had delved deeply into the subject, and had been Mayer's contact. Had she been hypnotized in her role as a courier? Why bother? Estabrooks's theory sounded exactly that—a theory.

MK-ULTRA and Project Bluebird—those CIA experimental programs of the sixties and early seventies that resulted in public and congressional outrage. Those projects had been abandoned, according to official proclamations from the agency. Had they? Was Mayer simply another experimental subject who'd gone out of control? Or had Estabrooks's theories, refined by the CIA, been put to practical use in her case?

For a moment, she lost concentration and her mind wandered. She'd soon need hypnosis to focus on the subject. Her eyes misted as she thought of Vern Wheatley—and then they opened wide. Why did Vern have Estabrooks's book at his bedside? Hank Fox had said that Wheatley was digging into the supposedly defunct ULTRA and Bluebird projects. Maybe Fox was right. Maybe Wheatley was using her as a conduit for information.

"Damn," she said to the back of the seat in front of her. She took a walk up and down the aisles of the aircraft, looking into the faces of other passengers, women and children, old and young, infants sleeping on mothers' laps, young lovers wrapped around each other, businessmen toiling over spread sheets and lap-top computers, the whole spectrum of airborne humanity.

She returned to her seat, loosely buckled her seat belt and, for the first time since she'd joined the CIA, considered resigning. The hell with them and their cops-and-robbers games, hiding behind vague claims that the fate of the free world depended upon their clandestine behavior. Destroy the village to save it, she thought. The Company's budgets were beyond scrutiny by any other branch of government because it was in "the national interest" to keep them secret. President Truman had been right when he'd eventually railed against the animal he'd created. It *was* an animal, free of all restraints, roaming loose in the world with men whose pockets were filled with secret money. Buy off someone here, overthrow someone there, turn decent people against their own countries, reduce everything to code words and collars turned up in the night. "Damn," she repeated. Send her off to dig into the lives of other people while, undoubtedly, people were delving into her life. Trust no one. A Communist threat exists under every pebble on the shore.

The flight attendant asked if Cahill would like a drink. "Very much," Cahill said; "a bloody Mary."

She drank half the drink and her thoughts went to the reason for her trip to the British Virgin Islands. That was the problem, she realized. Some things were important, not only for America but for people in other parts of the world. Like Hungary.

Banana Quick.

She hadn't been allowed access to all aspects of the plan— Need-to-know—but had learned enough to realize that the stakes were enormous.

She also knew that Banana Quick had been named after a tiny BVI bird, the bananaquit, and that someone within the CIA, whose job it was to assign names to projects, had decided to change it to Banana Quick. Quit was too negative, went the reasoning. Quick was more like it, positive, promising action and speed, more in line with the agency's vision of itself. There'd been laughter and snide remarks when the story had gotten around, but that was often the case in Central Intelligence. The international stakes might be high, but the internal machinations were often amusing.

Banana Quick was designed to set into motion a massive uprising by Hungarians against their Soviet keepers. The '56 attempt had failed. No wonder. It was ill-conceived and carried out by poorly armed idealists who were no match for Soviet tanks and troops.

Now, however, with the backing of the major powers— the United States, Great Britain, France, and Canada— there was a good chance that it would succeed. The climate was right. The Soviets had lost control over Hungary in a social and artistic sense. Hungarians had been gradually living freer lives, thumbing their noses at the young men in drab uniforms who wore red stars on their caps. What had Árpád Hegedüs told her when she asked how to distinguish Hungarian soldiers from Russian soldiers? "The dumb-looking ones are Russian," he'd answered.

Hungary had slowly turned in the direction of capitalism. Graft and corruption were rampant. Pay someone off and you'd have your new automobile in a month instead of six years. Condominiums were rising in the fashionable hills, available to anyone with enough hidden, hoarded illegal cash to buy in. More shops had been opened that were owned by individual entrepreneurs. They, too, had to pay some Russian, in some department, for the privilege, and that Russian was buying his own condo in the hills.

Banana Quick. A small bird flying free in the simple, excruciating beauty of the BVI. Stan Podgorsky had told her that they'd chosen the idyllic Mosquito Island as a planning center because, in his words, "Who'd ever think of looking there for planning a major uprising in an Eastern European country? Besides, we're running out of remote places to meet, unless we go to Antarctica or Ethiopia, and I, for one, am not going to those hellholes."

Who would look to the BVI for the brain trust behind a Hungarian uprising?

The Russians, for one. They'd taken over the private island because they knew something was up, knew the gray-haired men in dark suits flying in were anything but Canadian businessmen going over marketing strategies for a new product. The Soviets were many things; dumb wasn't one of them. Something was up. They'd play the game, too, lie, claim they needed a place for their weary bureaucrats to unwind in the sun. They'd watch. We'd watch.

Eric Edwards. He was there to *watch*. To look into their telescopes through his own, eye to eye, think one step ahead, as each man reported back to the dark suits in his own country.

Games.

"Games!" she said as she finished her drink.

As she deplaned in San Juan, she'd come to peace with the fact that she was a player in this game, and would give her all. After that, she'd see. Maybe . . .

Maybe it was time to get out of the business.

In the meantime, she'd apply her father's philosophy. "You take someone's money, you owe them a decent day's work."

20

"Hello, my name is Jackie, I work for Mr. Edwards," the slight native girl said in a loud voice.

"Yes, he told me you'd be here," Cahill said. Edwards had also told her during the telephone conversation that the girl he was sending for her was almost totally deaf. "Talk loud and let her see your lips," he'd said.

Jackie drove a battered yellow Land Rover. The back seat was piled high with junk, so Cahill sat in front with her. Edwards needn't have bothered instructing her how to communicate with Jackie. There was no conversation. The girl drove on the left side of the road with a race car driver's grim determination, lips pressed together, foot jamming the accelerator to the floor, one hand on the wheel, the heel of the other permanently against the horn. Men, women, children, dogs, cats, goats, cattle and other four-legged animals either heeded the horn or were run over.

The ride took them up and over steep hills. The views were spectacular—water like a painter's palette, every hue of blue and green, lush forests that climbed the sides of mountains and, everywhere, white slashes in the water that were yachts, big and small, sails raised or lowered. It was, at times, so breathtaking—their perch so high—that Cahill gasped.

They came down into Road Town, skirted Road Harbor, and then headed up a steep incline that took them through a clump of trees until reaching a plateau. A single house stood on it. It was one story and pristine white. The roof was covered with orange tiles. A black four-door Mercedes stood in front of a black garage door.

Collette got out and took a deep breath. A breeze from the harbor below rippled her hair and the elephant ears, kapok, white cedar, and manalikara trees that surrounded the house. The air was heavy with hibiscus and bougainvillea, and with the sound of tree frogs. Bananaquits flew from tree branch to tree branch.

Jackie helped bring the luggage into the house. It was open and airy. Furniture was at a minimum. The floors were white and yellow tile, the walls stark white. Flimsy yellow curtains fluttered in the breeze through the open windows. A huge birdcage that stood floor to ceiling housed four brilliantly colored, large parrots. "Hello, goodbye, hello, goodbye," one of them repeated over and over.

"It's just beautiful," Cahill said from behind Jackie. She remembered, came around in front of the girl, and said, "Thank you."

Jackie smiled. "He'll be back later. He said for you to be comfortable. Come." She led her to a rear guest bedroom with a double bed covered in a white-and-yellow comforter. There was a closet, dressing table, two cane chairs, and a battered steamer trunk. "For you," Jackie said. "I have to go. He'll be here soon."

"Yes, thanks again."

"Bye-bye." The girl disappeared. Cahill heard the Land Rover start and pull away.

Well, she thought, not bad. She returned to the living room and talked to the parrots, then went to the kitchen, opened the refrigerator, and took out one of many bottles of club soda. She squeezed half a lime into it, walked to a terrace overlooking the harbor, closed her eyes, and purred. No matter what was in store for her, this particular moment was to be cherished.

She sat on a chaise longue, sipped her drink, and waited for Edwards to arrive.

It was a longer wait than she'd anticipated. He rolled in an hour later on a Honda motorcycle. He'd obviously been drinking. Not that he was overtly drunk, but there was a slur to his speech. His face glowed; he'd been in the sun.

"Hello, hello, hello," he said, taking her hand and smiling.

"As long as you don't say, 'Hello, goodbye, hello, goodbye,' " she said with a laugh.

"Oh, you met my friends. Did they properly introduce themselves?"

"No."

"Bad manners. I'll have to speak to them. Their names are Peter, Paul, and Mary."

"The fourth?"

"Can't decide. Prince, Boy George, some bloody rock-'n'-roll star. I see you've helped yourself and are well into limmin'."

"Limmin'?"

"Native for loafing. Pleasant trip?"

"Yes, fine."

"Good. I've made plans for dinner."

"Wonderful. I'm famished."

They left an hour later in his Mercedes and drove to a small local restaurant ten minutes away where they dined on native food; she passed up what he ordered as a main course, souse, a boiled pig's head with onion, celery, hot peppers, and lime juice. She chose something more conventional, *kallaloo*, a soupy stew of crab, conch, pork, okra, spinach, and very large pieces of garlic. The soup was *tannia*, their before-dinner drinks rum in a fresh coconut split open at the table.

"Delicious," she said when they were through, and after she'd tasted "bush tea," made of soursop.

"Best cure for a hangover ever invented," he said.

"I may need it," she said.

He laughed. "I think I probably spill more in a day than you drink."

"Probably so."

188

"Game for a little sightseeing?"

She looked through the window at darkness. Only a few flickering lights on distant hills broke the black.

"Beautiful time to be out on the water. Can't sail . . . wind's always down about now, but we can loaf along on the engine. I think you'd like it."

She looked down at the slinky white dress she was wearing. "Hardly sailing clothes," she said.

"No problem," he said, getting up and pulling out her chair. "Plenty of that on board. Let's go."

During the short drive to where Edwards's yachts were docked, Cahill pleasantly realized that she was totally relaxed, something she hadn't been in far too long a time. She was all for limmin' if it made you feel the way she felt at that moment.

The man behind the wheel, Eric Edwards, had a lot to do with it, she knew. What was it in men like him that made a woman feel important and secure? His thoroughly masculine and slightly dissipated looks contributed, of course, but there was more to it. Chemical? Some olfactory process at work? The climate, the sweet fragrances in the tropical night air, the food and rum in the belly? Who knew? Cahill certainly didn't, nor did she really care. Pondering it was just a way of intensifying the feeling.

Edwards helped her to board the Morgan 46. He started the engine and generator, and turned on a light in the cabin. "Take what you want from under that bench," he said.

Cahill picked up the bench top and saw an assortment of female clothing. She smiled; along with everything else, he was practiced at enticing women on impetuous nighttime sailings. She pulled out a pair of white terrycloth shorts and a sleeveless, navy blue sweatshirt. Edwards had gone up on deck. She quickly kicked off her shoes, slipped out of her dress, and put on the shorts and shirt. She hung her dress behind a door that led to a lavatory and joined him as he freed his dock lines.

Edwards skillfully manipulated engine and wheel and backed away from the dock, then reversed power and slowly guided the large, sleek vessel past other secured boats until reaching open water. "Here, you take it," he said, indicating the wheel. She started to protest but he said, "Just keep aiming for that buoy with the light on it. I'll only be a minute." She slid behind the wheel as he went forward and took a breath against her nervousness, then smiled and relaxed into the seat cushion.

If she'd felt relaxed before, it had been nothing compared to the euphoria she now experienced.

He came back to her a few minutes later and they settled into a leisurely sightseeing journey, moving smoothly on an eastern tack through Sir Francis Drake Channel, the lights of Tortola, and the silhouette of the "Fat Virgin"—Virgin Gorda Island—their land markers.

"What are you thinking?" he said in a soft voice.

Her smile was one of pure contentment. "I was just thinking that I really don't know how to live."

He chuckled. "It isn't always this peaceful, Collette, not when I have a charter with three or four couples all hell-bent on having a good time and guzzling booze as fast as I can stock it."

"I'm sure that's true," Cahill said. "But you have to admit it isn't always that way. Obviously, you have time to . . ."

"Time to take moonlight sails with beautiful young women? True. You don't hold that against me, do you?"

She turned and looked into his face. He was wearing a broad smile. His teeth, very white, seemed phosphorescent in the light of the moon. She said, "How could I hold it against you? Here I am enjoying it to the hilt." She was about to throw in a disclaimer that she wasn't necessarily a "beautiful woman," but she decided not to bother. She'd never felt more beautiful in her life.

They continued their cruise for another hour, then headed back, reaching the dock at two in the morning. She'd fallen asleep next to him, her head on his shoulder. She helped him secure the Morgan and they went to the house, where he poured nightcaps of straight Pusser's Rum into large brandy snifters.

"You look tired," he said.

"I am. It's been a long day . . . and night."

"Why don't you get to bed? I'll be out early, but you sleep in. The house is yours. We'll catch up when I get back.

I'll leave the keys to the Mercedes in the kitchen. Feel free."

"That's generous, Eric."

"I like having you here, Collette. Somehow, it makes me feel a little closer to Barrie." He studied her face. "You aren't offended at that, are you? I don't want you to feel used, if you understand what I mean."

She smiled, stood, and said, "Of course not. Funny, but while we were out on the water I thought a lot about Barrie and realized that I was feeling closer to her, too, by being here. If there is any using, we're both guilty. Good night, Eric. Thanks for a lovely evening."

21

She heard Edwards leave and took his advice: rolled over and went back to sleep. When she awoke again, she didn't know what time it was but the room had become hot. She looked up into a gently revolving ceiling fan, then slipped on her jumpsuit and strolled out to the kitchen. A heavy black woman was polishing countertops. "Good morning," Collette said.

The woman, who wore a flowered dress and straw sandals, smiled and said in a singsong voice, "Good morning, lady. Mr. Edwards, he gone."

"Yes, I know. I heard him. My name is Collette."

The woman evidently did not want to extend the conversation to that level of intimacy because she turned away and went back to making circles on the counter.

Collette took a pitcher of fresh-squeezed orange juice from the refrigerator, filled a large glass, and took it to the terrace. She sat at a round white table with an orange umbrella protruding from a hole in the middle and thought about the exchange in the kitchen. Her interpretation was that Edwards had so many young women walking into the kitchen and introducing themselves that the housekeeper

192

had decided it wasn't worth getting to know them. Chances were they never stayed around long enough to become part of the household.

The marina and harbor below bustled with activity. Cahill squinted against the sun and picked out the section of the complex where Edwards's yachts were situated. She was too far away to see whether he was there, but she assumed he'd left early to take out a charter. Then again, he hadn't specified that, so maybe he had other business on the island.

She got the Estabrooks book on hypnotism from the bedroom and returned to the terrace, settled in the chair, and picked up reading where she'd left off on the plane.

She was fascinated as she read that certain people have a heightened ability to enter the hypnotic state, and that these people, according to the author, were capable of remarkable feats while under hypnosis. Estabrooks cited examples of men and women undergoing major surgery, with hypnotism as the only anesthesia. To such special people, total amnesia about the hypnotic experience was not only possible, it was easily accomplished by a skilled hypnotist.

She also learned that contrary to popular perception, those who enter a hypnotic state are anything but asleep. In fact, while under hypnosis, the subject enters a state of awareness in which it is possible to focus most intently, and to block out everything else. Memory "inside" is enhanced; it's possible under hypnosis to compress months' worth of material into an hour and to retain virtually everything.

Collette found particularly fascinating the chapter on whether it was possible to convince someone under hypnosis to perform a degrading or illegal act. She remembered high school chatter when boys used to kid about hypnotizing girls to get them to take off their clothes. One boy had sent away for a publication advertised on the back of a comic book promising "total hypnotic, seductive power over women." The girls in school had giggled, but the boys kept trying to get them to submit to their new-found power. No one did, and it was forgotten in the wake of the next fad which was, as she recalled, the ability to "throw your voice through ventriloquism."

According to Estabrooks, it was not possible to blatantly

convince people in hypnosis to act against their moral and ethical codes. It was, however, possible to achieve the same end by "changing the visual." He went on to explain that while you could not tell a moral young lady to take off her clothes, you could, with the right subject, convince that person under hypnosis that she was alone in an impossibly hot room. Or, while you could not persuade someone, even the most perfect hypnotic subject, to murder a close friend, you could create a visual scenario in which when that friend came through the door, it was not that person. Instead, it was a rabid bear intent upon killing the subject, and the subject would fire in self-defense.

Cahill looked up into the vivid blue sky. The sun was above her; she hadn't realized how long she'd been reading. She returned the glass to the kitchen, took a shower, dressed in the loosest, coolest clothing she had, and got into the Mercedes, through the wrong door. The steering wheel was on the right side. She'd forgotten that the islands were British. No problem, she thought. She'd had plenty of experience driving on the other side of the road in England.

She drove off without the slightest idea of where she was going. That pleased her. The lack of destination or timetable would give her a chance to leisurely explore the island and to find her own adventures and delights.

She drove into Road Town, the BVI's only thoroughly commercial area, parked, and strolled its narrow streets, stopping to admire classic examples of West Indian architecture painted in vivid colors, hip roofs glistening in the midday sun, heavy shutters thrown open to let in air and light. She stopped in shops, many of which were just opening, and bought small gifts to bring home.

At two, she drove on again. Once she left the town, she was lost, but it didn't bother her. The vistas in every direction were spectacular, and she stopped often along the side of a mountain road to drink in their natural beauty.

Rounding a sharp curve, she looked to her right and saw a large sign: PUSSER'S LANDING. She'd forgotten what Hank Fox had told her. She checked her watch; it was almost three, but she reasoned that since everything else started late on the island, lunch hour would probably still be in progress. She parked, entered beneath the sign, passed a gift shop, and reached the outdoor dining deck that overlooked a gentle, protected bay.

As she headed for a vacant table near the water, she came to a large birdcage. In it was a big, docile parrot. She glanced around. There were perhaps twenty people on the deck, some at tables, others standing in small clusters sipping rum drinks. She decided to go to the table first and order, then feed the bird to see if someone approached her. She ordered a hamburger and a beer and went to the cage. "Hello there, fella," she said. The bird looked at her with sleepy eyes. A tray of bird food was in front of the cage. She picked up a piece of fruit and extended her hand through the open cage door. The bird took the fruit from her fingers, tasted it, then dropped it to the cage floor.

"Fussy, huh?" she said, picked up some seed, and extended her open palm. The bird picked at the seed and swallowed it. "Want some more?" she asked. She was so engrossed in feeding the bird that she'd forgotten the real reason for doing it.

"Like him?" a male voice asked.

The voice startled her, and the snap of her head toward it testified to that fact. So she smiled. "Yes, he's beautiful."

The man to whom the voice belonged was tall and heavy. He wore baggy overalls and a soiled tan shirt. His black hair was thinning and swirled over his head without direction. His round face bore the scars of childhood acne. He was light-skinned, obviously the child of mixed parentage, and his eyes were pale blue. An interesting-looking man, Cahill thought.

"I call him Hank," the man said.

"He looks like a fox to me," she said intuitively.

The man laughed. "Yes, a Fox called Hank. Are you visiting the islands?"

"Yes, I'm from the States."

"Have you found our people pleasant and helpful?"

"Very." She fed the bird more seeds.

"We have that reputation. It's important for tourism. If there's anything I can do for you while you visit us, please do not hesitate to let me know. I have lunch here every day."

"That's kind of you. Your name is . . . ?"

He grinned and shrugged. "Call me Hank."

"Like the fox."

"Look at me. Bear would be more like it. Have a good day, miss, and enjoy your stay."

"Thank you; now I know I will."

22

"Have a good day?" Eric Edwards asked as he came to the terrace where Collette was sitting. She'd bathed and slipped into her caftan, found a glass pitcher in the refrigerator filled with a dark liquid and decided to try it. "What is this?" she asked Edwards as he joined her at the table.

"Oh, you found my daily supply of *maubi*. The housekeeper whips it up for me. It's non-alcoholic, but if you let it age long enough it ferments into something that knocks your socks off. It's got tree bark, ginger, marjoram, pineapple, stuff like that in it."

"It's delicious."

"Yeah, only I'm ready for a real drink. Let me get it and I'll brief you on the next couple of days of your vacation."

When he returned, he carried a large vodka martini on the rocks. "How would you like a *real* sail?" he asked.

"I'd love it," she said. "What does a *real* sail mean?"

"Two days and a night. Jackie's provisioning the boat first thing in the morning. We'll spend the day with sails up and I'll really show you the BVI. We'll find a pleasant place to anchor overnight, and spend the days catching beautiful winds and seeing one of God's gifts to the world. Sound good?"

"Sounds religious," she said. This didn't reflect what she was thinking at first. The sail would mean being out of touch, particularly with her contact at Pusser's Landing. Somehow, that brief encounter had been comforting.

Still, she knew that her job was to stay close to Edwards and to find out what she could. So far, she'd been successful only in discovering that he was handsome, charming, and a generous host.

He took her for dinner that night to the Fort Burt Hotel, and they stopped for a drink at Prospect Reef before returning to the house. She assumed this warm, pleasant evening would culminate in some attempt at seduction. Later, she had to laugh quietly in bed when she realized that the absence of any attempt at seduction left her ambivalent. She didn't want to be seduced by Eric Edwards. On the other hand, there was a side of her, part psychological and part physical, that yearned for it.

She heard Edwards walking about the house and tried to determine from her bedroom what he was doing. She heard him go outside, then return, listened to the dishwasher start and begin its cycles. She closed her eyes and focused on sounds from outside her window. The tree frogs were especially noisy. A pleasant sound. She allowed waves of contemplation of two days on that magnificent yacht to carry her into a blissful sleep.

Edwards, who'd poured himself a glass of rum over ice, sat on the terrace. The harbor below was peaceful and dark, except for occasional lights shining through tiny portholes on the yachts docked there. One of those lights came from his Morgan. Inside, Edwards's shipmate, Jackie, was putting the finishing touches on a vegetable tray she'd prepared for the sail. She covered it with plastic wrap and placed it in the galley's refrigerator along with the other food and drinks Edwards had ordered.

She went to the companionway, took two steps up, and surveyed the deck and dock. Then she returned to the cabin and went to a low door that led to a large hanging locker containing extra gear, flotation cushions, and snorkeling equipment. She opened the door. A flashlight's movement threw a sudden ray of light on her. "Are you done yet?" she asked.

A young native scrambled toward her on his knees, shone the light on his face, and nodded. She motioned for him to come. He took a final look back into the black corner of the stowage locker. She, of course, could hear nothing, but if he concentrated hard enough, he could hear the regular, rhythmic ticking in the silence of the night.

He joined her in the main cabin and they turned out the interior lights. She went up the companionway again, looked around, saw that it was clear, waved for him to follow, and they quickly climbed onto the dock. They looked at each other for a moment, then separated, Jackie heading in the direction of the main buildings, the young man following a narrow strip of wooden walkway until he reached a small beach and disappeared into the trees.

23

"Good job, Jackie," Eric Edwards said, as the slender girl in tight shorts and a T-shirt tossed him the last line from the dock.

She smiled and waved.

Once Edwards had backed the yacht away from the dock and was proceeding toward the same water they'd traveled two nights ago, he turned over the wheel to Cahill. This time she took it with confidence, eager to guide the sleek vessel with enough proficiency to make him proud.

"I don't know how much you know about sailing," Edwards said, "but you're going to have to help me."

"I don't know much," Cahill said, raising both hands in defense, "but I'll do what you tell me to do."

"Fair enough," Edwards said. "Let's kill that noisy engine and get some sail up."

The difference between sailing up Sir Francis Drake Channel in the daytime and at night, Cahill realized, was literally as different as day and night. The sun on the water turned it into a glistening turquoise and silver fantasy. She sat at the helm and watched Edwards, who wore only white duck pants, scurry back and forth over the coach roof and foredeck adjusting halyards and running rigging. The huge white sails billowed in the wind, the sound of them flapping against the yacht's spar like a giant bird's wings. When Eric was satisfied, he stood, hands on hips, and looked up at the full white sheets pressed into perfect symmetry by the 20-knot Caribbean breeze. Like something out of a movie, Cahill thought, as she took deep breaths and raised her face to the sun. A spy movie—or a romance?

"Where are we going?" she asked as he joined her at the wheel.

"We'll go right up the channel past Beef Island—that's where you flew in—and then up through the Dogs."

"The dogs?"

"Yeah. Why they're called that depends on who you talk to. Somebody told me once Sir Francis Drake dropped his dogs off on them. Some people think the islands look like dogs. The way I figure it, they named them the Dogs the way they name most things down here. Somebody just liked the name. There's three of them. Once we're past them, we'll be up off the northwest tip of Virgin Gorda. I thought we'd come around and go into Mosquito Island."

Was he testing her? Cahill wondered. Looking for a sign of recognition when he mentioned Mosquito Island? It didn't seem that way because the minute he finished telling her of their sailing plans, he left her side and busied himself again up front.

They reached the Dogs a little after three and anchored near Marina Cay, where they took a swim in the warm, incredibly clear water and had lunch. Eating made her sleepy, but once they were under way again, her spirits and energy picked up and she threw herself into the role of mate. They sailed between West Dog and Great Dog, came around a tiny bump in the water that Edwards said was Cockroach Island, then sailed almost due east toward Anguilla Point, which jutted out from the Fat Virgin. Far in the distance was Mosquito Island.

"See that island over there?" Edwards said, pointing to his left. "That's really the dogs, or gone to the dogs." Cahill shielded her eyes and saw a small island dominated by a large house built on its highest point. Edwards handed her a pair of binoculars. She peered through them and adjusted the lenses until the island and its structure were sharp. Virtually the entire island was surrounded by a high metal fence, with barbed wire stretched along its top. Two large black Dobermans ran along the perimeter of the property. On top of the building were elaborate antennas, including a huge dish.

She lowered the binoculars to her lap. "Is that a private island?"

Edwards laughed. "Yes, privately owned. The owner leased it out to the Soviet Union not long ago."

Collette feigned surprise. "Why would the Soviet Union want an island down here?"

Another laugh from Edwards. "They say it's to provide rest and recreation for its top bureaucrats. There's some debate about that."

Cahill looked at him quizzically. "Do people think it's a military installation?"

Edwards shrugged and returned the binoculars to the clip on the taffrail. "Nobody knows for sure," he said. "I just thought you'd be interested in seeing it."

"I am," she said.

He guided the vessel around Anguilla Point and approached Mosquito Island from the south. He went below and called Drake's Anchorage, the only resort on Mosquito, on VHF Channel 16 to inform them they would be mooring in the bay and would like a launch to bring them in for drinks and dinner. The pleasant female voice asked Edwards what time he estimated dropping anchor. He looked at his watch. "About an hour, hour and a half," he said. He flicked off the microphone switch, said to Cahill, "Feel like another swim before we go ashore?"

"Love it," she said.

"Make it an hour and a half," Edwards said to the young woman on the other end of the radio.

Ordinarily, Edwards would have brought the Morgan in closer, but he wanted Cahill to see a prime snorkeling reef a few miles to the east, near Prickly Pear Island. He headed for it, dropped anchor, went below, opened the door to the stowage locker, and pulled out two sets of masks and flippers. He helped Collette fit her feet into her flippers, adjusted the mask on her face, then put on his own set. "Ready?" he asked.

She nodded.

"Let's go."

Edwards climbed up onto the stanchion and threw himself over backwards into the water. Cahill managed a minor variation on the technique and soon they were paddling along, side by side, toward the coral reef he'd pointed out.

Edwards moved in front of her and began pointing beneath the water to a spectacular staghorn reef, its multicolored polyps beckoning as though they were millions of fingers. A thick school of yellow snapper appeared from behind the reef and crossed below them, so close that Cahill was able to probe the middle of the school with her hand.

Edwards brought his head out of the water and spit the breathing tube from his mouth. Cahill raised her head, too. He said, "Let's go around the reef that way," indicating the direction with his head. "There's a great . . ."

The sound started with a low rumble that was more felt than heard from where they were. Thunder? On such a day? They looked around, then back in the direction from which they had come. A microsecond later, Edwards's 46-foot Morgan rose into the brilliant blue BVI sky in a giant, ferocious fireball. Out of the top of the cloud came thousands of shreds and shards of what had been a magnificent sailing vessel.

The explosion was deafening, but more potent was what the impact did to the water below the surface. Cahill and Edwards were suddenly engulfed in a swirl of water gone mad. She was flipped on her back and water rushed into her mouth. Her arms and legs flailed for something to grab on to, something to help her combat the violent force in which she was trapped.

Then, as quickly as it had begun, the water's surge ebbed. Debris rained down from the sky above, flaming pieces of the yacht hitting the water with a vicious sizzle, large hunks of fiberglass and wood, steel and plastic falling like meteorites. A piece of burning material struck Cahill on her back, but she quickly turned over and the pain was gone.

She'd now regained enough of her senses to begin to think about what had happened, and about what to do next. She looked for Edwards, saw him close to the reef. He was on his side. One hand reached into the sky as though looking for a hook to grasp. There was blood coming from the exposed side of his face, and his mouth was open like that of a dying fish.

Cahill swam to him. "Are you all right?" she asked foolishly, her hand instinctively going to the wound on his temple.

His whole body heaved as he discharged water from his mouth and throat. He shook his head and said, "I think my arm is broken."

Cahill turned in the water and looked back to where the yacht had been. All that was left were random pieces, smoke drifting lazily from them. A large motor launch pierced the smoke, skirted the debris, and came directly at them.

The three young natives in the launch helped Cahill into it, then carefully brought Edwards on board. Cahill looked at his arm and asked, "Can you move it?"

He winced as he tried to extend the arm. "I think I can. Maybe it isn't broken."

Now, safe in the launch, Cahill was suddenly assaulted by the mental and physical horror of what had happened. She fell against the back of one of the wooden seats and began to breathe deeply and quickly. "Oh, my God. My God, what happened?"

Edwards didn't answer. His eyes were wide and fixed upon the remains of the Morgan.

"We take you back?" one of the natives asked.

Edwards nodded and said, "Yes, take us to the island. We need to make a phone call."

24

After Cahill applied first aid to his arm and head in the manager's office of Drake's Anchorage, Edwards made a call to his office on Tortola and told them to send a motor launch to pick them up on Virgin Gorda. The Mosquito Island shuttle boat took them there and they went to a clinic where more sophisticated aid was given Edwards, including an X-ray of his arm. It wasn't broken. The gash on his head, the result of a falling piece of metal, was deeper than they'd realized. It took eleven stitches to close.

They were driven to a dock where one of Edwards's native staff was waiting with a large powerboat. An hour later they were back at Edwards's house.

Throughout the return to Tortola, they said little to each other. Collette was still in mild shock. Edwards seemed to have his wits about him, but he made the journey with his face set in a pained, brooding expression.

They stood together on his terrace and looked down on the harbor.

"I'm sorry," he said.

"Yeah, sorry, me, too," she said. "I'm just glad to be alive. If we hadn't taken that swim . . . "

205

"There are a lot of *ifs*," he mumbled.

"What could have caused it?" Cahill asked. "A gasoline leak? I've heard about that happening with boats."

He said nothing, stared instead at the marina far below. Then he slowly turned his head and said, "It was no gasoline leak, Collette. Somebody wired the yacht. Somebody planted explosives on a timer."

She took a few steps back until her bare calves touched a metal chair. She collapsed into it. He continued looking out over the harbor, his hands on the terrace railing, his body hunched over. Finally, he turned and leaned against the rail. "You damn near lost your life because of things you don't know, and I'm going to tell you about them, Collette."

As much as she wanted to hear what he had to say, she was gripped with a simultaneous, overwhelming wave of nausea and shaking, and her head had begun to pound. She stood and used the arm of the chair for support. "I have to lie down, Eric. I don't feel well. Can we talk later?"

"Sure. Go rest. Whenever you feel up to it we'll sit down and hash out what happened."

She gratefully climbed into bed and fell into a troubled sleep.

When she awoke, she was facing the window. It was dark outside. She sat up and rubbed her eyes. The tree frogs were performing their usual symphony. They provided the only sound.

She looked toward the door, which was open a crack. "Eric?" she said in a voice that could be heard by no one. "Eric," she said louder. No response.

She'd slept in what she'd been wearing that day, removing only her shoes. She placed her bare feet on the cool tile floor, stood, and tried to shake away her lingering sleepiness and the chill that had turned her flesh into a pattern of tiny bumps. She said it again: "Eric?"

She opened the door and stepped into the hallway. A light from the living room spilled over to where she stood. She followed it, crossed the living room, and went to the open terrace doors. No one. Nothing.

She was met with the same situation when opening the

front door. The Mercedes and motorcycle were there, but no sign of their owner.

She went to the car and looked inside, then walked to the side of the house where a large tree created a natural roof above a white, wrought-iron love seat.

"Sleep good?"

A burst of air came from her mouth. She turned and saw Eric standing behind the tree.

"All rested?" he asked as he approached her.

"Yes, I . . . I didn't know where you'd gone."

"Nowhere. Just enjoying the evening."

"Yes, it's . . . lovely. What time is it?"

"Nine. Feel like some dinner?"

"I'm not hungry."

"I'll put it out anyway, nothing fancy, a couple of steaks, local vegetables. A half hour okay?"

"Yes, that will be fine, thank you."

A half hour later she joined him on the terrace. Two plates held their dinner. A bottle of Médoc had been opened, and two delicately curved red wineglasses stood on the table.

"Go ahead, eat," he said.

"Funny, but I am hungry now," she said. "Some people eat when they're upset, others can't bear the thought of it. I was always an eater."

"Good."

She asked how his arm felt, and he said it was better. "A bad sprain," the doctor at the clinic had said. Edwards had been told to keep it in the sling the doctor had provided, but he'd discarded it the minute they left the clinic. There was a large compression bandage on his left temple. A spot of dried blood that hadn't washed off remained on his cheek.

Cahill pushed her plate away, sat back, and said, "You said you wanted to share something with me. Sorry I wasn't in any shape to listen before, but I'm ready now. Do you still want to tell me?"

He leaned forward, both forearms on the table, took a breath and looked down into his plate, as though debating what to say.

"You don't have to," she said.

He shook his head. "No, I want to. You almost lost your

life because of me. I think that deserves an explanation."

Cahill thought: Barrie Mayer. Had *she* lost her life because of him?

He repositioned his chair so that there was room for him to cross his legs and to face her. She adopted a similar posture, her hands in her lap, her eyes trained on his.

"I really don't know where to begin." A smile. "At the beginning. That makes sense, doesn't it?"

She nodded.

"I suppose the best way to get into this, Collette, is to tell you that I'm not what I appear to be. Yes, I have a yacht-chartering service here in the BVI, but that's a front." She told herself to offer nothing, take in what he had to say and make decisions later.

He continued. "I work for the Central Intelligence Agency."

It struck her that he was being completely honest, that he had no idea that she knew about his involvement. Obviously, Barrie hadn't told him what her close friend Collette did for a living. That realization was refreshing. On the other hand, it put Cahill in a position of being the dishonest one. It made her squirm.

Her turn to say something. "That's . . . interesting, Eric. You're an . . . agent?"

"I suppose you could call it that. I'm paid to keep my eyes and ears open down here."

Cahill took a moment to appear as if she were looking for the next question. In fact, she had a list of a dozen. She said, "The CIA has people everywhere in the world, doesn't it?" She didn't want appear too naive. After all, he knew she had once worked for the CIA. She certainly would be somewhat knowledgeable about how things worked.

"It's more than just having people plopped in places around the globe to report back on what's going on. I was sent down here for a specific purpose. Remember the island I pointed out to you, the one the Russians have taken over?"

"Yes."

When he didn't say anything else, she leaned forward. "Do you think the Russians blew up the yacht?"

"That would be the logical explanation, wouldn't it?"

"I suppose it's possible, considering you're an agent for the other side. But you don't seem convinced."

Edwards shrugged, poured more wine into each of their glasses, held his up in a toast. "Here's to wild speculation."

She picked up her glass and returned the gesture. "What wild speculation?"

"I hope you don't misunderstand why I would say something like I'm about to say. I mean, after all, we both work for the United States government."

"Eric, I'm not a recent college graduate having her first taste of bureaucracy."

He nodded. "Yeah, well, here goes. I think the CIA set the charge aboard the yacht, or arranged for someone to do it."

It hadn't occurred to her for a moment since the incident that the people *she* worked for would do such a thing. She'd thought of the Russians, of course, and also wondered whether it hadn't been the act of a competing yacht-chartering company. She'd also had to question whether anyone else *had* been involved at all. There was no more evidence to link the explosion to a plot than there was to rule out a natural cause.

But those thoughts had little value at the moment. She asked the only obvious question: "Why do you think that?"

"I think it because . . . because I know things that the CIA would prefer not be told to anyone else."

"What things?"

"Things about individuals whose motivations are not in the best interests of not only the Central Intelligence Agency but the United States as well. In fact . . ."

Collette's body tensed. She was sure he was about to say something about Barrie Mayer's death.

He didn't disappoint her. "I'm convinced, Collette, that Barrie was murdered because she knew those same damaging things." He pulled his head back a little and raised his eyebrows. "Yes, she knew them from me. I suppose that's why I'm talking to you this way. Being responsible for the death of one person is bad enough. Seeing a second person come this close"—he created a narrow gap between his thumb and index finger—"to losing her life is too much."

Cahill leaned back and looked up into a sky that had, like her mind, clouded over. Her brain was short-circuited with thoughts and emotions. She got up and went to the edge of the terrace, looked down on the harbor and dock. What he was saying made a great deal of sense. It represented the sort of thing her instincts had pointed to from the beginning.

A new thought struck her. Maybe he was wrong. Assuming that the explosion had been the result of someone's having planted a device on board, who was to say the intended victim hadn't been herself? She turned to him again. "Are you suggesting that someone from the CIA murdered Barrie?"

"Yes."

"What about Dave Hubler, her associate at the literary agency?"

He shook his head. "I don't know anything about that, unless Barrie gave him the same information she'd gotten from me."

Collette returned to her chair, took a sip of wine, and said, "Maybe I was to be the victim."

"Why you?"

"Well, I . . . " She'd almost stepped over the line she'd drawn for herself in terms of how much she would reveal to him. She decided to stay on her side. "I don't know, you were the one who toasted 'wild speculation.' Maybe somebody wanted to kill me instead of you. Maybe the engine just blew up by itself."

"No, nothing blew up by itself, Collette. While you were sleeping, the authorities were here questioning me. They're filing a report that the destruction of the yacht resulted from an accidental electrical discharge into a fuel tank because that's what I want them to think. No, I know better. It was deliberate."

Cahill was almost afraid to ask the next question but knew she had to. "What was it that Barrie learned from you that caused her death, and that prompted somebody to try to kill you?"

He gave forth a throaty laugh, as though saying to himself, "My God, I can't believe I'm doing this." Collette felt for him. Obviously, the event near Mosquito Island, and Barrie's death, had brought him to a level of candor that every bit of his training cautioned against; in fact, prohibited. Her training, too, for that matter. She touched his knee. "Eric, what was it that Barrie knew? It's terribly important for me to know. As you said, I came this close to losing my life."

Edwards closed his eyes and puffed out his cheeks. When he exhaled through his lips and opened his eyes again, he said, "There are people within the CIA whose only interest is their own *self*-interest. Ever hear of Project Bluebird?"

Back to that again. Jason Tolker. Was that what he was getting at? She said, "Yes, I've heard of it, and MK-ULTRA, too." The minute she'd said it, she knew she'd offered too much.

His surprised look indicated she was right.

"How do you know about those projects?" he asked.

"I remember them from my training days with the CIA, before I quit and went to work for the embassy."

"That's right, they did talk about such projects in training, didn't they? You know, then, that they involved experimentation on a lot of innocent people?"

She shook her head. "I don't know the details of it, just that those projects had been operative and were abandoned because of public and congressional pressure."

Edwards narrowed his eyes. "Do you know how Barrie got involved with the CIA?"

Collette did a fast mental shuffle. Should she acknowledge knowing about Mayer's life as a courier? She decided to continue playing the surprised role.

"Did Barrie ever mention someone named Tolker?"

Cahill raised her eyes as if thinking back, then said, "No, I don't think so."

"He's a psychiatrist in Washington. He was the one who recruited her."

"Really?"

"You didn't know that? She never told you any of this?"

"No, I don't remember anyone named Tolker."

"How much did she tell you about what she was doing for the CIA?"

Her laugh was forced. "Not much. It certainly wouldn't have been professional for her to tell me, would it?"

211

Edwards shook his head. "No, it wouldn't, but Barrie wasn't necessarily the most professional of intelligence couriers." He seemed to be waiting for Cahill to respond. When she didn't, he said, "I suppose it doesn't matter what she told you. The fact is that she'd been seeing this guy Tolker professionally. She was a patient of his. He used that opportunity to bring her into the fold."

"That isn't so unusual, is it?" Cahill asked.

"I suppose not, although I really don't know a hell of a lot about that end of the business. The point is, Collette, that Dr. Jason Tolker was deeply involved in Operation Bluebird and MK-ULTRA—and continues to be involved in experimentation programs that spun out of those projects."

"The CIA is still doing mind-control experimentation?"

"Sure as hell is, and Tolker is one of the top dogs. He manipulated Barrie, brought her into the CIA as a courier, and that's why she's dead today. More wine?"

It seemed an absurd thing to say considering the tenor of the conversation, but she said, "Yes, please." He poured.

Collette thought about what she'd read in the book by G. H. Estabrooks, about how people could be persuaded to do things against their will if the hypnotist changed the visual scenario. Was that what Edwards was suggesting, that Barrie had been seduced into the role of CIA courier against her will? She asked him.

"Barrie evidently was an unusual hypnotic subject," Edwards answered, "but that really isn't important. What *is* important is that when she left on her most recent trip to Budapest, she carried with her information that would hang Jason Tolker by his thumbnails."

"I don't understand."

"Tolker is a double agent." He said it flatly and matter-of-factly. It left Cahill stunned. She got up and crossed the terrace.

"He's a goddamn traitor, Collette, and Barrie knew it."

"How did she know it? Did you tell her?"

Edwards shook his head. "No, she told me."

"How did *she* learn he was a double agent?"

He shrugged. "I really don't know, Collette. I pumped her, but all she'd say was that she had the goods and was going to blow him out of the water." He grinned. "That's an apt way to put it considering our little snorkeling excursion today, huh?"

Her smile was equally rueful. She asked the next obvious question. Who was Barrie going to tell about what she knew of Tolker's supposedly traitorous acts?

He answered, "My assumption was that she'd tell somebody back in Washington. But it didn't take me long to realize that that didn't make any sense. She didn't know anybody at Langley. Her only contact with the CIA *was* Jason Tolker. . . ."

"And whoever her contact was in Budapest."

Edwards nodded and joined her at the edge of the terrace. The strains of a fungee band, with its incessant island rhythms, drifted up to them.

They stood close together, their hips touching, both lost for a time in their individual thoughts. Then Edwards said in a monotone, "I'm getting out. I don't need boats blown out from under me."

She turned and looked into his face. Lines that had always been there now seemed more pronounced. "Was the yacht insured?" she asked.

His face broke into a wide smile. "Insured by the richest insurance company in the world, Collette, the Central Intelligence Agency."

"That's something to be thankful for," she said, not meaning it. It was something to say. Money meant nothing in this scenario.

He turned grim again. "The CIA is run by evil men. I never wanted to accept that fact. I never even acknowledged it until recently. I was filled with the sort of patriotism that leads people into working for an intelligence agency. I believed in it and its people, *really* believed in what the CIA stood for and what I was doing." He shook his head. "No more. It's filled with the Jason Tolkers of this world, people who only care about themselves and who don't give a damn who gets trampled in the process. I . . ." He placed his hand on her shoulders and drew her to him. "You and I have lost something very special in Barrie Mayer because of these people. I didn't know David Hubler, but he just joins the list of people who've had to pay with their lives because of them."

She started to say something but he cut her off. "I told Barrie to stay away from Tolker. The projects that he's involved in are at the root of what's rotten about the Company and the government. It uses innocent citizens as guinea pigs without any regard for their fate. They've lied to everyone, including Congress, about how they abandoned Operation Bluebird and MK-ULTRA. Those projects never missed a beat. They're more active today than they ever were."

Cahill was legitimately confused. "But what about funding? Projects like that cost money."

"That's the beauty of an organization like the CIA, Collette. There's no accountability. That's the way it was set up in the beginning. That was one of the reasons Truman had serious thoughts about establishing a national intelligence-gathering organization. The money is given to individuals and they're free to spend it any way they want, no matter who it hurts. There's got to be a thousand front groups like mine, shipping companies and personnel agencies, little airlines and weapons brokers, university labs and small banks that do nothing but launder Company money. It stinks. I never thought I'd get to this point but it *does* stink, Collette, and I've had it."

She stared at him for a long time before saying, "I understand, Eric, I really do. If you're right, that whoever blew up the yacht today did it on orders from people in my own government, I don't know how I can keep working for it, even in State."

"Of course you can't. That's the whole point. I'm glad to be an American, always have been, always considered it a rare privilege to have been born American, but when I end up as part of a series of systematic abuses that result in the murder of a woman I loved very much, it's time to draw the line."

The band down the hill began a slow, sensuous rendition of an island song. Edwards and Cahill looked at each other until he said, "Care to dance?"

Again, the absurdity of the request, considering the circumstances, caused her to burst out laughing. He joined her, slipped his right arm around her waist, took her left hand in his, and began leading her across the terrace.

"Eric, this is ridiculous."

"You're right, it is so ridiculous there is only one thing left to do—dance."

She stopped protesting and gracefully followed his lead, thinking all the while of how ludicrous it was yet at the same time how romantic and beautiful. The feel of his hardness against her sent a succession of tiny sexual electric bursts through her body. He kissed her, tentatively at first, then with more force, and she returned his hunger.

As they danced by the table, he deftly took the wine, led her through the open doors and into the bedroom. There, he released her and his fingers began opening the buttons on the front of her blouse. She knew it was the last opportunity to protest, or to step away, but she moved closer. They made love, and soon her intensely pleasurable response merged with his, and with visions of the fireball in the blue skies of the British Virgin Islands.

The next day, Edwards was out early. He said he had a number of officials on the island with whom he had to speak about the explosion.

After he was gone, Cahill grappled with conflicting thoughts. What he'd said last night had caused her to rethink everything she'd done since coming to work for Central Intelligence. She certainly didn't share his passionate disgust with the CIA. She wasn't even sure that what he'd said was true. All she knew was that it was time to do some serious thinking, not only about this assignment, but about who she was.

She considered placing a call to Hank Fox in Washington but was afraid of breaching security. Phone calls from the islands went to the United States via satellite; conversations were open to the world, including the Russians on their small, private island.

Pusser's Landing.

She drove Edwards's Mercedes there at noon, took a table, ordered a sandwich and a Coke, then went to the birdcage where she fed the parrot. She'd noticed the big man from the day before. He was down on the dock repairing an outboard engine on a small runabout. Soon, he had casually made his way to her side.

"I thought I'd come back for lunch again," she said. "It was so pleasant last time."

"It is a pleasant place, miss," he said. He looked about to ensure no one was near them before adding, "It is even nicer in Budapest. You should go there immediately."

"Budapest? Who . . . ?"

"As quickly as possible, miss. Today."

Cahill asked, "Does my travel agent know about this?"

The big man smiled and said, "Ask him yourself. You are to go to Washington first."

She left Pusser's Landing, telling the waiter that an emergency had arisen, found her way back to Edwards's house, quickly packed, and left him a note.

Dear Eric,
I won't even try to explain why I've rushed away but I assure you it's urgent. Please forgive me. There are so many things I want to say to you about last night, about feelings it generated in me, about—well, about a lot of things. There's no time now. Thank you for providing a wonderful vacation in your beloved BVI. I hope I'll be able to share it with you again soon.

Collette

25

Cahill got off the plane at Dulles Airport, rented a car, and drove directly to her mother's house where she was met with a barrage of questions about where she'd been and why she was running off again in such a rush. Cahill explained, "They're having some kind of a budget crisis at the embassy at Budapest and I have to get back right away."

"What a shame," her mother said. "I thought I might get to see you for at least a day."

Collette stopped rushing for a moment, hugged her, said she loved her and yes, she would have coffee, and ran upstairs to pack.

She shared the next hour with her mother in the kitchen and felt a desperate yearning to stay, to retreat into childhood where the world was wondrous and the future bright when viewed from the protective custody of family and home. She had to force herself to say goodbye, leaving her mother standing at the front door with a poignant expression on her face. "I'll be back soon," Cahill yelled through the open car window. She knew her mother's smile was forced but she appreciated the effort.

She drove back to Washington, went to a phone booth,

and dialed the special number Hank Fox had given her. When a young woman answered, Cahill said, "This is Dr. Jayne's office calling for Mr. Fox." The woman told her to hold. A minute later Fox came on the line and said, "I heard about the accident. I'm glad you're all right."

"Yes, I'm fine. I made friends with someone at Pusser's Landing. He told me . . . "

Fox said sharply, "I know what he told you. The Fisherman is restless in Budapest."

"The Fisherman?" Then, it dawned on her. Code name Horgász—Árpád Hegedüs. She said, "I thought he went to . . . ?"

"He didn't, and he wants to talk to his friend. It's important that he see her as soon as possible."

"I understand," she said.

"How is your boyfriend in the British Virgin Islands?"

"He's . . . he's not my boyfriend."

"How is he?"

"Fine." She started to think of the last conversation she'd had with Edwards but Fox didn't give her enough time to complete the thought.

"You can leave tonight?"

Cahill sighed. More than anything she didn't want to get on a plane for Budapest. What she really wanted was to return to the BVI and be with Eric Edwards, not only because of the intimacy that had developed between them, but because she wanted to talk more about this thing she was doing, this organization she'd placed so much trust in. That trust wasn't there anymore. Now she knew: She wanted out, too.

"I'll be hearing from Joe," Fox said. Breslin.

"I'm sure you will. I have to go. Goodbye." She slammed the receiver into its cradle, gripped the small shelf beneath the phone and shook it, muttering as she did, "The hell with you, the hell with it all."

She caught a flight out of Washington to New York and barely made the Pan Am flight to Frankfurt, Germany, where she could make a direct connection for Budapest. She'd called Vern Wheatley at his brother's apartment but there was no answer. She needed to talk with him. Somehow, she had the sense that if she didn't talk to someone outside the organization, someone who wasn't intrinsically bound up in its intrigues, she'd go to pieces. And that, she knew, would be the worst thing that could happen.

By the time she left the plane in Budapest she was exhausted but, at least, more in control of herself and her circumstances. She realized as she went through Customs that she was now back in her official status as an employee of the United States Embassy. It didn't matter that her real employer was the CIA. What *did* matter was that things were familiar now; not quite as comforting as the bosom of her mother, but certainly better than what she'd been through the past week.

She took a cab to her apartment and called Joe Breslin at the embassy.

"Welcome back," he said. "You must be beat."

"I sure am."

"It's five o'clock. Think you can stay awake long enough for dinner?"

"I'll make myself. Where?"

"Légrádi Testvérek."

Cahill managed a smile despite her fatigue. "Going fancy, are we? Is this in honor of my return?"

"If it makes you feel good thinking that, then that's what it's for. Actually, my stomach is in need of a good meal, and I get a kick out of the chubby little violin player."

"I'll consider it in my honor. What time?"

"I prefer late but, considering your condition, maybe we should make it early. How's eight sound?"

"Eight? I'll be dead to the world by then."

"Okay, tell you what. Take a good long nap and meet me there at ten."

She knew there was little sense in trying to negotiate a different time. He said he'd make a reservation under his name. She opened the door of her small refrigerator and remembered she'd cleaned it out before leaving. The only thing in it was two bottles of Szamorodni, the heavy dessert white wine, a half dozen bottles of Köbanyai világos beer, a tin of coffee, and two cans of tuna fish her mother had sent in a "care package" a month ago. She opened the tuna fish, realized she was out of bread, ate it directly from the can, stripped off her clothing, set her alarm clock, climbed into bed, and was asleep in seconds.

They sat across from each other in a small room at Légrádi Testvérek. The oval table betwen them was covered with a white lace tablecloth. Their chairs were broad, had high backs covered in a muted tapestry. A single silver candle epergne with ruffled glass dishes on two protruding arms dominated the center of the table. One of the dishes held fresh grapes and plums, the other apples and pears. The walls were stark white, the ceiling low and curved. Gypsy music emanated from a short, fat violinist and a tall, handsome cimbalom player who used tiny mallets to delicately strike the strings on his pianolike instrument.

"You look good," Breslin said, "considering the schedule you've been on."

"Thank you. Nothing like a can of American tuna fish and a nap to put color back in a girl's cheeks."

He smiled and looked up at the owner, who'd come to take their order. They decided to share a dish of assorted appetizers—caviar, tiny shrimps on salmon mousse stuffed into an egg, three kinds of pâté, and marinated oysters. Breslin ordered beef with pâté as his entrée; Cahill opted for chicken layered with a paprika sauce and little pools of sour cream. They skipped wine; Breslin had a Scotch and soda, Cahill mineral water.

"So?" he asked.

"So?" she mimicked. "You don't want a litany here, do you?"

"Why not?"

"Because . . ." She made a small gesture with both hands to indicate the public nature of the restaurant.

"Skip the names, and I don't need details. First, what about your boyfriend in the pretty place?"

She shook her head and sat back. "Joe, what do you and Hank do, talk every twenty minutes?"

"No, just two or three times a day. What about him? Did you enjoy your vacation?"

"Very much, except for a minor mishap out in the water."

"I heard. What were you doing, snorkeling or something?"

"Exactly, and that's why I'm sitting here tonight. As for my so-called boyfriend, he's terrific. Want to know something? A lot of our *friends* have said bad things about him. . . ." She raised her eyebrows and adopted an expression to reinforce she was talking about her employer. "People are wrong. If there's a problem, it's not with my 'boyfriend.' "

"I see," Breslin said, scratching his nose and rubbing his eyes. "We can discuss that at length another time. Did you see your shrink while you were back?"

"My— Oh, you mean Dr. Jayne."

"Who?"

"Don't worry, Joe, we're talking about the same person. I didn't see him again after I saw you in Washington. I felt no need to. My mental health is getting better all the time."

He narrowed his eyes as he scrutinized her across the flickering candle. "Something up with you, Collette? You okay?"

"I think I'm beginning to be more than okay, Joe. I think I grew up this past week."

"What does that mean?"

"It means . . ." She realized she was on the verge of tears and told herself that if she cried, she would never forgive herself. She looked around the restaurant. A waiter brought the appetizers on a white china platter. He filled their glasses with water and asked if they needed anything else.

"No, *köszönöm szepen,*" Breslin said politely. The waiter left and Breslin gave his attention to Cahill. "You're not happy, are you?"

Cahill shook her head in wonder and laughed. She leaned forward so that her face was inches from the candle's flame and said, "What the *hell* am I supposed to be happy about, Joe?"

He held up his hands and said, "Okay, I won't press it. You've been under a lot of strain. I realize that. Come on, enjoy the food. It's costing me a month's salary."

Throughout the meal, Cahill was on the verge a dozen

times of telling him how she felt. She resisted the temptation and contented herself with light conversation.

The doorman got Breslin's car for him. When he and Cahill were in it, Breslin asked, "Feel up to a little nightlife?"

"Joe, I . . . the Miniatur?"

"No, I ran across another spot while you were away. Change is good for the soul, right?"

"If you say so, Joe. Might as well catch up on what's new in Budapest, but not too late, huh? One drink and get me home."

"Trust me."

She always had, but wasn't so sure anymore.

He drove slowly through the narrow, winding streets of the Pest side of the city until reaching Vörösmarty tèr, with its statue of the famed Hungarian poet for whom the square was named. They passed a succession of airline offices and government buildings until they reached Engels Square and its large bus terminal. Ahead of them was St. Stephen's basilica. Breslin made a sharp turn north and, five minutes later, entered an especially narrow street made worse by cars hanging off their sidewalk parking spots. He found a place, wedged his small Renault between two other cars, and they got out. Cahill looked up the street to the huge red star atop the Parliament Building. She was back. Hungary. Budapest. Red stars and Soviet tanks. She was glad. Oddly, it was as close to home as she'd ever be outside of her mother's house in Virginia.

The bar wasn't marked, no sign, no windows. Only the faint tinkling of a piano heralded its location, and that was confused by a dozen dark doors set into the long concrete wall that formed the front of the street's buildings.

Breslin rapped with a brass knocker. The door opened and a large man in a black suit, with long greasy black hair and sunken cheeks, scrutinized them. Breslin nodded toward Cahill. The man stepped back and allowed them to enter.

Now the music was louder. The pianist was playing "Night and Day." Female laughter in the air mingled with his notes.

Cahill looked around. The club was laid out much like

the Miniatur—bar as you entered, a small room just off it in which customers could enjoy the piano.

"*Jó napot* (How are you?)," Breslin said to an attractive woman with hair bleached white, wearing a tight red satin dress.

"*Jó estét* (Good evening)," she said.

"*Fel tudya ezt váltani?* (Can you change this?)" Breslin asked, handing her a Hungarian bill of large denomination.

She looked at the bill, at him, then stepped back to give them access to a door hidden in shadows beyond the bar. Breslin nodded at Cahill and she followed him. He hesitated, his hand poised over the knob, then turned it. The door swung open. Breslin indicated that Cahill should enter first. She took a step into a small room lighted only by two small lamps on a battered table in the middle. There were no windows, and heavy purple drapes covered all walls.

Her eyes started to adjust to the dimness. A man, whose face was vaguely familiar, was the first object she focused on. He had a thick, square face. Bones beneath bushy eyebrows formed hairy shelves over his cheeks. His black hair was thick and curly and streaked with gray. She remembered—Zoltán Réti, the author, Barrie Mayer's author.

Next to Reti sat Árpád Hegedüs. One of his hands on the table covered a female hand. A plain, wide-faced woman with honest eyes and thin, stringy hair.

"Árpád," Cahill said, the surprise evident in her voice.

"Miss Cahill," he said, standing. "I am so happy to see you."

26

Collette looked across the table at Hegedüs and Réti. Hegedüs's presence was the more easily understood. She'd known that the purpose of her return to Budapest was to meet with him. Réti was another matter. She'd forgotten about him in the rush of the past weeks.

"Miss Cahill, allow me to introduce you to Miss Lukács, Magda Lukács," Hegedüs said. Cahill rose slightly and extended her hand. The Hungarian woman reached out tentatively, then slipped her hand into Cahill's. She smiled; Cahill did, too. The woman's face was placid, yet there was fear in her eyes. She wasn't pretty, but Cahill recognized an earthy female quality.

"I mentioned Miss Lukács to you the last time we were together," Hegedüs said.

"Yes, I remember," said Cahill, "but you didn't mention her name." She again smiled at the woman. Here was Hegedüs's lover, the woman Cahill had fervently hoped would not deter him from continuing to provide information. Now, as she observed the happiness in Hegedüs's face, she was glad he'd found Magda Lukács. He was happier and more relaxed than Cahill could ever remember seeing him.

As for Réti, she knew him only from photographs, and from having seen him on Hungary's state-controlled television network. Barrie had often spoken of him but they'd never met. "I'm glad to finally meet you, Mr. Réti," she said. "Barrie Mayer spoke so often and enthusiastically of you and your work."

"That is flattering," said Réti. "She was a wonderful woman and a fine literary agent. I miss her very much."

Cahill turned to Breslin. "Joe, why are we here?"

Breslin glanced at the others before saying, "First of all, Collette, I should apologize for not telling you up front how the evening would play. I didn't want to lay a lot of tension on you at dinner. From what I've heard, there's been enough of that in your life already."

She half smiled.

"Mr. Hegedüs has come over to our side."

Collette said to Hegedüs, "You've defected?"

He gave her a sheepish smile. "Yes, I have. My family is in Russia and I am now one of you. I am sorry, Miss Cahill. I know that was not what you or your people wished."

"No need to apologize, Árpád. I think it's wonderful." She looked at Magda Lukács. "You have defected, too?"

Lukács nodded. "I come with Árpád."

"Of course," said Cahill. "I'm sure that . . ." She swung around to Breslin. "But that isn't why we're sitting here, is it?"

Breslin shook his head. "No, it's not. The defection has already taken place. What we *are* here for is to hear what Mr. Hegedüs and Mr. Réti have to tell us." He smiled. "They wouldn't say a word unless you were here, Collette."

"I see," Cahill said, taking in the table. "Well, go ahead. Here I am, and I'm all ears."

When no one spoke, Breslin said, "Mr. Hegedüs."

Now Hegedüs seemed more like his old nervous self. He cleared his throat and squeezed his lover's hand. He ran a finger beneath his shirt collar and said with a forced sense of gaiety, "We are in a bar, yes? Could I possibly have some whiskey?"

His request visibly annoyed Breslin, but he got up with a sigh and went to the door, opened it, and said to the woman in the red satin dress who was seated at the bar, "Could we have a bottle of wine, please?"

Hegedüs said from behind Breslin, "Would bourbon be all right?"

Breslin turned and screwed up his face. *"Bourbon?"*

"Yes, Miss Cahill always . . ."

Breslin shook his head and said to the woman in red, "A bottle of bourbon." He then laughed and added, "And some Scotch and gin, too." He closed the door and said to Cahill, "Never let it be said that Joe Breslin didn't throw as good a defector party as Collette Cahill."

"You're a class act, Joe," Collette said. She looked at Zoltán Réti and asked, "Have you defected too, Mr. Réti?"

Réti shook his head.

"But have you . . . ?" She checked Breslin before continuing. His expressionless face prompted her to go ahead. "Have you been involved with our efforts all along, Mr. Réti, through Barrie Mayer?"

"Yes."

"Were you Barrie's contact here in Budapest?"

"Yes."

"She would hand you what she was carrying for us?"

He smiled. "It was a little more complicated than that, Miss Cahill."

There was a knock at the door. Breslin opened it and the woman in red carried in a tray with the liquor, a bucket of ice and glasses. After she'd placed it on the table and left, Collette cocked her head and listened to the strains of piano music and the laughter of patrons through the wall. Was this place secure enough for the sort of conversation they were having? She was almost ashamed for even questioning it. Breslin had a reputation of being the most cautious intelligence employee within the Budapest embassy.

"Maybe I'd better lead this conversation," Breslin said.

Cahill was momentarily taken aback, but said, "By all means."

Breslin pointed a finger across the table at Zoltán Réti and said, "Let's start with you." To Hegedüs, "You don't mind, do you?"

Hegedüs, busy pouring a tall glass of bourbon, quickly shook his head and said, "Of course not."

Breslin continued. "Mr. Réti, Miss Cahill has been back in the United States trying to find out what happened to Barrie Mayer. I don't know if you're aware of it, but they were best of friends."

"Yes, I know that," said Réti.

"Then you know that we've never believed that Barrie Mayer died of natural causes."

Réti grunted. "She was assassinated. Only a fool would think otherwise."

"Exactly," said Breslin. "One of the pieces we've had trouble with has to do with what she could have been carrying that was important enough for her to have been murdered. Frankly, we weren't even aware of her final trip to Budapest until after the fact. We expected nothing from Washington. But you evidently knew she was coming."

Réti nodded, and his heavy eyebrows came down even lower over his eyes.

Cahill said, "But you weren't *here*, Mr. Réti. You were in London."

"Yes, I was sent there by the Hungarian Arts Council to make an appearance at an international writers' conference."

"Didn't Barrie know that you wouldn't be here to meet her?" Cahill asked.

"No, I had no time to contact her. I was not allowed access to any means of communication with her before she left the United States."

"Why?" Cahill realized she had taken the meeting from Breslin. She cast a glance at him to see if he were annoyed. The expression on his face showed that he wasn't.

Réti shrugged. "I can only assume that they . . . the government had become aware that she and I were more than simply agent and author."

Cahill processed what he'd said, then asked, "And they didn't do more to you than just keep you from telling Barrie that you wouldn't be here to meet her? They knew that you were involved in some sort of activity on our behalf, but only kept you from calling her?"

227

Réti smiled, exposing a set of widely spaced teeth. He said, "That is not so surprising, Miss Cahill. The Russians . . . and my government . . . they are not so foolish to punish someone like myself. It would not look so good in the world, huh?"

His explanation made sense to Cahill, but she said, "Still, if Barrie *had* arrived and didn't find you here, what would she do with what she was carrying? Who would she hand it to?"

"This time, Miss Cahill, Barrie was not to hand me anything."

"She wasn't?"

"No."

"What was she to do, then?"

"She was to tell me something."

"Tell?"

"Yes. This time what she carried was in her head."

"Her mind, you mean."

"Yes, in her mind."

The room was hot and stuffy, yet a chill radiated through Collette that caused her to fold into herself. Was it all coming true now—Jason Tolker, Estabrooks's theories on using hypnosis to create the perfect intelligence courier, programs like Operation Bluebird and MK-ULTRA, supposedly scrapped years ago but still going strong—everything Eric Edwards had told her, every bit of it?

She looked at Breslin. "Joe, do you know what Barrie was supposed to tell Mr. Réti?"

Breslin, who'd just lighted his pipe, squinted through the smoke and said, "I think so."

Cahill hadn't expected an affirmative answer. Breslin said to Hegedüs, "Perhaps it's time for you to contribute to this conversation."

The Hungarian psychiatrist looked at Magda Lukács, cleared his throat with a swallow of bourbon, and said, "It has to do with what I told you last time, Miss Cahill."

Collette said it quietly, almost to the table: "Dr. Tolker."

"Yes, your Dr. Tolker . . ."

"What about him?"

A false start from Hegedüs, then, "He had given Miss

228

Mayer information of the gravest importance to the Banana Quick project."

"What sort of information?" Cahill asked.

"The source of the leak in the British Virgin Islands," Breslin said.

Cahill raised her eyebrows. "I thought that . . ."

Breslin shrugged. "I think you're beginning to understand, Collette."

"You told me the last time we were together, Árpád, that Tolker was not to be trusted."

"That is correct."

"But now I'm to understand that he's the one who is identifying a security leak in Banana Quick."

"Right," said Breslin. "You know who we're talking about, Collette."

"Eric Edwards."

"Exactly."

"That's ridiculous," Collette said.

"Why?" Breslin asked. "Edwards has been a prime suspect from the beginning. That's why you were . . ." He stopped. The rules were being broken. Take everything you could from the other side but offer nothing.

Collette was having trouble controlling her emotions. She didn't want to mount an impassioned defense of Edwards because it would only trigger in Breslin the question of why she was doing it. She imposed calm on herself and asked Breslin, "How do you know what Barrie was carrying? Maybe it had nothing to do with Banana Quick . . . or Eric Edwards."

Breslin ignored her and nodded at Hegedüs, who said regretfully, "I was wrong, Miss Cahill, about Dr. Tolker."

"Wrong?"

"I was misled, perhaps deliberately by certain people within my professional ranks. Dr. Tolker has not been disloyal to you."

"Just like that," Cahill said.

Hegedüs shrugged. "It is not such a crime to be wrong, is it, not in America?"

Cahill sighed and sat back. "Collette," Breslin said, "the

facts are written on the wall. Barrie was coming here to . . ."

She said, "Coming here to deliver a message that had been implanted in her mind by Jason Tolker."

"That's right," said Breslin. "Tell her, Mr. Réti."

Réti said, "I was to say something to her when she arrived that would cause her to remember the message."

"Which was?" Collette asked.

"That this Eric Edwards in the British Virgin Islands has been selling information to the Soviets about Banana Quick."

"How do we know that's what she was carrying?"

"Tolker has been contacted," Breslin said.

Cahill shook her head. "If Tolker can simply tell us what he knows about Eric Edwards, why did he bother sending Barrie with the information? Why didn't he just go to someone at Langley with it?"

"Because . . ." Breslin paused, then continued. "We can discuss that later, Collette. For now, let's stick to what Mr. Réti and Mr. Hegedüs can provide us."

"Well?" Cahill said to the two Hungarians.

"Miss Cahill," Réti said, "first of all, I did not know what Barrie was to tell me when I said to her the code words."

"What were those words?" Cahill asked.

Réti looked to Breslin, who nodded his approval. "I was to say, 'The climate has improved.' "

"The climate has improved," Cahill repeated.

"Yes, exactly that."

"And she was then to open up to you like a robot."

"I do not know about that. I was simply following instructions."

"Whose instructions?"

"Mr. . . ." Another look at Breslin.

"Stan Podgorsky," Breslin said. "Stan's been the contact for Barrie and Mr. Réti since the beginning."

"Why wasn't I told that?" Cahill asked.

"No need. Barrie's courier duties had nothing to do with you."

"I wonder about that."

"Don't bother. It's the way it is. Accept it."

"Árpád, who has caused you to change your opinion of Jason Tolker?"

"Friends." He smiled. "Former friends. There are no longer friends for me in Hungary."

"Collette, Mr. Réti has something else to share with us," Breslin said.

Everyone waited. Finally, Réti said in a low, slow monotone, "Barrie was bringing me money, too."

"Money?" Cahill said.

"Yes, to pay off one of our officials so that the earnings from my books could reach me here in Hungary."

"This money was in her briefcase?"

"Yes."

"Joe, Barrie received her briefcase from Tolker. Why would he . . . ?"

"He didn't," Breslin said. "The money wasn't from Mr. Réti's fund in the States. It was Pickle Factory money."

"Why?"

"It's the way it was set up."

"Set up . . . with Barrie?"

"Right."

"But she had Réti's own money, didn't she? Why would she need CIA money?"

Breslin lowered his eyes, then raised them. "Later," he said.

"No, not later," Cahill said. "How about now?"

"Collette, I think you're becoming emotionally bound up in this. That won't help clarify anything."

"I resent that, Joe."

What she was really feeling was a sense of being a woman, and disliking herself for it. Breslin was right. He'd read her; she wasn't taking in and evaluating what was being said at the table like a professional. She was bound up in protecting a man, Eric, a man with whom she'd slept and, incredibly, with whom she'd begun to fall in love. It hadn't seemed incredible at the time, but it did now.

She took in everyone at the table and asked, "Is there anything else?"

Hegedüs forced a big smile, his hand still resting on his lover's hand. He said, "Miss Cahill, I would like you to

231

know how much I appreciate . . . how much Magda and I appreciate everything you have done for us."

"I didn't do anything, Árpád, except listen to you."

"No, you are wrong, Miss Cahill. By spending time with you, my decision to leave the oppression of the Soviets was made clear, and easier." He stood and bowed. "I shall be forever grateful."

Cahill found his demeanor to be offensive. "What about your family, Árpád, your beautiful daughter and bright young son? Your wife. What of her? Are you content to abandon them to the tenuous life you know they'll lead in Russia?" He started to respond but she went on. "You told me you wanted more than anything else for your son to have the advantage of growing up in America. What was that, Árpád, all talk?" Her voice was now more strident, reflecting what she was feeling.

"Let's drop it," Breslin said with finality. Collette glared at him, then said to Réti, "What happens to you now, Mr. Réti? The money never reached you."

Réti shrugged. "It is the same now as it was before. Perhaps . . . "

"Yes?"

"Perhaps you could be of help in this matter."

"How?"

"We're working on it, Mr. Réti," Breslin said. To Cahill, "It's one of the things I want to discuss with you when we leave here."

"All right." Collette stood and extended her hand to Magda Lukács. "Welcome, Miss Lukács, to freedom." Hegedüs beamed and offered his hand to Cahill. She ignored it, said to Breslin, "I'm ready to leave."

Breslin got up and surveyed the bottles on the table. "Souvenirs?" he asked, laughing.

"If you would not be offended I would . . . "

"Sure, Mr. Hegedüs, take it with you," Breslin said. "Thank you for being here, all of you. Come on, Collette, you must be exhausted."

"That, and more," she said, opening the door and walking into the smoky barroom. The lady in red was standing at the door.

"*Jó éjszakát*," Breslin said.

"*Jó éjszakát*," she said, nodding at Cahill.

Collete said "Good night" in English, walked past her, and stood in the cool, refreshing air outside the club. Breslin came to her side. Without looking at him, she said, "Let's go somewhere and talk."

"I thought you were beat," he said, taking her arm.

"I'm wide awake and I'm filled with questions that need answering. Are you up to that, Joe?"

"I'll do my best."

Somehow, she knew his best wouldn't be enough, but she'd take what she could get.

They'd driven out of the city to the Római fürdö, the former Roman baths that now constituted one of Budapest's two major camping sites. The sky had clouded over and was low. It picked up the general glow of the city's lights and was racing over them, pink and yellow and gray, a fast-moving scrim cranked by an unseen force.

"You said you had questions," Breslin said.

Cahill had opened her window and was looking out into the dark. She said into the night, "Just one, Joe."

"Shoot."

She turned and faced him. "Who killed Barrie Mayer?"

"I don't know."

"Know what I think, Joe?"

"No, what?"

"I think everybody's lying."

He laughed. "Who's *everybody*?"

"*Everybody!* Let's start with Réti."

"Okay. Start with him. What's he got to lie about?"

"Money, for one thing. I knew Barrie was supposed to pay off some government bigwig on Réti's behalf, but I didn't know until tonight that Barrie was actually carrying the money with her in the missing briefcase. Oh, that's right, you said you'd discuss with me later why the Company used its money to buy off the official, instead of Barrie using what she'd already collected of Réti's earnings. This is later, Joe. I'm ready."

He scrutinized her from where he sat in the driver's seat, ran his tongue over his lips, then pulled a pipe from his raincoat pocket and went through the ritual of lighting it. This was all too familiar to Cahill, using the pipe to buy thinking time, and tonight was especially irritating. Still, she didn't interrupt, didn't attempt to hasten the process. She waited patiently until the bowl glowed with fire and he'd had a chance to inhale. Then she said, "Réti's money. Why the Company?"

"To make sure he knew who he owed," Breslin answered.

"That doesn't make sense," she said. "Why would he owe anyone? The money is his. His books earned it."

"That's what he said, but we educated him. He's Hungarian. His big money is earned out of the country. Puts him in a tough position, doesn't it? All we did was to set up a system to help him get his hands on some of it."

"If he played the game with us."

"Sure. He thought Barrie would take care of it as his agent." Breslin smiled. "Of course, he didn't know up front that she worked for us, and would do what we told her to do. We struck a nice deal. Réti cooperates with us, and we see that he gets enough money to live like a king here."

"That is so . . . goddamned unfair. He earned that money."

"I suppose it is unfair, unless you're dealing with a Socialist writer and a capitalist agent. Come on, Collette, you know damn well that nothing's fair in what we're called upon to do."

" 'Called upon to do.' You make it sound so lofty."

"Necessary. Maybe that's more palatable to you."

She drew a sustained, angry breath. "Let's get to Hegedüs and Jason Tolker. Why do you buy Hegedüs's change of mind about Tolker?"

"Why not buy it?"

"Why *not*? Joe, hasn't it occurred to you that Árpád might have come over to feed us disinformation? What if Tolker has been cooperating with the other side? How convenient to have Hegedüs defect and get us to look the other way. No, I can't buy it. When Hegedüs told me earlier that Tolker was not be to trusted, he meant it. He doesn't mean what he's saying now. He's lying."

"Prove it."

"How do you prove anything in this stupid game?"

"Right, you don't. You look at everything you've got—which sure as hell never amounts to much—and you feel what your gut is saying and listen to what your head says and you make your decisions. My decision? We've got ourselves a defector, a good one. Sure, we'd all prefer he'd stayed in place so he could keep feeding us from the inside, but it's okay that he's with us now. He's loaded with insight into the Soviet and Hungarian psychological fraternity. You did a good job, Collette. You turned him nicely. He trusted you. Everybody's pleased with the way you've handled him."

"That's terrific. Why don't *you* trust me?"

"Huh?"

"Why can't you put some stock in what my gut feels and my head says? He's lying, Joe, maybe to protect his family back in the Soviet Union, maybe to play out his own brand of patriotism to his government. Don't you question why the Soviets have let him off the hook? He was supposed to go back to Russia because they didn't trust him. He doesn't go, and he neatly defects. He's lying. They've plopped him into the middle of us, and one of his jobs is to get Jason Tolker off the hook."

"Pure speculation, Collette. Ammunition. Give me something tangible to back it up."

She spread her hands. "I don't have any, but I know I'm right."

"What about Réti?" Breslin asked. "What's he got to lie about?"

"I don't know. But remember, he was in London when Barrie died."

"Meaning?"

"Meaning maybe he killed her because he knew her briefcase was loaded with cash."

"His cash. Why kill her for it?" A long, slow drag on his pipe.

"Did he know how much she was bringing to him?"

"Not sure. Probably not."

"Maybe Mr. Réti figured out that he was never going to get a square count from us. Maybe he figured out that he'd only get a small piece of what she was carrying. Maybe he wanted to get his hands on the money while he was outside Hungary and stash it."

"Interesting questions."

"Yes, aren't they?"

"What about Hubler back in Washington? Réti sure as hell didn't kill him, Collette."

"He could have arranged it if Hubler knew what had happened. The Soviets could have done it. Then again, maybe it was pure coincidence, nothing to do with Barrie."

"Maybe. What other theories do you have?"

"Don't dismiss what I'm saying, Joe. Don't treat me like some schoolgirl who's spewing out plots from bad TV shows she's watched."

"Hey, Collette, back off. I'm a white hat, remember? I'm a friend."

She wanted to question what he'd said but didn't. Instead, she asked if he had a cigarette.

"You don't smoke."

"I used to, back when I was a schoolgirl watching bad TV shows. Got any?"

"Yeah, in the glove compartment. Every once in a while I get the urge."

She opened the compartment and reached inside, found a crumpled pack of Camels, and pulled one from the pack. Breslin lighted it for her. She coughed, exhaled the smoke, then took another drag, tossed the cigarette out the window, and said, "You think Eric Edwards is a double agent?"

"Yes."

"Do you think he killed Barrie?"

"Good chance that he did."

"Why would he do that? He was in love with her."

"To save his skin."

"What do you mean?"

"Barrie knew he was a double agent."

"Because Tolker told her."

"No, because she told Tolker." He reached across the seat and grabbed her arm. "You ready for some heavy stuff, Collette?"

"Heavy stuff? The last week hasn't exactly been light-weight, Joe, has it?"

"No, it hasn't." He paused, used his pipe to fill a few seconds, then said, "Your friend Barrie sold out, too."

"Sold out? What do you mean? Sold out to whom?"

"The other side. She was in it with Edwards."

"Joe, that's . . ."

"Hey, at least hear me out."

She didn't, jumped in with, "If she was in it with Edwards, why would she be off to Hungary to blow the whistle on him?"

"Ever hear of the woman scorned?"

"Not Barrie."

"Why not?"

"Because . . . she wouldn't do something like that." Now there was only a modicum of conviction behind her words. What spun through her mind was the kind of control some-one like Jason Tolker could exercise over a good subject like Barrie Mayer. What she'd read in Estabrooks's book was there, too, about changing the "visual" in order to get people to behave in a manner foreign to their basic person-ality and values.

"What if Tolker programmed her to come up with a story about Eric Edwards out of . . . I don't know, out of jealousy or pique or to save his own hide? Maybe Tolker is a double agent and used Barrie to cover up. Maybe he poisoned Barrie against Edwards."

"Yeah, maybe, Collette. Who poisoned you against Tolker?"

"I'm not . . ."

"Put another way, how come you're so hell-bent on de-fending Edwards?"

"I'm not doing that, either, Joe."

"I think you are."

"Think again, and get off treating me like some pathetic woman defending a lover to the death. I am a woman, Joe, and I am an agent of the CIA. Know what? I'm good at both."

"Collette, maybe . . ."

"Maybe nothing, Joe. You and Stan have wrapped everything up in what you think is a neat little package, no loose ends, no doubts. Why? Why is it so damn important to resolve Barrie's murder by laying it on Edwards?" He raised his eyebrows as though to say, "There you go again." She shook her head. "I don't buy it, any of it, Joe."

"That's a shame," he said quietly.

"Why?"

"Because that attitude will get in the way of your next assignment."

She stared quizzically at him, finally asking, "What assignment?"

"Terminating Eric Edwards."

She started to speak but all that came out was breath.

"You understand what I'm saying, don't you?"

"Terminate Eric? Kill him."

"Yes."

It was hardly an accurate reflection of what was on her mind, but it happened anyway: She laughed. Breslin did, too, and continued until she stopped.

"They mean it," he said.

"They?"

"Up top."

"*They* . . . they told you to assign me to kill him?"

"Uh-huh."

"Why me?"

"You can get close to him."

"So can lots of people."

"Easier and neater with you, Collette."

"How do 'they' suggest I do this?"

"Your choice. Go by Tech in the morning and choose your weapon."

"I see," she said. "Then what?"

"What are you talking about, what happens after it's done?"

"Right."

"Nothing. It's over, the double agent in Banana Quick is no longer a problem and we can get back to normal, which can't be too soon. Banana Quick is close to popping."

"Back to normal for me, here in Budapest?"

"If you wish. It's customary for anyone carrying out a wet

affair to have their choice of future assignment, even to take a leave of absence, with pay, of course."

"Joe, I'm sorry but . . ." She started to laugh again, but it did not become laughter, and this time he didn't join her. Instead, he puffed on his pipe and waited for her nervous, absolutely necessary reaction to subside.

"They're serious, Collette."

"I'm sure they are. I'm not." She paused, then said, "Joe, *they* blew up the yacht, didn't they?" When he didn't respond, she added, "Eric knew it."

Again, no reply from him.

"I was on that yacht, Joe."

"It wasn't us."

"I don't believe you."

"It was the Soviets."

"Why would they do that if he's on their side?"

A shrug from Breslin. "Maybe he started holding out for more money. Maybe they thought he was feeding them bad information. Maybe they didn't like him carousing around with a pretty CIA agent."

Cahill shook her head. "You know what's remarkable, Joe?"

"What?"

"That 'they' means the same people . . . the Soviets, the CIA . . . all the same, same morality, same ethics, same game."

"Don't give me the moral equivalency speech, Collette. It doesn't play, and you know it. We've got a system to preserve that's good and decent. Their system is evil. I'll tell you something else. If you do want to view it that way, keep it between us. It wouldn't go over too big with . . . "

"The hell with *them*."

"Suit yourself. I've given you the assignment. Take it?"

"Yes."

"Look, Collette, you realize that . . . ?"

"Joe, I said I'd do it. No need for more speeches."

"You'll really do it?"

"Yes, I'll really do it."

"When?"

"I'll leave tomorrow."

"I get the feeling that . . . "

"Take me home, Joe."

"Collette, if there's any hesitation on your part, I'd suggest you sleep on it."

"I'll do that. I'll sleep just fine."

"Why?"

"Why what?"

"Why the sudden willingness to kill Edwards?"

"Because . . . I'm a pro. I work for the CIA. I do what I'm told. It's obviously for the good of the country, *my* country. Someone has to do it. Let's go."

He pulled up in front of her apartment building and said, "Come talk to me in the morning."

"What for?"

"To go over this a little more."

"No need. You'll tell Tech I'll be by?"

He sighed, said, "Yes."

"Know something, Joe?"

"What?"

"For the first time since I joined the CIA, I feel part of the team."

27

She awoke the next morning feeling surprisingly re-freshed. There was no hangover from jet lag or from the late evening and its drinks. She showered quickly, chose her heather wool tweed suit and burgundy turtleneck, and called for a taxi. A half hour later she walked through the front door of the United States Embassy on Szabadság tér, flashed her credentials at the security guard who knew her well, was buzzed into the inner lobby, and went directly to the transportation office. There she booked an afternoon Malev flight to London, and a connecting flight to New York the following evening.

"Good morning, Joe," she said brightly to Breslin as they approached each other in the hall.

"Hello, Collette," he said somberly.

"Can we get this over with now?" she asked.

His was a deep, meaningful sigh. "Yeah, I suppose so," he said.

He closed the door to his office. "Got a cigarette, Joe?" she asked pleasantly.

"No. Don't start the habit."

"Why not? Looks like I'm about to start a whole new set of bad habits."

"Look, Collette, I talked to Stan late last night. I tried to . . ." He looked up at the ceiling. "Let's take a walk."

"No need. You've arranged for me to go to Tech this morning?"

"Yes, but . . ." He got up. "Come on."

She had little choice but to follow him out of the embassy and across Liberation Square to a bench on which he propped a foot and lighted his pipe. "I tried to get you off it, Collette," he said.

"Why? I didn't balk."

"Yeah, and that worries me. How come?"

"I thought I explained myself last night. I want to be a pro, part of the team. You join an organization like this because, no matter how much you want to—need to—deny your fascination with James Bond movies, it's always there. Right, Joe?"

"Maybe. The point is, Collette, I went to Stan's house after I dropped you and tried to persuade him to cancel the order from Langley."

"I wish you hadn't. I don't want to be treated different from anyone else because I'm a woman."

"That wasn't what I pegged my request upon," Breslin said. "I don't think you're the one to go after our friend in the BVI because of your relationship with him."

"I don't have a *relationship* with him, Joe. I went down there on business and did what I was told to do. I got close to him and damn near ended up fish food in the bargain. It makes perfect sense for me to do this."

"Hank thinks so, too."

"Fox? I'm flattered. All I seem to end up with are father figures, and want to know something, Joe?"

"What?"

"I don't need a father, and that includes you."

"Thanks."

"No gratitude necessary. All my fathers seem to do—including you—is to send their daughters into battle. New definition of fatherhood, I guess. Female liberation. I'm glad. Now, let's get back to basics. You tried to get me off, you failed. That's good because I'm committed to this. Everything is right in my mind. One thing I don't need is a set of doubts implanted." She laughed. "Besides, I'm a lousy hypnotic subject. It's a shame Barrie wasn't."

Breslin nodded toward a far corner of the square where two men in overcoats and hats stood, conspicuously not watching them. "I think we've talked enough," Breslin said.

"I think you're right," Cahill said. "I have a plane reservation for this afternoon. Better get inside and pick up my supplies."

"All right. One other thing, though." He walked away from her and toward a corner where a line of taxicabs waited for fares. He slowed down and she caught up with him. "When you get home, Collette, contact no one involved with us. No one. Understand?"

"Yes." The order didn't surprise her. The nature of her mission would preclude touching base with anyone even mildly associated with the CIA and Langley.

"But," he said, "if you need help in a real emergency, there's been a control established for you in D.C."

"Who?"

"It doesn't matter. Just remember that it's available in an emergency. You make contact any evening for the next two weeks at exactly six o'clock. The contact point is the statue of Winston Churchill just outside the British Embassy on Massachuetts Avenue. Your contact will hold for ten minutes each evening, no more. Got it?"

"Yes. Do I still have my contact in the BVI, at Pusser's Landing?"

"No."

"All right."

She had nothing more to say, just followed him back inside the embassy, went to her office, closed the door, and stood at the window peering out at the gray, suddenly bleak city of Budapest. Her phone rang but she ignored it. She realized she was in the midst of an unemotional void: no feelings, no anxiety or anger or confusion. There was nothing, and it was pleasant.

Ten minutes later she went to the embassy's basement where a closed door bore the sign TECHNICAL ASSISTANCE.

She knocked; a latch was released and Harold Sutherland opened the door.

"Hi, Red," she said.

"Hi. Come on in. I've been expecting you."

Once the door was closed behind them, Sutherland said, "Well, kid, what do you need?"

Cahill stood in the middle of the cramped, cluttered room and realized he was waiting for an answer. What was the answer? She didn't know what she "needed." Obviously, there were people who did for a living what she was about to do. For a death. *They* knew what was needed in their job. She didn't. It wasn't her job to kill anyone, at least not in the lengthy job description that accompanied her embassy employment. But those specifications were a lie, too. She didn't work for the embassy. She worked for the Central Intelligence Agency, the CIA, the Company, the Pickle Factory, whose stated purpose was to gather and assimilate intelligence from all over the world and . . . and to kill when it was necessary to keep doing its job.

She'd had courses during her CIA training at the Farm that dealt with killing, although it was never labeled as such. "Self-protection," they called it. There were other terms— "Termination Techniques," "Neutralization," "Securing the Operation."

"You flying somewhere?" Sutherland asked.

His gravel voice startled her. She looked at him, forced a smile, and said, "Yes."

"Come here."

He led her past his desk, past rows of floor-to-ceiling shelving stocked with unmarked boxes and to a tiny separate room at the rear. It was a miniature firing range. She didn't even know it existed. She'd participated in firing exercises on the embassy's main range, which wasn't much bigger, just longer.

There was a table, two chairs, and a thick, padded wall ten feet away. The pads were filled with holes. She glanced up; the ceiling was covered with soundproofing material. So were the other walls.

"Have a seat," Sutherland said.

She took one of the chairs while he disappeared back into

the shelves, returning moments later carrying a white card-board box. He placed it on the table, opened it, and removed a purple bag with a drawstring. She watched as he opened the bag and lifted from it a piece of white plastic that was shaped like a small revolver. He pulled a second bag from the box. It contained a plastic barrel. The only metal item was a small spring.

"Nine millimeter," he said as he weighed the components in his large, callused hand. "It's like the Austrian Glock 17, only the barrel is plastic, too. It's U.S.-made. We just got it last week."

"I see."

"Here, put it together. Simple."

He watched as she fumbled with the pieces, then showed her how to do it. When it was assembled, he said, "You stick the spring in your purse and pack the rest in your suitcase. Wrap it in clothes, only that's not even necessary. X-ray picks up nothing.

She looked at him. "Bullets?"

He grinned. "Ammunition, you mean? Pick it up in any sporting goods store where you're traveling. Want to try it?"

"No, I . . . Yes, please."

He showed her how to load it and told her to shoot at the padded wall. She placed two hands on it and squeezed the trigger. She'd expected a kick. There was virtually nothing. Even the sound was small.

"You need a silencer?"

"Ah, no, I don't think so."

"Good. It's developed but we don't have it yet. Break it down. I'll watch."

She disassembled and assembled the small plastic weapon four times.

"Good. You've got it down. What else?"

"I . . . I'm not sure, Red." What she wanted to say was that she was about to go off on an assignment to kill someone, to kill a man she'd slept with, to terminate him for the good of her country and the free world. She didn't say anything, of course. It was too late for that. It wouldn't be professional.

"Red."

"Yeah?"

"I'd like some prussic acid and a detonator."

His eyebrows went up. "Why?" he asked.

"I need it for my assignment."

"Yeah? I ought to . . ." He shrugged and heaved his bulk to its feet. "Joe said give you anything you wanted. Sure you want this?"

"Yes, I'm sure."

It took him a few minutes to assemble her request. When he handed it to her, she was amazed at the smallness of it. "Know how to use it?" he asked.

"No."

He showed her. "That's all there is to it," he said. "You get it close to the nose and trip this spring. Make sure it's not your own nose. By the way, if it is, use this stuff fast." He handed her a package of two glass ampules. "Nitro. If you get a whiff of the prussic, break this under your nose or . . ." He grinned and patted her on the shoulder. "Or I lose a favorite of mine."

His words cut into her, but then she smiled, too, and said, "Thanks, Red. Any last words of wisdom?"

"Yeah, I got a few."

"What are they?"

"Get out of the business, kid. Go home, work for a bank, get married and raise a couple of good citizens."

She wanted to cry but was successful in fighting the need. "Actually," she said, "I was going to become the Attorney General of the United States."

"That's not much better than what you're doing now." He shook his head and asked, "You want to talk?"

She did, desperately, but what she said was, "No, I have to get going. I haven't packed. The other stuff, that is." She looked down at the white box she held in her hands. Sutherland had put the revolver, the prussic acid vial, and detonator in it, packing it carefully, like a bridal gift.

"Good luck, kid," he said. "See you back here soon?"

"Yeah, I guess so. Unless I decide to go work for a bank. Thanks, Red."

"You take care."

28

It was a running joke among embassy employees—Malev airlines, the national Hungarian airline, sold a first-class section on its flights, but its seats, food, and service were identical to those in the rear of the plane. A Communist compromise with free enterprise.

It was also unusual, Cahill knew, for her to be flying first class. Company policy put everyone in coach, with the exception of chiefs-of-station. But when Cahill had walked into the Transportation Department, she was handed first-class tickets on every leg of the trip. The young woman who handled embassy travel arrangements lifted a brow as she handed the tickets to Cahill. It had amused Cahill at the time, and she was tempted to say, "No, there hasn't been a mistake. Assassins always ride first class."

Now, at thirty thousand feet, between Budapest and London, it was not as amusing. It carried with it a symbolism that she would have preferred to ignore, but couldn't. Like a last meal, or wish.

She passed through Heathrow Customs and went to the approximate place where Barrie would have been standing when the prussic acid was shoved beneath her nose. She stared at the hard floor for a long time, watching hundreds of pairs of shoes pass over it. Didn't they know what they were walking on? What a horrible place to die, she thought as she slowly walked away, took a taxi outside the terminal, and told the driver to go to 11, Cadogan Gardens.

"Yes, we have a room," the manager on duty told her. "I'm afraid the room you enjoyed last time isn't available, but we have a nice single in the back."

"Anything will be fine," Cahill said. "This was a last-minute trip, no time to call ahead."

She ordered a dinner of cold poached salmon and a bottle of wine. When the hall porter had left, she securely latched the door, undressed, removed the small plastic revolver from her suitcase, did the same with the spring and prussic acid detonator from her purse, and placed everything on the table next to the tray. She tasted the white wine the porter had uncorked. It was chilled and tart.

She ate the salmon with enthusiasm, and finished half the wine, her eyes remaining for most of the meal on the mechanical contraptions of death with which she'd traveled.

The phone rang. "Was dinner satisfactory?" the porter wished to know.

"Yes, fine, thank you," said Cahill.

"Do you wish anything else?"

"No, no, thank you."

"Shall I remove the tray, madam?"

"No, that won't be necessary. In the morning. Will you arrange a wake-up call for me at ten, please?"

"Yes, madam."

"And breakfast in the room. Two eggs over easy, bacon and toast, coffee, orange juice."

"Yes, madam. Have a pleasant evening."

"Thank you."

She stood at the window and watched a brisk wind whip leaves from the trees on the street below. People walked their dogs; someone was attempting to squeeze a too-large automobile into a too-small parking space.

She went to the table and picked up the white plastic revolver, assembled its components and, with two hands, aimed at an oil of a vase of roses that hung on the far wall.

There was no ammunition in the weapon; she'd have to buy it when she got to the British Virgin Islands. She'd never bought bullets before and wondered whether she'd be able to do it with aplomb. Like a teenage boy sheepishly buying contraceptives, she thought.

She squeezed the trigger several times, sat on the couch and took the weapon apart, put it back together again, and repeated the process a dozen times. Satisfied, she carefully picked up the detonator and tested the spring, making sure before she did that the ampule of prussic acid wasn't in it.

She dialed a local number. It was answered on the first ring.

"Josh, this is Collette Cahill."

"Collette, great to hear your voice. How've you been?"

"It's good to hear your voice, too, Josh. I've been fine. I'm in London."

"Hey, that's great. Can we get together? How about dinner tomorrow? I'll round up some of the troops."

"I'd love it, Josh, but I'm here on business and have to leave early tomorrow evening. Actually, I'm calling for a favor."

"Anything. What is it?"

"I need a photograph."

"You're looking for a photographer?"

"No, I need an existing photograph of someone. I thought maybe you could pull one out of the files for me."

He laughed. "Not supposed to do that, you know."

"Yes, I know, but it really would be a tremendous help to me. I won't have to keep it, just have it for an hour or so tomorrow."

"You've got it—if we have it. Who do you want a picture of?"

"A literary agent here in London named Mark Hotchkiss."

"I don't know whether we'd have anything on a literary agent, but I'll check. You'd probably do better through a newspaper morgue."

"I know that, but I don't have time."

"I'll check it out first thing in the morning. Where can I meet up with you?"

She gave him the address of the hotel. "At least I'll get to see you tomorrow," he said. "If I come up with the photo, you owe me the chance to buy you a quick lunch."

"That'll be great. See you around noon."

Josh Moeller and Collette had worked closely together during her previous CIA assignment to the listening post in England. They'd become fast friends, sharing a mutual sense of humor and a quiet disdain for much of the bureaucratic rules and regulations under which they lived and worked. Their friendship evolved into a brief affair shortly before Cahill's reassignment to Budapest. Her move concluded the affair with finality, but they both knew it had effectively died by its own hand before that, one of those situations in which the friendship was stronger and more important to both parties than the passion. They'd initially kept in touch, mostly through letters delivered by way of the diplomatic pouch between Budapest and London. But then their correspondence tapered off, too, as will happen with the best of friends, especially when the friendship is strong enough to preclude any need for frequent contact.

Her next call was long-distance. It took ten minutes for it to go through to the BVI. Eric Edwards's secretary answered.

"Is Mr. Edwards there?" Cahill asked, glancing at her watch to reconfirm the time difference.

"No, ma'am, he is not. He is in the United States."

"Washington?"

"Yes, ma'am. Is this Miss Cahill?"

Cahill was surprised to be asked. "Yes, it is."

"Mr. Edwards told me that if you called I should inform you that he is staying at the Watergate Hotel in Washington, D.C."

"How long will he be there?"

"One more week, I think."

"Thank you, thank you very much. I'll contact him there."

One final call, this one to her mother in Virginia.

"Collette, where are you?"

"London, Mom, but I'll be coming home in a few days."

"Oh, that will be wonderful." A pause: "Are you all right?"

"Yes, Mom, I'm fine. I think . . . I think I might be coming home for good."

Her mother's gasp was audible even over the poor connection. "Why?" she asked. "I mean, I'd love for that to happen but . . . are you sure everything is all right? Are you in some sort of trouble?"

Collette laughed loudly to help make the point that she wasn't. She simply said, "Lots of things have been happening, Mom, and maybe the best of them all is to come home and stay home."

The connection was almost lost, and Cahill said quickly, "Goodbye, Mom. See you in about a week."

She knew her mother was saying something but couldn't make out the words. Then the line went dead.

She stayed up most of the night, pacing the room, picking up and examining the weapons she'd brought with her—thinking—her mind racing at top speed, one person after another in her life taking center stage—Barrie Mayer, Mark Hotchkiss, Breslin, Podgorsky, Hank Fox, Jason Tolker, Eric Edwards—all of them, the chaos and confusion they'd caused in her small world. Was it that simple to restore order, not only to her life but to so complex and important a geopolitical undertaking as Banana Quick? The ultimate solution, they said, lay on the coffee table—a white plastic revolver that weighed ounces and a spring-loaded device that cost a few dollars to make, devices whose only purpose was to snuff out life.

She could almost understand now why men killed on command. Women, too, in this case. What value has a single human life when wrapped in multiple layers of "greater good"? Besides, eliminating Eric Edwards wasn't her idea. It didn't represent what she was really all about, did it? "But wait, there's more," she told herself as she paced the room, stopping only to look out the window or to stare at the tools of the trade on the table. She was avenging the death of a good friend. Barrie had died at the hand of someone who viewed life and death from the same perspective as she was being called upon to accept. In the end, it didn't matter who the individual was who'd taken Barrie's life—a Soviet agent, a doctor named Tolker, very different characters like Mark

Hotchkiss or Eric Edwards—whoever did it answered to a different god, one it was now necessary for her to invoke if she were to go through with this act.

As she continued trying to deal with the thoughts that had invaded her ever since Joe Breslin told her to kill Eric Edwards, she became fascinated with the process going on inside her, as though she were a bystander watching Collette Cahill come to terms with herself. What she'd been asked to do—what, in fact, she was actually setting out to do—represented so irrational an act that had it been suggested to her at any other point in her life, it would have immediately gotten lost in her laughter. That was no longer true. What had evolved, to the bystander's amusement and amazement, was a sense of right and reason responsive to the act of murder. More important, it could be done. *She* could do it. She hadn't thrown up her hands, raced from Breslin's car, hid in her apartment, or hopped the first flight out of Budapest. She'd accepted the mission and chosen her weapons carefully, no different from selecting a typewriter or pencil sharpener for an office job.

She was numb.

She was confused.

And she was not frightened, which was the most frightening thing of all for the bystander.

In the morning, a series of taps on her door. She'd forgotten; she'd ordered breakfast. She scrambled out of bed and said through the door, "Just a minute," then went to the living room and hastily took the tools from the coffee table and slid them into a desk drawer.

She opened the door and a hall porter carried in her tray. He was the same porter she'd talked to during her last visit to the hotel, the one who'd told her about the three men coming to collect Barrie Mayer's belongings. "Will you be on duty all day?" she asked him.

"Yes, madam."

"Good," she said. "I'd like to show you something a little later."

"Just ring, madam."

Josh Moeller arrived at a quarter of twelve carrying an

envelope. After they'd embraced, he handed it to her, saying in slight surprise, "We had this in our own files. I don't know why, although there's been a push for the past year to beef up the general photo files. You'd think Great Britain had become the enemy the way we've been collecting on everybody."

Collette opened the envelope and looked into the black-and-white glossy face of Mark Hotchkiss. The photo was grainy, obviously a copy of another photograph.

Moeller said, "I think this came from a newspaper or literary magazine."

Cahill looked at him and said, "Any dossier on him?"

Moeller shrugged. "I don't think so, although I have to admit I didn't bother checking. You said you wanted a photograph."

"Yes, I know, Josh, that's all I needed. Thanks so much."

"Why are you interested in him?" he asked.

"A long story," she replied, "something personal."

"Got time for the lunch you promised me?"

"Yes, I do. I'd love it, but first I have to do one thing."

She left him in the suite and went downstairs to where the hall porter was sorting mail. "Excuse me," she said, "do you recognize this man?"

The porter adjusted half-glasses on his large nose and moved the photo in and out of focus. "Yes, madam, I believe I do, but I can't say why."

She said, "Do you remember those three men who came to collect the belongings of my friend, Miss Mayer, right after she died?"

"Yes, that's it. He was one of the gentlemen who came here that day."

"Is this a photograph of Mr. Hubler, David Hubler?"

"Exactly, madam. This is the gentleman who introduced himself as a business associate of your lady friend. He said his name was Hubler, although I can't quite recall what his first name was."

"It doesn't matter," Cahill said. "Thank you."

Cahill and Moeller had lunch in a pub on Sloane Square.

They promised to keep in touch, and hugged before he climbed into a taxi. She watched him disappear around the corner, then walked briskly back to the hotel where she carefully packed, had the desk call a taxi, and went directly to Heathrow Airport for a first-class ride home.

29

Cahill deplaned in New York and went to the nearest public telephone where she dialed Washington, D.C., information. "The number for the Watergate Hotel," she asked.

She placed the call and said to the hotel operator, "Has Mr. Eric Edwards changed suites yet?"

"Pardon?"

"I'm sorry. I'm here in Washington with the French contingent of Mr. Edwards's investors. When I tried to reach him before, I realized he'd changed suites. Is he still in 845?"

"Well, I . . . no, he's still in 1010 according to my records. I'll connect you."

"Oh, don't bother. I just didn't want to bring the French group to the wrong suite." She laughed. "You know how the French are."

"Well . . . thank you for calling."

Collette hung up and sighed. Hotel operators didn't give out room numbers, but there were ways. Dazzle 'em with confusion. She picked up the phone again, dialed the Watergate number, and asked whether there were any suites available.

"How long will you be staying?" she was asked.

255

"Three days, possibly more."

"Yes, we have two diplomat suites available at $410 a night."

"That will be fine," Cahill said. "Do you have one on a low floor? I have a phobia about high floors."

"The lowest we would have is on the eighth floor. Our diplomat suites are all higher up."

"The eighth floor? Yes, I suppose that will be all right." She gave her name, read off her American Express card number, and said she would be taking the shuttle to Washington that evening.

It took her longer to get from Kennedy Airport to La Guardia than it did for the flight to Washington's National Airport. The minute she stepped off the plane, she went to a telephone center, pulled out a Washington Yellow Pages, and scanned the listing for sporting goods stores. She found one in Maryland within a few blocks of the district line and took a cab to it, catching the owner as he was about to close. "I need some bullets," she told him sheepishly, the teenager buying condoms.

He smiled. "Ammo, you mean."

"Yes, ammunition, I guess. It's for my brother."

"What kind?"

"Ah, let's see, ah, right, nine millimeter, for a small revolver."

"Very small." He rummaged through a drawer behind the counter and came up with a box. "Anything else?"

"No, thank you." She'd expected questioning, a demand for an address, for identification. Nothing. Just a simple consumer purchase. She paid, thanked him, and returned to the street, a box of bullets in her purse.

She walked to the Watergate and checked in, her eyes scanning the lobby.

The moment she was in her suite, she unpacked, took a hot shower and, wearing a robe provided by the hotel, stepped out onto a wraparound balcony that overlooked the Potomac River and the oversized, gleaming white Kennedy Center. It was a lovely sight, but she was too filled with energy to stand in any one place for more than a few seconds.

She went to a living room furnished with antique reproductions, found a scrap of paper in her purse, and dialed the number on it. The phone at Vern Wheatley's brother's apartment rang eight times before Wheatley answered. The minute he heard her voice, he snapped, "Where the hell have you been? I've been going crazy trying to find you."

"I was in Budapest."

"Why didn't you tell me you were leaving? You just take off and not even tell me?"

"Vern, I tried to call but there was no answer. It wasn't a leisurely trip I took. I had to leave immediately."

His voice indicated that he'd ignored her words. He said flatly, "I have to see you right away. Where are you?"

"I'm . . . why do you want to see me?"

He snorted. "Maybe the fact that we slept together is good enough. Maybe just because I want to see you again. Maybe because I have something damned important to discuss with you." She started to say something but he quickly added, "Something that might save both our lives."

"Why don't you just tell me on the phone?" she said. "If it's that important . . ."

"Look, Collette, there are things I haven't told you because . . . well, because it wasn't the right time. The right time is *now*. Where are you? I'll come right over."

"Vern, I have something I have to do before I can talk to you. Once it's done, I'll *need* to talk to someone. Please try to understand."

"Damn it, Collette, stop . . ."

"Vern, I said I have other things to do. I'll call you tomorrow."

"You won't catch me here," he said quickly.

"No?"

"I'm getting out right now. I was on my way when the phone rang. I almost didn't bother answering it."

"You sound panicked."

"Yeah, you might say that. I always get a little uptight when somebody's looking to slit my throat or blow up my car."

"What are you talking about?"

"What am I talking about? I'll tell you what I'm talking about. I'm talking about that freaky outfit you work for.

257

I'm talking about a bunch of psychopaths who start out ripping wings off flies and shooting birds with BB guns before they graduate to people."

"Vern, I don't work for the CIA anymore."

"Yeah, right, Collette. That one of the courses down on the Farm? Lying 101? Goddamn it, I have to see you right now."

"Vern, I . . . all right."

"Where are you?"

"I'll meet you someplace."

"How about dinner?"

"I'm not hungry."

"Yeah, well I am. I'm in the mood for Greek. Like drama or tragedy. Meet me at the Taverna in an hour."

"Where is it?"

"Pennsylvania Avenue, Southeast. An hour?"

She almost backed out but decided to go through with the date. After all, she'd called him. Why? She couldn't answer. That weakness coming through, that need to talk with someone she knew and thought she could trust. Talk about *what*, that she was back in Washington to assassinate someone? No, there'd be no talk of that. He sounded desperate. It was *he* who needed to talk. Okay, she'd listen, that's all.

As she dressed, she went over in her mind what she'd been told about Vern by Joe Breslin. He'd come to Washington to do an exposé of one sort or another on the CIA, particularly its mind-control experimentation programs. If that was true—and she was sure it was, based upon their brief conversation a few minutes ago—he was to be as distrusted as the rest of them. Nothing was straightforward anymore. Living a life of simple truth must be reserved for monks, nuns, and naturalists, and it was too late to become any of those.

She rode the elevator to the tenth floor and walked past Suite 1010, her heart tripping in anticipation of running into Edwards. It didn't happen; she retraced her steps, got in the elevator, and went to the lobby. The Watergate was bustling. She stepped through the main entrance to where a long line of black limousines stood, their uniformed drivers waiting for their rich and powerful employers or customers to emerge. A cab from another line moved forward. Cahill got in and said, "The Taverna, on Pennsylvania Avenue, South. . . ."

The driver turned and laughed. "I know, I know," he said. "I am Greek."

She walked into what the cabbie had said was a "goud Grick" restaurant and was immediately aware of bouzouki music and loud laughter from the downstairs bar. She went down there in search of Wheatley. No luck. He hadn't specified where he would meet her but she assumed it would be the bar. She took the only vacant stool and ordered a white wine, turned and looked at the bouzouki player, a good-looking young man with black curly hair who smiled at her and played a sudden flourish on his instrument. She was reminded of Budapest. She returned his smile and surveyed others in the room. It was a loud, joyous crowd and she wished she were in the mood—wished she were in the position—to enjoy something festive. She wasn't. How could she be?

She sipped her wine and kept checking her watch; Wheatley was twenty minutes late. She was angry. She hadn't wanted to meet him in the first place but he'd prevailed. She looked at the check the bartender had placed in front of her, laid enough money on it to take care of it plus tip, got up and started for the stairs. Wheatley was on his way down. "Sorry I'm late," he said, shaking his head. "I couldn't help it."

"I was leaving," she said icily.

He took her arm and escorted her up the stairs to the dining room. Half the tables were vacant. "Come on," he said. "I'm starved."

"Vern, I really don't have time to . . ."

"Don't hassle me, Collette, just spend an hour while I get some food for my belly and feed you some food for your thoughts."

The manager showed them to a corner table that put them at considerable distance from other patrons. Collette took the chair that placed her back against the wall. Wheatley sat across from her.

After they'd ordered a bottle of white wine, Wheatley shook his head and grinned. "You could drive a guy crazy."

"I don't mean to do that, Vern. My life has been . . ." She smiled. "It's been chaotic lately, at best."

"Mine hasn't been exactly run-of-the-mill, either," he said. "Let's order."

"I told you I'm not hungry."

"Then nibble."

He looked at the menu, motioned for the waiter, and ordered moussaka, stuffed grape leaves, and an eggplant salad for two. After the waiter was gone, Wheatley leaned across the table and said, his eyes locked on hers, "I know who killed your friend Barrie Mayer, and I know why. I know who killed your friend David Hubler, and I know why he was killed, too. I know about the people you work for but, most of all, I know that you and I could end up like your dead friends if we don't do something."

"You're going too fast for me, Vern," she said, her excitement level rising. A large "What if?" struck her. What if Breslin and the rest of them were wrong? What if Eric Edwards was not, in fact, a double agent, had not killed Barrie Mayer? It was the first time since she left Budapest that she acknowledged to herself how much she hoped it was the case. . . .

Wheatley said, "All right, I'll slow down for you. In fact, I'll do even better than that." He had a briefcase on the floor at the side of his chair. He pulled from it a bulging envelope and handed it to her.

"What's this?" she asked.

"That, my friend, is the bulk of an article I'm writing about the CIA. There's also the first ten chapters of my book in there."

She immediately thought of David Hubler and the call that brought him to Rosslyn and to his death. She didn't have to ask. Wheatley said, "I was the one who called Hubler and asked him to meet me in that alley."

His admission hit her hard. At the same time, it wasn't a surprise. She'd always questioned the coincidence of Wheatley having been there at the time. The look on her face prompted him to continue.

"I've been working through a contact in New York for months, Collette. He's a former spook—I hope that doesn't offend you, considering you're in the same business. . . ." When she didn't respond, he continued. "This contact of mine is a psychologist who used to do work for the CIA. He broke away a number of years ago and almost lost his life in the bargain. You don't just walk away from those people, do you?"

"I don't know," Cahill said. "I've never walked away," which was only half true. She'd left Budapest committed to never returning, not only to that city but to any job within Central Intelligence once her present assignment was completed.

"When someone tried to kill my contact, he did some fast thinking and came to the conclusion that his best protection was to offer up everything he knew for public consumption. Once he did that, why bother killing him? Eliminating him would only make sense if it were to avoid disclosure."

"Go on," she said.

"A mutual friend got us together and we started talking. That's what brought me to Washington."

"Finally, some simple honesty," Cahill said, not particularly proud of the smugness in her voice.

"Yeah, that must be refreshing for you, Collette, considering that you've been dishonest with me all along."

She was tempted to get into that discussion but resisted. Let him continue talking.

"My contact put me in touch with a woman who'd been an experimental subject in the Operation Bluebird and MK-ULTRA projects. They pulled out all the stops with her and, in the process, manipulated her mind to the extent that she doesn't know who she is anymore. Ever hear of a man named Estabrooks?"

"A psychologist who did a lot of work with hypnosis." She said it in a bored tone of voice.

"Yeah, right, but why should I be surprised? You probably know more about this than I ever imagined."

She shook her head. "I don't know much about those CIA projects from the past."

He guffawed. "From the *past*? Those projects are going

on stronger than ever, Collette, and someone you know pretty well is one of the movers and shakers in them."

"Who would that be?"

"Your friend Dr. Jason Tolker."

"He's not a friend. I simply . . . "

"Simply slept with him? I don't know, maybe I've got my definition of friendship all screwed up. You slept with me. Am I your friend?"

"I don't know. You used me. The only reason you got together with me again was to get close to someone involved with the . . . "

"The CIA?"

"You were saying?"

"What you just said, about me making contact with you because you're with the CIA, is only partially true. You're acknowledging that you're with the CIA, right? The embassy job is a front."

"That doesn't matter, and I resent being put in the position of having to explain what I do with my life. You have no right."

He leaned toward her, and there was a harsh edge to his voice. "And the CIA has no right to go around screwing up innocent people, to say nothing of killing them, like your friend Barrie, and Hubler."

Collette leaned away from him and glanced about the restaurant. The sounds of the bar crowd downstairs mingled with the strains of the bouzouki music as it drifted up the stairs. Upstairs, where they sat, it was still relatively quiet and empty.

Wheatley sat back. His was a warm, genuine smile and his voice matched it. "Collette, I'll level with you one hundred percent. After that, you can decide whether you want to level with me. Fair enough?"

She knew it was.

"This woman I mentioned, the one who was a subject in the experimentation, is a prostitute. The CIA is big on hookers. They use them to entice men into apartments and hotel rooms that have been wired for sight and sound. They slip drugs in their drinks and the shrinks stand behind two-way mirrors and watch the action. It's a nasty game, but I suppose they rationalize it by saying that the other side does it, too, and that 'national defense' is involved. Whether those things are true or not I don't know, but I do know that a lot of innocent people get hurt."

Cahill started to add to the conversation but stopped herself. She simply cocked her head, raised her eyebrows, and said, "Go on."

Her posture obviously annoyed him. He quickly shook it off and continued. "I came down to Washington to see what I could find out about whether these experimental projects were still in operation. The day before Hubler was killed, I got a call from this lady, the prostitute, who told me that someone within the CIA was willing to talk to me. No, that isn't exactly accurate. This person was willing to *sell* information to me. I was told to meet him in that alley in Rosslyn. I figured the first thing I ought to do was to test the waters with a book publisher, see if I could raise the money I needed to pay the source. I knew the magazine wouldn't pay, and I sure as hell don't have the funds.

"I was trying to think of people back in New York to call when Dave Hubler came to my mind. You'd told me all about him, how Barrie Mayer put a lot of faith in him and had actually left the agency to him. I figured he was my best move, so I called him. He was very receptive. In fact, he told me that if the kind of information I was talking about was valid, he could probably get me a six-figure advance. The problem was he wanted to hear with his own ears what this source was selling. I invited him to meet with me. I knew the minute I hung up that it was a mistake. Having two of us show up would probably scare the guy off, but I figured I'd go through with it anyway. Want to know what happened?"

"Of course."

"I ran late, but Hubler got there on time. Obviously, there was nobody selling information. It was a setup, and if I'd arrived when I was supposed to and alone, I would have had the ice pick in my chest."

His story had potency to it, no doubt about that. If what he'd said were true, it meant . . . . "You've got problems," she told him.

"That's right," he said. "I'm being followed everywhere I go. The other night I was driving through Rock Creek Park and a guy ran me off the road. At least he tried to. He botched it and took off. I think they've thrown a tap on my brother's phone, and my editor back in New York told me he'd received a call from a personnel agency checking my references for a job I was applying for with another magazine. I didn't apply for a job with another magazine. There's no legitimate personnel agency checking on me. These guys will stop at nothing."

"What do you plan to do?" she asked.

"First of all, keep moving. Second, I'm going to adopt the philosophy of my shrink friend back in New York, get everything I know on paper, and make sure it's in the proper hands as fast as possible. No sense killing somebody once they've spilled what they know."

Cahill looked down at the heavy envelope. "Why are you giving me this?"

"Because I want it in someone else's hands in case anything happens to me."

"But why *me*, Vern? You seem filled with distrust where I'm concerned. I'd think I'd be the last person you'd give this to."

He grinned, reached across the table, and held her hand. "Remember what I wrote in the yearbook, Collette?"

She said softly, "Yes, of course I do. I'm the girl in this world who would never sell out."

"I still feel that way, Collette. You know something else I feel?"

She looked in his eyes. "What?"

"I'm in love with you."

"Don't say that, Vern." She shook her head. "You don't know me."

"I think I do, which is why I'm throwing in with you. I want you to hold on to this, Collette," he said, tapping the envelope. "I want you to read it and look for any gaps."

She shoved the envelope back across the table at him. "No, I don't want that responsibility. I can't help you."

His face, which had settled into a slack and serene expression, now hardened. His voice matched it. "I thought you took some oaths when you became a lawyer, silly things like justice and fairness and righting wrongs. I thought you cared about innocent people being hurt. At least, that was the line you used to give. What was it, Collette, high school rhetoric that goes down the drain the minute you hit the real world?"

She was stung by his words, assaulted by hurt and anger. Had she succumbed to the hurt, she would have cried. Instead, her anger overrode the other feeling. "Don't preach to me, Vern Wheatley, about ideals. All I'm hearing from you is journalist's rhetoric. You're sitting here lecturing me about right and wrong, about why everybody should jump on your bandwagon and sell out our own government. Maybe there is justification for what an organization like the CIA does. Maybe there are abuses. Maybe the other side does it, only worse. Maybe national defense *is* involved, and not just a slogan. Maybe there are things going on in this world that you or I have no idea about, can't even begin to conceive of the importance of them to other people—people who don't have the advantages we have in a free society."

The eggplant salad had gone untouched. Now the waiter brought the stuffed leaves and moussaka. The moment he left, Collette said to Vern, "I'm leaving."

Wheatley grabbed her hand. "Please don't do that, Collette," he said with sincerity. "Okay, we've each made our speech. Now let's talk like two adults and figure out the right thing to do for both of us."

"I already have," she said, pulling her hand away.

"Look, Collette, I'm sorry if I shot off my mouth. I didn't mean to, but sometimes I do that. The nature of the beast, I guess. If spies are out in the cold, journalists need friends, too." He laughed. "I figure I have one friend in this world. You."

She slumped back in her chair, stared at the envelope, and suffered the same sensation she'd been feeling so often lately, that she had become increasingly dishonest. She was perfectly capable of taking a stand at the table, yet, more than anything, she wanted that envelope and its contents. She was desperate to read it. Maybe it contained factual answers to events that had shrouded her in confusion.

She deliberately softened as she said, "Vern, maybe you're right. I'm sorry, too. I just . . . I don't want, alone, the responsibility for that envelope."

"Fine," he said. "We'll share the responsibility. Stay with me tonight."

"Where?"

"I've taken a room in a small hotel over in Foggy Bottom, around the corner from Watergate. The Allen Lee. Know it?"

"Yes, friends who used to visit me at college stayed there."

"I figured it was low class enough that they wouldn't look for me there, although that's probably naive. I used a phony name when I checked in. Joe Black. How's that for a pseudonym?"

"Not very original," she said, realizing that she shouldn't have checked into the Watergate under her own name. Too late to worry about that now. "Vern, I think it's better if I left now and we both did some thinking on our own." He started to protest but she grabbed his hand and said earnestly, "Please. I need time alone to digest what you've said. I can use it to read your article and book. Okay? We'll catch up tomorrow. I promise."

Dejection was written all over his face but he didn't argue.

He slid the envelope back toward her. She looked at it, picked it up, and cradled it in her arms. "I'll call you at the Allen Lee, say around four tomorrow afternoon?"

"I guess that's the way it will be. I can't call you. I don't know where you're staying."

"And that's the way it will have to be until tomorrow."

He forced himself to lighten up, saying pleasantly, "Sure you don't want some food? It's good."

"So my cab driver said. He told me this was 'goud Grick.' " She smiled. "I'm not a fan of Greek food, but thanks anyway." When his expression sagged again, she leaned over and kissed him on the cheek, said into his ear, "Please, Vern. I've got a lot of thinking to do and I'll do it best alone." She straightened up, knew there was nothing more to say, and quickly left the restaurant.

A taxi was dropping off a couple. Cahill got in.

"Yeah?"

266

"I'd like to go to . . ." She'd almost told him to take her to Dr. Jason Tolker's office in Foggy Bottom.

How silly. Like giving the name of an obscure restaurant and expecting the driver to know it.

She spelled out Tolker's address.

30

Lights were on in Tolker's building. Good, she thought, as she paid the driver. She hadn't wanted to call ahead. If he weren't there, she'd go to his house. She'd find him someplace.

She rang the bell. His voice came through the intercom. "Who is it?"

"Collette. Collette Cahill."

"Oh. Yes. I'm tied up right now. Can you come back?" She didn't answer. "Is it an emergency?" She smiled, knew he was asking it for the benefit of whoever was with him. She pressed the "Talk" button: "Yes, it is an emergency, Doctor."

"I see. Well, please come in and wait in my reception area, Miss Cahill. It will be a few minutes before I can see you."

"That will be fine, Doctor. Thank you."

The buzzer sounded. She turned the knob and pushed the door partially open. Before entering, she patted her raincoat pocket. The now familiar shape of the small revolver resisted her fingers' pressure. A deep breath pumped any lost resolve back into her.

She stepped into the reception area and looked around. Two table lamps provided minimal, soft lighting. A light under his office door, and muffled voices, indicated at least two people in there. She stepped close and listened. She heard his voice, and then a woman. Their words were only occasionally audible: ". . . Can't help that . . . Hate you . . . Calm down or . . ."

Collette chose a chair that allowed her to face the office door. She'd started to pull the revolver from her raincoat pocket when the office door suddenly opened. She released the weapon and it slid back to its resting place. A beautiful and surprisingly tall young Oriental girl, dressed in tight jeans, heels, and wearing a mink jacket, came into the reception area, followed by Tolker. The woman strained to see Collette's face in the room's dimness. "Good night," Tolker said. The girl looked at him; there was hatred on her face. She crossed the room, cast a final, disapproving look at Collette, and left. Moments later the front door closed heavily.

"Hello," Tolker said to Collette.

"Hello. A patient?"

"Yes. You thought otherwise?"

"I thought nothing. It's nice of you to see me on such short notice."

"I try to accommodate. What's the emergency?"

"Severe panic attack, free-floating anxiety, paranoia, an obsessive-compulsive need for answers."

"Answers to what?"

"Oh, to . . . to why a friend of mine is dead."

"I can't help you with that."

"I disagree."

He conspicuously looked at his watch.

"This won't take long."

"I can assure you of that. Ask your questions."

"Let's go inside."

"This is . . ." He stopped when he saw her hand come out of her raincoat holding the revolver. "What's that for?"

"A persuasive tool. I have a feeling you might need persuasion."

"Put it away, Collette. James Bond never impressed me."

"I think I can . . . *impress* you."

He blew through his lips and sighed resignedly. "All right, come in, *without* the gun."

She followed him into his office, the revolver still in her hand. When he turned and saw it, he said sharply, "Put the goddamn thing away."

"Sit down, Dr. Tolker."

He made a move toward her. She raised the weapon and pointed it at his chest. "I said sit down."

"You've gone off the deep end, haven't you? You're crazy."

"That's professional."

"Look, I . . ." She nodded toward his leather chair. He sat on it. She took the matching chair, crossed her legs, and observed him. He certainly hadn't overreacted, but she could discern discomfort, which pleased her.

"Go ahead," she said. "Start from the beginning, and don't leave anything out. Tell me all about Barrie, about how she came to you as a patient, how you hypnotized her, controlled her, got her involved in the CIA and then . . . I'll say it . . . and then killed her."

"You're crazy."

"There's that professional diagnosis again. Start!" She raised the revolver for emphasis.

"You know everything, because I told you everything. Barrie was a patient. I treated her. We had an affair. I suggested she do some courier work for the CIA. She gladly and, I might add, enthusiastically agreed. She carried materials to Budapest, things she got from me, things I didn't know. I mean, I would hand her a briefcase, a *locked* briefcase, and off she'd go. Someone killed her. I don't know who. It wasn't me. Believe that."

"Why should I?"

"Because . . ."

"When Barrie made her last trip to Hungary, whatever it was she carried wasn't in a briefcase. It was in her mind, because you implanted it there."

"Wait a minute, that's . . ."

"That's the truth, Dr. Tolker. I'm not the only one who knows it. It's common knowledge. At least it is now."

"What of it? The program calls for it."

"What was the message?"

"I can't tell you that."

"I think you'd better."

He stood. "And I think you'd better get out of here."

Collette held up the envelope she'd been given by Vern. "Know what's in this?"

He tried for levity. "Your memoirs of a clandestine life."

She didn't respond in kind. "A friend of mine has been researching the projects you're involved with. He's done quite a job. Want an example?"

"You're talking about Vern Wheatley?"

"Right."

"He's in deep water."

"He's a strong swimmer."

"Not with these tides. Go ahead. I know all about him, and about you. Bad form, Collette, for an intelligence agent to sleep with a writer."

"I'll let that pass. Vern knows, and so do I, that you programmed Barrie to claim that Eric Edwards, from the BVI, was a double agent. Correct?"

To her surprise, he didn't deny it. Instead, he said, "That happens to be the truth."

"No, it's not. You're the double agent, Doctor."

The accusation, and the weight of the envelope despite neither of them knowing what was in it, stopped the conversation. Tolker broke the silence by asking pleasantly, "Drink, Collette?"

She couldn't help but smile. "No."

"Coke? The white kind?"

"You're disgusting."

"Just trying to be sociable. Barrie always enjoyed my sociability."

"Spare me that again."

"Like to spend some intimate moments with our deceased friend?"

"What?"

"I have her on tape. I'm reluctant to expose myself to you because, naturally, I'm on the tape, too. But I will."

"No thanks." Collette didn't mean it. Her voice betrayed her true feelings.

271

He did exactly the right thing. He said nothing, simply sat back down, crossed his legs, folded his hands in his lap, and smirked.

"What kind of tape? While she was hypnotized?"

"No, nothing concerning therapy. That would be highly unprofessional of me. The tape I'm talking about is more *personal*."

"When she was . . . with you?"

"When she was very much with me, right here in this office, after hours."

"You recorded it?"

"Yes. I'm recording us, too."

Cahill's head snapped left and right as she took in the room in search of a camera.

"Up there," Tolker said casually, pointing to a painting at the far end of the room.

"Did Barrie know?"

"Shall we see it?"

"No, I . . ."

He went to bookshelves where hundreds of videotapes were neatly lined up and labeled. He pulled one from the collection, knelt before a VCR hooked up to a 30-inch NEC monitor, inserted the tape, pushed buttons, and the screen came alive.

Collette turned her head and watched the screen from an angle, like a child wanting to avoid a gruesome scene in a horror movie, yet afraid to miss it. Tolker resumed his seat and said smugly, "You came here demanding answers. Watch closely, Collette. There's lots of answers on the screen."

Cahill looked away, her eyes going to where Tolker indicated there was a camera recording them. Out of the corner of her eye, a naked form appeared on the TV monitor. She focused on the screen. It was Barrie, walking around Tolker's office, a glass in her hand. She went to where he sat fully dressed in his chair. "Come on, I'm ready." Her words were slurred; her laugh was that of a drunken woman. When he didn't respond, she sat on his lap and kissed him. His hands ran over her body. . . .

"You slime," Collette said.

"Don't judge me," Tolker said. "She's there, too. Keep watching. There's more."

A new scene appeared on the screen. Barrie was seated cross-legged on the carpet, still nude. A man's naked form—presumably Tolker—was in shadows. He obviously knew where to position himself so that he was out of the camera's direct focus, and out of the lighting.

Barrie held a clear plate on which cocaine was heaped. She put a straw to her nose, leaned forward, placed the other end in the powder, and inhaled.

Cahill stood. "Turn that damn thing off," she said.

"It's not over. It gets even better."

She went to the VCR and pushed the "Stop" button. The screen went blank. She was aware that he'd come up behind her. She quickly fell to her knees, spun around, and pointed the revolver up at his face.

"Easy, easy," he said. "I'm not out to hurt you."

"Get away. Back up."

He did as she requested. She stood, was without words.

"See?" he said. "Your friend was not the saint you thought she was."

"I never considered her a saint," Collette said. "Besides, this has nothing to do with how she died."

"Oh, yes, it does," Tolker said. He sat in his chair and tasted his drink. "You're right, Collette, this is kid's stuff. Ready for the adult version?"

"What are you talking about?"

"Barrie was a traitor. She sold out to Eric Edwards, and to the Soviets." He sighed and drank. "Oh, God, she was so innocent in that situation. She didn't know a Soviet from a Buddhist monk. A great literary agent, a lousy intelligence agent. I should have known better than to get her involved. But that's water over the dam."

"She wasn't a traitor," Collette said, again without conviction. The truth was that she knew little about her close friend. The video she'd seen—so unlike the image she had of Barrie—caused anger to swell in her. "How dare you record someone in their . . ."

Tolker laughed. "In their *what*, most intimate moments? Forget the tape, think about what I just told you. She was going to turn Edwards in, and that's what got her killed. I tried to stop her but . . ."

"No you didn't. You were the one who poisoned her against Eric."

"Wrong. You're wrong a lot, Collette. Sure, she told me that Edwards was working both sides of the street, and I encouraged her to blow the whistle on him. Want to know why?" Cahill didn't answer. "Because it was the only way she had a chance to get herself off the hook. They knew about her."

"Who?"

"The British. Why do you think that buffoon, Hotchkiss, came into the picture?"

Cahill was surprised. "What do you know about him? Why . . . ?"

"You came here for answers," Tolker said, standing. "I'll give them to you, *if* you give me the gun, sit down, and shut up!" He extended his hand; his expression said he'd lost patience.

For a moment, Collette considered handing the revolver to him. She started to, but when he went to grab it from her hand, she yanked it away. Now his expression indicated he'd progressed beyond impatience. He was angry. He would do whatever he had to do. He would hurt her.

Collette glared at him; there was an overwhelming desire to use the small plastic revolver—to kill him. It had nothing to do with having determined his responsibility for Barrie's death, nor was it bound up in some rational thought process involving her job or mission. Rather, it represented what had become an obsession to take action, to push a button, place a phone call, pull a trigger to put an end to the turmoil in her life.

Then again, it occurred to her, there *was* a certain order to what was being played out, a Ramistic logic that said, "Enjoy the pragmatic role you're in, Collette. You're a CIA agent. You have the authority to kill, to right wrongs. Nothing will happen to you. You're expected to act with authority because it is your country that is at stake. You're a member of law enforcement. The gun has been given to you to use, to enforce a political philosophy of freedom and opportunity in order to keep evil forces from destroying a precious way of life."

The thoughts cleared her mind and calmed her down. "You underestimate me," she said.

"Get out."

"When I'm ready. Hotchkiss. What role did he play?"

"He . . ."

"Why are you knowledgeable about him?"

"I have nothing more to say to you."

"You said the British knew about Barrie being a . . . traitor. That's why Hotchkiss is here?"

"Yes."

"You convinced Barrie to become his partner?"

"It was best for her. It was the understanding."

"Understanding?"

"The deal. It saved her. Our people agreed with it."

"Because they believed you, that she and Eric Edwards were traitors."

"No, Collette, because they *knew* they were. They gave Barrie's mother money not to pursue any interest in the agency. Barrie's will left operating control to Hubler, but her mother was to receive Barrie's share of profits. The old bitch was happy for cash."

"How much?"

"It doesn't matter. Any amount was too much. She created the person Barrie became, a muddled, psychotic, pathetic human being who spent her adult life hiding from reality. It's not unusual. People with Barrie's high capacity for hypnotic trance usually come out of abused childhoods."

A smirk crossed Collette's face. "Do you know what I want to do, Dr. Tolker?"

"Tell me."

"I either want to spit on you, or kill you."

"Why?"

"You never tried to help Barrie get over her abused childhood, did you? All you were interested in was exploiting it, and her. You're despicable."

"You're irrational. Maybe it's a female thing. The agency ought to reconsider hiring women. You make a good case against the policy."

Collette didn't respond. She wanted to lash out. At the same time, she couldn't mount an argument against what he'd said. Somehow, defending equality between the sexes didn't seem important.

His voice and face had been cold and matter-of-fact up until now. He softened, smiled. "Tell you what," he said. "Let's start over, right now, this night. No silly guns, no nasty remarks. Let's have a drink, dinner. Good wine and soothing music will take care of all our differences. We are on the same side, you know. I believe in you and what you stand for. I like you, Collette. You're a beautiful, bright, talented, and decent woman. Please, forget why you came in here tonight. I'm sure you have other questions that I can answer, but not in this atmosphere of rancor and distrust. Let's be friends and discuss these matters as friends, the way you used to discuss things with Barrie." His smile broadened. "You *are* incredibly beautiful, especially when that anger forces its way to the surface and gives your face a . . ."

He went for her. She'd shifted the revolver to her left hand minutes before. As he lunged, she dropped Vern's envelope, stiffened her right hand, and brought the edge of it against the side of his neck. The blow sent him sprawling to the carpet. A string of four-letter words exploded from him as he scrambled to his feet. They stood facing each other, their breathing rapid, their eyes wide in anger and fear.

Collette slowly backed toward the door, the revolver held securely in two hands, its tiny barrel pointed directly at his chest.

"Come here," he said.

She said nothing, kept retreating, her attention on controlling the damnable shaking of her hands.

"You've got it all screwed up," he said. She sensed the tension in his body as he prepared to attack again, a spring being compressed to give it maximum velocity and distance when released. The restraint on the spring was disengaged. It uncoiled in her direction. Her two fingers on the trigger contracted in concert; there was an almost silly "pop" from the revolver—a Champagne cork, a dry twig being snapped, Rice Krispies.

She stepped back and he fell at her feet, arms outstretched. She picked up the envelope, ran through the door and to the street where, once she realized the revolver was still in her hands, she shoved it into her raincoat and walked deliberately toward the nearest busy intersection.

The message light on her telephone was on when she returned to her suite at the Watergate. She called the message center. "Oh, yes, Miss Cahill, a gentleman called. He said"—the operator laughed. "It's a strange message. The gentleman said, 'Necessary that we discuss Winston Churchill as quickly as possible.' "

"He didn't leave a name?"

"No. He said you'd know who he was."

"Thank you."

Collette went to the balcony and looked out over the shimmering lights of Foggy Bottom. What had Joe Breslin told her? She could make contact with someone at the Churchill statue any evening for the next two weeks at six o'clock, and that the contact would remain there for no more than ten minutes.

She returned to the living room, drew the drapes, got into a robe, and sat in a wing chair illuminated by a single floor lamp. On her lap was Vern Wheatley's envelope. She pulled the pages from it, sighed, and began reading. It wasn't until the first shaft of sunlight came through a gap in the drapes that she put it down, hung the DO NOT DISTURB sign on the door, and went, soberly, to bed.

31

Sleep. It was what she'd needed most. The small travel alarm clock on the nightstand next to her bed read 3:45. She'd slept almost ten hours, and it had been easy. The events earlier in the evening seemed not to have happened or, at least, had happened to someone else.

It was four-thirty when she got out of the shower. As she stood in front of the bathroom mirror drying her hair, she remembered she was supposed to call Vern. She found the number for the Allen Lee Hotel and dialed it, asked for Mr. Black's room. "Sorry to be late calling," she said. "I slept all day."

"It's okay. Did you read what I gave you?"

"Read it? Yes, two or three times. I was up all night."

"And?"

"You make some remarkable accusations, Vern."

"Are they wrong?" he asked.

"No."

"Okay, talk to me. How did you react to . . . ?"

"Why don't we discuss it in person?"

He whooped. "This is called progress. You mean you're actually going to initiate a date with me?"

"I wasn't suggesting a date, just some time to discuss what you've written."

"Name it. I'm yours."

"I have to meet someone at six. How about getting together at seven?"

"Who are you meeting?" he asked. It irked her but she said nothing. He said, "Oh, that's right, Miss Cahill operates incognito. Known in high school as the girl most likely to succeed dressed in a cloak and dagger."

"Vern, I'm in no mood for your attempts at sarcasm."

"Yeah, well, I'm not in any mood for jokes, either. You ever hear of Operation Octopus?"

She had to think. Then she started to mention Hank Fox, cut off her words, and said, "No."

"It's a division of the CIA that keeps computer tabs on writers, at least the ones who don't carry briefs for the goddamn agency. I'm at the top of the list." When she didn't respond, he added, "And they take care of writers like me, Collette. Take care." He guffawed. "They goddamn kill us, that's what they do."

"Where shall we meet at seven?" she asked.

"How about picking me up here at the hotel?"

"No, let's meet at the bar in the Watergate."

"You buying? Drinks there cost the national debt."

"If I have to. See you here . . . there at seven."

She found a vacant cab and told the driver to take her to the British Embassy on Massachusetts Avenue. As they approached it, she kept an eye out for a statue. There it was, less than a hundred yards from the main entrance, set into clumps of bushes just off the sidewalk. The driver made a U-turn and let her off in front of the embassy gate. It had started to rain, and the air had taken on a distinct chill. She brought the collar of her raincoat up around her neck and slowly walked toward the statue of Winnie. It was imposing and lifelike, but the years had turned Churchill green, blending into the foliage. He would not have liked that.

Traffic was heavy on Massachusetts Ave. It was raining harder, too, which slowed the traffic. There were few pedestrians, those scurrying past her coming from jobs at the British Embassy. She checked her watch; exactly six. She looked up and down the street in search of someone who might be interested in her but saw no one. Then, across the broad avenue, a man emerged from Normanstone Park. It was too dark and he was too far away for her to see his face. His trench-coat collar was up, his hands deep in his pockets. It took him some time to cross the street because of the traffic but, eventually, there was a break and he took advantage of it with long, loping strides. Good.

She sensed someone approaching from her right, turned, and saw another man coming down the sidewalk. He wore a hat, and had hunched his shoulders and lowered his head against the rain. She'd forgotten the rain and realized her hair and shoes were soaked. She quickly looked to her left again. The man from the park was gone. Another look to the right. The man in the hat was almost abreast of her. She poised, waiting for him to look up and say something. Instead, he walked by, his head still lowered, his eyes on the sidewalk.

She took a deep breath and wiped water from her nose and eyes.

"Miss Cahill." It came from her left. She knew immediately who it was from the accent. British. She turned and looked into the long, smiling face of Mark Hotchkiss.

"What are you doing here?" she said quickly. The question represented the only thought on her mind at the moment. What *was* he doing there?

"You arrived precisely on time," he said pleasantly. "Sorry I'm a few minutes late. Traffic and all that, you know."

As difficult as it was to accept, she had no choice. The contact who was to meet her here at the Winston Churchill statue. "I suggest we get out of this bloody rain and go somewhere where we can talk."

"You left the message at my hotel?"

"Yes, who else? Let's go to my office. I have some things to say to you."

"Your office? Barrie's, you mean?"

"As you wish. It's one and the same. Please, I'm getting damn well drenched standing here. Not much of a Londoner, forgetting my umbrella this way. Too long in the States, I suppose."

He took her arm and led her back toward the entrance of the British Embassy. They passed it and turned left on Observatory Lane, the U.S. Naval Observatory on their right, and walked a hundred yards until reaching a champagne-colored Jaguar. Tolker's Jaguar. Hotchkiss unlocked the passenger door and opened it for her. She became rigid and stared at him.

"Come on, now, let's go." His voice was not quite as pleasant as earlier.

She started to bend to get in, stopped and straightened, took a few steps back, and fixed him in a hard look. "Who *are* you?"

His face testified to his exasperation. "I don't have time to answer your silly questions," he said harshly. "Get in the car."

She backed farther away, her right hand up in a gesture of self-defense. "Why are you here? You have nothing to do with . . ." He'd been standing with his hands outstretched as he attempted to convince her. Now his right hand slipped into his raincoat pocket.

"No," she said. She spun around and ran back toward Massachusetts Avenue. She stumbled; one shoe fell off but she kept going, an increasing wind whipping her face with water. She looked over her shoulder without breaking stride, kicked off her second shoe, and saw that he had started after her but had stopped. He shouted, "Come back here!"

She kept going, reached the avenue and ran, retracing her route toward the statue of Winston Churchill, passing other embasssies and racing through puddles that soaked her feet. She kept going until she was out of breath, stopped, and looked back. Hotchkiss's Jaguar came up to the corner and waited for a break in traffic to make a right. A vacant taxi approached her. She leaped into the gutter and frantically waved it down. The driver jammed on his brakes, causing others behind him to do the same. Horns blew and muffled curses filled the air. She got in the back, slammed the door, and said, "The Watergate, please, the hotel, and if a light Jag is behind us, please do everything you can to lose him."

"Hey, lady, what's the matter? What's going on?" the young driver asked.

"Just *go*—please."

"Whatever you say," he said, slapping the gearshift and hitting the accelerator, causing his wheels to spin on the wet pavement.

Cahill looked through the rear window. Vision was obscured but she could see a dozen car-lengths behind. The Jaguar wasn't to be seen.

She turned around and said to the driver, "Get off this street, go through the park."

He followed her order and soon drove up to the main entrance to the Watergate Hotel.

Cahill was drained. Once she was certain that Hotchkiss wasn't behind them, her energy had abandoned her and she slumped in the back seat, her breath still coming heavily.

"Lady, you all right?" the driver asked over the seat.

She'd closed her eyes. She opened them and managed a small smile. "Yes, thank you very much. I know it all seems strange but . . ." There was no need to explain any further. She handed him a twenty-dollar bill and told him to keep the change. He thanked her. She got out and suddenly realized the condition she was in. Her shoeless feet were bleeding from cuts on the soles. The bottoms of her stockings were in shreds.

"Evening," the doorman said from beneath the protection of a canopy.

Cahill mustered all the dignity she could and said, "Messy night," proudly walked past him and into the lobby, aware that he'd turned and was taking in her every step.

The lobby was busy as usual which, Cahill reasoned, was to her advantage. People were too engaged in coming and going and in conversations to care about a shoeless, wet woman.

She went to the elevator bank serving her floor and pushed the "Up" button. Because she was in a hurry, it was a series of eternities as she watched the lights above the elevator door indicate a slow descent from the top of the hotel. "*Damn*," she muttered as she glanced left and right to see whether there was any interest in her. There wasn't. She looked up again; the elevator had stopped at the tenth floor. She thought of Eric Edwards and Suite 1010. Had it stopped to pick him up? Coincidence but . . .

She moved away from the door so that she was not in the line of anyone's vision coming through it. She could still see the lighted numbers. The elevator had stopped at Five, had skipped Four and stopped at Three. A large party of conventioners who'd flooded the center of the lobby ever since Cahill entered moved out en masse, affording her a clear view of a cluster of small tables and stuffed chairs at which well-dressed people enjoyed pre-dinner cocktails. The sight didn't seem real at first, but it took her only a second to realize that it was. He was sitting at a table by himself, a glass in his hand, legs casually crossed, his attention directed at a woman seated at an adjacent table. Cahill quickly turned her head so that only her back was visible to him.

The sudden opening of the elevator door startled her. A dozen people filed out. Collette faced the wall and took each of them in with her peripheral vision. No Eric Edwards.

The moment the elevator was empty, she sidestepped into it, her back still to the cocktail area. She pushed Eight, then the "Close Door" button. She kept punching it, silently cursing the fact that it had no effect on what the elevator did. Like "Walk" buttons at intersections, she thought. Placebos.

A man in a tuxedo and a woman in a gown and furs joined her in the elevator. She ignored their glances at her feet and kept her eyes trained on the control buttons. The doors started to close; a man suddenly reached in and caused them to open again. He stepped in, followed by two teenage girls. One of them looked down at Cahill's shoeless dishabille, nudged her friend, and they both giggled.

The doors finally closed and the elevator made its ascent. The teenagers got off first, glancing back, then the man who'd stopped the doors with his arm. At the eighth floor, Cahill hobbled out. The man in the tux and the woman in furs whispered something unintelligible to each other. Oh, to be respectable.

She went to her door and opened it. A maid had been in and turned down the bed, leaving two small pieces of foil-wrapped chocolate on the pillow. Cahill locked the door from inside and attached the chain. She quickly got out of her raincoat, which was soaked through, and dropped it on the floor. The rest of her clothes followed. A tiny smear of blood on the carpet from her foot was dissolved by the wet clothing. She turned on the shower and, when it was as hot as she could stand it, stepped in. Ten minutes later she emerged, dried herself, found a Band-Aid in her purse and applied it to the small cut on her foot.

She hadn't noticed upon entering her room that her message light was on. She picked up the phone and identified herself. "Yes, Miss Cahill, you have a message from a Dr. Tolker. He said he was anxious to speak with you and would be in the hotel this evening. You can have him paged."

"No, I . . . Yes, thank you very much, I'll do that later, not now."

The message from Tolker was no surprise. Seeing him sitting in the lobby with a glass of wine had been. She'd assumed she'd killed him. Unless his CIA-funded research had resulted in perfect clone development, he was very much alive. She was glad for that. And frightened.

She picked up the phone again, dialed the number for the Allen Lee Hotel, and asked for Mr. Black's room. There was no answer. Then the operator asked, "Do you happen to be Miss Collette Cahill?"

"Yes, I am."

"Mr. Black had to run out but he left a message in case you called. He said he would return at ten. He said he had some urgent business that came up at the last minute."

Collette's sigh of frustration was, she was certain, audible to the operator even without the benefit of a telephone. She closed her eyes and said dejectedly, "Thank you."

Naked while on the phone, she suddenly felt cold and vulnerable. She pulled out a pair of jeans from the suitcase that she hadn't bothered to unpack, and a furry pink sweater. She got into them and slipped her feet into white sneakers.

She turned on all the lights, looked at the suitcase on the floor, hesitated, then went to it and unlocked an inside compartment. She reached in and came out with the ampules of prussic acid and nitro, and the cigar-shaped detonator. She sat in a chair beneath a lamp and assembled it, then reloaded the small white plastic revolver. She slipped everything into her purse and sat quietly, her fingers playing with the purse's shoulder strap, her ears cocked for sound, her eyes skating over every inch of the large room.

It was intensely quiet, which unnerved her. She was getting up to turn on the television set when the phone rang. The sound of it froze her in the middle of the room. Should she answer? No. Obviously, Tolker and Mark Hotchkiss knew that she was staying at the Watergate, and she didn't want to speak to either of them. Vern didn't know where she was. "How stupid," she chided herself. Why had she played it so secret with him? He loomed large as the only human being in Washington that she could trust. That was ironic, she realized, considering how deceitful he'd been up until their dinner last night.

What suddenly imbued him with trustworthiness was that of everyone in her recent life, only Vern was outside the Company. In fact, he was outside trying to break in, dedicated to exposing and harming it. So much of what he'd written was accurate, at least to the best of her knowledge. Although he hadn't stated it in so many words, the pattern that emerged from his pages gave considerable weight to the idea that it was Jason Tolker who was responsible for Barrie Mayer's and David Hubler's deaths. It all seemed so clear to her now, as though a brilliant light illuminated the truth as she stood in the center of the room.

Árpád Hegedüs *had* lied in that small bar in Budapest. What he'd told her earlier in their relationship was the truth, and what she'd suggested to Joe Breslin made sense. Hegedüs had come over as a defector in order to spread disinformation to the Americans. Tolker had been selling information to the Soviets about the results of mind-control experimentation in the United States. More than that, according to Wheatley's manuscript, he'd used various hypnotized subjects to transmit that information.

Wheatley hadn't mentioned Eric Edwards in his pages. Chances were he didn't even know about him. But Cahill quickly created a scenario in which Tolker, viewing Edwards as a threat because of his close relationship with the too-chatty Barrie, had convinced those involved in Banana Quick that Edwards was a double agent selling information to the other side. What other explanation could there be for his having been accused of double-dealing? Again, there was no tangible evidence to support her thesis, but the cumulative weight of everything that had happened, of every scrap of input she'd taken in, supported her notion.

She knew that she might be justifying her initial instincts about Tolker, but that didn't matter now. The picture she'd painted was good enough. The paramount thing in her mind at this point was to avoid Tolker and Hotchkiss, find Vern and, together, make contact with someone within the CIA who could be trusted. Who could that be? she wondered. The only name she could come up with was Eric, but that posed a risk. He was surrounded by controversy. Still, he represented for Cahill the one person besides Wheatley who seemed to deal with things in a straightforward manner. Hank Fox also came to mind but she dismissed the thought. He was too much one of *them*, despite his fatherly approach.

The phone stopped ringing. Collette returned to the chair, opened her purse, and ran her fingers over the revolver's smooth, plastic finish. Mark Hotchkiss! The confrontation with him had shaken her. What was he, MI-6? A contract agent. There were lots of them in the global system. Hotchkiss's obvious close working relationship with Tolker both puzzled and dismayed her. It made sense, in a way, she reasoned. Tolker wouldn't have physically killed Barrie and Dave Hubler. Too messy, not his style, or role. But Hotchkiss might have been the actual killer, working under Tolker's direction. Yes, that played for her.

She squeezed her eyes shut and shook her head. Why was she bothering trying to make sense out of a system that depended, to a great extent, upon being nonsensical? Too many things in the gray world of intelligence were inscrutable, begging answers, defying the common man's logic. Friends. Enemies. You needed a scorecard to tell the players on opposing teams. Hotchkiss had been in place geographically to kill both Barrie and David. Of course, it was possible that he had no connection with Tolker at all. If he'd killed Mayer and Hubler, he might have been acting strictly on behalf of British intelligence. They'd preached during her training days that there were no allies in the spy business, no forbidden, hands-off nations. The Israelis had proved that recently, and it was well known that the British had dozens of agents in place within the United States.

The phone rang again. Cahill ignored it for a second time. Then another sound intruded upon her thoughts.

Someone was knocking at her door.

32

She went slowly, quietly to the door and placed her ear against it. A male voice said, "Collette?" She couldn't place it. It wasn't Hotchkiss; no trace of a British accent. "Collette."

She remained silent and motionless, the small revolver at her side, her senses acutely tuned. She pressed her eye against the peephole in the door, saw no one. Whoever had been calling her name was against a wall, out of range of the wide-angle lens. She had no way of knowing whether he was still there. The halls were carpeted; no footsteps to give a clue.

She went to the phone and called Vern again on the chance that he might have returned early. He hadn't.

Pacing the living room of her suite, she tried to sort out her next move. She was tempted to abandon the safety of the locked room, but that very safety kept her from doing it, at least for now. Still, she knew she'd have to leave sometime to go to the Allen Lee. Should she, could she wait until Wheatley returned and ask him to come to the Watergate? She answered no to both questions.

She looked down at the phone and read the instruction

for calling another room in the hotel. She debated it, then picked up the receiver, dialed the required prefix, and punched in 1010. It rang a long time. She was about to hang up when Eric Edwards came on the line. He sounded out of breath.

"Eric. It's Collette."

"I don't believe it. Mystery lady surfaces. Let me get my breath. I've been working out. Where are you?"

"I'm . . . I'm in the vicinity."

"I knew you were in Washington. My secretary told me. How long will you be here?"

She wanted to say forever, said instead, "I really don't know. I'd like to see you."

"I hoped you'd want to see me," he said. "I was really upset the way you disappeared on me down in the BVI."

"I couldn't help it. I'm sorry."

"Nothing to be sorry about, and thanks for the note. I have a dinner engagement later this evening but . . ."

"I really need to see you tonight, Eric."

"Could you come by now? We can have a drink before I have to get dressed."

Collette paused before saying, "Yes, I can be there in ten minutes."

"Hope you don't mind a sweaty host."

"I won't mind that at all. Will we be alone?"

"Sure. What are you suggesting?"

"Nothing. Ten minutes."

"Fine, I'm in Suite 1010."

"Yes, I know."

After hanging up, she put on her raincoat and slipped the revolver into its pocket. She slung her purse over her shoulder and went to the door, her ear again cocked against the cool metal. There wasn't a sound outside. Then she heard the rattling of dishes and someone whistling—a hotel employee going past her room with a serving cart. She listened to the jangle as it faded into the distance, and until everything was silent again. She undid the chain as quietly as possible, turned the lock on the knob and opened the door, looking out into the hallway right and left. Empty. She made sure she had her key, stepped through the opening, and closed the door behind her.

The elevators were to her left, about a hundred feet away. She started swiftly toward them when Mark Hotchkiss stepped from around a bend in the hallway beyond the elevators. She stopped, turned, and saw Jason Tolker approaching from the opposite direction. His right arm was in a sling, that side of his suit jacket draped over his shoulder. She hadn't noticed that downstairs. "Collette," Tolker said. "Please, I want to talk to you."

"Get away," she said, backing toward the elevators, her hand slipping into her pocket.

Tolker continued to walk toward her, saying, "Don't be foolish, Collette. You're making a big mistake. You must listen to me."

"Shut up," she said. Her hand came out of the pocket holding the revolver and she pointed it at him. It stopped him cold. "I won't miss you this time."

"Miss Cahill, you're being bloody unreasonable," Hotchkiss said from behind.

She glanced over her shoulder and showed him the weapon. "I'm telling you to stay away from me or I'll kill you both. I mean it."

Both men stopped their advance and watched as she moved toward the elevators, her head moving back and forth like a spectator's at a tennis match, keeping them both in view.

"Get her," Tolker yelled.

Hotchkiss extended his arms and stumbled toward her. She waited until he was about to grab her, then brought her knee up sharply into his groin. His breath exploded from him as he sank to his knees, his hands cupping his wounded genitals.

Collette ran to the elevators and pushed the "Down" button. Almost immediately one of the doors opened. The elevator was empty. She backed into it. "Don't come after me," she said, the doors sliding closed and muffling her words.

She looked at the control panel and pushed Seven. The elevator moved a floor lower. She got out, ran along the hall, and turned a corner until she came to another bank of elevators. She frantically pushed the button until one of them arrived. In it were two couples. She stepped inside and pressed Ten.

The couples got out with her at the tenth floor. She waited until they'd entered a room, then walked past it and went directly to 1010. She knocked. The door was immediately opened by Eric Edwards. He wore blue gym shorts and a gray athletic shirt with the sleeves cut off at the shoulders. His hair was damp with perspiration and hung over his tanned forehead.

"Hello, Eric," she said.

"Hello to you," he said, stepping back so that she could enter. He closed the door and latched it.

She went to the center of the room and looked down at a pair of hotel barbells and a couple of towels tossed in a pile on the floor. She kept her back to him.

"Not even a kiss hello?" he asked from behind. She turned, sighed, lowered her eyes, and her body began to shake. Large tears instantly ran down her cheeks.

He put his arms around her and held tight. "Hey, come *on* now, it can't be that bad. Some reaction to me. I should be offended."

She controlled herself, looked up, and said, "I'm so confused, Eric, and frightened. Do you know why I'm here in Washington?"

"No, except you said you had some business to attend to."

"But do you know what that business was?"

He shook his head and smiled. "No, and unless you tell me, I never will."

"I was sent here to kill you."

He looked at her as though she were a small child caught in a lie. She said, "It's true, Eric. They wanted me to kill you, and I said I would."

"Telling you to kill me is one thing," he said as he went to a chair near the window, "agreeing to it is another. Why would you want to kill me?"

She tossed her raincoat on a couch. "I don't. I mean, I didn't. I never intended to."

He laughed. "You're incredible, you know that?"

She shook her head, went to him, and sank to her knees

291

in front of the chair. "Incredible? No, I'm anything but. What I am is a terribly mixed up and disillusioned woman."

"Disillusioned with what, our good friends at Langley?"

She nodded. "The so-called Company, everyone in my life, life itself I guess." She took a deep breath. "They wanted me to kill you because they think you're a double agent, selling information to the Soviets about Banana Quick."

He grunted, shrugged.

"When I came to you and asked for advice about a vacation in the BVI, it was all a lie. They told me to do it. They wanted me to get close to you so that I could find out what you were doing down there."

He leaned forward, touched her cheek, and said, "I knew that, Collette."

"You did?"

"Well, not for certain, but I had a pretty strong feeling about it. It really didn't bother me for a couple of reasons. One, I fell in love with you. Two, I figured that when you almost went up with me and the yacht, you'd lost your taste for doing their dirty work. Was I right?"

"Yes."

"Having something like that happen puts things in perspective, doesn't it? You can see how little you or I mean to them. We can go out and put our necks on the line for their crazy sense of duty and patriotism, but when push comes to shove, we're all expendable. No questions asked, just 'terminate' some people and get on with the sham."

His words had considerable impact on her, as words always do when they say what you've already been thinking. She thought of Tolker and Hotchkiss and their confrontation. "There are two men in the hotel who tried to stop me in the hall."

He sat up. "Who are they? Do you know them?"

"Yes. One is Jason Tolker, the psychiatrist who was Barrie's control. He brainwashed her, Eric. The other is an Englishman named Mark Hotchkiss, the one who took over Barrie's agency."

Edwards's placid face turned grim as he looked out the window. "You know him?" Collette asked.

"I know of him. He's British intelligence, an old buck who supposedly did some hits for MI-6, the Middle East, I think."

Cahill said, "I think Tolker is the one who killed Barrie and David Hubler, maybe not directly, but I'm convinced he was behind it."

Edwards continued to stare silently at the window. Finally, he turned to her and said, "I have a proposal for you, Collette."

"A proposal?"

He managed a thin smile. "Not that kind of proposal, although maybe that's in the cards down the road. As it would have been with Barrie if . . ." She waited for him to finish his thought. Instead, he said, "For all her intelligence, Barrie didn't have one tenth the smarts you have, Collette."

"If there's one thing I don't consider myself these days, it's smart."

He placed his hands on her shoulders and kissed her gently on the forehead. "You've seen more in your lifetime than most people can only imagine. You've not only witnessed the rotten underbelly of the CIA, what they call Intelligence, you've been a victim of it, like me. Barrie didn't understand that. She never realized how she was being used by them."

Cahill sat back on her haunches. "I don't understand," she said.

"I suppose it doesn't matter anymore about Barrie. She's dead. It's different for you, though. You could . . . you could step in where she left off, sort of in her memory." His face lit up as though what he'd just said represented a profound revelation. "That's right, you could view it that way, Collette, as doing something in Barrie's memory."

"View *what* that way?"

"Doing something to right wrongs, to avenge all the things that have happened because of them, including the loss of your good friend, and that young man who worked for her. You could do something very worthwhile for the world, Collette."

"What do you mean?"

"Come in with me," he said.

She had no idea what he meant, and her face indicated it.

He hunched forward and spoke in low, paternal tones. "Collette, I want you to think carefully about everything that's happened over the past weeks, beginning with the death of Barrie Mayer." He scrutinized her face. "You know why Barrie died, don't you?"

"Sometimes I think I do, but I've never been sure. Do you know . . . for sure?"

His expression was one of bad taste in his mouth. He said in the same measured tones, "Barrie died because she wouldn't listen to me. She did in the beginning, and it was good for her, but then she started listening to others."

"Tolker?"

"Yes. He had remarkable control over her. I warned her. I tried to reason with her, but every time she'd see him, he'd capture another small piece of her mind."

"I knew that was the case, but . . . "

"But what?"

"Why would he have killed her if she were so obedient to him?"

"Because that's the flaw in their whole stupid mind-control program, Collette. They spend millions, screw up one life after the other, but still can't—and never will—create a person they can *totally* control. It's impossible, and they know it."

"But they . . . "

"Yeah, they keep spending and trying. Why? The freaks who work in those projects, like Tolker, get off on it. They exaggerate results and keep promising a breakthrough, while the ones who control funding rationalize the millions by claiming the other side is doing it, and in a bigger way. Barrie might have been manipulated by Tolker, but he didn't own her. Maybe it would have been better if he did. Or thought he did."

Collette said nothing as she thought about what he'd said.

"Tolker filled Barrie with a lot of lies that turned her against me," Edwards continued. "It was a tragic mistake on her part. She didn't know who to trust, and ended up putting all her cards in the wrong player's hand."

Cahill went to a table. She leaned her hands on it and peered down at its surface. As hard as she tried, she couldn't fully process what he was saying. Everything was so indirect, raising more questions than answers.

"Eric, why was Barrie killed? What did she know that made it necessary to murder her? Who would have been so hurt if she stayed alive that they'd be driven to such an act?"

He came closer to her. "You have to understand, Collette, that Barrie knew the risks involved in what she was doing."

"Being a courier? Occasionally carrying things to Budapest shouldn't pose that much of a risk, Eric."

"Not unless what she was carrying could be construed as being destructive to the Company."

"Why would it be destructive? She was working *for* it, wasn't she?"

"In the beginning, then . . . Look, let me level with you, Collette, the way I've been doing right along. I won't try to soften it, mince words. Barrie eventually saw the wisdom in cooperating with—the other side."

Collette shook her head. "No, I can't believe that Barrie would double-deal. No, sorry, I can't accept that."

"You have to, Collette. Open your mind. Don't automatically make it negative. What she was doing was noble in its own way."

"Noble? You're saying she was a traitor."

"Semantics. Is trying to achieve a balance of sanity in this world a traitorous act? I don't think so. Is saving the lives of thousands of innocent people, Hungarians in this case, traitorous? Of course it isn't. Banana Quick was ill-conceived from the beginning, doomed to failure, like the Bay of Pigs and the rescue attempt in Iran and all the other misguided projects we undertake in the name of freedom. If Banana Quick is implemented, it will only result in the death of innocent people in Hungary. Barrie didn't see that at first, but I eventually convinced her of it."

"*You* convinced her?"

"Yes, and I want to convince you of the same thing. This is something I've wanted to do ever since I met you, but I was never sure you'd be receptive. Now I think you will be, just as Barrie was, once she understood."

"Go ahead."

"I want you to work with me to fend off this madness. I want you to pick up where Barrie left off. I want you to . . . to help me feed information to where it will do the most good, to what you call 'the other side.' "

Cahill's stomach churned and she felt light-headed. What they'd said was true. He *was* a double agent, and had recruited Barrie. She didn't know what to say, how to respond, whether to lash out at him physically or to run from the room. She held both instincts in check. "I defended you at every turn. I told them they were wrong about you. I was the one who was wrong." She'd said it with a calm voice. Now she exploded. "Damn it, damn you! I thought Tolker was the double agent leaking information about Banana Quick. I really believed that, but now you're admitting to me that you are. You bastard! You set Barrie up to be killed, and now you want me to put myself in the same position."

He shook his head slowly. "Collette, you have a lot more to offer than Barrie did. She was so naive. That's what got her in trouble, what led to her death. When I took Barrie into my confidence, I had no idea of her potential for control by someone like Tolker. She told him everything, and he convinced her to inform on me. She'd learned too much. I never should have let her get that close, but I fell in love. I do that too easily and often for my own good."

"Love? You call it love for a woman to recruit her into selling out her country?"

"Love comes in all forms. It was a nice partnership, personally and professionally, until Tolker soured everything. Barrie made a lot of money from our partnership, Collette, a lot more than she was getting from the CIA."

"Money? That matters to you?"

"Sure. It mattered to her, too. There's nothing inherently evil with money, is there? Let me suggest something. Climb down off your high horse and hear me out. I'll cancel my date tonight and we'll have dinner right here in the room. We'll get to know each other better." He laughed. "And we can pick up where we left off in the BVI. No strings,

Collette. You don't have to fall in with me. Nothing lost by talking about it."

"I don't want to talk about it," she said.

"You don't have much choice."

"What do you mean?"

"You're already in because you know too much. That makes sense, doesn't it?"

"Not at all."

He shrugged, leaned over and picked up a barbell, lifted it a few times over his head. "I'll make a deal with you. All you have to do is go back to Budapest and tell them I'm clean. I'll give you materials that make a case against Tolker as having thrown in with the Soviets. That's all you have to do, Collette, tell them you dug up this material and are turning it over like a good Company employee. They'll take care of Tolker and . . . "

"And what, terminate him?"

"That's not our concern. You knew, didn't you, that Barrie was carrying almost two hundred thousand dollars to pay off some Hungarian bureaucrat?"

She didn't reply.

"I have it."

"You took it from her after you killed her." She was amazed at how matter-of-factly she was able to say it.

"It doesn't matter how I got it. What's important is that half is yours for clearing me. After that, there'll be plenty more if you decide to help me on a long-term basis. Think about it, lots of money stashed away for your retirement." Another laugh as he did curls with the barbell. "I figure I've got maybe another year at best before it's time for me to get out. I want enough money to start my own charter service, not a front I don't own. What do you want in a year, Collette? A house in Switzerland, an airplane, enough money in a foreign bank so that you'll never have to work again? It's yours." He dropped the barbell to the floor and said, "How about it? Dinner? Champagne? We'll toast anything you want, anybody, and then we can . . . "

"Make love?"

"Absolutely. I established a rule with myself years ago that I'd never let anything get in the way of that, especially

when it's a beautiful and bright woman like you who . . . "
He shook his head. "Who made me fall in love again."

She went for her raincoat on the couch. He jumped in
front of her and gripped the back of her neck, his fingertips
pressing hard against her arteries. She could see the muscles
rippling in his bare arms, and the red anger on his face.
"I'm through being nice," he said, pushing her across the
room and into the bedroom. He flung her down on the bed,
grabbed the front of her sweater, and tore it off.

She rolled off the bed and scrambled across the floor
toward the door, got to her feet, and raced into the living
room. She swiped at her raincoat and tried to get behind
the couch where she'd have time to retrieve the revolver.
He was too quick; she'd barely managed to pull the weapon
from the pocket when he grabbed her wrist and twisted, the
white plastic gun falling to the floor.

"You bitch," he said. "You would kill me, wouldn't you?"

His ego was so damaged momentarily that he relaxed his
grip on her wrist. She sprang loose and ran to where she'd
left her purse on top of a large console television set, grabbed
it, and tried to find something to get behind, a haven where
she could catch her breath and ready the detonator. There
wasn't any such place—her only escape route was into the
master bedroom. She ran there and tried to slam the door
behind her, but he easily pushed it open, the force sending
her reeling toward the bed. Her knees caught it, and she
was suddenly on her back, her hands frantically seeking the
device in her purse.

He stood over her and glared. "You don't understand the
game, do you? What did you think would happen when you
decided to get some excitement in your life by joining up?
What did you think, you can play spy but run home to
Mommy when it hurts?"

"I'm . . . please don't hurt me," she said. Her purse had
fallen to the floor, but she'd grasped the loaded detonator
and cupped it in her right hand, her arms flung back over
the edge of the bed.

"I don't want to," he said. "I don't hurt people for fun.
Sometimes, though . . . sometimes it's necessary, that's all.
Don't make it necessary for me to hurt you."

"I won't." His eyes were focused on her bare breasts. He smiled. "A beautiful woman. You'll see, Collette, we'll end up together. It'll be nice. We'll stash the money, then go away somewhere and enjoy the hell out of it—and each other."

He leaned forward and put a hand on either side of her head. His face was inches from her face. He kissed her on the lips, and she managed to return it, mimicking the memory of their night together, until he pulled his head back and said, "You're beautiful."

Then she brought her hand up and jammed the detonator against his lips. Her thumb pulled the switch and the ampule exploded, sending the acid and a thousand fine fragments of glass into his face. He gasped and fell back to his knees, his hands ripping at his sweatshirt, his face contorted.

Cahill, too, felt the effect of the acid. Her face had been too close to his. She reached down and shoved her hand into her open purse, found the small glass vial of nitro and broke it beneath her nose, breathing deeply, praying it would work.

"Me . . . " Edwards said. He was now writhing on the floor, one hand outstretched, his last living expression one of pleading. Cahill lay on her stomach, her head at the foot of the bed, her eyes wide as she watched him breathe and then, with one last convulsion, his head twisted to one side and he was dead, his open eyes looking up at her.

33

She made her final trip to Budapest a week later, to process out and to arrange for the shipment of her things back to the United States.

Joe Breslin met her Malev flight and drove her to her apartment. "I really don't have much," she said. "It was probably silly for me even to come here."

"You didn't have to bother with packing," Breslin said, lighting his pipe. "We would have done it for you. Got a beer?"

"Go look. I don't know."

He returned from the tiny kitchen with a bottle of the Kőbányai világos and a glass. "Want one? There's plenty."

"No."

He sat on a deep window bench and she leaned against a wall, her arms folded across her chest, ankles crossed, her head down. She sighed, looked at him, and said, "I'll hate you and everybody in the CIA for the rest of my life, Joe."

"I'm genuinely sorry about that," he said.

"So am I. Maybe if I grow up someday and begin to understand everything that's happened, I won't feel quite so filled with hatred."

"Maybe. You know, none of us likes doing what we have to do."

"I don't believe that, Joe. I think the agency's filled with people who love it. I thought I did."

"You did a good job."

"Did I?"

"Your handling of Hegedüs was as masterful as any I've ever seen."

"He was telling the truth about Tolker, wasn't he?"

"Yeah. I wish the Fisherman were still in place. He's no good to us now."

She made a sound of displeasure.

"What's the matter?" he asked.

" 'He's no good to us now.' That's the way it is, isn't it, Joe? People are only worthwhile as long as they have something to give. After that . . . instant discard."

He didn't respond.

"Tell me about Hotchkiss," she said.

Breslin shrugged and drew on his pipe. "MI-6, an old-timer who hung in. They—the Brits—set Hotchkiss up in the literary agency business years ago. Nice cover, good excuse to travel and get a pulse on what's happening in the literary fraternity. In most countries, literary means political. Having him in that business paid off for them. They're not talking, at least to us, but somehow they got wind that Barrie had turned, and was working with Edwards. They sicced Hotchkiss on her." Breslin's laugh was one of admiration. "Hotchkiss did a better job than they'd hoped for. He actually got Barrie to consider going into partnership."

"Consider? They did become partners."

"Not really. The papers were bogus. We figure your friend told Hotchkiss to get lost the night before she died. That eventuality had been considered for a long time. Those papers were drawn, and her signature forged, in anticipation of the deal going down the tube."

"But why . . . ?"

"Why what? Go through all that? The British have been complaining from the first day about Banana Quick. They felt we were running the show, and that they were being left in the dark about too many things. Answer? Get some-

301

one on the inside, in this case Barrie Mayer. Knowing what she was up to was as good as sleeping with Edwards."

"And Jason Tolker?"

A long draw on his pipe. "Funny about Tolker. He really was in love with Barrie Mayer, but he found himself between a rock and a hard place. The British suspected she was double-dealing, but never knew for certain. Tolker knew. He was the only one, besides Edwards, but what does he do with the information? Turn them in and destroy the woman? He couldn't do that, so he went to work on her and tried to convince her to drop Edwards, turn him in, and hope that they'd let her off the hook. He was effective, *too* effective. She finally decided to do it. Edwards couldn't allow that. That's why he killed her. All such a waste. They've scrapped Banana Quick."

Cahill stared at him incredulously, then quickly went to a closet. She would not allow him to see that her eyes were moist. She waited until she was under control before pulling out a blue blazer and slipping it on over her white blouse. "Let's go," she said.

"Stan wants to talk to you before you leave," said Breslin.

"I know. What is it, a debriefing?"

"Something like that. He'll lay down the rules. He has to do that with anyone leaving. There are rules, you know, about disclosure, things like that."

"I can live with rules."

"What about your friend, the journalist?"

"Vern? Don't worry, Joe, I won't tell him what happened, what *really* happened."

"The book he's writing."

"What about it?"

"You've seen it. Is it damaging?"

"Yes."

"We'd like to know what's in it."

"Not from me."

"Do him a favor, Collette, and get him to drop it."

"That sounds like an order."

"A strong request."

"Denied."

She started to open the door but he stopped her with

"Collette, you sure you want to make such a clean break? Hank Fox told you what your options were before you came here. The outfit takes good care of those who do special service, and do it well. You could have six months anywhere in the world with all expenses paid, a chance to get your head together and for enough time to pass so that it all doesn't seem so terrible. Then a nice job back at Langley, more money, the works. People who . . ."

"People who carry out an assassination are taken care of. Joe, I didn't assassinate Eric Edwards. He tried to rape me. I was like any other woman—except I had a plastic gun, a vial of lethal acid, and the blessing of my country's leading intelligence agency. I killed him to save myself, no other reason."

"What does it matter? The job got done."

"I'm glad that makes everyone happy. No, Joe, I want ten thousand miles between me and the CIA. I know there are a lot of good people in it who really care about what happens to their country, and who try to do the right thing. The problem is, Joe, that not only are there lots of people who *aren't* like that, but the definition of 'right thing' gets blurred all the time. Come on. Let me go and have the rules explained to me, and then let's have dinner. I'm really going to miss Hungarian food."

Murder in the House

"Trees, though they are cut and lopped, grow up again quickly, but if men are destroyed, it is not easy to replace them."

—PERICLES

PROLOGUE

"The chaplain will offer the prayer."

"We ask you, the creator of all men and institutions, to generously dispense this day the wisdom and courage necessary to do the nation's business. And we seek your divine counsel in order that we may govern wisely, and with compassion. Amen."

The Speaker pro tem, named by the Speaker to rule that day over the House of Representatives, next announced, "The gentlelady from Florida will lead us in the pledge."

Two dozen right hands pressed against two dozen bosoms as the Pledge of Allegiance was spoken. Few members attended opening ceremonies. The first vote of the day would bring the rest running from their offices across the street.

The day's Speaker brought down the gavel sharply: "The Chair will entertain morning-hour speeches. For what purpose does the gentleman from Oregon seek recognition?"

"To address the House for one minute, and to revise and extend my remarks."

"Without objection. The gentleman is recognized for one minute."

The representative from Oregon stepped to "the well"— a podium and microphone on his side of the aisle; the other political party had its own well—and spent his allotted sixty seconds praising the University of Oregon's baseball team for having won the state's collegiate championship. Other speakers would follow, taking advantage of morning hours, during which any of the 435 members of the House were free to speak for a minute on any subject, even baseball.

Later, more serious debate would take place, with each side having an hour to present its speakers' views on a pending bill that would, if passed, strengthen environmental laws. Not that the debate would change anyone's mind. Each member's vote on the legislation had been determined days ago, along strict party lines. But emoting with passion on one side of the issue or the other played well back home, especially now that C-SPAN carried the business of the House of Representatives into millions of homes across America.

The visitors gallery contained a hundred or so people watching the proceedings in person. They included Jack Marx, retired from a large insurance company and a Republican, and his friend and neighbor Oliver Jones, a retired schoolteacher and lifelong Democrat. They'd traveled to Washington, D.C., from North Carolina with their wives, and had obtained passes to the House chamber from their congressman.

They left after an hour and went downstairs, where they hooked up with a tour group. Eventually, they wandered outside and sat on a small bench in a pocket park, a few hundred feet from the Capitol Building.

"Whew!" Marx said, wiping sweat from his brow and lowering his large camcorder to the grass. "Some hot. Hot air."

"Inside," his friend Jones said, laughing.

"Yeah. They're all full of hot air."

"But they eventually get things done."

"If it suits some lobbyist, some big-money contributor," said Marx. "I don't trust any of 'em."

"Push for term limits. Write a letter to the editor."

"Lot of good that would do. Jesus, Ollie, how can you watch those guys on C-SPAN all the time?"

"Keeps him busy," Diane Jones answered for him. "Out of my hair since he retired."

"Amen," Roberta Marx chimed in.

"All they do is talk," Marx said.

"Just some of them. Notice how few were there?"

"Yeah."

"Most of them work behind the scenes. Work hard," Jones said. "There's that small group who spend all their time on the floor making speeches. Same ones every day."

"Blowhards."

Oliver Jones laughed, slapped his friend and neighbor on the back. "You'd agree with Mark Twain," he said.

"I liked him."

"Mark Twain? You know what *he* said about Congress."

"What did he say?"

"Something like 'There's no distinctively native American criminal class, except Congress.' "

"I always liked him."

"Ready to go?" Roberta asked.

"The House really does represent us. America," her husband said as he picked up his camcorder and slung it over his shoulder. "Think about it. Four hundred thirty-five men and women. We send them up here to make decisions."

They slowly walked in the direction of their hotel.

"Good guys, bad guys," Jones continued. "Drunks and womanizers, religious zealots and do-gooders. Black and white. Hispanic. Men and women. Wife beaters and devoted husbands. Left wing, right wing. Middle-grounders. America."

Marx pondered his friend's comment.

"And I'll tell you one thing," Jones said as they waited for a traffic light to change.

"What's that?" his wife said.

"As dumb as the system seems sometimes, there's no better one on earth. Ask any Russian about that."

1

MOSCOW—EARLY SEPTEMBER

It was a sour morning.

Yvgeny Fodorov, naked, looked through his crusted apartment window to the British Embassy across *Ulitsa Solyanka*, near where Moscow's infamous *Khitrov* meat market had once festered.

He tasted bile; his eyes, open only a few minutes, itched. His fingers went to them, rubbing. A headache pounded at his temples, causing him to place his fingertips against them as though it would help.

A trim young woman dressed in a navy suit and red high heels entered the embassy. He'd seen her before, an employee, certainly British. She showed her pass to the guard and disappeared inside.

The kettle whistled from the pullman kitchen at the other end of the long, narrow room that had been his home for six months. He made tea, sliced two pieces from a loaf of black bread bought the day before at his local *khleb*, one of a chain of recently privatized bread stores, and made a sandwich of tongue and tomato.

After slipping into a pair of stained white gym shorts and eating his sandwich, he returned to the window, teacup in hand. The sun was rising like a hot orange; the city's pollution, now visible in daylight, blanketed everything, gauze over the lens through which Yvgeny observed the city of his birth that morning.

People came and went on the street below his window. He sat on a rickety wooden chair and watched them impassively, the raising of the cup to his thin lips his only motion. But his thoughts were on last night. Not pleasant thoughts.

Considering the importance of this day, he was stupid to have stayed out half the night. Too much vodka. The incessant beat and blare of the rock music, so loud it hurt. And then the argument with Sofia to top off the night. He'd wanted to be alone with her, discuss things, bring her back to his apartment to make love.

But she wanted to be with her friends, damn them. How he detested their arrogant, trendy ways, so influenced by the rush of Western values and styles since the collapse of the Soviet Union, vapid creatures whose only interests were clothes and dancing and drugs. He'd put up with them for most of the evening at Night Flight, one of Moscow's many discos.

At two in the morning—or was it three?—he'd tried to convince Sofia to leave with him. She'd just laughed, and continued gyrating on the dance floor. The others laughed, too. "The night is just starting," one said.

He hadn't planned to hit her. But the rage had been

building inside all night as she and her friends taunted him. "Don't be such an old man," one had said. "Loosen up, Yvgeny. Smile. You look like you sucked on a lemon." More laughter. And then Sofia came to where he stood at the edge of the dance floor, tossed a hip in his direction, held her face inches from his, and said, mirth in her voice, "What are you, Yvgeny? An *apparatchik*? *B-o-r-i-n-g!*"

He'd lashed out with his fist, bloodying her lip and knocking her to the floor. She'd scrambled away from him on all fours, screaming, cursing so loud her voice was heard above the music, dancers tripping over her.

Fearing an attack from Sofia's male friends, Yvgeny ran from the club and went home, where he sat shaking and finishing what was left of a bottle of vodka, hearing their jibes over and over: "Apparatchik?" Yes, and proud to be. What were their loyalties? To decadence. Softness. Wasted, narcissistic lives.

His continued commitment to the Communism that had been pushed aside by Yeltsin and other so-called reformers was a source of pride. It had been since he was a teenager, enthusiastically joining *Komsomol*, the youth movement of the Communist Party, in which the drinking of large amounts of vodka proved one's comradeship, and by extension political unity. That wasn't long ago; Yvgeny was only twenty-two.

Yvgeny Fodorov had volunteered in Gennady Zyuganov's campaign for president, and shared with his fellow believers the bitter disappointment of losing to the fat fool, Yeltsin.

"There will be another day for us," Zyuganov had said to a rally of campaign workers following his defeat. And he repeated what he had written in his book, *Beyond the*

Horizon, which Yvgeny had read so many times he'd virtually committed it to memory: "Capitalism does not fit the flesh and blood, the customs of the psychology of our society. Once already it caused a civil war. It is not taking root now, and it will never take root."

Yvgeny was determined that Zyuganov's words would hold true. Communism had made the Soviet Union a great power. Capitalism had destroyed it, turned it into an impotent Third World nation adrift without moral compass or dedication to a common, shining goal.

He finished his tea and lifted weights, observing his efforts in a mirror. He'd always been ashamed of his thin, pale, undefined body and the thick glasses he was forced to wear. But since beginning his exercise regimen four months ago, there had been a discernible hardening of his arms and stomach. At least it looked that way to him in the glass. The stale hot air in the apartment caused sweat to run freely down his face, chest, and back. He added an extra weight to each side of the dumbbell, resumed his prone position on the bench, and struggled to lift it. He managed to do it once, lowered it into its stand, got up breathing hard, and posed for the mirror, the way bodybuilders posture during their competitions. He knew he would look funny to others. But in his eyes, his efforts were succeeding. He was readying himself for the great tests he'd been called upon to face.

Beginning today.

An hour later, after a bath, and dressed in his favorite outfit—black suit, pearl-gray shirt, black tie and shoes—Yvgeny Fodorov walked to where he'd parked his battered Lada around the corner, on *Ulitsa Varvarka.* He settled in the driver's seat, pulled a 9-mm semiautomatic pistol from the waistband of his trousers, and placed it on top of a large wrapped package in a thick red shopping bag. Reflecting sunglasses were taken from the glove box and placed on his small nose, the positioning of them carefully checked in the rearview mirror.

The engine came to life with a series of coughs. Yvgeny pulled from the curb, cutting off a Mercedes speeding down *Ulitsa Varvarka*. Its driver, who was speaking on the car phone, leaned on his horn and cursed loudly out the window. Yvgeny placed his right hand on the revolver and smiled. "Go ahead. Make my day," he muttered in English. He'd learned the words from the American actor Clint Eastwood, who'd spoken them in a *Dirty Harry* movie Yvgeny had seen with Sofia. His aversion to all things American didn't extend to the imported gangster and cop movies proliferating in Moscow theaters.

He'd managed to displace his anger of the previous evening by focusing on the day ahead. But as he drove through Moscow, swerving to avoid gaping potholes or to give way to large red-and-white buses, it returned, as it did with regularity these days. Everything he saw caused his belly to churn and his throat to burn. Gone was the Soviet red flag with hammer and sickle, which had once flown proudly over the city, replaced by the Russian red, white, and blue tricolor.

He passed American fast-food outlets with long lines of customers, gaudy billboards touting American products and services, men on every corner holding cell phones to their ears. A traffic light stopped him in front of G.U.M., the department store, which had recently extended its hours to accommodate more of the fashionably dressed women passing through its doors. At another corner, a knot of teenagers, ears pierced, hair colored purple and orange and green, stood in defiant postures, openly smoking marijuana and making fun of passersby.

Yvgeny's anger elevated to fury; he wanted to get out with his gun and blow them away.

As he reached Moscow's northern outskirts and the Yaroslavl Highway, the city's oppressive, humid heat was gradually replaced by cooler air coming through the Lada's open windows. Traffic thinned. His anger abated, replaced by a growing anxiety that caused him to roll his fingertips on the steering wheel, and to hum the melody of an old Stalin-era song, "My Motherland Spreads Far and Wide," over and over.

He'd been driving more than an hour when the cathedral domes of Zagorsk, also known by its pre-revolutionary name of Sergiev, told him he was close to his destination. Once the center of Russian Orthodoxy, Zagorsk still drew thousands of the faithful each year, bearing bottles to fill with holy water.

Yvgeny slowed as he passed a procession of black-shrouded women shuffling slowly along the highway's shoulder. Old fools, he thought. That was the problem with the Communist Party. There were too many old people at its core, feeble, ineffective old people. That was why Yvgeny knew he was important to the party. It needed dedicated youth like him, willing to do whatever was needed to set the nation back on the right track.

He turned onto a crumbling asphalt road and slowed to spare his aging car's shocks and tires. Ten minutes later he left that road to take a narrow dirt lane running through farmland until ending at a river. He stopped beneath a clump of trees and turned off the engine, lit a cigarette, and fixed his eyes on a small cottage at the river's edge. The air was cool and moist. The sound of singing birds merged with the gentle rippling of the water.

He sat there for five minutes, finishing two cigarettes, which he tossed through the open window. If she was watching, she'd probably criticize him for littering the land near her house. If not for that, for something else.

He exited the Lada and stretched against a dull ache in his back. The Lada was no fun to drive for long periods. But that would soon end. He'd been promised. Hopefully a Zhiguli. Red, if he had his say.

After a few deep breaths, Yvgeny opened the passenger door and removed the shopping bag. His back to the cottage, he slipped the weapon into his waistband, secured his jacket over it, and slowly walked to the front door. He peered through the screen, saw no one. He knocked on the door frame. "*Zdrastvuitye?* Mother? Hello?"

He saw her shadow before she came into view. She opened the door, stood back, hand on hip, head cocked, small smile on her lips: "Well, well, look who's here."

"Hello, Mother. I said I was coming."

"That's right. You did. Sorry. Come in. You'll have to excuse the mess. I was working all night. This morning, too." She stepped back to allow him entry.

Yvgeny entered the large, spare room that served as living room, dining room, and kitchen. There were few windows, and no lights were on. It was cool inside, and still.

Vani Fodorov went to the kitchen and busied herself at the sink. Yvgeny stood in the center of the room, unsure of where to move next. She turned. "How have you been?" she asked, wiping her hands on a towel.

"Good. Fine. You?"

"Working hard. I'm finishing a novel."

"Oh?"

"Perhaps you'd like to read it when I'm done."

He didn't respond. Instead, he put the shopping bag down next to a chair and went to an open door at the opposite end of the room. It was his mother's office. A computer screen glowed blue. The desk was piled high with books, some open, some closed. Others were on the floor, surrounding a green office chair. Free-standing bookcases sagged under the weight of the volumes they contained. One wall featured framed photographs.

"Go ahead." His mother had come up behind; the closeness of her voice startled him. "Afraid to enter my capitalistic den?" She laughed.

Yvgeny faced her. "I'm not afraid—of anything."

"Of course not. Look at the photos on the wall. They're some of your favorite people." Her tone was sarcastic.

Yvgeny pushed past his mother into the living room, her laughter following. Then, silence. She came to him and placed her hands on his arms, looked into his eyes. "Yvgeny, Yvgeny, poor Yvgeny. Don't you understand the wonderful thing that has happened to us? We're free now, Yvgeny. Free."

"Free to do what?" he said.

"Free to—"

"Free to starve? Free to let the Americans and the British and all the rich bastards of the world own us? You call that freedom?"

"Yes, I do," Vani said. "You don't remember what it was like under Stalin and Lenin, under the Communists. Your father was arrested and sent to the camps because they didn't like what he wrote. I had to write in secret, with pencil and paper because they refused to register my typewriter and took it away. Don't you see? We're free to be who we are and what we wish to be. You're young, Yvgeny. There is now such promise in Russia for young people."

He guffawed and pulled away.

"Communism is over, Yvgeny. It is finished. Gone. Things are hard because we've never experienced freedom and capitalism. But in time—"

"Capitalism does not fit the flesh and blood, the customs of the psychology of our society, Mother. Once already it caused a civil war. It is not taking root now, and it will never take root."

"Good God," she said, leaning against a table. "You're still spouting that garbage. And look at you. The way you dress. You want to be a Communist? Dress like one, like a Communist peasant content to work for the State. What are you, a gangster now? That suit. Is that what you take from our new freedom, to join a gang? To be a criminal?"

Yvgeny turned from her and clenched his fists, breathed against the heaviness in his chest. He couldn't look at her. She was dressed in a thin white T-shirt; no bra kept her nipples from pressing against the fabric. Her jeans were tight over her lithe figure, American designer jeans with the name on them. She didn't look Russian. She looked to him like some French trollop or American prostitute.

Writing a novel! he thought.

Trash, undoubtedly. Like the articles she and her friends wrote for rags like *Moskovskiy Komsomolets* and *Nezavisimaya Gazeta*. She had such pretensions about her writing. Vani Fodorov idolized the iconoclast Soviet writer Ivan Turgenev, who'd indicted serfdom in his writings and was banished to exile in Europe as a result. Yvgeny's father, also a writer, preferred the writings of Gogol; as a child, Yvgeny sat through nightly dinner table debates of the relative merits of those writers and others.

Yvgeny was a young boy when they took his father away. He didn't understand it then—something about having written things that were illegal. He never saw him again. From the moment his mother told him his father had died, less than a year after he'd been arrested, everything about Vani Fodorov changed in Yvgeny's eyes. New friends seemed always to be at their Moscow flat, secretive people drinking all night and talking in hushed voices, most of them members of the Soviet Writers' Union, of which his mother was an active, enthusiastic member. Some became her lovers, the sounds of their copulating causing him to hold the pillow over his ears.

When the painful process of *perestroika*, the restructuring of the Soviet Communist system, commenced in 1988 under Gorbachev—and *glasnost* followed, allowing free discussion of all issues without fear of State reprisal—Yvgeny again saw his mother change. He was fourteen, a sullen, angry teenager who viewed his now gay and vibrant mother as the cause of all his problems, his lack of friends, slowness in school, and wan, sickly looks.

It was as though she'd been reborn and he had begun his death spiral. They fought. He dropped out of school and stayed away from home for days at a time.

On his seventeenth birthday, Vani confronted him with an ultimatum: either he change his ways and begin to build his life, or he could live elsewhere.

Yvgeny moved in with an older friend, Felix, who shared his views of what was happening all around them in Moscow. Felix earned money by running errands for local mobsters, who promised he would move up in the ranks one day. He introduced Yvgeny to his employers, and they gave him chores to do.

Yvgeny rarely saw his mother during the ensuing five years. She kept the apartment in Moscow, but bought the *dacha* in Zagorsk, where she spent most of her time, returning to the city only when the winter became too foul to enjoy the countryside.

This visit represented the first time they'd seen each other in almost a year. Vani had been surprised when Yvgeny called to say he intended to visit. Had she been totally honest, she would have said that she did not want to see her only child. His involvement with the burgeoning criminal element of Moscow—of every Russian city—disgusted her.

Still, he was flesh and blood. Was he coming to Zagorsk to announce a change of heart, to tell her that he realized the error of his ways and intended to set a new course in his life before it was too late?

"I would love to see you, Yvgeny," she'd said. "Yes. I look forward to it very much."

And now here he was, as defiant as ever, dressed in his silly black suit and mouthing tired Communist clichés.

"Yvgeny," his mother said, "why did you come here today? Would you like to have lunch and talk about pleasant things? You can tell me about what you've been doing with your life. I'll tell you about my novel, what it's about and why I have such high hopes for it." Her laugh was forced. "I suppose you won't agree with its . . . politics . . . but there's much more to it than that. It really isn't a political novel, although there is some. Yvgeny, I would like this to be a happy visit. I haven't seen you in too long a time. You look well. I must admit I do not like that sort of suit, but it's your choice. You are an adult. I've met someone. He's an artist, a very good one." When he said nothing, she added, "I mean I've met someone I'm falling in love with. His name is—"

"I brought you a present," Yvgeny said.

"Oh?" She looked to the red shopping bag on the floor. "Is that it? May I open it?"

"Da."

She removed the wrapped gift from the bag and took it to the kitchen, where she slowly began to undo the green ribbon, out of habit not wanting to cut it, to save it for another day. As she did, her back to him, she said, "It was sweet of you to bring me a gift. I think, Yvgeny, this might be the day we put our lives together again. I mean, as mother and son. There's so much I want to share with you. I was thinking just this morning that you come from the blood of two writers. You showed writing promise in school. I wish you hadn't dropped out, but it isn't too late to go back."

She was as careful and deliberate with the wrapping paper as she had been with the ribbon.

"What would you think if I suggested that we—?"

Her fingers stopped peeling the tape from the wrapping. She sensed that he'd come up behind her, that something was wrong.

She started to turn but never had the opportunity. Yvgeny touched the 9-mm to the base of her skull and pulled the trigger, causing Vani Fodorov's head to erupt in an explosion of blood the color of cardinals.

2

WASHINGTON, D.C.—A FEW DAYS LATER

"I don't care what the Chinese ambassador said, Sandy. The fact is they're trying to do an end-run around the treaty and I'll be damned if they'll get away with it. Put it in the strongest possible terms at the press briefing. Put it in Chinese if you have to. . . . What? You don't speak Chinese? I suggest you remedy that as soon as possible. . . . Sure. Thanks. Check in with me after the briefing."

Joseph Scott hung up on his press secretary and pushed a button on the intercom. "Is Congressman Latham here yet? . . . Good. Send him in."

An aide opened the door, and United States Representative Paul Latham strode into the Oval Office. Scott got to his feet and came around the desk to greet him. "Welcome back, Congressman."

"Thank you, Mr. President."

The two men were tall, but that was where physical similarities ended. Joe Scott was a strong, beefy man, six feet five inches tall and solidly built, with brown hair tinged with red and just the right touch of gray at the temples. Everything was oversized about him; people on the receiving end of his handshakes often commented on the size of his hands.

Paul Latham was six feet tall, but slender in body and face. Although both men needed glasses to read, the president was reluctant to wear them, especially when in public or facing a camera. Latham's half-glasses were perpetually perched at the end of his aquiline nose. "Professorial" was the term often used by the press to describe him, causing him to laugh and say, "If that's true, anybody wearing glasses would automatically be smart. And we all know that's a crock." He looked more professorial than he sometimes spoke.

"Sit down," Scott said, settling into his leather chair and indicating the seat he wanted Latham to take. "Coffee?"

"No, thank you," Latham replied. "It might keep me awake."

"We can't have that. So, Congressman, how did things look to you on your latest jaunt to the riddle wrapped in a mystery inside an enigma?"

"Pretty much as Winnie said it, Mr. President. The Russians may have officially opened up to the rest of the world, but that doesn't translate into letting it all hang out. Depends on who you talk to. Yeltsin's people say everything is fine. But our intelligence people at the embassy have a different take."

18

"I spoke to Yeltsin last night," the president said. "He sounded drunk."

"He doesn't drink anymore since the surgery."

"According to the press releases. How's Ruth?"

"Fine. Mrs. Scott?"

"Complaining that the White House is aging her prematurely. Other than that, she's top-notch. Always asks for you."

The president of the United States and the California congressman went back a long way together. Both Democrats, although not always in agreement, they'd been through the political mill. That Joe Scott would one day run for and win the presidency was never a surprise to his friend. He had a bigger-than-life quality about him, star power that drew people to him, made them want to touch him, lose their hand in his, be the recipient of his engaging smile and fast, firm slap on the back. Paul Latham, eight terms in Congress and going for his ninth, had backed Scott at every step of his rise from Chicago ward politics to the House of Representatives, then on to the Senate and finally, firm possession of the White House.

Latham had been especially helpful a year ago when Scott ran for the presidency. The towering Joe Scott was known as a domestic candidate, comfortable and effective with issues at home, but lacking experience—lacking understanding, according to his opponent—of foreign affairs. Latham's leadership as chairman of the House International Relations Committee, and his special interest in that committee's Subcommittee on Economic Policy and Trade—coupled with his being in the enviable position of having Scott's ear—helped balance the voters' perception of the man who would become president.

Naturally, there was speculation that Scott would nominate Paul Latham as his secretary of state. But once Scott became president, there were other debts to be paid. The nomination went instead to the distinguished international attorney Jacob Baumann, who was easily confirmed by the Senate, and who'd done so far what most Washington pundits felt was a credible job.

What most people didn't know was that President Scott had approached Latham first about the job, and that Latham had politely declined. The odd fact was that Paul Latham loved his position in the House of Representatives. Chairing a committee as important as International Relations, with the particular emphasis he placed upon economic policy and trade, was immensely fulfilling to the former college professor, attorney, and think-tank advisor.

"I appreciate the confidence behind the offer, Joe," he'd said, "but it's not for me. Go with Baumann. He's a good man, will sail through confirmation and do the job for you."

That was the last time he'd called his old friend "Joe." From that moment on it was "Mr. President," even when they shared quiet moments together and the president suggested Latham drop the formality. Formality, ritual, and precedence were important to the congressman from California.

"So, Mr. Chairman, tell me about your trip," the president said.

Latham pulled a sheet of paper from the inside breast pocket of his conservatively cut blue suit and consulted it while giving the president a thumbnail report, ending with "The single thing I found most disturbing, Mr. President, was what our intelligence people told me at a briefing just before I left. It's their opinion that an unholy alliance is being forged between the Communists and the *mafiya*. All those out of work KGB types are becoming Russian mobsters. The ranks are swelling."

Scott's eyebrows went up. "Why would the Communists and the blackbread mob join hands, for Christ's sake?"

A small shrug from Latham. "Desperation. The Communists are becoming increasingly desperate while Yeltsin bullies the economy into some semblance of success. He may be the duly elected leader of Russia, but he runs things like he was still a Communist bureaucrat. A few embassy people feel there's a calculated reason for the Russian mob to hook up with the Communists. Here it is: Yeltsin's biggest problem is crime. You can't do business there without paying off some goon or gang. They call it *krisha*. 'Cover.' Built into the budget like rent and paper clips. The more crime, goes the theory, the harder for Yeltsin to make things work. The bigger he fails and the worse off people become, the better the chances for the Communists in the next election."

Scott grunted. "You buy the theory?"

"It's as good as any I've heard lately."

"The FBI's East European unit briefed Justice a couple of days ago. Here's a synopsis." He slid it across the desk to Latham.

"Can I take this?"

"Sure. Anything devious going on over on the Hill I should brace for?"

Latham smiled. "I'm sure there is, Mr. President, but I haven't been back long enough to tap in. If there is, you'll be the first to know, as usual."

"Glad you're back, Paul. Staying in town a few days?"

"Exactly. Just a few. I'll be heading back home for the election."

"If you need anything, let me know."

"Things are good there," Latham said, standing.

His district in Northern California, which included a large area of San Francisco, was known as one of the more solid districts in Congress. There had been an occasional threat to his reelection over the years, but nothing to cause him sleepless nights. Still, you couldn't take anything for granted. The voters wanted to see you on your home turf, press the flesh, hear your answers at town hall meetings and on TV debates with your opponent. Local issues. That was what it was all about. The minute you lost sight of it, you lost elections. Paul Latham believed in what President Harry Truman once said about running for office: "When there's a hundred people applauding you, look for the one who isn't, and find out why."

"Thanks for seeing me, Mr. President," Latham said. "You're looking good. Rested."

Scott laughed and came to where Latham stood. "I wish I could say the same to you. You look like you need two days of sleep."

"As usual, you're right. I—"

The door opened, causing Scott to scowl at the intruder. It was a senior aide. "What is it?" the president asked.

"Sir, this just came in. It's . . . very important." He crossed the room and handed Scott a piece of paper.

The president frowned as he read it, lowered his head, and mumbled an obscenity.

"Mr. President?" Latham said.

"Thank you," Scott said to the aide. "I want the crisis

group together in a half hour. Fifteen minutes. Get Sandy in here now!"

The aide left the Oval Office. "From Hopkins in Ops," Scott said, handing the paper to Paul Latham. He read its terse message: URGENT. AIR FORCE AIRCRAFT CARRYING SECRETARY BAUMANN AND GROUP REPORTED DOWN IN CHINA. CAUSE UNKNOWN. INITIAL REPORT NO SURVIVORS.

3

THE NATIONAL CATHEDRAL—FIVE
DAYS LATER

Secretary of State Jacob Baumann's funeral was held in
the cathedral's tenth-of-a-mile-long nave. It was attended
by six hundred people, two dozen of whom eulogized him.

The religious portion of the service was conducted by
the Right Reverend George St. James, bishop of Washington and dean of the cathedral, imposing in his purple,
black, and white clerical garments, a pectoral cross resting comfortably on his chest. St. James spoke directly to
God on behalf of Baumann's soul.

Those who stepped forward wearing secular attire
directed their flowery comments to Baumann's family,
friends, and to the television cameras and sizable press
contingent among the mourners. In Washington, D.C.,
you grabbed your photo ops where you found them.

Members of President Joe Scott's cabinet spoke, as did leaders of the House and Senate, and close personal friends of the deceased secretary.

"Go in peace," St. James said, sending the temporarily bereaved out of the cathedral and back to their busy lives. Baumann would be buried in the presence of a small group of people, immediate family and specially invited friends, which included Congressman Paul Latham and his wife, Ruth, a short, trim, neat brunette with well-turned calves, testimony to her pre-Latham life as a dancer. It was virtually impossible for her to wear anything that didn't look good on her.

Baumann's body was lowered into the ground with appropriate ceremony. The honored few left the gravesite and walked across the peaceful, verdant cemetery to waiting limos. Baumann's wife, Patricia, guided Latham away from the group.

"Anything I can do, just call," Latham said.

"I know that, Paul. You've been a good friend."

"There'll be hearings into the crash," he said, seeking words of encouragement to offer. "I thought after Ron Brown died, the air force would get its act together and upgrade the navigational equipment on its planes. It's been over four years now. It's just not happening fast enough. If Jake's death has any meaning, it will prompt them to—"

"Paul," Patricia Baumann said, hand on his arm, "I know that. What I wanted to say was that if the president asks you to replace Jake as secretary of state, I hope you'll accept. It's what he would have wanted."

"The president hasn't offered anything, Pat."

"But he will. That's what I hear. All I ask is that if he does, you seriously consider it. For Jake. Please?"

"I will."

"So much good has been initiated by the Scott administration. It would be a tragedy if that work isn't carried forward."

"I understand. I'll keep in touch."

"I know you will, Paul. Thanks."

They hugged, and climbed into their respective limousines.

"Are you going back to the Hill?" Ruth Latham asked her husband as they headed for Washington.

"Yes. I have a committee hearing at one. I'll be late tonight. Two fund-raisers to drop in on, and that reception for Giles Broadhurst."

"When does the president get back from the G-Seven meeting?"

"Tonight. He hated to miss Jake's service. I'm glad the veep was there."

"Will you have a chance to speak with the president tonight about—?"

"I don't think so." Latham visually confirmed that the partition between the driver and passenger compartments was closed. He whispered to his wife, "I promise, Ruth, I won't make a decision about the nomination until we've had a good long stretch of time to discuss it. I won't do anything without your support."

"I know." She managed a small smile and gripped his hand. "We'll talk."

Congressman Latham's administrative office was in the Rayburn House Office Building, south of the Capitol Building at Independence and First Street, N.W., built in 1965, the newest of three buildings accommodating the offices of the 435 elected members of the House of Representatives. Shortly after its completion, *New York Times* architectural critic, Ada Louise Huxtable, described it as "profligate, elephantine . . . the apotheosis of humdrum," concluding her review with "to be both dull and vulgar may be an achievement of sorts."

Paul Latham usually agreed when friends commented negatively about the building's jumble of columns, pediments, cornucopias, and other marble overkill. But the Rayburn Building, named after famed Texas House Speaker Sam Rayburn—whose statue greeted you when you came through the main entrance—provided the most modern facilities of the three buildings. The statue of Rayburn had originally been installed with its back to the entrance, perhaps to mirror the former Speaker's disdain for ostentatious, expensive, and complicated architecture. (The Rayburn Building was one of the most costly public buildings ever constructed in the nation's capitol.) But enough people complained about the deceased Speaker's apparent rudeness, and he was turned.

Because Latham had sufficient seniority, he enjoyed one of the building's 169 suites, giving him and his staff room in which to function. His suite was situated on the north side of the building, its splendid view of the Capitol more than making up for the suite's drab, tan walls, the color of all offices on the north and west sides of the building. East- and south-side offices were painted robin's egg blue. It was the rule. Why? No one knew. The Congressional Building Committee operated behind closed doors, answering to no one.

"How was the funeral?" Bob Mondrian asked as he followed his boss into the imposing office.

"Tough," Latham replied. He tossed his jacket on a

leather couch and, standing, scanned papers neatly arranged on his desk. Mondrian hung the jacket on an antique coat tree.

"What's this?" Latham asked, holding up a sheet of paper.

Mondrian came around the desk and looked over Latham's shoulder. "Jack Emerson brought it over this morning," he said. Emerson was staff director of the International Relations Committee, chaired by Paul Latham.

"Where did *he* get it?" Latham asked.

"Kelley at Ops and Rights." International Operations and Human Rights was one of five subcommittees under control of the full committee.

Latham sat heavily and directed a stream of air through pursed lips. "The Commies won't give it up, will they?" he said.

"If the analysis is correct," Mondrian said.

Robert Mondrian had been Latham's chief of staff for twelve years. He was considered by other congressional staffers to be one of the best in the House, bright and insightful, hard-nosed when necessary, conciliatory at other times, and fiercely loyal to his boss, one of the most powerful members of Congress because of his chairmanship of the International Relations Committee.

Mondrian was divorced, his marriage a casualty of the often insane demands of the job. The father of two teenage daughters, he was a short, squat, swarthy man who'd suffered male pattern baldness at an early age, and did nothing to compensate for it. His square build rendered suits shapeless; he never took offense at jibes by fellow staffers that he'd been voted worst-dressed by a nonpartisan House panel.

Prior to joining Latham as chief of staff, Mondrian had worked for the Export-Import Bank in its international business development division, and had put in six years as a Washington lobbyist. He'd been around, and knew how to get things done on the Hill. More important, he knew how to keep them from happening. And he was fully aware of his importance to the legislative process. Every survey of Washington lobbyists confirmed that their number-one target was always congressional staff members, so potent was their input into their elected bosses' decisions.

Latham's appointment secretary, Marge Edwards, entered the office. "Good morning, Paul," she said, handing him his schedule for the rest of the day. Latham glanced at it. "How did this Asian-American group get on the slate?" he asked.

Mondrian answered: "Just five minutes, Paul. A quick give-and-take, a shot or two, they're gone. They carry a lot of weight back home—in California."

"All right." He looked at the antique grandfather clock, a gift many years ago from his mother-in-law. One o'clock. He was due at his committee meeting.

They turned their attention to side-by-side color TV sets. One was tuned to C-SPAN 1, offering gavel-to-gavel coverage of the House of Representatives. The other, C-SPAN 2, carried debate from the Senate. Mondrian turned down the sound on the House, and boosted volume on C-SPAN 2. Republican Senate minority whip Frank Connors, a three-term senator from Southern California, had stepped into the well: "It is no secret to any of my colleagues in this body, on both sides of the aisle, that while my personal admiration and respect for Jacob

Baumann was great, my view of this administration's foreign policy, as carried out by the secretary of state, was not as generous. The president will soon nominate someone to replace Jake Baumann. I take this opportunity to extend my sincerest sympathy to Secretary Baumann's fine family—and to put the White House on notice that the soft policy generously granted our enemies in this volatile world will not be allowed to be repeated. . . ."

"Great timing," Mondrian said. "Baumann isn't even cold."

"The meeting," Marge said. As she left the office, both men cast admiring glances at her nicely turned body, and long, shapely legs extending from a black leather miniskirt.

Latham grabbed his jacket from the coat tree and headed for the door, saying over his shoulder, "Get me a list of who'll be at Broadhurst's reception tonight. And check up on Molly, see if she moved into the page dorm. She was supposed to this afternoon." Molly, the Lathams' youngest daughter, had been accepted as a House page for that session of Congress. Because he was a prudent man, believing in protocol, he'd asked another member, close to the House leadership, to arrange for Molly's appointment. In return, that member's son was granted an internship on Latham's International Relations Committee. *Entre nous.* The way of the House.

He went to the Rayburn Building's basement, where the subway connected all House and Senate office buildings, and with the Capitol itself. He was the only elected representative in the open car, sharing it with a dozen tourists. A woman recognized him: "You're Congressman Latham."

30

Latham grinned, said, "For better or worse. Enjoying your visit to D.C.?"

"Sure are," her husband replied, " 'cept for the heat. Hottest damn place I've ever been."

The short ride ended and Latham bounded off, papers under his arm, a farewell wave for his fellow passengers. A few minutes later he came through the door of H 139, on the southwest corner of the Capitol's ground floor in a cluster of House committee offices. Jack Emerson was waiting.

"Sorry I'm late," Latham said. "The funeral."

"Everybody seems to be running late today," Emerson replied. He was a veteran of House and Senate committee staffs, minority or majority, depending on which party dominated Congress during any given period. Latham knew he'd hired a top staff director in Emerson; the young man's reputation was pristine.

"Did Bob give you that report from Russia?"

"Yes. I have it with me. It's shocking—if true. Is it? True?"

"No reason not to think so," Emerson answered. "The four murders happened, Mr. Chairman. That's fact. All four were members of the old Soviet Writers' Union. Still exists, different name—Russian Writers' Union."

"All of them shot?"

"Execution style, according to the report."

"Why the assumption it was the Communists? Sounds more like the mob. I don't recognize any of these names, Jack."

"No reason you should, Mr. Chairman. None of the four were widely published. Wannabe writers, I suppose. Mr. Stassi wants to hold hearings on it."

Congressman Mario Stassi, a Republican, was the

31

ranking minority member of both the International Operations and Human Rights Subcommittee and Latham's International Relations Committee.

"It doesn't warrant a hearing," Latham said.

"I told Stu that," Emerson said, referring to Stassi's subcommittee staff director.

"And?"

"He says Mr. Stassi is adamant. He's talking about going to the floor to ask for a resolution calling for hearings on human rights abuse in Russia. Widen the scope, but use these four killings as the pivot."

"I'll talk to him. He still wants the tariff reduction for that manufacturer in his district. If he pushes for hearings, he can kiss that good-bye. Who are we meeting with this afternoon?"

"Mr. Brazier's advisors. They have reservations about some of the provisions the policy and trade staff want included in the bill."

"Can't staff resolve it?"

"We've tried, Mr. Chairman. I think it needs your direct input at this point. Frankly, I don't see it getting out of subcommittee without you putting on the screws."

"Are they here?"

"Yes."

"Then let's get on with it."

An hour later, Latham rode the subway back to his office. He'd no sooner arrived when Molly called.

"Hi, sweets," he said. "You get moved in all right?"

"Uh-huh."

"Sorry I couldn't help. Mom get you settled?"

"Uh-huh. Are you coming with us to the shore this weekend?"

"I can't, sweets. All tied up. But you and Mom enjoy

yourself. Maybe in a few weeks when things slow down."

"I understand. I think I told you before, Dad, but I really appreciate your getting me into the page program. It'll look great on college applications."

"And it's good real-world experience. Or as close as Washington ever gets to the real world. Besides, I'll be able to see you every day."

She laughed. "So you can keep your eye on me."

"That's my job, isn't it? I'm your father."

Bob Mondrian poked his head through the open door. "The A-A group is here, Paul."

"Got to run, Molly," Latham said. "Picture time with some voters. Love you."

"Love you, Dad."

He spent fifteen minutes with his Asian-American visitors, the session ending with a photo taken on the Capitol steps. He had just settled back behind his desk when Marge Edwards appeared. "Here's the guest list for Mr. Broadhurst's reception tonight."

Latham perused it. Quickly. "Oh, Mac Smith will be there. Good. Time we scheduled a little tennis to let me get even for the last match. Nice man, wicked backhand. Probably illegal. Thanks, Marge. Everything good with you? You don't look happy."

Her lovely, full mouth broke into a smile. "Considering my love life is on hold, everything's great."

"I thought you were dating that exec from Brazier's office."

"Anatoly? I am. I mean, we go out now and then. But nothing heavy. Russian guys are strange."

Latham laughed. "They come out of a very different experience, Marge."

"I know. Which makes them strange. Hear from Martin?"

Latham's son, Martin, who now crafted wood furniture in upstate New York, as distant geographically and philosophically from politics as he could take himself, had briefly dated Marge when she first came to work for Latham. Latham wasn't especially pleased with that arrangement, convinced that Martin had done it deliberately to nettle him. But he did nothing to get in the way of the relationship, which ended abruptly two months after it had commenced when Martin moved away. Being dumped, as Marge put it, had upset her. But she had seemed to bounce back quickly, much to Latham's relief.

"Yes, as a matter of fact. He'll be in town for a week."

"Say hello for me."

"Say hello yourself. He'll be stopping by the office."

Don't count on it, she thought. She said, "Okay. I will."

"Well," Latham said, "any time you want to vent, come on in, close the door, and let it all hang out, as they say."

"I just may do that."

"By the way, Marge—now that Molly's going to be here on the Hill every day, and I never know where I'll be, I thought you wouldn't mind keeping an eye on her. You know, sort of be the one she can come to if she has a problem, and I'm not available."

"Happy to, Paul. Don't worry about it."

Latham thought about Marge Edwards after she left.

She'd been his scheduler for almost two years. It was one of the toughest jobs on the Hill, keeping track of members' hectic days and nights, fielding requests for "just a minute of his time," and managing the office as well, juggling the $900,000 budget allotted each House member.

Most of Latham's colleagues complained about their appointment secretaries, not because they didn't do a good job; they blamed them for their busy schedules. A no-win situation was the way Latham viewed it.

Marge Edwards was good at her difficult job, and Latham knew it. He also knew firsthand how volatile she could be when under personal stress. Her emotions seemed always to be on the edge, or out in the open, and he'd ended up becoming her father-confessor on more than one occasion. He never resented that additional duty. Marge reminded him in some ways of his oldest daughter, whom he seldom saw these days.

Did Marge view *him* as a father figure? He assumed she did.

Did counseling her about her personal trials and travails, including some highly personal aspects of her life, provide him with a psychological substitution for the time he didn't have for his own daughter? Help assuage his guilt?

He hoped not.

He just wished he had more time to figure it out.

4

Annabel Reed-Smith pulled the blue Chevy Caprice up to the curb in front of the National Democratic Club on Ivy Street, S.E. The Republican hangout on the Hill was the Capitol Hill Club on First Street, S.E. The two clubs were closer in geographic proximity than political philosophy, but Mac commented that the top-shelf liquor served in both was distinctly nonpartisan.

"How late will you be?" Annabel asked her husband.

"A few hours," Mackensie Smith said. "I'll be home before you, unless the concert drives you out early."

"Not likely. The National Symphony seldom disappoints."

Smith smiled, leaned over, and kissed his wife on the cheek. It was one of those moments that occurred for him with regularity since marrying Annabel Reed. He was immensely grateful to her for having said yes to his proposal.

* * *

They were practicing attorneys when first introduced at a British Embassy party, she specializing in matrimonial law, he one of Washington's most respected criminal lawyers.

Annabel had never married. (How could this be? Mac mused after that initial introduction, and a long, pleasant conversation over glasses of white wine.) Her face was open and lovely, framed by hair the color of burnished copper. Her five-foot-seven-inch figure was nicely proportioned. Most appealing at that first meeting was her ready, wide smile and sincere interest in everything he said. An impressive package, Mac thought at first.

No. More than that.

Annabel Reed was quite simply the most beautiful woman he'd met since losing his wife and son years ago in a Beltway head-on collision, a drunken Agriculture Department employee crossing the line to take from him everything that was good and precious.

That defining moment in his life changed Mac Smith forever. His passion for criminal law dimmed, and he began to question whether he should continue to pursue it. What would he do instead? Retire? Politics? Teach? The last became increasingly appealing.

At the time of their introduction, Annabel, too, had started to wonder whether the practice of law, especially her emotionally wrenching specialty of divorce and child custody, was worth the pain. Deciding to become a lawyer had been a pragmatic move. Prior to law school, she'd been an art major, focusing on the pre-Columbian. Launching a career in the art world as an assistant curator in some small museum—if she could even find such an entry-level job—would not, she knew, provide the material things she wanted at that stage of her life.

Law proved to be a good choice in that regard. Her practice flourished, she surrounded herself with well-chosen, lovely things, and eventually there was money in the bank for her future, no matter what it held.

But there was, at once, an emptiness inside. She suspected it could be filled only by following her dream: opening a gallery specializing in pre-Columbian art. Now that she was financially secure, that goal was certainly reachable.

After Mac and Annabel fell in love—it happened surprisingly fast, considering they were lawyers—and as their conversations dug deeper into their inner selves, their mutual dissatisfaction with their profession increasingly took center stage. One night, over succulent Maryland crab cakes at La Chaumière, they made some fateful decisions.

"I just feel that since I don't want to do it anymore," Mac said, "I can't do justice to my clients."

"Of course you can't. I feel the same way."

"What's your dream, Annabel?"

"To own a gallery. To surround myself with artifacts I love."

"Might that include *this* artifact?"

"Mackensie Smith?"

"Yes."

"Hmmmm."

"I've been offered a teaching position at GW. In the law school, of course."

"Of course."

"I don't know much about art," Mac said. "But I know even less about pre-Columbian art."

She laughed. "You don't have to know anything about it. *I* have to know about it. All you have to know is what your law students need to know."

"But I wouldn't want to appear stupid about what you do each day."

"The one thing you could never appear to be, Mackensie Smith, is stupid. About anything."

"Thanks for the vote of confidence."

"It isn't that. I believe that if two people are satisfied with their individual lives, they stand a better chance of being satisfied in their relationship."

"No argument. But you're leaving the law. I'll still be involved with it. Granted, as a teacher, not an advocate. But your life will revolve around art, and I'll—"

"Mac, I think what we each do with the rest of our lives doesn't mean a damn thing, as long as we respect what it is that each of us does."

"I can be cantankerous."

"I can be difficult. But adorable."

"The older I get, the more liberal I become despite knowing I'm supposed to become more conservative because I have more to conserve."

"And?"

"And, I become more accepting of the human condition with each passing year."

"I like that."

"Annabel."

"Yes, Mackensie?"

"Would you consider a contract? Would you consider marrying me?"

"Be more direct."

"More direct? All right. *Will* you marry me?"

"Of course."

"Why?"

She sat back and laughed. "*Why?* You sound like you're back in the courtroom. *Why?* Because I love you, about-to-be former counselor and soon-to-be distinguished professor of law at George Washington University, pipe, bow tie, and all, I assume. I love the image."

"You're beautiful, Annabel."

"Thank you. You're handsome."

"Thank you. Let's do it. You open your art gallery—with my enthusiastic encouragement—and I'll become a mentor of future Supreme Court justices."

"It's a deal." They shook hands across the table.

"And we'll be married. Soon."

"Of course."

"Of course."

Annabel watched her husband enter the building and experienced her own twinge of gratitude. Although Mac was decisive and self-assured, he moved his angular, fit, and lanky frame with appealing modesty. Entering a room on his arm was always a pleasure.

She pulled away from the curb and headed for a night of Mozart, Haydn, and Bruckner at the Kennedy Center. But she was on his mind as Mac came through the door of the National Democratic Club and went to the third-floor O'Neill Room. "Mac, hello," Congressman Paul Latham said as he spotted his friend.

"Congressman," Smith said, shaking Latham's hand. "I see you're still spending your life on airplanes."

"Fortunately, planes with more up-to-date navigation systems than Jake Baumann's. Did you know him?"

"We shook hands a few times. Any word on who the president will nominate to replace him?"

"Your guess is as good as mine."

"I doubt that," Smith said, smiling.

Latham went to greet other arrivals, leaving Smith to make his way to where the reason for the gathering, Giles Broadhurst, talked with well-wishers. Next to Broadhurst was an attractive, big-boned blond woman in a yellow suit. She spotted Smith approaching and came directly to him, hand outstretched. "Professor Smith," she said. "I heard you were coming. How great to see you."

"Always nice to see one of my favorite students again. How have you been, Jessica?"

"Terrific. I'm coming with Giles to the CIA."

"Really? Congratulations. Life there will be a lot different than over at ITC."

At the U.S. International Trade Commission, Giles Broadhurst headed up its Office of Executive and International Liaison. He was leaving that position to establish a new division within the CIA, devoted to using the spy agency's intelligence-gathering ability to enhance America's overseas industrial competitiveness. In actuality, such a division had been in operation for years, ever since the Cold War ended. But the spy agency had recently gotten caught on two occasions doing industrial espionage, and decided it would be politic to, as Le Carré put it, come in from the cold.

"I'm braced for it," Jessica Belle said brightly.

Smith laughed. "At least you won't be spying on spies anymore. Makes sense, using our intelligence agency to help American industry—legitimately."

"That's the way Giles sees it. Me, too, of course. How's Mrs. Smith?"

"Tip-top."

She plucked a miniature quiche from a fast-moving tray, took a tiny bite, and said, "Are you still teaching the class?" She'd been a nonmatriculated student in a special six-session course Smith had taught on the difference between systems of jurisprudence in the United States and Russia, a recent and compelling interest of his.

"No."

"Then I was lucky I took it when I did. I learned a lot."

"Glad to hear it. That's what you were there for."

Broadhurst joined them, looking every bit the academic he was: floppy red-and-white bow tie, natural-shoulder tweed jacket despite the city's heat, modified crew cut, and horn-rimmed glasses. He was considerably shorter than Mac Smith and Jessica Belle, and had a tendency to bounce on his toes while speaking.

Jessica introduced the men.

"My pleasure," Giles Broadhurst said. "Jess says you taught her everything she knows."

"Fortunately, that's not true," Smith replied. "Congratulations on the new post. I've been reading about it, followed the House hearings pretty closely."

Broadhurst launched into a discourse on why such an economic intelligence gathering division was officially needed, and what he hoped to accomplish. His youthful enthusiasm was pleasing to Smith. This was a smart guy, Smith knew, as evidenced by what he'd crammed into his forty-five years—attorney, Ph.D. in economics, a master's in sociology. Quite a résumé.

Others gathered about Broadhurst, freeing Smith to head for the bar, where he ordered a single-barrel bourbon and soda and wandered to an unoccupied corner to enjoy it. As he sipped, he was able to observe the hundred or so people milling about the large room. What a remarkable city, he thought, politics its major industry and seemingly only topic of interest at such gatherings. Along with a little sex and real estate. He wished he'd gone to the concert with Annabel. He'd reached a point in his life where the sort of intrigues routinely played out in Washington didn't hold the interest they once did. Annabel was intriguing enough to last him the rest of his life.

He checked his watch. Another half hour, say hello to a few more people, and he could make his escape, go home and walk Rufus, who'd appreciate the gesture, and wait with the Great blue Dane for Annabel to return.

He was considering a refill from the bar when three latecomers arrived. Smith recognized the group's leader from his picture on the cover of newsmagazines and on television. He also knew a few things about the man, learned from Paul Latham.

His name was Warren Brazier, out of Northern California, one of the country's richest and most influential business leaders and a Latham backer since Latham's first run for Congress sixteen years ago.

But Brazier's notoriety was not limited to the billions he'd amassed from his far-flung industrial empire. He'd become a potent political force in America. There was constant speculation that he would one day use his wealth to launch a third political party, à la Perot, although his denials were consistent, and forceful, like everything else he did. Those close to him were quick to point out that Warren Brazier reveled in his behind-the-scenes power, supporting elected officials in whom he believed, and devoting energy—more important, money— to ridding the nation of others whose political philosophy butted heads with his own.

Brazier was a small man, almost diminutive. Smith judged him to be no taller than five feet four, five-five at best. But he exuded largeness. He was accompanied by two younger men, whom Mac took in with interest. One was clearly not American. Eastern European, perhaps, judging from the cut of his suit and hair. The other man had the distinct look of government; FBI? INS?

Brazier went directly to Congressman Latham. He laughed at something Brazier said. After a few seconds of banter, Latham looked past Brazier to where Mac stood and waved for him to join them.

"Mac Smith, say hello to Warren Brazier."

"Mr. Brazier. A pleasure."

Brazier took Mac's outstretched hand and shook it with energy. The industrialist's smile displayed good, strong white teeth, made more dazzling against a muddy tan. "The pleasure is mine," Brazier said.

"Mac was this city's top defense lawyer," Latham said. "Get in big trouble, call Mac Smith."

"*Was?* What do you do now, Mr. Smith?"

"Teach law."

"Where?"

"George Washington University."

"Well, all I can say is I'm glad I didn't have any reason to meet you in your earlier career. I've devoted my life to staying out of trouble."

"And staying clear of lawyers," Mac said.

"That, too."

"It was nice meeting you, Mr. Brazier," Mac said. To Latham: "I have to run, Paul. Another commitment."

"How's your stroke these days?" Latham asked.

"My stroke? Oh, tennis?"

"Yes. Steal some time this weekend?"

44

"Sure."

"I'll call."

"Look forward to it."

"Play golf?" Brazier asked Smith.

"No."

"Shame. Thought we could put together a foursome."

"I'll teach him," Latham said. "Safe home, Mac."

As Mac turned to leave, he glanced at the young men standing slightly behind Brazier. Their faces were blank, lacking affect. Humorless young men, Smith thought as he snaked through the crowd to say good-bye to Jessica Belle and Giles Broadhurst. Unpleasant young men.

Mac took Rufus for a long walk that night after returning to the house he and Annabel shared in Foggy Bottom, near the exciting Kennedy Center, the infamous Watergate complex, the enigmatic State Department, and Mac's benevolent employer, George Washington. As usually happened, he fell into a dialogue with the dog—he considered it a dialogue despite its one-way nature—about many things on his mind, glancing about from time to time to make sure his conversation with an oversized canine wasn't being observed.

The walk lasted a half hour, ample time for Smith to make all the points he wished to make without argument from the Dane. That's what made Rufus "Great," he thought. Once back in the house, he poured himself a brandy and turned on the television set to CNN. Rufus sprawled at his feet.

President Scott's arrival back in Washington from the G-Seven meeting in France dominated the news. Scott gave a brief statement at the foot of Air Force One's boarding stairs, stressing the need for the United States to become a full partner in the burgeoning global economy of which it was an intrinsic part, despite those who would wish otherwise.

Mac smacked his lips and shifted position in the red leather chair. The president was an impressive speaker, which had served him well during his campaign for the White House. Mac had voted for him, but not without reservations. Scott's Republican opponent, the governor of Texas, was a good man with a number of views with which Smith agreed. Still, Scott possessed a leadership quality the law professor considered important in moving the country forward. That Paul Latham, for whom Smith had nothing but unbridled respect and personal fondness, believed fervently in Scott helped tip the scales in the Democrat's favor.

A reporter asked the president whether he'd given more thought to who would replace Jacob Baumann as secretary of state.

Scott said, "I can't give it more thought because I'm always thinking about it."

"Who's on the list?" another reporter asked.

"I'll have an announcement soon." He started to walk away from the cluster of microphones.

"Congressman Latham still your first choice?" he was asked.

The president leaned back and said into the mikes, "He'd be a great one, wouldn't he?"

Annabel arrived home and gave her husband a lingering kiss on the lips.

"How was the concert?" Mac asked.

"Wonderful, although Bruckner takes some getting used to."

"Brandy?" Mac asked.

"Love some. I'll get changed."

Mac joined her in the bedroom. They returned to the study in pajamas and robes and toasted each other, as was their custom: "To us."

"How was the reception?" she asked.

"Typical. I'm impressed with Broadhurst. Paul was there."

"And how is he?"

"Fine. We're trying to schedule a tennis match this weekend."

"Sounds like fun. You beat him last time."

"Barely. Paul's benefactor, Warren Brazier, was there, too."

"You met him?"

"Yeah. Pleasant enough guy, although I suspect he can turn on being pleasant when it doesn't pose any threat to him. He had two dour young guys with him. Why do young people today have such trouble smiling?"

"I suppose because they aren't happy."

"Why aren't they happy?"

"You'll have to ask them. I am."

"Happy?"

"Very. You?"

"Happier than usual. Taking a sabbatical this semester was a stroke of genius."

She laughed. "You're so modest."

"Realistic. I'm really looking forward to the project, the trip to Russia, all of it."

Smith had been granted a sabbatical to research and further develop his course on the differences between the American and Russian justice systems, especially in light of Russia's halting, painful struggle to democratize. Accompanied by Annabel, he and a half-dozen other law professors from around the country were scheduled to take a three-week trip to Russia in October, during which Mac and his colleagues would meet with Russian lawyers, judges, and bureaucrats charged with bringing the system in line with the nation's desperate need for legal reform.

"I'm excited, too," she said. "Want to practice?"

"Sure."

"Vy govoritye pa angliski?"

"Ya nye govoryu pa russki."

"Not bad," she said.

"We'll have to learn more Russian than that before we go. Asking whether I speak English and saying you don't speak Russian won't hack it."

She giggled. "We'll get by. You and me, we go to bedski now?"

"Bedski? To sleepski?"

"Nyet. To fool aroundski."

"Da. You betski."

Communicating those needs—in any language—had never been a problem for Mr. and Mrs. Smith.

5

Mac Smith and Congressman Paul Latham met for their tennis match at seven o'clock Saturday morning at Mt. Vernon College, on Foxhall Road. Ted Koppel and Maria Shriver were playing on the adjacent court. Latham and Shriver eked out victories.

"I should say I let you win," Smith said, "your being a congressman and all. But I didn't."

"That's good to hear. We should do this more often, then." They walked to their cars.

"How about coming back to the house for some breakfast?" Latham asked.

"Thought I'd grab something at home," Mac said. "With Annabel. She was sleeping when I left."

"Ruth and Molly are down at the shore for the weekend," Latham said. "I'm tied up this afternoon and tomorrow. Sure I can't entice you? I make a world-class omelette, Mac. Besides, there's something I'd like to discuss with you."

"All right. I'll call Annabel from there."

The Latham family home in Washington was one of the more modest houses in the predominantly wealthy Foxhall section of the city, north of Georgetown and Glover Park. When he'd first come to Washington as a freshman congressman from California, Latham rented a small apartment on Capitol Hill, seeing Ruth and the kids only on occasional weekend trips home, and during congressional recesses. But as his personal finances grew along with his political clout, they purchased the Foxhall house and virtually made it their permanent home, keeping the house in Northern California and adding to their real estate holdings later by purchasing a two-bedroom condo on the Maryland shore. Paul Latham had not become rich on his congressional salary of $133,600. But, as he sometimes said, "We're not missing any meals."

After calling Annabel to tell her he'd be home in an hour, Smith settled at the kitchen table with a cup of coffee while Latham put together the makings of a cheese and mushroom omelette.

"Where are you off to next?" Smith asked. "Good coffee."

"Thanks. California. Do a little politicking. Ruth's coming with me."

"What about Molly?"

"She's now officially in the House page program. Living in the page dorm."

"Good for her," Mac said.

"Yeah. She's a good kid. Wish I saw more of her."

Latham served them and joined Mac at the table. After

50

tasting his breakfast—"You're right, Paul. Olympic-class omelette"—Smith said, "There's something you wanted to discuss with me?"

"That's right. I've only shared this with Ruth and a few close advisors. It'll stay in this kitchen?"

"If you've shared it with others, I can't promise that. Ben Franklin had it right: Three people can keep a secret if two of them are dead. It won't come from me, Paul."

"The president wants to nominate me to replace Jake Baumann as secretary of state."

Smith took another bite of omelette. "I hope you weren't hoping to surprise me, Paul. You haven't."

Latham laughed.

"The bigger question is whether you'll accept."

"I have to make that decision this afternoon. I'm meeting with the president at five."

"You're still undecided?"

"Not really. Ruth's behind me if I decide to do it."

"What's keeping you from just saying you will?"

"I don't know. The Senate confirmation process can be tough. You heard what Clarence Thomas said the other day when asked whether he'd consider becoming chief justice."

"One confirmation process was enough for a lifetime."

"That's right."

"You aren't concerned, are you, that you wouldn't be confirmed?"

"A lawyer asks me that question? Since when is anything certain? Never been surprised by a jury?"

"Too many times. Well, Paul, all I can say is that if you decide to say yes, the country's foreign affairs will be in exceptionally good hands."

"Thanks. Mac, would you consider being my counsel if I'm nominated?"

"At your confirmation hearing?"

"Yes."

"Why me?"

"Stature. You don't carry a brief for any party, as far as I know. You're my friend. That's why."

"I'm not sure I'd have the time, Paul."

"I thought you were on sabbatical."

"I am, and never busier. Annabel and I head for Russia in October. Three weeks there. And a ton of book research."

"I understand."

"That's not to say I couldn't be your counsel. From where I sit, you'll breeze through. Your staff will do all the preliminary work. All I'd have to do is sit there and look lawyerly."

"Does that mean you will?"

"What that means, Paul, is that I'll think about it, run it by Annabel, mull it over. But I won't start that process until you decide to accept."

"Will you be home this evening?"

"I expect to be, unless we run out for dinner."

"I'll call you after I meet with the president."

"I'll look forward to hearing from you. Hell of a breakfast, Paul. If the nomination doesn't work out, you can always open a ham-'n'-egg joint. Have to run. Good luck with your meeting."

Latham and the president of the United States sat in the Oval Office.

"Well?" Scott said.

"I'd be honored to serve as your secretary of state, Mr. President."

"Good. I'll announce it Monday morning. I have a press conference scheduled at ten. This should spice it up. You'll have a statement ready?"

"If you wish."

"I wish. Run it by Sandy tomorrow night."

"All right."

"Ruth's onboard?"

"Yes, sir."

"We've been friends a long time, Congressman."

"That we have."

"We know a lot about each other."

Latham nodded.

"But we don't know *everything* about each other."

"We can't know everything about *anyone*, Mr. President."

President Scott swiveled in his chair so that he looked out the window.

"Mr. President, I know what you're getting at. Is there anything in my life, personal or professional, that might be used against me during the confirmation process?"

The president again faced his friend. "Is there?" he asked, his face without expression.

"No."

"No pretty little girls coming out of the woodwork to claim you dipped their pigtails in the inkwell?"

Latham laughed and snapped his fingers. "I forgot about them, Mr. President," he said, his voice still carrying the laugh. "Ruth and I planned to go back to California on Monday. I suppose we'd better cancel."

Scott nodded, stood, stretched, and came around the

53

desk to shake Latham's hand. "Welcome to the cabinet, Mr. Secretary."

"A little premature."

"Piece a cake. Love to Ruth."

"Mac. Paul Latham."

"Hello."

"Where did you have dinner?"

"How did you know we did?"

"Got the machine."

"There was no message."

"I didn't want to leave one. My meeting went well."

"We ate at Pesce. The rockfish with artichoke and escarole was wonderful. Glad to hear it. It's all set?"

"Looks like it. Ruth's coming back from the shore first thing in the morning. I'll be huddled all day with staff. Writing a statement, that sort of thing."

"When's it being announced?"

"Monday morning at a press conference."

"Well, all I can say is congratulations. Deeply felt."

"Thank you. What did Annabel have to say?"

"Nothing. I didn't mention it."

"You didn't?"

"No. But now I will. Feel like stopping over? I pour a mean brandy."

"Another time. We've canceled the trip home. I'll stay in touch. Let me know what you decide."

"I certainly will. Again, congrats, Paul. It's much deserved. You'll make a world-class secretary of state."

Smith's conversation with Annabel about functioning as Latham's counsel during Senate hearings lasted five minutes.

"I think it's wonderful," she said.

"No reservations?"

"None. It's great that Paul will be secretary of state, and I'm excited you'll sit with him during the hearing. I may even see you on C-SPAN."

"You see me in person all the time."

"But TV has a certain cachet. I always wanted to be married to a media star."

Rufus plopped his large head on Mac's lap. "What do you think, my friend?" he asked the Dane.

Rufus pulled back, leaving drool on Mac's pants.

"That's what I love about Rufus, Annabel. He lets you know exactly what he thinks. Come on, big guy, time for a walk. She's too easy. I need to discuss this further with you."

6

FOUR DAYS LATER

A white stretch limousine with darkened windows delivered Warren Brazier and two of his aides to the sector of San Francisco International Airport servicing private and corporate aircraft. The industrialist set a brisk pace across the tarmac to his private jet, an Airbus 300A model commercial aircraft that had been modified to carry enough fuel to reach almost any point on the globe. BRAZIER was emblazoned in red along both sides of the black fuselage. A red *B* rose up along the vertical tail surface.

When the aircraft was in commercial use, its spacious interior accommodated more than two hundred passengers. Brazier Industries' transformation of it for private use took advantage of the space to create two large bedrooms, a boardroom, a dining room, two marble baths, a kitchen, and conventional airline seating for twenty. Its interior was a rich amalgamation of lemon and orange wood, leather and gold.

At various times during the flight to London, aides were summoned to meet with "the boss" to discuss specific business issues. Executives of Brazier Industries learned early on to have their facts straight, and to present them concisely and speedily; leave the adjectives at home. Brazier was equally terse and quick with his decisions. He hadn't built one of the world's most prosperous industrial empires by being indecisive.

After a two-hour layover at Heathrow for Brazier to meet onboard with staff from his London office, the group, augmented by two employees of the London office, left for Moscow, where they were met at Sheremetevo-2 airport, twenty-five miles outside of the city, by three men in Mercedes limousines. Besides the drivers, there were three armed plainclothes private security guards. Brazier and entourage were driven to the National Hotel, on the corner of *Tverskaya Ulitsa*, across the street from Red Square. The National, built in 1903, was reopened in 1995 after years of painstaking renovation. Whether it or the venerable Metropole represented Moscow's finest hotel was the subject of ongoing debate. Brazier preferred the National because of its top-floor fitness center and swimming pool. He was fond of swimming there late at night when the crenellated top of the Kremlin and the cupolas and domes of its multiple cathedrals were awash in light.

The Brazier contingent always reserved rooms on the same high floor, with Brazier occupying a corner suite. The security men took up positions in the hallway. After an hour of freshening up, everyone met in the rococo lobby at the foot of the sweeping marble staircase, climbed into the waiting limos, and were driven to a modern high-rise building across from the new American Embassy, on the banks of the Moscow River near Presnia Station. Brazier Industries had been a major partner in an American-British-Canadian consortium that had financed the building's construction in 1994. Prior to moving into its new quarters, Brazier Industries' Moscow office, and its hundred employees, had been housed in an old brick building near Red Square.

People stood at their desks when Brazier stepped off the elevator and strode through the offices of the company bearing his name. He greeted them warmly but quickly—"hello" or *"zdrastvuitye"*—not stopping to chat. The staff who'd traveled with him kept pace, eyes straight ahead, smug authority dispensed with each step.

Brazier's private Moscow office was kept vacant in his absence. Knowing he was coming, his staff had placed vases of colorful flowers in it, as well as a tea and coffee service, and a plate of *blinchiki s'varenem*, jam pancakes, for which Brazier had developed a taste. There was never any alcohol served in his presence. He was a teetotaler. Nor did he smoke, presenting an especially difficult situation for his Russian employees, for whom tobacco was an integral part of life. They sneaked their cigarettes outside, out of sight.

He secluded himself in his office, allowing staff members who'd traveled with him to catch their breath. They were bone-weary from the long trip. Brazier, who'd just turned sixty, operated from a seemingly bottomless well of energy. He'd trained himself to stave off fatigue with frequent catnaps—no longer than ten minutes—an ability those on his staff had not been able to master, although God knows they tried. For them, staying awake and alert on such trips was more a matter of dogged determination than acquired skill.

Twenty minutes after arriving, Brazier buzzed for Elena, his personal assistant, a solidly constructed middle-aged Russian woman who'd sat poised outside his door. "Get everyone in the conference room," he said. "Ten minutes."

It wasn't a difficult directive for her to follow. Brazier's traveling staff had already camped in the conference room, joined there by four of the Moscow office's senior execs. But her announcement prompted them to remove their feet from chairs and the edge of the twenty-foot-long leather-inlaid conference table, check their clothing, and sit at attention.

"Good afternoon," Brazier said crisply as he took his seat at the head of the table. "Everyone feeling fresh?"

There was muffled laughter.

"I suggest you suck it up. We have a lot to accomplish in the next twenty-four hours."

A half hour was spent with Brazier receiving updates on company projects underway in Russia. The reports were short and to the point: a new shopping center on *Tverskaya Ulitsa*, the road from Moscow to St. Petersburg; a hotel in the *Kitai Gorod* area of the city; a joint oil-drilling venture with the French and Russians on *Yuzhno-Sakhalinsk*, a Russian island north of Japan and site of the Russian Far East's only known offshore energy field (it wasn't going well; the report on its progress was a few minutes longer than the others); and assorted smaller ventures.

Brazier listened passively, interrupting only to ask an occasional question delivered with the sharpness of a surgical knife. After everyone at the table had had their say,

Brazier issued a series of orders. He looked at his watch, stood abruptly, and walked from the room, four of his staff following, two who'd traveled to Moscow with him from San Francisco, and two from the Moscow office. They were joined by four heavyset men carrying automatic weapons under their suit jackets. Warren Brazier was, among many things, a careful man. The rampant crime in Russia had generated a thriving industry for security consultants to businessmen traveling there. Brazier Industries had on retainer one of the world's best security firms, augmented by the company's own large and well-trained security staff.

Not a word was said as they descended to the lobby and climbed into the waiting Mercedes. Brazier turned to one of his Russian aides. "He knows why we're meeting?"

"Yes, sir. I made it clear."

"His reaction?"

"Noncommittal. Simply said he would be there."

"Have the funds been moving freely?"

"*Da.*"

"His position is still secure?"

"*Da.* As far as I know."

Brazier looked at him hard. " 'As far as you know?' And how far is that?"

"I am reasonably sure that—"

"I don't pay you to be reasonably sure, Misha. I pay you to be certain."

Misha coughed and glanced nervously at the other two aides in the back of the limo before replying, "I am certain, Mr. Brazier, that the deputy prime minister's position is secure."

Brazier directed a question at another staff member. And another. The Q-and-A was cut short when the limousine pulled up in front of the Radisson *Slavjanskaya*, next to the Kiev Railway Station, its western amenities making it the hotel of choice for many American business travelers.

Surrounded by the four armed men, Brazier and his small group walked past two guards at the entrance and into the imposing two-story lobby lined with restaurants and shops. An assistant manager had been awaiting Brazier's arrival. He quickly crossed the lobby and extended a nervous hand, matched by a tentative smile. "*Dobry vecher,* Mr. Brazier. Good evening. Welcome. Welcome."

They rode in silence to the eleventh floor. The door to a corner suite was open. The manager stepped aside, bowing annoyingly. The security men waited in the hall as Brazier and his aides entered the large living room and stopped in the middle of the green-carpeted floor.

Two men sat in a corner, one young, one older. A smoky haze hung over them like an aura; the younger man smoked a long black cigar, the older gentleman a cigarette. A half-dozen glasses and a silver bucket containing ice and a bottle of vodka were on a table between their chairs. A platter of *zakuski*—sliced sturgeon and fatty sausage hors d'oeuvres—appeared to be untouched. An ashtray overflowed with cigarette butts.

For a moment, it appeared that neither group would acknowledge the other. But then the older Russian stubbed out his latest cigarette and stood. "*Zdrastvuitye,* Brazier," he said, extending his arms as though about to hug his visitor.

Brazier shook hands with Platon Mikhailov, deputy minister of finance in the Commonwealth of Independent States' Congress of People's Deputies, the government that had taken the place of the former Soviet Union.

Mikhailov, a lifelong Communist, had managed to sustain his power through the party's forty percent hold on the new Congress. Yeltsin might have won the presidential election, but the Communists still controlled a majority in the legislature, as slim as it was.

"Sit. Have a chair," Mikhailov said. To his young aide, sternly: "A chair for my guest."

Platon Mikhailov was an imposing man physically, especially when compared with Brazier's diminutive stature. Approaching seventy, he'd held a variety of positions within the party throughout his life. Born in 1927, three years after the death of Lenin, he first became active as a teenager in the party's youth movement. He was a zealous Communist, happiest when playing a direct role in the brutal *Cheka*, Stalin's version of Ivan the Terrible's *Oprichniki*, a militia and intelligence agency answering only to its leader. Even as a teen, Mikhailov firmly believed in the *Cheka*'s creed: "No other measures to fight counter-revolutionaries, spies, speculators, ruffians, hooligans, saboteurs and other parasites than merciless annihilation on the spot of the offence."

Unlike many of his young friends, Mikhailov pursued higher education, majoring in finance at Moscow's coveted Academy of Economics. As his educational credentials grew, so did his positions of responsibility within the party.

When Gorbachev came to power in 1985 and speeded up the process that would result in the Soviet Union's collapse, Mikhailov and fellow hard-line Communists labored to thwart attempts at *perestroika* and *glasnost*. They failed, at least on paper and at the polls. But the Communist Party held out hope that one day the nation would be returned to its former glory through a reinstated Socialist system. Platon Mikhailov believed it would.

He told his aide to wait outside. "Your people, too," he said to Brazier, who waved his aides from the room. When they were gone, Mikhailov said, "*Vodichka,* Brazier?" He pulled the bottle from the ice bucket.

"No," Brazier replied.

"Something to eat?" He gestured to the platter of *zakuski.* "Maybe you would prefer *ikra.*"

"I don't want caviar, Platon. I'm here to talk."

Mikhailov broke into a smile, exposing teeth that looked like corn on the cob. "Of course. You are well?"

Brazier ignored the pleasantry. "What is the status of the sale?" he asked, his voice low and monotone, his eyes trained on the big Russian.

Mikhailov shrugged and poured himself a drink. Brazier sat impassively and watched as Mikhailov downed half the vodka in the glass, smacked his lips, and laughed. "You don't know what you're missing," he said, finishing the drink and pouring another.

"I'm losing patience, Platon," Brazier said.

"Are you? What is the saying? Patience is a virtue. For a Russian who must deal in this new era, it is more than a virtue. It is a necessity, Brazier."

"For some. But I was led to believe you had the ability to cut through it."

The Russian filled his glass; a hand went up in a gesture of ambivalence. "It is not easy these days, you know, my friend. It was better before, huh? But then there was not so much to gain."

Brazier knew only too well what the deputy minister meant.

"I might need more from you to finalize the sale,"

Mikhailov said through the smoke of another cigarette. Again, a gesture of resignation with his hand. "It's not as easy as it once was, Warren. More competition for businesses being privatized by the State."

"You mean bigger payoffs being paid," Brazier said softly, narrowing his eyes against the smoke wafting in his direction.

Mikhailov laughed, and coughed. "Not only a matter of money," he said. "Favors to be dispensed. Loyalties to be remembered and rewarded. Remember, Yeltsin was an *apparatchik*, too, until he decided to love democracy and the free market." He chuckled at his comment.

Brazier had had enough. He stood and went to a floor-to-ceiling window overlooking the train station.

"I'm sure we can work it out," Mikhailov said from where he remained seated. "How is your friend, Congressman Latham?"

"He's fine," Brazier said to the window.

"Will he be able to deliver the bill, now that he will be distracted because of his nomination as secretary of state?"

Brazier slowly turned and faced Mikhailov. He was suddenly consumed with disgust for what he saw—the hulking deputy minister of finance, cigarette in one hand, glass of vodka in the other, lips parted in a crooked smile.

"It will be a shame to lose him," Mikhailov said. "Committee chairmen are so powerful in your Congress. Secretary of state? A figurehead. Am I right?"

Brazier's response was to go to the door. He turned and asked, "When will I know whether you've paved the way for the sale of Kazan Energy to Brazier Industries?"

Mikhailov had picked up a sausage from the *zakuski* platter and had taken a bite. He finished it, licked his fingers, picked up his vodka, and extended it as a toast. "To when all is resolved, Warren. To when your Congress has passed the Russian Trade and Investment Bill, and to when Kazan Energy becomes part of your family of businesses. When do you leave Moscow?"

"In the morning."

"Call me at my office. Perhaps I will have something additional to report."

Brazier left the suite and swiftly led his administrative and security entourage to the lobby and into the waiting limousines. Unlike the trip to the hotel, he occupied one limo by himself. Two of the security men were instructed to follow in another, leaving Brazier's aides, and the other two guards, to make use of the one remaining vehicle.

Brazier was delivered to the National Hotel, where he changed into bathing trunks, robe, and slippers and went to the top-floor health club. It was more crowded than he preferred—ideally, he would have the pool to himself. He ignored the four other men, dove in, and swam energetic laps until his shoulders ached.

He dried himself, put on his robe and slippers, and looked out over the Kremlin, once the symbol of Soviet power, now nothing more than a center of bureaucratic confusion. He was seething when he had left Mikhailov; the swim hadn't fully exorcised the anger from his tightly wound body.

He muttered an obscenity in Russian. What a mess reformers like Gorbachev, Yeltsin, and their cronies had made of what had once been an equally corrupt but assuredly more orderly system to navigate, especially if you knew what you were doing.

Warren Brazier had been navigating the old Communist system since 1965. He knew it well, how the bureaucrats thought and reacted, their individual weaknesses, the greed that prevailed, and especially the chains of command you had to go through to get what you wanted.

He'd suffered countless frustrations in attempting to gain an industrial foothold in the Soviet Union. His ventures there had never been as lucrative as others in different areas of the globe. But he hung on, developing his friends in high places, building his own personal list of those who'd prospered through his generosity, and who owed him.

He'd been calculating his moves in the Soviet Union with one goal: Be the individual they turned to when the inevitable happened, the collapse of the economic system and the Soviet Union itself. His prognosis had been on the money: The system and government had collapsed.

But instead of Warren Brazier being in the right place at the right time, being the one in the best position to prosper by the collapse—being first in line to snap up formerly State-owned industries at bargain-basement prices—he'd been forced to compete with Russian business interests with longer tentacles into the reformed government, some of them in the government itself.

Brazier and Deputy Minister of Finance Platon Mikhailov went back a long way, to when Brazier made his first business foray into what was then the Soviet Union. Khrushchev had been deposed by party leaders less than a year earlier, and the Ukrainian, Leonid Brezhnev, was in power. Difficult as it was, Warren Brazier had done business with the Communists for twenty years—through the Brezhnev era, and those of Andropov and Chernenko after Brezhnev died in 1982—succeeding where few other outsiders had, or could. From his perspective, it didn't matter who was in charge of the totalitarian state. Business, Soviet style, went on as usual.

But the economy was a disaster. Technology hadn't progressed much beyond the 1950s, except in space, while the West forged ahead to develop the computer age, and toward such exotic military concepts as the so-called Star Wars defense.

Through his highly publicized efforts to create profitable industries within the Soviet Union, Warren Brazier became known as America's unofficial ambassador to it. His views on U.S.-Soviet relations were sought by congressional committees, think tanks, and even presidents of the United States. His picture appeared on the covers of *Time* and *Newsweek*. Would he launch a third political party? Brazier never said yes, never said no, encouraging grassroots attempts to draft him as a candidate one day, protesting he was too busy running his company to become mired in politics on another. Observers felt he reveled in the power such ambivalence generated, and they were right. Warren Brazier's short stature was more than compensated for by an ego of gargantuan proportions.

While his staff, except for the on-duty security men in the hall outside, drank and danced to American hip-hop music in one of many Western-style discos springing up all over the city, Brazier solemnly ate dinner alone in his suite. He'd developed over the years a taste, at times even a love, for Russian food, especially Georgian fare.

But this night, his dark mood precluded anything Russian. He ordered steak well done, and a salad, and washed it down with mineral water.

He awoke the following morning with as much anger as when he'd gone to bed.

Clearly, certain changes had to be made.

7

In Washington, D.C., there are as many jurisdictional disputes each day as there are tourists daily during cherry blossom time. The investigation of Congressman Paul Latham as nominee for secretary of state, though assumed to be a shoo-in, would not be an exception.

The FBI wanted preliminary questioning to take place at its headquarters on Pennsylvania Avenue. President Scott's chief of staff suggested that the White House would provide a more conducive setting. Latham preferred his own office. Mac Smith, as the congressman's counsel, reluctantly intervened with all the parties, and prevailed on behalf of his client.

Smith, Latham, a White House attorney, two FBI special agents, and a stenographer sat in a semicircle in Latham's office in the Rayburn House Office Building. It was eleven in the morning. The mood was relaxed. The participants exchanged quips about things in the so-called news. The two C-SPAN channels, volume off, provided silent pictures over Latham's shoulder of the House and Senate in action.

"Well, let's get to it," Latham said. "I haven't missed a vote in ten years and don't intend to now."

"I wouldn't want you to miss the vote on executive-branch appropriations," Dan Gibbs, the White House attorney, said. "I'm hoping for a raise." He didn't smile.

"Post office funding, too," Latham said. "The day of the dollar stamp is not far off."

One of the FBI agents asked the stenographer if she was ready. She confirmed that she was with a nod, then remembered and said, "Yes." He said to Latham, "You know, Congressman Latham, that this is routine."

"Of course. I assume you've already started digging into my background."

"That's right. Actually, this will probably be a lot faster than most cabinet nominee investigations. Hard to find anything controversial in your life."

"That's because I've avoided controversy. Maybe not here in the House, but certainly in my personal life."

"Let's go back a bit," the agent said. "You taught political science at U of California at Berkeley."

"Briefly," Latham said.

"Two years?"

"A few months shy of that."

"A very liberal university."

"A very open-minded and challenging university," Latham countered.

The agent turned to his colleague and asked lightly,

"What did they call the university at Berkeley? The People's Republic of Berkeley?"

The second agent nodded.

Mac Smith looked at Latham for a response; his client didn't seem to be annoyed at the flippant comment.

"We managed to track down some of your students," the lead agent said.

"You're in trouble now," Smith said.

"I assume you were impressed with their educational credentials," Latham said.

"Very," said the agent. "They said you ranked among their most popular teachers."

"Glad to hear it."

"One of them said you had some pretty unorthodox theories about international relations."

"Oh? Obviously not one of my brighter students."

"She said you seemed to be sympathetic to the Soviet Union."

Latham looked at Smith and laughed. "I'm about to be called a fellow traveler." To the agent: "Don't give her name to Senator Connors. Christ, he'll call her in as a witness against me."

The questioning lasted until 11:45, when the sound of a bell from Latham's office clock announced that a fifteen-minute floor vote had been called.

"If you want to continue this after the vote, I'll be happy to—"

"No need, Congressman," the agent said. "We're pretty much finished up here. There is one area we have to explore a little, but it can wait."

Latham, who'd gotten up and gone to his desk in search of papers relating to the vote, asked absently, "What area is that?"

The agent answered with equal casualness, "Your relationship with Warren Brazier."

Latham looked up, his brow furrowed. "Nothing to tell you about that," he said, scooping up the papers and heading for the door. "Mac, will you hang around until I get back?"

"Sure," Smith said.

Latham's chief of staff, Bob Mondrian, poked his head in the door. "Mr. Frank's on the phone."

"What does he want?"

"The vote. He says Sanders might come around to our side."

The clock's bell sounded again, indicating ten minutes left to vote. A recorded male voice reported the substance of the bill. Republican offices had their own recorded voice, which usually put a different spin on each piece of legislation up for vote.

Latham and Mondrian left the office suite. The FBI special agents closed their briefcases and said good-bye. The stenographer packed up her portable equipment and followed them out, leaving Smith and Dan Gibbs alone in Latham's office.

"Nice to hear the Bureau thinks this will be a fast investigation," Smith said. "Do you?"

Gibbs, a scholarly-looking middle-aged man with soft black hair that flopped in conflicting directions, and whose black-rimmed glasses were oversized, reclined in his chair, slung an arm over its back, and said, "Yeah, it is. Only, that doesn't necessarily translate into easy sledding with the committee. Senator Connors is no fan of Congressman Latham."

"So I hear. And read."

Gibbs got up and closed the door, took his seat, leaned

toward Smith, and lowered his voice. "This question about the congressman's relationship with Warren Brazier could be problematic. I know I can raise this with you as his counsel."

"Of course. Better raised now than later. How much of a problem?"

"We're not certain. As you know, the FBI's check into his background won't amount to much. They look for obvious areas of conflict, things that might cause the president to withdraw the nomination." He laughed. "That's about as likely as the president resigning from office. But we have our own investigators dredging up everything and anything Connors and the committee's investigators might come up with—and use."

Smith grunted. "I'm sure that by the time this is over, we'll know everything we don't want to know about Congressman Latham's life, including at what age he was toilet trained and his favorite fast food. It's a brutal process."

Gibbs chewed his cheek, asked, "What do you know about the congressman's relationship with Brazier?"

Mac didn't immediately respond. He'd been around Washington long enough to know that casually sharing information with anyone, even those who presumably were in your camp, like Gibbs and the White House he represented, wasn't prudent.

So Smith did what all savvy Washingtonians did. He replied without offering anything Gibbs didn't already know.

"Warren Brazier and Paul Latham have been friends for years."

"I know that Mr. Brazier has been a big financial contributor to Latham's campaigns," Gibbs said.

"I wouldn't know about that," Smith said. "But it doesn't surprise me. I'm sure any financial help Brazier gave Paul was well within legal guidelines."

Gibbs smiled, more of a facial tic, and shrugged. "Brazier's business history in Russia is interesting. Isn't it?"

"I've found it interesting over the years. I mean, I've enjoyed reading about his adventures and successes."

"Do you know him?"

"Warren Brazier? I've met him once. A week or so ago. We shook hands."

"Congressman Latham has put through some legislation over the years that was beneficial to Brazier."

"Has he?"

This time, Gibbs's smile said something—that he realized Smith was not about to offer much. He said, "I have to get back to the White House. I've enjoyed talking to you, Mac. You have quite a reputation in this town. The congressman is lucky to have you as counsel."

"Any lawyer would do. He'll be confirmed with ease."

"I'm sure you're right." He stood and arched his back against an unseen pain. "Do me a favor?"

"If I can."

"If you come up with anything that might—well, that would give ammunition to Senator Connors and others who might not want to see the congressman confirmed—you'll let me know?" He didn't give Smith a chance to respond, adding, "I'm sure you wouldn't want to see the president embarrassed in any way."

Smith stood and shook Gibbs's hand. "I enjoyed meeting you, Dan."

"Same here. We'll be in touch." He handed Smith a business card with his White House direct line on it, and left, leaving the door to Latham's office open.

Marge Edwards entered the outer office cradling a sheaf of papers in her arms. The appointment secretary spotted Smith, dropped the papers on a desk, and stood in the doorway. "Hi, Mr. Smith. How are you?"

"Fine, Marge. Yourself?"

"Okay, I guess. Busy. Things are going nuts here with Paul up for State."

"I can imagine. How's the confirmation process seem to you to be going?"

"Proceeding at its predictable, plodding pace."

She glanced up at the clock on Latham's wall. "Oops," she said, "got to get out of here. I'm meeting Molly for lunch."

"Molly Latham?"

"Yup. I promised Paul I'd keep an eye on her now that she's a page. You know, be sort of a big sister."

"Sounds like pleasant duty."

"Always happy to help Paul. He gave me some things to give her at lunch. Books about Congress, some of his speeches." She laughed. "I think he's grooming her to become the first female president." ·

"The time has come."

"Want to join us for lunch?"

"Can't, but thanks. I'm meeting my wife."

"Well, another time. Great seeing you. I'm sure you'll be a familiar face around here."

"Sorry about that."

Her spirited laughter trailed behind as she bounced from the outer office, almost bumping into Latham returning from the vote. He came directly into his office, closed the door, and turned up the volume on both TV sets. A veteran Democratic representative from New York was delivering an impassioned speech from the well on wasteful defense spending. In the Senate, a controversial Republican senator from Georgia, twice divorced, spoke about the need to restore family values.

Latham pointed to C-SPAN 1's screen. "He's right, Mac. Instead of fixing what we have, the Pentagon just wants to keep developing exotic new weapons."

"That's good for you and your Silicon Valley voters, isn't it?" Smith said.

"Only if those exotic new weapons get built in my district. They left, I see."

"Yes."

"Waste of time, wasn't it? A student from twenty years ago says I was controversial. Think that'll derail my nomination?"

"I hope not. The White House lawyer, Gibbs, asked about you and Warren Brazier."

"Did he? What did he ask?"

"About campaign contributions, and legislation you've sponsored that was beneficial to Brazier."

Latham sat heavily behind his desk, slapped it, and said, "Warren Brazier is one of the greatest men this country has ever produced, Mac. He opened up the Soviet Union years before anyone else. He's a great American, and I'll be damned if I'll see his name dragged through the mud. I'd rather tell the president to find another nominee."

Smith went to a photograph on the wall of Latham and President Joe Scott together. He smiled, turned, and said, "Mind if I use this moment to offer my first piece of advice as your counsel?"

"Of course not."

"Warren Brazier is bound to come up during the hearings. You'll be pounded about him, questioned from every angle, most of it with political overtones. I suggest you tone down your defense of him. Keep your answers about your relationship with him short and factual. I know he's your friend, and has been your leading supporter for years, Paul. He's also controversial. And you can't know everything about him. Or me. Nothing to be gained by singing his praises. Keep it factual."

"Good advice, Mac. I'll heed it. I'm meeting with Warren this afternoon. He flew in from New York last night."

"Have to run, Paul. Lunch with Annabel. Talk later today?"

"What?"

"Talk later today?"

"Oh. Sure. Call me. Thanks for being here."

Mac and Annabel joined up at their favorite hangout, the Foggy Bottom Cafe in the River Inn. Over mushroom soup and Caesar salad with grilled chicken, they compared mornings.

"I really think he might buy the feather ornaments," she said, excited. "All three pieces. He didn't blink when I told him the price."

"I blink every time you mention the price," Mac said. "In fact, I flutter my eyes. How did you leave it with him?"

"He said he'd get back to me in a few days." She frowned. "I almost hate to sell those ornaments," she said. "They're among my favorites."

"Everything in your gallery is 'among your favorites,' " Smith said as a young waitress removed their soup plates. "If he meets your price, sell the feathers. Flutter your eyes. You are, after all, in business, Mrs. Smith."

"Feather *ornaments*. And I know, I know, it's good you're around to remind me I'm in business. I'd never sell anything otherwise. How did it go with Paul?"

"All right. The FBI questioned him. A White House lawyer named Gibbs sat in. Paul's friendship with Warren Brazier looms."

"Oh? How so?"

Over the next ten minutes, Mac filled her in.

"What does Paul say?" she asked.

"Gave me a speech. It was a little off-putting. Sort of a God-and-country speech, touting Brazier as being worthy of another D.C. monument. I suggested he tone it down at the hearings."

The waitress brought coffee and the dessert menu.

"Share a sour cream chocolate cake?" Mac asked.

"God, no. You go ahead. I'll have a bite."

Which, Mac knew, would result in losing more than half.

They stood in the sunshine outside the restaurant on Twenty-fifth Street, two blocks from their home. "Walk me back to the gallery?" Annabel asked.

"Sure. I'm free this afternoon. I told Paul I'd call him later."

Mac lingered at Annabel's gallery in Georgetown to examine two new pieces she'd recently purchased from a New York dealer. As he was leaving, she asked, "Sorry you got involved with Paul's confirmation?"

"No. It's a fascinating process, blatantly political but useful. At least that's the way the Founding Fathers saw it."

"I'm glad you're not sorry. I think it's great you're in the middle of something this important." She kissed his cheek, then laid another on his mouth. "See you at dinner."

"I'll be there. Sorry you weren't in the mood for sour cream chocolate cake."

"It was so good."

Mac smiled. "When will I learn to not buy that 'I'll just have a bite' routine? Enjoy the afternoon, Annie. Love you."

8

Marge Edwards and Molly Latham lingered over large glasses of lemonade in the Rayburn Building's spacious, bustling cafeteria. Molly, whose voluble personality held her in good stead on her high school debating team, was on a roll.

"... and I can't believe I'll be a page in the House of Representatives. I love my roommate—she's from Mississippi and has this amazing accent—my mom wanted me to live at home, but living in the dorm is part of the experience, don't you think, Marge?"·

"I know how proud your dad is of you," Marge said.

"More luck than anything," Molly said. "The Democrats are in the majority—there are only sixty-six pages—the Democrats get to appoint fifty-four of them—I'd never have made it if the Republicans were the majority. It's awesome, Marge—I'm getting paid more than a thousand dollars a month. Do you know what they used to pay pages? I mean, ages ago—three hundred dollars a month. They take three hundred from me for the room and meals—five dinners and five breakfasts—but that's not much. I'll be working in the cloakroom—the Democratic cloakroom, of course. Know what I heard? Years ago only the majority could appoint pages, and some reporters—I think it was Drew Pearson or somebody like that—maybe not—these reporters paid some pages to tell them what was going on in the majority cloakroom—wow—I mean, that's awesome—and when somebody found out about it, they changed all the rules so both parties could assign pages. . . ."

Marge listened patiently, a bemused smile on her face. Now, she laughed. Molly's enthusiasm was contagious. But there was a parallel sadness in sitting across the table from Molly Latham, whose life was all in front of her. She was sixteen years old, a junior in high school, born to a privileged family with the inherent advantages that situation creates. She was bright and pretty—golden, silky hair pulled back into an old-fashioned ponytail, face unblemished and glowing, a fit and trim figure, solid and firm.

Marge Edwards's self-image was not nearly as generous. At thirty-five, she often wondered during those dark moments alone, which seemed to have been occurring with increasing frequency, where the first thirty-five years had gone—and what was left. She hadn't married, although she'd come close a few times. At least she preferred to think marriage had been on the horizon, but had fallen through for reasons beyond her control. Men were so immature these days, she told friends, so afraid to commit and to assume responsibility.

"I can't wait to bring a message from the cloakroom to Dad on the floor. What a hoot."

"Your father is a wonderful man," Marge said.

"Hmmmm," said Molly.

"I mean, really a special man. We're very close, you know."

Molly took a long swig of her lemonade.

"It's like—well, it's almost like being man and wife, you know, working so closely together. That's what they call it"—a chuckle —"office wife."

"Uh-huh."

"You're very fortunate to have him as a father."

"I wish I saw him more. He's so busy."

"What he's doing is so important to the country."

Suddenly, Molly seemed more drawn into the conversation. "He'll be the secretary of state. In the president's cabinet."

"Yes. Unless—"

"He will be, won't he?"

"I'm sure he will. Unless something crazy happens. You never know in politics, Molly. That's one thing you learn working on the Hill."

"I guess I'd better go," Molly said, draining her cup.

"Me, too," Marge said. "Oh, here are some things from your dad. And from me." She handed Molly two packages. One was wrapped in yellow and green floral paper, and sported a large green bow. The other, which she'd hurriedly wrapped in the office before coming to lunch, was secured with brown paper and string.

Molly weighed the brown package in her hands. "It's heavy. What's in it?"

"Books, papers. Things your dad wants you to read. The other is a little present from me."

Molly unwrapped the smaller package to reveal a

pretty red, white, and blue silk scarf. "It's beautiful," she said. "What's it for? It's not my birthday or anything."

Marge smiled. "Just congratulations to Congress's newest and best page."

Molly put the scarf about her neck and checked her image in the reflection from a nearby stainless-steel surface. "It's beautiful, Marge. I can wear it with my uniform—we can only wear navy blue jackets, white blouses—they let us wear slacks—or skirts—but no slits, they told us—I guess a scarf is okay."

"I'm sure it is," said Marge.

They parted in sunshine in front of the building.

"Keep a secret, Molly?"

The teen's giggle was nervous. "Sure."

"I may not be around much longer."

"Why? What do you mean?"

"I may, ah—I may take another job."

"Really?" Her eyes opened wide. "What other job?"

"It's not definite yet. *P-l-e-a-s-e,* not a word to anyone, especially your father. It would be wrong if he found out from anyone but me."

"Sure. Okay. I wish you wouldn't . . . take another job."

"Maybe I won't. But we'll stay friends, won't we?"

"Sure. Thanks for the present."

"My pleasure."

They shook hands and went their separate ways, Marge back into the building, Molly down the street in the direction of the Page Residence Hall, on the third and fourth floors of the O'Neill House Office Building, an annex to the three main House buildings. Originally the Congressional Hotel, it was purchased in 1957 and converted to office use, as well as a residence hall for pages. Girls occupied the fourth floor, boys the third.

She skirted the Cannon House Office Building, gave a Capitol police man on patrol a big wave, entered the O'Neill Building, named for former Speaker of the House "Tip" O'Neill, gave an equally expansive greeting to the officer manning the lobby desk, and went upstairs to her room, where her roommate, Melissa, had just come from the shower and was brushing long, brunette hair in front of a mirror. Molly put the package she'd been given by Marge on her dresser and plopped on the bed.

The room was surprisingly large for a dorm. Each girl had covered her twin bed with a pretty floral spread, and had hung pictures on the wall over them, mostly of family, some of rock and movie stars.

"Hi, y'all," Melissa said, not missing a stroke with the brush.

"Hi," Molly said. "I had lunch in the Rayburn Building. Cool cafeteria. My dad always says it's a lot better than the one in Longworth. He calls that a hellhole. We'll have lunch. Not this weekend. The cafeterias are closed on weekends."

The brush kept moving. "Your daddy arrange that?" Melissa asked.

"No. Anybody can go there. But it's, like, interesting. A lot of the congressmen go there 'cause it's quick and cheap."

"You don't care about cheap, do you?"

"Sure I do."

Melissa's laugh was sardonic. "You don't have to worry about money. Your daddy's going to be secretary of state." Melissa's father owned a clothing store in Biloxi, and was active in local politics.

"Maybe he won't be," Molly said, brow furrowed.

The brush stopped and Melissa turned. "What do you mean? The president wants him."

"I don't know. Sometimes crazy things happen in politics."

The brush in motion again. "Did you see that neat guy from New York at the briefing?"

"John? He's cute."

But Molly's mind was not on the cute male page from upstate New York. Marge Edwards's words kept coming back to her—that her father might not be confirmed as secretary of state, and that Marge might be leaving for another job. What was that all about? Molly wondered. Her father wouldn't be happy losing his scheduler; he always spoke highly of Marge, sometimes too highly and too often.

The Lathams seldom argued, for which Molly was grateful. So many of her friends' parents seemed always to be bickering, and ended up divorced. Her brother, Martin, once said to her when she'd commented how well their parents got along, "It's because he's never home." Molly was overtly angry at Martin for being so flippant and disrespectful about their mother and father, and told him so. Down deep she wondered whether he might be right.

She had overheard occasional sharp words between her parents where Marge Edwards was concerned. Although Ruth Latham had never said it directly—at least not within Molly's earshot—Molly sensed that her mother suspected her husband of having an affair with Marge, a notion Molly refused even to consider. As far as she was concerned, her father, the congressman from California and soon to be the nation's secretary of state, was the most moral man in the world. The idea of him in the arms of a woman other than her mother—any woman—was anathema. Not that she was naive. She'd heard all the gossip about unfaithfulness among her friends' mothers and fathers, the occasional scandal when an elected official was caught in a compromising position, men in Washington who made their adulterous goals known, and married women at parties hosted by the Lathams who openly flirted with other women's husbands.

But not Paul Latham. Not Molly Latham's father.

"What are you doing tonight?" Melissa asked, dropping her robe and walking naked to her dresser, where she pulled out fresh underwear. Her casual nudity made Molly uncomfortable.

"I don't know. I thought I might read after dinner. My father gave me—"

"Y'all read too much," said Melissa. "We've got till ten. A few days now we'll be so tired goin' to school and runnin' all over the House floor, we'll be lucky if we can stay awake to study. What's that?" She pointed to the package wrapped in brown paper and string.

"From my father. Books and speeches. He's always after me to read more."

"Not now," Melissa said. "Come on, girl." She laughed wickedly. "Maybe we can coax John to come with us for a burger, a little dancing."

"All right," Molly said. "You really like him, huh?"

"Who?"

"John, silly. From New York."

"Oh, him. I like him well enough. I like 'em all well enough, Molly Latham. I think bein' a page in the United States Congress is goin' to be a ton a fun."

9

Senate minority whip Frank Connors was generally described as resembling an Irish pit bull with a boil, although those close to him were quick to say that his scowl and gravelly bark were considerably more menacing than his bite. Still, he was quick to snap. Once in his jaws, it was tough to shake loose unless he decided you'd finally seen things his way.

He'd just come from a Republican fund-raiser for two freshman representatives from Southern California. "Arrogant young bastards," he said to an aide as they left the Capitol Hill Club. His sentiments weren't reserved for only young House Republicans. Senator Connors found first-term representatives from both sides of the aisle to be arrogant, at best, and dumb at worst.

The aide pulled into the underground parking garage of the Russell Senate Office Building, on the north side of the Capitol, and came to a stop in Connors's reserved space. The senator set a fast pace to his office, where members of his staff awaited his arrival.

In a corner of the reception area, a bulky man with a nose of the formerly broken variety and a shadowy beard line browsed that day's copy of the *Congressional Monitor.* He glanced up as Connors burst through the door and went directly to his office, followed by his chief of staff, Dennis Mackral. Once inside, Connors asked, "Who's that out there?"

"The private investigator."

"What's his name?"

"Perrone. James Perrone."

"Is he legit?"

"According to Morris and Kellerman." Kyle Morris and Mitch Kellerman were full-time investigators on the Senate Foreign Relations Committee, the body that would hold hearings into Paul Latham's nomination as secretary of state. Connors was the ranking minority member. If the committee approved Latham's nomination, it would recommend to the Senate at large that he be confirmed.

Connors pulled a Don Lino Havana Reserve cigar from the humidor on his desk and examined it. "They say there's Cuban tobacco in these," he said, "but don't you believe it. If there was, you wouldn't catch me smoking it."

Mackral had heard the denial before. He didn't care whether banned Cuban tobacco was in the rope his boss smoked or not. That the company making them claimed the tobacco was one hundred percent Honduran, and that the wrappers were from Connecticut, was good enough. What did it matter?

Connors lit the cigar with care, making sure the

lighter's flame didn't touch the cigar's end. There was a time early in his political career when he smoked in public. But as his Southern California constituents led the way in the antismoking crusade—anti-everything and anything pleasurable, Connors thought—he adjusted his public posture: no smoking in public; a daily jog, especially if there was a camera to record it; plenty of pasta, vegetables, fruit, and chicken with its skin removed; and an attempt to change his approach from square-cut gray and blue suits to an occasional tan number, blue blazers over chino slacks when he felt it appropriate, and even open-neck shirts for selected photo ops.

Dennis Mackral, on the other hand, had found it necessary to become a little *less* Southern California when first coming aboard as Connors's COS, chief of staff. A year shy of forty, he'd arrived in Washington a dozen years ago as administrative assistant (same job as a COS, different title) to a California representative, a first-termer whose previous career had been in the movies. But his freshman boss was no Ronald Reagan. His being sent to Washington to represent his conservative district was considered an electoral aberration, and he was soundly defeated after one term by a conservative Republican woman, a breeder of show dogs, who convinced voters in overwhelming numbers to reject what she repeatedly called "Hollywood hedonism," which most voters didn't fully understand, but knew it sounded bad.

Mackral decided to stay in Washington after his boss packed up and headed west. He changed his California style to better conform with dark-suit D.C., although his natural coppery tan, gelled dirty-blond hair, and laid-back, beachy heritage betrayed his origins. At first, he was viewed as nothing more than a displaced Californian who'd come to town with a loser. But there was a substantive side of Dennis Mackral that eventually became known to staffers on the Hill with whom he became friends. He was hired by a House member as press secretary, was promoted to AA six months later, then joined Senator Connors's team as deputy chief of staff. Others on the staff were surprised to see the gruff, hard-nosed senator take to the boyishly handsome Mackral, increasingly relying on him to handle important legislative assignments. When the COS resigned, Connors tapped Mackral to replace him. As skeptical as other staff members had been of Mackral, they soon had to agree that he was up to the demands of being chief aide to one of the Senate's most powerful members.

"You hear from Stassi?" Connors asked from behind a sheaf of papers.

"We're set to meet at six."

"Where?"

"Judiciary conference room."

"We bringing this Perrone with us?"

"No. He's strictly unofficial, on assignment for Morris and Kellerman. Anything he comes up with is through them."

"Then why is he here?"

"I wanted you to meet him. Know what you're paying for."

"What *I'm* paying him? I thought he was getting private money."

"He is. The Yucca Valley fund. Still—"

"Bring him in," Connors said.

Perrone was even bigger than he'd appeared while seated. He wore an ill-fitting brown suit, green shirt, and yellow tie, and carried a tan raincoat over his arm.

"Say hello to Senator Frank Connors," Mackral said. They shook hands. "Have a seat," Mackral said, indicating a chair in front of the desk.

"Well, now, Mr. Perrone," Connor said from his leather chair, "Dennis says you might have uncovered some information to share with us."

Perrone shifted in his chair; his eyes were in constant motion, glancing left, right, lighting on Connors, then resuming movement again. He looked up at Mackral, who leaned against a wall, arms crossed, head cocked.

"Well, Mr. Perrone?" Connors said.

"No offense," Perrone said, "but Kellerman never did tell me what I'm being paid."

Connors looked to Mackral for the answer. The AA said, "Because you're not staff, Mr. Perrone—because you're not officially investigating Congressman Latham— it takes some time to set up the pay. But I assure you—"

Connors said, "Dennis told me a little about the direction your investigation is taking, Mr. Perrone. I'm interested. It's important to the country and the American people that such information be made public. I'm sure your fee will be worked out to your satisfaction. You have my word on that."

Perrone, relaxed in his chair, one leg slung over the other, a crooked, satisfied smile on his inelegantly handsome face, shifted position, leaned forward, and said, "I don't especially trust politicians, Senator. Any politician. Nothing personal. No offense."

Connors returned the smile: "No offense."

"What I want is some assurance that if what I'm going after pans out—you know, supports what you want—that I get paid what it's worth. I mean, I can just let it drop— or keep it quiet."

"Or get paid by the other side." Connors's voice mirrored his impatience. "What's your politics, Mr. Perrone?"

"What's that got to do with anything?"

"Dennis tells me you share my views of certain things—and people."

"If you mean I don't like liberals, you're right. I was a cop in this city for fourteen years. The liberals made it tough for us to do our job. Arrest a perp, he walks. Book a black, he's out in an hour. Judges. Politicians. Yeah, I don't like liberals."

"That means we'll get along just fine." To Mackral: "Work this out with Mr. Perrone at another time. Thanks for coming in, Mr. Perrone. It was a pleasure meeting you."

Mackral motioned Perrone from the office. He walked him into the hallway and said, "Go ahead with your investigation into the allegation you say has been made. Don't worry about money. You deliver and you'll be paid accordingly." He flashed Perrone a wide smile. "You can trust me, Jim. I'm not a politician. I just work for one." He slapped the investigator on his broad back and sent him on his way.

Mackral spent the next hour preparing a position paper for the senator. Pleased with the result, he left it on Connors's desk and exited the Russell Senate Office Building through a delivery entrance. He drove to a McDonald's in the Adams-Morgan section of the city, where he ate a Big Mac and sipped a soft drink until the person he was to meet joined him in the booth.

"Something to eat?" Mackral asked.

"No." Jules Harris, a freelance investigative reporter, took out a long, spiral-bound reporter's notebook and a pen from his tan safari jacket, and laid them on the table. "What've you got?" he asked.

"This is strictly between us," Mackral said. "We owe you from that piece you did on the senator."

The reporter picked up the pen. "Shoot."

Mackral finished the last bite of his hamburger, drank some soda, and said, sotto voce, "Latham's confirmation is in big-time trouble."

"I came all the way here to be told that? Warren Brazier. Right?"

"Right. But there's more."

"Oh, yeah?"

"How about a charge of sexual harassment?"

The reporter whistled, said, "You in a rush?"

"No."

"I'm hungry."

A few minutes later, a half-eaten cheeseburger in front of him, Harris said, "Proceed. My stomach's stopped growling. Mind is fed, too. Sexual harassment? Who?"

Mackral's hand went up. "First, an understanding. I want this out ASAP. Within a day."

"Hold on," said Harris, holding up his hand for emphasis. "What's the rush?"

"That's for me to know, Jules."

"I can't just go with this without *some* corroboration."

"I'll give it to you. But you've got to find an outlet within twenty-four hours."

"I'll do my best."

"That's all I can ask. We have an understanding?"

"Sure. Give it to me. Who's making the charge?"

Molly, Melissa, John from New York, and another page from Ohio went to Georgetown that evening. They would have preferred to have burgers in one of the trendy bars—J. Paul's, Houston's, Martin's, or the Grog and Tankard—but their ages precluded that. So they sat upstairs in the American Cafe and ate sandwiches and salads and drank Cokes, and talked and laughed and kidded one another. Melissa was open in her flirtation with John, although the other young male page, Peter, had also captured her attention at times.

"Aren't you ever afraid?" Peter asked Molly after another round of Cokes had been delivered.

"Afraid of what?"

"You know, being the daughter of a famous congressman. Don't you have security?"

Molly laughed as she stripped paper from a fresh straw and plunged the straw into her glass. "Congressmen don't have security," she said. "I mean, I guess some do. The Speaker, people like that. But my dad doesn't."

"But when he's secretary of state, he will," Melissa said.

"I guess he will," Molly said.

"I guess *you* will," John said.

"I hope not," Molly said.

"It'd be fun," Melissa said. "Havin' all those cute Secret Service agents around." She lightly touched John's hand on the table. "Don't you feel like dancin'?"

Molly looked at her watch. It was after nine. The weekday curfew for pages was ten, midnight on weekends. They'd signed a binding code of conduct, and were told any breach of it called for strict sanctions. "We have to get back," Molly said.

Melissa made a pouty face.

"Yeah, we have to get back," John said. "What time is the school briefing tomorrow?"

"Six forty-five," Peter said.

"That's cruel and unusual punishment," Melissa said, "having classes start that early every day. I need my beauty sleep."

John laughed, and waved for a check. "Better get used to it."

He was right.

Once school started in the attic level of the Library of Congress Jefferson Building, they'd be taking five forty-minute classes, five days a week, the curriculum accredited by the Middle States Association of Colleges and Secondary Schools. Immediately following the final class of the day, they would report to the page supervisor, where the first order of business might be filing the *Congressional Record* from the previous day's proceedings. After that, they'd be busy delivering correspondence and legislative material within the congressional complex, answering phones in the members' cloakroom and delivering those messages to them on the floor, and manning a telephone bank of incoming requests for page services. They'd be expected to be on duty until five, or until the House adjourned for the day, whichever was later, many times working far into the night. And then, back to their dorm rooms to study and to get ready for the next day. Weekends were relatively free, except for alternate Saturdays, when they were expected to attend a seminar called WISP, the Washington Interdisciplinary Studies Program.

They arrived at the O'Neill Building at five minutes before ten and were met in the lobby by one of five assistants to the dorm director. She narrowed her eyes and said, "Cutting it close, aren't you?"

Melissa made a show of looking at her watch. "It's not ten," she said sweetly.

"I'd suggest you plan your evenings a little better,"

said the dorm monitor. With that, she disappeared, leaving Melissa, Molly, and the two male pages alone with the security guard behind the reception desk, a heavyset black man with a wide smile, who said in a deep baritone, "Better play by the rules, ladies and gentlemen. They're taken seriously around here."

Molly and Melissa went to their room and got ready for bed. In pajamas, they sat in their beds and read, Molly the book of rules for pages, Melissa that morning's copy of *The Washington Post.*

"Look at this," Melissa said, tossing a section of the paper to Molly in which a picture of Molly's father with industrialist Warren Brazier appeared, taken a few months earlier when both were in Moscow on a trade mission led by Latham.

The photo illustrated an article reporting that Congressman Latham's long-standing personal relationship with Warren Brazier was being closely scrutinized by the Senate Foreign Relations Committee as it prepared for confirmation hearings. According to the reporter, Senate minority whip Frank Connors, chairman of the committee, was especially interested in Brazier's contributions to Latham's campaigns over the years, and legislation Latham had sponsored in the House benefitting the California businessman.

"Do you know him?" Melissa asked.

"Mr. Brazier? Sure. He's *s-o-o-o* rich. He sends me expensive birthday and Christmas gifts every year."

"He looks sort of mean."

"Some people say that, but he's real nice to me and Dad and the rest of the family. We don't see him much. He's always traveling. Always in Russia or some other place."

"I suppose to get that rich, you have to be tough," Melissa said. "What's the story about?"

"Oh, that the confirmation committee wants to find out whether my dad did anything wrong. You know, take illegal campaign funds from Mr. Brazier, that sort of thing."

"Did he?"

"Did he what? My father? Take illegal money from Mr. Brazier? Of course not."

"That's good. Well, quarter a seven's almost here. Night."

"Good night."

Melissa fell asleep immediately, but Molly stayed awake. For the first time, she wished her father hadn't been nominated by President Scott. She had an idea from the beginning, of course—from the moment he announced to her that he'd accepted the nomination—that it meant intense examination of him as a politician and as a man. The family, too. Like his election campaigns back home in Northern California, but magnified a thousand percent. Everything about them would come under a microscope, especially one focused by his enemies. She heard that neighbors had been questioned by the FBI. So had the principal of Molly's school; what *he* could offer was beyond her.

But as sleep slowly came, her thoughts turned more positive. It would be exciting to be the daughter of the country's secretary of state. She didn't know how her brother, Martin, felt about it because they hadn't had much contact since the nomination. Her sister, Priscilla, was even more emotionally remote than Martin, living in New York where she was public relations director for a leading steamship line.

Her final thoughts were of Marge Edwards and their lunch. Would she really leave her job as her father's appointment secretary? She hoped not. In some ways, Marge was more of a sister to her than Priscilla, and certainly a more simpatico figure in her life than Martin.

She decided to call Marge the next morning and urge her to stay with her father, at least until the confirmation process was over and Paul Latham was secretary of state. She knew her father had made enemies over the course of his career in the House of Representatives, individuals unhappy with votes he cast and legislation he championed. What he needed now were all his good, loyal friends to come forward and stand beside him. Good, loyal friends like Marge Edwards.

Paul and Ruth Latham sat side by side on a cushioned glider on a small screened porch at the rear of their Foxhall home. They were in robes and pajamas. It was after midnight. Two citronella candles cast a silent, flickering sense of peace and well-being over the small space. A neighbor's TV, played too loud, had annoyed them a half hour ago. Now, with the neighbor in bed, the chirping of crickets and the drone of cicadas were the only sounds from beyond the screens. Fireflies in the yard provided their miniature fireworks display.

"I still wish she'd decided to live here," Ruth said.

"I can understand why she wants the dorm," he said.

"I can, too. But I get nervous when I think about her on her own for the first time. Capitol Hill isn't the safest part of town."

Latham smiled and patted his wife's hand. "She'll be fine. Security at the dorm and school is heavy. Besides, if she had to get up here in time to make her six forty-five class, there'd be war in the house."

Ruth laughed softly. "Speaking of wars, Martin's due tomorrow."

"I know. I hope the chip has fallen off his shoulder."

"That's funny. The chip. He's knee-deep in wood chips every day."

"I wish he were a chip off the proverbial old block."

"Don't start on that, Paul."

"I won't. It's just that he's always so damn angry. It'll be good to see him. Heard from Priscilla?"

"She called this afternoon. She's off on another trip. Transatlantic. With a group of travel writers."

"I met with Warren this afternoon."

"Oh? A problem?"

"Yes."

Her silence said she was listening.

"I told him I was backing off on the Russian Trade and Investment Bill."

Ruth Latham had never delved too deeply into details of her husband's political activities. She was a solid campaigner for him every two years in California, and was an active participant in a variety of Washington charities, which was sincere on her part and also reflected positively on him. But the nitty-gritty of the Hill held little interest for her.

"Isn't that the bill you said a few months ago was the most important Russian trade bill in your career?"

"Yeah. I said that. And it would be. But there's something about it that's off. . . . It feels wrong. Warren's staff keeps pushing for amendments to it that—well, frankly, that would distort its original intent. He's looking for the moon in the bill—earmarked tax breaks, protection against nationalism, accelerated depreciation. Yeah. The moon."

"Was he angry?"

"He was angry before I even told him. Evidently, things aren't going well for him in Russia. He's trying to buy Kazan Energy from the Russian government."

"I've never understood that," she said. "How a government sells industries."

"Because the government doesn't own industries, for the most part, in this country. The Soviet government used to own everything. Now that it's opened up, the government is selling off its holdings to raise money, and to give credence to its new free-market economy."

"And Warren wants to buy this Russian energy company?"

"Right. If it were a fair bidding process, he wouldn't have a problem. But the people in the Yeltsin government responsible for selling its industries are on the take big-time. That's why the bill in committee is so important to Warren. He told me that if he can deliver that bill, it will grease the skids for buying Kazan Energy."

"That's awful."

"Sure it is. The Yeltsin government is—"

"I don't mean that. Wanting you—this government—to pass a bill to help him get richer sounds . . . sounds wrong, as you said."

It was a reassuring, somewhat condescending laugh he offered. "Nothing really wrong with it, Ruth, as long as it benefits this country, along with helping out an American business or industry. I admire your black-and-white view of things, but nothing gets done without compromise. When both sides benefit from a bill, it's a good deal. All the legislation I've sponsored over the years that helped

Warren's business also advanced our global competitiveness, especially in Russia."

"I'm sure it has."

"Which is why I have to back off with this new legislation, unless Warren backs off, too."

"The nomination?"

"What about it?"

"Is that playing a role in your decision?"

"Sure. My relationship with Warren is looming large with Connors and his committee. Dan Gibbs, one of the president's lawyers who's handling my nomination for the White House, called just before I met with Warren. He says the president wants me to pull back on any legislation even potentially involving Warren. At least until the hearings are over."

She squeezed his hand and said, "That sounds smart to me." She kissed his cheek. "Come on, Mr. Secretary. My, that has a nice ring to it. Time for bed."

He returned the kiss, lightly, on her lips. "Not sleepy. You go on. I'll be up in a while."

He sat on the porch for another half hour before going to a dressing room separate from the master bedroom. He showered there, then went to the kitchen and brewed a half pot of strong coffee. He returned to the dressing room and put on a suit and tie, buffed his black shoes with an electric buffing machine, went to the kitchen, and left a note on the table: *Couldn't sleep, so figured might as well get an early start. Call you later. Me.* He drew a crude heart with their initials in it, and added an arrow.

He left through the front door and stood in the driveway, next to the silver Lexus that was his car; Ruth drove the white Plymouth Voyager. He looked up to their bedroom window, where his wife of thirty-one years slept soundly, at peace with herself and their life together. Somehow, in some way, he knew, his decision to accept the president's bid to become secretary of state threatened to shatter that peace. He forced the thought from his mind, got into the Lexus, and drove faster than was his custom over the empty streets of the nation's capital.

10

Bill Fadis had been a member of the Capitol police force for almost twenty years.

The force had been started in 1801 with a single night watchman, but grew rapidly over the years—exponentially after 1954, when four Puerto Rican terrorists opened fire from the gallery into the House chamber, wounding five representatives. Seventeen years later, a bomb exploded in the wee hours in a men's room of the old Senate wing, propelling the Capitol police into a highly professional law enforcement agency, incorporating state-of-the-art K-9 bomb detection capability, hostage negotiation teams, and a large contingent of plainclothes detectives.

More recently, with the increased threat of terrorist attacks on government institutions, two new units had been created—a Containment and Emergency Response Team trained by the FBI's Hostage Rescue Team, and the

First Responder Unit, specially equipped to lock down the Capitol should a terrorist attack be launched.

Nothing like crisis to prompt action.

Even with the increase in manpower (currently more than thirteen hundred)—womanpower, too (almost two hundred women)—the force was spread thin, providing round-the-clock security seven days a week for the forty-block, 250-acre complex of congressional buildings. Its clients? The 435 representatives, 100 senators, and the more than 25,000 people working for the elected officials.

An unambitious, placid man, Fadis had been content to remain a uniformed officer assigned to guard building entrances. This day, he'd been on duty since midnight at the southeast entrance to the Capitol. He enjoyed the midnight shift. It was quiet at night, even tranquil without the thousands of sweaty, noisy tourists streaming in each day to see their government in action, or for some, in inaction, plus congressional staffers and members coming and going, making demands.

He was surprised to see one of those members arrive that morning.

"Congressman Latham," he said, pulling in his stomach and smiling.

"Good morning, Bill."

Fadis glanced at a clock on the wall: a little after 2 A.M. It wasn't unusual to see members of the House working late, all night at times when Congress was immersed in tricky, controversial legislation, or in times of national crisis. But things had been slow that week.

Rather than walking by, Latham paused next to Fadis. "Rainy day in the forecast," he said.

"So they say."

"You've been here a long time, haven't you?"

"Twenty years in two months, Congressman."

"A little longer than I have."

"Not by much. How's the family?"

"My daughter's a page this term."

"Oh?"

"You'll be seeing her around. Her name's Molly."

"I'll . . . be looking for her, Mr. Latham."

Latham, too, checked the wall clock. Four minutes had passed.

"Good to see you, Officer Fadis."

"Yes, sir. Have a good day."

Fadis watched Latham walk slowly in the direction of Statuary Hall, the former House chamber, refurbished for the 1976 bicentennial as a repository of two statues from each of the fifty states. During normal hours, as many as 25,000 visitors would pass through it—more this day, with rain in the forecast.

Latham thought of Shakespeare—"hush as death"—as he walked across the vast black-and-white marble floor, his steps coming back at him. The hall's quiescence was deafening. It had unique acoustics. Latham had brought each of his three children there when they were little to demonstrate how by standing in a certain place on the floor and whispering, people across the hall, also stationed in a special place, could hear the words. All three kids had been astounded and delighted.

Latham went to the south door and paused beneath the statue depicting Liberty, then turned to take in Clio, the "Muse of History," riding in a winged chariot and recording passing events in a large tablet. A gilded clock attached to the chariot had been keeping time there since 1819, the Capitol's "official" timepiece.

He drew a deep breath. The clock said two-thirty. They were to meet at three. A half hour to kill.

He spent the next twenty minutes admiring art in the Capitol's hallways. At ten minutes before three, he headed for the door that led to a small, parklike area surrounded by trees and shrubbery. On good-weather days, he and dozens of fellow House members would walk past the pocket park on their way to and from their offices when a vote had been called on the House floor.

The guard at the door, a young black man with military bearing, didn't recognize Latham and asked for his pass.

"New?" Latham said, showing him his ID.

"Yes, sir. Sorry."

"Better you do your job. Thought I'd get some air."

"Humid."

"Yes, it is. Thank you."

Latham stepped into the outside air, heavy with humidity, gray, almost green, the moon attempting to bore a hole through low, turbid clouds.

For some unexplained reason, Latham wanted a cigarette. He'd quit smoking a dozen years ago, but still had sporadic urges, usually during theater intermissions.

He sat on a small concrete bench and looked up at the illuminated twenty-foot, seven-and-a-half-ton bronze figure, the Statue of Freedom, rising into the mist from atop the Capitol dome like some ethereal figure ascending from the grave.

He stood and looked at his watch. Five past three. The urge for a cigarette was stronger. He thought of Ruth sleeping at home, unaware he'd left the house to wait in this picturesque little oasis from the strife and turmoil of Congress.

* * *

Another five minutes passed.

Angry now, he decided to wait for only another five.

Two minutes went by.

And three.

"Hello."

Latham turned in the direction from which the nearby voice came.

The discharge sound from the weapon was small and almost noiseless, a tiny *pop*.

Latham fell to his knees, his right hand involuntarily going to his right temple, where the bullet had entered. Blood ran freely down his fingers and over his hand. He pitched forward, twisting as he did so, his final living action. He landed on his back, eyes open wide, arm outstretched, more blood seeping from his partially open, crooked mouth.

A figure stepped from the shrubbery, came directly to the body, went down on one knee, and with gloved hand placed the instrument of Latham's death, a 9-mm Uzi, silencer removed, in the dead congressman's right hand, curling his sticky, red fingers around it. It took only seconds to accomplish. The figure stood, looked left and right, and disappeared into the bushes, leaving the lifeless body to be viewed only by the Statue of Freedom, looking down on it from her position on the Capitol dome, the crown of the building symbolizing the American dream, which had inspired Hawthorne to write during an 1862 visit, "the world has not many statelier or more beautiful edifices."

Paul Latham, eight-term congressman from Northern California, nominee for secretary of state, would never see it again.

11

Paul Latham's body was found at five-seventeen by a member of the Patrol Division of the Capitol police's Uniform Services Bureau. He immediately notified a dispatcher in the communications room beneath the Russell Senate Office Building, who in turn passed the message on to the Contingency Emergency Response Team (CERT), housed in headquarters a block from the Hart Office Building.

"Member down," the CERT commander on duty yelled. "Congressman Latham. Let's go."

The commander and two other officers, wearing camouflage pants, white T-shirts and sneakers, pulled on camouflage shirts and bulletproof jackets and ran upstairs to the roll-call room, where a gun rack was unlocked. Each was handed an M-249 automatic weapon, capable of firing more than a thousand rounds a minute.

The watch commander joined them. "He's in the pocket park, southeast corner. He's not in succession."

An important piece of information.

Had the victim been the Speaker of the House, or the president pro tempore of the Senate—in the line of succession to the presidency—the Secret Service's CAT, or Counter Assault Team, would immediately be brought in. The Capitol police's CERT unit and the Secret Service's CAT held periodic joint drills to prepare them for such situations.

As the CERT team headed for the scene, news of Latham's death reached every division of the Capitol police. Its chief, Henry Folsom, raced to the park after issuing orders to seal off all Capitol Building entrances, and to do the same with the crime scene. As an afterthought, he ordered patrol cars to shut down the six intersections marking the perimeter of Capitol Hill. By the time he arrived at the park, it had been draped with yellow plastic tape: CRIME SCENE—DO NOT CROSS. The crime scene unit under his command was on its way. It had started to rain, as promised.

Latham had been covered with a blue blanket. Folsom reached down and slowly, gingerly folded it back to reveal the head, upper torso, right arm, and hand. He stared at Latham for what seemed to others to be a very long time. Finally, he turned to his assistant chief, Vic Lombardo. "Have the architect and sergeants-at-arms been notified?"

Lombardo lowered the cell phone from his ear. "Yes, sir. They've just gathered in the architect's office waiting for you."

Folsom sighed and pressed his lips tightly together.

As chief of the Capitol police, which he'd headed for

six years after a long but undistinguished career in the FBI, he answered to the Capitol Police Board, consisting of three people—the architect of the Capitol, and the sergeants-at-arms of the House and Senate, both political appointees. Folsom really couldn't be critical of political patronage. He was the beneficiary of it, a long friendship with two powerful senators leading to his job on Capitol Hill.

As for the "architect": His name was Jack Goss. Goss was not an architect. There was a time when those holding the position possessed that credential. But that was when the job focused upon how things *looked* on Capitol Hill. Now, the architect was responsible for keeping things running, a building superintendent of sorts, charged with the technical and physical operations of the Capitol and its House and Senate office buildings, the Supreme Court and Library of Congress, even the ten thousand species of flowers and plants in the U.S. Botanic Garden. In a word, everything federal within the confines of the Hill.

Folsom carried no brief for Goss, and was disappointed when he was chosen to replace the previous architect, with whom Folsom had a better, certainly more cordial relationship. The problem, Folsom often told his wife, was that the Capitol police answered to three people who knew little if anything about law enforcement and security. At least at the FBI, you reported to pros. Folsom's first and foremost priority from the day he became chief was to continue the process of turning his force into one as capable and advanced as any other police department in Washington, of which there were many, too many as far as he was concerned.

There was—he could recite the list in his mind—the

CIA's own security cops protecting Langley; the National Institutes of Health private force; D.C.'s MPD, with more than 3,500 armed cops; the FBI; 469 park police; 345 uniformed Secret Service officers; 286 Metro transit police; 159 U.S. marshals; 100 armed Federal Protective Service agents; 68 drug cops with the Drug Enforcement Agency; the Bureau of Alcohol, Tobacco and Firearms; Immigration and Naturalization; the State Department's 1,000-person force protecting Washington's vast foreign diplomatic community.

Even the Washington aqueduct boasted its own police force.

And Folsom's 1,300-strong Capitol police.

Small wonder the heads of these agencies spent half their days trying to resolve jurisdictional disputes.

Folsom said to Lombardo, "Keep everybody out of here except for the crime scene people. Everybody! No exceptions."

"Got it."

"I'll be with Goss."

"Okay."

The architect of the Capitol occupied a large, handsomely appointed office on the fourth, or attic, floor of the Capitol. Folsom, dressed in his dark blue uniform with gold buttons, the six stripes on his left sleeve and gold on his cap's visor designating his leadership rank, was immediately ushered into the office and asked to take a chair across from Goss's expansive mahogany desk. The two sergeants-at-arms and a few assistants sat in chairs to either side of Goss.

"What do we know?" Goss asked, not bothering with preliminaries.

Folsom ran it down for him. Not much to tell.

Congressman Latham found at five-seventeen in the pocket park outside the southeast entrance. Possible suicide. Gun in right hand. Fatal wound to right temple.

"What's the status of the investigation?" Goss asked, hands forming a tent beneath his narrow chin. He was bald—he shaved his head each day—and wore round glasses from another era. Jack Goss was fifty years old. He had a habit of chewing on his lower lip; Folsom sometimes wondered why he didn't bite through it. His voice was unpleasantly high.

"Status? Of the investigation? We haven't even thought about that phase, Jack. We've just secured the body and the scene. Crime lab personnel are there going over everything. We've shut off the building at all entrances. Same with the intersections."

"I know about the intersections," Goss said. "The mayor called a few minutes ago. He's concerned about rush hour."

"Rush hour? That's his concern? I—"

"Hardly seems necessary to create a traffic snarl, considering it's a suicide. Where's the threat?"

Folsom told himself not to demonstrate annoyance. He said in an even voice, "We don't know if it's a suicide, Jack. We don't know much of anything at this moment. It's prudent to seal off the Capitol until we know more."

"The press?" the House sergeant-at-arms asked.

"Gathering rapidly," Folsom answered. "We're herding them into the plaza."

The Senate sergeant-at-arms said, "You've notified the FBI." Folsom would have preferred that it be put as a question.

"No," he said.

"Why not?" Goss asked.

112

"Premature," Folsom replied.

"What about the medical examiner?" Goss asked.

"I want the crime scene people to finish up first."

"Why?" asked Goss.

"It makes sense," Folsom said. "There's nothing to be gained calling in MPD's crime scene techs. Nothing they can do that we can't. Besides, the faster the scene is examined, the better. Less evidence to lose, or screw up."

"Washington MPD has to be called in anyway," the House sergeant-at-arms said. "It's in the code."

"Using the D.C. medical examiner is in the code," Folsom said. "Nothing about MPD."

"Disagree," the sergeant-at-arms said, holding up a piece of paper. "The MPD is authorized to help the medical examiner. That means they're part of the investigation."

"Wonderful," Folsom muttered, more to himself. "We'll be tripping over each other."

Goss's phone rang. He picked it up, listened, then slowly lowered the receiver into its cradle. "The FBI is on its way over. No need to call."

Folsom stood. "I'd better get back to the scene," he said. "Anything else?"

"Now that the FBI is involved, there is nothing else," Goss said.

Folsom returned to the park, where his people were finishing up. The rain fell harder now. The body had been covered again, this time by a sheet of plastic on top of the blanket. Folsom took another look at Latham, quicker this time. Pictures had been taken; the gun had been removed from the deceased's right hand, to be examined in the lab. If the popular congressman had killed himself, the FBI wouldn't hang around long.

But would anyone accept a suicide ruling after the

Vince Foster death, investigated by the park police? Political detractors of the Clinton White House had kept the possibility of murder open, primarily through the media. The park police took a ton of criticism for having been the agency charged with the investigation, lacking homicide expertise and personnel as it did.

The Capitol police had its own homicide unit, and a good one as far as Folsom was concerned: small by MPD standards, but manned by men and women with previous city police experience.

Folsom was torn as he left the crime scene and returned to his office, on the top floor of the seven-story Capitol police headquarters, to further coordinate things. Vic Lombardo had been left in charge at the park to handle on-site coordination with the other agencies that would soon arrive.

On the one hand, he wanted the investigation of Latham's death to remain within his jurisdiction. On the other hand, there was a relief factor in having the Federal Bureau of Investigation take over.

By the time he reached his office and had settled behind his desk, he found dozens of phone messages to be returned, noted on pink slips in front of him. Jack Goss had overridden Folsom's order to block off all streets leading to the Capitol. Traffic would flow again.

A number of other decisions were made, and actions taken, in the next hour.

Latham's body was removed to the Washington MPD morgue for an autopsy.

Ruth Latham was notified of her husband's death by the Speaker of the House, who led a small contingent to the Latham home with the grim news.

A hastily called press briefing, blessed by the architect,

saw Chief Folsom give a brief, factual statement of what was known to date. He declined to answer questions, saying more than once, "We have nothing more to give you at this time. We have told you everything we know."

Three members of Congress joined Folsom at the press briefing, and took the opportunity to praise the deceased member and Cabinet nominee. Their opportunistic attitude dismayed Folsom, but he reminded himself that were he an elected official, he'd probably do the same—gravitate to any microphone or reporter with a pad to say hello to the voters back home. "Man is by nature a political animal." Who'd said that? Folsom wondered. Yogi Berra? Probably not.

The president of the United States issued a terse message through his press secretary, Sandy Teller: "This is a tragedy of not only personal proportions for the family, but for the nation. We have lost a loyal, courageous, and effective representative of the American people. And I have lost a dear friend."

And Mac Smith, secluded in his study at home, poring over computer printouts on recent legal developments in Russia, got the call from Paul Latham's chief of staff, Robert Mondrian.

"I'll be there in a half hour," Smith said.

12

Rather than waste time looking for a parking space, Smith took a taxi to the Rayburn House Office Building. Each time he climbed into a D.C. cab—or one in New York—he thought of London and its fleet of clean, efficient vehicles driven by knowledgeable, proud drivers. At moments, he considered moving there for that reason alone.

A knot of journalists and TV cameras were on the sidewalk outside the building. A reporter recognized Smith and stepped in his path. "What's new on this, Mr. Smith?"

"I know less than you do," Smith said.

"They're keeping us outside. Hell, some of us are trying to go in to see other members."

"Excuse me," Smith said, aware that the rain, which had abated, now fell with renewed conviction.

On an ordinary day, entering a House or Senate office

building involved only passing through a metal detector as found at any airport, and allowing hand luggage to go through a similar device. This morning, three Capitol police uniformed officers—there was usually only one—stopped Smith to ask what business he had there.

"I was called by Mr. Mondrian, chief of staff to Congressman Latham. I'm—I was his legal counsel. Name is Smith. Mackensie Smith."

One of the officers called the office: "Okay," he said.

Bob Mondrian was waiting, along with others on the staff. A female staffer cried quietly at her desk. Two young men huddled in a corner, discussing the tragic news.

"Hello, Mac," Mondrian said, shaking his hand. "Come on in."

They entered Latham's office, where two plainclothes investigators from the Capitol police were talking with Latham's press secretary, Harry Davis. Smith was introduced as Latham's counsel for the confirmation hearings.

The investigators, a man and a woman, each in their thirties, returned to their conversation with Davis. Smith and Mondrian listened in.

"That press conference this morning was uncalled for," the female investigator said. "Chief Folsom has been instructed to release nothing further to the press without prior clearance from the White House."

"Nothing?" Davis said. "Stonewall them? For how long?"

"Until the White House gives the go-ahead. Congressman Latham was up for secretary of state. This obviously has ramifications beyond the House."

"Sure, I understand that," said Davis. "But—"

"Look," the male investigator said, "this incident is out of our hands—out of *everyone's* hands—except for the

117

White House. The autopsy is being performed downtown as we speak." He turned to Mondrian. "The FBI will be here shortly to start going through the office. We'll be working with them."

"How thorough a search?" Mondrian asked.

The investigators looked at each other like two children who'd been asked a silly question by an adult. "As thorough as it has to be," the male investigator said. "Right now, you and the staff will have to vacate. We're sealing this office off."

Mondrian laughed, said to the investigators, "We can't just vacate. There's a ton of work to be done here. Besides, Paul—Congressman Latham has a number of files that are classified. He's been reviewing them for his confirmation hearing."

The man said, "I understand all that, Mr. Mondrian. But we have our orders. The White House has dispatched representatives to be here when the office is searched. State Department, too, I believe."

"On whose authority?" Davis asked.

"The White House."

"This is a congressional matter, at least for the moment," Davis said.

"Let's not get into a debate on jurisdiction," said the woman. "The president has already called the Speaker and asked for an 'understanding.' The Speaker gave it to him. Look, don't make this more difficult than it has to be. Ask everyone to leave the office immediately. Nothing is to be removed by the staff except personal belongings—handbags, umbrellas, that's it."

Mondrian looked to Smith for support of his position. What he received was Mac's laconic, "They're within their rights, Bob. Where can we all gather?"

Mondrian thought for a moment. "Paul's committee office, in the Capitol."

"That's been sealed, too," said the woman investigator. She went into the large outer office and announced to the staff that they would have to leave—"Immediately!"

"Let's go," Mondrian said, coming up behind her. "Just take your purses, umbrellas. Nothing else." He returned to Latham's office, picked up the phone, and after a brief conversation announced, "The hearing room directly above us is free. We'll go there."

The male investigator said, "We'll want to be questioning each of you. Along with the FBI. I suggest you stay in that room until we contact you." Mondrian gave them the hearing-room number, and led the staff and Mac Smith to their temporary nesting place. Once there, and settled at a large conference table in front of the tiered section at which House members sat when conducting hearings, Mondrian took a pen from his jacket pocket, pulled closer a yellow lined legal pad on the table, and said, "Before they start questioning, maybe we should discuss this together. You know, get a sense of what anyone of us knows."

Glances all about, shoulders shrugged, muttered denials of knowing anything of interest.

Smith said, "I'm probably more in the dark than any of you. All Bob told me when he called was that Congressman Latham was dead, and that it was an apparent suicide." He turned to Mondrian. "A gun, you said?"

Mondrian filled Smith in, to the extent he was able, on the discovery of Latham's body and events occurring since then.

"Anyone have an inkling that Paul was depressed, anxious, *suicidal*?" Smith asked.

"He's been uptight," a young woman said. She was part of a team that answered Latham's constituent mail.

"Natural," Mondrian said. "The nomination on top of everything else he was juggling."

"Beyond that," Smith said. "Any unusual pressures on him? Any threats?"

"Threats?" Harry Davis said. "It's a suicide."

"Allegedly," Smith said. "Even if it is, there might have been some threat that drove him to take his life."

No one knew of any.

"What about you, Mac?" Mondrian asked. "You've been staying close to Paul lately."

"I spoke with him late yesterday afternoon. He sounded—well, under the gun. Even a little angry."

"About what?" Davis asked.

"I have no idea. The conversation was brief. No more than a few minutes."

The door opened. "Congressman Latham's staff?"

"Yes," Mondrian replied.

"We're FBI. Mind if we come in?"

"Please do," Mondrian said.

Four special agents of the Federal Bureau of Investigation entered the room and were introduced by the agent in charge. "We'd like to talk to each of you individually about the death of the congressman. The House clerk told us there's an adjacent empty room over there." He pointed. "We can use that."

"I have a question," one of Latham's staff said. "Why are we being questioned by the FBI? Paul—Congressman Latham—killed himself."

"We have to investigate any unusual death on the Hill, ma'am. It won't take long."

"I'm Mackensie Smith," Mac said. "I was counsel to

Congressman Latham for his confirmation hearings. I assume I'm free to go."

The lead agent chewed his cheek and consulted a paper he'd taken from his briefcase. "We'd like to speak with you, too, Mr. Smith. But we can do that later today, if you'll make yourself available."

"Of course." Smith slid a business card to the agent. "Call me. I'll be at this number all afternoon."

The light on Smith's answering machine was blinking when he returned to his Foggy Bottom home. Annabel had called twice. She'd heard the news on the radio. "Where *are* you?" she said through the tiny speaker.

Smith realized he should have called her at the gallery before racing to Latham's office. He did so instantly.

"Was it suicide?" she asked.

"That's what they're saying—now. He had a gun in his right hand. The wound was to his right temple."

"Can it be?"

"Who knows? He was under a lot of stress. The FBI and Capitol police have sealed off his office. They're doing the autopsy at the MPD morgue."

"Have you talked to Ruth yet?"

"No. Dreading the call."

"Want me to make it?"

"Let's let it go until tonight. We'll make it together. I'm sure she doesn't need us intruding so soon."

"Mac."

"Yes?"

"Is there any talk of murder?"

"If there is, I haven't heard it. But after Vince Foster, I don't think anybody in this town will take suicide for granted again. They'll nail it down, and quickly, I imagine. At least I hope so."

"The president is speaking in a half hour."

"Oh? I'll turn on the TV."

"Will you be there the rest of the day?"

"Expect to be, unless something comes up. Sorry I didn't call you this morning before going to Paul's office. I'll let you know if I leave again."

The majority of other calls on his machine were from media people, requesting interviews, comments, etc. But the call that captured his attention to the extent that he returned it immediately was from Jessica Belle, former student in his class on Russian-U.S. legal systems, who'd followed Giles Broadhurst to his new position at the CIA. She answered on the first ring of the direct number she'd left.

"Thanks for getting back so fast, Professor. I—"

"Make it Mac. Okay?"

"Sure. Can we get together?"

"Of course. What about?"

"Paul Latham."

"I should have assumed. What do you hear about it?"

"Probably more than you have, or than I want to."

"What does *that* mean?"

"When can we meet?"

"I'm free right now."

"I'm into a meeting in ten minutes. Four?"

"All right. Where?"

"The Marriott at National?"

"All right."

"The bar? At four."

"I'll be there."

He called Annabel and told her where he'd be later that afternoon.

"Any idea what she wants?" Annabel asked.

"Not a clue."

"The president's on in ten minutes."

"I'll watch."

"Call after he's through."

"Shall do."

The president spoke from the White House briefing room. Joseph Scott's broad, handsome face was drawn and sad as he placed notes on the lectern, issued a flat greeting to the reporters, and said, "This is a very sad day for me personally, for the nation, and for the entire world. Congressman Paul Latham was not only a dear and trusted friend, he was one of the most able members of Congress. I nominated him to be our secretary of state because the nation and world need the sort of steady hand on the rudder he would have provided.

"I urge each of you not to speculate on the circumstances of the congressman's untimely death until more is known. This is a dreadful blow to his family. Speculation will only add to their grief. Thank you."

He walked away from a barrage of questions hurled at him.

Mac called Annabel. "Tough on the president," he said.

"Have you heard anything else?"

"No. There are calls on the machine from the press. I don't intend to return them."

"I agree. But look out the door before you leave. They'll probably track you down at home."

"Yeah. Well, I'll try to get in an hour or so on the Russian project before heading for Rosslyn."

"Okay. I'll be home early. 'Bye. Love you."

The FBI man called and asked if they could get together with Mac the following morning. They would be at the house at ten.

He tried to concentrate on the U.S.-Russian legal project, but gave up after a series of false starts.

He left the house at three-thirty, relieved to see no reporters camped outside the door. It was while passing over the Theodore Roosevelt Bridge on his way to Rosslyn, Virginia, that it struck him for the first time: Latham's appointment secretary, Marge Edwards, hadn't been at the office that morning. Was she sick? Or was she so distraught at the news that she couldn't bring herself to be there? He remembered Marge's comment about Paul asking her to keep an eye on Molly. She's probably with the daughter, he thought. Tough duty, beyond the call of appointment secretary.

The question came and went, replaced by the larger and more meaningful question of why he was meeting Jessica Belle.

13

The Washington, D.C., press corps was stretched thin that day trying to get a handle on the death of Representative Paul Latham—so many friends and colleagues to corner and question, so many places to be at the same time.

By four that afternoon, their ranks had swelled as reporters from other cities, and from national and international wire services and publications, arrived in the capital to follow up on the initial news.

Everyone who'd ever had dealings with Paul Latham, for any reason and in any capacity, was fair game. The reporters and photographers, remote TV trucks, cameramen, familiar on-air TV anchorpeople, and hundreds of support staff camped in front of the Lathams' Foxhall home, the Rayburn House Office Building, the White House, and the State and Justice departments. The home addresses of Latham's staff were ferreted out, and correspondents dispatched to them. Neighbors of the Lathams were interviewed for clues into the dead congressman's state of mind: "Notice anything unusual about him lately?" "Now that I think of it, yes. I saw him last weekend in the yard. I don't know, he had a funny look on his face."

No surprise either that a sizable press contingent sought out Warren Brazier, or anyone from his organization willing to speak to the media. The best that could be determined was that the industrialist was in Washington, probably in his office on the top two floors of an eight-story office building on New Jersey Avenue, within shouting distance of the Capitol and Union Station.

As with other administrative centers of Brazier Industries—Moscow, San Francisco, New York, Singapore, and New Delhi—a large corner office was kept empty for the company's dynamic leader, flowers changed each day, his favorite beverages and snacks on hand, personal staff poised to serve. Each office had a large, private marble bath with sauna and Jacuzzi, a small bedroom area, and a closet containing a full wardrobe.

Brazier had been there since five that morning. He received word at six from an aide, who'd been monitoring local television, that Latham's body had been found.

"Are you sure?" Brazier had responded.

"Yes, sir."

"I see. Thank you. Please inform the staff, and make it clear there is to be no comment, from anyone, to the press."

"Yes, sir."

Brazier tuned the TV in his office to CNN. His timing was good; the anchor had just begun an update on the story. He intoned over a still photo of Latham, "As reported earlier, Congressman Paul Latham of California, eight terms in the House of Representatives, highly respected chairman of the powerful House International Relations Committee, and nominated by President Scott to become secretary of state, is dead. . . . His body was discovered earlier this morning by a member of the Capitol police, who came across Representative Latham in a small park near the Capitol. According to our information, he was found with a revolver gripped in his right hand. Death resulted from a gunshot to the temple. An autopsy is being conducted by the district medical examiner.

"A source close to CNN tells us that Congressman Latham had recently been depressed over allegations of impropriety stemming from his friendship with the industrialist Warren Brazier. Our source further informs us that the Senate Foreign Relations Committee, chaired by California Senator Frank Connors, the committee that would have conducted Latham's confirmation hearing, had developed evidence of alleged wrongdoing by the deceased Congressman. We'll continue to bring you this breaking story as more information becomes available."

Now, at four in the afternoon, Brazier remained secluded in his office. He'd spent much of the day conferring with top aides, including his chief lobbyist, Tom Krouch. Krouch was a veteran Washington hand on the Hill, a switch-hitter, having worked for a number of senators and representatives, Republican and Democrat, both on their office staffs and on committees. His extensive network of congressional contacts trusted him, a lobbyist's most precious commodity. He ran Brazier Industries' lobbying effort by the book, which meant he knew how to walk that fine line between legal and illegal lobbying, crossing it only when he was confident he'd get away with it.

The other member of Brazier's senior staff with whom he spent considerable time that day was Aleksandr Patiashvili. Patiashvili, headquartered in Moscow, had flown into Washington two days earlier. He headed up the company's Russian executive corps, including the dozen or so in the Washington office whose responsibility was, among other things, to advise Krouch's lobbying group on matters of direct interest to the company's Russian projects, and to maintain liaison with various embassies in Washington representing nations of the CIS, the Commonwealth of Independent States, which had replaced the Soviet Union. As a group, they were young and well educated, with the exception of Patiashvili, who'd been with Brazier for more than twenty years.

Before joining the company, he'd been an old-line Communist, a general in the *Komitet Gosudarstvennoi Bezopasnosti*, the KGB. Many eyebrows were raised when he left that post to become a Brazier Industries' employee. You didn't just walk away from the feared and powerful Soviet intelligence agency to join an American company without the move having been blessed from high up. Speculation was that Brazier had paid handsomely, not to Patiashvili, but to leaders within the Soviet government to bring onboard someone with Patiashvili's heavy credentials.

While these meetings took place, Russian executives on the floor below assigned to Brazier's Washington office caught up on things back home with the three young men who'd accompanied Patiashvili from

Moscow. They sipped tea and nibbled on an overflowing platter of *blinchiki s'varenem*, the jam pancakes favored by the boss, that were flown in regularly from Russia. They commented on the news that the boss's friend, the American congressman from California, Paul Latham, had committed suicide that morning. But none of them knew just how close—more important, how interdependent— Brazier and Latham had been. It was a Warren Brazier management technique never to let anyone else in his organization know the big picture. That, he reserved for himself.

Soon, talk among the young Russian men turned from suicide to more pleasant things. There was laughter and good-natured kidding, the latest jokes told, most of them sexual, but one of the young men in the room did not seem to be enjoying the banter. Anatoly Alekseyev, thirty-four, an employee of Brazier Industries for two years, left the room twice to make a phone call. When asked whom he was calling, he replied, "A friend. Just a friend."

Alekseyev's area of responsibility was in the energy division of the company. Brazier's joint oil-drilling venture with the French and Russians on *Yuzhno-Sakhalinsk* had been receiving most of his attention the past six months. What had started as a relatively forthright project had deteriorated into a bureaucratic morass, complicated by a falling-out between Brazier and his French partners. Adding to Alekseyev's daily burdens was the recent attempt by the company to buy Kazan Energy from the Russian government. He'd been working twelve- and fourteen-hour days, seven days a week, which cut annoyingly into his social life as a Washington bachelor. He enjoyed America's capital city, especially

Georgetown and its many pubs and nightclubs, where singles gathered to perform the mating dance.

He was a handsome young man, tall and angular with thick black hair worn short, and a serious, dedicated, olive-skinned face. He'd gradually replaced the suits he'd brought with him from Moscow with Western-style clothing, which draped neatly on his slender, muscular body. He did nicely at those watering holes frequented by singles, if such success was determined by not going home alone. Upon arriving in Washington, he lived in a one-bedroom apartment in a building constructed on upper Wisconsin Avenue to provide housing for employees of what was then the new Soviet Embassy, built on the city's highest point, Mount Alto, and providing a troublingly direct line of sight into the White House. But after a year there, Alekseyev moved away from this Russian conclave to a decidedly fancier and certainly more American apartment complex on the banks of the Potomac River, in lively Georgetown. He was much happier there.

Alekseyev and the others waited to be summoned by Brazier. But at five-thirty, to their surprise, the boss's personal secretary entered the room and said, "You must be living good. He says everyone can go home except for a few people. Enjoy your evening. He wants the staff here at seven in the morning. There is to be no comment to any member of the press. Anyone who violates that will be dismissed immediately." The young execs waited until she was gone before allowing sarcastic chuckles to surface.

Alekseyev and his Washington-based colleagues went to their offices to pack up for the night. Offices were to be spotless and uncluttered overnight; Brazier was known to wander through at odd hours, leaving caustic notes for those who violated that rule, one of many.

The three newcomers, who'd flown in from Moscow with Aleksandr Patiashvili, were unsure what to do. They lingered in the hall. "We can leave, too?" one asked another.

He shrugged. "I don't know."

Their question was answered by Brazier's secretary. She came to where they stood and said, "Wait here." She poked her head in Anatoly Alekseyev's office doorway and said, "He wants you to make sure they get dinner and arrive back at the hotel without incident."

"Me?" His voice mirrored his disappointment.

"Yes, Anatoly, you. And make sure they're back here by seven."

She returned to the three young men in the hallway and repeated, in surprisingly smooth Russian, the admonition about not speaking to the press.

Alekseyev led his three charges from the building, exiting through a back entrance leading from the building's basement. Although the majority of reporters were in front, there were a half-dozen waiting at the rear doorway. They shouted questions, but Alekseyev waved them off, saying as they walked, "No comment. No comment."

His car, a two-year-old Buick Le Sabre, was parked in the outdoor lot. The four piled in, and he pulled from the lot and into the street, almost hitting a young female reporter who'd followed them. One of the three muttered a comment in Russian about her breasts, causing the man seated next to him to laugh loudly. The third man's response was different. He kept his eyes on the young woman until she was out of view. The veins in his forehead and neck swelled like snakes devouring a meal; his mouth was a tight, straight line.

The one who'd made the suggestive comment poked his serious colleague in the ribs with an elbow. "Hey, Yvgeny, don't tell me you didn't notice those big ones."

Yvgeny Fodorov forced his thin, pale face to relax, even to smile as he said, "*Da*. She has nice big ones."

14

Mac Smith showed up at the Marriott Hotel at National Airport precisely at four and went to the bar, where he ordered a white wine. A TV set was tuned to a channel providing continuous stock market quotes at the bottom of the screen, while talking heads conversed with each other above the steady stream of symbols and prices.

When Jessica Belle hadn't arrived fifteen minutes later, he considered calling her office. But as he was about to head for a phone, she came through the door with a flourish, flashed an "I'm sorry" smile, and shook his hand.

"I got hung up in traffic coming out of Langley," she explained, sitting on an adjacent stool. "I think they call it the Puzzle Palace because of the parking lots. Insane."

"Drink?" Smith asked.

"Something soft." To the bartender: "Club soda, please, and lots of lime."

"Well," Smith said after she'd been served, "what brings us together at the airport for this seminar?"

"Hope you didn't mind driving over here, Mac. I'm catching a flight in an hour. Thanks for indulging my schedule."

"Obviously more harried than mine. Settling in at the CIA?"

"No time for that. Giles and I have hit the floor running, as that dreadful cliché goes. Head is swimming."

"You sounded anxious when you called," Smith said, sipping his wine.

"Anxious to talk to you. That's for sure." She glanced up and down the bar; they could talk without being overheard, provided they did it *pianissimo*.

"I'm waiting," he said.

"Okay. First, know that I'm here with Giles's blessing."

"Why is that important?"

"Because I'm not here to debate whether the District should be given statehood. Irrelevant issues like that. I'm here, Mac—funny, I have trouble calling my former professor by his first name—I'm here because of something we've learned at Langley about Congressman Latham and Warren Brazier."

"I see." Another sip of wine, longer this time to allow time to think. "Jessica, why would you be telling *me* such a thing?"

"Two reasons, and I had to convince Giles it was important that you be rung in. First, you were one of Latham's closest friends. Second, you were his counsel for the hearings."

"But I no longer enjoy either role. He's—dead. As opposed to deceased, or passed away."

"But his reputation still lives. And there's the president's reputation."

"The president? I can't keep up with these grand leaps you're making. Let's stick to *Paul's* reputation. Something's about to besmirch it?"

"Yes. Warren Brazier."

"I'm with you so far."

"Mac, Giles and I have spent almost every waking moment since arriving at Langley poring over intelligence reports from Russia. You know we're charged with helping American industry overseas."

"Yes."

"Warren Brazier is a major player in American business development in Russia—*the* major player."

"That's not new, Jessica. Doesn't take the CIA to know that."

She smiled. "Of course it doesn't. But it does take an agency like the CIA to get beyond what the media reports about Brazier's Russian activities, and what's *really* going on there."

"Okay. What's *really* going on?"

She leaned closer to his ear. "Warren Brazier had Paul Latham in his pocket since Latham first ran for Congress. All the strings from Latham have been in Brazier's hands, and he's pulled them every inch of the way."

Smith winced, but not at what she'd said. He was due for a visit to the dentist. A sudden pain from a tooth that had been giving him trouble confirmed it.

"Jessica, let's accept that Paul Latham was influenced by Warren Brazier, maybe even to what some would consider an unreasonable level. But that's nothing new in American politics. Influence peddlers like Brazier are always on the lookout for up-and-coming political stars.

They toss their weight and offer financial support to them in return for having the politicians' ear. Lots of legislation gets passed to benefit some special interest. Maybe most of it. An unpleasant reality, perhaps, but reality nonetheless."

"You're right, of course. Paul Latham wasn't the only committee chair influenced by Brazier. He's pumped money into Connie Dailey's campaigns for years." Congressman Cornelius Dailey chaired the powerful Ways and Means Committee, which had joint jurisdiction where tax breaks for businessmen like Warren Brazier were involved. But Dailey, one of Latham's closest allies in Congress, was known to follow Latham's lead on most international issues.

"Fast forward for me, Jessica," said Smith. "The president. What's this have to do with him?"

"He's known about it."

"And?"

"Still puts Latham up as secretary of state."

"Have you considered—?"

"The Russian trade bill Latham's been pushing through committee is a total sellout to Brazier."

"Have you considered that the bill might benefit this country as well as Warren Brazier? A strong market economy in Russia is good for us."

"Maybe. Maybe not. There's more."

"Oh?"

She checked her watch, finished her drink. "Have to run pretty soon. All the new airport security. No more last-minute sprint for a plane."

"Then you'd better talk fast."

"Latham was about to be charged with sexual harassment."

Smith's eyes widened, and he directed a stream of air through pursed lips. "Who's making the charge?"

"A female employee. A—" She screwed up her broad, pretty face in thought. "A Marge Edwards."

"That's nonsense."

Why hadn't Marge been at Latham's office this morning?

"Maybe," she said. "But that's a personal thing. Not important now that he won't be facing confirmation hearings."

Tell that to Ruth Latham and the kids.

"The second revelation has a lot more significance, certainly for the country. We believe Warren Brazier has been funneling large sums of money into the Communist movement in Russia."

"Why would he do that?"

"To see them come back to power. The Yeltsin government hasn't been especially cooperative with Mr. Brazier. He's trying to buy a company, Kazan Energy. You've heard of it?"

"Yes. An industrial giant."

"Brazier always had easy access to the powers that be when the Communists were in control."

"Wait a minute, Jessica. Are you saying that legislation Latham championed benefiting Brazier also benefited the Communists, not the free-market democratic leaders like Yeltsin?"

"*I'm* not saying it, Mac. That's what our intelligence indicates."

"I'm not convinced."

"You don't have to be. Brazier and the Communists are cozy with the Russian mafia."

"According to your intelligence."

"According to our intelligence. Brazier routinely uses them as security."

"Buys security from them?"

"Uses them."

"Lots of American businessmen buy security when doing business in Russia. In any of the independent states. Crime is rampant there."

"There's buying security—and then there's *hiring* Russian thugs and mobsters."

She checked her watch again. "Gotta run."

Smith smiled, then laughed. "I love this," he said. "Former student joins the CIA, calls me, meets me at the airport, and drops a series of provocative charges on the bar. Then runs for a plane. Why have you told me these things?"

"Because you might be in a position to find out more for us."

" 'For us'? For the CIA?"

"Not exactly. Look, we're on the same side, want the same thing. If Paul Latham was used by Brazier—and that's probably what happened—at least I hope that's what happened, that he was duped—and this comes out—which it undoubtedly will—"

"If someone wants it to."

"—Latham's sterling reputation will be badly tarnished. Think of his family. President Scott's reputation will take a hit, too, by extension."

"Assuming that's true, why do you think I'm in a position to find out more about it?"

She stood and straightened her white skirt, checked her appearance in the bar mirror. "You've made lots of contacts within the Russian legal system. Latham's family could be a source. His staff." She raised her pretty blond eyebrows and cocked her head. "Just a thought. Giles is all for it. Thanks for indulging me, and sorry to run like this."

Smith stood, too, and they shook hands. "Where are you off to?" he asked.

"L.A."

"Business?"

"Of course. Thanks again. Oh, let me buy." She opened her purse, but Mac placed his hand over it. "My contribution to national security. Safe trip."

" 'Bye."

He watched her exit through the door, a bag slung over her shoulder. He couldn't help but smile. He always took particular pride in seeing former students, especially female ones, go out and conquer the world—or think they have—with a few ideas of his included in their arsenal of knowledge. Bright, scrubbed young women striding down a city street, briefcase in hand, clothing stylish yet appropriate to their careers, never failed to provide a pulse of pleasure. He sometimes wished he'd had a daughter, as well as the son who'd died.

He paid the check, went to his car, and headed home. It was during the ride, slowed by rush-hour traffic, that the impact of the conversation he'd just had hit him. He was being recruited by the CIA, through a former student, to feed that agency information, even as journalists, athletes, academics, businessmen, and even run-of-the-mill American travelers had been asked to do for decades.

Marge Edwards charging Paul Latham with sexual harassment? That had to take first and immediate priority. As Latham's counsel, he owed it to his dead client's family to ascertain the truth about the allegation he'd just heard, and to do what he could to put it to rest.

The dome of the Capitol came into view, so proudly emblazoned against the sky, the dignified, harmonious, utilitarian center of the democracy that was America. Inside, members of the House proved it was aptly named the House of Representatives, 435 American men and women representing the nation's citizens at their best, and worst.

This day tilted toward the latter category.

15

Washington's medical examiner's office and MPD's forensic laboratories were housed in a salmon-colored building on the grounds of the District's general hospital, at Nineteenth and Massachusetts Avenue, S.E. It had been a relatively quiet night in a city where the homicide rate rose as fast as the city's coffers declined. A disgrace, the nation's capital struggling to stay afloat like some Third World city, was the nonpartisan view. How to fix it was another story, one that brought out party labels and histrionic bickering—political fiddling while America's Rome burned.

But the building's quiet had been shattered that morning when Congressman Latham's body was wheeled into the building from a rear loading ramp. Unlike routine homicides, in which the body is accompanied by a couple of med techs and maybe a uniformed MPD officer, Latham's wheeled stretcher was surrounded by dozens of people, including members of the Capitol police, FBI, MPD, Secret Service, and the House of Representatives' deputy sergeant-at-arms. The parking area was clogged with press vehicles; the scene was thoroughly captured by TV cameras and still photographers. Shouted questions from reporters were ignored.

The medical examiner, Cooley Ashburn, alerted to Latham's imminent arrival, had put into motion preparations for the autopsy to be performed. Dr. Ashburn was a stooped man with sleepy eyes that seemed unusually large through his round, thick glasses. His hair was mouse colored and lifeless. The staff always said, out of his hearing, that Ashburn didn't look much more alive than the bodies over which he labored. He, of course, became aware of such comments, but dismissed them as not being worthy of reaction. There was little in the ME's life other than his job. The place of the dead was his life, you might say, his virtual home; he lived alone in a small apartment two blocks from the office. He was divorced, no children. When he smiled, about twice a year, there seemed to be pain behind it, as though he had to struggle to rearrange his facial muscles into what would pass as pleasantness.

His assistant entered Ashburn's office that morning and said, "He's downstairs."

"Prepped?" Ashburn asked as though not expecting an answer.

"In the process. I took a quick look."

"And?"

"Clean entry, right temple."

Ashburn slowly nodded. "Clean?"

"Appears that way to me."

"I'll be there in a few minutes. Who'll be observing?"

"I don't know. There's plenty of people."

The ME yawned, not bothering to cover his mouth with a hand. "Not *too* many," he said.

The assistant left, and Ashburn resumed reading a new textbook on homicide investigation. No matter what others thought of him as a person, no one questioned his dedication to his specialty, nor his constant attempt to stay abreast of the field. In time, he made his way downstairs.

Latham's body was naked, plastic bags secured over his head, hands, and feet. He was wheeled into the examining room and placed on a stainless-steel table with a lip to catch bodily fluids before they dripped to the floor. Ashburn, his assistant, and representatives from the Capitol police, FBI, and Secret Service, all wearing green surgical gowns, masks and hats, and latex gloves, stood over the body. The assistant ME carefully removed the plastic bag from Latham's head. Ashburn turned it so that the right temple was exposed, illuminated by the overhead fluorescent lights and a headband he wore containing a high-intensity light. With the light from his forehead leading the way, he slowly, carefully pushed aside hair to better uncover the entry wound. As he proceeded with his examination, he gave a running commentary into a tiny microphone pinned to his gown.

"... entry of bullet clean, skin has closed over it— slight grease ring from bullet—circular discoloration around circumference of entry—bruising—no sign of gross destruction of surrounding tissue—no scorching— no sign of gases undermining skin—no visual sign of powder."

He turned Latham's head to the other side, where the bullet would have exited. It had not.

"No exit wound—bullet undoubtedly in skull—X-ray confirmation needed."

He said to his assistant, "We have the weapon?"

"Yes."

"Test fired?"

"Not yet."

"Please do."

After another ten minutes of visual inspection of Latham's head and body, and an X ray of his skull, the ME announced, "I'm going in after the bullet. You might want to leave."

No one moved.

Ashburn shrugged. "Give me the saw," he said to his assistant, as though asking for the salt to be passed.

An hour later, after the bullet had been retrieved from Latham's brain—impact with bone matter on its way in had severely flattened it—and with only the FBI observer still in the examining room, Ashburn and his assistant discarded their gowns, masks, caps, and gloves and went to Ashburn's office, where they conferred for another half hour. The interested parties had increased by three, much to Ashburn's chagrin—Senator Frank Connors's administrative assistant, Dennis Mackral; Capitol Police Chief Henry Folsom; and White House attorney Dan Gibbs. What the hell can you contribute? Ashburn thought. Political vultures . . .

"Look," the ME said in a weary, reedy voice, "it's my professional opinion, based upon my visual examination of the deceased, that he did not take his own life. The weapon was fired from at least eighteen inches away, probably further."

"But you can't be certain without conducting the rest of the autopsy, can you?" Mackral said.

"The rest of the autopsy, as you put it, will shed no light on whether the shot was fired close enough for him to have inflicted the wound himself, or whether it came from a distance. The test firing of the weapon doesn't conflict with my finding." He shoved the report of the weapons test across his metal desk.

"Did he have any drugs in his system?" Mackral asked.

"We haven't gotten that far yet," Ashburn responded.

"Why would you ask that?" Dan Gibbs asked Mackral.

Senator Connors's AA shrugged. "Maybe he took some medication that depressed him."

Gibbs turned to Dr. Ashburn. "As you're aware, Doctor, there's a blackout on information concerning Congressman Latham's death, including from this office."

Ashburn nodded, and yawned.

Gibbs looked at Capitol Police Chief Folsom, Dennis Mackral, and the others in the cramped office. "That's understood by everyone?" Their lack of response said to Gibbs that they understood. But he raised it again to Mackral. "Senator Connors understands this?"

Mackral responded with a smile. "Of course. He was on the phone with the president right after Latham's body was discovered. He urged the president to buy as much time as possible—in the event it *wasn't* suicide."

An FBI agent chimed in: "We're in agreement with the president. If what you say is accurate, Dr. Ashburn, that it wasn't a suicide, then we've got the murder of a leading member of Congress to deal with."

"The problem is," said Chief Folsom, "does anyone in this room really think this can be kept under wraps for very long?"

145

"We can try," the representative from the Secret Service said. "At least keep it quiet for a day or two."

Gibbs said to Ashburn, "I think we're agreed, Doctor. You won't be releasing information because you don't have it all. Correct?"

"I have enough to know that—"

"Doctor, all that's being asked of you is that you say what is the truth, that the cause of the congressman's death has still not been determined with any certainty. How long will the rest of the autopsy take?"

A long, pointed sigh from Ashburn. "A day at the most."

"Two days," Gibbs said. "Because he was such an important person—hell, he was up for secretary of state—your office, Doctor, has undertaken a precise, careful, and painstaking examination of the deceased."

"Yes. I understand."

"All right," Gibbs said, patting an errant strand of hair back in place as he stood, briefcase in hand. "We have two days' grace. Dr. Ashburn, I think it would make sense for you to come outside with us and give a brief statement along the lines I've suggested."

Ashburn's expression said he was, at once, surprised and reluctant.

"Just say the autopsy of Congressman Latham is going on as you speak, and that there will not be a determination of cause of death for two days. No questions. Just say it, and get back inside."

"I'd really rather not," Ashburn said.

They left the office, Gibbs leading the way, and went to the rear loading dock, where reporters and cameras waited. The group's sudden appearance provided a surprise for the press. When Ashburn stepped forward and raised his hands, prompted by a gentle nudge from Dan Gibbs, a hush fell over the parking lot.

"The autopsy of Congressman Paul Latham has started. It will be two days before it is completed. Thank you."

Ashburn walked away from his "handlers" in the direction of the door. The press merged into a solid block of followers, tossing a stream of questions at him. Gibbs and the others took the opportunity to head for their cars. A few reporters split from the main group and pursued them. "No comment," they said, almost as a chorus. Only Dennis Mackral stopped long enough to say, "Dr. Ashburn just told you the situation. That's it."

"What's his name?" a young reporter asked.

"Ashburn. Washington medical examiner." He spelled "Ashburn" for them. "Excuse me. You're in my way."

Now, at the end of the day, Cooley Ashburn sat alone in his office. The impromptu appearance on the loading dock had unnerved him. Each time he thought of it, his heart tripped. An occasional tic in his left eye was more pronounced.

The continuation of the autopsy on Latham had been conducted by members of his staff, including the removal of all relevant organs for lab testing. Ashburn spent the rest of the day taking phone calls from a variety of people, all of them unwelcome.

The mayor called twice, congratulating him on his aplomb in handling the press, and reminding him to say nothing else.

The chief of police called three times, once to ask how he was holding up, once to receive an update on the autopsy—he was dismayed that all roads led to murder rather than suicide—and finally to warn Ashburn that he would be hounded by the press when he left the building, and to stand firm in his public silence.

Dan Gibbs called from the White House: "Nice job, Doctor. Keep it up. The president is appreciative of your discretion. There is a great deal at stake here. National security. That sort of thing."

His former wife called. She'd seen him on TV, and told him he should speak slower if he was going to be making public appearances. Hearing her voice was strangely comforting, but she hung up before he could continue the conversation.

All calls from the press—there were more than a hundred, according to the switchboard—were answered by the operators, who'd been briefed by an MPD public affairs officer to say that there would be no statement until the autopsy was completed.

Ashburn's wasn't the only phone ringing that day. Every person who might know something, anything, and be willing to share it was contacted repeatedly by the burgeoning, frustrated press corps. Rumors grew like weeds. But anyone who could provide a definitive answer kept it close to the vest.

Dennis Mackral returned to Senator Connors's office in the Russell Building and made a series of calls. He'd placed the last of them and was about to leave when another staffer answered a ringing phone, held her hand over the mouthpiece, and said to Mackral, "For you."

"Who?"

"Petrone? Perone?"

Mackral picked up the extension on his desk, waited until the female staffer had hung up, and said, "Yeah? What's up?"

"We better talk."

"Okay. But why?"

"She's gonesville, man."

"What the hell are you talking about?"

"Your Ms. Edwards. She's split."

"You sure?"

"Yeah. I'll find her, but that wasn't part of the deal. That costs more."

"The McDonald's in Adams-Morgan. Eighteenth and Columbia. A half hour."

"McDonald's? I don't do business in McDonald's. The Palm in a half hour. I got this sudden yen for lobster."

16

"Why don't they just turn the damn boat around?"

Martin Latham, dressed in jeans, a yellow T-shirt, and sandals, angrily tossed the question out from where he sat at the kitchen table. With him were his mother and younger sister, Molly. Two dozen visitors milled about in other parts of the house. Outside, clots of law-enforcement and media personnel blanketed the lawn and street.

"Because they can't," Ruth Latham said.

"Because they won't," Martin snapped.

"Pris will fly home the minute they reach port," said his mother. "The last place she wants to be at a time like this is in the middle of the North Atlantic. How are you doing, Molly?"

"All right, I guess," she said, breaking into tears as the words tumbled out. Ruth pulled up a chair and wrapped her arms about the youngest of her three children.

When Molly stopped crying, she said, "I think I'll go to my room."

"Okay, sweetie," her mother said.

Ruth and Martin Latham watched the young girl walk from the kitchen and up the stairs to the second floor.

"She was so excited about being a House page," she said.

"She still can be," Martin said. "She'll get over this."

Her son's coldness caused Ruth Latham to close her eyes against it. You just don't "get over" a parent's death in a hurry. He was so unlike every other member of the family, who were quick to hug and to praise, and to use terms of endearment, even silly ones. Not Martin.

Latham's chief of staff joined them. "Ruth. A minute?"

Ruth followed the boxlike Mondrian into the den, where the Speaker, two other members of Congress, the deputy secretary of state, and the White House counsel Gibbs stood in a corner talking. The arrival of Latham's widow caused conversation to cease. Mondrian nodded at Dan Gibbs, who excused himself from the group and accompanied the COS and Ruth to the screen porch, where she and her husband had spent their final moments together. Mondrian shut the door. Ruth and Mondrian sat on the cushioned glider. Gibbs chose a red director's chair on which Congressman Paul Latham's name had been stenciled in white. A matching chair with Ruth's name on it occupied a far corner.

"Sorry to talk business at a time like this, Ruth," Mondrian said, "but there are things that need to be covered."

"Of course. Please, don't worry about me. I'm fine. It'll take a few days before I fall apart." She tried a laugh, instead swallowed hard and wiped a tear from her cheek. "What is it?"

"First," said Mondrian, "you're going to have to identify Paul's body."

"Identify it? Why? . . . Why, Bob? Is there any doubt
it's him?"

"Strictly a formality, Ruth," said Gibbs. "Required by
law."

"When?"

"Tomorrow. We'll go with you," Mondrian said.

"All right. I'll brace for that. Next?"

"Paul's office has been sealed," Gibbs said. "We have
representatives there during the search. The White House,
I mean."

"Of course."

"The house is next."

"The house? *This* house? Why, for heaven's sake?"

"To look for anything indicating Paul was in a frame
of mind that might have led to taking his own life,"
Gibbs said.

"I assure you there's nothing here that would bear on
that."

Gibbs nodded, smiled. "I'm sure you're right, Ruth,
but again, it's—"

"A formality."

"Yes."

"Why is the White House so involved?" Ruth asked,
pique in her voice. "Paul was a member of Congress. He
never made it to the Cabinet."

"They'll also be looking for any files Paul brought
home with him from the office," said Mondrian.

"And there's the funeral," Ruth said to her lap.

"The National Cathedral," Gibbs said.

"And a special memorial service in the Capitol.
Statuary Hall, most likely," Mondrian said.

"That would be nice. Paul would have . . . liked that."

"Have you heard from Mr. Brazier?" Gibbs asked.

"Warren? No. Not yet. He's probably out of the country."

"He's here in Washington," Gibbs said, hoping it didn't sound as though he was challenging her.

"Then I'm sure he'll be calling soon," Ruth said.

Gibbs and Mondrian looked at each other before Gibbs spoke. "Ruth, did Paul say anything lately about his relationship with Brazier?"

Her cocked head said she wondered why the question had been asked.

"They'd been working closely on legislation in the economic policy and trade subcommittee," said Gibbs. "There's scuttlebutt; they had a falling out over it."

This time, Ruth's laugh came through. "Scuttlebutt? In Washington, D.C.? I can't believe it."

The men laughed gently.

"I've heard rumors that Paul was murdered."

Another glance between Gibbs and Mondrian. No comment.

"I don't believe he killed himself. It wasn't Paul. You asked about Warren. The answer is no. I don't know of any rift between them."

But then the conversation she'd had with her husband the night before came back to her:

HE: "I met with Warren this afternoon."

SHE: "Oh? A problem?"

HE: "Yes. . . . I told him I was backing off on the Russian Trade and Investment Bill."

SHE: "Isn't that the bill you said a few months ago

was the most important Russian trade bill in your career?"

HE: "Yeah. I said that. And it would be. But there's something about it that's . . . wrong. Warren's staff keeps pushing for amendments to it that—well, frankly, that would distort its original intent. . . ."

SHE: "Was he angry?"

HE: "He was angry before I even told him. . . ."

And Paul had told her the president wanted him to pull back on any legislation involving Warren Brazier until the conclusion of the confirmation hearings.

She made a decision on the spot not to mention that conversation. She'd been in Washington, had been around government long enough, if only as a leading congressman's wife, to have developed the inherent, reflexive sense to think before speaking to anyone in an official capacity. Paul had been fond of quoting from a song to make that point, a blues tune by the pianist and singer Mose Allison: "Your mind is on vacation, your mouth is working overtime." He even sang it on occasion when in a scampish mood at parties, and given an extra bourbon and soda.

"The president called," Ruth said.

"I know," said Gibbs. "They were good friends."

"Mutually respectful," Ruth said. "Paul really believed in Joe Scott. The day of his inauguration, Paul was happier than I've ever seen him. He really felt Joe was the right person to lead the country."

"He was right," Gibbs said.

"When will they search the house?" she asked.

"They wanted to do it today," Mondrian said. "We

154

convinced them it would be barbaric to do that to the family."

Ruth sighed. "No more barbaric than Paul being dead. He did not commit suicide!"

"That will be determined at the autopsy, Ruth," Mondrian said.

Martin Latham opened the door and said, "Mac Smith and his wife are here."

Mac and Annabel stood at the entrance to the living room. Ruth approached them, arms outstretched.

"I'm so sorry," Annabel said, embracing her.

"A terrible shock," Mac said. "How are you holding up?"

"Best we can, Mac. Come in. There's coffee and Danish. The bar is open. Paul would have wanted me to be the perfect hostess, no matter what the circumstance. A requisite for a congressman's wife."

They followed her into the large room, where others greeted them. New arrivals streamed into the house. Ruth shut drapes against the harsh lights from TV crews outside.

Mac and Annabel had coffee. As they sipped, Mac stuck out his hand to intercept Bob Mondrian on his way across the room. "A word?" Mac said.

"Sure."

"Just the two of us?"

"Okay."

Mondrian led Mac to the porch, which was empty. Alone, door closed, Mondrian said, "Ruth's doing pretty well. Martin and Molly, too. Priscilla's on a ship, but she'll be home in a couple of days."

"Bob, I have to ask you something."

"Go ahead."

"Where's Marge Edwards?"

"Marge? I—she's home, I suppose."

"She wasn't at the office this morning."

"No, she wasn't. I never even thought about that in the confusion. Why do you ask? Is there a problem?"

"There may be. Look, Bob, I have to do something I always dislike when others do it. I was told something today about Marge by someone whose identity I can't reveal. I don't know whether it's true or not, and I'm not asking you for verification. But I'm compelled to bring it up."

"Sounds serious."

"Not as serious as Paul's death, but damned unpleasant for Ruth and the kids."

"I'm listening."

"Marge was about to level a charge of sexual harassment against Paul."

If Smith's flat statement had an impact on Latham's chief of staff, his broad face didn't reflect it. He stared at Mac with unblinking eyes.

"Were you aware of this?" Smith asked.

"No."

"No hint of it? You and Marge work closely together."

"If I knew anything about it, I would have acted immediately." He scowled. "You aren't suggesting I knew about it and did nothing, are you?"

"Of course not."

"Assuming there's any validity to it."

"Yes. There's only the assumption. But let's say there *is* truth to what I was told. Let's say Marge did intend to bring such a charge against Paul. Have you ever witnessed anything that might give credence to her claim?"

He guffawed. "Of course not. Paul is—was—the

classic straight arrow. Office hanky-panky? Fanny-patting? 'Gimme a kiss' by the watercooler? Come on, Mac. Paul Latham was the consummate gentleman, maybe not always when taking on another member of Congress, or an administration, but always the gentleman in his personal life."

"Of course, that's my read, too," Smith said. "Still, I had to bring it up with you. I'd like to talk to Marge before this rumor grows legs. You assumed she was at home. Can we give her a call?"

"Sure, only . . ."

"Only what?"

"Only I think it would be inappropriate to make that call from here. Ruth. The kids."

Smith nodded. "You're right. Annabel and I will be leaving soon. I tried Marge from home a few hours ago. There was no answer. I'll try again."

"Good. Anything else?"

"No. Heard anything on the autopsy?"

"Nope. Ruth's convinced he didn't kill himself. I agree."

"If he didn't—"

"Yeah. *If he didn't.* Thanks for bringing up this Marge thing, Mac. Sorry if I reacted badly at first. It's so ludicrous, it's almost laughable."

They were unsmiling as they prepared to leave the porch.

"I'll tell you one thing," Mondrian said. "If there is any truth to what you've told me, that Marge was considering making a ridiculous charge like this against Paul, it could only be because she's so damned unstable."

"I wasn't aware of that," Smith said.

"Some day I'll fill you in. This isn't the time."

Mac and Annabel left the house at nine. He tried Marge Edwards's number several times from home, to no avail.

Annabel had held off asking her husband what he and Mondrian discussed. She knew, of course, why Mac had cornered Latham's COS; he'd told her about Jessica Belle's allegation the moment he returned home from Rosslyn. Now, she asked.

He recounted the conversation with Mondrian.

"And?" she said when he'd finished.

"I can't help but be concerned, Annie. There's no reason for Jessica to have told me about it, other than being sincerely worried about the negative impact it might have on the Scott administration. Paul dies of a gunshot wound, and Marge can't be reached. Mondrian lays on me the idea that Marge is unstable. Is that true, or is it spin control in the event Marge *was* intending to charge Paul? Yeah, I'm concerned. It would devastate Ruth."

"But now that Paul is dead," Annabel said, "there's no reason for Marge to make such a charge. Is there? I mean, if she intended it to derail his confirmation—and that's assuming she ever intended anything—that goal is not to be gained any longer."

"True. But maybe she wasn't intending it to spike his confirmation. Maybe she really believes she's been a victim of sexual harassment, has some noble purpose for making it public."

"You know what, Mac?"

"What?"

"Here we are talking as though Jessica was right, that Marge did intend to bring such a charge. *We're* giving it legs."

Smith smiled. "Exactly what I told Mondrian I wanted to avoid. And that's what we'd better try and do before it takes off at a sprint."

The last person left the Latham house at midnight. Friends had offered to stay with Ruth and her two children, but she declined. "I think we'll do better if we can just be together alone," she told those who offered. They understood, having spent the night projecting themselves into her shoes.

Martin turned on the television, leaving Ruth to sit with Molly in the young girl's bedroom. They said nothing for a while, content to sit quietly and chew on their individual thoughts. It was Molly who broke the silence.

"Daddy didn't kill himself, did he?"

"We'll know that in a day or so," Ruth replied. "But no, I do not think he did."

"I mean, why would he? Everything was going great." She sat up on her bed, more animated. "He was going to be secretary of state. And he knew we loved him. Didn't he?"

This time, it was Molly's turn to comfort her mother, who broke down and sobbed softly.

"Didn't he know that?" Molly repeated.

"Of course he did, Molly. And we know he didn't kill himself. Someone—someone shot him. God."

"Who?" Molly asked.

"I don't know, Rabbit. Some evil, warped person. But they'll find out. In the meantime, we have to be as strong as Daddy would want us to be. We have to be dignified, and celebrate the wonderful life we've had with him. And that means we all need to get our sleep."

She hugged her daughter, running her hand through her silky blond hair. "I love you," she said.

"I love you, too, Mom. I even love Martin."

They both laughed quietly. Ruth said, "Martin just has trouble accepting our love. But down deep he loves this family as much as you and I do. Good night, sweetie. It'll be a tough day tomorrow."

As Ruth Latham went to the door, she noticed a package wrapped in brown paper and string on Molly's dresser. "What's that?" she asked.

"Oh, that? Just some books Dad gave me to read."

"Well, you won't be reading much for a few days. But once you're back in the page dorm, you'll have time to read again. Night."

She closed the door to Molly's bedroom, leaned against the wall, and wrapped her arms about herself to stem the shaking.

It *had* been murder. Her husband, Paul Latham, congressman from California, lover, father, companion, had been taken from them by another human being.

A murderer.

That realization doubled her over, and sent her to the bathroom, where she fell to her knees in front of the toilet.

17

Anatoly Alekseyev's mood hadn't improved since being designated tour guide and baby-sitter for the three young Russians who'd flown into Washington with former KGB general Aleksandr Patiashvili.

After leaving Brazier's Washington offices, he'd driven them to where they were staying, the Holiday Inn on Capitol Hill, and waited in the lobby while they freshened up. They came down and said they were in the mood for seafood, so he took them for dinner to the appropriately touristy Hogate's, on the District's southwest waterfront.

Now, it was close to midnight. Alekseyev had wanted to drop them back at the hotel after dinner, but two of them, already tipsy from vodka consumed during dinner, insisted upon going to an American disco. Anatoly pointed out that discos were no longer the rage in America, which didn't dissuade them; they were popular in Russia. He decided on Georgetown's Deja Vu, one of many popular

161

hangouts for Washington's young professionals, and where he often ended up after a night of pub crawling.

Deja Vu was crowded, as usual, and the rock music was played loud. They found space at the bar and ordered more *vodichka*, "darling little water" in Russian.

Alekseyev had twice excused himself during dinner at Hogate's to make phone calls. And he excused himself at Deja Vu for the same purpose.

He rejoined the three at the bar and tried to participate in their drunken conversation. It wasn't easy. The two outgoing members of the group had grown increasingly boisterous and aggressive with young women seated next to them, fueled by the seemingly unending shots of vodka they'd downed. Alekseyev was uncomfortable with their behavior, and wished he'd taken them to a bar where he wasn't known. Too late for that. Getting them to leave took center stage.

He found an ally in the third member of the trio, Yvgeny Fodorov. Fodorov was obviously one of those people for whom alcohol generated depression, perhaps even anger, certainly not expansiveness. Unlike his flamboyant friends, Yvgeny had sunk deeper into morose drunkenness, his thin, sallow face set in a perpetual scowl, corners of his mouth drawn down, eyes watery from the alcohol.

"Hey, you all right?" Anatoly asked him.

"*Nyet*. I want to leave."

Alekseyev laughed. "Good. So do I." He slapped Yvgeny on the back and said to the others, "Come on, my friends, let's go."

They agreed to leave, but only if Anatoly would join them for a final drink at the hotel. "Okay," he said. Anything to get them out of Deja Vu.

The bar at the Holiday Inn was closed, but Alekseyev knew one a block away that would be open.

"*Nyet,*" Yvgeny said as they left the lobby. "I am going to bed."

Alekseyev envied him.

Later, at the bar, a quiet, neighborhood place with swing era big-band music coming softly from a jukebox, the two young Russians, new to Washington, quieted down considerably, to Anatoly's relief. Although they continued to drink, they seemed to sober up to some extent, and talk turned to topics other than sex and drinking—*dusha a dushe,* heart-to-heart talk.

"So, what do you do for Brazier Industries?" Alekseyev asked.

"Finance," one said. "Dealing with Russian banks."

"You?" Alekseyev asked the other.

"The same. The Central Bank must do something to avoid a liquidity crisis. We're trying to influence the bankers in this direction." He snickered. "The old man, Brazier, is going nuts, huh, trying to deal with Yeltsin and his cronies?" He lowered his voice as though to pass on a confidence. "You know what? He wants to buy Sidanco."

"Oh?" said Alekseyev.

"*Da.*"

"I would have known," Anatoly said. "It produces oil. My area."

A loud laugh this time. "Why should you know? No one knows what the next person is doing in this company. Am I right?"

His friend agreed.

"*Da.* He wants to buy Sidanco, but the government auction—some auction—the rules mean that only Oneximbank can buy it. Some auction, huh?"

"Some auction," Alekseyev agreed. He wasn't anxious to get into a lengthy debate over auctions, or banks, or anything, for that matter. Not at that hour.

He changed the subject. "What about Yvgeny?" he asked.

The two looked at each other and laughed. "The fag?" one said.

"Weird," said the other.

"What does he do for Brazier?" Alekseyev asked.

They shrugged. One said, "I asked him on the flight. He said he worked for security. I think it was the only thing he said the whole trip."

"Security," the other said scornfully. "We have more security than anything else. They're everywhere. Like the KGB, huh? Idiots!"

"He doesn't look like a security man to me," Alekseyev said, putting money on the bar and standing. "Tomorrow at seven." He checked his watch. "Almost two. Come on, or we'll be here all night."

He walked them back to the hotel, got in his car, and drove to his apartment.

Across town, in the Holiday Inn on Capitol Hill, Yvgeny Fodorov was too busy to think of sleep.

There had been an envelope in his room when he arrived after their night out. He opened it and removed the airline ticket it contained, the note, and the five hundred dollars in American money, which he put in his wallet.

The ticket was for the Delta Shuttle from Washington's National Airport to New York's LaGuardia.

The note, written in Russian, instructed him to take the first flight the following morning, and to contact a person in Brighton Beach, Brooklyn, whose phone number was included.

The final line of the note was: *You are to stay there until contacted. Everything you need will be supplied.*

The note wasn't signed.

Fodorov paced the room. Every light burned brightly; the television was on, loud. His mind raced. So much had happened to him in such a short period of time.

Yvgeny Fodorov's mother, Vani, had stipulated in her will that she was to be cremated, and that there was to be no religious service. Instead, she asked that her closest friends gather in a favorite restaurant, and eat and drink in her memory. She earmarked a small sum from her estate to pay for this.

The party to celebrate Vani Fodorov's life was held in B. B. King Blues Club on *Sadovaya-Samotyochnaya*, which had opened to considerable fanfare because of the appearance of the American blues master for whom the club was named. Vani's party was attended by a few dozen men and women, who feasted on American-style ribs and cornbread, augmented by Russian *shashlik*—grilled spicy lamb—and *pelmeni*—stuffed cabbage leaves—with *vodichka*, a Russian champagne called *shampanskoye*, and later, *konyak*, brandy from Georgia.

Yvgeny, of course, was there as the grieving son, receiving words of condolence from his mother's friends and fellow writers, hearing the expressions of horror at how she died: "The *mafiya*," they said. "Pigs! Killers!"

"And all of them writers. Killed. In one day. Why?"

Yvgeny told them he didn't have an answer. "Maybe it

wasn't the *mafiya*," he said. "Maybe it was a sick, demented individual. A nut."

His suggestion was met with a firm, "*Nyet!* How could it be one person? Four writers murdered in the same day, many miles from each other. I tell you, it was the damned *mafiya*."

The arguments were short-lived because there was too much food and alcohol, and dancing to the infectious blues music coming through massive loudspeakers, to enjoy.

Privately, there were comments made about Yvgeny, few of them complimentary. His brooding, cold nature was well known to those at the party, if not through direct experience with him, certainly because of stories told over the years by his mother. Guests made remarks behind his back about his black suit and shirt and skinny white tie. Some at the gathering were aware of his friendship with the lower echelons of Moscow's criminal society. They, of course, were not the ones espousing to his face the theory that Vani Fodorov and three other writers had been murdered by the mafia.

The party started at four and lasted into the night. Most stayed—Vani Fodorov's celebratory party would have made her happy—but Yvgeny left at six, saying good-bye to no one. He wasn't missed.

He took a city bus to the Mezhdunarodnaya Hotel, got off, and walked along *Krasnopresnenskaya-Naberezhnaya* until reaching the floating casino, the Alexander Blok, permanently moored there. It was one of dozens of casinos that had sprung up in Moscow, feeding on the inflationary climate of the city and the former Soviet Union.

The gaming tables were already busy when he arrived.

He walked through the main room to a door leading to a set of stairs down to a small dock area, where a half-dozen men sat at a makeshift table playing cards. They glanced up at Yvgeny as he descended the wooden stairs, but paid him no more attention than that, returning to their game.

Yvgeny lit a cigarette and leaned against a wooden railing. Below, small craft bobbed in the brown wake of excursion boats. The sky was clear and blue, marred only by fast-moving cirrus clouds high above. A gentle breeze came off the water, carrying the smell of the waterway's pollution to his nostrils.

He'd been there ten minutes—three cigarettes—when the door opened and his friend, Felix, came through it, followed by an older, heavyset man. The card players laid down their hands and watched. The older man, the second to come down the stairs, waved for them to leave, which they did immediately, and without discussion.

Felix and Yvgeny embraced, awkwardly, as men tend to do. The older man watched, heavy legs planted solidly on the weathered gray wood of the dock, a cigarette jutting from his lips in an ivory holder, giving his crude, large features an odd touch of elegance.

Felix stepped back from Yvgeny and said, "My friend, please meet Mr. Pralovich." He stepped aside for Yvgeny to shake Pralovich's large hand.

"Yvgeny Fodorov," Pralovich said, as though deciding whether he liked the sound of it. "*Da.* I know of you. From Felix. From others."

Yvgeny knew Gennady Pralovich by reputation. He was a Moscow *mafiya* boss, a *rukovodstvo*, a made man, with dozens of street gangs reporting to him through a cadre of underbosses. He lived in a mansion, was driven in an armor-plated Mercedes 500, and was fond of Fendi fur coats and Hennessy cognac at such favored bars as the Up and Down Club.

Like other mafia organizations in other countries, the Russians didn't limit their criminal schemes to street-level bullying. Their influence and power reached into the highest echelons of government, into the offices of the secretaries of the party district committees, the Central Committee, and the Council of Ministers. Pralovich, it was claimed, controlled more than a hundred Moscow business enterprises, seemingly legitimate, but firmly directed by him and his lieutenants; a small percentage, perhaps, of more than forty thousand *mafiya*-controlled businesses in Russia—an estimated half of the country's one hundred stock exchanges, sixty percent of its 2,200 banks—but lucrative enough to rank him as a leading criminal boss.

It was also said of Gennady Pralovich that when other *mafiya* bosses needed an assassin for a particularly difficult assignment, they turned to Pralovich. His small group of hitmen, many of them Chechens imported from the Caucasus to Moscow, were considered the best. They'd made a solid contribution to the dramatic rise in Moscow's premeditated murders, from a little over one hundred in 1987 to almost fifteen hundred in 1993— eight and a half murders a day, more than half of them never solved.

"Felix tells me you are a good man, Yvgeny Fodorov, a good soldier."

Yvgeny didn't know what to say.

"I know from others, too, about what you have been doing for us. Impressive. Very impressive." He pulled a cigarette pack from the pocket of the tight-fitting gray suit he wore, and offered it to Yvgeny.

"*Nyet,*" Yvgeny said. "*Spasiba.*" *Don't offend him by failing to say thank you.*

Pralovich said to Felix, "Go get a drink or something. Your friend here and I have something to discuss."

Yvgeny was uncomfortable seeing his friend go up the stairs and disappear through the door, leaving him alone with Gennady Pralovich. The *mafiya* boss leaned on the railing and looked out over the water, drawing deeply on his cigarette. Yvgeny lighted up, too, not sure whether by choosing his own brand, he would offend. It didn't seem to matter.

Pralovich continued to smoke in silence, increasing Yvgeny's discomfort. Then, in a voice void of emotion or inflection, he said into the breeze that had picked up, "You killed your own mother."

"I was told—"

"Yes, I know, Yvgeny Fodorov. You were told to do it. What is impressive to me is that you followed that order. Your own mother. Flesh and blood. You came from her womb."

"I want to please," said Yvgeny, wishing Pralovich would turn and face him.

"Of course you do. So do many other young men like yourself. But most would not . . ." Now, he turned slowly and smiled. "Most would not follow orders to kill their mother."

"I—"

"But you did."

"*Da.*"

"Did you love her?"

The question stunned Yvgeny. Love her? Why would he ask that?

"Did you? Love your mother, Yvgeny?"

What should the answer be? Which answer would please him?

"I am used to having my questions answered," Pralovich said.

"I loved her."

"Did you? I am glad to hear that. We should love our mothers, *da*? They give us life."

Yvgeny said nothing.

"It must have been even more difficult for you to kill her, loving her as you did."

"It was."

Pralovich now leaned his back against the railing. He looked up into the sky and smiled, drew an audible deep breath. "Today is a good day. A clear day."

"It is a clear day," Yvgeny parroted.

"Have you ever been away from the Soviet Union, Yvgeny?"

Yvgeny was surprised that Pralovich used that name for his country. It was pleasing to his ear.

"*Nyet,*" Yvgeny replied. "Never."

"Would you like to take a trip?"

"Yes."

"Are you free to leave immediately?"

"Yes."

"If I decide to choose you for this very important job, you must realize the great danger you will face."

Yvgeny's blood pulsed strong. His heart pounded.

Please, let it be me he chooses.

"We have a customer, Yvgeny, a client who pays us

well. He has asked that we do him a great service. It will be difficult to satisfy him, but with the right person—"

"Yes, Mr.—Comrade Pralovich. I am ready to serve."

"Are you?"

"Yes, sir."

"But you do not know what you must do. Do you not care?"

"*Da,* I care, but I am willing to do anything."

"Yes, I suppose you are. You killed your beloved mother to prove that to us. I mustn't forget that. It was necessary to send a message from our Communist friends to the fools in power, huh? Necessary. Your mother, and others whose interests were different from our friends', wrote bad things about them. Our customers. It will happen to others, I can assure you."

Pralovich returned his attention to the water. A sight-seeing boat passed, and passengers waved. Pralovich returned their greetings. Yvgeny started to, but kept his hands at his sides.

The *mafiya* boss turned and looked through Yvgeny's thick glasses into his anxious eyes. He nodded. "Yes, I think you are the one, Yvgeny Fodorov. Here." He handed Yvgeny an envelope. "In it you will find everything you need. You are to contact the person mentioned in this envelope immediately. He will provide you with other things. You leave tomorrow."

Yvgeny wasn't sure he could get the words out. "Yes, tomorrow. Where am I going?"

"America. Washington, D.C. The capital of that powerful country."

"And when I am there?"

"You will be told when it is necessary for you to know.

171

Go now. The person mentioned in the envelope waits for you. *Dobry vecher,* Yvgeny Fodorov."

"Yes, sir. Good evening."

"Do your job well."

"I will. I will."

"One final thing."

"Yes?"

"Buy a better suit before you leave. You look like a fool in that."

By midnight, Yvgeny had purchased a more conservative suit and accessories, and had met with the man mentioned in the envelope, who gave him a passport, instructions on who to contact upon arrival in the United States, and emergency numbers to call in the event of trouble. His flight would leave from Moscow at ten in the morning, not much time for most people to pull together last-minute things. But for Yvgeny Fodorov, there was nothing to pull together.

When he met Felix for a drink at one in the morning, his small bag was packed and he was ready to go.

"What are you to do?" his friend asked.

"I don't know," Yvgeny answered truthfully. "I will be told."

"It must be very important, Yvgeny. *Very* important."

"Da."

"I envy you."

"Yes."

"Good things will be yours—if all goes well." He managed to keep the resentment he felt from his voice. He'd brought Yvgeny into the gang. It should have been him, Felix, chosen for such an important assignment.

"I know."

Yvgeny then did something uncommonly gregarious

for him. He raised his glass in a toast. Felix touched his rim to Yvgeny's.

"To my only friend, Felix."

"And to a safe journey for you, Yvgeny."

As Felix said it, he knew he would never see Yvgeny Fodorov again.

18

By the time Mac and Annabel got up the next morning, an hour before their clock radio went off at seven, the Washington press corps was reporting two startling, unsettling stories.

According to "reliable sources," Congressman Paul Latham had not taken his own life. The autopsy showed that the bullet had been fired from a distance.

And, according to another reliable source, a charge of sexual harassment was to have been leveled against the congressman by a female employee, his scheduling secretary, Marge Edwards.

The latter story broke in that morning's edition of the conservative Washington *Standard*, and was reported on local TV. The article had been written by Jules Harris, a freelance journalist, who said in his piece that repeated attempts to contact Ms. Edwards had been unsuccessful.

Harris's timing had not been good. The thrust of his

story was that the sexual harassment charge had been a factor in Latham's decision to take his life.

But the other story—that Latham *hadn't* killed himself—rendered the Harris article itself unreliable, despite its so-called unimpeachable source.

Over melon and berries, toast and coffee, Mac and Annabel watched the early morning news in their kitchen.

"Well," Mac said, "it's out."

"Marge Edwards, you mean?"

"Yeah. I can only imagine what Ruth is feeling."

"And it was murder."

"If the 'reliable source' is right, which I suspect he or she is. 'Suicide' wasn't in Paul's vocabulary."

Annabel shivered against a sudden internal chill. "Murder! A U.S. congressman gunned down. It had to have been a professional killing, an assassination."

"Certainly looks that way. Whoever shot Paul took the time to place the gun in his hand. Still, not a very smart assassin. Any fool knows that even the most inept medical examiner can determine whether a shot was fired close enough to have been suicide."

"Maybe he did it to cause confusion, buy some time."

"Or he decided to improvise. . . . Why do we keep saying 'he'?"

"Assassins are usually men," Annabel said.

"*That* sort of assassin, at least."

She let it pass.

"Marge Edwards. I'll try to reach her again. This story that she was going to charge Paul with sexual harassment might be just that, a story. All she has to do is deny it. That'd put an end to it."

"If she's willing to come forward. Looks like she's gone underground."

"To avoid having to comment."

"Do you think your friend Jessica Belle might be the source of this reporter's story?"

"Can't imagine why."

"She was *your* source."

"Hmmmm."

"You've been reasonably close to Paul all these years, especially recently. Who would have wanted him dead?"

"No idea. He was one of the most revered members of the House."

"Powerful, too."

"Meaning?"

"Power makes enemies."

"Sounds like something Kissinger might say."

"He probably has. Mac, this is all just now hitting me. The meaning of it."

"Me, too."

The phone rang. Mac reached for the kitchen extension.

"Hello, Jessica. Yes, I've heard. Where are you?"

"Still in L.A."

"It's three in the morning for you."

"I haven't been to bed. Anything you can tell me from that end?"

"No. Annabel and I have been watching the news. We've been to see Ruth Latham."

Mac realized he was *reporting* to Jessica.

"I'm flying back this morning. I'd like to talk to you again."

"All right. Any idea who leaked the rumor about Marge Edwards?"

She said nothing right away; time to think? he wondered.

"No. You?"

"No."

"The allegation that he was murdered hasn't been verified, has it?"

"Not as far as I know, Jessica. But it makes sense, doesn't it?"

"I don't think murder ever makes sense," she said.

"I meant that it was highly unlikely he took his own life. I'll look forward to your call."

When Smith hung up, Annabel said, "You seem angry."

"Not angry. Perplexed is more accurate."

The phone rang again. A reporter. Another called ten minutes later.

"Want me to answer while you shower?" Annabel asked.

"No. Let technology handle it. Come on, this promises to be a splendid day I'm sure we'll both rather forget."

After showering and dressing, Mac called Bob Mondrian at Latham's Rayburn Building office.

"How goes it?" he asked the COS.

Mondrian answered with an audible exhalation. "They turned the offices upside down, Mac. Walked out of here with boxes of materials."

"To be expected. Have you been in contact with Marge Edwards?"

"No answer at her apartment. She hasn't shown up here."

"That's cause for concern, isn't it?"

"Sure. I've got a couple of my people looking for her. I talked to her father in Indiana. Mother's dead. Her father says he hasn't heard from her."

"Did he have anything to say about the story?"

"No. And I didn't raise it. He said he'd have her call me if she showed up."

"The autopsy leak. I assume it's true," Mac said.

"Right. For some reason, the ME is dragging his feet in releasing the results. I heard this morning that Senator Connors is behind it."

"I heard the president is."

"I doubt that, Mac. The faster Paul's death is verified as murder, the faster this ridiculous rumor that Marge was about to charge him with sexual harassment vaporizes. Anything new on your end?"

"No. The FBI is due here at ten. Spoken with Ruth yet about the stories?"

"Yeah. She's a strong lady. She dismissed the Marge Edwards thing with 'That's nonsense.' End of comment."

"Good for her. I'd like to come down after my session with the FBI. You'll be there?"

"I expect to be, trying to put this place back in order."

"Noon. Free for lunch?"

Mondrian laughed. "Lunch? What's that? Sure. I'll order sandwiches up."

Annabel joined her husband in the den.

"The FBI's due here in an hour," he said.

"I don't have to be here, do I?"

"I don't see any reason why you should be. Unless you want to."

"I don't want to. I think I'll head for the gallery, catch up on some paperwork."

"I'm going to Paul's office at noon."

"Oh? Why?"

"Talk to Mondrian. See if I can learn more about the Marge Edwards story. Mondrian says she's still missing."

Annabel's face took on a worried look.

"I'm sure Marge has simply decided to lay low for a while, stay out of the spotlight," he said.

"I hope you're right."

Fifteen minutes later she reappeared in the den dressed to leave. They kissed. "Keep in touch," she said.

"I will."

He walked her to the door and opened it. Outside, a half-dozen media types milled about. Two uniformed MPD officers in a marked car kept an eye on them.

"Ready?" Mac asked.

"Sure."

They greeted the press and walked past them, down the street to the garage they rented from an elderly neighbor. Reporters followed.

"Any comment about the sexual harassment charge against Latham?" one asked.

"No," Mac replied. "No comment."

"He was your client."

"Right."

"They say he was murdered."

"I'd prefer to wait for the official autopsy report," Mac said.

"Mrs. Smith, have you talked to Mrs. Latham?"

Annabel ignored the question.

"What's the mood over there?" the reporter followed up.

Annabel stopped, started to express her dismay at the question, shook her head, and followed Mac into the garage. " 'What's the mood over there?' " she said disgustedly. "Joyous, of course."

"Ignore them," said Mac, opening the driver's-side door for her. "They're just doing their job."

She started the engine.

"Drive careful, Annabel," Mac said, a sudden, fleeting vision of his wife and son being hit head-on causing him to wince.

"I will. And you take care."

Mac went to the sidewalk, where the press stood in front of the open garage door. "Better get out of the way," he said. "She has trouble backing up."

The two FBI agents who questioned Mac that morning were efficient, polite, and on time. Their questions were short, well prepared, and to the point. Mac told them what he knew, which wasn't much. The only question that piqued his interest was about Marge Edwards. One of the agents said, "We've put out an all-points on Ms. Edwards, Mr. Smith. You haven't heard from her, have you?"

"No, nor would I expect to. I knew her, but only as someone working in Congressman Latham's office. His scheduling secretary. I didn't know her outside of her office capacity."

The agent jotted his reply in a notebook.

The questioning went on for another ten minutes. Satisfied Smith had nothing to offer beyond what he'd already told them, they thanked him for his time and were gone by ten-thirty.

He again tried to concentrate on research for the Russian project, but couldn't get more than ten minutes into it each time before the phone would ring.

His boss, dean of GW's law school, called "just to chat," eventually getting around to asking Mac what was *really* going on in the Latham case.

A woman from a local library called to see whether Mac would be the guest speaker at an October program.

He said he'd be in Russia, but thanked her for thinking of him.

Annabel called just to see how he was.

He let Rufus out in the postage-stamp-sized fenced yard long enough for the dog to mark his favorite tree, called for a taxi, and waited in the foyer for its arrival. The phone rang. The cab pulled up. Mac locked the door behind him, waved off questions, climbed into the back of the cab, and told the driver to take him to the Rayburn Office Building.

Inside the Smith residence, the answering machine gave out Mac's message: "I can't take your call right now, but please leave your name, number, and a brief message after the tone and I'll return the call as soon as possible." He'd recently added to the message: "And please, either repeat your number, or say it slowly the first time." Callers who rattled off numbers had joined what was becoming a long list of Mackensie Smith's pet peeves.

Marge Edwards listened to Smith's outgoing message. When it was finished, she slowly, quietly hung up.

19

Yvgeny Fodorov had gotten to National Airport three hours before the first Delta Shuttle flight to New York. He sat stoically on a bench until a coffee shop opened, and ordered two jelly doughnuts and tea, into which he poured four sugars.

He was first in line when the flight was called, his only luggage the small carry-on he'd traveled with from Moscow. As with the flight to the United States, he felt naked without the gun. He had it with him always back home. But one of his instructions before leaving Moscow was that he was never to attempt to carry a weapon aboard any flight. There would always be another weapon, he was assured, at his various destinations.

The driver of his taxi was a black man. Yvgeny hated black people even more than Jews. Being in America was uncomfortable enough without having to be close to so many of them. There were few blacks in Russia, but too many Jews. You had to get rid of them, or at least keep them in their place, if any country was to be successful.

He showed the driver the address in Brighton Beach, and settled into the backseat.

The cabbie, one of New York's friendlier, more talkative ones, tried to engage Yvgeny in conversation, asking him where he was from—"Soviet Union"—what it was like there—"Nice, good"—and what he thought of America—"Nice, good." But that was the extent of it. Most of the trip into Brooklyn was made in silence, with Yvgeny staring out the window at the striking visual mosaic that was New York, crossing the river by bridge and proceeding into the borough of Brooklyn, down Ocean Parkway, turning off onto Coney Island Avenue until the outlines of the Cyclone roller-coaster and the rusting, abandoned steel skeleton of the parachute jump came into view. A few minutes later, they were on Brighton Beach Avenue, and soon Yvgeny felt more at home. They passed shops heralding Russian food— *kasha*, black bread, herring, sturgeon, and caviar—on signs written in Russian. People on the streets looked Russian. There were no black faces.

The cab came to a stop in front of a peeling, two-story gray building. Yvgeny leaned closer to the window and squinted through his thick glasses to read the sign above the door: BRIS AVROHOM. The driver said, "Here you are, my man," and pointed to the meter. Yvgeny dug money from the envelope in his jacket pocket and handed it to the smiling driver, who counted off the fare and handed back the change. "Welcome to the good ol' USA, my man," he said. "Glad we're not at war with you guys no more." He laughed heartily.

Yvgeny said nothing as he exited the taxi and slammed the door. The driver leaned across the front seat and said, "What's the matter, man? I didn't give you a nice ride?"

Yvgeny stared at him.

"This is America, buddy. We tip cabbies in America." He extended his hand, palm up, through the open window.

"Nyet," Yvgeny said. *"Ya nye panimahyu!"* But he *did* understand what the driver wanted. Before the collapse of the Soviet Union, tipping was rarely practiced. But with the influence of the West, that had changed.

"Da svidanye," Yvgeny said, turning away and entering the building, his curt good-bye prompting a loud and vigorous string of obscenities from the driver, ending with "You Commie bastard!"

The driver couldn't know how right he was.

Yvgeny shut the building door against the tirade and looked about the small room that he'd entered. There was a metal desk and two chairs, a long wooden bench along one wall, a four-drawer steel file cabinet, and a small red and yellow braided rug that needed to be cleaned.

He observed the few pictures on the wall, photographs of Russia, he judged, pastoral scenes of mountains and rivers taken in the good weather.

There was a closed door behind the desk. Should he open it? Fodorov wondered. His question was answered when the door was opened by someone else.

A slender man dressed in a heavy wool three-piece suit, white shirt, and narrow red tie entered the room. His hair was wet, and combed from ear to ear across a tan, pitted bald pate. He wore glasses tethered around his neck by a black cord. His mustache was a thin line across his upper lip.

Fodorov greeted him in Russian. The man returned the greeting. "You are?" he asked.

"Yvgeny Fodorov. Here."

Fodorov handed him a piece of paper included in his envelope of instructions.

The man moved his glasses lower on his nose and read the note. His expression was pained, as though the note had wounded him. He handed it back to Fodorov and said, "Come."

They went through the door and up a narrow stairway to the second floor. The man opened a door and stepped back for Yvgeny to enter.

The room into which Fodorov stepped was as plush as the downstairs had been spartan. The floor was covered with thick Oriental carpets, one on top of the other. The furniture was oversized, chairs with wide wooden arms and heavy brocade red and yellow cushions and backs. The smell of incense and the scent of fried foods hung heavy in the air.

A small kitchen was off the main room. The shadow of someone in it moved like an ethereal vision across the walls.

"Sit there," Fodorov's greeter said, pointing to one of the chairs and leaving the room.

Yvgeny tried to see who was in the kitchen, but the shadow prevailed. Then, the open doorway to the kitchen was filled by a hulking man with a huge belly, whose shaved head almost touched the top of the frame. He wore a black T-shirt, brown cardigan sweater secured by a single button, baggy black pants, and carpet slippers. A massive cross sat on his bulging stomach, secured to his thick neck by a leather thong. Large gold rings studded

185

with diamonds on both hands caught the light, tossing their brilliance at Fodorov.

Fodorov stood, mumbled hello.

"Zdrastvuitye," the man echoed in a deep, gravelly voice. He stepped into the room and extended his hand; Yvgeny's hand disappeared into it. "I am Pavel Bakst. Welcome."

"Thank you," said Fodorov.

"Sit. Some coffee? Tea? Vodka? Beer?"

Fodorov asked for tea with sugar.

Bakst disappeared into the kitchen. A minute later a tea kettle's whistle sounded. Bakst reappeared carrying a tray with tea, a sugar bowl, milk, and a plate of *vetchina*, sliced ham, a salted cheese called *suluguni*, and blini, small, traditional Russian pancakes.

Yvgeny ate eagerly while Bakst, who'd settled in a facing chair, watched, his thick lips set in an amused smile. When Yvgeny had finished, Bakst said, "So, Mr. Yvgeny Fodorov, you work for Brazier Industries."

"Da. But only temporary. On a special assignment."

"I see. I am told you are an associate of Gennady Pralovich in Moscow."

Fodorov wanted to agree, but was anxious not to stretch the truth. "Associate? *Nyet.* I am only a soldier."

"But he sends you on such an important assignment. He must think highly of you."

"I like to think so, Mr. Bakst."

Bakst shifted his bulk in the chair. "Well," he said, "it is our pleasure to host you until you are needed again. We will do everything to make your stay pleasant."

Yvgeny felt an inner glow. To be treated with such respect was warming. He suppressed a smile of satisfaction.

"Do you know what they call this Brighton Beach, Yvgeny?"

"*Nyet.*"

"Little Odessa. Twenty, maybe thirty thousand fellow Russians here. Like being home, huh?" He laughed.

"It feels good," Fodorov said. "I do not like America."

"Oh? You do not like the land of opportunity?"

"I do not."

"The streets are paved with gold here, Fodorov."

Yvgeny's laugh was scoffing.

"You laugh. But it is true. We do very well here. Better than in Russia."

Yvgeny's face was serious. "How can that be?" he asked.

"There is more money here to be gotten," Bakst said. "We have made excellent inroads in America. Millions from our gasoline-tax projects alone. America is ripe for the taking."

Fodorov nodded. "I see," he said.

"Of course, we have had to make certain business arrangements with the local Italians. They have had it all to themselves for many years. Now, they have become weak, their leaders sent away. And we are here to step in."

"One day . . ."

"One day what, Fodorov?"

"One day when Yeltsin is gone and we are again in power in Russia—when it is the Soviet Union again—there will be gold on our streets, too."

Bakst had wrapped a blini around some ham and cheese, and had just bitten into it when Yvgeny issued his proclamation. The large man laughed, coughed, and spit the food onto the rugs. He continued laughing. Fodorov felt anger, but quickly told himself not to show it. He waited until the coughing and laughing had subsided before asking, "I am sorry if I said something wrong, Mr. Bakst."

"Who are you talking about?" Bakst asked, kicking the food aside with his slipper.

"Who? I meant the Communists."

"The Communists?" He fell into another laughing and coughing fit.

Fodorov decided to say nothing.

"The Communists? An *apparatchik*, are you, Fodorov? A loyal believer."

"*Da*. Aren't you?"

"*Nyet*, Fodorov. I hold no beliefs for any political party. It does not matter who sits in the *Kreml*. They call it the Kremlin here. Americans want to go to Moscow to see the Kremlin. For what? To spend their money? To look at something that never worked? Communism. Democracy. What does it matter? It is only the *Organizatsiya* that matters, my young, idealistic friend. Only us, the *mafiya*. The Italians call it 'our thing.' It is no longer their thing. Now, it is *our* thing."

Fodorov fought himself to keep from extending the conversation. He was confused, but did not want to admit it.

In Moscow, he and his colleagues worked for the Communists, did they not? Was it not the same here? The Communists paid for his services, for the services of everyone in the organization. He'd been paid by them to kill his own mother. Not directly, of course, but he knew why he'd been instructed to do it. To send a message, the way they'd sent a message by taking away his father so many years ago for his traitorous writings, or refusing to register his mother's typewriter.

Killing his mother had been surprisingly easy. He'd hated her for what seemed to be his whole life. Still, while driving back to Moscow after leaving her lifeless body in the *dacha*, he'd suffered a wave of sadness, even self-loathing. It didn't last long. By the time he reached the city, an exaltation had consumed him, and he couldn't wait to report that he'd accomplished his mission, and to receive their praise, slaps on the back, shots of vodka to down in celebration for having taken on such a difficult assignment. That's exactly what did happen upon his return to Moscow, and he hadn't felt sadness or self-loathing again.

"It is very good tea, Mr. Bakst," Yvgeny said.

"Thank you. It is time to take you to where you will stay. Tonight, you will join us for dinner. We have some fine restaurants here, Yvgeny. Authentic. Good Russian food and drink. Music. Entertainers. Later, there will be a woman for you."

Bakst brought Fodorov downstairs to where the little man with the mustache sat at a desk. He instructed him to have someone pick Yvgeny up immediately, and to take him "to Misha's house."

"I would like to have a weapon," Yvgeny said quietly. "For protection. They would not let me bring mine."

"Of course they wouldn't, because they are smart. But you won't need protection here, my friend." He slapped Fodorov hard on the back. "We take care of each other. Go now. Rest. There is plenty to drink and eat at Misha's. Not far from here."

Fodorov stood on the sidewalk with Bakst until the car arrived. Many people passing greeted Bakst. He must be very important, Yvgeny thought. A leader. A boss.

189

He looked back at the sign above the front door. BRIS AVROHOM. "What is that?" he asked.

"A fine organization to welcome our Russian citizens to America, help them settle, find work, housing. We are not—how shall I say it?—we are not an official part of it. But we raise money for it. The sign is good, huh? It says we care, to the authorities at least." A laugh. "We have our own ways to welcome our fellow Russians to this country. The sign? No one tells us to take it down, so it stays up. Ah, here is your car. I will see you tonight, Fodorov. Take a nap. Nights last a very long time in Little Odessa."

The party at Rasputin, one of Brighton Beach's most popular Russian restaurants, lasted until four the next morning. A band played loud dance music, augmented during its intermissions by strolling minstrels. The first course was served at eleven—*borscht,* containing real red beets, Yvgeny was told, as opposed to the borscht of the old Soviet Union, consisting mainly of cabbage. Crab and shrimp dishes followed, then lamb smothered in a succulent sauce of mushrooms and cranberries, accompanied by stuffed cabbage leaves and rice and potatoes and overflowing green salads. Fodorov had never seen so much food at one sitting, and he took advantage of it, stuffing his face while attempting to engage in the spirited, raucous conversations around him.

A pretty young girl asked him to dance. He didn't want to because he didn't know how. She laughed when he told her that, and said she would teach him.

On the dance floor, she said in a giddy voice, "My father says you are a very important person from Moscow."

Fodorov wasn't sure how to respond, so he laughed.

"Who is your father?" he asked, stumbling over his feet as she led him to the beat of the music.

"Bakst," she said.

"Bakst. Oh. He is your father?"

"Yes. He says you are here on an important job."

"I—I cannot talk about that," Yvgeny said.

She giggled. "Of course you can't. Now watch, follow me. It's easy."

Yvgeny kept his eyes on Bakst's daughter, Trina, all night. He liked her. She was pretty, like Sofia, but without Sofia's silly ways. Trina had called her father by his last name. Strange, thought Yvgeny. It must be the way *mafiya* bosses are referred to in America. Each time Fodorov thought of what Trina had said, that her father considered him an important person from Moscow, he was filled with pleasure he dared not exhibit.

After all, he was now a hardened, paid killer.

Hardened, paid killers did not smile.

At five in the morning, Yvgeny lay in bed with a prostitute Bakst had dispatched to Misha's house for the visitor's pleasure. He knew he was not a skilled lover, so sought to compensate by treating the short, pale, chubby girl roughly. She didn't complain, simply went through her motions as quickly as possible and left the small room.

Outside, she climbed into her Russian pimp's Cadillac. The sun was rising over Coney Island and Brighton Beach. She gently touched her breasts through the fabric of her dress, where Yvgeny had hurt her.

The pimp had told her that her final customer for the night would be an important visitor from Moscow, according to Bakst.

"How was he?" the pimp asked, lighting a cigarette and starting the engine.

"Creepy," she replied. "A faggot."

Her pimp laughed as he pulled away from the curb. "Next time we should send him a boy," he said.

"Next time," she said, "send him a dog."

20

Mac Smith walked into the office of former congressman Paul Latham and went directly to where Bob Mondrian sat at a computer. Mondrian held up his index finger, and went back to his task. Smith waited patiently. Finally, Mondrian stood, shook Smith's hand, and suggested they go into the congressman's office.

"Getting squared away?" Smith asked once the door was closed behind them.

"In a manner of speaking," Mondrian said. "The official ME's autopsy report is about to be announced. I got the call a few minutes ago."

"No surprises, I assume."

"No. It was murder. That's a definite. The FBI is holding a news conference in a half hour."

"Murder's no novelty in Washington," Smith said, more to himself than to the chief of staff. "But a congressman . . ."

"Presidents have fallen to the bullet," Mondrian said, settling behind Latham's desk and gesturing to a chair across from it.

Smith sat.

"Another blow to the country," Mondrian said. "Every time a leader is killed, the whole nation loses another thread in its moral fabric."

Smith looked across the desk at Bob Mondrian. He was aware of the high regard in which Latham had held his COS. Mondrian, besides being a skilled and effective staffer, was a keen student of history. Latham had once told Smith, "Sometimes I feel downright inferior to Bob. I love history, but he really *knows* it. Quotes Thucydides all the time. Considers him the greatest of all the historians. Spends his vacations traveling to major historical sites. He'd make a hell of a professor, if he wasn't such a good pol."

Smith asked Mondrian, "Any leads that you know of?"

Mondrian shook his head. What he then said gave credence to his reputation. "I spent a few weeks this summer in Albania, Mac. On a CODEL."

"CODEL?"

"Congressional Delegation trip. Never got close to Corfu, though, where the Peloponnesian War took place between Athens and Sparta. It settled the question of who would dominate Greece. Once Athens lost its navy, it was no contest." Mondrian smiled. "Don't mean to ramble."

"Feel free."

"The minute I heard about Paul's death, all I could think of was what Pericles said about leaders being killed."

"What did Pericles say? My history's not up to yours."

" 'Trees, though they are cut and lopped, grow up

194

again quickly, but if men are destroyed, it is not easy to replace them.' "

"As true now as back then, before the coming of Christ," Smith said.

"Maybe even more so now," Mondrian said gruffly.

"The FBI interviewed me this morning," Smith said.

"Right. You said they would be. Painless?"

"Relatively. They've put out an all-points on Marge Edwards."

"So I understand. Her father called here this morning."

"And?"

"He was upset. He now knows about the story that Marge was poised to charge Paul with sexual harassment. Some local press out there are bugging him for a statement. And he was visited last night by a guy billing himself as a private detective."

"Who's this detective working for?"

A shrug from Mondrian. "I didn't ask. Her father said his name was Petrone. Something like that."

"Uh huh. Any word on who'll fill Paul's seat?"

"The leadership wants Ruth to push for it."

"Oh?"

"She won't, of course. A great congressman's wife, but basically apolitical."

Smith smiled. "That might be one of her most endearing attributes."

Mondrian raised his eyebrows, then allowed a half smile to surface. "Not a fan of the political process, Mac?"

"Depends upon who's doing what in that process. Bob, when I told you at Paul's house about the Marge Edwards rumor, you dismissed it, then said that if it were true, it was because she's so—how did you put it?—because she's so 'damned unstable.' Care to elaborate on that?"

Mondrian chewed his cheek, sat back, and rubbed his eyes. He came forward again and ran his hand through his thinning hair. "What I'd rather do, Mac, is wait to see if she was, in fact, going to charge Paul. No sense telling Marge Edwards tales out of school unless necessary."

"You already have," Smith said, slightly annoyed at Mondrian's sudden concern for her reputation. "You've told me she's unstable. I'd like to have some examples of what leads you to that conclusion."

Mondrian sighed. "I understand what you're saying, Mac. But I also know that with Paul's murder, you don't have an official reason for staying involved. As I understand it, your only role was as Paul's counsel at his confirmation hearings."

Smith didn't allow the comment to nettle him. He replied, "That's right. But I feel a continuing obligation to Paul's family. That's not hard to understand, is it?"

Mondrian shook his head. "No, it's not. Forgive me. I've been under the gun."

Smith acknowledged that he understood; no forgiveness necessary, despite the overly apt expression. He also knew that Mondrian was not about to offer more about Marge Edwards. He stood. "Thanks for your time, Bob."

"Lunch? I'll order the sandwiches."

"No, thanks. By the way, how about giving me Marge's father's number?"

Mondrian thought for a second, then said, "Sure. I have it outside. Anything else I can do for you?"

"I don't think so. Not for the moment anyhow."

"Amazing," Mondrian said as he walked Smith to the outer offices. "It's only been a day since Paul was murdered, and all the focus is back on politics. Who'll run for his seat? Who will the president nominate now for State? Who will the leadership put up for Paul's chairmanship of International Relations?"

"Just business as usual, D.C. style," Smith said, accepting the slip of paper from Mondrian on which Marge Edwards's father's number was written.

"Just a word of caution, Mac," Mondrian said.

"Yes?"

"I'd think twice about contacting the father."

"Why?"

"He didn't sound—I don't know—maybe he's old, losing it. Just a thought."

Just a thought, like his off-hand comment about Marge's stability was "just a thought."

"Thanks, Bob. Stay in touch."

Smith meant—with reality.

21

Congressman Paul Latham's funeral service was held at night in the National Cathedral, where former secretary of state Jake Baumann's death had been officially mourned. His body would be flown to California for burial.

The day after the funeral, a tribute to him was held in the Capitol's Statuary Hall. A succession of congressmen and senators offered words of praise and sadness, and directed their condolences to Ruth Latham and her three children, who sat erect and proud in the front row. Priscilla had flown in from London, arriving just in time for the National Cathedral service.

When it was over, the Latham family formed a receiving line of sorts, and greeted the hundreds of friends and colleagues who'd shown up, Mac and Annabel Smith among them.

"They were touching and fitting tributes," Smith said to Ruth Latham.

"Paul would have been proud," she replied, dry-eyed.

Smith shook Martin's hand. The only Latham son, hair tied in a long ponytail, wearing one of his father's suit jackets over a T-shirt, chino pants, and black sneakers, thanked Mac for coming.

"Your father was a good friend," Smith said. "And a good man."

"Your tennis partner."

"Among other things."

As they spoke, Annabel chatted briefly with Priscilla Latham. She hadn't seen Priscilla in at least two years, and was struck by the young woman's radiant beauty. She carried her nicely cut English suit and simple silk blouse with grace; she spoke with parallel aplomb.

". . . I suppose the hardest part, Mrs. Smith, is knowing my father was murdered. That happens to other families, inner-city families, poor families."

"I'm sure they'll find the person responsible soon," Annabel said, continuing to hold Priscilla's hand.

"I hope so. We could use some closure."

Smith had moved on to Molly Latham. He wasn't sure what to say to the sixteen-year-old, whose expression told him she was trying to balance a desire to appear composed with the need to bawl her brains out.

"As sad as all this is, Molly," Smith said, "I find myself celebrating all the years your father was my friend. Hard to do sometimes, but it's the way he would want it. At least that's the way I choose to view it."

She nodded and forced a small smile. "He always said such nice things about you and Mrs. Smith."

"That's good to hear."

"I remember when he and mom came back from your wedding." She glanced at Annabel. "I remember he said you were the best-looking couple in Washington, except for him and Mom."

Smith laughed, squeezed her hand, and moved to the next person in line. Molly introduced her: "This is my roommate in the page dorm, Melissa Marshall."

"Pleased to meet you," Smith said, noticing that Annabel was now in front of Molly.

"Mah pleasure," Melissa said.

Smith turned and asked Molly, "When will you be getting back to being a page?"

She shrugged.

Melissa answered for her, "As soon as possible, Mr. Smith. Ah certainly do miss her."

The Smiths left the Capitol and stood in the sunshine, as far from the hundreds of press people as possible. Security was heavy. The Lathams had twenty-four-hour-a-day MPD escort. Capitol police seemed to be everywhere. FBI agents, trying to be unnoticed, were obvious in their attempt.

"Lovely day."

"As far as the weather goes," Annabel said.

"They seem to be holding up quite well."

"The collapse will come later. What time is your flight?"

"Four. Out of National."

"Still sure you want to go?"

"Yes. I've been chafing ever since Bob Mondrian told me I basically didn't have any business asking questions about Marge Edwards. When I called her father, he came off to me as a rational, intelligent man. Mondrian said he was losing it, as he put it. Why?"

"Maybe that's the way the father came off to *him.*"

"Possibly. His name is Jim. The father. I didn't intend

to go out to Indiana to see him. But when he said the last time Marge called him, she said that if she were ever in trouble in Washington she'd call me, I figured I owed her this."

"You no longer think she's simply gone underground to get away from the glare?"

"Still a possibility, Annie. But I have this gut feeling that—"

"Which you tend to trust more than I trust mine, women's intuition aside."

"I have this feeling that Marge Edwards is in trouble beyond simply claiming her boss sexually harassed her. If that's even true."

Annabel said, "Go to Indiana and talk to . . . Jim, is it? I just hope you're wrong."

22

Jim Edwards picked him up at the Indianapolis Airport. He was not what Smith expected him to be.

For some reason, since his conversation with Bob Mondrian, and during the flight from Washington, Smith had conjured a vision of an old, crusty Indiana farmer.

Instead, he was greeted by a handsome, youthful gentleman dressed in sport coat and tie. He had a full head of bushy brown hair, with some gray at the temples. Mac judged him to be in his mid-fifties—maybe a few years older than that, considering lines in his ruddy face. His smile was wide and genuine, his handshake firm.

They drove to Edwards's home in his red Jeep Grand Cherokee. His home wasn't far from the airport, a well-kept small tract house with a manicured lawn and pretty white front porch. As they approached, Edwards slowed down and pointed to a TV satellite van and four or five people leaning against it.

"The press caught up with you, I see," said Smith.

"Yes. I don't know how people in the public eye stand it, the constant scrutiny, the interference in your life."

"It's a negative perk," Smith said. "Goes with being a public figure."

They pulled into the driveway. Smith, carrying his small overnight bag, walked with Edwards across the lawn and to the porch. The reporters cut them off before they had a chance to go up the four steps.

"Any word from your daughter?" Edwards was asked.

"No," he responded. "No word."

"Who are you?" a reporter asked Smith.

Smith smiled against the questioner's bluntness. "Mackensie Smith."

Another reporter said, "Congressman Latham's lawyer."

"Former counsel," Smith corrected.

"Why are you here, Mr. Smith?"

"Just visiting," Mac said. To Edwards: "Can we?"

They stepped up onto the porch. Edwards opened the screen door, used his key to unlock the inner door, and ushered Smith inside.

They stood in the living room, a square space with sheets on the chairs and couch. "I keep the furniture covered, Mr. Smith, because of the dogs and cats."

Smith looked about. "My dog would be all over a guest," he said.

"So would mine, if I let them. I keep them in a small apartment over the garage when guests are coming. The cats are probably frightened. One of them will venture out in a while. Please. Sit." He whipped the sheet from the couch. "Can I get you something? You haven't had dinner, have you?"

"Peanuts and a Coke on the flight," Mac said. "That's

what seems to pass for a 'snack' these days with the airlines. But I'm not hungry. I'll eat later at the hotel."

"I made a reservation for you at the Holiday Inn. Only a few miles away. The invitation to stay here is still open. It's just me and the animals these days."

"Thanks, but I don't want to intrude. A cup of coffee would be fine, if it's no trouble."

"Never any trouble with instant coffee, Mr. Smith."

Smith, a self-acknowledged coffee snob, said, "Any tea?"

"Sure. Only be a minute."

Smith used Edwards's absence to stroll and to take in the living room. Mondrian had said Edwards's wife was dead; a dozen pictures of a woman, obviously her, helped to preserve the memories for her widower.

There were also pictures of Marge; as a small child cuddling a puppy, at high school graduation, on prom night, and a more recent one taken in front of the Capitol Building. She looked happy in all of them.

Smith had just picked up a book from a table—surprised to find a collection of short stories by Arturo Vivante that had appeared in *The New Yorker*; Smith also had a copy, which rested in a section of a bookcase reserved for favorite works—when Edwards reappeared with tea and a small plate of vanilla cookies.

"Perhaps you'd prefer a drink. Liquor, I mean," Edwards said.

"No, thank you. Tea is fine."

"You don't mind if I do? It's that time."

"Sure. Go ahead," Smith said.

They passed the next few minutes talking about Vivante's book and others. Edwards said he and his deceased wife, Sue, had always been ravenous readers despite jobs that were distinctly not literary. Sue Edwards had worked as a secretary at a small manufacturing plant. Jim was employed as a maintenance supervisor at a rental car's Indianapolis office.

Smith finished his tea and addressed his reason for being there. "Jim," he said, "Paul Latham was a dear friend of mine. His family, too, has always been close. As you know, a rumor surfaced that Marge was considering— I suppose that's the accurate way to put it—she was considering bringing a sexual harassment charge against Latham, which conceivably could have caused a serious problem with his confirmation hearings as secretary of state."

Edwards, who sipped from a glass, said nothing, simply nodded as Mac made his points.

Smith continued. "Then, of course, as you know, Congressman Latham was murdered."

"That's definite?" Edwards asked. "It wasn't suicide?"

"No. The autopsy confirms it was murder. It was on the news."

Edwards sounded defensive. "I don't watch much of the news. Everything's so grim these days. I prefer to read."

"I can certainly understand that," Smith said. "Naturally, with Paul Latham dead, the question of whether Marge was, indeed, intending to bring the charge changes considerably. A question for you, Jim. Did she ever indicate, in any way, that Paul Latham had demonstrated sexual, romantic interest in her?"

Edwards thought before responding. "No," he said. "Never. The gentlemen from the FBI asked about that, too."

"They interviewed you?"

"Yes. A man and a woman from the Indianapolis office. They were very nice. Very polite."

"That's always been my experience. Unless, of course, you give them a hard time."

"I would never do that," Edwards said.

"I'm sure you wouldn't," Smith said. "How much has Marge discussed with you about her job as Latham's scheduling secretary?"

"Not much." He drank. "Sure I can't tempt you?"

Smith shook his head. "What did she say when she *did* discuss it? Her job, that is."

"Oh, I don't know. She complained a lot about how hard it was. But she liked the congressman. Liked him very much, the way I heard it."

"What about her colleagues in the office? She like them, too?"

"Oh, yes. Well, there is a chap—name is, ah, Bob—"

"Bob Mondrian, Latham's chief of staff."

"Yes, that's right. It seems Marge and this Bob didn't get along all that well."

"Any reason for it?"

"Not that she ever said. I gather he's a bit of a dictator."

"The pressure in those jobs is intense," Smith offered. "Anything else Marge might have said about the people she works with?"

Edwards shook his head. "I'm ready for a refill," he said.

"I will join you," Mac said. "Scotch, bourbon? With water?"

"Either one."

"Bourbon. Light."

Glasses in their hands, Smith continued.

"Do you have any idea, Jim, where Marge might be?"

"No."

206

"Other family she might have gone to? Close friends?"

"I've talked with other family members as recently as this afternoon. They haven't heard from her."

"Has she disappeared like this before?"

"Not that I recall. No, never. Oh, we fall out of touch from time to time, but—"

"For how long at a stretch?"

"A month, sometimes. About a month. She's real busy in Washington. Nice city. I've visited her a few times since she moved there."

"She's a pretty, vivacious young woman. An active social life, I imagine."

"Marge always had lots of beaus. Real popular in high school and college." It was a small, rueful laugh. "She's like most women her age, I suppose. Hears the biological clock ticking and wonders why she isn't married and doesn't have kids. She came close a few times."

"Really?"

"Funny, asking before about whether she had any problems with people she works with . . . The maddest I've ever seen her—I mean, since she became an adult; lots of temper tantrums in high school, like most teenagers—was when she was going out with the congressman's son."

"Martin Latham?"

"That's right. She was really in love with him, I can tell you. Called every other night to tell me how happy she was. I thought I was about to have a son-in-law."

"What happened?" Smith asked.

"It broke up. Martin left Washington and went someplace to become a woodworker, I think. Some craft like that. Marge wanted to go with him, but he wanted to go alone. She was very hurt, very angry."

"I see." Smith tried to recall whether Paul Latham had

ever mentioned to him that Martin was dating Marge
Edwards. He hadn't. Interesting pairing, Smith thought.
Martin had to be eight or ten years younger than Marge.

"I wasn't aware they'd dated."

"She was never quite the same after that episode in her
life," Jim Edwards said. "There was a bitterness that
crept in. Not overt. Not a big deal. But I could tell whenever we spoke."

Smith had been waiting ever since his arrival at Jim
Edwards's house for the right moment to bring up Mondrian's contention. Was there ever such a right time? This
was as good a time as any, he decided. Jim Edwards was
a nice man, open and candid. Unlikely he would take
offense at such a question.

So Smith asked, "As Marge's father, you obviously
know her as well as or better than anyone else. Would
you consider her unstable?"

The question caused Edwards to pause. He squeezed
his eyes shut as though forcing the right answer to emerge
through his mouth. He opened his eyes, inhaled, let the air
out, and said, "I suppose you could say that. No, let me
clarify it. Marge has always been high-strung. Very much
like her mother was. Emotional. Feelings always on the
surface. She's capable of flying off the handle, even
when it isn't in her best interests. But so are a lot of
people. Is that a definition of unstable? Maybe it is. I'll
leave it up to you."

Smith said, "I'm really not in a position to judge your
daughter, Jim, nor would I want to be. I'm here because I
care about her, and want to know where she is so that I
might be able to help her."

"That's what she said, you know. She said if she ever
got in trouble in Washington, she'd want to talk to you.

And I appreciate you coming all the way out to Indiana. May I ask you a question?"

"Sure."

"Do you think something terrible has happened to Marge?"

"I—"

"I've tried not to worry. I prefer to think she's just gone away for a few days because of this damned stupid rumor about the congressman and her. She's a big girl, all grown up. Still, I do worry. I guess you never stop being a father."

Smith thought of his son. Sometimes you do stop, because you're forced to.

"No, you never do, Jim. I'm glad I made this trip. I wasn't sure why I wanted to come, couldn't come up with a tangible reason for it. But I'm glad I did. To answer your question: No, I don't think anything terrible has happened to Marge. Probably exactly what you said. She got away for a few days, and will probably be calling in any day to say she's okay and to put to rest the rumor. By the way, I understand a private detective visited you, asking about Marge."

"That's right. A big fellow named Petrone."

"Did he say why he was looking for her?"

"No. Well, he said he knew her. Was a friend."

"A private detective. He didn't say he was here on behalf of a client?"

"No. I have his card."

Edwards dug it out from a pile of papers on a small desk in the corner, and handed it to Smith.

"James Perrone."

"Yes. Perrone. Not Petrone."

"Mind if I take this with me?"

"Not at all. I don't intend to call him if Marge gets in touch."

Edwards offered another drink, but Smith said he was tired and wanted to get to the hotel.

"Have you there in no time," Edwards said. "You're flying back tomorrow?"

"Yes."

"I'd drive you to the airport but I have to be at work."

"A cab will do just fine. But thanks for thinking of it."

They stood up to leave and the phone rang. Edwards looked at Smith with a questioning expression.

"Go ahead," Smith said. "I'm in no rush."

"Hello? Yes, he's right here, Mrs. Smith. Just a moment." He handed the phone to his guest.

"Hello, Annabel. Anything wrong?"

"No. But I'm glad I caught you. Marge Edwards just called."

Smith glanced at Edwards, who was in the process of taking their glasses to the kitchen.

"Where is she?" Mac asked quietly.

"I don't know. She wanted to speak with you. I started to tell her where you were, but she said she'd call again and hung up."

"At least she's alive. How did she sound?"

"Too brief a conversation to tell. How's it going there?"

"Good. Ironic, huh?"

"What's ironic?"

"I come to Indiana, and she calls me in Washington."

"Life's a series of ironies."

"I know, I know. And most of them I could do without. How are you?"

"Fine. The press has decamped from in front of the house. They fly out with you? How's Mr. Edwards?"

"Nice guy. He'll be happy to hear about the call. He's driving me to the hotel. I'll call later from there."

"Okay. And—oh, yes. Love you, Mac."

Smith sensed Edwards had entered the room and stood just behind him.

"Me, too," he said, returning the phone to its cradle.

Smith told Jim Edwards about the call from Marge as they drove to the hotel.

He could hear the man literally breathe easier.

"That's a relief," Edwards said. "I wish she'd called me."

"I'm sure she will. Sometimes when you're under pressure, you don't want to bring your family in on it until it's over." He didn't know whether that was true or not, but it seemed the thing to say.

They shook hands at the entrance to the Holiday Inn.

"Thanks for all your Hoosier hospitality, Jim."

"No. Thank you for caring so much about my daughter. You'll let me know when you talk to her?"

"Count on it."

23

Smith had a light dinner in the Holiday Inn's coffee shop, and spent the next few hours reading a book he'd brought with him, *How Russia Became a Market Economy,* published by the Brookings Institution. He checked in with Annabel before turning in for the night. Marge Edwards had not called again.

The next morning, he took the first flight to Washington, and had the taxi drop him in Georgetown at Annabel's gallery.

After a serious embrace, she said, "I really missed you. You were gone weeks, not overnight."

"Glad to be back. I swung by here because I'm not sure what to do with the knowledge that Marge Edwards is alive and presumably well."

"I was thinking the same thing. Maybe you should report her attempt to reach you."

"I suppose I should. Still, I didn't speak with her. We

have no idea where she is. No, I think it can wait till I actually talk to her."

"It's your call. Tell me more about Jim Edwards."

Smith gave her a thumbnail sketch of his time with the father.

"So, he confirmed that his daughter might be termed unstable at times," Annabel said.

"Not in so many words, Annie. But he didn't paint her as a rock of emotional stability."

He handed her the card given Edwards by the private investigator, James Perrone, and explained why he had it.

"Hmmmm. Based here in Washington," Annabel said, noting a suite number at an address on New Jersey Avenue.

"Yeah. He told Edwards he knew Marge. I wonder if he did, or if he went out to Indianapolis for a client."

"Who would that client be?" she asked. "Has Paul's staff, maybe Bob Mondrian, hired him?"

Mac shrugged. "I might drop in on Mr. Perrone."

Her eyebrows arched. "Why?"

"To follow up in every possible way on Marge's disappearance. As long as this sexual harassment rumor floats out there, I think I owe it to Ruth and the kids. Spoken with Ruth?"

"Yes. She sounded okay."

"Well, looks like nothing is new here," he said, gesturing within the gallery. "Mind if I take the car?"

"Nope." She handed him the keys; he knew the garage she used.

He drove home and unpacked. Mac Smith was as meticulous at unpacking as he was at packing. That applied to his briefcase, too. His first action upon returning home each evening was to empty it, put things away, and repack for the next day. Obsessive-compulsive? Certainly about his briefcase and luggage; he wore the badge proudly. He walked Rufus, had a bowl of soup, locked up, and headed for New Jersey Avenue.

He'd considered calling ahead to Perrone's office, but opted instead simply to drop in on the PI. He didn't know what he was seeking from Perrone. Knowing why someone might have hired a private investigator to find Marge Edwards would be interesting, but to what use? He wasn't even sure why he was continuing this quest to find her. He could easily rationalize it—and had done so to Annabel more successfully than he had to himself—by his concern for Paul Latham's reputation in death. The family. Bad enough to have lost a husband and father, but even worse to have a cloud of sleaze hanging over the loss. Like finding evidence of infidelity in a dead husband's desk drawers at the office.

By the time Smith parked, and entered the building on New Jersey Avenue, he no longer grappled with motivation. You could spend your life questioning why you wanted to do something, and end up never doing it.

The sign on the door read J. PERRONE, PRIVATE INVESTIGATIONS. There was a button to push, and a squawk box to the right of the handle. Smith pushed the button. A distorted female voice said, "Yes?"

"I'm here to see Mr. Perrone. Mackensie Smith."

"Do you have an appointment?"

"No. I'm—I was Congressman Latham's legal counsel."
A prolonged pause.

A buzz sounded. Smith opened the door and stepped inside a small, cramped reception area. A receptionist sat behind a desk. "Mr. Smith?" she said.

"Yes. Is Mr. Perrone in?"

"Yes, but he's in conference."

A fancy way to say he's busy, Smith thought. Or does not want to see me.

"If you'd like to make an appointment, Mr. Smith, I'll be happy to do that."

"Actually," Smith said, "I'm only looking for a few minutes of Mr. Perrone's time. I'm not here as a potential client. It has to do with Congressman Latham's murder"—the word came out hard—"and the disappearance of Ms. Marjorie Edwards."

Smith sensed as he spoke that his words were being piped into Perrone's private office. It didn't take long for that to be confirmed. The door opened and Perrone came through it, an unlighted cigar jutting from his mouth, a brace of red and yellow suspenders holding up his pants. He wore a mustard-colored shirt and wide black-and-white tie. The investigator was no fashion plate.

"Mr. Smith?" he said.

"Yes. I take it you're Jim Perrone."

"Right." They shook hands.

"Sorry to barge in like this, but I thought I might get lucky."

Perrone smiled. "If seeing me is good luck, Smith, your luck's running bad. Come on in."

"I don't want to disturb your . . . conference."

"It's over."

He stepped back to allow Smith to enter.

It was a pleasantly furnished and decorated office, nothing Raymond Chandler would have created for his hard-boiled, lean-and-mean, honor-driven private eye, Philip Marlowe. There was a softness to the pastel walls, thick wall-to-wall rose-colored carpeting, and mauve drapes. A woman's touch, Mac thought.

"Sit down, Mr. Smith," said Perrone. He took a high-back leather chair behind a teak desk on which there were few papers or files. The office was a lot neater than the man. "You were Latham's lawyer, huh?"

"That's right." No need to qualify, Smith decided.

"And you're wondering where Marge Edwards went."

"Right again." He'd heard every word from the reception area.

"So, why are you here talking to me?"

"Because you've been looking for her, too."

Perrone's hand went to his heart. "I have?" he said with exaggerated surprise.

"According to Marge Edwards's father, Jim. Indianapolis?"

Perrone lighted his cigar. "You don't mind, huh?"

"Not at all." The suit was due for the cleaners anyway, Smith told himself.

"Jim Edwards told me that you claimed to be Marge's friend. Or at least knew her."

Perrone nodded.

"How did that come about?"

"What do you mean?"

"How did you become friends with her?"

Perrone dismissed the question with a smoky wave of the cigar.

Smith knew he would have to justify his questions if he hoped to receive any useful answers. He said, "Because Marge Edwards can't be contacted, the rumor that she claims to have been sexually harassed by Paul Latham stays alive. I care about the Latham family, and want to put a stake through the rumor's heart. I thought you might help me."

216

"Maybe I would," Perrone said. "Tell me why I should."

"A sense of decency. You say you know Marge. Maybe you can tell me—"

"*You* say I know her."

"*You* told her father you know her."

"I met her a couple of times."

"She ever tell you that Congressman Latham harassed her? Sexually, that is."

Perrone nodded, drew smoke.

"She did?"

"Yeah."

"When?"

"I don't know. A month, two months ago."

"Where did she tell you?"

Perrone stood and stretched.

Smith asked, "Why did she tell *you*?"

"Where? When? Why? What is this, the Inquisition?"

"You've heard of that."

"Yeah, I—look, Smith, thanks for stopping in. If you want to hire me to find Marge Edwards, the fee is two-fifty a day and expenses. Interested?"

"Is that what your other client is paying you?"

"Have a nice day, Smith."

Smith stood. "You, too, Perrone. Good of you to see me on such short notice."

Mac got into his car and drove home. His brief encounter with James Perrone had angered him. At the same time, he found the exchange to have been of interest, perhaps even useful. He didn't believe for a minute that Marge Edwards had claimed to Perrone that Paul Latham had sexually harassed her. And he seriously doubted they even knew each other, although he had nothing upon which to base that belief. Marge and Perrone would have had little in common, nothing to cause her to open up to a PI, if he was a PI.

Unless—unless it was money, that great social leveler. He picked up the phone in his den office.

"You have reached the offices of Anthony Buffolino," said a woman via the answering machine. "We are unable to take your call right now. Please leave your name, number, and a message if you wish and we will return your call as soon as possible. Thank you."

"This is Mackensie Smith," Mac said, "calling at—"

"Mac?"

"Tony? Don't interrupt. I was talking to the machine."

"Yeah. That time of the month. Everybody wanting to get paid. Great gadget, the answering machine. You get to answer—or not answer. Some calls I pick up, some I don't. You, I pick up for even before you call. If you know what I mean."

Mac Smith and Tony Buffolino (with an *O*) went back a long way together. Buffolino had been a Washington MPD detective, and a good one. His fifteen-year record was clean; a desk drawer was filled with citations of merit and letters of appreciation from local politicians and citizens groups.

Then, after taking three bullets in his right leg, two in the thigh and one in the knee, in a shootout during a bank robbery, he was retired on full pay.

But retirement wasn't on Buffolino's agenda. Despite the objections of his second wife, and the gibes of fellow officers who only dreamed of being retired at full salary, he undertook extensive physical rehabilitation, passed the physical, and was reinstated as part of a special task force formed to combat Washington's burgeoning drug trade.

In retrospect, it was the wrong decision.

A year after joining the D.C. drug task force, one of his children from his first marriage developed leukemia, and the medical bills mounted, soared, until he made a fateful move that would forever change his life. He crossed the line between cop and criminal to cut a one-time deal with a notorious Washington-based Colombian drug dealer named Garcia. He would take Garcia's dirty money only once, he rationalized, and simply turn it all over to his first wife so she could pay the doctors and labs and hospitals. Just a one-shot indiscretion.

Once was all that was needed for the MPD to set up a sting, with Garcia's cooperation in return for leniency on a previous arrest. It occurred in a Watergate suite, and Tony Buffolino, with an *O*, was marched through the lobby in cuffs, forever disgraced, the fifteen years of heroic service, all the citations and awards nothing more than a measure of how far he had fallen.

Enter eminent Washington criminal attorney Mackensie Smith, through an intermediary for whom Smith had considerable respect. As abhorrent as drugs were to Mac, there was, at once, a mitigating set of feelings he developed for Buffolino. The cop had been stupid in seeking money from a drug dealer. He'd broken the code and dishonored himself. At the same time, having used a vicious drug dealer like Garcia to nail an otherwise good cop was anathema to Smith. And there was Buffolino's motivation. Not to get rich or to live the high life. Separated, and eventually divorced from his second wife, he lived in an industrial area of Baltimore in a hovel he called an apartment, and drove a faded red 1978 Cadillac with a cracked white landau roof and white leather interior grimy from age and too many greasy cheeseburgers and spilled sodas.

Smith interceded with the MPD and local prosecutors and cut a deal for Buffolino: no criminal prosecution, but a dishonorable discharge from the force, loss of pension and other rights, and a public confession of wrongdoing.

It was a good deal for Tony. But although he accepted its terms, he viewed Smith as having sold him down the river, and treated him that way. Until one day, Smith needed the services of a private investigator, thought of Buffolino, who'd set up shop in Baltimore as a private eye, called him, and they got together.

The friendship they forged from that moment certainly wasn't based upon common interests. They moved in vastly different circles. But there was a shared respect, Tony for the great trial attorney-turned-learned-professor-of-law, Mac for the gritty resolve of the private investigator whose street smarts and sometimes skewed view of life made him the most effective private eye Smith had ever known.

Buffolino married again, to a supportive and understanding woman named Alicia. Mac and Annabel often said Alicia had "tamed" Tony, which was true to an extent. That she'd managed to accomplish the feat without taking from him his spirit, or charming rough edges, was a tribute to her skill at wielding a whip, and a feather.

"I was going to give you a call, Mac, about this Latham case I've been reading about."

"I beat you to it, Tony. How's things?"

"Tip-top, Mac. I'm taking the high road these days. No more peeping in motel windows to nail a roving husband for some wife who's probably in some other motel down the road. Strictly business investigations these days."

"Glad to hear it," Smith said, remembering that Tony was screening calls to avoid creditors. "How's Alicia?"

"Good. Sometimes you get lucky. Drives me up the wall now and then, but she's a woman. And a good driver, if you get my meaning."

Smith smiled, asked, "What do you know about a colleague named James Perrone?"

"Colleague? Not even in the same league as me."

"But you do know him?"

"Yeah. A lowlife. Wears funny clothes, always has his big hand out for a payoff."

Wears funny clothes? Smith thought. Buffolino did not exactly define *haute couture*, although Alicia had managed to spruce him up a bit.

"A clean record?" Smith asked.

"I guess so. Nobody yanked his license I know of. Hey, Mac, you aren't thinking of hiring that *schmuck*, are you? What'd I do to lose your business?"

Smith laughed. Alicia, who was Jewish, had obviously substituted a little Yiddish for Tony's usual Italian slang. "No, Tony, I'm not looking to hire Perrone. I just want to know more about him."

"Having to do with the Latham murder, I suppose."

"Yes."

"You need me, Mac?"

"I could use you to come up with hard information on Perrone. Maybe even to keep an eye on him for the next few days. But since you're now taking the high road, as you put it, I suppose that would be out of the question."

"Yeah, it's not what I've been doing lately. Still, for you, I'd make an exception. I am busy. Up to my neck, you might say. But just for a few days? Shadow him? Yeah, I'll do it. My rates went up, I should inform you. Inflation."

"Of course. Can you get on it right away?"

"I'll make a point of it. How's the gorgeous redhead?"

"Annabel's very well, thank you. She often asks for you."

"Yeah, well, give her a big kiss for me. You'll be around?"

"Yes."

"You'll hear from me."

24

President Joseph Scott's press secretary, Sanford Teller, fielded a question about Paul Latham at the daily White House press briefing:

"Some sources are saying the president knew when he nominated his friend Congressman Latham for secretary of state that the sexual harassment charge by a female employee was about to be leveled. Any truth to that?"

Teller, aptly named for a spokesman, showed his anger in his pale blue eyes. He cast them over the reporters in the briefing room and said, "Those so-called sources give your profession a bad name. The rumor that a female employee of Congressman Latham was going to bring such a charge is just that, a rumor. As for the president, I can tell you that as a close friend of Congressman Latham, he's pretty upset—no, amend that—he's pretty damn mad about the rumor. Those on the Hill who seek political gain from perpetuating this slander against

Congressman Latham are not only prolonging his family's lingering grief, they're feeding the public's already negative perception of politics. Until and unless the young lady in question comes forth, that question's off the table here. Next? Helen?"

Mac Smith switched from C-SPAN to CNN, then to MSNBC, and finally turned off the set. Good for the president, he thought. Maybe if more people displayed outrage about rumors, they would diminish.

Senator Frank Connors, the Senate minority whip, had also watched the White House briefing. With him in his Russell Senate Office Building suite were his AA, Dennis Mackral, and Republican Congressman Mario Stassi, the ranking member on what used to be Paul Latham's House International Relations Committee and its subcommittee on International Operations and Human Rights.

Connors said over Teller's voice, "Since when does the president's press secretary get to spout his personal opinions? I'd fire the son of a bitch if he did that to me."

"It reflects the president's views, Frank," Stassi said.

"That comment of his was pointed at me," said Connors, lighting a cigar. He looked at Mackral. "Am I right?"

"I'd say so," Mackral replied. "The statement we issued yesterday was pretty blunt."

"I wish you'd run it past me before it went out," Stassi said. "The majority leaders are pressing for Jessup to take Latham's committee chair. Bad enough we're the minority without causing undue antagonism with the other side."

"We're still looking for her," Mackral said.

"Why?" Stassi asked, not attempting to disguise his annoyance. "Latham's dead. There's not going to be any confirmation hearings. This sexual harassment thing should have been dropped the minute he died."

"Dropped where?" Connors asked, his tone belligerent. "In my lap? We're taking enough heat about it without folding our tent and slinking away. You just heard Teller—the president—hell, they're out to paint us as irresponsible rumor mongers. They've turned it into their advantage—the heartless Republicans, spreading false accusations to derail a great nominee for State. I think it's more important than ever to find Marge Edwards and get her to confirm the story."

"*Get* her to?" Stassi said. "You have to *get* her to confirm it?"

"You know what I mean, Mario. Put her in front of a camera to tell everybody it happened. Latham played grab-ass with her. Then she says that now that the poor man is dead, there's no need for her to go any further with it. Let him rest in peace. But at least confirm it, for Christ's sake."

"And you have no idea where she is?"

"We're working on it."

Mackral walked Stassi to the hallway. Stassi stopped, turned, looked hard at Mackral, and said, "I think this stinks, Dennis. It has all the aroma of a phony setup. We're taking a lot of heat on the House side. Paul Latham was a leader. And he was one of us. If I were you, I'd push your boss to drop the whole thing before it really backfires."

Mackral shrugged, said, "You know Frank, Mario. He won't budge. Frankly, I agree with you. But there's not a lot I can do, although I'll keep trying."

"Yeah, do that," Stassi said. "You know what the first polls say? What my voters back home say? They don't give a damn about some missing, neurotic woman claiming Paul Latham kissed her or whatever. They *do* care that somebody murdered him."

"Of course," Mackral said.

"Level with me, Dennis. How did Marge Edwards get to you and Frank, tell you that Paul harassed her?"

"I'm not at liberty to say at the moment," Mackral responded. "But it was through a reliable source."

Stassi guffawed.

Mackral shot him a California smile. "Trust me, Mario. The source was good."

"I'm sure it was. And nobody cares, except Frank Connors. Look, Dennis, I butted heads with Paul every day. He ran the committee with an iron hand in a velvet glove. Do it his way or no way. Cross him, you kissed off your own constituent needs. But he was a hell of a man. A good and decent man. He would have made an excellent secretary of state. Sure, I would have gone along with the minority and tried to keep Scott from getting what he wanted. Not that I could have done much. Confirmations are a Senate prerogative. I would have made some speeches on the floor about his cozy relationship with Warren Brazier. Hell, as you know, the offensive against Paul's confirmation was all scripted by our leadership. But this sexual charge. It's scummy, Dennis. Ranks right up there with Dick Morris on the slime meter."

As he spoke, Stassi became red in the face. He started to say something else, abandoned it, and walked away.

Mackral started back to the office, changed his mind, left the building, and went to a phone booth two blocks away. Perrone took the call. "What's up?" he asked.

"We need to talk."

"Come on over."

"No. You know the rules. The Monocle. A half hour."

"You know, Mackral, you're taking up one hell of a lot of my time. Time's money, they say. All I've got to sell is time."

"Just be there, huh? There'll be enough money to pay for your goddamn time."

The Monocle, on D Street, N.E., between First and Second streets, just north of Capitol Hill, was within a few blocks of both the Capitol and the Supreme Court. Its location had made it a favorite hangout for years of staffers from both institutions, especially Senate aides. Slightly south of the Capitol was another venerable watering hole, Bullfeathers, which appealed more, for no apparent reason, to staffers from the House.

Mackral was there within minutes. Although he seldom frequented the Monocle, he was recognized as he entered by some people at the bar. After returning their greetings—slaps on the back, squeezes of the arm, and quick one-liners—he headed for a table at the rear of the room adjacent to the bar. He ordered a Diet Coke and waited, his eyes on the door.

He saw a man enter a few minutes later, obviously no staffer, but paid no further attention to him. Tony Buffolino took a seat at the ten-stool bar, sat back, and surveyed the room. "Nice place you got here," he said to the bartender, a chain-smoking older gentleman wearing a red-and-white-striped shirt, red tie, and suspenders.

The bartender introduced himself in a southern accent as Robert. He looked over half-glasses and asked Buffolino what he wanted to drink.

"A beer. Rolling Rock."

Tony sipped his beer and waited for Perrone to arrive. He'd followed him from Perrone's office building on

New Jersey Avenue to the Monocle's parking lot, parked his silver Ford Taurus at the opposite end (things had improved since his rusty red Cadillac days, including his level of taste), and used other vehicles for cover on his way to the bar's door. What was Perrone doing out there? he wondered. Had he changed his mind and taken off? Did he become aware he was being followed?

All around him at the bar, the conversation was politics. Nothing but politics. Political jokes. Political insight. Political BS, he thought. And enough cigars to call it a Te-Amo convention.

He was poised to go outside in search of Perrone when the bulky PI came through the door. Buffolino turned so that his face wasn't visible. He and Perrone didn't know each other well, but they had met on a few occasions. Perrone lumbered by him and joined a man at a nearby table. Buffolino shifted position so that he could keep an eye on them without revealing himself.

From Buffolino's perspective, the two men knew each other but weren't especially friendly. A visible tension manifested itself in rigid body language. If he hadn't been afraid of being recognized by Perrone, he might have considered taking a table closer to them. But that was out of the question. Besides, from the way they were speaking to each other, it seemed to Buffolino that they were trying to keep their words private. An intrusion into their space might cause them to leave.

So he continued to sit at the bar, nursing his beer and wishing he'd learned to read lips.

Perrone and Mackral conferred for twenty minutes. Buffolino was on his second beer when Mackral left the table and headed for the front door. A young man seated next to Buffolino grabbed Mackral's arm. "Hey, Dennis, how goes it?"

"Okay," Mackral replied, a little angrily, from Buffolino's perception. This was a guy who'd just had an unpleasant conversation and was anxious to get out of there.

The bar patron insisted upon telling Mackral a joke. He listened patiently, smiled—this guy's either an actor or a displaced California beach bum, Buffolino decided—said good-bye, and was out the door.

"Dennis," Buffolino said under his breath, noting the name on a cocktail napkin.

He returned his attention to the table, where Perrone was in the process of placing an order with a waiter. Buffolino wondered whether he should follow this Dennis, but ruled it out. Mac Smith had been specific: Follow Perrone.

Perrone had ordered a shrimp cocktail, steak, fries, and a side order of pasta.

" 'Nother beer?" Robert, the bartender, asked in a deep baritone.

"Yeah. And some snacks. Peanuts, maybe?"

It took Perrone an hour to finish his meal. A third beer for Buffolino. He noticed that Perrone hadn't paid when he left the table. Dennis must have picked up the tab.

Buffolino again turned so Perrone wouldn't get a clear look at his face. The minute Perrone was out the door, Buffolino dropped money on the bar and stood. "Thanks, Robert," he said.

The bartender nodded, drawled, "Y'all come back."

"You should be on the radio," Buffolino said, smiling and waving as he left.

He fell in behind Perrone, headed across the city in the

direction of the Theodore Roosevelt Bridge. Traffic was heavy, the going slow. When he was a cop, Buffolino took pride in his driving ability when following someone, knowing how far he could hang back to avoid being noticed without losing his target.

Perrone, driving a sand-colored, almost new Dodge sedan, took them over the bridge into Virginia. He continued through the small cities on that side of the Potomac until turning at Route 66 West, which he stayed with until joining the Dulles Toll Road, settling into a steady sixty miles per hour. Buffolino adjusted his cruise control to remain a comfortable distance behind.

Eventually, Perrone left the highway at Exit 9, which Buffolino noticed put them on Sully Road. Five traffic lights later, Perrone turned left onto Waxpool Road; they were in the town of Ashburn. Buffolino followed Perrone to a residential street called Rising Sun Terrace, which wound through a development of single-family homes and town houses, creating the sort of typical planned community popular in Virginia and the greater Washington area.

Perrone pulled into a driveway. Buffolino stopped a block away. Perrone got out of his car, went to the front door of a town house, and rang the bell. A woman answered. Perrone and the woman talked for a minute. It appeared to Buffolino they were arguing. Then, Perrone entered the town house, and the door closed.

Buffolino waited a few minutes before slowly driving past the house. He noted the number on the door and the cross streets before coming around the block and resuming his watchful position.

He was aware that another woman had been peering at him through her front window. He didn't need someone calling the police, or the enclave's private security force to report a stranger in a car, so he drove away, toward a sales office he'd noticed when entering the complex.

He parked, bounded up the steps, and entered the model home, where a middle-aged woman sat behind a desk piled high with brochures.

"May I help you?" she asked pleasantly.

"I hope so," he said, slipping into his best Detective Columbo hesitant imitation. "I've been thinking of buying something here in the development—I like it here. I work only a couple of miles away, but—"

"I'd be happy to show you some vacant models," the woman said, standing.

"Well, actually, I've already looked at one that appeals to me."

"You have? Who showed it to you?"

"The owner."

"Ah, a current resident."

"Yeah. Number eleven-eleven."

"Eleven-eleven? I didn't know Ms. Craig was thinking of selling. She's only been here a year."

"Something about a new job someplace. Out of the state. Ms. Craig . . ." He slapped the side of his head. "I never can remember her first name."

"Maureen."

"Of course. Maureen Craig. Sometimes I think I'm losing it, you know?"

"Yes, I do. My mother has Alzheimer's. It's such a terrible disease. Physically, she's fine. But mentally . . ." She squeezed her eyes shut and shuddered.

"Yeah, I know what you mean. Thanks a lot."

The woman opened her eyes and asked, "What did you

want? We don't get involved in private sales by current residents."

Buffolino shrugged. "I guess I just wanted to get a feel for the community. Overall, you know. It's nice here, huh?"

"Very nice. Peaceful. Good people. Very few children or animals."

Not like the Congress, Buffolino thought.

He thanked her again and left, hoping she wouldn't pick up the phone and call Maureen Craig, whoever she was. He found a different spot from where he could observe the car in the driveway of 1111, thankful Perrone hadn't left while he was conning the sales agent. Now that he was back in position, he wished Perrone would get going. He was hungry; a search of the glove compartment confirmed he'd finished the last of the candy bars he kept in it as emergency rations.

Forty-five minutes later, Perrone came through the front door, down the steps and got into his car. He carried a manila envelope. The woman hadn't come to the door with him, as far as Buffolino could see. Perrone retraced his route back to Washington, where he pulled into the underground parking garage of the apartment building in which he lived.

No sense hanging out here, Buffolino decided. He went to his office and called.

"Something to report?" Smith asked.

"Maybe. I just left Perrone at home. Been with him most of the day. He spent time in that bar on the Hill, the Monocle."

"Pleasant place. Did you meet Robert?"

"The bartender? Yeah."

232

"Fascinating man," Smith said. "He's been there over twenty years. Seen it all."

"I bet he has. I've seen half of it. So anyway, Mac, Perrone sits with a guy at a table. They're together maybe twenty minutes. Then this guy leaves, and Perrone stays almost an hour pigging out. Steak. Pasta. The works. This other guy evidently paid 'cause Perrone didn't."

"Good friend to have. Do you know who Perrone met with?"

"Just the name Dennis. Some guy called him that at the bar."

"Dennis?" Smith ran the name through his memory. He came up with only one, Dennis Lambert, a respected senior staffer on the Hill with whom Smith had been friends for a number of years. "What did he look like, Tony?"

"Like Troy Donahue."

"Who?"

"The actor. A California type. Blond hair all slicked back, big-time tan. A salon, I figure, considering the weather here."

Dennis Mackral. Senator Frank Connors's administrative assistant.

"Catch anything they said?" Smith asked.

"No. I followed Perrone after he finished his meal. Took me all the way out into Virginia. Ashburn. Know it?"

"I've heard of it. That's pretty far. What did he do there?"

"Visited somebody named Maureen Craig."

"Know anything about her?"

"No. Here's her address."

"You've been busy, Tony."

233

"I got to be, Mac. Like I told you, I'm shoehorning this assignment in for you."

"And I appreciate it. Can you spend another day on Perrone's back?"

"Sure."

"And I know you'll keep good track of your hours."

"Course I will. But you get the professional discount."

"Still an extra two percent if in cash?"

"Better. Three."

25

The minute Smith hung up, he called Jim Edwards in Indianapolis. No answer. Smith checked his watch. Marge's father was probably still at work.

Next, he called Ruth Latham.

"Everybody holding up all right?" Smith asked.

"Yes, although we'll feel a lot better when Paul's murderer has been brought in. Have you heard anything new on that front?"

"Afraid not."

"Marge Edwards?"

Smith sighed. "Still don't know where she is."

Should he tell her that Marge had tried to call him? He couldn't come up with a compelling reason to do it, so he let his statement stand.

"How are the kids?"

"Good. Martin has decided to stay around a bit longer.

That pleases me. Pris had to get back to her job in New York, which I understand."

"And that vivacious teenager of yours?"

Ruth laughed. "Molly is doing just great. I'm taking her back to the page dorm this afternoon. She agrees with me that the sooner we all get back to living normal lives, at least to the extent that's possible with Paul gone, the better off we'll be. Some will say it's irreverent. I don't."

"A grown-up philosophy."

"Mac, there's something I learned recently from Molly that I thought you might want to know."

"What's that?"

"Just before Paul was killed, Molly had lunch with Marge Edwards."

"I know," Mac said. "I spoke with Marge as she was leaving Paul's office for that lunch."

"Molly told me that when they parted on the street, Marge said she might be leaving the office."

"Really? She'd promised Paul she'd keep an eye on Molly. No hint of thinking of leaving. Did she say why?"

"Something about another job. Molly was upset when she heard it. Ever since the rumor surfaced about Marge's intention to accuse Paul, Molly's reaction has been disbelief. She really liked Marge. Never bought it that Marge would even consider such a thing. I suppose that's why Marge's offhand comment about possibly leaving didn't register with her until now."

"Interesting, Ruth."

"Is it?"

"Yes."

"Why?"

"Oh, nothing major. I've been doing some checking of my own into Marge's whereabouts."

"You have?"

"Yup. I want to see this vague smear on Paul's character stamped out. As quickly as possible."

"So do I. Thanks, Mac, for so many things."

"Please give the family my best. *Our* best."

"Get together soon?" she asked.

"Whenever you're up to it."

He called Virginia Information and asked for the number in Ashburn of Maureen Craig. It was unlisted.

Smith called Buffolino at his office. Alicia answered. After preliminary pleasantries—she was fine, Tony was driving her batty; they were thinking of going to Italy, or going bankrupt—she put him on the phone.

"Any chance of getting hold of this Maureen Craig's number?" Smith asked. "It's unlisted."

Buffolino gave forth with a satisfied laugh. "I'm way ahead of you, my lawyer friend." He reeled off the number, which Smith wrote down on a pad. "Anything else I can do for you?"

"You've done quite enough, my detective friend. Good hearing Alicia's voice again. She says you're driving her batty."

"Yeah, I know. But what can you expect?"

"She's a woman," Smith said, wincing as he did.

"You got it, man. *Ciao.*"

Annabel arrived home as Smith was about to try Jim Edwards again.

"What's new?" she asked after kicking off her shoes and settling on the small couch in the den.

He filled her in on what the day had offered so far.

"Tony's amazing," she said.

"He's good, that's for sure. Now I want to find out

whether Marge ever mentioned a Maureen Craig to her father."

He tried Edwards's number again.

"Just walked through the door," Edwards said, slightly out of breath. "Did you have a good trip home?"

"Fine, thank you. A question. Did Marge ever mention to you a woman by the name of Maureen Craig?"

"Maureen?"

Judging from his tone, he knew who she was.

"Why do you ask about her?"

"It seems that the private detective who visited you, James Perrone, knows Ms. Craig. I'm trying to establish a link between her and your daughter—if one exists."

Smith waited.

"Jim?"

"Yes, I'm here. Surprised, that's all."

"Why?"

"I haven't heard Maureen's name for a very long time. I think about her, though."

"Oh? What's her relationship with you?"

"Maureen is my stepdaughter from my wife's first marriage."

"I see," Mac said. "Were Marge and Maureen Craig close?"

"Closer than *I* was to Maureen. Had nothing but trouble with her. Headstrong and arrogant. No, I had little use for her, aside from respecting her as my wife's daughter. I tried to be a good stepfather, but stepparenting is tough and she didn't make it easy."

"When's the last time you spoke with her?"

"Oh, hard to say. Ten years? Twelve?"

"That's a long time," Smith said. "What about Marge? Has she stayed in touch with Maureen?"

"I believe so. Marge never talked much about it, but she did mention a few times—last time she was here, as a matter of fact—that she'd seen Maureen. Had dinner with her, something like that."

"Do you think there's any chance that Marge is staying with her half sister?"

"I wouldn't know."

"Think you could call Maureen and ask if she's seen Marge?"

"I'd rather not. Would you?"

"I'll consider it. Anything else you can tell me, Jim, about Maureen? Did she go to college? Does she work? Is she married?"

"She went to college. Somewhere in New York."

"But she ended up in the Washington area. A job? A boyfriend or husband?"

"I just don't know, Mac. Wish I could be more helpful."

"You've been very helpful, Jim. Can we keep this conversation between us, at least for the moment?"

"Sure."

"The press still camped at your door?"

"No. They've left. Bigger and better fish to fry."

"Not better. But I'm glad they're gone."

"I take it Marge hasn't tried to call you again."

"No, she hasn't."

"I want you to know, Mac, that I haven't mentioned to a soul that she did try to reach you."

"I appreciate that. Well, Jim, I'll let you pour yourself a drink and have some dinner. I'll keep in touch."

Annabel, who'd been listening, said after the conversation concluded, "What now?"

"I thought you'd help me decide that, Annie."

239

"The man this character Perrone met was Dennis Mackral?"

"According to Tony. No, strike that. I came to that conclusion based upon Tony's description of him. If it was Mackral, that raises the question of why he'd be meeting with a private detective, whose assignment seems to be to find Marge Edwards."

"Senator Connors has never kept it a secret that he was against Paul becoming secretary of state," said Annabel.

"He's never been subtle about it," Smith said. "Possible, I suppose—and troubling—that Connors's office—Mackral—might have wanted Marge Edwards to testify at his hearings that Paul had sexually harassed her."

"Yes. Troubling to even contemplate."

"But Paul's dead. Why bother now?"

"Maybe it's a case of not being able to stop the snowball once it heads downhill. Or not wanting to," said Annabel.

"Ummm. Or maybe that bullheaded Senator Connors wants to smear the administration, and Paul Latham, dead or alive."

"This rumor that Marge Edwards was going to charge Paul with sexual harassment was reported by a single reporter, this—what was his name?"

"Harris. Something Harris."

"Jules Harris. He breaks the story, basing it on the usual so-called reliable source. Everybody else picks up on it. Paul is murdered. Marge disappears. Now, Paul's enemy in the Senate, Connors—his top aide—is working with a private detective to try and find Marge. Why?"

"Your analysis was as good as any," Smith said. "Or mine."

"Who was Harris's source? Marge Edwards herself?"

"If so, why has she run? Guilt? Embarrassment?"

"Dennis Mackral, on Senator Frank Connors's behalf—he might have leaked it to Harris to derail the confirmation."

"What do you suggest I do next?" Smith asked.

"See if Marge Edwards is staying with Maureen Craig."

"My guess is she's not. Perrone was there. If she's with her half sister, he wouldn't have gone out to Indianapolis looking for her. By the way, Ruth says Marge told Molly just before Paul's murder that Marge told her that she was thinking of leaving Paul's office."

"She give a reason?"

"Another job. Very vague."

"It seems to me the next step is to find out more about Maureen Craig, and then approach her, see what she knows about Marge's whereabouts."

"Tony can help."

"Who's paying his bill?" Annabel asked.

"I am."

"Big spender."

"I'm getting the professional discount."

"Tony Buffolino. With an *O*. What a guy."

"In the meantime," Smith said, "I've got to get back to the Russian project. It's slipping away from me."

"The trip there is getting closer."

"I know. Bring something in for dinner?"

"I'll call. Chinese?"

"Sounds good."

Smith worked into the night, breaking only for the dinner delivered to the door. His wife secluded herself in the bedroom with a fat novel she'd started, but had put aside.

The phone rang at ten.

"Hello, Jessica. I was waiting for you to call."

"Why?"

"Because you said we'd talk again after you got back from Los Angeles."

"Right. Can we talk?"

"I'm listening."

"Not on the phone. Meet you for a drink?"

"Out of the question. Breakfast? You an early riser?"

"Not when I can help it. Sure, breakfast will be fine. Where?"

"Bread and Chocolate, on Twentieth? Seven-thirty?"

"Too busy."

"Too public, you mean?"

"Uh-huh. Washington Harbor? Bagels on me. Seven-thirty in front of Tony and Joe's?"

"Okay."

Annabel appeared in the doorway. "Who was that?"

"Jessica Belle. I'm having breakfast with her."

"Where?"

"Washington Harbor. Bagels. Her treat."

"On the promenade?"

"Yes. All very hush-hush. She's picked up the true CIA spirit."

"Any idea what she wants to talk to you about this time?"

"Not a clue. Let's catch the news."

Paul Latham's murder occupied a sizable portion of that evening's newscast—two minutes amid five-second sound bites. The FBI was in charge of the ongoing investigation; all statements would come from the Bureau. There were no leads.

The Marge Edwards story was still alive but received

brief mention—only that Latham's alleged accuser was still missing.

But then the news anchor wrapped up the story with "Mackensie Smith, formerly a prominent Washington criminal lawyer, more recently a law professor at GW, and counsel to Paul Latham, returned today from meeting with the missing Marge Edwards's father at his Indianapolis home. Smith had no comment on his trip."

"I'll be damned," Smith said, leaning forward in his chair and slapping his hands on his thighs. "No comment? Nobody asked me anything. What kind of journalism is that?"

The phone rang.

"Hello," Annabel said. Smith waved his hands. "No, he's not here. Who's calling? I don't know. Yes, I expect him back tonight. Yes, of course. I'll give him the message."

The caller was the producer of the newscast they'd just watched.

The phone rang again. Annabel took another message from a reporter. And another.

"Go to the tape," Smith said, pointing to the answering machine.

A flashing light probed the drapes over the front window. They went to it and looked outside. A TV news truck was parked in front of the house.

They looked quizzically at each other.

"What did Jack Paar say?" Smith asked. "They can't hurt you under the covers?"

"My sentiments exactly," Annabel said, turning off the television set. "The bedroom phone gets shut off, too."

"I like the way you think, Annie."

She grinned.

26

Molly Latham's return to the page dorm was harder than she'd anticipated.

Her mother drove her there as the other pages were gathering for dinner. The welcome was overwhelming, causing her to break into tears with each hug and expression of sympathy.

Her roommate, Melissa, gushed at having Molly back. "Mah, how I missed you, girl," she said. "Not the same without you. Come on, dinner's served. At least that's what they call it."

"I want to walk my mom to the car," Molly said. "Back in a minute."

"You okay, Rabbit?" Ruth Latham asked as they stood on the sidewalk in front of the O'Neill House Office Building.

"I think so. Gee, they're great, huh?"

"Yes, they are. They seem to really care. Well, you go on back in and I'll head home."

"Mom."

"What?"

"Are *you* okay?"

Ruth wiped a tear from her cheek. "I'm fine, sweetie. As long as I have you, Pris, and Martin, I'll always be fine. Go on, now. Get to dinner. Call me tonight before you go to bed."

After dinner in the page dining room, Molly and Melissa went upstairs.

"It must be tough losin' your daddy like that," Melissa said.

Molly had braced for such reminders of her loss, even when raised by the well-meaning. But her roommate's sincere and certainly accurate comment released her tears again.

Melissa came to where Molly sat, bent over, and hugged her. "Maybe Ah shouldn't have said that."

"No, no," Molly said, wiping her cheeks with the back of her hand. "It's okay. It'll be this way for a while, I know, and then it won't be. How've you been?"

"Wiped out. They run us ragged. That school's rougher than anything back home, I can say. But bein' on the floor is fun, in the cloakroom, deliverin' messages to the most powerful people in the country. I'm glad Ah'm here."

Molly smiled. She liked Melissa despite their overt differences in background and style, and felt warm and comfortable being back with her. Since dinner, she'd experienced a sense of positive anticipation at getting into the swing of things, actually working as a page in the House of Representatives, where her father had served with distinction for so many years.

"How's John?" Molly asked.

"Heavenly," Melissa said, "although boys from New York sure are different than boys from back home. They talk funny, they walk funny, and they do everything else funny, too."

Molly smiled and nodded. The more Melissa talked, the more Molly liked her.

Eventually, the girls stopped chatting and slipped into their evening activities. Melissa complained about the amount of homework facing her—"How much can one girl's brain absorb?"—but turned to it, leaving Molly to take a look at some of Melissa's textbooks, the ones she wasn't using at the moment. She glanced over often at her roommate, whose back was to her as she sat hunched over her desk, an occasional grunt of despair from her lips.

At ten, Molly announced she was going to call her mother from one of the pay phones. As she padded down the hallway in bare feet, a dorm counselor stopped her. "You had a call late this afternoon, Molly," she said.

"Who?"

"A woman. Sorry I didn't tell you right away." She handed Molly a pink telephone message slip. Notations on it indicated the call was for Molly Latham, had been received at 4:30 P.M., that the caller did not leave a number at which she could be reached, and that she would call again.

All of which was irrelevant to Molly compared with the name of the caller written on the paper.

Marge.

27

A chilly mist slapped Mac Smith's face as he left the house early the next morning to meet with Jessica Belle.

He'd slept fitfully, getting up twice to pace the house, thoughts spawned in the twilight of waking fleeing his mind no matter how he tried to capture them for further evaluation.

Annabel woke once, and came to where her husband sat behind the desk in the den, a pencil's eraser tapping out an impatient paradiddle on a yellow legal pad.

"What's keeping you awake? As if I had to ask."

"Maybe it's not what you think," he said.

"Oh?"

"I've been so totally focused on Marge Edwards and her alleged charge that Paul's murder itself has taken a backseat. But not tonight. The obvious fact that he was assassinated is keeping me up. If he'd been killed by a street criminal, a disgruntled constituent, an escapee from a mental institution, spurned lover, even a member of his own family, it would make some perverted sense. But an *assassination*? If you rule out personal or impersonal personal motives for shooting him, you're left with only politics as a possible reason. Cold-blooded. Calculating. On Capitol Hill, Annie!"

"It's a chilling realization, isn't it? Worthy of insomnia."

"I'm proving that tonight, Annabel. Ruling out other possible suspects, it leaves someone who viewed Paul Latham as a big enough political problem to warrant being killed."

"Maybe it wasn't politics. Maybe it was business."

"Paul wasn't a businessman. He had investments. We even shared investment ideas from time to time. But not business in the usual sense."

"What about Warren Brazier?" Annabel said.

Mac sat forward at the desk. "He's at the top of the list of people keeping me awake. But I can't come up with any rational reason he'd want Paul dead. Paul was his protégé in Congress, maybe too much so, if some people are to be believed. He worked closely with Brazier on opening up the Soviet Union, forging alliances there that undoubtedly played a role in bringing down Communism and opening up a free, more or less democratic market."

"Did he profit financially from his ties to Brazier?"

"I'm sure he didn't, unless you consider retaining his seat in Congress to be 'profiting.'"

"It is, you know."

"Sure. And I'm fully aware we can never know everything about a person, even those close to us. But no, Annabel, Paul Latham was not the sort of man—not the sort of elected official—who would sell out to a businessman like Brazier. To anyone."

"No argument from me. What about someone determined that Paul not become secretary of state?"

"A possibility. But a pretty dramatic way to block a nomination." Smith narrowed his eyes. "The same person, maybe, who floated the sexual harassment rumor?"

"Who was?"

"My money's on Senator Connors."

"Or his aide."

"One and the same, wouldn't you say?"

"Not necessarily. He wouldn't be the first congressional staffer to take matters into his own hands. Step over the line to help his boss. Protect the chief from direct knowledge of a nasty act."

Smith grunted. "I'm going back to bed."

"One more question. Do you think Paul's family is in any danger?"

"No. Why would they be? If we're right in assuming Paul was killed for political or business reasons, the family wouldn't be brought into it."

"Unless they know something they shouldn't."

"Something that Paul knew?"

"Yes."

Smith yawned, stretched, looked at the clock on the wall. "Five o'clock. Maybe I should just stay up. Bagels with Jessica is at seven-thirty."

"Come back to bed, Smith. I like to feel you next to me."

"An offer I can't refuse."

The TV remote truck was gone when Smith left the house and went to where he and Annabel garaged their car. Had the weather been better, he would have walked to Georgetown, not very far from Foggy Bottom. But the mist was a precursor to steady rain, the radio weatherman had promised as Smith shaved. No matter how often such meteorological promises were broken, Smith tended to heed them.

He retrieved the car, drove to the revitalized Georgetown waterfront, parked on Thirty-first Street, and checked his watch. He was fifteen minutes early. Carrying a small black pop-up umbrella, he got out of the car and entered the complex of expensive high-rise condominiums, beneath which a variety of shops and restaurants offered their wares and services to the thousands of visitors, locals and tourists, who enjoyed the views across the Potomac of the Kennedy Center to the south, and the Key Bridge to the north, leading into the busy Virginia city of Rosslyn.

The area was deserted at that hour, except for an occasional jogger detouring down the steps and running along the promenade until emerging again on K Street. The mist was thicker at Washington Harbor; fog, in fact, spreading an eerie charm along the waterfront.

Jessica Belle stood at the railing separating the promenade from the Potomac. Smith saw her through the haze and started in her direction. As he approached, a second person, who'd been behind her, stepped into Smith's line of vision. A few steps closer revealed that it was Jessica's boss at the CIA, Giles Broadhurst.

"Hello," Smith said.

"Hi, Mac," said Jessica.

"Hope we didn't get you up too early," Broadhurst added, smiling and shaking Smith's hand. He and Jessica wore what appeared to be matching tan trench coats, collars up.

"You didn't." Smith looked around. "Is this where you usually hold power breakfasts?"

Broadhurst laughed, a little too energetically for Smith's taste.

"It's a nice, quiet spot to meet," Jessica said.

"Quiet—and damp," said Smith. It had started to rain. Smith opened his umbrella.

"Let's go over there," Broadhurst suggested, indicating an overhang in front of the string of restaurants.

"Better?" Broadhurst asked.

"I suppose so. Look, Jessica," Smith said, "I'm here because you asked me to be, just as I met with you last time—under dryer circumstances. I asked you then why you told me—with your apparent encouragement, Giles— a number of things: that Paul Latham was unduly beholden to Warren Brazier, that Latham was pushing through a massive Russian trade bill to benefit Brazier, and that Brazier was funneling money to the Communists in Russia to help them return to power. Right?"

"That's right," Jessica said.

"Okay," Smith said. "I also think you said that what was important to you was the damage this could do to the president's reputation."

"Right again," said Jessica.

"Well, here I am, assuming there's something *else* you want to tell me."

Broadhurst ran his fingertips over a faint blond mustache on his upper lip. "First, Mac, let me say how appreciative we are of your cooperation and help."

"I have no idea what you're talking about," Smith said. "I feel like old Admiral Stockdale during those vice-presidential debates—who am I, and why am I here? Meeting in the fog and rain early in the morning. Secrets being whispered. That's your game, not mine."

251

Broadhurst's hand went up, meaning that he understood, but wanted to explain.

But Smith pressed on. "I met with Jessica the last time because she said it had something to do with my friend Paul Latham. And it did. You were the first one to tell me about the sexual harassment charge. Which leads me to a question, Jessica. Were you the reporter's source for that story?"

"No," she said.

"Where did you hear it?"

"Mac," Broadhurst said, "it really doesn't matter where we hear such things. The agency is like a sponge, soaking up thousands of pieces of information every day. Gathering it isn't difficult. Evaluating it is."

"I think we should get to the reason I asked you to meet me again," Jessica said to Smith. To Broadhurst: "Agree?"

A nod from Broadhurst. "Mac, to be right up front with you, we're here this morning to ask for your help."

"Jessica asked for my help the last time," Smith said. "She asked me to drip a few more drops of information about Paul onto your sponge. I don't have any to offer."

"This time, Mac, we have more information to offer *you*," said Broadhurst.

"To what end?" Smith asked.

"To see whether you'd be willing to do something with this new information on our behalf."

"That depends," Smith said.

"On?" Broadhurst asked.

"On whether there's a reason for me to do it. I'm a law professor. My involvement came about only because a close friend, Paul Latham, had been nominated for secretary of state and asked me to be his counsel during confirmation hearings. The only reason I ended up speaking with you was because Jessica was one of my students. When she asked that we get together, I immediately agreed. But when I left the bar, Jessica, and was driving home, I felt I was being used."

"Oh, Mac, that isn't true," she said, touching his arm. "I just thought—*we* thought because you were so close to Congressman Latham, you might pick up on something useful to help clear his name."

"Maybe even to get to the bottom of who killed him," Broadhurst added.

"Used?" she said. "The last thing I would ever do is try to use someone like you, Mac."

"I accept that. So why am I being asked to do something for the CIA?"

"For Paul Latham," Broadhurst said. "For the country."

Smith pinched off an expletive before it was audible.

Broadhurst continued: "It was never my intention when I took this job to get involved in anything but helping American industry flourish globally. I came over from ITC with that as my mission, one with which I fervently agree. But Congressman Latham's murder immediately put me in a position I couldn't foresee."

"How?" Smith asked.

"How? Warren Brazier."

"More about his allegedly pumping money into the Russian Communists?"

Broadhurst and Belle looked at each other. It was Jessica who spoke. "No," she said. "This time it's about murder. Paul Latham's murder."

"Why you?" Smith asked. "Why the CIA? Paul's murder is an FBI matter."

"It is," said Broadhurst. "But that's just a bureaucratic

necessity. One agency, one voice. It doesn't mean other agencies, including ours, aren't involved. Sharing information. Feeding what we all know into a central source."

Smith looked across the empty plaza. He couldn't help but smile as he said, "I don't mean to be critical, but the three of us standing here in the rain, the two of you in trench coats with collars turned up, me holding a black umbrella, is more conspicuous than if we were having coffee in the lobby of the Four Seasons."

Broadhurst laughed, said, "You're right, Mac. We're new to this."

"Forget I said it," Smith said, "and let's get on with this meeting. What's the new information you claim has bearing upon Paul's murder?"

"Intelligence from Russia," Broadhurst said. "Concerning Brazier."

"I'm listening," Smith said.

"First, Mac," Broadhurst said, "I need to know whether you're willing to do something with the information."

"What is the information? Once I know that, I'll decide whether to 'do something with it,' as you put it."

Another set of glances between Jessica and her boss.

Smith waited.

Broadhurst spoke. "What we ask of you, Mac, is to take the information to Brazier. Tell him you came into possession of it through your close personal and professional relationship with Latham."

"And why would I do that? More to the point, what is it intended to accomplish?"

"Prompt Brazier to take some action that will help prove what we are alleging."

"And what is that?"

"That he ordered Congressman Latham to be eliminated."

Warren Brazier had stayed in his Washington office overnight. He'd managed to delay questioning by the FBI on the Latham murder until this morning. The special agents were due at nine.

He'd slept only two hours, spending most of the night poring over financial reports received that day via a secure fax line from his Moscow office.

Now, at 8:45, dressed in a pearl-gray suit, white shirt, midnight-blue tie, and black wingtip shoes, all from favorite London custom clothing shops, he walked into the conference room, where three members of his Russian staff awaited his arrival.

"Good morning, sir," Anatoly Alekseyev said, standing quickly along with his two fellow executives.

"Good morning," Brazier said, sitting in his chair at the head of the table and opening a file folder he'd carried with him. "These figures. I'm not happy with them."

The three younger men said nothing.

"It is not my intention to see everything I've worked for in the Soviet Union come to this!" He slammed his fist on the table, remarkably without moving the rest of his body.

"Mr. Brazier," Alekseyev said, "you're quite right. But the numbers are misleading when you factor in the Sidanco negotiations."

If Brazier was surprised, dismayed, or angry that his young Russian executive was aware of what had been, to date, a secret undertaking, he did not demonstrate it. Instead, he ignored the comment and turned to another project that was, in his judgment, a new example of ineptitude on the part of his staff.

Alekseyev and his two colleagues sat glumly, taking their boss's verbal blows without expression. Brazier ended with "I'm replacing the three of you at this office. You'll return to Moscow. There will be lesser jobs for you there."

"Mr. Brazier," Alekseyev said, "if I might say something."

Brazier's personal assistant knocked.

"In!" Brazier said.

She opened the door and said the visitors for his nine o'clock appointment had arrived, and were waiting in his office.

"Thank you," Brazier said, closing the file folder and leaving the room without another word.

The Bureau had assigned two of its most senior special agents to interview Brazier that morning, Matthew Miller and Kenneth Wahlstrom, both from a division formed after the collapse of the Soviet Union to deal with the new challenges presented by that dissolution.

Brazier's greeting of them was abrupt. He sat behind his desk and said, "I trust this won't take long. I have meetings scheduled all day."

The agents had dealt with difficult individuals long enough not to be put off by such behavior. Miller said, his face void of expression, "We're here to ask questions of you in the matter of Congressman Paul Latham's murder. You're free to have counsel present, if you wish."

"I don't need any lawyers here," Brazier shot back. "Ask your questions. Let's not waste time with needless preliminaries."

Again, Miller ignored it. "Where were you, Mr. Brazier, the morning Congressman Latham was shot?"

Brazier met the special agent's steady, unblinking stare. "Here," he said. "In my office."

"At that early hour?"

"I don't keep bureaucrat's hours," Brazier said. "Next?"

"Was anyone here with you?"

"No."

"There's no one to verify your statement?"

"My word is good enough." Brazier made the checking of his Rolex a conspicuous action.

The two agents had decided before confronting Brazier to allow Miller to do the questioning, and for Wahlstrom to make notes, not only of Brazier's responses, but to characterize his demeanor.

The picture Wahlstrom presented externally was as noncommittal as his partner's. Inside, he seethed with dislike for this cocky, arrogant little man whose power stemmed only from money. Unlike Miller, who tended to shrug off such people, Wahlstrom actively disliked them to the extent that he felt the excessive, even obscene wealth of industrial leaders—garnered on the backs of working people, whose relatively meager salaries were increasingly considered impediments to their leaders' bottom line—was the greatest threat the nation faced. Of course, he seldom expressed those sentiments. The Bureau tended not to react favorably to special agents with mildly socialist-sounding views.

"When was the last time you saw Congressman Latham, Mr. Brazier?"

Brazier's shrug was barely discernible.

"I'll repeat the question," Miller said.

"I saw him that afternoon."

"*That* afternoon? You mean the previous afternoon."

"I mean the afternoon of the day before he died."

"What time was that?"

"Late. Four o'clock, maybe. Four-thirty."

"You don't keep records of your meetings, especially with members of Congress?"

Brazier narrowed his eyes.

"Sir?"

"We were friends. I don't keep records of getting together with friends."

"Where did you and Congressman Latham meet?"

"His office."

"A social visit?"

"It was to discuss a few things."

"And what were they?"

"I don't think that's of concern to anyone but Paul Latham and me."

"The FBI is officially charged with investigating the murder of Congressman Latham," said Miller. "What things did you and the congressman discuss?"

"I really don't recall."

Agent Wahlstrom thought back to his pre-Bureau days, when he was a police officer in Los Angeles. Anyone displaying Brazier's swagger during questioning might have been made more cooperative with a fist to the face. He wanted to go over the desk at the contemptuous industrialist, his impatience magnified by what he and Miller had been told prior to coming to interview Brazier. Warren Brazier had become a prime suspect in Congressman Latham's murder. If Brazier had been behind it, Wahlstrom looked forward to playing a part in nailing it down. But as frustrating as it was, he knew he'd have to wait for that satisfaction. He wrote on his pad that Brazier did not recall what had been discussed during his last meeting with Latham.

"No idea?" Miller followed up. "Not even one thing that came up during your meeting?"

"No. It was a social call. Idle conversation. Sports. Movies. Family."

"Family? Did you talk about your family? His?"

"Both."

"Did the congressman seem upset about anything that afternoon?"

"No. He was in good spirits."

"Did anything he said indicate that he intended to be in that pocket park at such an early hour the next morning?"

"No." Another overt look at his watch.

"Did he indicate to you during that social call, or during any previous meetings, that there might have been someone with enough of a grudge against him to contemplate killing him?"

"Of course not."

"Why do you say 'of course not'? A man in his position of leadership would naturally make enemies."

"I wasn't one of them."

Brazier's response piqued the interest of both agents, but they said nothing to indicate it.

"You and Congressman Latham worked together closely over the years, didn't you? On legislation regarding your business interests in Russia?"

"You don't 'work closely' with a congressman. You help a congressman think through a piece of legislation, provide him and his staff with needed, helpful facts, point out the potential impact of legislation."

Miller dismissed Brazier's capsule education on congressional lobbying, and asked his next question: "Did you have an argument with Congressman Latham during that last social visit?"

"No."

A buzzer sounded. Brazier pushed a button on a compact intercom unit on his desk. His assistant's voice said, "You're running late for your next meeting, sir."

"Thank you," Brazier said. He removed his finger from the button and said to the special agents, "You'll have to wrap this up. As you can see, I have nothing to offer, except to again extend my condolences to Congressman Latham's fine and grieving family."

He stood. The interview was over, as far as he was concerned.

Neither agent left his seat. Wahlstrom continued writing as Miller asked, "Have you been in touch with the congressman's family?"

"Of course," Brazier said.

The agents knew he hadn't. Ruth Latham had informed other agents who'd interviewed her late the previous afternoon that she was disappointed at Brazier's lack of communication with her.

Miller pressed on. "Where, when, and how did you learn of Congressman Latham's death?"

"Sorry, but I must leave . . . gentlemen."

Special Agent Wahlstrom broke his silence. "How long will you be in your next meeting?" he asked.

"I don't know."

"We'll wait," Wahlstrom said.

"If you wish," Brazier said, going to the door and gesturing for them to follow. "You can wait in the reception area. You might be there awhile. A few days, perhaps."

The agents stepped into the hallway. Brazier said,

"Good day." With that, he set off at a quick pace, turned a corner, and was gone.

Wahlstrom swore under his breath.

Miller smiled, placed his hand on his colleague's shoulder, and said, "Just goes to show money doesn't buy class. Or honesty. Let's get out of here."

At two that afternoon, Dr. Giles Broadhurst, head of the CIA's new division to foster American business competitiveness abroad, attended a meeting at FBI headquarters, in the J. Edgar Hoover Building on Pennsylvania Avenue between Ninth and Tenth streets, N.W. Its ironic location, two blocks south of the Martin Luther King Memorial Library, wasn't lost on Broadhurst. Hoover had tried to bring King down, yet the monuments to both shared that small parcel of land. If it was any consolation to Dr. King, his building was clearly superior in architecture—to say nothing of public sentiment—to the controversial former FBI chief's memorial. *It* was sometimes termed Washington's major contribution to the new design "Brutalism."

The meeting took place in a windowless office. With Broadhurst in the room was the Bureau's special agent in charge of the Latham case, Gerry Lakely.

"How did it go?" Lakely asked.

"Good," Broadhurst replied.

"He'll do it?"

"I think so. No commitment from him this morning, but my guess is he will. He's a careful, prudent man. Lawyer, you know. Professor."

"What questions did he ask?"

"Oh, why we were asking him. Why you and your people didn't simply confront Brazier with the information yourselves."

"And you said?"

"I said what we'd agreed I'd say. That his close relationship with Latham, professional and personal, made it more likely Brazier would buy what he was saying—and offering."

"Good."

"A question."

"Yes?"

"Why *are* you taking this approach, using him?"

Lakely, whose reputation within the Bureau was that of a cold, methodical agent with the ability to create elaborate scenarios in which to trap suspects, rubbed his hands together as though they were cold. He thought for a moment before replying, "If we actually had the evidence against Brazier, we'd take it to him. But since we don't physically have possession of it—although I'm sure we will in due time—we don't want this agency, or yours for that matter, to be out there swinging in the breeze. Better someone without official connection to either body. Don't you agree?"

"Of course. No progress on locating Ms. Edwards?"

"None. But there will be. Any problem with your assistant, Ms. Belle?"

"No. Should there be?"

"Only because she brought Smith into the picture. Her teacher, pedagogue, and preceptor, man to look up to. No problem that might cause her to balk? Maybe tip him off to what we're doing?"

"No. No problem."

"Good. Then I think this should move along smoothly. Thanks, Giles."

"Happy to help, although I'll be glad to get back to what I was hired for—boost American business abroad."

"I think you're doing precisely that, Giles. Let's face it. Warren Brazier, and the way he does business overseas, doesn't do anyone any good. Let me know when Smith gets back to you."

At three that afternoon, Warren Brazier's secretary took a phone call.

"My name is Mackensie Smith. I was counsel to former congressman Paul Latham."

"Yes, Mr. Smith. How may I help you?"

"I would like to make an appointment to see Mr. Brazier at his earliest convenience."

"I see. May I ask what it's in reference to?"

"Well, that's hard to explain on the phone. You might simply tell Mr. Brazier that I've come into possession of certain information regarding Congressman Latham that I know will be of great interest to him."

Smith waited while she wrote down every word.

"How can we get back to you, Mr. Smith?"

Mac gave her his number.

"I'm sure Mr. Brazier will return your call shortly. Thank you, Mr. Smith."

"I'm sure he will. Thank *you*."

28

Anatoly Alekseyev's attempts to arrange a meeting with Warren Brazier had been a resounding failure. Once he accepted the reality that Brazier would not allow him to plead personally to stay in Washington, he sent him a long, detailed memo pointing to contributions he'd made to the company's success, his loyalty to the firm's goals and its leader, and reasons why a sudden transfer back to Russia would pose a personal hardship for him. The latter reason for remaining in Washington was weak, he knew. Brazier never made personnel decisions based upon individual needs, which Alekseyev understood from a management perspective. Still, he felt he had to pull out all the stops.

There hadn't been any response from Brazier to the memorandum, nor did the young executive hold out much hope there would be. He and his two colleagues had been instructed by Human Resources to be prepared to depart within four days. The thought of leaving a city and lifestyle he'd grown to love was anathema.

This day, after starting the process of cleaning out his desk, and having made a few calls to friends in search of another job that would keep him in Washington, he left the office at four. He didn't want to stop in at any of his regular Georgetown haunts because he wasn't in the mood for idle chat. Instead, he chose the Hotel Washington, where he sat alone in the Sky Terrace Lounge, nursing vodkas on the rocks and contemplating his situation. He'd been to the hotel's rooftop before, once with friends to observe the city's Fourth of July celebrations; its panoramic views of Washington were unrivaled.

Feeling the effects of the vodka, but not drunk, Alekseyev retrieved his car from a parking garage and headed for his apartment complex, stopping on the way at Jaimalito's to take out two orders of enchiladas.

By the time he walked into his apartment, a pervasive sense of desperation had set in, fueled, to some extent, by the alcohol. He sensed he had to do something, and do it fast.

But what *could* he do?

Finding a new job would take weeks, perhaps months. He hadn't saved any money to sustain him through a prolonged search. Too, there was the fear that Brazier would put out unfavorable references about him. Or worse. The man was capable of that, Alekseyev knew. A brilliant businessman—and a ruthless one, with little or no regard for people.

"Hello," he called out, shutting the door behind him and putting the shopping bag of food on a nearby table. "Marge?"

Marge Edwards, dressed in a bathrobe and slippers,

emerged from the bedroom. Her disheveled hair and puffy eyes said she'd been sleeping.

"Hi," she said in a husky voice.

"Hi," he said. "Any calls?"

"No. I don't think so. I was sleeping."

Alekseyev checked the answering machine. No tiny red blinking light.

He tossed his jacket on a chair and brought the take-out dinners into the kitchen. She followed. "Anything new with Brazier?"

"No." He removed the aluminum-foil dishes from the brown shopping bag and pulled two plates from a cupboard. "Wine?" he asked.

"I'll get it. White?"

"Yes."

They sat at the kitchen table. Alekseyev's disposition was not gregarious. He ate in silence, chewing aimlessly, drinking his Pouilly-Fuissé without tasting it.

Marge Edwards respected his mood, and silence. She knew what a blow Warren Brazier had dealt her lover. And she was not oblivious to what Brazier's decision might mean to her, at least in the short haul.

She refilled their glasses.

"I don't know what to do," Alekseyev said.

"Nothing from him?"

"No. Just Human Resources. Pack up and be gone in four days."

She covered his hand on the table with hers. "You don't have to go back to Moscow," she said. "Quit. Tell Warren Brazier to stuff it."

"And live on what? If he fired me, I could collect from the unemployment insurance. If I resign, I have nothing. And there is my status in this country."

"You have your dignity, Anatoly. You'll be able to find another job and stay here, if you work at it."

His face was drawn, sad, as he said, "The man is insane, Marge. To blame me and the others for his bad deals in Russia . . . it is wrong. Unfair. I have always done good work. I have been so damn loyal, even though I know things about him and his company that would put him in jail."

Up until being told he was being sent back to Russia— *exiled* there—Alekseyev had told Marge little about the inner workings of Brazier Industries. Nor had she confided in him what she knew about her boss, Congressman Paul Latham, and his dealings with Warren Brazier. They tended to leave work at their offices each evening, content to revel in the newfound pleasures each gave the other. What had begun as a one-night sexual fling had quickly developed into a deeper, more caring union.

They kept their relationship low-key. Their being romantically involved—sharing pillow talk—would be viewed negatively by their employers. Once, and only once had Marge casually mentioned to Latham that she'd been seeing someone who worked for Brazier Industries: "A nice guy, pleasant to have dinner with once in a while. A little strange at times. Nothing serious." Latham didn't press for further details.

But by then it had become serious. Marge Edwards, daughter of Jim and Sue Edwards of Indiana, and Anatoly Alekseyev, born, raised, and educated in the Soviet Union, now enjoying the rewards of working for a multinational company, had found each other, and had even begun to talk of spending their lives together.

She cleaned up the kitchen while Anatoly changed into his pajamas and slippers. They sat side by side on the couch and watched a television sitcom, the only laughter in the room the show's laugh track.

When the program was almost over, Alekseyev clicked off the set with the remote control, turned, and looked into her eyes. "Marge," he said, "we have to take steps now. Even if I was not being sent home, you could not stay hidden here forever. What sort of life is this? You stay in these four walls day and night, afraid to go out, to walk in the sun, drink a cup of coffee in a café."

"Are you trying to get rid of me?" she asked, lightening her tone to indicate she was being playful.

He took her seriously. "You know that is not true."

"Anatoly, you know why I'm here. I'm afraid to face the world because of what's happened. I want to leave. I want to walk in the sun and sip that coffee in a café. But you know what certain people will want of me."

He slapped his hands to the sides of his head and stood. "Marge, this silly thing about sexual harassment means nothing. Stand tall, tell them it is not true. You make such a statement and walk away. It is over. What are you so afraid of? Of telling the truth?"

"It's not that simple," she said, an edge to her voice.

"Why? Is there someone who can say that it happened? Is there someone who can prove it?"

"No. I mean, there is something that can be twisted to make it look as though it's true."

She'd never before mentioned such a "thing" in their conversations. He frowned while waiting for her to continue. When she didn't, he asked, "What are you talking about?"

She swallowed hard. "A diary," she said.

"A diary? Whose diary?"

"Mine."

The word stung him. He went to the kitchen and poured himself a glass of vodka, then returned to where Marge continued to sit, her lips pressed together, eyes focused on the rug's geometric pattern.

"You kept a diary about how Latham made sexual advances to you?"

"Yes. No, it was not that. It was not a diary of facts."

"Then what was it?" he asked angrily.

"It was . . ." She wept softly. "It was my fantasy."

Alekseyev glared at her, his focused dark eyes mirroring what he was feeling. "Fantasy?" he repeated. "What fantasy could you have?"

She turned from his hard stare, pressed her knuckles to her mouth. "Anatoly," she said quietly, "I was in love with Paul Latham."

He muttered in Russian.

She faced him. "I was in love with him from the first day I went to work in his office. This man represented everything I wanted from life. I met his wife and children, and I won't deny the envy I felt for them. I saw how he treated them, with love and respect. Not like so many men I've been involved with. Paul was gentle and kind, like a father to me."

"And you were in love with your father?" A Russian curse came from him.

"No, Anatoly. I wasn't in love with Paul Latham because he was like a father to me. I was in love with him as a man. God, how I wanted to change places with his wife, be there at home for him after a difficult day in Congress, counsel and soothe him, proud to be on his arm at parties and political functions. Love him. Is that so difficult to understand?"

"And you wrote down these feelings? These fantasies?"

"Yes. Almost every night. Just a word sometimes. Other nights, many pages."

Alekseyev poured another drink.

"Would you get me one, too?" she said.

He did, reluctantly, spilling some as he handed it to her because his hand shook.

"Where is this diary?" he asked.

"Someplace safe."

"Where?"

"I can't tell you."

"Why? I thought we cared for each other."

She forced a smile onto her quivering lips. "I thought we loved each other."

"How can you love me, Marge. You love him. A dead man."

"God!" She stood, hands held up in frustration as she crossed the room. "Can't you understand what I mean when I say I *loved* Paul Latham? Is there something in the Russian mentality that makes it impossible to accept a love based upon fantasy and wishing? Yearning for something better?" She spun around to face him. "I fell in love with my science teacher in junior high school, Anatoly. I had a crush on my college psych professor. Haven't you ever fantasized about a woman you couldn't have?"

"*Nyet!*"

His use of Russian startled her. They'd spoken only English to each other since meeting.

"Then you aren't human," she said.

That charge further angered him.

She came to where he stood and placed her hands on his arms, spoke softly to him: "Please try to understand, Anatoly."

The deep breaths he'd drawn had been calming. He stepped back and said, "I am trying to understand, Marge. But how can you expect me to—what?—to stand by you if you tell me only some of the story? This diary of your false love for him."

"Not false, Anatoly."

"False. Fantasy. Whatever. You share just so much of it with me, yet do not trust me to know where the diary is. To see it so that I can help you."

Her pause seemed an eternity.

"I just want to help," he repeated.

"Let's sit down." She went to the couch. He joined her.

"One of my diaries ended up with my half sister," she said.

"Half sister?"

"My mother's daughter. From her first marriage."

"How did she get the diary?"

"Does it matter?"

"I think it matters. Did you give it to her, Marge?"

"No. Of course not. She and I were not friendly. We didn't speak for years. Then, one day, she called me. She'd moved to this area, and thought it was time for us to get together. We shared the same mother, she said, and should try to honor our blood tie.

"I agreed, and we started seeing each other, a few lunches, dinner, then weekends together, usually at her house in Ashburn. That's in Virginia."

"And you gave her this diary?"

She shook her head. "No. But I showed it to her one weekend. Silly, I know, but we'd become very close in a short period of time. I told her about it because . . . girl kind of talk. Do you understand?"

"Girl talk?"

"Something girls do when they're together." She smiled. "I told her about my fantasy of being married to Paul. She . . . Well, we had a good laugh over it."

"And then what happened?"

"I left the diary at her house by mistake. Completely forgot about it for a few days. We were so busy at the office, major legislation being prepared, everyone wanting some of Paul's time." A small laugh. "No time for fantasizing."

"Call her and tell her to give it back."

"I did."

"And?"

"She said she didn't have it."

"How could she say that?"

"She said it disappeared."

"Impossible."

"I asked if I could come help her look. She said she was too busy for that and hung up. Each time I call, she refuses to talk to me."

"I could go there and demand she give it to me."

"Anatoly, I'm sure she means what she says. She doesn't have it. Someone else has it, the same someone who's using it to back up the claim that I was sexually harassed by Paul Latham."

"Who?"

"I don't know. Someone she gave it to. Someone she sold it to. What does it matter?"

He poured another drink in the kitchen, saying when he returned, "If the diary is nothing more than what you say is fantasy, then it does not prove that Congressman Latham made advances to you."

"Of course," she said. "But how do you think I'll look, writing a schoolgirl diary about my crush on my boss, one of the leading members of Congress? I was explicit at times about my sexual fantasies. I'll be disgraced."

"And if the diary is released, even without you? You'll be disgraced also. Your name."

She pulled her knees up to her chin and wrapped her arms about them. He looked at her. "So, Marge, what will you do?"

"I don't know." Then, almost inaudibly, "There's more."

"What did you say?"

"I said there's more."

"Tell me."

She twisted and looked into his earnest olive face and soft brown eyes. "There is another diary, Anatoly. A second diary. A report, actually. A very important one."

29

"Mr. Brazier will see you now, Mr. Smith."

He followed the secretary down a hallway to Brazier's private office. Although the morning was cool—the city's unrelenting summer heat was fast becoming an unpleasant memory—the air-conditioning blasted frigid air into the office. Mac Smith decided as he stepped through the door that Warren Brazier either had an out-of-whack internal body thermostat, or cranked up the AC to freeze unwelcome visitors.

"Mr. Smith, how nice to see you." Brazier, in shirt-sleeves and tie, came from behind his desk, smiling broadly, hand extended. Smith shook it. "Sit down, sit down. Coffee? Tea?"

"Nothing, thank you. I've had my caffeine ration for the morning." More accurately, he didn't trust anyone else's hand at coffee.

When both were seated, Brazier said, "I'm intrigued at

your reason for being here, Mr. Smith. Let me refer to my notes of our brief phone conversation. You said—and I think I took it down verbatim—'I have information to share with you that I think you'll be vitally interested in.' " He looked up, eyebrows arched. "Accurate?"

"Yes."

"You also said, and I quote, 'I think you should hear what I have to say before the information goes to other people.' Right again?"

"Right again," Smith said, smiling.

Brazier pushed aside the paper, extended his hands palms up, and said, "I'm listening with great interest."

Smith had spent two hours that morning going over in his mind the "script" suggested to him by Giles Broadhurst and Jessica Belle. After they'd given him a thumbnail sketch of what they hoped to accomplish, and he'd agreed to listen, they left the soggy Washington Harbor complex for the warmth and dryness of a nearby luncheonette. Over cups of remarkably bad coffee, Broadhurst went into more detail on the mission they hoped Smith would undertake for them.

Instead of going home after the meeting, Smith stopped by Annabel's gallery.

"How did your clandestine meeting go?" she asked.

Smith grinned. "I feel like a character in an Eric Ambler novel. Almost comical, if the ramifications weren't so dire."

"What did Jessica want?"

"It wasn't just her. Her boss, Giles Broadhurst, was there, too."

"What does that mean?"

"It means Jessica just acted as the go-between," Smith

275

replied. "Broadhurst wants me to take on an assignment for him."

"For the CIA."

"For the CIA. And the FBI."

"The heavy-hitting alphabet soups. What do they want you to do, Mac?"

"It could help get to the bottom of Paul's murder, Annabel."

"Oh? How?"

"If what I do is successful, it might flush out Paul's killer."

"Why the CIA? It's an FBI case."

"Because the information they're acting upon came through Broadhurst and his people. They're cooperating. Rare, indeed."

"Mac."

"What?"

"You haven't told me what it is they want you to do."

"Oh. Right. It's not terribly difficult. Not a big deal."

"Why do I have the feeling you don't want to tell me?"

"I can't imagine . . . why you'd feel that way. Interesting, how Broadhurst's division of the CIA came up with what they have."

"Mac!"

"They want me to . . ."

It took him ten minutes to explain the scheme set forth by Broadhurst and Belle. When he was finished, Annabel's furrowed brow and tight lips spoke volumes about what she thought.

"That's it," he said. "That's what they want me to do."

"And you agreed to do it."

"Yes."

"I am not happy, Mac."

"Funny how I sensed that right away."

"Do you realize what you're getting into?"

"I think so. I deliver this message to Brazier, and walk away. If he reacts the way Broadhurst hopes he will, he might provide the proof they need that he was behind Paul's murder. If he doesn't, I did my part and can forget about it."

"Mac."

"I wish you wouldn't say my name with that tone, Annie. It sets my teeth on edge."

"I'd like to set something else on edge."

"Like what?"

"Your head."

"Are we about to have an argument?"

"No, Mac. We are not about to have an argument. We are about to have a *war*!"

"Why?"

"Because what you've agreed to do is dangerous. What if Brazier *was* behind Paul's murder? You confront him, claiming you were given information by Paul that points to Brazier as a crook, a traitor to his own country, and a menace to society. What do you think he does then?"

"I have no idea what he'll do."

"He'll have you killed, too."

"Oh, Annie, that's stretching things."

"No, it's not. Have you stopped to think that this scheme—I love the word—this *farchadat* scheme—this crazy idea has been cooked up by the Central Intelligence Agency? They go around trying to kill Castro by poisoning his cigars. The northern Iraq fiasco. Running drugs. Crazy mind-control experiments. They tell you there's information enough to implicate Brazier in a number of criminal acts, but they also tell you they don't have 'physical possession' of it." Her tone was derisive.

"Yet."

"Yet. Maybe they don't have a thing."

"They say someone close to Paul and Brazier documented all of Brazier's illegal acts."

"Sell *that* to a jury."

"There's more. The CIA has been delving into Brazier's Russian operations for years, way back before the breakup of the Soviet Union. According to Broadhurst, they've amassed a huge file on his wrongdoings."

"Good for them. Mac, don't do it. Call Jessica and say you've thought it over and have decided not to become involved."

"Tell her my wife doesn't approve?"

"What's wrong with that?"

"Nothing. Look, ever since Paul was killed, my life has been on hold and will stay that way until his murder is solved. If I can do something to speed up that process, I want to do it. Make sense?"

"Sure it does. But to put yourself out front like this, be the messenger for the CIA? That's asking too much of anyone."

"I want to play a role in finding Paul's killer, Annie."

Her face and voice softened. "I know how important that is to you, Mac. And I'm also aware that I have a role to play, too, to support you in it. Just as you supported me when I went undercover to recover that Caravaggio masterpiece. You weren't happy when I did that, but you understood, and stood by me."

"Yes, I did. And I'd do it again."

"I love you, Mackensie Smith, more than anything in

this world. I don't want to see a single hair on your head injured. You—"

"I don't have as many hairs as I used to have to worry about. Was that what you were about to say?"

Her laugh was cathartic.

They talked for another half hour. He left the gallery, secure in her support for what he was about to do, and more madly in love with her than ever.

Now, the following morning, he was about to put into play what he'd been asked to do by Broadhurst and Belle.

"Mr. Brazier," Smith said, "you're aware, I'm sure, that I was very close to Paul Latham, personally and professionally."

"Yes, I am, Mr. Smith."

"Our relationship went back many years."

"How many years?"

He's taking the offensive, Smith thought. Brazier's arrogance wasn't surprising, or off-putting. Smith had dealt with enough rich, powerful, contumelious men to understand it was their style to attempt to turn things around, to bully others into submission.

"Paul shared a great deal with me, Mr. Brazier," Smith said, ignoring his question.

Brazier held up his left arm and studied his Rolex for longer than it took to tell the time.

"And he was open with me regarding some of his dealings with you."

"Cold, Mr. Smith?"

It took Smith a second to realize Brazier was referring to the air-conditioning. "Not at all," he said. "I'm quite comfortable in here with you."

Brazier's expression was blank. He sat back and formed a tent with his hands beneath his chin.

"You go back a long way with Paul Latham, too. Lots of legislation that benefited you, lots of deals in the Soviet Union and Russia."

"Are you looking to be my biographer, Mr. Smith?"

"You've been known to hire some people whose résumés aren't what might be called mainstream."

No reaction.

"Security people, they're called."

A stare.

"And then there's your involvement in Russian politics."

"I don't get involved in politics," Brazier said. "In Russia or anywhere else."

"As I understand it, Mr. Brazier, things were better for you when the Communists were in power."

"Things are good for me now."

"That's not what I hear."

Brazier abruptly stood, went to a window behind the desk, and sat on its deep sill. He folded his arms across his chest, lowered his head, and looked at Smith from that perspective.

Smith met his gaze and said nothing.

"Paul often spoke of you, Mr. Smith, and always with the highest praise."

"The feeling was entirely mutual."

"You were a big-time attorney in this town, Mr. Smith. Darrow, Nizer, and Bennett rolled into one."

"You put me in good company."

"Obviously, you didn't achieve your success by being imprecise."

"A lack of precision was useful at times."

"But this isn't one of them."

"You'd like me to be precise about what Paul told me and gave to me about you."

"I like people who pick up on cues. I don't mean to be rude, but I do have other commitments."

"Of course."

It took no more than ten minutes for Smith to deliver to Brazier the information provided by Broadhurst and Belle. Brazier didn't interrupt, his face painted with indifference. When Smith concluded his remarks, Brazier said, "How much do they pay you to teach law, Mr. Smith?"

"GW is generous with me, Mr. Brazier."

"Not as much as when you were burning up the courtroom."

"Too much of that was blood money," Smith said. "I'm content to be out of that fire."

"I've always paid men of your caliber generously," Brazier said. "You come with pristine references."

"From a dead friend. I'm not here looking for a job, Mr. Brazier."

"Well, perhaps we can meet again."

"Whenever you wish. You'll think about what I've said this morning?"

Brazier grinned. "Oh, yes, Mr. Smith. I'll give it considerable thought. Thank you for stopping by. My secretary will show you out."

As Smith passed through the reception area on his way to the elevator—he was tempted to blow on his hands—he noticed a handsome young man sitting in a chair. He looked vaguely familiar to Mac, but he didn't know why.

Smith got in his car and breathed a sigh of relief, and satisfaction. He'd played many roles in the courtroom, but none like this. He was glad he'd done it, and at once was glad it was over.

Solving the assassination of Paul Latham was not his responsibility, he knew. But by having contributed something to the process, perhaps a closure of sorts had been accomplished. He now felt free to resume his life, especially the challenge of completing his analysis of differences between the American justice system and its counterpart in Russia, and coming up with ideas in advance of his trip to Russia as to how the Russian system could be improved.

This sudden, newfound sense of liberty consumed him as he drove to Foggy Bottom, so much so that he never noticed the two men in the car that followed him home.

The chair in which Smith had sat in Warren Brazier's office was now occupied by Marge Edwards's lover, Anatoly Alekseyev. Brazier granted him a half hour. When it was over, Alekseyev, stifling a smile, shook his boss's hand and quickly departed the building. Once outside, he allowed the smile to erupt, and he stabbed a fist into the air, the way athletes do when winning.

His exuberance was short-lived, however, lasting only long enough for him to return to his apartment.

"Hello?" he called once inside. "Marge?"

There was no response, but a note was on the dining room table:

Dear Anatoly:

Getting everything off my chest to you was cleansing, therapeutic. Now that you know what really caused me to run and to hide—and I will never be able to thank you enough for being my protector during this awful period—I've developed the backbone to do something about it, to take action. I'm going to meet with Bob Mondrian and hash everything out. Then, I'll see to it that the report on Brazier Industries is placed in the right hands. I don't want to involve you any further because you have your own problems with Brazier. Maybe if I finally do the right thing, I'll be better able to help you stay here in Washington. I want that because I don't want to lose you. I will call and keep in touch. I love you (one day I'll learn to say it in Russian). Marge.

Brazier summoned his chief of Russian personnel, Aleksandr Patiashvili, to his office. A minute later, Patiashvili returned to his own office, where he placed a call to Brighton Beach, Brooklyn. Pavel Bakst answered. They spoke in Russian.

"Hello, Alek," Bakst said.

"Hello, Pavel. All is well?"

"Very well," the Russian mob boss replied. "You?"

"Problems."

"Oh?"

"The young man we sent, Fodorov. He is with you?"

"No, but close by. A strange one, Alek. A real *zhopachnik*, huh?"

Patiashvili wasn't interested in Yvgeny Fodorov's sexual orientation. "He wants him here in Washington this afternoon."

They both understood who "he" was. Brazier. The boss of bosses.

"All right. I'll put him on a plane myself. If I can wake him. He's a lazy *zhopachnik*. Better to be with you than me. *Ciao*, Alek."

30

Washington-area McDonald's were busy that day.

Dennis Mackral sat in a booth at the Adams-Morgan fast-food outlet with James Perrone. The private investigator ate a Big Mac as if it were an hors d'oeuvre and sipped a giant soda. Mackral had nothing in front of him; he was too angry to ingest anything but air.

"I'm telling you straight out, Perrone, we won't pay a penny more for this joke you call a diary. In fact, we ought to get back what we've already given you."

"Don't push me," Perrone responded, chewing.

"Don't push you? The senator and I read the diary from cover to cover. It's nothing you represented it to be. Nothing! Just the schoolgirl fantasies of Marge Edwards. It doesn't prove a damn thing."

"That's not my problem."

"The hell it isn't. You told me—and I stuck my neck out with the senator—you told me that you knew this woman who had a diary belonging to a friend who worked for Latham, and that the same diary documented his sexual overtures to her over a period of years."

"That's what *she* told *me*," Perrone said, wiping ketchup from his mouth with a small white paper napkin.

"I thought you looked at the diary."

"I did. She showed it to me. I didn't read the whole thing, but it had a lot of sexual stuff in it about Latham."

"Her sexual *fantasies*. That's all they were. Christ, the diary paints Latham as a saint."

Perrone shrugged. "What you do with it is your business. All I promised was to deliver it to you. I did. And you owe me money."

"No, we don't." Mackral held up his right index finger to reinforce his statement.

Perrone grabbed the finger and pressed it back, hard. "You owe me money," the investigator repeated. He released the finger. "You think this was easy, cozying up to this Craig broad?"

"You *bought* the diary from her."

"Yeah, but how do you think I even knew the damn thing existed? I had to get close."

"How much of the money have you paid her?"

"All of it."

"All of it?"

"How come you keep repeating what I say?"

"I thought you were paying her in installments."

"That's how I started. But when you put the screws on me to see the diary, I pressed her. She wouldn't budge. She's as tight when it comes to a buck as she is ugly. She wanted the rest of the ten, so I gave it to her."

"Ten thousand dollars. For nothing. My job's on the line."

"Why? You said the money came from a private fund."

Mackral leaned across the table. "A private fund that can't afford losing ten thousand dollars. We have to account for that money to . . . them."

"Twenty thousand, Dennis."

"No. We've given you, what? Six?"

"Which means you owe me four."

"Forget it."

Perrone hunched his shoulders, as though getting ready for a physical act. "Dennis," he said, "either you pay me the four grand you owe me, and do it fast, or there'll be some people, like people in *press* people, who'll enjoy knowing you and your politico boss paid money out of a secret slush fund to buy a diary smearing Congressman Paul Latham so he wouldn't become secretary of state. Understand?"

Perrone left the restaurant.

A defeated Dennis Mackral sat back in the booth, less tan than a half hour before.

Molly Latham and a group of fellow pages ate takeout from the McDonald's on Capitol Hill. Dressed in their uniforms, they sat on the grass in a park on Constitution Avenue, comparing notes about their classes that morning.

Molly was happy to be back. There were sudden, unpredictable moments of sadness, especially when someone mentioned her father during a floor speech, or when a member of the House made a special fuss over her. She wanted to be treated like everyone else, and hoped it wouldn't be long before that was the case.

Molly and her new friends eventually turned to what had become their favorite pastime when together, evaluating members of the House they served each day.

"Does Mr. Schumer ever stop talking?" Melissa asked.

"He's okay," said John. "At least he doesn't go off the deep end like Mr. Dornan used to. Mr. Traficant's the one cracks me up. He even dresses funny. Those ties."

"Beam me up, Mr. Speaker," they said in unison, laughing as they mouthed Traficant's favorite phrase.

"The one who scares me is Mr. Solomon. What a temper," another member of the group offered. "He blew up at me because I didn't get a message from the cloakroom to him fast enough."

"He's not as mean as Bonior or DeLay" was another opinion, voiced between bites of sandwiches.

"Mr. Dreier's so cute," said Melissa. "Wish Ah were older."

"You notice the women members are the nicest?" John asked.

"No, they're not," someone said.

"They are," John said, defending his observation. "Ms. Kelly and Jackson Lee and Waters? They're terrific."

"I like Ms. Molinari" was tossed into the conversation. "But I guess I like Republicans better anyway."

"Maybe we ought to write a book when this session is done," John said. "You know, take a poll and rate everybody in the House."

"Who's your favorite so far, Molly?" John asked, immediately wishing he hadn't. Would she feel compelled to name her father?

"They've all been okay," she replied. "Mr. Jessup's been real nice. He's going to take over my dad's chairmanship of International Relations."

"Ah like him, too," said Melissa.

Everyone else agreed.

"We'd better get back," Molly said, getting up from the grass and brushing crumbs from her skirt.

"That's a pretty scarf," another female page said.

Molly touched it. Marge Edwards had given it to her the last time they saw each other. *Where is she?* Molly wondered as she led the group back into the Capitol.

Molly was assigned that afternoon to the Democratic coatroom, her favorite posting. She'd spent the morning after classes running dozens of small American flags up and down the flagpole outside the building. Members liked giving the flags to visiting constituents, proudly proclaiming that each had flown over the nation's Capitol.

The coatroom provided more challenge, and was certainly more interesting. The phones seemed never to stop ringing, especially when there was a debate on the floor of sufficient interest to entice a large number of members to it. This was one of those afternoons; the session promised to go well into the night.

In addition, Molly noticed on the day's schedule of events that the International Relations Committee's subcommittee on Economic Policy and Trade had scheduled a meeting at seven that night. Must be an important issue being discussed, she surmised, to be slated at the last minute, and to start that late.

A rush of memories of her father engulfed her. He loved his committee chairmanships more than the House of Representatives itself, often saying it was in committee where the truly important legislation was shaped and drafted. He was fond of quoting Woodrow Wilson on the subject: "Congress in session is Congress on public exhibition, whilst Congress in committee rooms is Congress at work."

That thought triggered another—the package Marge Edwards had given her containing books and papers her father wanted her to read.

Ruth had visited the Capitol that morning, her first appearance there since the moving memorial tribute to her husband in Statuary Hall. She'd stopped in at Paul's office to collect personal items packed by Bob Mondrian and other staffers, said hello to House colleagues with whom Paul had been especially close, and swung by the page room to leave for Molly the package Paul had asked Marge Edwards to deliver to her. Knowing her mother was coming to the Capitol, Molly had called first thing to remind her to bring the materials.

Thinking about her father, and his desire that she read what he considered important, brought a lump to her throat. With a solitary tear running down her cheek, she gulped water from a fountain and headed for the page room.

The McDonald's at National Airport did a brisk business, too.

Yvgeny Fodorov got off the Delta Shuttle and went directly into the restaurant, ordering two bacon cheeseburgers, a large fries, and a chocolate milk shake. He'd been told to wait there until someone from Brazier Industries' security staff picked him up. He had time for an apple pie and another shake before his driver appeared, tapping him on the shoulder and greeting him in Russian.

Fodorov was driven directly from the airport to the company's Washington offices, where he was told to wait in an empty room next to Aleksandr Patiashvili's office. He was edgy, couldn't sit still.

His stay in Brighton Beach had been confusing.

On the one hand, he was treated with respect by most

members of the Russian mob. But he was also aware of the scorn some demonstrated toward him. One in particular, about Fodorov's age, had nettled him, laughing when he saw him undressed, and once even calling him a *zhopachnik*, a fag. Fodorov considered killing him. Perhaps if he'd stayed in Brooklyn longer, he might have acted upon the impulse. And enjoyed it.

He'd found killing to be pleasurable since shooting his mother. That had been his first act of murder, but not his last. Shortly after murdering her, he'd been ordered to kill a Moscow drug dealer who'd held out on money. Remarkable, Fodorov thought as he shot the man in the head in front of his apartment building and slowly walked away, how exciting it was to plan a murder, stalk the victim, and complete the act, especially when you did it professionally, under orders, and were congratulated afterward.

He seriously considered shooting Sofia and some of her friends. But by then he'd decided that murdering for profit and praise was the only worthwhile reason for doing it. Killing those around him simply because they annoyed him rendered the act frivolous. He now viewed himself as having an occupation, a profession: Yvgeny Fodorov, professional assassin, killer for hire, cold and calculating, feared by those who deserved to die, respected by those who employed him.

He didn't know why he'd been summoned back to Washington.

The first time, it had been to kill that congressman, Latham.

How easy that had been.

Fodorov didn't know who arranged for Latham to be at the tiny park at such an odd hour, but he'd shown up, on time, alone and vulnerable. No guards. No security. What kind of country was this to allow elected officials to wander anywhere, day and night? It wouldn't have happened in the old Soviet Union.

Placing the weapon in the dead congressman's hand had been a spur-of-the-moment decision. Fodorov wasn't even sure why he'd done it, and after being sternly criticized, he wished he hadn't. It just made sense to him at the time. What did it matter? he rationalized. He was told the weapon wasn't traceable. In doing it, he delayed the official finding of murder, which gave him extra time to leave the city. What had been the harm?

But he hadn't voiced those arguments when Patiashvili chastised him: "You do what you're told, Fodorov, only what you're told, and do it the way you are told."

Fodorov had agreed, sullenly. He'd been smarting at Patiashvili's harsh words ever since.

It was almost five o'clock when Brazier Industries' head of Russian personnel summoned Fodorov to his office. Patiashvili pulled a revolver from his desk drawer and slid it across the desk to Fodorov. "Put it in here." Next to cross the desk was a slim leather briefcase.

Fodorov weighed the weapon in his hand, then opened the briefcase and slid the semiautomatic in with papers already inside.

"Thank you," Fodorov said. "What do you wish me to do?"

Fifteen minutes later, Fodorov left the building and hailed a taxi.

"Yes, sir?" the Arab driver said.

Fodorov handed him a slip of paper with an address in Georgetown written on it, sat back, lighted a cigarette, and looked through the window at the workers of Washington, D.C., on their way home after doing the nation's business.

A small smile crossed his thin lips. His work was just beginning.

Robert Mondrian met in what had been Latham's office with Jack Emerson, staff director to the House International Relations Committee, soon to be chaired by Spencer Jessup, Democrat from North Carolina. The purpose for getting together was the scheduled meeting of the committee.

"You say Brazier himself is coming?" Mondrian said.

"According to the list Brazier Industries sent over. Twelve names, one of them Brazier's."

"Twelve? It's not a hearing, Jack. It's a meeting to hash over some of the amendments. Who's on the list?"

"A bunch of his staff. Economic and banking types, I guess. There's more than a hundred amendments to the bill, Bob. Stassi wants to tack on hearings into crime in Russia. I suppose Brazier feels he needs this many people with knowledge in the areas addressed by the amendments."

"Yeah, I understand that," said Mondrian. "But why is Brazier coming along? He hasn't shown his face around here before."

"Maybe to massage Jessup. You know, he lost his angel when Paul died. Wants to cozy up to the new chairman."

Mondrian resented Emerson's characterization of his former boss but let it slide.

"Look, Bob," Emerson said, chewing on a pencil's eraser, "there's a chance of gutting this legislation before it comes out of committee. Jessup doesn't stand behind it the way Paul did. Businesses in Paul's district had a lot to gain from it. Spence's district is barely impacted."

"Maybe Paul wasn't as solidly behind it as you think," Mondrian said.

Emerson looked at him quizzically. "Explain?"

Mondrian shrugged. "Just that Paul wasn't in Brazier's camp to the extent too many people believed he was."

A staffer knocked, opened the door, and said, "Bob, a call for you."

"Get a name. I'll call back."

Her response was to motion for him to join her in the outer office.

"Sorry," Mondrian said to Emerson.

"Bob," Sue said when they were outside. "It's a woman. She says she has to talk to you."

"Who is she?"

"She wouldn't give her name."

"Tell her to—"

"She says it's a matter of life or death."

Mondrian laughed involuntarily. "Is it, now?"

He went to his desk, picked up the receiver, and punched the lighted button. "Bob Mondrian."

"Bob. It's Marge."

He sat up straight and cupped the mouthpiece with his hand. "Marge? Where are you?"

"I have to see you."

"Yeah. Sure. Where the hell did you go?"

"That's not important. Are you free now?"

"No. Meetings. I have people here."

"When?"

Mondrian looked around the office. The committee meeting was at seven. He wouldn't be there because only

293

committee staff was involved. Others in the office would be gone by six. He'd see to it that they were.

"Here?" he said softly. "Seven-thirty? Eight?"

"The office?"

"Yeah."

She exhaled loudly into her mouthpiece, audibly sending air into Mondrian's ear.

"Okay? You still have your pass? Yeah, you do. I've never rescinded it."

"Okay," she said. "Seven-thirty. You'll be alone?"

"Yes. I know what you want, Marge."

"I'm sure you do. All I want to do is talk about it with you."

"Seven-thirty."

"I'll be there. Make sure we're alone. Okay?"

"Okay."

Mondrian returned to where Jack Emerson waited.

"Problem?" Emerson asked.

"Everything's a problem," Mondrian replied. "Where were we?"

The moment Marge Edwards hung up on Mondrian, she called Anatoly, reaching him at home.

"Where are you?" he asked.

"That's not important," she said. "It's where I'm going to be that matters." She told him of her scheduled meeting that evening with Bob Mondrian.

"What do you hope to accomplish?" he asked.

"I'm not really sure, Anatoly. But if I can get him to come forward with me, corroborate what I know, I'll have that much more credibility."

There was silence on the other end.

"Anatoly?"

"Yes. I'm here. It sounds good, Marge. You will let me know what happens?"

"Of course. I love you, Anatoly."

"And I—I love you, too."

The click in her ear said the conversation was over. And maybe more.

31

Since the murder of Paul Latham, Mac and Annabel Smith's routine had been anything but that. Which was why they decided on the phone late that afternoon to meet for drinks in pleasant surroundings, and to indulge themselves with an early dinner at their favorite Washington steakhouse, Ruth's Chris, on Connecticut Avenue, N.W. The Smiths ate little red meat, but when the mood struck, they wanted the real thing.

They started their evening at the Hay-Adams Hotel, settling into comfortable stuffed chairs in the handsome John Hay Room. They toasted each other with perfect martinis, straight up, and reveled in the soothing refrains of a pianist.

"I could use a week here," Annabel said.

"A week anywhere but Washington," Smith said.

He'd filled her in earlier on his meeting with Warren Brazier.

"How did he react when you told him Paul had confided in you about Brazier's illegal activities? Money laundering? Contract killings? I'm surprised he didn't shoot you on the spot. And grateful he didn't."

Smith shrugged. "He suggested I come to work for him."

"And?"

"I told him I was gainfully employed, happily. Arrogant bastard."

"Is this the end of it, then?" she asked in the genteel surroundings of the richly appointed room.

"Of my involvement? Absolutely."

"Have you heard from Jessica Belle or her boss?"

"No."

"So you don't know whether confronting Brazier accomplished anything."

"That's right, although it's a little early for results—if there are any. I'm still wondering whether I should drive out to Ashburn to see Marge Edwards's half sister."

"For what purpose?"

"Just to follow up on what Tony uncovered."

"The fact that this private investigator Perrone met with her doesn't mean anything, at least on the surface. I thought your involvement was over."

Smith laughed, took her hand. "I guess I forgot. I actually was able to focus this afternoon on the Russian project. It felt good."

"Glad to hear it. Which reminds me, I'd better start thinking about what to pack for Moscow."

"Maybe we'd better pack guns first," he said. "The crime problem there is staggering, from everything I read."

297

"But we'll be safe, won't we?"

"Of course, provided we follow sensible security precautions. Let's not worry about it." They finished their drinks with yet another toast. "Hungry?" Smith asked.

"Famished."

"I think I'll check the machine before we head out."

"Expecting an important call?"

"No. Just like to keep in touch." He went to the hotel lobby in search of a pay phone.

Annabel's smile said many things. Her husband was hardly finished with Paul Latham's murder. But who could blame him for wanting to follow through? Once he'd made the decision to inject himself into the case, it was a natural tendency to want to keep tabs on progress, if only out of curiosity. Or to help make progress.

"Any calls?" she asked when he returned.

"Marge Edwards," he said, sitting.

Annabel sat up a little straighter. "Did she say where she was?"

"No. Said she'd call again tonight."

"How did she sound?"

"Breathless. Anxious."

"Want to call off dinner, go home in case she does call again?"

Smith thought about it.

"Red meat isn't good for us anyway," Annabel said bravely.

"Yes, it is, in moderation. Besides, nobody seems to know what really is good or bad for us. Next thing we know they'll be selling cholesterol pills to get the levels up. Come on. I'm famished."

Annabel had mixed emotions about going through

with their plans. On the one hand, it had been a while since they'd gone out to dinner together, just the two of them. She loved the restaurant and its homey atmosphere. And, she was hungry.

On the other hand, she knew Mac would be distracted by Marge Edwards's latest attempt to reach him.

"You're concerned I'll be distracted at dinner," he said.

"We haven't been married long enough to read each other's minds," Annabel said.

"But you were thinking that."

"Yes."

He grinned. "My mind is only on a rare fillet, Annabel, shared with an even rarer woman."

"Who is it?" Alekseyev asked, going to his apartment door in response to a knock.

"Fodorov. From Brazier."

Alekseyev peered through the security peephole and recognized the distorted face of the creepy young man he'd taken to dinner a few nights ago.

"What do you want?" Alekseyev asked through the closed door.

"Mr. Brazier wants for me to give to you a message. It is a very important message."

"So, tell me."

Fodorov said nothing.

Alekseyev reconsidered his response toward Fodorov. Better to be polite and cooperative with someone sent by Brazier. He was hardly in a position to be surly with the boss's emissary.

Alekseyev had barely managed to save his job in Washington with Brazier Industries. He did it by telling its leader he knew of a report that could prove extremely damaging to the company, and to Warren Brazier himself.

"And what do you expect me to do with this startling information, Mr. Alekseyev?" Brazier had asked.

Alekseyev responded with a speech he'd rehearsed while waiting his audience. He spoke of his loyalty to the company and its goals, emphasizing that what he'd learned of the report would remain with him. When Brazier didn't respond, Alekseyev went so far as to promise to use his best efforts to obtain the report from the person who'd told him about it.

"And who might that be?" Brazier had asked.

Alekseyev hesitated. He hadn't intended to mention Marge.

But when he did, Brazier's recognition of the name was obvious. He thanked Alekseyev for coming forth, and said he would reconsider the transfer back to Moscow.

"Come in," Alekseyev said, opening the door to allow Fodorov to enter the apartment. When he was inside, Alekseyev said, forcing a smile, "Good to see you again, Yvgeny. A drink?"

"*Nyet.*"

"Okay. What's the message from Mr. Brazier?"

Yvgeny slid the weapon from his waistband so quickly and smoothly that Alekseyev wasn't immediately aware what was happening. But when Fodorov raised the gun, a silencer extending the barrel, and aimed it at Alekseyev's face, the reality screamed out. Alekseyev's reflex action was to raise his hands in front of his face. The first shot tore through the back of his hand and into his cheek. The wounded hand pressed against the gaping hole in his face. Blood ran freely down his wrist and drizzled to the floor.

Alekseyev's mouth and eyes opened in pain and shock. Before he could do or say anything else, the second slug entered his mouth and smashed through the back of his head, carrying with it skull and brain and a streamer of crimson blood. Alekseyev's body followed, stumbling back six feet until falling into a heap on the floor.

Fodorov replaced the weapon in his waistband, looked at his watch, cast a final, fleeting glance at the lifeless body of Alekseyev, and left the apartment. Ten minutes later he was back at the Washington headquarters of Brazier Industries, just in time to join Brazier and his contingent of janissaries as they piled into cars and drove to the Capitol, where they were met in the underground garage by a staffer from International Relations. The staffer handed them visitor badges, led them past security, and up to the committee room.

Jack Emerson, majority staff director of the House International Relations Committee, left his meeting with Bob Mondrian and rode the subway back to the Capitol Building. He walked into Room H 139, where other committee staffers, and some House members, waited for the meeting to start.

"Where's Mr. Jessup?" Emerson asked.

"On the floor. He'll be here soon," an assistant answered.

Tom Krouch, Brazier Industries' chief lobbyist, entered the room. His reputation in Washington, built over years of service to House and Senate committees, as well as to individual House members and senators, was considerable and deserved. His decision two years ago to join Brazier Industries raised a few of his colleagues' eyebrows, but no one questioned his motivation. Speculation was that Warren Brazier had given Krouch an offer he couldn't refuse, making him the highest-paid lobbyist in Washington. He'd earn his pay, they knew. Not only was Brazier's autocratic, often brutal management style well known, his executives were on call twenty-four hours a day, seven days a week.

Krouch called Emerson aside. "We'll need another room, Jack, for staff."

"Yeah, I heard you were bringing an army. Why?"

"Brazier wants his troops here. You know, feed him economic data if we get into technical areas."

Emerson screwed up his face. "What's your boss doing here in the first place? The glitches in the bill don't need him to get fixed."

Krouch leaned close to Emerson's ear. "A last-minute decision, Jack. You know how he is. I wouldn't be surprised if he didn't show up. It's minute-to-minute with him. If he does show, it's probably because he wants to press the new chairman's flesh, let him know how strongly he personally feels about this bill."

"He'll accomplish that, I suppose."

"Level with me," Krouch said.

A smile from Emerson: "Of course. This is Washington. Remember?"

"Jessup. What's his view of Brazier and Brazier Industries?"

"Want it straight?"

"Sure."

"He's no Paul Latham when it comes to championing your boss's agenda."

"Against this bill?"

"You know he is."

"All of it?"

Emerson shrugged. "Enough to gut it."

"Thanks for being candid. Anything I can do to soften him?"

"Yeah."

"And?"

"Put Brazier in a box and keep him away after tonight. Jessup dislikes him even more than the bill."

"Advice noted. What room can staff use?"

"Over here." Emerson led him to an adjacent, empty conference room with a dozen chairs around an oblong teak table. "This do?"

"Perfect."

The arrival of Warren Brazier caused a speculative buzz among the staffers, some of whom had never seen him in person. Brazier's own staff hung back as he shook hands with members of the committee. Tom Krouch knew his boss's style well, and was impressed at how the generally pugnacious Brazier could, in a blink, like Khrushchev, become friendly and outgoing when the situation called for it. Twenty minutes ago, he'd been cruelly tyrannical with everyone.

"Sure you brought enough people with you?" Congressman Jessup asked.

Brazier laughed, said, "I can get another dozen here with a phone call."

Jessup, a tall, courtly North Carolinian with silvery, senatorial hair and an easy, slow southern manner of speaking, laughed. "Please don't do that, Mr. Brazier. No place to put 'em. I wasn't expectin' you personally to attend this meeting. But now that you're here, I'm sure you'd like to get down to business."

"That makes sense, Congressman."

The large room seemed smaller once the many participants took their seats. Brazier was flanked by Tom Krouch, his chief lobbyist, and a pudgy, middle-aged gentleman wearing a plastic-looking toupee, who was introduced by Brazier as the company's vice president of banking. Joining Congressman Jessup were five other members of the committee, and six of the more than eighty committee-staff members, including director Jack Emerson.

Jessup said, "This committee is in a little bit of flux, Mr. Brazier, as you can imagine. The tragic and damnable murder of Paul Latham, a good friend of yours, I know, and my good friend, too, has caused us to hold up on any further consideration of this bill."

"And I can certainly understand a certain amount of confusion," said Brazier. "I just hope that the fine work Paul Latham did all these years on this committee, and especially on this critical piece of legislation, which, I hasten to add, will advance America's vital interest in seeing Russia become a successful free-market economy and vibrant democracy, wasn't in vain."

Tom Krouch kept a watchful eye on Congressman Jessup for signs of reaction. His read as the meeting progressed was that as hard as Jessup tried to be courteous— to be political—his distrust of the truculent Brazier, indeed his dislike, was evident in subtle facial expressions and body language.

The meeting, everyone knew, was unusual. Brazier had testified on occasion before the committee and its subcommittees in the past. But to gather like this, at night, with so many interested parties present, was unprecedented, at least from Krouch's perspective, and he was surprised that his last-minute request for it had been granted by the majority and minority leadership.

As the meeting progressed, the discussion widened to include others in the room. But it was Jessup who got to the meat when he said, "Mr. Brazier, I have some serious reservations about this legislation, especially the amendments you advocate."

"I'm listening," Brazier said.

Jessup went on to cite two amendments that had been pushed by Krouch and his lobbying staff. Brazier asked his banking chief to provide figures on the financial impact of those amendments on the International Monetary Fund, World Bank, and the Russian central banking system. That prompted the banking expert to ask for two of his staff from the adjacent room to join them.

In the smaller room, the ten remaining representatives of Brazier Industries continued to while away the time. They weren't sure why they were there, but that wasn't unusual. Working for Warren Brazier often meant waiting around, killing time until summoned by the boss. But you'd best remain focused and sharp, ready to respond when the call to do something came.

Yvgeny Fodorov, glum and uncommunicative, not a usual member of the group, sat stoically, picking at skin on his hands. Resting against his chair was the slim briefcase given him by Aleksandr Patiashvili earlier that afternoon. He felt superior to the others in the room, hated them for their smug disdain of him. Inside, he felt satisfied. It had been a good evening so far.

Not so for Warren Brazier.

As the meeting in the main room droned on, he continued to present his reasons why the legislation pending before the International Relations Committee was not only good for his company, but for the United States as well. His tone answering the long, drawn-out questioning had become more arrogant and impatient, which was not lost on the others. He leaned heavily on the late Paul Latham's supposed commitment to the bill, and Latham's unparalleled understanding of its U.S.-Russian ramifications.

Krouch hoped the meeting would end soon, before Brazier allowed more of his true nature to surface. The lobbyist's professional respect for Brazier tempered his privately held personal view—that his boss was the most unpleasant man he'd ever met.

Marge Edwards took a deep breath as she stood on Independence Avenue, in front of the Rayburn House Office Building. It was twenty minutes to eight; she was ten minutes late.

She went up the steps and entered the building, relieved that the uniformed Capitol police officer on duty was not one of the regulars who might recognize her. A conveyor belt passed her bag into the X-ray machine as she stepped through the archway without causing beeps from the metal detector. She thanked the officer when he handed her bag back to her, and headed for Congressman Paul Latham's office.

She paused outside the office. Hopefully, Mondrian was alone. The click of high heels on the marble hallway floor prompted her to open the door and step inside. The door closed behind her. Latham's private office was open.

"Bob?" she called, her voice lacking strength.

"Come on in," he replied from Latham's office.

She stood in the doorway. He sat behind Latham's desk, one foot propped up on it. He was in shirtsleeves. His tie, pulled loose from his neck, was a muted montage of game birds in a green forest.

"Hi," she said, giving a little wave.

"Hi," he said, not moving.

"Well . . ." She entered the office and stood across the desk from him. "Surprised to see me?"

"No. Close the door."

She did what he asked.

"Sit down," he said. His stare was hard, his voice firm and angry.

Once she'd pulled up a chair, he lowered his foot from the desk, leaned forward, rested his chin on his clasped hands, and said, "Where is it?"

"It's safe, Bob."

"Safe?"

"Yes. Safe from you."

He cocked his head. "Marge," he said, "I don't know where you got it into that crazy head of yours, but Paul's investigation and report doesn't have to be kept from me. We're on the same side."

She locked eyes with him. "No, we're not," she said. "And you know it. That report on Warren Brazier and Brazier Industries was meant to go to the Justice Department. Paul spent the last year of his life compiling information on Brazier for Justice. And it *cost* him his life."

"It probably did," Mondrian said. "So why did you run off with it? The least we can do in Paul's memory is to make sure Justice gets it."

"Exactly. And if I left it here with you, it never would arrive there."

"Marge, I—"

She stood and placed her palms on the desk, jutted her chin at him. "Bob, I know about the overture Brazier made to you through his intermediaries. What were you offered? Fifty thousand? Was it more? No matter what it was, it was cheap, Bob. Cheap to sell out a man like Paul."

"I don't need a lecture, Marge. Being offered and taking are two different things."

"You didn't take money from Brazier Industries?"

"No. Not *that* money."

"Not *that* money? What does it matter what money you took from them? Even if you took a dollar from that sleazebag Brazier, you sold Paul out. If you'd do it for one thing, Bob, you'll do it for another, in this case the report. That's why I grabbed it from Paul's safe and ran."

He glared at her.

"How could you?"

"Who the hell are you to lecture me, Marge? You ever have to scrape just to get by?"

"That doesn't justify anything." She softened. "Bob, I don't care that you sold out to Brazier Industries in the past, in some—in some goddamn moment of weakness. That's human. *You're* human. But it isn't too late. Let's take the report to Justice together, in Paul's memory, as you put it. I'll forget you ever took a nickel from Brazier."

He sat back and exhaled. "Why didn't *you* just take it to Justice, Marge?"

"I would have. But then Paul was murdered. I didn't know what to do. And there was the story that I would charge Paul with sexual harassment. Nonsense! That's all it was. But—"

"There was a diary," Mondrian said. "Wasn't there?"

"I don't care about that, Bob. Maybe it was just as well that everyone thought I ran because of the harassment rumor. No one knows about Paul's investigation and report except you, me, and the people at Justice who set it in motion a year ago."

"God, you are naive, Marge. Justice didn't set it up. It was CIA. They had Broadhurst working on this back when he was with the trade commission. *He's* the one who approached Paul. Once he and his people started putting together the case against Brazier—and God knows there was enough to make that case—he saw Paul as the perfect insider. No one was closer to Brazier than Paul. He knew every dirty deal Brazier was involved with."

"And you'd sell out to someone like that." Her tone wasn't one of disgust. Fatigue more accurately described it.

"What about Paul, Marge? He knew about Brazier for years, but kept right on working with him. How many times did you hear him defend Brazier, praise him as some goddamn gift to free economy and the democratic process? All those bills he ramrodded through. Did *he* sell out to Brazier? You bet he did. And you and I did, too, every time we advanced trade legislation to benefit Brazier."

"Paul really believed in Brazier, at least until a year ago," she said. "Sure, he knew he owed Brazier for all his support over the years, the fund-raising, the contributions, the influence on voters in Paul's district. But give Paul credit, Bob. When he realized what Brazier was really like—the huge payoffs in Russia, his covert support of the Communists, his use of mobsters—God, the man is a godfather of Russian mobsters here. Once Paul saw this, had it pointed out by Broadhurst and the others, he didn't hesitate to cooperate, to document everything he could in the report. To even consider protecting Brazier is to spit on Paul's grave."

"I never intended to cooperate with Brazier on the report, Marge. You know that. Hell, when Paul confronted Brazier at their meeting the day before Paul died, told him what he intended to do, he put his life on the line."

"Literally," she said.

"As it turned out. Where is the report, Marge?" he asked.

"Where I know it won't go to Warren Brazier."

Mondrian sighed. "Okay," he said. "Wait here." He left the office, returning a minute later with a small envelope, which he handed to her.

"What's this?" she asked.

"Open it. You'll see."

Inside was the check from Brazier Industries, written to Robert Mondrian.

"When did you get this?" she asked.

"Earlier today."

"And you—"

"Go ahead, Marge. Tear it up."

She hesitated, then tore the check into four pieces, placed them in the envelope, and handed it to him.

"Satisfied?" he asked.

She looked down at the floor, then up at him. She smiled. "I guess I get carried away sometimes," she said.

His smile was broad, but not as spontaneous as hers had been. "Look, Marge," he said, "I'm really glad you're okay, and that you're here. It's easy to get carried away in this insane place, isn't it?"

Her response was a stream of air directed at an errant strand of hair on her forehead.

"You're right," he said, coming around the desk and placing his large hands on her shoulders. "Let's take the report to Justice together. Lay it all out for them. Do right by Paul."

She nodded.

"Where is the report? You have it with you?" He glanced at her oversized shoulder bag.

"No," she said.

"Well?"

"I put it in a package of books and papers I gave Molly."

"Molly? Molly Latham?"

"Yes."

"Why? What did you expect her to do with it?"

"Nothing. Frankly, I didn't think she'd even open it."

"And if she did . . . open it?"

Marge shrugged. "I didn't think that far ahead. All I knew was that I wanted it out of here. Paul gave me the books and some of his speeches to package up for her, so I included the report in with it."

"And she's had it all along."

"Yes. She would have gotten hold of me if she had opened it and saw what it was."

"How could she? You disappeared."

"I know. The sexual harassment thing. The report. I—I just panicked, Bob. That simple. Excuse me. Nature calls."

"Molly's probably on page duty. I'll try to call her. They're still in session. We'll find her and put this thing to rest."

"Yes," Marge said. "That's what we'll do."

* * *

"It's time for your other meeting."

Yvgeny Fodorov picked up his briefcase from the floor and stood. Another young Russian also stood; he, too, held a leather briefcase in his hand. The others in the room watched with interest as they left the room. "Where are they going?" one asked.

"A meeting. A related topic," Patiashvili said.

"A security meeting?" another said, his tone skeptical.

Patiashvili trained his black eyes on the questioner.

There were no further questions.

Fodorov and his colleague from security approached a uniformed Capitol Hill police officer in the hall just outside H 139. They nodded.

"Good evening," the officer said, eyeing the official visitor badges hanging from their jacket handkerchief pockets.

They proceeded down the hall to a stairway leading to the basement, where the Capitol subway system linked the building to the House and Senate office buildings. They climbed aboard the sleek, open tram, operated by a young black man in white shirt and tie. Others boarded, too. When the cars were full, the subway left the loading ramp and, in a few minutes, came to a stop beneath the Rayburn House Office Building.

Fodorov and his partner joined the flow of passengers riding the escalator to the floor above. They paused at an intersection of hallways. Fodorov had been given a map of the building to study. Still, it was confusing.

"Where?" the other man said.

"This way," Fodorov replied, choosing one of the halls and leading them down it.

They reached the outer door to the office suite with

Paul Latham's nameplate still on it. Looking left and right, they opened the briefcases, removed the weapons, and secured them in the waistband of their pants. A glance at each other, a nod, and a hand on the doorknob.

32

Molly Latham had returned to the Democratic cloak-room after delivering a message on the House floor to Congressman Barney Frank, when the phone rang again. Melissa looked at Molly, who'd rolled her eyes up in an expression of fatigue and frustration. Melissa laughed. "Ah'll get it, hon," she said.

Melissa wrote down the message—"For Mr. Skelton," she said, waving to Molly and heading for the floor.

Molly sat heavily in one of the many leather chairs.

"Got you running, huh?" a congresswoman said pleasantly.

"I have to get better shoes," replied Molly.

Phones started ringing again.

"Relax," another page said. "Take a break."

As her fellow pages answered phones, and ran messages to the floor, Molly picked up the wrapped package from her father, plopped it on her lap, and slowly began to undo it.

"Present, Molly?" a congressman asked.

She smiled and shook her head. "Just some dull reading," she said, wondering whether she dishonored her father by saying it.

The ringing phones were now a discordant chorus. Molly dropped the partially opened package to the floor and started answering calls again. She hoped the House finished its business soon. A pile of homework awaited her back at the dorm.

This was shaping up to be a longer night than she had thought.

"Democratic cloakroom," she said, answering yet another call.

"I'm trying to reach Molly Latham."

"This is Molly."

"Molly. Bob Mondrian."

"Oh, hi, Mr. Mondrian. You're looking for *me*?"

"Yes. I—I'm in your dad's office with Marge Edwards."

Molly's eyes widened. "Marge is there?"

"Yes. It's very important that we talk with you."

"Right now? I'm real busy."

"Is your supervisor around?"

"Yes."

"Molly, do you remember a package Marge gave you?"

Molly's hand went to the scarf she wore, Marge's gift to her at lunch. "I'm wearing it," she said.

Mondrian's momentary silence testified to his confusion. "Wearing it?"

"The scarf she gave me."

"No, Molly. Another package, with books and—"

"From my dad. I have it here with me. Mom dropped it off this morning."

"Have you opened it?"

Molly laughed. "I started to, but the phones went crazy again and—"

"Look, can you hop on the subway and come over here to the office? Bring the package with you."

"All right. Where has Marge been? Is she all right?"

"She's just fine, Molly. Put your supervisor on."

"That was wonderful," Smith said, sitting back and admiring his empty plate. He'd opted for a porterhouse steak. Annabel had chosen a smaller version.

"I'm stuffed," she said. "Nothing but apples and water for the next few days."

Smith made a face. "Dessert?" he asked.

"You jest, of course."

"No, I—"

Their waiter came to the table. "An after-dinner drink, compliments of the manager?" he asked.

They looked at each other.

"We really shouldn't," she said.

"No, we shouldn't," he said. To the waiter: "That is, cognac, please."

Annabel laughed.

The manager, whom they knew, joined them. "Still planning your trip to Russia?" he asked.

"Planning it," Annabel replied. "Whether we'll ever get there is another question."

"I can put you in the mood," the manager said.

"Oh?"

"A special after-dinner drink. The Commissar. Equal amounts of vodka and Triple Sec. Very smooth."

"No, I—"

"Try it," said Mac.

"All right."

"And as long as we're going this far—"

"Bread pudding with whiskey sauce?" the manager asked, knowing of their fondness for the restaurant's special dessert.

"Mac!"

"Just one to share," Mac said.

And so they lingered over their cordials, and dipped spoons into the heavenly pudding, content to be together sharing the meal, one hand occasionally touching the other's, the problems of Washington, especially of murder, kept at bay by the window separating them from Connecticut Avenue.

"I'm getting sleepy," she said.

"I'll be tucking you in very soon, Annie," he said. "How's the Commissar?"

"Good. He sends his best."

She delivered the message with a light kiss on his lips.

33

From the private bathroom in Paul Latham's office suite, Marge Edwards heard the door open, and close. "Damn," she said softly. It didn't strike her as strange that someone else had arrived at that hour, but it was dismaying. She wanted to talk alone with Bob Mondrian. She reacted by putting on lipstick and fluffing her hair.

Yvgeny Fodorov and his colleague, Vladimir Donskoi, stepped into Latham's private office, where Mondrian had just hung up on Molly Latham.

"Can I help you?" Mondrian asked, standing behind the desk.

Fodorov and the other man, Donskoi, answered by drawing their weapons.

"Who the hell are you?" Mondrian said, starting around the desk.

"Where is the report?" Donskoi said in almost flawless English.

"Report? Hey, come on. Put those down. I'm—"

Fodorov swore in Russian as he squeezed the trigger, sending three bullets into Mondrian's chest. The chief of staff fell back against the desk, his hands desperately attempting to stem the sudden rush of blood and searing pain.

Donskoi turned to Fodorov. "Fool," he shouted. "Imbecile."

Fodorov ignored him, pushed Mondrian's lifeless body to the floor from where it was sprawled over the desk, and started going through piles of paper in a frenzy, sending files flying.

Donskoi was tempted to shoot him. Their orders were to go to the office and demand of the man and woman who would be there that they turn over the report. Donskoi was in charge. He'd been shown photographs of Marge Edwards and Robert Mondrian, and had been briefed on the nature of what they were looking for. It was only after they'd gotten their hands on the report, or couldn't, that they were to kill both people.

In frustration, Donskoi joined Fodorov in his haphazard search.

The sounds from the office froze Marge Edwards in the bathroom. What could be happening? Should she remain there until the intruders left? She decided she couldn't. They might search the entire office. Who'd been shot? Bob Mondrian? Why? Who?

She opened the bathroom door an inch and peered through the gap. Sounds came from Latham's office—muttered voices, things being thrown about.

She opened the door farther, wide enough to slip through, drew a deep, desperate breath, and crossed the office to the door leading to the hallway. Should she stop to see what had happened to Mondrian? No. There was nothing she could do by herself. She had to find help, the Capitol police, let them know.

The door to the suite had a heavy latch bolt that made a loud metallic sound whenever the door was opened and closed. Marge Edwards paused, held her breath, and opened the door, the noise sounding to her like a cell door in prison movies. She glanced at Paul's office. No one responded, thank God.

She stepped into the hallway and allowed the door to slam shut behind. "Oh, God," she gasped, again gripped with inertia as she tried to decide in which direction to run. She looked back at the door. It opened. A face appeared—and a revolver.

She bolted toward an intersecting hallway, slipped as she turned the corner, retained her balance with one hand on the marble floor, and ran as fast as she could to a stairway leading down to the building's main lobby. She was afraid to look back, but did, only for a second. A man holding a weapon stood at the intersection of hallways. He'd stopped there. No matter. Marge stumbled down the stairs two at a time, grasping the railing to keep from making the descent headfirst.

She reached the main floor and went to where the uniformed security guard sat behind a table.

"Please," she said. "There are men with guns in Congressman Latham's office."

He stood. "What are you saying? Men with guns?"

"Yes." She looked over her shoulder, then back at the officer. "Someone's been shot there. Mr. Mondrian, I think."

"Slow down," the officer said. "Who are they?"

A puff of exasperation came through her lips; she

slapped her hands against her thighs. "Call for help," she said. "Please."

The officer took a battery-powered radio from his belt and spoke into it, giving his name and location: "Report of armed individuals in the building. Congressman Latham's office. Request immediate backup to investigate."

A wave of relief caused Marge to relax. Help was on its way. She shut her eyes tight and said a silent prayer that Bob Mondrian was all right—that everyone was all right.

"Did you see them up close?" the security officer asked.

"No. I was in the bathroom and—"

The front doors to the building opened and a half-dozen members of the Capitol police, armed with M-249s, burst through. The building security officer told them the problem had been reported by the young lady standing next to him, and that it had occurred in Congressman Latham's office, one floor up.

"How many armed men?" the group's leader asked Marge.

"I don't know. I only saw one, but I think I heard two. Talking. I think there were two different voices."

"What sort of weapons?"

"I don't know," she said, wishing they would just go and see for themselves.

The group leader used his radio to call the communications room, asking for a CERT team to secure the building. That request delivered, he said to the other officers, "Let's go, but slow." To Marge: "You'd recognize the one you saw?"

"I think so."

"Stick close. Keep quiet. If you see him, say so."

Marge fell in behind as they made their way from the entrance lobby, the stone eyes of former Speaker Sam Rayburn peering down at them.

Vladimir Donskoi made an instant decision after seeing the woman disappear down the stairs. He ran past Latham's office door in the direction of stairs on the other side of the building, leaving Yvgeny Fodorov alone. He'd no sooner rounded the corner when Molly Latham approached from the opposite direction, carrying the package Mondrian had asked her to bring.

She paused to knock at her father's door, placed her hand on the knob, and opened it.

"Bob?" she called as the door closed behind her. "Marge?"

Fodorov appeared from the inner office. The sight of him caused Molly to start. "Where's—?"

He pointed his gun at her. "Shud up!" he said in broken English.

"Where's Marge—and Mr. Mondrian?"

The sound of multiple footsteps outside captured Fodorov's attention. As he listened, Molly backed away and reached for the doorknob. But Fodorov was too quick. He grabbed her arm and pushed her against the door.

The thud of Molly's body stopped everyone outside in their tracks; anxious looks were exchanged.

"Who's in there?" the officer in charge asked Marge.

"I don't know."

But then it hit her: Mondrian had said he would try to call Molly. Did he reach her while Marge was in the bathroom? *Was Molly Latham in there with a killer?*

"It might be Congressman Latham's daughter," Marge said. "She's a House page. She was coming here tonight."

More armed officers arrived. The leader of the second group conferred with the initial force's leader. They turned to Marge.

"She knows you?" one asked.

"Yes."

"Call her name."

"I—all right."

Marge put her mouth close to the door. "Molly," she said, too softly to penetrate the wood. "Molly," she repeated, louder this time.

Two shots splintered the door inches from Marge Edwards's head, accompanied by an agonized female scream from inside.

Marge fell to her knees; the officers pressed themselves against the walls. "Jesus," one said. "Who the hell is in there?"

"It's Molly," Marge said, crawling to where a knot of police congregated. "What are you going to do?"

"What's the phone number in there?"

Marge gave it to him. After ordering another officer to contact headquarters to declare an emergency alert for the entire Capitol, he dialed the number Marge had given him on a cellular phone. They heard it ring in the office. It went unanswered. The officer slid along the wall to the door, checked the position of his fellow officers, then said in an authoritative voice, "This is Lieutenant Shuttee. Capitol police. You can't leave. There are dozens of armed officers here in the hall. The building is surrounded. Put down your weapons, open the door, and come out with your hands raised."

They waited for a reply. There was none.

The officer repeated his order.

Seconds that seemed like minutes passed.

The door slowly opened.

Molly was the first to be seen. Her eyes, red and wet, were wide with fright. Fodorov stood directly behind her, one hand gripping her blond hair, the other pressing his weapon against her temple. He said something in Russian, then again in fractured English: "Away! Ged away! This girl dead if you do not go away."

"Molly," Marge said.

Molly's mouth opened, but no words came out.

"Back off," the officer in charge said.

"I will kill her," Fodorov said.

"Who the hell is he?" an officer whispered to Marge.

"I don't know. He's Russian."

"His accent. You sure?"

She thought of Anatoly. "Yes," she said softly.

Fodorov slowly maneuvered Molly through the door and into the hall.

"It's the congressman's kid," an officer said.

"I know, I know," the lead officer said. "Everybody stay calm. Calm, cool, and collected."

Another officer at the rear of the pack called communications to order a hostage negotiation team be sent to the Rayburn Building. The phone at communications was immediately handed to Capitol Police Chief Henry Folsom.

"What's the status?" he asked.

The officer on the scene gave him a capsule rundown.

"What's he doing?"

"Just standing there with a gun to the kid's head."

"Any ID on him?"

"No. He's got an accent. He's Russian, we think."

Folsom immediately thought of the meeting going on in House committee room H 139: a dozen official visitor badges issued, most to a group of Russians from Brazier Industries.

"What's he doing now?"

The officer in the hall looked over others blocking his view. "He's starting to move with her. Down the hall. Real slow."

"No chance of getting a clean shot?"

"No. He's got her pressed right up against him, walking in lockstep. Got her by the hair, gun up against her head. He's got a crazy look about him."

"Don't spook him," Folsom said. "Hostage team'll be there in a few minutes."

The now sizable contingent of Capitol police followed Fodorov at a distance as he moved with Molly to stairs leading to the first floor. Two officers entered Latham's office and found Mondrian dead on the floor. They quickly passed word that the man holding Molly Latham hostage had already killed, and would kill again if cornered.

"Keep a distance," everyone was quietly instructed. "Don't push him."

It was assumed that Fodorov would take Molly to the lobby and out into the street.

Instead, he proceeded to another set of stairs leading down to the subway connecting the building with the Capitol.

"What's he going down there for?" an officer asked, not expecting an answer.

By now, Fodorov's route was lined with armed police. Their increasing presence visibly unnerved him. His eyes darted from face to face, blinking rapidly, mouth working as though chewing something. Molly's face, too, reflected the stress and tension. Her eyes seemed to plead with every other set of eyes to help, to do something for her.

By the time they arrived at the subway platform, a contingent of Capitol police were there, along with special agents of the FBI. The young black man running the subway that night had been shocked to see members of the CERT team swarm into the area. At first, he thought they'd come for him. "What'd I do?" he asked.

"Just stay where you are," he was told.

Seconds later, Fodorov and Molly appeared.

"Do what they tell you to do," the driver was ordered.

Fodorov, still with a painful grip on Molly's hair, stopped on the platform. His pinched, pale face mirrored his confusion. He was surrounded by heavily armed men and women wearing flak jackets, a hundred of them, maybe more. If he didn't have this hostage, he knew, he'd be gunned down. Despite the situation, he felt a certain superiority. He wouldn't hesitate to kill the girl, and they knew it. He'd take some of them down, too. Any fear he might have been feeling at the moment was tempered by a certain euphoria. They would never accuse him of being a coward. Not Yvgeny Fodorov. The adrenaline pulsing through his body was palpable.

He maneuvered Molly onto the empty subway car, and, in Russian, ordered the operator to move.

"Go on, take him," a senior officer said.

The operator tentatively activated a control, causing the small train to move away from the platform on a cushion of air. Police lined the pedestrian walkway and watched the car make its short, virtually silent journey to the Capitol. Other police, led by Chief Folsom, waited on the platform beneath the Capitol for its arrival.

Fodorov forced Molly from the car. Folsom instructed his men to step back and allow them access to the door. They went through it and moved to where two elevators stood with open doors. One had a sign above it indicating it was for the exclusive use of members of the House of Representatives. Fodorov shoved Molly into it. As he did, he created a momentary gap between them, prompting some police officers to raise their weapons. But the moment Fodorov and his hostage were in the elevator, he grabbed her again and pulled her to him. He pushed a button. The door slid closed.

"He's going to the floor," Folsom said. "What's the status there?"

"Secure, sir. They're still in session, but all entrances are secure, heavily guarded."

"Which won't do anybody any good as long as he has the Latham girl," Folsom said, more to himself. He spoke into his radio: "Suspect and hostage on their way up in members' elevator. Might be heading for the floor. Do nothing—repeat—do *nothing* to cause him to injure the hostage." Folsom headed for the stairs, dozens of officers following on his heels.

The elevator door opened, and Fodorov peered out at a circle of armed police. "Get back!" he shouted in Russian, then in English. He waved his gun for emphasis. "Back! Get back!" He moved in tandem with Molly from the elevator and in the direction of one of the doors leading to the floor of the House of Representatives.

"Does he know where he's going?" an officer asked Chief Folsom.

Folsom shrugged. Then, he saw the four officers guarding the door brace themselves, and raise their automatic weapons. "Stand down!" Folsom said in a booming voice. To one of his lieutenants: "Get around to another entrance. Clear the floor. Get the members out of there, into cloakrooms, whatever. Now!"

But it was too late to vacate the floor. Fodorov, who'd paused as though to gather his thoughts, made a sudden lunge toward the doors leading to the House chamber. The officers stepped back as the Russian assassin, Molly still in tow, pushed open the doors and disappeared behind them.

Folsom got on his radio. "They still there?" he asked an officer assigned to a three-person squad at Room H 139, where the House International Relations Committee met with Brazier Industries' Warren Brazier.

"Yes, sir."

"Get Mr. Brazier and put him on."

"Get—?"

"Damn it, just do what I say."

"Yes, sir."

Those attending the meeting had been told there was an emergency situation in the Capitol, and that they were to remain in the room until it was resolved. Questions of the officer went unanswered. "Orders are for you to remain here," he said. "That's the order."

"What's the emergency?" he was asked again.

"Orders are to remain here," he repeated. He walked from the room, a buzz of speculation following him.

Folsom waited until Brazier said, "Hello? Brazier here."

"This is Capitol Police Chief Folsom, Mr. Brazier."

"Yes?"

"Sir, there's an armed man holding hostage the daughter of Congressman Paul Latham."

"Molly Latham?"

"Yes, sir."

"Good God!"

"Sir, we believe the gunman is Russian. He's already

killed Mr. Latham's chief of staff, and he's holding a gun to the girl's head."

"I can't believe this."

"I know you have a number of Russian executives with you at the meeting."

"Yes?"

"Have any of them left you this evening?"

"I—I don't know. Some of my staff is in a separate room. You aren't suggesting that—?"

"All I'm suggesting is that I'm trying to save the girl's life, Mr. Brazier. Has any of your staff left the area?"

"I'll see," Brazier said.

A minute later he spoke into the radio again. "I'm afraid one of them is gone."

"Who?"

"One of my security men. Fodorov. Yvgeny Fodorov."

"Thin, pasty face, thick glasses?"

"Yes."

"Mr. Brazier, I'm afraid he's the one."

"I can't imagine . . . Why would he? What can I do?"

"I'd like you to come down here, sir. I'll have one of my men escort you."

"Yes, of course. This is shocking."

"Yes, sir, it is. Put the officer back on.

"Bring Brazier down here," Folsom said. "On the double."

At first, those inside the House chamber were unaware of Fodorov and Molly. Congressman J. C. Watts, former football star and second-term representative from Oklahoma, spoke from the well on a bill he'd sponsored that was being debated on the floor. Fifty or so other members milled about, and chatted with one another at their seats.

The visitors gallery contained a few onlookers. C-SPAN's cameras transmitted the debate live; the cable channel was pledged to carry every session of the House of Representatives gavel to gavel.

The realization that something was amiss started with those nearest Fodorov and Molly Latham, and spread in a ripple. At first, the response was quiet shock, and disbelief. But as it expanded, voices became louder. A woman screamed. A member slid down to the floor in front of his chair. The Speaker *pro tempore*, Democratic representative from Hawaii Neil Abercrombie, unaware of what had caused the upset, repeatedly rapped his gavel and called for the House to be in order.

"Get down!" the clerk, seated in front and below Abercrombie, shouted. The Speaker disappeared behind the raised desk, the gavel flying from his hand.

The C-SPAN camera operator couldn't believe what he was seeing. Nor could those members of the press who'd stayed late to follow the evening's debate. They rushed out of the expansive congressional press room to the press gallery, overlooking the House floor. "The guy's got a gun." "The kid he's holding. She's a page." "That's Paul Latham's kid." "What the hell is he up to?"

Fodorov, uncomfortable with the small area to which he was confined just inside the door, moved toward the center of the huge, ornate chamber, 139 feet long and 93 feet wide, one of the largest legislative rooms in the world. Everyone else in the chamber froze, a few peeking through spread fingers at what was happening, the way they would watch a violent movie. Others refused to look. Still others were too stunned to do anything but gape open-mouthed.

Initially, Molly had struggled against Fodorov's grip.

Now, she was like a rag doll, drained, empty, literally being dragged by him from place to place.

Fodorov reached the well. He looked up to the visitors gallery, where a few people sat with their arms on the railing, their attention focused on the macabre scene playing out below them.

The setting was not lost on Fodorov. Since being in the United States, he'd seen C-SPAN's coverage of the House of Representatives. He was scornful of those who spoke: "Windbags," he said to himself in Russian.

Still, the majesty of the House chamber was not lost on him. Pomp and officialdom had always impressed Fodorov. The grandiose rituals of the Soviet Union, particularly those involving the military, stirred his blood. And now here he was, center stage in America's symbol of its arrogant democracy, all eyes on him, fear on the faces of those witnessing Yvgeny Fodorov's moment.

Those watching the spectacle in the House chamber included Ruth Latham.

She'd been in the kitchen, filling the dishwasher after dinner. Martin was in the family room clicking through channels on the television. He went right by C-SPAN, then went back to it. He came forward to the edge of his chair and extended his neck. It couldn't be. *"Mom!"*

Warren Brazier, accompanied by one of his staff and by Capitol Police Chief Henry Folsom, entered the chamber through the Republican cloakroom.

"That him?" Folsom asked.

"Yes," Brazier replied. "He must be insane."

"Think he'll listen to you, Mr. Brazier?"

"I don't know."

Margaret Truman

"Only if you don't think it'll set him off."

Brazier turned to his young staff member. "You are his friend. Right?"

"Yes."

When Folsom had asked Brazier why he was bringing the young man with him, Brazier had replied, "He and Fodorov are friends. He might be helpful."

Folsom said to the young man, "You want to talk to him?"

"Yes. I will talk to him." He looked at Brazier.

"Go ahead," Brazier said. To Folsom: "They work together in my security office."

Folsom looked around. Instinct told him time had run out.

The cloakroom door behind them opened, and two hostage negotiators joined them. Folsom looked to where Fodorov continued to hold Molly, his gun pressed to her temple. "This guy's going to try to talk to him," Folsom told the negotiators. "They're friends."

"Go ahead," Brazier said. "Go on!"

Folsom glanced at the industrialist, taken slightly aback at his having taken charge.

Vladimir Donskoi, who'd returned to the meeting in H 139 after running from Latham's office, walked slowly in Fodorov's direction. As he did, he spoke in Russian, his tone friendly, almost joking. "Hey, Yvgeny, calm down, man." He raised his hands to show they were empty. "It's all worked out. We can leave here. Diplomatic immunity. No problem."

"What's he saying?" Folsom asked one of his negotiators.

"Beats the hell out of me."

Donskoi continued toward Fodorov. "Hey, Yvgeny,

cool it, man. Brazier worked everything out. We're out of here, on his private goddamn jet back to Moscow."

He stopped six feet from Fodorov and Molly. Fodorov's eyes were open wide—frightened, confused eyes. He stared at Donskoi, then said, "Brazier? We can leave?"

"*Da.*"

Donskoi broke into a wide smile. "Everything's okay, man. Everything's cool."

He closed the gap between them and stood at Fodorov's side.

"Who's he?" one of C-SPAN's camera operators asked another as they zoomed in, Donskoi's face filling the screen.

"I don't know. Widen the shot."

It happened so fast no one saw it coming, especially Yvgeny Fodorov. Donskoi's hand came up holding a revolver. In one continuous motion, it moved from his belt to beneath Fodorov's chin. The weapon's discharge was picked up and magnified by the microphone at the podium. Simultaneously, Fodorov's jaw and a portion of his face erupted in a vivid red cloud of blood. The hand holding the gun next to Molly's head flew up in the air, Fodorov's finger squeezing tightly against the trigger in a reflexive action, sending a hail of bullets from the automatic weapon up to the visitors gallery, where onlookers dove for cover.

Molly Latham, now free of her abductor's grasp, slumped to the floor, on top of Fodorov's lifeless body. They were immediately surrounded by Capitol police, two of whom lifted Molly and ran with her to the front row of the Republican side of the aisle. They gently laid her across the seats. "Get a doctor!" one yelled.

Molly opened her eyes. Her fingers went to her bosom,

then came away with Yvgeny Fodorov's blood on them. She shuddered, allowed a cry of anguish that had been bottled up to come forth, and then began to sob.

Vladimir Donskoi handed his weapon to Chief Folsom.

"Nice going," Folsom said. He turned to Warren Brazier. "Thanks for the help, Mr. Brazier."

"I'm just glad the girl wasn't hurt. Her father was one of my best friends."

34

"Wonderful, as usual," Mac Smith said to the manager as he and Annabel prepared to leave the restaurant.

"Always good to see you," the manager said. "Safe home."

The Smiths had parked their car a half block away. They stepped out onto the street and took deep breaths. "Lovely evening," Smith said.

"Delightful. Care to carry me to the car?" Annabel asked. "I'm so full I'm not sure I can walk."

"Of course," he said, grabbing her around the waist and pretending to try and lift her.

"I was only kidding," she said, giggling. "Mac, stop it!"

The two men who'd waited across Connecticut Avenue for them to leave the restaurant crossed the street and approached. They held weapons.

But before they could reach the couple, four armed men emerged from a car parked two removed from the

Smiths' Chevy. They ran into the street: "Drop the guns," one commanded.

The two men crossing stopped in the middle of the avenue.

"What the hell—?" Mac said.

He was interrupted by the sound of a single gunshot, then the sting of a bullet entering his thigh. As he fell to the sidewalk, the usually peaceful Connecticut Avenue became a battleground. The four men opened fire on the other two. One fell to the street, mortally wounded. The other attempted to flee, but was cut down by a fusillade of bullets ripping across his legs. His weapon flew from his hand and skidded across the avenue. He swore in Russian.

Annabel crouched over her husband. "Mac, are you all right?"

"My leg," he said, grimacing against the pain.

Annabel stood and shouted, "Help! My husband's been shot!"

Two of the four men came to her side. "We've called for an ambulance, Mrs. Smith," one said.

"Good. You know who I am?" she said.

"Yes, ma'am." He held out his badge for her to see. "FBI."

"FBI? You just happened to—?"

"Annabel," Smith said. He was now in a sitting position, his hands gripping his thigh.

"Yes?" she said, her hand lightly resting on his cheek.

"It was a good dinner."

"Yes, it was," she said, a large lump in her throat. "A very good dinner."

35

Mac Smith was taken to the George Washington University Medical Center, where emergency room physicians treated his wound. The bullet had passed cleanly through the fleshy portion of his thigh; no damage to muscles or nerves. He wanted to go home, but doctors prevailed upon him to stay overnight.

He sat up in bed. Annabel perched on its edge and held his hand. They watched the news on TV. Footage from C-SPAN had been provided to other stations, which ran special programs on the events that evening at the House of Representatives.

The station they watched reported that the murderer of Robert Mondrian, and abductor of Molly Latham, Yvgeny Fodorov, had been killed by another employee of Brazier Industries, Vladimir Donskoi. Donskoi was hailed as the hero of the evening. He declined to be interviewed. But Warren Brazier faced reporters outside the Capitol:

"This has been a tragedy of immense proportions," he said. "That an employee of Brazier Industries would turn into such a demented villain is beyond my comprehension. I'm just thankful that another of my people bravely intervened, and that the daughter of my good friend, Congressman Paul Latham, was spared."

The replay of how Yvgeny Fodorov's threat to Molly Latham was resolved was run over and over as interviews continued to be aired. One was of Ruth Latham, flanked by Martin and Molly.

"I just thank God that it ended the way it did," Ruth said.

"Does it bother you that an employee of your late husband's good friend Warren Brazier almost took your daughter's life?" a reporter asked.

"No," she replied. "A crazy person can work for any company. All the shootings in post offices by disgruntled employees proves that."

Another question: "Your husband was murdered, Mrs. Latham. Now his chief of staff. And your daughter is kidnapped. Do you see a pattern here?"

"No. Please, we just want to get home."

Melissa had been standing just behind Molly. She said quickly, leaning into the camera, "When I heard Molly—she's my roommate at the page dorm; we're both pages—when Ah heard what was happening to her, I could just have died right on the spot."

The program shifted to a statement by Capitol Police Chief Henry Folsom, who said all circumstances of the evening would be investigated thoroughly by the appropriate law enforcement agencies.

Smith shifted his position in the bed and growled, "Ruth doesn't see a pattern? What else can you see?"

"Once the attack on *you* becomes part of the mix, Mac, that pattern will become painfully clear."

A doctor entered the room. "How are you feeling?" he asked.

"Not bad," Smith replied.

"Up to some visitors?"

"Who?" Annabel asked.

The doctor consulted a piece of paper. "A Ms. Belle and a Mr. Broadhurst. There are two FBI agents with them. I assume they're with the Bureau, too."

Mac looked at Annabel and smiled. "At least they're not asking me to meet them in a rowboat on the Potomac." He said to the doctor, "Sure, send them up. But have them check their guns at the door."

An hour later, Belle, Broadhurst, and the two special agents left Mac and Annabel alone once again. They sat silently, each trying to sort out what they'd just been told. It was Annabel who broke the silence.

"The man is evil incarnate," she said of Warren Brazier. Smith nodded.

"He tried to eliminate every person who might know of his criminal acts. Paul. Bob Mondrian. Marge Edwards. And then you. Even Molly Latham."

"I know."

Annabel shook her head and sighed. "I never understand rich and powerful people resorting to crime to become even more rich and powerful."

"*Avaritia,*" Mac said.

"Spoken like a true lawyer, reverting to the Latin," said Annabel.

"I'd say it in Russian if I knew how. Greed. Money corrupting. Egos running amuck. What surprises me is the claim that Brazier is actually a major figure in the

Russian mob, here and in Moscow, laundering their dirty drug money and God knows what else. A man can be brilliant, even brilliantly criminal, brilliantly corrupt, and then finally stupid. What did he think—because he was in a meeting at the Capitol when the mayhem went on that he had a perfect alibi? Or had he stopped thinking? From what Giles and Jessica and the agents said, all the strings lead right back to Brazier. They have him dead-to-rights—the money laundering, payoffs, contract killings, the works. And he's not the least impenitent."

"Giles is confident that the FBI will make a solid case against him, based upon what the CIA has come up with over the past year, and Paul's investigation and report. I hope he's right."

At eleven, Annabel prepared to leave. "You'll be okay?" she asked.

"It's you I worry about," Smith said. "Hate to see you alone in the house."

"I'm never alone, not with the Beast there."

He smiled. "Give Rufus an ear rub for me."

The eleven o'clock news came on, updating the events in the House that evening. Annabel stopped to watch.

"We have two important additions to this ongoing story," the anchor said in dulcet tones. "First, we've learned that another murder attempt took place tonight in Washington, this also involving Russians. An attempt was made on the life of Mackensie Smith, former noted criminal attorney and professor of law at George Washington University. Smith was also counsel to murdered congressman Paul Latham. The incident took place outside a restaurant on Connecticut Avenue, when two men, Russian national citizens with alleged ties to organized crime, attempted to kill Smith and his wife. The FBI, which had been quietly protecting Smith because of his link to Latham, killed one of the assailants and severely wounded another. Smith, according to our source, received a superficial wound, and is spending the night in the GW Medical Center."

"The FBI protecting me," Smith muttered.

"I'm glad they were there," Annabel said.

"You were right."

"About what?"

"About not getting involved. If I hadn't, there never would have been any need to 'protect' me."

Their attention returned to the screen. The newscaster said, "In still another related development, an employee of Brazier Industries, Anatoly Alekseyev, was found shot to death in his Georgetown apartment. His body was discovered following the tense scene at the Capitol by Marge Edwards, an employee in Congressman Latham's office, who disappeared after it was rumored she intended to charge President Scott's nominee for secretary of state with sexual harassment, a rumor she emphatically denied tonight. Ms. Edwards, it's reported, was romantically involved with the murdered Brazier Industries employee, Mr. Alekseyev. She has been admitted to a local hospital."

Smith used the remote to click off the set. "It seems the cold war didn't end, Annabel," he said. "We've been invaded by the Russians."

"No, Mac. The invader was a sick individual named Warren Brazier. And he's been defeated." She kissed him on the lips. "Get some sleep, which is what I intend to do. I'll be back first thing in the morning."

The Smiths made their trip to Russia, where he met with a variety of legal experts. The corruption in the judicial and law enforcement communities there was more pervasive than he'd ever imagined from his research. There was much to be done before the former Soviet Union would become a true democracy, and where a free people and a free market could flourish. Mac and his colleagues promised to return to the United States and draw up a list of recommendations for their Russian hosts to consider.

They enjoyed the trip, although the ghost of Warren Brazier, and the havoc he created, followed wherever they went.

They returned to Washington and settled into their routines, Mac back to teaching at the university, Annabel to managing her art gallery.

Federal charges, ranging from money laundering to racketeering to murder, were filed against Warren Brazier and some of his associates. Brazier vowed to fight them, but the overwhelming legal opinion was that despite his money, the case against him was strong enough to assure a conviction.

Smith met with Marge Edwards only once, the day before she was to leave Washington to live with her father in Indianapolis: "Just until I put the pieces together," she told him.

"A smart move," he said.

"You know I never intended to hurt Paul," she said.

"Of course I know that. He was a good man. I miss him. The country misses him."

"Well, I'm sorry for all the upset I caused. I acted like a silly schoolgirl."

Smith smiled, said, "It's all in the past, Marge. Say hello to your father. I like him. It's a good place for you to be right now. And it will brighten his life."

Molly Latham, according to her mother, had settled

back into being a House page, and was thoroughly enjoying the experience. "I think she'll run for Congress one day," Ruth said.

"She'll have my vote," Smith replied. "Provided Annabel and I move to Northern California."

Senator Connors fired his AA, Dennis Mackral, who returned to California to attempt to build a base for his own run for Congress. His prospects were considered to be 15-watt, although it was, after all, California.

President Scott put up another nominee for secretary of state, a former ambassador to the Soviet Union whose reputation had been carefully built over the years to preclude the ruffling of feathers—anywhere, with anyone—including Senator Frank Connors. The nominee passed Senate scrutiny with ease.

That evening, Mac received a call at home from Jessica Belle.

"Hello, Jessica," he said.

"Hi, Mac. Giles and I were wondering if we could get together."

"Get together?"

"Maybe dinner? Our treat. There's something we wanted to bounce off you."

A twinge of pain in his thigh where he'd been shot caused him to wince. He slowly recrossed his legs.

"Mac?"

"Yes, I'm here."

"Dinner? Tomorrow?"

"I, ah—I'm tied up, Jessica. Will be for quite a while."

"Sure. I understand," she said. "How about giving me a call when things ease up?"

"A good suggestion."

Rufus placed his large canine head on Smith's lap.

Smith scratched him behind the ears, smiled, and said, "I'll get back to you, Jessica."

"In a year or so," he said to Rufus after hanging up. "And maybe later. Come on, big guy. I've got a few things to talk over with you. Need your advice. Need a walk."

Read on for a preview of Margaret
Truman's next thrilling novel,

Murder at the
Washington Tribune

Available at bookstores everywhere
Published by Ballantine Books

Another speaker came to the podium.

Joe Wilcox leaned close to his wife and muttered just loud enough
for her pretty ears only, "Another speaker." He shifted position in his
chair and twisted his neck against a growing stiffness, and full-blown
boredom. With them at a front table were three couples, others from *The
Washington Tribune* and their spouses who'd agreed to attend the
awards evening with the Wilcoxes out of friendship, or obligation, or
maybe a little of both.

The dinner was an annual event for the Washington Media Association, whose members came from the ranks of Washington, D.C.'s, print
and broadcast journalists. Like most such groups, its leadership was
fond of bestowing awards on deserving members and their chosen profession, giving that same leadership a reason for taking to the podium
and expressing their views on many things, mostly political. An occasional, usually accidental, bit of humor provided blessed audience relief
from those who spoke endlessly.

At least they're getting to the awards, Wilcox thought as the speaker
said "In conclusion" for the third time. Wilcox looked toward a table at
which his daughter, Roberta, sat. She was the reason Wilcox and Georgia were there.

The speaker at the podium finally concluded, and the bestowing
of awards commenced, twenty-two in all. Three weeks later—or so it
seemed—Roberta was the sixteenth recipient called to the podium to accept the award for Best Local Investigative Reporting—Broadcast, accompanied by the producer and the director of a TV series they'd done
on corruption within the Washington MPD.

"Doesn't she look beautiful?" Georgia said.

"Of course she does," Wilcox replied. "Because she is."

Roberta Wilcox did look stunning that evening in a stylish pantsuit the color of ripe peaches. But it was radiance from within that created a virtual aura around her, enhanced by a bright smile that had lit up the nightly news, since she joined the station three years earlier. "The best-looking newscaster in D.C." was the consensus. She usually wore her auburn hair pulled back when on the air, but this evening she'd let it down, framing an oval face with inquisitive raisin-brown eyes, her skin fair but not pale, her makeup tastefully underapplied. She thanked the station for having given her the freedom and support to pursue the exposé, read from a slip of paper the names of those who helped, including the producer's and the director's, and ended by crediting her parents for having instilled in her the natural curiosity necessary to get the job done. "Of course," she added, "I come from good reportorial stock. My father is as good a reporter as there is in this city." She watched him wince, tossed him a kiss off her fingertips, and led her fellow award winners back to their table.

It was announced from the podium that the evening had come to an end, and most of the three hundred men and women left their tables to mingle, gravitating to familiar faces and offering congratulations to the winners and their families.

"How'd an ugly guy like you end up with such a knockout of a daughter?" a *Trib* reporter asked Wilcox, the question accompanied by a laugh and then a slap on the back.

"Her mother's genes," Wilcox replied, nodding in the direction of his wife, who'd gone to Roberta's table to talk with her and her celebrating tablemates.

"Must be," Wilcox's friend said. He lowered his voice. "What do you think of Hawthorne getting an award?" Gene Hawthorne, a *Trib* Metro reporter, had been cited for a three-part series he'd done on a local bank's illegal payoffs to a District official.

Wilcox shrugged, which accurately reflected what he was thinking. Hawthorne, in his late twenties, did not rank high on Wilcox's list of favorite people. He wasn't alone in his negative view of the abrasive, aggressive young reporter who had a penchant for rubbing colleagues the wrong way, his knife always in search of an unprotected book, it seemed. Equally galling was the backing he received from the *Trib*'s ranking editors and management, who obviously viewed the young, smug, sandy-haired, self-possessed reporter as a rising star, which, of course, he was; a bit of news that wasn't lost on anyone at the *Trib*, Wilcox included.

He saw in the young reporter something of himself years ago, when he'd come to *The Washington Tribune* brimming with ambition and possessing the energy to fuel it. But it had been different at the paper twenty-three years ago. Then, there were still plenty of grizzled veteran reporters from whom to learn, men (almost exclusively) who lived the lives of reporters as portrayed in movies and plays, characters straight out of *The Front Page,* their heads surrounded by blue cigarette and cigar smoke, pints of whiskey in their desk drawers, the rattle and clank of their typewriters testifying to their daily output, spoken words tough and profane, written words sharp and to the point. There weren't many of them left. The younger *Trib* reporters, including Wilcox, had been hired to supplement that veteran staff. But eventually Gene Hawthorne and dozens of men and women like him had been brought in to replace the over-fifty crowd. There had been a flurry of buyouts offered over the past few years, and many newsroom veterans had jumped at the severance package with its generous cash settlement, pension options, and health and life insurance. In came the new blood, working at half the pay of the reporters who'd gone on to their retirement, or in many cases new jobs. One of the *Trib*'s top economics reporters had left on a Friday; his byline appeared over an article in the *Trib* the following Monday, written for a wire service that had eagerly hired him.

It just wasn't the same anymore for Joe Wilcox. He was now a member of the dinosaur club himself, viewed with a certain barely disguised scorn by Hawthorne and his cadre of young hotshots. Wilcox was two years from fifty-five, the buyout age, with the lapel pin certifying that he'd given *The Washington Tribune* the best twenty-five years of his life.

Roberta and Georgia approached and Roberta gave him a hug. She was taller than her father.

"Thanks for the plug," he said.

"I meant it," she said.

"You look great, honey. Congratulations. That was a hell of a piece you did."

"I wonder if anyone at MPD will ever congratulate me," she said.

Wilcox laughed. "I'm sure the police are preparing a proclamation as we speak, naming you honorary cop of the year."

"I know it was awkward for you," Roberta said, her expression as serious as her words.

"They'll get over it," he said. "I still have friends over there who agreed with you. They all suffer when a few foul balls taint the entire force."

"But if they knew you'd fed me some of the information I used—"

"Which they won't. Don't give it another thought, sweetie."

"Anything new on Kaporis?" she asked.

His response was a shake of his head, and a tiny smile for a thought that came and went. This daughter-journalist had not asked the question out of natural curiosity.

Like her father, Roberta Wilcox had been reporting on the killing of Jean Kaporis, a young woman who'd joined the *Trib* less than a year ago, fresh out of the University of Missouri's school of journalism. Kaporis had been assigned to the paper's "Panache" section, helping cover the city's vibrant social scene: the weddings of those whose names were well-known enough to justify coverage, fundraisers—a day didn't pass in Washington when someone wasn't raising money for something deemed worthy of their time and effort, important or whimsical—and, ideally, a scandal among the rich and famous and thin, a political faux pas, or a fatuous misstep that would leave readers tittering. It wasn't the sort of assignment she preferred, but she knew it represented a starting point for many newly hired female reporters and she threw herself into it, hoping her work would capture the attention of someone in a position to move her into hard news.

That kind of break hadn't happened during her time at the *Trib*. But she had one advantage. She was lovely. Male heads turned and pulse rates sped up whenever she sauntered through the newsroom wearing skirts, sweaters, and blouses that accented her ripe body, donning a linen blazer now and then as a nod to corporate correctness. No doubt about it, Jean Kaporis was a splendid example of young womanhood, every curve and bump properly placed, good genes in ample evidence, and especially a pleasant, willing personality to go with it, all of which attracted many people to her—including whoever had strangled her to death.

A maintenance man found her early one morning a month ago in a secluded second-floor supply closet at the far end of the main newsroom; bruises on her neck, pretty mouth going in the wrong direction as though someone had removed it and carelessly pasted it back on. The autopsy reported that she'd died from manual strangulation, her throat and larynx damaged from pressure exerted by her assailant's hands and fingers. The presence of petechial hemorrhages in the mucous membrane lining of the inner surface of her eyelids provided presumptive evidence of strangulation. She'd bitten her tongue, not an uncommon occurrence with victims of strangulation. The struggle with her attacker had been brief. Although laboratory analysis indicated that she'd engaged in sexual intercourse within twenty-four hours of death, there was no outward sign of having been sexually assaulted.

"No, nothing new," Wilcox told his daughter. "They've been questioning everyone at the paper. Makes sense."

"And?"

"No 'ands,' Roberta. That's all I know. Maybe you know something you'd like to share."

She shook her head.

"Let you know if anything breaks," he said.

She smiled and squeezed his arm. "And I'll do the same."

"Back to the house for a drink?" Georgia asked their daughter.

"Thanks, no, Mom. I promised the guys from the station I'd go out with them."

"Ah, youth," Wilcox said. *Wasted on the young.* To his wife: "What say we call it a night?"

Georgia nodded and kissed her daughter on the cheek. "Not too late," she said. "You need your beauty sleep."

"Mom!"

"I know, I know, but—."

"Not too late," Joe Wilcox echoed, a wide grin crossing his craggy face. "And eat breakfast. You should always start the day with a good breakfast. Diane Sawyer does."

As the Wilcoxes and hundreds of other people poured out of the Washington Hilton and Towers onto Connecticut Avenue NW, they were confronted with a chaotic crime scene. A half-dozen marked police cars lights flashing and radios crackling, had blocked off the wide thoroughfare. Yellow crime-scene tape marked an area of the sidewalk almost directly in front of the hotel's main entrance. A body covered by a white cloth lay on the sidewalk inside the taped-off section.

"Hey, Joe!"

A colleague from a competing paper, with whom Wilcox had covered myriad crime scenes, came up to the couple.

"What happened?" Wilcox asked.

"A drive-by. Middle-aged white guy."

"He's dead?" Georgia asked.

"Very." To Wilcox: "You covering?"

"No. Night off. This is the same spot where Hinckley shot Reagan back in eighty-one."

"That's right," said the reporter, making a note in his pad. "Forgot about that."

"Let's go," Georgia said.

Wilcox took a final look at the covered body, shook his head, took his wife's arm, and maneuvered through the crowd in the direction of the parking garage. As they pulled onto the street, Georgia said, "If you want to go back, Joe, I'll drive home. You can take a car service."

"Thanks but no thanks. I'm not missing anything. There'll be another murder to cover tomorrow. There always is. No, this is Roberta's night, and I don't want anything to spoil the memory of her up there getting her award. Damn, she looked good."

It was, he knew, what his wife wanted to hear. She squeezed his thigh and said, "Let's stop for ice cream. I'm in the mood."

"Then ice cream it'll be."

MARGARET TRUMAN has won faithful readers with her works of biography and fiction, particularly her ongoing series of Capital Crimes mysteries, including her newest, *Murder at the Washington Tribune*. Her novels let us into the corridors of power and privilege, poverty and pageantry, in the nation's capital. She is the author of many nonfiction books, including *The President's House,* in which she shares some of the secrets and history of the White House where she once resided. She lives in Manhattan.